London County Council

awarded to ANDREW TURVEY

THE LOUGHBOROUGH SECONDARY (CENTRAL) SCHOOL, School

MINET ROAD, BRIXTON, S.W.9

for an excellent G.C.E. result and outstanding example as Deputy Boy Captain

date JUL 1955

John Brown. Education officer

FOUR TALES

The Thirty-Nine Steps
The Power-House
The Watcher by the Threshold
The Moon Endureth

FOUR TALES

The Thirty-Nine Steps
The Power-House
The Watcher by the Threshold
The Moon Endureth

BY

JOHN BUCHAN
(LORD TWEEDSMUIR)

William Blackwood & Sons Ltd.
Edinburgh and London
1952

First printed . .	*February* 1936 . . .	5,250 *copies*
Reprinted . . .	*September* 1936 . . .	5,250 ,,
Reprinted . . .	*November* 1939 . . .	5,250 ,,
Reprinted . . .	*March* 1942 . . .	2,150 ,,
Reprinted . . .	*October* 1942 . . .	2,200 ,,
Reprinted . . .	*June* 1943 . . .	3,200 ,,
Reprinted . . .	*August* 1944 . . .	2,750 ,,
Reprinted . . .	*December* 1946 . .	15,000 ,,
Reprinted . . .	*September* 1949 . . .	5,000 ,,
Reprinted . . .	*August* 1952 . . .	4,000 ,,

PRINTED IN GREAT BRITAIN

CONTENTS.

THE THIRTY-NINE STEPS

THE POWER-HOUSE

THE WATCHER BY THE THRESHOLD

THE MOON ENDURETH

I.

THE THIRTY-NINE STEPS

TO

THOMAS ARTHUR NELSON,

LOTHIAN AND BORDER HORSE.

MY DEAR TOMMY,

You and I have long cherished an affection for that elementary type of tale which Americans call the "dime novel," and which we know as the "shocker"—the romance where the incidents defy the probabilities, and march just inside the borders of the possible. During an illness last winter I exhausted my store of those aids to cheerfulness, and was driven to write one for myself. This little volume is the result, and I should like to put your name on it in memory of our long friendship, in these days when the wildest fictions are so much less improbable than the facts.

J. B.

CHAPTER I.

THE MAN WHO DIED.

I RETURNED from the City about three o'clock on that May afternoon pretty well disgusted with life. I had been three months in the Old Country, and was fed up with it. If anyone had told me a year ago that I would have been feeling like that I should have laughed at him; but there was the fact. The weather made me liverish, the talk of the ordinary Englishman made me sick, I couldn't get enough exercise, and the amusements of London seemed as flat as soda-water that has been standing in the sun. "Richard Hannay," I kept telling myself, "you have got into the wrong ditch, my friend, and you had better climb out."

It made me bite my lips to think of the plans I had been building up those last years in Buluwayo. I had got my pile—not one of the big ones, but good enough for me; and I had figured out all kinds of ways of enjoying myself. My father had brought me out from Scotland at the age of six, and I had never been home since; so England was a sort of Arabian Nights to me, and I counted on stopping there for the rest of my days.

But from the first I was disappointed with it. In about a week I was tired of seeing sights, and in less than a month I had had enough of restaurants and theatres and race-meetings. I had no real pal to go about with, which probably explains things. Plenty of people invited me to their houses, but they didn't seem much interested in me. They would fling me a question or two about South Africa, and then get on to their own affairs. A lot of Imperialist ladies asked me to tea to meet schoolmasters from New Zealand and editors from Vancouver, and that was the dismalest business of all. Here was I, thirty-seven years old, sound in wind and limb, with enough money to have a good time, yawning my head off all day. I had just about settled to clear out and get back to the veld, for I was the best bored man in the United Kingdom.

That afternoon I had been worrying my brokers about investments to give my mind something to work on, and on my way home I turned into my club—rather a pot-house, which took in Colonial members. I had a long drink, and read the evening papers. They were full of the row in the Near East, and there was an article about Karolides, the Greek Premier. I rather fancied the chap. From all accounts he seemed the one big man in the show; and he played a straight game too, which was more than could be said for most of them. I gathered that they hated him pretty blackly in Berlin and Vienna, but that we were going to stick by him, and one paper said that he was the only barrier between Europe and Armageddon. I remember wondering if I could get a job in those parts. It struck me that Albania was the sort of place that might keep a man from yawning.

About six o'clock I went home, dressed, dined at the Café Royal, and turned into a music-hall. It was a silly show, all capering women and monkey-faced men, and I did not stay long. The night was fine and clear as I walked back to the flat I had hired near Portland Place. The crowd surged past me on the pavements, busy and chattering, and I envied the people for having something to do. These shop-girls and clerks and dandies and policemen had some interest in life that kept them going. I gave half-a-crown to a beggar because I saw him yawn; he was a fellow-sufferer. At Oxford Circus I looked up into the spring sky and I made a vow. I would give the Old Country another day to fit me into something; if nothing happened, I would take the next boat for the Cape.

My flat was the first floor in a new block behind Langham Place. There was a common staircase, with a porter and a liftman at the entrance, but there was no restaurant or anything of that sort, and each flat was quite shut off from the others. I hate servants on the premises, so I had a fellow to look after me who came in by the day. He arrived before eight o'clock every morning and used to depart at seven, for I never dined at home.

I was just fitting my key into the door when I noticed a man at my elbow. I had not seen him approach, and the sudden appearance made me start. He was a slim man, with a short brown beard and small, gimlety blue eyes. I recognised him as the occupant of a flat on the top floor, with whom I had passed the time of day on the stairs.

"Can I speak to you?" he said. "May I come in for a minute?" He was steadying his voice with an effort, and his hand was pawing my arm.

I got my door open and motioned him in. No sooner was he over the threshold than he made a dash for my back room, where I used to smoke and write my letters. Then he bolted back.

"Is the door locked?" he asked feverishly, and he fastened the chain with his own hand.

"I'm very sorry," he said humbly. "It's a mighty liberty, but you looked the kind of man who would understand. I've had you in my mind all this week when things got troublesome. Say, will you do me a good turn?"

"I'll listen to you," I said. "That's all I'll promise." I was getting worried by the antics of this nervous little chap.

There was a tray of drinks on a table beside him, from which he filled himself a stiff whisky-and-soda. He drank it off in three gulps, and cracked the glass as he set it down.

"Pardon," he said, "I'm a bit rattled to-night. You see, I happen at this moment to be dead."

I sat down in an arm-chair and lit my pipe.

"What does it feel like?" I asked. I was pretty certain that I had to deal with a madman.

A smile flickered over his drawn face. "I'm not mad—yet. Say, sir, I've been watching you, and I reckon you're a cool customer. I reckon, too, you're an honest man, and not afraid of playing a bold hand. I'm going to confide in you. I need help worse than any man ever needed it, and I want to know if I can count you in."

"Get on with your yarn," I said, "and I'll tell you."

He seemed to brace himself for a great effort, and then started on the queerest rigmarole. I didn't get hold of it at first, and I had to stop and ask him questions. But here is the gist of it:—

He was an American, from Kentucky, and after college, being pretty well off, he had started out to see the world. He wrote a bit, and acted as war correspondent for a Chicago paper, and spent a year or two in South-Eastern Europe. I gathered that he was a fine linguist, and had got to know pretty well the society in those parts. He spoke familiarly of many names that I remembered to have seen in the newspapers.

He had played about with politics, he told me, at first for the interest of them, and then because he couldn't help himself. I read him as a sharp, restless fellow, who always wanted to get down to the roots of things. He got a little further down than he wanted.

I am giving you what he told me as well as I could make it out. Away behind all the Governments and the armies there was a big subterranean movement going on, engineered by very dangerous people. He had come on it by accident; it fascinated him; he went further, and then he got caught. I gathered that most of the people in it were the sort of educated anarchists that make revolutions, but that beside them there were financiers who were playing for money. A clever man can make big profits on a falling market, and it suited the book of both classes to set Europe by the ears.

He told me some queer things that explained a lot that had puzzled me—things that happened in the Balkan War, how one state suddenly came out on top, why alliances were made and broken, why certain men disappeared, and where the sinews of war came from. The aim of the whole conspiracy was to get Russia and Germany at loggerheads.

When I asked Why, he said that the anarchist lot thought it would give them their chance. Everything would be in the melting-pot, and they looked to see a new world emerge. The capitalists would rake in the shekels, and make fortunes by buying up wreckage. Capital, he said, had no conscience and no fatherland. Besides, the Jew was behind it, and the Jew hated Russia worse than hell.

"Do you wonder?" he cried. "For three hundred years they have been persecuted, and this is the return match for the *pogroms*. The Jew is everywhere, but you have to go far down the backstairs to find him. Take any big Teutonic business concern. If you have dealings with it the first man you meet is Prince *von und zu* Something, an elegant young man who talks Eton-and-Harrow English. But he cuts no ice. If your business is big, you get behind him and find a prognathous Westphalian with a retreating brow and the manners of a hog. He is the German business man that gives your English papers the shakes. But if you're on the biggest kind of job and are bound to get to the real boss, ten to one you are brought up against a little white-faced Jew in a bath-chair with an eye like a rattlesnake. Yes, sir, he is the man who is ruling the world just now, and he has his knife in the Empire of the Tzar, because his aunt was outraged and his father flogged in some one-horse location on the Volga."

I could not help saying that his Jew-anarchists seemed to have got left behind a little.

"Yes and no," he said. "They won up to a point, but

they struck a bigger thing than money, a thing that couldn't be bought, the old elemental fighting instincts of man. If you're going to be killed you invent some kind of flag and country to fight for, and if you survive you get to love the thing. Those foolish devils of soldiers have found something they care for, and that has upset the pretty plan laid in Berlin and Vienna. But my friends haven't played their last card by a long sight. They've gotten the ace up their sleeves, and unless I can keep alive for a month they are going to play it and win."

"But I thought you were dead," I put in.

"*Mors janua vitæ,*" he smiled. (I recognised the quotation: it was about all the Latin I knew.) "I'm coming to that, but I've got to put you wise about a lot of things first. If you read your newspaper, I guess you know the name of Constantine Karolides?"

I sat up at that, for I had been reading about him that very afternoon.

"He is the man that has wrecked all their games. He is the one big brain in the whole show, and he happens also to be an honest man. Therefore he has been marked down these twelve months past. I found that out—not that it was difficult, for any fool could guess as much. But I found out the way they were going to get him, and that knowledge was deadly. That's why I have had to decease."

He had another drink, and I mixed it for him myself, for I was getting interested in the beggar.

"They can't get him in his own land, for he has a bodyguard of Epirotes that would skin their grandmothers. But on the 15th day of June he is coming to this city. The British Foreign Office has taken to having International tea-parties, and the biggest of them is due on that date. Now Karolides is reckoned the principal guest, and if my friends have their way he will never return to his admiring countrymen."

"That's simple enough, anyhow," I said. "You can warn him and keep him at home."

"And play their game?" he asked sharply. "If he does not come they win, for he's the only man that can straighten out the tangle. And if his Government are warned he won't come, for he does not know how big the stakes will be on June the 15th."

"What about the British Government?" I said. "They're not going to let their guests be murdered. Tip them the wink, and they'll take extra precautions."

"No good. They might stuff your city with plain-clothes detectives and double the police and Constantine would still be a doomed man. My friends are not playing this game for candy. They want a big occasion for the taking off, with the eyes of all Europe on it. He'll be murdered by an Austrian, and there'll be plenty of evidence to show the connivance of the big folk in Vienna and Berlin. It will all be an infernal lie, of course, but the case will look black enough to the world. I'm not talking hot air, my friend. I happen to know every detail of the hellish contrivance, and I can tell you it will be the most finished piece of blackguardism since the Borgias. But it's not going to come off if there's a certain man who knows the wheels of the business alive right here in London on the 15th day of June. And that man is going to be your servant, Franklin P. Scudder."

I was getting to like the little chap. His jaw had shut like a rat-trap, and there was the fire of battle in his gimlety eyes. If he was spinning me a yarn he could act up to it.

"Where did you find out this story?" I asked.

"I got the first hint in an inn on the Achensee in Tyrol. That set me inquiring, and I collected my other clues in a fur-shop in the Galician quarter of Buda, in a Strangers' Club in Vienna, and in a little bookshop off the Racknitz-strasse in Leipsic. I completed my evidence ten days ago in Paris. I can't tell you the details now, for it's something of a history. When I was quite sure in my own mind I judged it my business to disappear, and I reached this city by a mighty queer circuit. I left Paris a dandified young French-American, and I sailed from Hamburg a Jew diamond merchant. In Norway I was an English student of Ibsen collecting materials for lectures, but when I left Bergen I was a cinema-man with special ski films. And I came here from Leith with a lot of pulp-wood propositions in my pocket to put before the London newspapers. Till yesterday I thought I had muddied my trail some, and was feeling pretty happy. Then . . ."

The recollection seemed to upset him, and he gulped down some more whisky.

"Then I saw a man standing in the street outside this block. I used to stay close in my room all day, and only slip out after dark for an hour or two. I watched him for a bit from my window, and I thought I recognised him. . . . He came in and spoke to the porter. . . . When I came back from my walk last night I found a card in my letter-box. It bore the name of the man I want least to meet on God's earth."

I think that the look in my companion's eyes, the sheer naked scare on his face, completed my conviction of his honesty. My own voice sharpened a bit as I asked him what he did next.

"I realised that I was bottled as sure as a pickled herring, and that there was only one way out. I had to die. If my pursuers knew I was dead they would go to sleep again."

"How did you manage it ?"

"I told the man that valets me that I was feeling pretty bad, and I got myself up to look like death. That wasn't difficult, for I'm no slouch at disguises. Then I got a corpse—you can always get a body in London if you know where to go for it. I fetched it back in a trunk on the top of a four-wheeler, and I had to be assisted upstairs to my room. You see I had to pile up some evidence for the inquest. I went to bed and got my man to mix me a sleeping-draught, and then told him to clear out. He wanted to fetch a doctor, but I swore some and said I couldn't abide leeches. When I was left alone I started in to fake up that corpse. He was my size, and I judged had perished from too much alcohol, so I put some spirits handy about the place. The jaw was the weak point in the likeness, so I blew it away with a revolver. I daresay there will be somebody to-morrow to swear to having heard a shot, but there are no neighbours on my floor, and I guessed I could risk it. So I left the body in bed dressed up in my pyjamas, with a revolver lying on the bed-clothes and a considerable mess around. Then I got into a suit of clothes I had kept waiting for emergencies. I didn't dare to shave for fear of leaving tracks, and besides, it wasn't any kind of use my trying to get into the streets. I had had you in my mind all day, and there seemed nothing to do but to make an appeal to you. I watched from my window till I saw you come home, and then slipped down the stair to meet you. . . . There, sir, I guess you know about as much as me of this business."

He sat blinking like an owl, fluttering with nerves and yet desperately determined. By this time I was pretty well convinced that he was going straight with me. It was the wildest sort of narrative, but I had heard in my time many steep tales which had turned out to be true, and I had made a practice of judging the man rather than the story. If he had wanted to get a location in my flat, and then cut my throat, he would have pitched a milder yarn.

"Hand me your key," I said, "and I'll take a look at the corpse. Excuse my caution, but I'm bound to verify a bit if I can."

He shook his head mournfully. "I reckoned you'd ask for that, but I haven't got it. It's on my chain on the dressing-table. I had to leave it behind, for I couldn't leave any clues to breed suspicions. The gentry who are after me are pretty bright-eyed citizens. You'll have to take me on trust for the night, and to-morrow you'll get proof of the corpse business right enough."

I thought for an instant or two. "Right. I'll trust you for the night. I'll lock you into this room and keep the key. Just one word, Mr Scudder. I believe you're straight, but if so be you are not I should warn you that I'm a handy man with a gun."

"Sure," he said, jumping up with some briskness. "I haven't the privilege of your name, sir, but let me tell you that you're a white man. I'll thank you to lend me a razor."

I took him into my bedroom and turned him loose. In half an hour's time a figure came out that I scarcely recognised. Only his gimlety, hungry eyes were the same. He was shaved clean, his hair was parted in the middle, and he had cut his eyebrows. Further, he carried himself as if he had been drilled, and was the very model, even to the brown complexion, of some British officer who had had a long spell in India. He had a monocle, too, which he stuck in his eye, and every trace of the American had gone out of his speech.

"My hat! Mr Scudder——" I stammered.

"Not Mr Scudder," he corrected; "Captain Theophilus Digby, of the 40th Gurkhas, presently home on leave. I'll thank you to remember that, sir."

I made him up a bed in my smoking-room and sought my own couch, more cheerful than I had been for the past month. Things did happen occasionally, even in this God-forgotten metropolis.

I woke next morning to hear my man, Paddock, making the deuce of a row at the smoking-room door. Paddock was a fellow I had done a good turn to out on the Selakwi, and I had inspanned him as my servant as soon as I got to England. He had about as much gift of the gab as a hippopotamus, and was not a great hand at valeting, but I knew I could count on his loyalty.

"Stop that row, Paddock," I said. "There's a friend of mine, Captain—Captain" (I couldn't remember the name) "dossing down in there. Get breakfast for two and then come and speak to me."

I told Paddock a fine story about how my friend was a great swell, with his nerves pretty bad from overwork, who wanted absolute rest and stillness. Nobody had got to know he was here, or he would be besieged by communications from the India Office and the Prime Minister and his cure would be ruined. I am bound to say Scudder played up splendidly when he came to breakfast. He fixed Paddock with his eyeglass, just like a British officer, asked him about the Boer War, and slung out at me a lot of stuff about imaginary pals. Paddock couldn't learn to call me "sir," but he "sirred" Scudder as if his life depended on it.

I left him with the newspaper and a box of cigars, and went down to the City till luncheon. When I got back the lift-man had an important face.

"Nawsty business 'ere this morning, sir. Gent in No. 15 been and shot 'isself. They've just took 'im to the mortiary. The police are up there now."

I ascended to No. 15, and found a couple of bobbies and an inspector busy making an examination. I asked a few idiotic questions, and they soon kicked me out. Then I found the man that had valeted Scudder, and pumped him, but I could see he suspected nothing. He was a whining fellow with a churchyard face, and half-a-crown went far to console him.

I attended the inquest next day. A partner of some publishing firm gave evidence that the deceased had brought him wood-pulp propositions, and had been, he believed, an agent of an American business. The jury found it a case of suicide while of unsound mind, and the few effects were handed over to the American Consul to deal with. I gave Scudder a full account of the affair, and it interested him greatly. He said he wished he could have attended the inquest, for he reckoned it would be about as spicy as to read one's own obituary notice.

The first two days he stayed with me in that back room he was very peaceful. He read and smoked a bit, and made a heap of jottings in a note-book, and every night we had a game of chess, at which he beat me hollow. I think he was nursing his nerves back to health, for he had had a pretty trying time. But on the third day I could see he was beginning to get restless. He fixed up a list of the days till June 15th, and ticked each off with a red pencil, making remarks in shorthand against them. I would find him sunk in a brown study, with his sharp eyes abstracted, and after those spells of meditation he was apt to be very despondent.

Then I could see that he began to get edgy again. He listened for little noises, and was always asking me if Paddock could be trusted. Once or twice he got very peevish, and apologised for it. I didn't blame him. I made every allowance, for he had taken on a fairly stiff job.

It was not the safety of his own skin that troubled him, but the success of the scheme he had planned. That little man was clean grit all through, without a soft spot in him. One night he was very solemn.

"Say, Hannay," he said, "I judge I should let you a bit deeper into this business. I should hate to go out without leaving somebody else to put up a fight." And he began to tell me in detail what I had only heard from him vaguely.

I did not give him very close attention. The fact is, I was more interested in his own adventures than in his high politics. I reckoned that Karolides and his affairs were not my business, leaving all that to him. So a lot that he said slipped clean out of my memory. I remember that he was very clear that the danger to Karolides would not begin till he had got to London, and would come from the very highest quarters, where there would be no thought of suspicion. He mentioned the name of a woman—Julia Czechenyi—

as having something to do with the danger. She would be the decoy, I gathered, to get Karolides out of the care of his guards. He talked, too, about a Black Stone and a man that lisped in his speech, and he described very particularly somebody that he never referred to without a shudder—an old man with a young voice who could hood his eyes like a hawk.

He spoke a good deal about death, too. He was mortally anxious about winning through with his job, but he didn't care a rush for his life.

"I reckon it's like going to sleep when you are pretty well tired out, and waking to find a summer day with the scent of hay coming in at the window. I used to thank God for such mornings way back in the Blue-Grass country, and I guess I'll thank Him when I wake up on the other side of Jordan."

Next day he was much more cheerful, and read the life of Stonewall Jackson much of the time. I went out to dinner with a mining engineer I had got to see on business, and came back about half-past ten in time for our game of chess before turning in.

I had a cigar in my mouth, I remember, as I pushed open the smoking-room door. The lights were not lit, which struck me as odd. I wondered if Scudder had turned in already.

I snapped the switch, but there was nobody there. Then I saw something in the far corner which made me drop my cigar and fall into a cold sweat.

My guest was lying sprawled on his back. There was a long knife through his heart which skewered him to the floor.

CHAPTER II.

THE MILKMAN SETS OUT ON HIS TRAVELS.

I SAT down in an arm-chair and felt very sick. That lasted for maybe five minutes, and was succeeded by a fit of the horrors. The poor staring white face on the floor was more than I could bear, and I managed to get a table-cloth and cover it. Then I staggered to a cupboard, found the brandy and swallowed several mouthfuls. I had seen men die violently before; indeed I had killed a few myself in the Matabele War; but this cold-blooded indoor business was different. Still I managed to pull myself together. I looked at my watch, and saw that it was half-past ten.

An idea seized me, and I went over the flat with a small-tooth comb. There was nobody there, nor any trace of anybody, but I shuttered and bolted all the windows and put the chain on the door.

By this time my wits were coming back to me, and I could think again. It took me about an hour to figure the thing out, and I did not hurry, for, unless the murderer came back, I had till about six o'clock in the morning for my cogitations.

I was in the soup—that was pretty clear. Any shadow of a doubt I might have had about the truth of Scudder's tale was now gone. The proof of it was lying under the table-cloth. The men who knew that he knew what he knew had found him, and had taken the best way to make certain of his silence. Yes; but he had been in my rooms four days, and his enemies must have reckoned that he had confided in me. So I would be the next to go. It might be that very night, or next day, or the day after, but my number was up all right.

Then suddenly I thought of another probability. Supposing I went out now and called in the police, or went to bed and let Paddock find the body and call them in the morning. What kind of a story was I to tell about Scudder? I had lied to Paddock about him, and the whole thing looked desperately fishy. If I made a clean breast of it and told the police everything he had told me, they would simply laugh at me. The odds were a thousand to one that I would be charged with the murder, and the circumstantial evidence was strong enough to hang me. Few people knew me in England; I had no real pal who could come forward and swear to my character. Perhaps that was what those secret enemies were playing for. They were clever enough for anything, and an English prison was as good a way of getting rid of me till after June 15th as a knife in my chest.

Besides, if I told the whole story, and by any miracle was believed, I would be playing their game. Karolides would stay at home, which was what they wanted. Somehow or other the sight of Scudder's dead face had made me a passionate believer in his scheme. He was gone, but he had taken me into his confidence, and I was pretty well bound to carry on his work.

You may think this ridiculous for a man in danger of his life, but that was the way I looked at it. I am an ordinary sort of fellow, not braver than other people, but I hate to see a good man downed, and that long knife would not be the end of Scudder if I could play the game in his place.

It took me an hour or two to think this out, and by that time I had come to a decision. I must vanish somehow, and keep vanished till the end of the second week in June. Then I must somehow find a way to get in touch with the Government people and tell them what Scudder had told me. I wished to heaven he had told me more, and that I had listened more carefully to the little he had told me. I knew nothing but the barest facts. There was a big risk that, even if I weathered the other dangers, I would not be believed in the end. I must take my chance of that, and hope that something might happen which would confirm my tale in the eyes of the Government.

My first job was to keep going for the next three weeks. It was now the 24th day of May, and that meant twenty days of hiding before I could venture to approach the powers that be. I reckoned that two sets of people would be looking for me—Scudder's enemies to put me out of existence, and the police, who would want me for Scudder's murder. It was going to be a giddy hunt, and it was queer how the prospect comforted me. I had been slack so long that almost any chance of activity was welcome. When I had to sit alone with that corpse and wait on Fortune I was no better than a crushed worm, but if my neck's safety was to hang on my own wits I was prepared to be cheerful about it.

My next thought was whether Scudder had any papers about him to give me a better clue to the business. I drew back the table-cloth and searched his pockets, for I had no longer any shrinking from the body. The face was wonderfully calm for a man who had been struck down in a moment. There was nothing in the breast-pocket, and only a few loose coins and a cigar-holder in the waistcoat. The trousers held a little penknife and some silver, and the side-pocket of his jacket contained an old crocodile-skin cigar-case. There was no sign of the little black book in which I had seen him making notes. That had no doubt been taken by his murderer.

But as I looked up from my task I saw that some drawers had been pulled out in the writing-table. Scudder would never have left them in that state, for he was the tidiest of mortals. Someone must have been searching for something —perhaps for the pocket-book.

I went round the flat and found that everything had been ransacked—the inside of books, drawers, cupboards, boxes, even the pockets of the clothes in my wardrobe, and the sideboard in the dining-room. There was no trace of the book. Most likely the enemy had found it, but they had not found it on Scudder's body.

Then I got out an atlas and looked at a big map of the British Isles. My notion was to get off to some wild district, where my veldcraft would be of some use to me, for I would be like a trapped rat in a city. I considered that Scotland would be best, for my people were Scotch and I could pass anywhere as an ordinary Scotsman. I had half an idea at first to be a German tourist, for my father had had German partners, and I had been brought up to speak the tongue pretty fluently, not to mention having put in three years prospecting for copper in German Damaraland. But I calculated that it would be less conspicuous to be a Scot, and less in a line with what the police might know of my past. I fixed on Galloway as the best place to go to. It was the nearest wild part of Scotland, so far as I could figure it out, and from the look of the map was not over thick with population.

A search in Bradshaw informed me that a train left St Pancras at 7.10, which would land me at any Galloway station in the late afternoon. That was well enough, but a more important matter was how I was to make my way to St Pancras, for I was pretty certain that Scudder's friends would be watching outside. This puzzled me for a bit; then I had an inspiration, on which I went to bed and slept for two troubled hours.

I got up at four and opened my bedroom shutters. The faint light of a fine summer morning was flooding the skies, and the sparrows had begun to chatter. I had a great revulsion of feeling, and felt a God-forgotten fool. My inclination was to let things slide, and trust to the British police taking a reasonable view of my case. But as I reviewed the situation I could find no arguments to bring against my decision of the previous night, so with a wry mouth I resolved to go on with my plan. I was not feeling in any particular funk; only disinclined to go looking for trouble, if you understand me.

I hunted out a well-used tweed suit, a pair of strong nailed boots, and a flannel shirt with a collar. Into my pockets I stuffed a spare shirt, a cloth cap, some handkerchiefs, and a tooth-brush. I had drawn a good sum in gold from the bank two days before, in case Scudder should want money, and I took fifty pounds of it in sovereigns in a belt which I had brought back from Rhodesia. That was about all I wanted. Then I had a bath, and cut my moustache, which was long and drooping, into a short stubbly fringe.

Now came the next step. Paddock used to arrive

punctually at 7.30 and let himself in with a latch-key. But about twenty minutes to seven, as I knew from bitter experience, the milkman turned up with a great clatter of cans, and deposited my share outside my door. I had seen that milkman sometimes when I had gone out for an early ride. He was a young man about my own height, with an ill-nourished moustache, and he wore a white overall. On him I staked all my chances.

I went into the darkened smoking-room where the rays of morning light were beginning to creep through the shutters. There I breakfasted off a whisky-and-soda and some biscuits from the cupboard. By this time it was getting on for six o'clock. I put a pipe in my pocket and filled my pouch from the tobacco jar on the table by the fireplace.

As I poked into the tobacco my fingers touched something hard, and I drew out Scudder's little black pocket-book. . . .

That seemed to me a good omen. I lifted the cloth from the body and was amazed at the peace and dignity of the dead face. "Good-bye, old chap," I said; "I am going to do my best for you. Wish me well, wherever you are."

Then I hung about in the hall waiting for the milkman. That was the worst part of the business, for I was fairly choking to get out-of doors. Six-thirty passed, then six-forty, but still he did not come. The fool had chosen this day of all days to be late.

At one minute after the quarter to seven I heard the rattle of the cans outside. I opened the front door, and there was my man, singling out my cans from a bunch he carried and whistling through his teeth. He jumped a bit at the sight of me.

"Come in here a moment," I said. "I want a word with you." And I led him into the dining-room.

"I reckon you're a bit of a sportsman," I said, "and I want you to do me a service. Lend me your cap and overall for ten minutes, and here's a sovereign for you."

His eyes opened at the sight of the gold, and he grinned broadly. " Wot's the gyme ? " he asked.

" A bet," I said. " I haven't time to explain, but to win it I've got to be a milkman for the next ten minutes. All you've got to do is to stay here till I come back. You'll be a bit late, but nobody will complain, and you'll have that quid for yourself."

" Right-O ! " he said cheerily. " I ain't the man to spoil a bit of sport. 'Ere's the rig, guv'nor."

I stuck on his flat blue hat and his white overall, picked up the cans, banged my door, and went whistling downstairs. The porter at the foot told me to shut my jaw, which sounded as if my make-up was adequate.

At first I thought there was nobody in the street. Then I caught sight of a policeman a hundred yards down, and a loafer shuffling past on the other side. Some impulse made me raise my eyes to the house opposite, and there at a first-floor window was a face. As the loafer passed he looked up, and I fancied a signal was exchanged.

I crossed the street, whistling gaily and imitating the jaunty swing of the milkman. Then I took the first side street, and went up a left-hand turning which led past a bit of vacant ground. There was no one in the little street, so I dropped the milk-cans inside the hoarding and sent the hat and overall after them. I had only just put on my cloth cap when a postman came round the corner. I gave him good-morning and he answered me unsuspiciously. At the moment the clock of a neighbouring church struck the hour of seven.

There was not a second to spare. As soon as I got to Euston Road I took to my heels and ran. The clock at Euston Station showed five minutes past the hour. At St Pancras I had no time to take a ticket, let alone that I had not settled upon my destination. A porter told me the platform, and as I entered it I saw the train already in motion. Two station officials blocked the way, but I dodged them and clambered into the last carriage.

Three minutes later, as we were roaring through the northern tunnels, an irate guard interviewed me. He wrote out for me a ticket to Newton-Stewart, a name which had suddenly come back to my memory, and he conducted me from the first-class compartment where I had ensconced myself to a third-class smoker, occupied by a sailor and a stout woman with a child. He went off grumbling, and as I mopped my brow I observed to my companions in my broadest Scots that it was a sore job catching trains. I had already entered upon my part.

"The impidence o' that gyaird!" said the lady bitterly. "He needit a Scotch tongue to pit him in his place. He was complainin' o' this wean no haein' a ticket and her no fower till August twalmonth, and he was objectin' to this gentleman spittin'."

The sailor morosely agreed, and I started my new life in an atmosphere of protest against authority. I reminded myself that a week ago I had been finding the world dull.

CHAPTER III.

THE ADVENTURE OF THE LITERARY INNKEEPER.

I HAD a solemn time travelling north that day. It was fine May weather, with the hawthorn flowering on every hedge, and I asked myself why, when I was still a free man, I had stayed on in London and not got the good of this heavenly country. I didn't dare face the restaurant car, but I got a luncheon-basket at Leeds and shared it with the fat woman. Also I got the morning's papers, with news about starters for the Derby and the beginning of the cricket season, and some paragraphs about how Balkan affairs were settling down and a British squadron was going to Kiel.

When I had done with them I got out Scudder's little black pocket-book and studied it. It was pretty well filled with jottings, chiefly figures, though now and then a name was printed in. For example, I found the words "Hofgaard," "Luneville," and "Avocado" pretty often, and especially the word "Pavia."

Now I was certain that Scudder never did anything without a reason, and I was pretty sure that there was a cypher in all this. That is a subject which has always interested me, and I did a bit at it myself once as intelligence-officer at Delagoa Bay during the Boer War. I have a head for things like chess and puzzles, and I used to reckon myself pretty good at finding out cyphers. This one looked like the numerical kind where sets of figures correspond to the letters of the alphabet, but any fairly shrewd man can find the clue to that sort after an hour or two's work, and I didn't think Scudder would have been content with anything so easy. So I fastened on the printed words, for you can make a pretty good numerical cypher if you have a key word which gives you the sequence of the letters.

I tried for hours, but none of the words answered. Then I fell asleep and woke at Dumfries just in time to bundle out and get into the slow Galloway train. There was a man on the platform whose looks I didn't like, but he never glanced at me, and when I caught sight of myself in the mirror of an automatic machine I didn't wonder. With my brown face, my old tweeds, and my slouch, I was the very model of one of the hill farmers who were crowding into the third-class carriages.

I travelled with half a dozen in an atmosphere of shag and clay pipes. They had come from the weekly market, and their mouths were full of prices. I heard accounts of how the lambing had gone up the Cairn and the Deuch and a dozen other mysterious waters. Above half the men had lunched heavily and were highly flavoured with whisky, but they took no notice of me. We rumbled slowly into a land of little wooded glens and then to a great wide moorland place, gleaming with lochs, with high blue hills showing northwards.

About five o'clock the carriage had emptied, and I was left alone as I had hoped. I got out at the next station, a little place whose name I scarcely noted, set right in the heart of a bog. It reminded me of one of those forgotten little stations in the Karroo. An old station-master was digging in his garden, and with his spade over his shoulder sauntered to the train, took charge of a parcel, and went back to his potatoes. A child of ten received my ticket, and I emerged on a white road that straggled over the brown moor.

It was a gorgeous spring evening, with every hill showing as clear as a cut amethyst. The air had the queer, rooty smell of bogs, but it was as fresh as mid-ocean, and it had the strangest effect on my spirits. I actually felt light-hearted. I might have been a boy out for a spring holiday tramp, instead of a man of thirty-seven very much wanted by the police. I felt just as I used to feel when I was starting for a big trek on a frosty morning on the high veld. If you believe me, I swung along that road whistling. There was no plan of campaign in my head, only just to go on and on in this blessed, honest-smelling hill country, for every mile put me in better humour with myself.

In a roadside planting I cut a walking-stick of hazel, and presently struck off the highway up a bypath which followed the glen of a brawling stream. I reckoned that I was still far ahead of any pursuit, and for that night might please myself. It was some hours since I had tasted food, and I was getting very hungry when I came to a herd's cottage set in a nook beside a waterfall. A brown-faced woman was standing by the door, and greeted me with the kindly shyness of moorland places. When I asked for a night's lodging she said I was welcome to the "bed in the loft," and very soon she set before me a hearty meal of ham and eggs, scones, and thick sweet milk.

At the darkening her man came in from the hills, a lean giant, who in one step covered as much ground as three paces of ordinary mortals. They asked no questions, for they had the perfect breeding of all dwellers in the wilds, but I could see they set me down as a kind of dealer, and I took some trouble to confirm their view. I spoke a lot about cattle, of which my host knew little, and I picked up from him a good deal about the local Galloway markets, which I tucked away in my memory for future use. At ten I was nodding in my chair, and the "bed in the loft" received a weary man who never opened his eyes till five o'clock set the little homestead agoing once more.

They refused any payment, and by six I had breakfasted and was striding southwards again. My notion was to return to the railway line a station or two farther on than the place where I had alighted yesterday and to double back. I reckoned that that was the safest way, for the police would naturally assume that I was always making farther from London in the direction of some western port. I thought I had still a good bit of a start, for, as I reasoned, it would take some hours to fix the blame on me, and several more to identify the fellow who got on board the train at St Pancras.

It was the same jolly, clear spring weather, and I simply could not contrive to feel careworn. Indeed I was in better spirits than I had been for months. Over a long ridge of moorland I took my road, skirting the side of a high hill which the herd had called Cairnsmore of Fleet. Nesting curlews and plovers were crying everywhere, and the links of green pasture by the streams were dotted with young lambs. All the slackness of the past months was slipping from my bones, and I stepped out like a four-year-old. By-and-by I came to a swell of moorland which dipped to the vale of a little river, and a mile away in the heather I saw the smoke of a train.

The station, when I reached it, proved to be ideal for my purpose. The moor surged up around it and left room only for the single line, the slender siding, a waiting-room, an office, the station-master's cottage, and a tiny yard of gooseberries and sweet-william. There seemed no road to it from anywhere, and to increase the desolation the waves of a tarn lapped on their grey granite beach half a mile away. I waited in the deep heather till I saw the smoke of an east-going train on the horizon. Then I approached the tiny booking-office and took a ticket for Dumfries.

The only occupants of the carriage were an old shepherd and his dog—a wall-eyed brute that I mistrusted. The man was asleep, and on the cushions beside him was that morning's 'Scotsman.' Eagerly I seized on it, for I fancied it would tell me something.

There were two columns about the Portland Place Murder, as it was called. My man Paddock had given the alarm and had the milkman arrested. Poor devil, it looked as if the latter had earned his sovereign hardly; but for me he had been cheap at the price, for he seemed to have occupied the police the better part of the day. In the latest news I found a further instalment of the story. The milkman had been released, I read, and the true criminal, about whose identity the police were reticent, was believed to have got away from London by one of the northern lines. There was a short note about me as the owner of the flat. I guessed the police had stuck that in, as a clumsy contrivance to persuade me that I was unsuspected.

There was nothing else in the paper, nothing about foreign politics or Karolides, or the things that had interested Scudder. I laid it down, and found that we were approaching the station at which I had got out yesterday. The potato-digging station-master had been gingered up into some activity, for the west-going train was waiting to let us pass, and from it had descended three men who were asking him questions. I supposed that they were the local police, who had been stirred up by Scotland Yard, and had traced me as far as this one-horse siding. Sitting well back in the shadow I watched them carefully. One of them had a book, and took down notes. The old potato-digger seemed to have turned peevish, but the child who had collected my ticket was talking volubly. All the party looked out across the moor where the white road departed. I hoped they were going to take up my tracks there.

As we moved away from that station my companion woke up. He fixed me with a wandering glance, kicked his dog viciously, and inquired where he was. Clearly he was very drunk.

"That's what comes o' bein' a teetotaller," he observed in bitter regret.

I expressed my surprise that in him I should have met a blue-ribbon stalwart.

"Ay, but I'm a strong teetotaller," he said pugnaciously. "I took the pledge last Martinmas, and I havena touched a drop o' whisky sinsyne. No even at Hogmanay, though I was sair temptit."

He swung his heels up on the seat, and burrowed a frowsy head into the cushions.

"And that's a' I get," he moaned. "A heid hetter than hell fire, and twae een lookin' different ways for the Sabbath."

"What did it?" I asked.

"A drink they ca' brandy. Bein' a teetotaller I keepit off the whisky, but I was nip-nippin' a' day at this brandy, and I doubt I'll no be weel for a fortnicht." His voice died away into a stutter, and sleep once more laid its heavy hand on him.

My plan had been to get out at some station down the line, but the train suddenly gave me a better chance, for it came to a standstill at the end of a culvert which spanned a brawling porter-coloured river. I looked out and saw that every carriage window was closed and no human figure appeared in the landscape. So I opened the door, and dropped quickly into the tangle of hazels which edged the line.

It would have been all right but for that infernal dog. Under the impression that I was decamping with its master's belongings, it started to bark, and all but got me by the trousers. This woke up the herd, who stood bawling at the carriage door in the belief that I had committed suicide. I crawled through the thicket, reached the edge of the stream, and in cover of the bushes put a hundred yards or so behind me. Then from my shelter I peered back, and saw the guard and several passengers gathered round the open carriage door and staring in my direction. I could not have made a more public departure if I had left with a bugler and a brass band.

Happily the drunken herd provided a diversion. He and his dog, which was attached by a rope to his waist, suddenly cascaded out of the carriage, landed on their heads on the track, and rolled some way down the bank towards the water. In the rescue which followed the dog bit somebody, for I could hear the sound of hard swearing. Presently they had forgotten me, and when after a quarter of a mile's crawl I ventured to look back, the train had started again and was vanishing in the cutting.

I was in a wide semicircle of moorland, with the brown river as radius, and the high hills forming the northern circumference. There was not a sign or sound of a human being, only the plashing water and the interminable crying of curlews. Yet, oddly enough, for the first time I felt the terror of the hunted on me. It was not the police that I thought of, but the other folk, who knew that I knew Scudder's secret and dared not let me live. I was certain that they would pursue me with a keenness and vigilance unknown to the British law, and that once their grip closed on me I should find no mercy.

I looked back, but there was nothing in the landscape. The sun glinted on the metals of the line and the wet stones in the stream, and you could not have found a more peaceful sight in the world. Nevertheless I started to run. Crouching low in the runnels of the bog, I ran till the sweat blinded my eyes. The mood did not leave me till I had reached the rim of mountain and flung myself panting on a ridge high above the young waters of the brown river.

From my vantage-ground I could scan the whole moor right away to the railway line and to the south of it where green fields took the place of heather. I have eyes like a hawk, but I could see nothing moving in the whole countryside. Then I looked east beyond the ridge and saw a new kind of landscape—shallow green valleys with plentiful fir plantations and the faint lines of dust which spoke of highroads. Last of all I looked into the blue May sky, and there I saw that which set my pulses racing. . . .

Low down in the south a monoplane was climbing into the heavens. I was as certain as if I had been told that that aeroplane was looking for me, and that it did not belong to the police. For an hour or two I watched it from a pit of heather. It flew low along the hill-tops, and then in narrow circles over the valley up which I had come. Then it seemed to change its mind, rose to a great height, and flew away back to the south.

I did not like this espionage from the air, and I began to think less well of the countryside I had chosen for a refuge. These heather hills were no sort of cover if my enemies were in the sky, and I must find a different kind of sanctuary. I looked with more satisfaction to the green country beyond the ridge, for there I should find woods and stone houses.

About six in the evening I came out of the moorland to a white ribbon of road which wound up the narrow vale of a lowland stream. As I followed it, fields gave place to bent, the glen became a plateau, and presently I had reached a kind of pass where a solitary house smoked in the twilight. The road swung over a bridge, and leaning on the parapet was a young man.

He was smoking a long clay pipe and studying the water with spectacled eyes. In his left hand was a small book with a finger marking the place. Slowly he repeated—

> "As when a Gryphon through the wilderness
> With wingéd step, o'er hill and moory dale
> Pursues the Arimaspian."

He jumped round as my step rung on the keystone, and I saw a pleasant sunburnt boyish face.

"Good evening to you," he said gravely. "It's a fine night for the road."

The smell of peat smoke and of some savoury roast floated to me from the house.

"Is that place an inn?" I asked.

"At your service," he said politely. "I am the landlord, sir, and I hope you will stay the night, for to tell you the truth I have had no company for a week."

I pulled myself up on the parapet of the bridge and filled my pipe. I began to detect an ally.

"You're young to be an innkeeper," I said.

"My father died a year ago and left me the business. I live there with my grandmother. It's a slow job for a young man, and it wasn't my choice of profession."

"Which was?"

He actually blushed. "I want to write books," he said.

"And what better chance could you ask?" I cried. "Man, I've often thought that an innkeeper would make the best story-teller in the world."

"Not now," he said eagerly. "Maybe in the old days when you had pilgrims and ballad-makers and highwaymen and mail-coaches on the road. But not now. Nothing comes here but motor-cars full of fat women, who stop for lunch, and a fisherman or two in the spring, and the shooting tenants in August. There is not much material to be got out of that. I want to see life, to travel the world, and write things like Kipling and Conrad. But the most I've done yet is to get some verses printed in 'Chambers's Journal.'"

I looked at the inn standing golden in the sunset against the brown hills.

"I've knocked a bit about the world, and I wouldn't despise such a hermitage. D'you think that adventure is found only in the tropics or among gentry in red shirts? Maybe you're rubbing shoulders with it at this moment."

"That's what Kipling says," he said, his eyes brightening, and he quoted some verse about "Romance bringing up the 9.15."

"Here's a true tale for you then," I cried, "and a month from now you can make a novel out of it."

Sitting on the bridge in the soft May gloaming I pitched him a lovely yarn. It was true in essentials, too, though I altered the minor details. I made out that I was a mining magnate from Kimberley, who had had a lot of trouble with I.D.B. and had shown up a gang. They had pursued me across the ocean, and had killed my best friend, and were now on my tracks.

I told the story well, though I say it who shouldn't. I pictured a flight across the Kalahari to German Africa, the crackling, parching days, the wonderful blue-velvet nights. I described an attack on my life on the voyage home, and I made a really horrid affair of the Portland Place murder. "You're looking for adventure," I cried; "well, you've found it here. The devils are after me, and the police are after them. It's a race that I mean to win."

"By God!" he whispered, drawing his breath in sharply, "it is all pure Rider Haggard and Conan Doyle."

"You believe me," I said gratefully.

"Of course I do," and he held out his hand. "I believe everything out of the common. The only thing to distrust is the normal."

He was very young, but he was the man for my money.

"I think they're off my track for the moment, but I must lie close for a couple of days. Can you take me in?"

He caught my elbow in his eagerness and drew me towards the house. "You can lie as snug here as if you were in a moss-hole. I'll see that nobody blabs, either. And you'll give me some more material about your adventures?"

As I entered the inn porch I heard from far off the beat of an engine. There silhouetted against the dusky West was my friend, the monoplane.

He gave me a room at the back of the house, with a fine outlook over the plateau, and he made me free of his own study, which was stacked with cheap editions of his favourite authors. I never saw the grandmother, so I guessed she was bedridden. An old woman called Margit brought me my meals, and the innkeeper was around me at all hours. I wanted some time to myself, so I invented a job for him. He had a motor-bicycle, and I sent him off next morning for the daily paper, which usually arrived with the post in the later afternoon. I told him to keep his eyes skinned, and make note of any strange figures he saw, keeping a special sharp look-out for motors and aeroplanes. Then I sat down in real earnest to Scudder's note-book.

He came back at mid-day with the 'Scotsman.' There was nothing in it, except some further evidence of Paddock and the milkman, and a repetition of yesterday's statement that the murderer had gone North. But there was a long article, reprinted from 'The Times,' about Karolides and the state of affairs in the Balkans, though there was no mention of any visit to England. I got rid of the innkeeper for the afternoon, for I was getting very warm in my search for the cypher.

As I told you, it was a numerical cypher, and by an elaborate system of experiments I had pretty well discovered what were the nulls and stops. The trouble was the key word, and when I thought of the odd million words he might have used I felt pretty hopeless. But about three o'clock I had a sudden inspiration.

The name Julia Czechenyi flashed across my memory. Scudder had said it was the key to the Karolides business, and it occurred to me to try it on his cypher.

It worked. The five letters of "Julia" gave me the position of the vowels. A was J, the tenth letter of the alphabet, and so represented by X in the cypher. E was U = XXI, and so on. "Czechenyi" gave me the numerals for the principal consonants. I scribbled that scheme on a bit of paper and sat down to read Scudder's pages.

In half an hour I was reading with a whitish face and fingers that drummed on the table.

I glanced out of the window and saw a big touring-car coming up the glen towards the inn. It drew up at the door, and there was the sound of people alighting. There seemed to be two of them, men in aquascutums and tweed caps.

Ten minutes later the innkeeper slipped into the room, his eyes bright with excitement.

" There's two chaps below looking for you," he whispered. " They're in the dining-room having whiskys and sodas. They asked about you and said they had hoped to meet you here. Oh! and they described you jolly well, down to your boots and shirt. I told them you had been here last night and had gone off on a motor-bicycle this morning, and one of the chaps swore like a navvy."

I made him tell me what they looked like. One was a dark-eyed thin fellow with bushy eyebrows, the other was always smiling and lisped in his talk. Neither was any kind of foreigner; on this my young friend was positive.

I took a bit of paper and wrote these words in German as if they were part of a letter:—

. . . " Black Stone. Scudder had got on to this, but he could not act for a fortnight. I doubt if I can do any good now, especially as Karolides is uncertain about his plans. But if Mr T. advises I will do the best I . . ."

I manufactured it rather neatly, so that it looked like a loose page of a private letter.

" Take this down and say it was found in my bedroom, and ask them to return it to me if they overtake me."

Three minutes later I heard the car begin to move, and peeping from behind the curtain caught sight of the two figures. One was slim, the other was sleek; that was the most I could make of my reconnaissance.

The innkeeper appeared in great excitement. "Your paper woke them up," he said gleefully. "The dark fellow went as white as death and cursed like blazes, and the fat one whistled and looked ugly. They paid for their drinks with half-a-sovereign and wouldn't wait for change."

"Now I'll tell you what I want you to do," I said. "Get on your bicycle and go off to Newton-Stewart to the Chief Constable. Describe the two men, and say you suspect them of having had something to do with the London murder. You can invent reasons. The two will come back, never fear. Not to-night, for they'll follow me forty miles along the road, but first thing to-morrow morning. Tell the police to be here bright and early."

He set off like a docile child, while I worked at Scudder's notes. When he came back we dined together, and in common decency I had to let him pump me. I gave him a lot of stuff about lion hunts and the Matabele War, thinking all the while what tame businesses these were compared to this I was now engaged in. When he went to bed I sat up and finished Scudder. I smoked in a chair till daylight, for I could not sleep.

About eight next morning I witnessed the arrival of two constables and a sergeant. They put their car in a coach-house under the innkeeper's instructions, and entered the house. Twenty minutes later I saw from my window a second car come across the plateau from the opposite direction. It did not come up to the inn, but stopped two hundred yards off in the shelter of a patch of wood. I noticed that its occupants carefully reversed it before leaving it. A minute or two later I heard their steps on the gravel outside the window.

My plan had been to lie hid in my bedroom, and see what happened. I had a notion that, if I could bring the police and my other more dangerous pursuers together, something might work out of it to my advantage. But now I had a better idea. I scribbled a line of thanks to my host, opened the window, and dropped quietly into a gooseberry bush. Unobserved I crossed the dyke, crawled down the side of a tributary burn, and won the highroad on the far side of the patch of trees. There stood the car, very spick and span in the morning sunlight, but with the dust on her which told of a long journey. I started her, jumped into the chauffeur's seat, and stole gently out on to the plateau.

Almost at once the road dipped so that I lost sight of the inn, but the wind seemed to bring me the sound of angry voices.

CHAPTER IV.

THE ADVENTURE OF THE RADICAL CANDIDATE.

You may picture me driving that 40 h.p. car for all she was worth over the crisp moor roads on that shining May morning; glancing back at first over my shoulder, and looking anxiously to the next turning; then driving with a vague eye, just wide enough awake to keep on the highway. For I was thinking desperately of what I had found in Scudder's pocket-book.

The little man had told me a pack of lies. All his yarns about the Balkans and the Jew-Anarchists and the Foreign Office Conference were eyewash, and so was Karolides. And yet not quite, as you shall hear. I had staked everything on my belief in his story, and had been let down; here was his book telling me a different tale, and instead of being once-bit-twice-shy, I believed it absolutely.

Why, I don't know. It rang desperately true, and the first yarn, if you understand me, had been in a queer way true also in spirit. The fifteenth day of June was going to be a day of destiny, a bigger destiny than the killing of a Dago. It was so big that I didn't blame Scudder for keeping me out of the game and wanting to play a lone hand. That, I was pretty clear, was his intention. He had told me something which sounded big enough, but the real thing was so immortally big that he, the man who had found it out, wanted it all for himself. I didn't blame him. It was risks after all that he was chiefly greedy about.

The whole story was in the notes—with gaps, you understand, which he would have filled up from his memory. He stuck down his authorities, too, and had an odd trick of giving them all a numerical value and then striking a balance, which stood for the reliability of each stage in the yarn. The four names he had printed were authorities, and there was a man, Ducrosne, who got five out of a possible five; and another fellow, Ammersfoort, who got three. The bare bones of the tale were all that was in the book—these, and one queer phrase which occurred half a dozen times inside brackets. ("Thirty-nine steps") was the phrase; and at its last time of use it ran—("Thirty-nine steps, I counted them—high tide 10.17 P.M."). I could make nothing of that.

The first thing I learned was that it was no question of preventing a war. That was coming, as sure as Christmas: had been arranged, said Scudder, ever since February 1912. Karolides was going to be the occasion. He was booked all right, and was to hand in his checks on June 14th, two weeks and four days from that May morning. I gathered from Scudder's notes that nothing on earth could prevent that. His talk of Epirote guards that would skin their own grandmothers was all billy-O.

The second thing was that this war was going to come as a mighty surprise to Britain. Karolides' death would set the Balkans by the ears, and then Vienna would chip in with an ultimatum. Russia wouldn't like that, and there would be high words. But Berlin would play the peacemaker, and pour oil on the waters, till suddenly she would find a good cause for a quarrel, pick it up, and in five hours let fly at us. That was the idea, and a pretty good one too. Honey and fair speeches, and then a stroke in the dark. While we were talking about the goodwill and good intentions of Germany our coast would be silently ringed with mines, and submarines would be waiting for every battleship.

But all this depended upon the third thing, which was due to happen on June 15th. I would never have grasped this if I hadn't once happened to meet a French staff officer, coming back from West Africa, who had told me a lot of things. One was that, in spite of all the nonsense talked in Parliament, there was a real working alliance between France and Britain, and that the two General Staffs met every now and then, and made plans for joint action in case of war. Well, in June a very great swell was coming over from Paris, and he was going to get nothing less than a statement of the disposition of the British Home Fleet on mobilisation. At least I gathered it was something like that; anyhow, it was something uncommonly important.

But on the 15th day of June there were to be others in London—others, at whom I could only guess. Scudder was content to call them collectively the "Black Stone." They represented not our Allies, but our deadly foes; and the information, destined for France, was to be diverted to their pockets. And it was to be used, remember—used a week or two later, with great guns and swift torpedoes, suddenly in the darkness of a summer night.

This was the story I had been deciphering in a back room of a country inn, overlooking a cabbage garden. This was the story that hummed in my brain as I swung in the big touring-car from glen to glen.

My first impulse had been to write a letter to the Prime Minister, but a little reflection convinced me that that would be useless. Who would believe my tale? I must show a sign, some token in proof, and Heaven knew what that could be. Above all, I must keep going myself, ready to act when things got riper, and that was going to be no light job with the police of the British Isles in full cry after me and the watchers of the Black Stone running silently and swiftly on my trail.

I had no very clear purpose in my journey, but I steered east by the sun, for I remembered from the map that if I went north I would come into a region of coalpits and industrial towns. Presently I was down from the moorlands and traversing the broad haugh of a river. For miles I ran alongside a park wall, and in a break of the trees I saw a great castle. I swung through little old thatched villages, and over peaceful lowland streams, and past gardens blazing with hawthorn and yellow laburnum. The land was so deep in peace that I could scarcely believe that somewhere behind me were those who sought my life ; ay, and that in a month's time, unless I had the almightiest of luck, these round country faces would be pinched and staring, and men would be lying dead in English fields.

About mid-day I entered a long straggling village, and had a mind to stop and eat. Half-way down was the Post Office, and on the steps of it stood the postmistress and a policeman hard at work conning a telegram. When they saw me they wakened up, and the policeman advanced with raised hand, and cried on me to stop.

I nearly was fool enough to obey. Then it flashed upon me that the wire had to do with me ; that my friends at the inn had come to an understanding, and were united in desiring to see more of me, and that it had been easy enough for them to wire the description of me and the car to thirty villages through which I might pass. I released the brakes just in time. As it was, the policeman made a claw at the hood, and only dropped off when he got my left in his eye.

I saw that main roads were no place for me, and turned into the byways. It wasn't an easy job without a map, for there was the risk of getting on to a farm road and ending in a duck-pond or a stable-yard, and I couldn't afford that kind of delay. I began to see what an ass I had been to steal the car. The big green brute would be the safest kind of clue to me over the breadth of Scotland. If I left it and took to my feet, it would be discovered in an hour or two and I would get no start in the race.

The immediate thing to do was to get to the loneliest roads. These I soon found when I struck up a tributary of the big river, and got into a glen with steep hills all about me, and a corkscrew road at the end which climbed over a pass. Here I met nobody, but it was taking me too far north, so I slewed east along a bad track and finally struck a big double-line railway. Away below me I saw another broadish valley, and it occurred to me that if I crossed it I might find some remote inn to pass the night. The evening was now drawing in, and I was furiously hungry, for I had eaten nothing since breakfast except a couple of buns I had bought from a baker's cart.

Just then I heard a noise in the sky, and lo and behold there was that infernal aeroplane, flying low, about a dozen miles to the south and rapidly coming towards me.

I had the sense to remember that on a bare moor I was at the aeroplane's mercy, and that my only chance was to get to the leafy cover of the valley. Down the hill I went like blue lightning, screwing my head round, whenever I dared, to watch that damned flying machine. Soon I was on a road between hedges, and dipping to the deep-cut glen of a stream. Then came a bit of thick wood where I slackened speed.

Suddenly on my left I heard the hoot of another car, and realised to my horror that I was almost up on a couple of gate-posts through which a private road debouched on the highway. My horn gave an agonised roar, but it was too late. I clapped on my brakes, but my impetus was too great, and there before me a car was sliding athwart my course. In a second there would have been the deuce of a wreck. I did the only thing possible, and ran slap into the hedge on the right, trusting to find something soft beyond.

But there I was mistaken. My car slithered through the hedge like butter, and then gave a sickening plunge forward.

I saw what was coming, leapt on the seat and would have jumped out. But a branch of hawthorn got me in the chest, lifted me up and held me, while a ton or two of expensive metal slipped below me, bucked and pitched, and then dropped with an almighty smash fifty feet to the bed of the stream.

Slowly that thorn let me go. I subsided first on the hedge, and then very gently on a bower of nettles. As I scrambled to my feet a hand took me by the arm, and a sympathetic and badly scared voice asked me if I were hurt.

I found myself looking at a tall young man in goggles and a leather ulster, who kept on blessing his soul and whinnying apologies. For myself, once I got my wind back, I was rather glad than otherwise. This was one way of getting rid of the car.

"My blame, sir," I answered him. "It's lucky that I did not add homicide to my follies. That's the end of my Scotch motor tour, but it might have been the end of my life."

He plucked out a watch and studied it. "You're the right sort of fellow," he said. "I can spare a quarter of an hour, and my house is two minutes off. I'll see you clothed and fed and snug in bed. Where's your kit, by the way? Is it in the burn along with the car?"

"It's in my pocket," I said, brandishing a tooth-brush. "I'm a colonial and travel light."

"A colonial," he cried. "By Gad, you're the very man I've been praying for. Are you by any blessed chance a Free Trader?"

"I am," said I, without the foggiest notion of what he meant.

He patted my shoulder and hurried me into his car. Three minutes later we drew up before a comfortable-looking shooting-box set among pine-trees, and he ushered me indoors. He took me first to a bedroom and flung half a dozen of his suits before me, for my own had been pretty well reduced to rags. I selected a loose blue serge, which differed most conspicuously from my former garments, and borrowed a linen collar. Then he haled me to the dining-room, where the remnants of a meal stood on the table, and announced that I had just five minutes to feed. "You can take a snack in your pocket, and we'll have supper when we get back. I've got to be at the Masonic Hall at eight o'clock, or my agent will comb my hair."

I had a cup of coffee and some cold ham, while he yarned away on the hearth-rug.

"You find me in the deuce of a mess, Mr ——; by-the-by, you haven't told me your name. Twisdon? Any relation of old Tommy Twisdon of the Sixtieth? No? Well, you see I'm Liberal Candidate for this part of the world, and I had a meeting on to-night at Brattleburn—that's my chief town, and an infernal Tory stronghold. I had got the Colonial ex-Premier fellow, Crumpleton, coming to speak for me to-night, and had the thing tremendously billed and the whole place ground-baited. This afternoon I had a wire from the ruffian saying he had got influenza at Blackpool, and here am I left to do the whole thing myself. I had meant to speak for ten minutes and must now go on for forty, and, though I've been racking my brains for three hours to think of something, I simply cannot last the course. Now you've got to be a good chap and help me. You're a Free Trader and can tell our people what a wash-out Protection is in the Colonies. All you fellows have the gift of the gab—I wish to heaven I had it. I'll be for evermore in your debt."

I had very few notions about Free Trade one way or the other, but I saw no other chance to get what I wanted. My young gentleman was far too absorbed in his own difficulties to think how odd it was to ask a stranger who had just missed death by an ace and had lost a 1000-guinea car to address a meeting for him on the spur of the moment. But my necessities did not allow me to contemplate oddnesses or to pick and choose my supports.

"All right," I said. "I'm not much good as a speaker, but I'll tell them a bit about Australia."

At my words the cares of the ages slipped from his shoulders, and he was rapturous in his thanks. He lent me a big driving coat—and never troubled to ask why I had started on a motor tour without possessing an ulster—and, as we slipped down the dusty roads, poured into my ears the simple facts of his history. He was an orphan, and his uncle had brought him up—I've forgotten the uncle's name, but he was in the Cabinet, and you can read his speeches in the papers. He had gone round the world after leaving Cambridge, and then, being short of a job, his uncle had advised politics. I gathered that he had no preference in parties. "Good chaps in both," he said cheerfully, "and plenty of blighters, too. I'm Liberal, because my family have always been Whigs." But if he was lukewarm politically he had strong views on other things. He found out I knew a bit about horses, and jawed away about the Derby entries; and he was full of plans for improving his shooting. Altogether, a very clean, decent, callow young man.

As we passed through a little town two policemen signalled us to stop, and flashed their lanterns on us. "Beg pardon, Sir Harry," said one. "We've got instructions to look out for a cawr, and the description's no unlike yours."

"Right-O," said my host, while I thanked Providence for the devious ways I had been brought to safety. After that he spoke no more, for his mind began to labour heavily with his coming speech. His lips kept muttering, his eye wandered, and I began to prepare myself for a second catastrophe. I tried to think of something to say myself, but my mind was dry as a stone. The next thing I knew we had drawn up outside a door in a street, and were being welcomed by some noisy gentlemen with rosettes.

The hall had about five hundred in it, women mostly, a

lot of bald heads, and a dozen or two young men. The chairman, a weaselly minister with a reddish nose, lamented Crumpleton's absence, soliloquised on his influenza, and gave me a certificate as a "trusted leader of Australian thought." There were two policemen at the door, and I hoped they took note of that testimonial. Then Sir Harry started.

I never heard anything like it. He didn't begin to know how to talk. He had about a bushel of notes from which he read, and when he let go of them he fell into one prolonged stutter. Every now and then he remembered a phrase he had learned by heart, straightened his back, and gave it off like Henry Irving, and the next moment he was bent double and crooning over his papers. It was the most appalling rot, too. He talked about the "German menace," and said it was all a Tory invention to cheat the poor of their rights and keep back the great flood of social reform, but that "organised labour" realised this and laughed the Tories to scorn. He was all for reducing our Navy as a proof of our good faith, and then sending Germany an ultimatum telling her to do the same or we would knock her into a cocked hat. He said that, but for the Tories, Germany and Britain would be fellow-workers in peace and reform. I thought of the little black book in my pocket! A giddy lot Scudder's friends cared for peace and reform.

Yet in a queer way I liked the speech. You could see the niceness of the chap shining out behind the muck with which he had been spoon-fed. Also it took a load off my mind. I mightn't be much of an orator, but I was a thousand per cent better than Sir Harry.

I didn't get on so badly when it came to my turn. I simply told them all I could remember about Australia, praying there should be no Australian there—all about its labour party and emigration and universal service. I doubt if I remembered to mention Free Trade, but I said there were no Tories in Australia, only Labour and Liberals. That fetched a cheer, and I woke them up a bit when I started in to tell them the kind of glorious business I thought could be made out of the Empire if we really put our backs into it.

Altogether I fancy I was rather a success. The minister didn't like me, though, and when he proposed a vote of thanks, spoke of Sir Harry's speech as "statesmanlike" and mine as having "the eloquence of an emigration agent."

When we were in the car again my host was in wild spirits at having got his job over. "A ripping speech, Twisdon," he said. "Now, you're coming home with me. I'm all alone, and if you'll stop a day or two I'll show you some very decent fishing."

We had a hot supper—and I wanted it pretty badly—and then drank grog in a big cheery smoking-room with a crackling wood fire. I thought the time had come for me to put my cards on the table. I saw by this man's eye that he was the kind you can trust.

"Listen, Sir Harry," I said. "I've something pretty important to say to you. You're a good fellow, and I'm going to be frank. Where on earth did you get that poisonous rubbish you talked to-night?"

His face fell. "Was it as bad as that?" he asked ruefully. "It did sound rather thin. I got most of it out of the 'Progressive Magazine' and pamphlets that agent chap of mine keeps sending me. But you surely don't think Germany would ever go to war with us?"

"Ask that question in six weeks and it won't need an answer," I said. "If you'll give me your attention for half an hour I am going to tell you a story."

I can see yet that bright room with the deers' heads and the old prints on the walls, Sir Harry standing restlessly on the stone curb of the hearth, and myself lying back in an arm-chair, speaking. I seemed to be another person, standing aside and listening to my own voice, and judging carefully the reliability of my tale. It was the first time I had ever told anyone the exact truth, so far as I understood it, and it did me no end of good, for it straightened out the thing in my own mind. I blinked no detail. He heard all about Scudder, and the milkman, and the note-book, and my doings in Galloway. Presently he got very excited and walked up and down the hearth-rug.

"So you see," I concluded, "you have got here in your house the man that is wanted for the Portland Place murder. Your duty is to send your car for the police and give me up. I don't think I'll get very far. There'll be an accident, and I'll have a knife in my ribs an hour or so after arrest. Nevertheless it's your duty, as a law-abiding citizen. Perhaps in a month's time you'll be sorry, but you have no cause to think of that."

He was looking at me with bright steady eyes. "What was your job in Rhodesia, Mr Hannay?" he asked.

"Mining engineer," I said. "I've made my pile cleanly and I've had a good time in the making of it."

"Not a profession that weakens the nerves, is it?"

I laughed. "Oh, as to that, my nerves are good enough." I took down a hunting-knife from a stand on the wall, and did the old Mashona trick of tossing it and catching it in my lips. That wants a pretty steady heart.

He watched me with a smile. "I don't want proofs. I may be an ass on the platform, but I can size up a man. You're no murderer and you're no fool, and I believe you are speaking the truth. I'm going to back you up. Now, what can I do?"

"First, I want you to write a letter to your uncle. I've got to get in touch with the Government people sometime before the 15th of June."

He pulled his moustache. "That won't help you. This is Foreign Office business, and my uncle would have nothing to do with it. Besides, you'd never convince him. No, I'll go one better. I'll write to the Permanent Secretary at the Foreign Office. He's my godfather, and one of the best going. What do you want?"

He sat down at a table and wrote to my dictation. The gist of it was that if a man called Twisdon (I thought I had better stick to that name) turned up before June 15th he was to entreat him kindly. He said Twisdon would prove his *bona fides* by passing the word "Black Stone" and whistling "Annie Laurie."

"Good," said Sir Harry. "That's the proper style. By the way, you'll find my godfather—his name's Sir Walter Bullivant—down at his country cottage for Whitsuntide. It's close to Artinswell on the Kennet. That's done. Now, what's the next thing?"

"You're about my height. Lend me the oldest tweed suit you've got. Anything will do, so long as the colour is the opposite of the clothes I destroyed this afternoon. Then show me a map of the neighbourhood and explain to me the lie of the land. Lastly, if the police come seeking me, just show them the car in the glen. If the other lot turn up, tell them I caught the south express after your meeting."

He did, or promised to do, all these things. I shaved off the remnants of my moustache, and got inside an ancient suit of what I believe is called heather mixture. The map gave me some notion of my whereabouts, and told me the two things I wanted to know—where the main railway to the south could be joined and what were the wildest districts near at hand.

At two o'clock he wakened me from my slumbers in the smoking-room arm-chair, and led me blinking into the dark starry night. An old bicycle was found in a tool-shed and handed over to me.

"First turn to the right up by the long fir-wood," he enjoined. "By daybreak you'll be well into the hills. Then I should pitch the machine into a bog and take to the moors on foot. You can put in a week among the shepherds, and be as safe as if you were in New Guinea."

I pedalled diligently up steep roads of hill gravel till the skies grew pale with morning. As the mists cleared before the sun, I found myself in a wide green world with glens falling on every side and a far-away blue horizon. Here, at any rate, I could get early news of my enemies.

CHAPTER V.

THE ADVENTURE OF THE SPECTACLED ROADMAN.

I SAT down on the very crest of the pass and took stock of my position.

Behind me was the road climbing through a long cleft in the hills, which was the upper glen of some notable river. In front was a flat space of maybe a mile, all pitted with bog-holes and rough with tussocks, and then beyond it the road fell steeply down another glen to a plain whose blue dimness melted into the distance. To left and right were round-shouldered green hills as smooth as pancakes, but to the south—that is, the left hand—there was a glimpse of high heathery mountains, which I remembered from the map as the big knot of hill which I had chosen for my sanctuary. I was on the central boss of a huge upland country, and could see everything moving for miles. In the meadows below the road half a mile back a cottage smoked, but it was the only sign of human life. Otherwise there was only the calling of plovers and the tinkling of little streams.

It was now about seven o'clock, and as I waited I heard once again that ominous beat in the air. Then I realised that my vantage-ground might be in reality a trap. There was no cover for a tomtit in those bald green places.

I sat quite still and hopeless while the beat grew louder. Then I saw an aeroplane coming up from the east. It was flying high, but as I looked it dropped several hundred feet and began to circle round the knot of hill in narrowing circles, just as a hawk wheels before it pounces. Now it was flying very low, and now the observer on board caught sight of me. I could see one of the two occupants examining me through glasses.

Suddenly it began to rise in swift whorls, and the next I knew it was speeding eastward again till it became a speck in the blue morning.

That made me do some savage thinking. My enemies had located me, and the next thing would be a cordon round me. I didn't know what force they could command, but I was certain it would be sufficient. The aeroplane had seen my bicycle, and would conclude that I would try to escape by the road. In that case there might be a chance on the moors to the right or left. I wheeled the machine a hundred yards from the highway, and plunged it into a moss-hole, where it sank among pond-weed and water-buttercups. Then I climbed to a knoll which gave me a view of the two valleys. Nothing was stirring on the long white ribbon that threaded them.

I have said there was not cover in the whole place to hide a rat. As the day advanced it was flooded with soft fresh light till it had the fragrant sunniness of the South African veld. At other times I would have liked the place, but now it seemed to suffocate me. The free moorlands were prison walls, and the keen hill air was the breath of a dungeon.

I tossed a coin—heads right, tails left—and it fell heads, so I turned to the north. In a little I came to the brow of the ridge which was the containing wall of the pass. I saw the highroad for maybe ten miles, and far down it something that was moving, and that I took to be a motor-car. Beyond the ridge I looked on a rolling green moor, which fell away into wooded glens. Now my life on the veld has given me the eyes of a kite, and I can see things for which most men need a telescope. . . . Away down the slope, a couple of miles away, several men were advancing like a row of beaters at a shoot. . . .

I dropped out of sight behind the skyline. That way

was shut to me, and I must try the bigger hills to the south beyond the highway. The car I had noticed was getting nearer, but it was still a long way off with some very steep gradients before it. I ran hard, crouching low except in the hollows, and as I ran I kept scanning the brow of the hill before me. Was it imagination, or did I see figures—one, two, perhaps more—moving in a glen beyond the stream?

If you are hemmed in on all sides in a patch of land there is only one chance of escape. You must stay in the patch, and let your enemies search it and not find you. That was good sense, but how on earth was I to escape notice in that table-cloth of a place? I would have buried myself to the neck in mud or lain below water or climbed the tallest tree. But there was not a stick of wood, the bog-holes were little puddles, the stream was a slender trickle. There was nothing but short heather, and bare hill bent, and the white highway.

Then in a tiny bight of road, beside a heap of stones, I found the roadman.

He had just arrived, and was wearily flinging down his hammer. He looked at me with a fishy eye and yawned.

"Confoond the day I ever left the herdin'!" he said, as if to the world at large. "There I was my ain maister. Now I'm a slave to the Government, tethered to the roadside, wi' sair een, and a back like a suckle."

He took up the hammer, struck a stone, dropped the implement with an oath, and put both hands to his ears. "Mercy on me! My heid's burstin'!" he cried.

He was a wild figure, about my own size but much bent, with a week's beard on his chin, and a pair of big horn spectacles.

"I canna dae't," he cried again. "The Surveyor maun just report me. I'm for my bed."

I asked him what was the trouble, though indeed that was clear enough.

"The trouble is that I'm no sober. Last nicht my dochter

Merran was waddit, and they danced till fower in the byre. Me and some ither chiels sat down to the drinkin', and here I am. Peety that I ever lookit on the wine when it was red!"

I agreed with him about bed.

"It's easy speakin'," he moaned. "But I got a post-caird yestreen sayin' that the new Road Surveyor would be round the day. He'll come and he'll no find me, or else he'll find me fou, and either way I'm a done man. I'll awa' back to my bed and say I'm no weel, but I doot that'll no help me, for they ken my kind o' no-weel-ness."

Then I had an inspiration. "Does the new Surveyor know you?" I asked.

"No him. He's just been a week at the job. He rins about in a wee motor-cawr, and wad speir the inside oot o' a whelk."

"Where's your house?" I asked, and was directed by a wavering finger to the cottage by the stream.

"Well, back to your bed," I said, "and sleep in peace. I'll take on your job for a bit and see the Surveyor."

He stared at me blankly; then, as the notion dawned on his fuddled brain, his face broke into the vacant drunkard's smile.

"You're the billy," he cried. "It'll be easy eneuch managed. I've finished that bing o' stanes, so you needna chap ony mair this forenoon. Just take the barry, and wheel eneuch metal frae yon quarry doon the road to mak anither bing the morn. My name's Alexander Trummle, and I've been seeven year at the trade, and twenty afore that herdin' on Leithen Water. My freens ca' me Ecky, and whiles Specky, for I wear glesses, being weak i' the sicht. Just you speak the Surveyor fair, and ca' him Sir, and he'll be fell pleased. I'll be back or mid-day."

I borrowed his spectacles and filthy old hat; stripped off coat, waistcoat, and collar, and gave him them to carry home; borrowed, too, the foul stump of a clay pipe as an extra property. He indicated my simple tasks, and without more ado set off at an amble bedwards. Bed may have been his chief object, but I think there was also something left in the foot of a bottle. I prayed that he might be safe under cover before my friends arrived on the scene.

Then I set to work to dress for the part. I opened the collar of my shirt—it was a vulgar blue-and-white check such as ploughmen wear—and revealed a neck as brown as any tinker's. I rolled up my sleeves, and there was a forearm which might have been a blacksmith's, sunburnt and rough with old scars. I got my boots and trouser-legs all white from the dust of the road, and hitched up my trousers, tying them with string below the knee. Then I set to work on my face. With a handful of dust I made a water-mark round my neck, the place where Mr Turnbull's Sunday ablutions might be expected to stop. I rubbed a good deal of dirt also into the sunburn of my cheeks. A roadman's eyes would no doubt be a little inflamed, so I contrived to get some dust in both of mine, and by dint of vigorous rubbing produced a bleary effect.

The sandwiches Sir Harry had given me had gone off with my coat, but the roadman's lunch, tied up in a red handkerchief, was at my disposal. I ate with great relish several of the thick slabs of scone and cheese and drank a little of the cold tea. In the handkerchief was a local paper tied with string and addressed to Mr Turnbull—obviously meant to solace his mid-day leisure. I did up the bundle again, and put the paper conspicuously beside it.

My boots did not satisfy me, but by dint of kicking among the stones I reduced them to the granite-like surface which marks a roadman's foot-gear. Then I bit and scraped my finger-nails till the edges were all cracked and uneven. The men I was matched against would miss no detail. I broke one of the bootlaces and retied it in a clumsy knot, and loosed the other so that my thick grey socks bulged over the uppers.

Still no sign of anything on the road. The motor I had observed half an hour ago must have gone home.

My toilet complete, I took up the barrow and began my journeys to and from the quarry a hundred yards off.

I remember an old scout in Rhodesia, who had done many queer things in his day, once telling me that the secret of playing a part was to think yourself into it. You could never keep it up, he said, unless you could manage to convince yourself that you were *it*. So I shut off all other thoughts and switched them on to the road-mending. I thought of the little white cottage as my home, I recalled the years I had spent herding on Leithen Water, I made my mind dwell lovingly on sleep in a box-bed and a bottle of cheap whisky. Still nothing appeared on that long white road.

Now and then a sheep wandered off the heather to stare at me. A heron flopped down to a pool in the stream and started to fish, taking no more notice of me than if I had been a milestone. On I went, trundling my loads of stone, with the heavy step of the professional. Soon I grew warm, and the dust on my face changed into solid and abiding grit. I was already counting the hours till evening should put a limit to Mr Turnbull's monotonous toil.

Suddenly a crisp voice spoke from the road, and looking up I saw a little Ford two-seater, and a round-faced young man in a bowler hat.

"Are you Alexander Turnbull?" he asked. "I am the new County Road Surveyor. You live at Blackhopefoot, and have charge of the section from Laidlawbyres to the Riggs? Good! A fair bit of road, Turnbull, and not badly engineered. A little soft about a mile off, and the edges want cleaning. See you look after that. Good-morning. You'll know me the next time you see me."

Clearly my get-up was good enough for the dreaded Surveyor. I went on with my work, and as the morning grew towards noon I was cheered by a little traffic. A baker's van breasted the hill, and sold me a bag of ginger biscuits which I stowed in my trouser-pockets against emergencies. Then a herd passed with sheep, and disturbed me somewhat by asking loudly, "What had become o' Specky?"

"In bed wi' the colic," I replied, and the herd passed on. . . .

Just about mid-day a big car stole down the hill, glided past and drew up a hundred yards beyond. Its three occupants descended as if to stretch their legs, and sauntered towards me.

Two of the men I had seen before from the window of the Galloway inn—one lean, sharp, and dark, the other comfortable and smiling. The third had the look of a countryman—a vet, perhaps, or a small farmer. He was dressed in ill-cut knickerbockers, and the eye in his head was as bright and wary as a hen's.

"'Morning," said the last. "That's a fine easy job o' yours."

I had not looked up on their approach, and now, when accosted, I slowly and painfully straightened my back, after the manner of roadmen; spat vigorously, after the manner of the low Scot; and regarded them steadily before replying. I confronted three pairs of eyes that missed nothing.

"There's waur jobs and there's better," I said sententiously. "I wad rather hae yours, sittin' a' day on your hinderlands on thae cushions. It's you and your muckle cawrs that wreck my roads! If we a' had oor richts, ye sud be made to mend what ye break."

The bright-eyed man was looking at the newspaper lying beside Turnbull's bundle.

"I see you get your papers in good time," he said.

I glanced at it casually. "Aye, in gude time. Seein' that that paper cam' out last Setterday I'm just sax days late."

He picked it up, glanced at the superscription, and laid it down again. One of the others had been looking at my boots, and a word in German called the speaker's attention to them.

"You've a fine taste in boots," he said. "These were never made by a country shoemaker."

"They were not," I said readily. "They were made in London. I got them frae the gentleman that was here last year for the shootin'. What was his name now?" And I scratched a forgetful head.

Again the sleek one spoke in German. "Let us get on," he said. "This fellow is all right."

They asked one last question.

"Did you see anyone pass early this morning? He might be on a bicycle or he might be on foot."

I very nearly fell into the trap and told a story of a bicyclist hurrying past in the grey dawn. But I had the sense to see my danger. I pretended to consider very deeply.

"I wasna up very early," I said. "Ye see, my dochter was merrit last nicht, and we keepit it up late. I opened the house door about seeven and there was naebody on the road then. Since I cam' up here there has just been the baker and the Ruchill herd, besides you gentlemen."

One of them gave me a cigar, which I smelt gingerly and stuck in Turnbull's bundle. They got into their car and were out of sight in three minutes.

My heart leaped with an enormous relief, but I went on wheeling my stones. It was as well, for ten minutes later the car returned, one of the occupants waving a hand to me. Those gentry left nothing to chance.

I finished Turnbull's bread and cheese, and pretty soon I had finished the stones. The next step was what puzzled me. I could not keep up this road-making business for long. A merciful Providence had kept Mr Turnbull indoors, but if he appeared on the scene there would be trouble. I had a notion that the cordon was still tight round the glen, and that if I walked in any direction I should meet with questioners. But get out I must. No man's nerve could stand more than a day of being spied on.

I stayed at my post till about five o'clock. By that time I had resolved to go down to Turnbull's cottage at nightfall and take my chance of getting over the hills in the darkness. But suddenly a new car came up the road, and slowed down a yard or two from me. A fresh wind had risen, and the occupant wanted to light a cigarette.

It was a touring car, with the tonneau full of an assortment of baggage. One man sat in it, and by an amazing chance I knew him. His name was Marmaduke Jopley, and he was an offence to creation. He was a sort of blood stockbroker, who did his business by toadying eldest sons and rich young peers and foolish old ladies. "Marmie" was a familiar figure, I understood, at balls and polo-weeks and country houses. He was an adroit scandal-monger, and would crawl a mile on his belly to anything that had a title or a million. I had a business introduction to his firm when I came to London, and he was good enough to ask me to dinner at his club. There he showed off at a great rate, and pattered about his duchesses till the snobbery of the creature turned me sick. I asked a man afterwards why nobody kicked him, and was told that Englishmen reverenced the weaker sex.

Anyhow there he was now, nattily dressed, in a fine new car, obviously on his way to visit some of his smart friends. A sudden daftness took me, and in a second I had jumped into the tonneau and had him by the shoulder.

"Hullo, Jopley," I sang out. "Well met, my lad!"

He got a horrid fright. His chin dropped as he stared at me. "Who the devil are you?" he gasped.

"My name's Hannay," I said. "From Rhodesia, you remember."

"Good God, the murderer!" he choked.

"Just so. And there'll be a second murder, my dear, if

you don't do as I tell you. Give me that coat of yours. That cap, too."

He did as he was bid, for he was blind with terror. Over my dirty trousers and vulgar shirt I put on his smart driving-coat, which buttoned high at the top and thereby hid the deficiencies of my collar. I stuck the cap on my head, and added his gloves to my get up. The dusty roadman in a minute was transformed into one of the neatest motorists in Scotland. On Mr Jopley's head I clapped Turnbull's unspeakable hat, and told him to keep it there.

Then with some difficulty I turned the car. My plan was to go back the road he had come, for the watchers, having seen it before, would probably let it pass unremarked, and Marmie's figure was in no way like mine.

"Now, my child," I said, "sit quite still and be a good boy. I mean you no harm. I'm only borrowing your car for an hour or two. But if you play me any tricks, and above all if you open your mouth, as sure as there's a God above me I'll wring your neck. *Savez?*"

I enjoyed that evening's ride. We ran eight miles down the valley, through a village or two, and I could not help noticing several strange-looking folk lounging by the roadside. These were the watchers who would have had much to say to me if I had come in other garb or company. As it was, they looked incuriously on. One touched his cap in salute, and I responded graciously.

As the dark fell I turned up a side glen which, as I remember from the map, led into an unfrequented corner of the hills. Soon the villages were left behind, then the farms, and then even the wayside cottages. Presently we came to a lonely moor where the night was blackening the sunset gleam in the bog pools. Here we stopped, and I obligingly reversed the car and restored to Mr Jopley his belongings.

"A thousand thanks," I said. "There's more use in you than I thought. Now be off and find the police."

As I sat on the hillside, watching the tail-light dwindle, I reflected on the various kinds of crime I had now sampled. Contrary to general belief, I was not a murderer, but I had become an unholy liar, a shameless impostor, and a highwayman with a marked taste for expensive motor-cars.

CHAPTER VI.

THE ADVENTURE OF THE BALD ARCHÆOLOGIST.

I SPENT the night on a shelf of the hillside, in the lee of a boulder where the heather grew long and soft. It was a cold business, for I had neither coat nor waistcoat. These were in Mr Turnbull's keeping, as was Scudder's little book, my watch and—worst of all—my pipe and tobacco pouch. Only my money accompanied me in my belt, and about half a pound of ginger biscuits in my trousers pocket.

I supped off half those biscuits, and by worming myself deep into the heather got some kind of warmth. My spirits had risen, and I was beginning to enjoy this crazy game of hide-and-seek. So far I had been miraculously lucky. The milkman, the literary innkeeper, Sir Harry, the roadman, and the idiotic Marmie, were all pieces of undeserved good fortune. Somehow the first success gave me a feeling that I was going to pull the thing through.

My chief trouble was that I was desperately hungry. When a Jew shoots himself in the City and there is an inquest, the newspapers usually report that the deceased was "well-nourished." I remember thinking that they would not call me well-nourished if I broke my neck in a bog-hole. I lay and tortured myself—for the ginger biscuits merely emphasised the aching void—with the memory of all the good food I had thought so little of in London. There were Paddock's crisp sausages and fragrant shavings of bacon, and shapely poached eggs—how often I had turned up my nose at them! There were the cutlets they did at the club, and a particular ham that stood on the cold table, for which my soul lusted. My thoughts hovered over all varieties of mortal edible, and finally settled on a porter-house steak and a quart of bitter with a welsh rabbit to follow. In longing hopelessly for these dainties I fell asleep.

I woke very cold and stiff about an hour after dawn. It took me a little while to remember where I was, for I had been very weary and had slept heavily. I saw first the pale blue sky through a net of heather, then a big shoulder of hill, and then my own boots placed neatly in a blaeberry bush. I raised myself on my arms and looked down into the valley, and that one look set me lacing up my boots in mad haste.

For there were men below, not more than a quarter of a mile off, spaced out on the hillside like a fan, and beating the heather. Marmie had not been slow in looking for his revenge.

I crawled out of my shelf into the cover of a boulder, and from it gained a shallow trench which slanted up the mountain face. This led me presently into the narrow gully of a burn, by way of which I scrambled to the top of the ridge. From there I looked back, and saw that I was still undiscovered. My pursuers were patiently quartering the hillside and moving upwards.

Keeping behind the skyline I ran for maybe half a mile, till I judged I was above the uppermost end of the glen. Then I showed myself, and was instantly noted by one of the flankers, who passed the word to the others. I heard cries coming up from below, and saw that the line of search had changed its direction. I pretended to retreat over the skyline, but instead went back the way I had come, and in twenty minutes was behind the ridge overlooking my sleeping place. From that viewpoint I had the satisfaction of seeing the pursuit streaming up the hill at the top of the glen on a hopelessly false scent.

I had before me a choice of routes, and I chose a ridge which made an angle with the one I was on, and so would soon put a deep glen between me and my enemies. The exercise had warmed my blood, and I was beginning to enjoy myself amazingly. As I went I breakfasted on the dusty remnants of the ginger biscuits.

I knew very little about the country, and I hadn't a notion what I was going to do. I trusted to the strength of my legs, but I was well aware that those behind me would be familiar with the lie of the land, and that my ignorance would be a heavy handicap. I saw in front of me a sea of hills, rising very high towards the south, but northwards breaking down into broad ridges which separated wide and shallow dales. The ridge I had chosen seemed to sink after a mile or two to a moor which lay like a pocket in the uplands. That seemed as good a direction to take as any other.

My stratagem had given me a fair start—call it twenty minutes—and I had the width of a glen behind me before I saw the first heads of the pursuers. The police had evidently called in local talent to their aid, and the men I could see had the appearance of herds or gamekeepers. They hallooed at the sight of me, and I waved my hand. Two dived into the glen and began to climb my ridge, while the others kept their own side of the hill. I felt as if I were taking part in a schoolboy game of hare and hounds.

But very soon it began to seem less of a game. Those fellows behind were hefty men on their native heath. Looking back I saw that only three were following direct, and I guessed that the others had fetched a circuit to cut me off. My lack of local knowledge might very well be my undoing, and I resolved to get out of this tangle of glens to the pocket of moor I had seen from the tops. I must so increase my distance as to get clear away from them, and I believed I could do this if I could find the right ground for it. If there had been cover I would have tried a bit of stalking, but on these bare slopes you could see a fly a mile off. My hope must be in the length of my legs and the soundness of my wind, but I needed easier ground for that, for I was not bred a mountaineer. How I longed for a good Afrikander pony!

I put on a great spurt and got off my ridge and down into the moor before any figures appeared on the skyline behind me. I crossed a burn, and came out on a highroad which made a pass between two glens. All in front of me was a big field of heather sloping up to a crest which was crowned with an odd feather of trees. In the dyke by the roadside was a gate, from which a grass-grown track led over the first wave of the moor.

I jumped the dyke and followed it, and after a few hundred yards—as soon as it was out of sight of the highway—the grass stopped and it became a very respectable road, which was evidently kept with some care. Clearly it ran to a house, and I began to think of doing the same. Hitherto my luck had held, and it might be that my best chance would be found in this remote dwelling. Anyhow there were trees there, and that meant cover.

I did not follow the road, but the burnside which flanked it on the right, where the bracken grew deep and the high banks made a tolerable screen. It was well I did so, for no sooner had I gained the hollow than, looking back, I saw the pursuit topping the ridge from which I had descended.

After that I did not look back; I had no time. I ran up the burnside, crawling over the open places, and for a large part wading in the shallow stream. I found a deserted cottage with a row of phantom peat-stacks and an overgrown garden. Then I was among young hay, and very soon had come to the edge of a plantation of wind-blown firs. From there I saw the chimneys of the house smoking a few hundred yards to my left. I forsook the burnside, crossed another dyke, and almost before I knew was on a rough lawn. A glance back told me that I was well out of sight of the pursuit, which had not yet passed the first lift of the moor.

The lawn was a very rough place, cut with a scythe instead of a mower, and planted with beds of scrubby rhododendrons.

A brace of black-game, which are not usually garden birds, rose at my approach. The house before me was the ordinary moorland farm, with a more pretentious whitewashed wing added. Attached to this wing was a glass verandah, and through the glass I saw the face of an elderly gentleman meekly watching me.

I stalked over the border of coarse hill gravel and entered the open verandah door. Within was a pleasant room, glass on one side, and on the other a mass of books. More books showed in an inner room. On the floor, instead of tables, stood cases such as you see in a museum, filled with coins and queer stone implements.

There was a knee-hole desk in the middle, and seated at it, with some papers and open volumes before him, was the benevolent old gentleman. His face was round and shiny, like Mr Pickwick's, big glasses were stuck on the end of his nose, and the top of his head was as bright and bare as a glass bottle. He never moved when I entered, but raised his placid eyebrows and waited on me to speak.

It was not an easy job, with about five minutes to spare, to tell a stranger who I was and what I wanted, and to win his aid. I did not attempt it. There was something about the eye of the man before me, something so keen and knowledgeable, that I could not find a word. I simply stared at him and stuttered.

"You seem in a hurry, my friend," he said slowly.

I nodded towards the window. It gave a prospect across the moor through a gap in the plantation, and revealed certain figures half a mile off straggling through the heather.

"Ah, I see," he said, and took up a pair of field-glasses through which he patiently scrutinised the figures.

"A fugitive from justice, eh? Well, we'll go into the matter at our leisure. Meantime I object to my privacy being broken in upon by the clumsy rural policeman. Go into my study, and you will see two doors facing you. Take the one on the left and close it behind you. You will be perfectly safe."

And this extraordinary man took up his pen again.

I did as I was bid, and found myself in a little dark chamber which smelt of chemicals, and was lit only by a tiny window high up in the wall. The door had swung behind me with a click like the door of a safe. Once again I had found an unexpected sanctuary.

All the same I was not comfortable. There was something about the old gentleman which puzzled and rather terrified me. He had been too easy and ready, almost as if he had expected me. And his eyes had been horribly intelligent.

No sound came to me in that dark place. For all I knew the police might be searching the house, and if they did they would want to know what was behind this door. I tried to possess my soul in patience, and to forget how hungry I was.

Then I took a more cheerful view. The old gentleman could scarcely refuse me a meal, and I fell to reconstructing my breakfast. Bacon and eggs would content me, but I wanted the better part of a flitch of bacon and half a hundred eggs. And then, while my mouth was watering in anticipation, there was a click and the door stood open.

I emerged into the sunlight to find the master of the house sitting in a deep arm-chair in the room he called his study, and regarding me with curious eyes.

"Have they gone?" I asked.

"They have gone. I convinced them that you had crossed the hill. I do not choose that the police should come between me and one whom I am delighted to honour. This is a lucky morning for you, Mr Richard Hannay."

As he spoke his eyelids seemed to tremble and to fall a little over his keen grey eyes. In a flash the phrase of Scudder's came back to me, when he had described the man he most dreaded in the world. He had said that he "could hood his eyes like a hawk." Then I saw that I had walked straight into the enemy's headquarters.

My first impulse was to throttle the old ruffian and make for the open air. He seemed to anticipate my intention, for he smiled gently, and nodded to the door behind me. I turned, and saw two men-servants who had me covered with pistols.

He knew my name, but he had never seen me before. And as the reflection darted across my mind I saw a slender chance.

"I don't know what you mean," I said roughly. "And who are you calling Richard Hannay? My name's Ainslie."

"So?" he said, still smiling. "But of course you have others. We won't quarrel about a name."

I was pulling myself together now, and I reflected that my garb, lacking coat and waistcoat and collar, would at any rate not betray me. I put on my surliest face and shrugged my shoulders.

"I suppose you're going to give me up after all, and I call it a damned dirty trick. My God, I wish I had never seen that cursed motor-car! Here's the money and be damned to you," and I flung four sovereigns on the table.

He opened his eyes a little. "Oh no, I shall not give you up. My friends and I will have a little private settlement with you, that is all. You know a little too much, Mr Hannay. You are a clever actor, but not quite clever enough."

He spoke with assurance, but I could see the dawning of a doubt in his mind.

"Oh, for God's sake stop jawing," I cried. "Everything's against me. I haven't had a bit of luck since I came on shore at Leith. What's the harm in a poor devil with an empty stomach picking up some money he finds in a bust-up motor-car? That's all I done, and for that I've been chivvied for two days by those blasted bobbies over those blasted hills. I tell you I'm fair sick of it. You can do what you like, old boy! Ned Ainslie's got no fight left in him."

I could see that the doubt was gaining.

"Will you oblige me with the story of your recent doings?" he asked.

"I can't, guv'nor," I said in a real beggar's whine. "I've not had a bite to eat for two days. Give me a mouthful of food, and then you'll hear God's truth."

I must have showed my hunger in my face, for he signalled to one of the men in the doorway. A bit of cold pie was brought and a glass of beer, and I wolfed them down like a pig—or rather, like Ned Ainslie, for I was keeping up my character. In the middle of my meal he spoke suddenly to me in German, but I turned on him a face as blank as a stone wall.

Then I told him my story—how I had come off an Archangel ship at Leith a week ago, and was making my way overland to my brother at Wigtown. I had run short of cash—I hinted vaguely at a spree—and I was pretty well on my uppers when I had come on a hole in a hedge, and, looking through, had seen a big motor-car lying in the burn. I had poked about to see what had happened, and had found three sovereigns lying on the seat and one on the floor. There was nobody there or any sign of an owner, so I had pocketed the cash. But somehow the law had got after me. When I had tried to change a sovereign in a baker's shop, the woman had cried on the police, and a little later, when I was washing my face in a burn, I had been nearly gripped, and had only got away by leaving my coat and waistcoat behind me.

"They can have the money back," I cried, "for a fat lot of good it's done me. Those perishers are all down on a poor man. Now, if it had been you, guv'nor, that had found the quids, nobody would have troubled you."

"You're a good liar, Hannay," he said.

I flew into a rage. "Stop fooling, damn you! I tell you my name's Ainslie, and I never heard of anyone called Hannay in my born days. I'd sooner have the police than you with your Hannays and your monkey-faced pistol tricks. . . . No, guv'nor, I beg pardon, I don't mean that. I'm much obliged to you for the grub, and I'll thank you to let me go now the coast's clear."

It was obvious that he was badly puzzled. You see he had never seen me, and my appearance must have altered considerably from my photographs, if he had got one of them. I was pretty smart and well dressed in London, and now I was a regular tramp.

"I do not propose to let you go. If you are what you say you are, you will soon have a chance of clearing yourself. If you are what I believe you are, I do not think you will see the light much longer."

He rang a bell, and a third servant appeared from the verandah.

"I want the Lanchester in five minutes," he said. "There will be three to luncheon."

Then he looked steadily at me, and that was the hardest ordeal of all.

There was something weird and devilish in those eyes, cold, malignant, unearthly, and most hellishly clever. They fascinated me like the bright eyes of a snake. I had a strong impulse to throw myself on his mercy and offer to join his side, and if you consider the way I felt about the whole thing you will see that that impulse must have been purely physical, the weakness of a brain mesmerised and mastered by a stronger spirit. But I managed to stick it out and even to grin.

"You'll know me next time, guv'nor," I said.

"Karl," he spoke in German to one of the men in the doorway, "you will put this fellow in the storeroom till I return, and you will be answerable to me for his keeping."

I was marched out of the room with a pistol at each ear.

The storeroom was a damp chamber in what had been the

old farmhouse. There was no carpet on the uneven floor, and nothing to sit down on but a school form. It was black as pitch, for the windows were heavily shuttered. I made out by groping that the walls were lined with boxes and barrels and sacks of some heavy stuff. The whole place smelt of mould and disuse. My gaolers turned the key in the door, and I could hear them shifting their feet as they stood on guard outside.

I sat down in that chilly darkness in a very miserable frame of mind. The old boy had gone off in a motor to collect the two ruffians who had interviewed me yesterday. Now, they had seen me as the roadman, and they would remember me, for I was in the same rig. What was a roadman doing twenty miles from his beat, pursued by the police? A question or two would put them on the track. Probably they had seen Mr Turnbull, probably Marmie too; most likely they could link me up with Sir Harry, and then the whole thing would be crystal clear. What chance had I in this moorland house with three desperadoes and their armed servants?

I began to think wistfully of the police, now plodding over the hills after my wraith. They at any rate were fellow-countrymen and honest men, and their tender mercies would be kinder than these ghoulish aliens. But they wouldn't have listened to me. That old devil with the eyelids had not taken long to get rid of them. I thought he probably had some kind of graft with the constabulary. Most likely he had letters from Cabinet Ministers saying he was to be given every facility for plotting against Britain. That's the sort of owlish way we run our politics in the Old Country.

The three would be back for lunch, so I hadn't more than a couple of hours to wait. It was simply waiting on destruction, for I could see no way out of this mess. I wished that I had Scudder's courage, for I am free to confess I didn't feel any great fortitude. The only thing that kept me going was that I was pretty furious. It made me boil with rage to think of those three spies getting the pull on me like this. I hoped that at any rate I might be able to twist one of their necks before they downed me.

The more I thought of it the angrier I grew, and I had to get up and move about the room. I tried the shutters, but they were the kind that lock with a key, and I couldn't move them. From the outside came the faint clucking of hens in the warm sun. Then I groped among the sacks and boxes. I couldn't open the latter, and the sacks seemed to be full of things like dog-biscuits that smelt of cinnamon. But, as I circumnavigated the room, I found a handle in the wall which seemed worth investigating.

It was the door of a wall cupboard—what they call a "press" in Scotland—and it was locked. I shook it, and it seemed rather flimsy. For want of something better to do I put out my strength on that door, getting some purchase on the handle by looping my braces round it. Presently the thing gave with a crash which I thought would bring in my warders to inquire. I waited for a bit, and then started to explore the cupboard shelves.

There was a multitude of queer things there. I found an odd vesta or two in my trouser pockets and struck a light. It went out in a second, but it showed me one thing. There was a little stock of electric torches on one shelf. I picked up one, and found it was in working order.

With the torch to help me I investigated further. There were bottles and cases of queer-smelling stuffs, chemicals no doubt for experiments, and there were coils of fine copper wire and yanks and yanks of a thin oiled silk. There was a box of detonators, and a lot of cord for fuses. Then away at the back of a shelf I found a stout brown cardboard box, and inside it a wooden case. I managed to wrench it open, and within lay half a dozen little grey bricks, each a couple of inches square.

I took up one, and found that it crumbled easily in my hand. Then I smelt it and put my tongue to it. After that I sat down to think. I hadn't been a mining engineer for nothing, and I knew lentonite when I saw it.

With one of these bricks I could blow the house to smithereens. I had used the stuff in Rhodesia and knew its power. But the trouble was that my knowledge wasn't exact. I had forgotten the proper charge and the right way of preparing it, and I wasn't sure about the timing. I had only a vague notion, too, as to its power, for though I had used it I had not handled it with my own fingers.

But it was a chance, the only possible chance. It was a mighty risk, but against it was an absolute black certainty. If I used it the odds were, as I reckoned, about five to one in favour of my blowing myself into the tree-tops; but if I didn't I should very likely be occupying a six-foot hole in the garden by the evening. That was the way I had to look at it. The prospect was pretty dark either way, but anyhow there was a chance, both for myself and for my country.

The remembrance of little Scudder decided me. It was about the beastliest moment of my life, for I'm no good at these cold-blooded resolutions. Still I managed to rake up the pluck to set my teeth and choke back the horrid doubts that flooded in on me. I simply shut off my mind and pretended I was doing an experiment as simple as Guy Fawkes fireworks.

I got a detonator, and fixed it to a couple of feet of fuse. Then I took a quarter of a lentonite brick, and buried it near the door below one of the sacks in a crack of the floor, fixing the detonator in it. For all I knew half those boxes might be dynamite. If the cupboard held such deadly explosives, why not the boxes? In that case there would be a glorious skyward journey for me and the German servants and about an acre of the surrounding country. There was also the risk that the detonation might set off the other bricks in the cupboard, for I had forgotten most that I knew about lentonite. But it didn't do to begin thinking about the possibilities. The odds were horrible, but I had to take them.

I ensconced myself just below the sill of the window, and lit the fuse. Then I waited for a moment or two. There was dead silence—only a shuffle of heavy boots in the passage, and the peaceful cluck of hens from the warm out-of-doors. I commended my soul to my Maker, and wondered where I would be in five seconds. . . .

A great wave of heat seemed to surge upwards from the floor, and hang for a blistering instant in the air. Then the wall opposite me flashed into a golden yellow and dissolved with a rending thunder that hammered my brain into a pulp. Something dropped on me, catching the point of my left shoulder.

And then I think I became unconscious.

My stupor can scarcely have lasted beyond a few seconds. I felt myself being choked by thick yellow fumes, and struggled out of the debris to my feet. Somewhere behind me I felt fresh air. The jambs of the window had fallen, and through the ragged rent the smoke was pouring out to the summer noon. I stepped over the broken lintel, and found myself standing in a yard in a dense and acrid fog. I felt very sick and ill, but I could move my limbs, and I staggered blindly forward away from the house.

A small mill-lade ran in a wooden aqueduct at the other side of the yard, and into this I fell. The cool water revived me, and I had just enough wits left to think of escape. I squirmed up the lade among the slippery green slime till I reached the mill-wheel. Then I wriggled through the axle hole into the old mill and tumbled on to a bed of chaff. A nail caught the seat of my trousers, and I left a wisp of heather-mixture behind me.

The mill had been long out of use. The ladders were rotten with age, and in the loft the rats had gnawed great holes in the floor. Nausea shook me, and a wheel in my head kept turning, while my left shoulder and arm seemed to be stricken with the palsy. I looked out of the window and saw a fog still hanging over the house and smoke escaping from an upper window. Please God I had set the place on fire, for I could hear confused cries coming from the other side.

But I had no time to linger, since this mill was obviously a bad hiding-place. Anyone looking for me would naturally follow the lade, and I made certain the search would begin as soon as they found that my body was not in the store-room. From another window I saw that on the far side of the mill stood an old stone dovecot. If I could get there without leaving tracks I might find a hiding-place, for I argued that my enemies, if they thought I could move, would conclude I had made for open country, and would go seeking me on the moor.

I crawled down the broken ladder, scattering chaff behind me to cover my footsteps. I did the same on the mill floor, and on the threshold where the door hung on broken hinges. Peeping out, I saw that between me and the dovecot was a piece of bare cobbled ground, where no footmarks would show. Also it was mercifully hid by the mill buildings from any view from the house. I slipped across the space, got to the back of the dovecot and prospected a way of ascent.

That was one of the hardest jobs I ever took on. My shoulder and arm ached like hell, and I was so sick and giddy that I was always on the verge of falling. But I managed it somehow. By the use of out-jutting stones and gaps in the masonry and a tough ivy root I got to the top in the end. There was a little parapet behind which I found space to lie down. Then I proceeded to go off into an old-fashioned swoon.

I woke with a burning head and the sun glaring in my face. For a long time I lay motionless, for those horrible fumes seemed to have loosened my joints and dulled my brain. Sounds came to me from the house—men speaking throatily and the throbbing of a stationary car. There was a little gap in the parapet to which I wriggled, and from which I had some sort of prospect of the yard. I saw figures come out—a servant with his head bound up, and then a younger man in knickerbockers. They were looking for something, and moved towards the mill. Then one of them caught sight of the wisp of cloth on the nail, and cried out to the other. They both went back to the house, and brought two more to look at it. I saw the rotund figure of my late captor; and I thought I made out the man with the lisp. I noticed that all had pistols.

For half an hour they ransacked the mill. I could hear them kicking over the barrels and pulling up the rotten planking. Then they came outside, and stood just below the dovecot, arguing fiercely. The servant with the bandage was being soundly rated. I heard them fiddling with the door of the dovecot, and for one horrid moment I fancied they were coming up. Then they thought better of it, and went back to the house.

All that long blistering afternoon I lay baking on the roof-top. Thirst was my chief torment. My tongue was like a stick, and to make it worse I could hear the cool drip of water from the mill-lade. I watched the course of the little stream as it came in from the moor, and my fancy followed it to the top of the glen, where it must issue from an icy fountain fringed with cool ferns and mosses. I would have given a thousand pounds to plunge my face into that.

I had a fine prospect of the whole ring of moorland. I saw the car speed away with two occupants, and a man on a hill pony riding east. I judged they were looking for me, and I wished them joy of their quest.

But I saw something else more interesting. The house stood almost on the summit of a swell of moorland which crowned a sort of plateau, and there was no higher point nearer than the big hills six miles off. The actual summit, as I have mentioned, was a biggish clump of trees—firs mostly, with a few ashes and beeches. On the dovecot

I was almost on a level with the tree-tops, and could see what lay beyond. The wood was not solid, but only a ring, and inside was an oval of green turf, for all the world like a big cricket-field.

I didn't take long to guess what it was. It was an aerodrome, and a secret one. The place had been most cunningly chosen. For suppose anyone were watching an aeroplane descending here, he would think it had gone over the hill beyond the trees. As the place was on the top of a rise in the midst of a big amphitheatre, any observer from any direction would conclude it had passed out of view behind the hill. Only a man very close at hand would realise that the aeroplane had not gone over but had descended in the midst of the wood. An observer with a telescope on one of the higher hills might have discovered the truth, but only herds went there, and herds do not carry spy-glasses. When I looked from the dovecot I could see far away a blue line which I knew was the sea, and I grew furious to think that our enemies had this secret conning-tower to rake our waterways.

Then I reflected that if that aeroplane came back the chances were ten to one that I would be discovered. So through the afternoon I lay and prayed for the coming of darkness, and glad I was when the sun went down over the big western hills and the twilight haze crept over the moor. The aeroplane was late. The gloaming was far advanced when I heard the beat of wings and saw it volplaning downward to its home in the wood. Lights twinkled for a bit and there was much coming and going from the house. Then the dark fell, and silence.

Thank God it was a black night. The moon was well on its last quarter and would not rise till late. My thirst was too great to allow me to tarry, so about nine o'clock, so far as I could judge, I started to descend. It wasn't easy, and half-way down I heard the back door of the house open, and saw the gleam of a lantern against the mill wall. For some agonising minutes I hung by the ivy and prayed that whoever it was would not come round by the dovecot. Then the light disappeared, and I dropped as softly as I could on to the hard soil of the yard.

I crawled on my belly in the lee of a stone dyke till I reached the fringe of trees which surrounded the house. If I had known how to do it I would have tried to put that aeroplane out of action, but I realised that any attempt would probably be futile. I was pretty certain that there would be some kind of defence round the house, so I went through the wood on hands and knees, feeling carefully every inch before me. It was as well, for presently I came on a wire about two feet from the ground. If I had tripped over that, it would doubtless have rung some bell in the house and I would have been captured.

A hundred yards farther on I found another wire cunningly placed on the edge of a small stream. Beyond that lay the moor, and in five minutes I was deep in bracken and heather. Soon I was round the shoulder of the rise, in the little glen from which the mill-lade flowed. Ten minutes later my face was in the spring, and I was soaking down pints of the blessed water.

But I did not stop till I had put half a dozen miles between me and that accursed dwelling.

CHAPTER VII.

THE DRY-FLY FISHERMAN.

I SAT down on a hill-top and took stock of my position. I wasn't feeling very happy, for my natural thankfulness at my escape was clouded by my severe bodily discomfort. Those lentonite fumes had fairly poisoned me, and the baking hours on the dovecot hadn't helped matters. I had a crushing headache, and felt as sick as a cat. Also my shoulder was in a bad way. At first I thought it was only a bruise, but it seemed to be swelling, and I had no use of my left arm.

My plan was to seek Mr Turnbull's cottage, recover my garments, and especially Scudder's note-book, and then make for the main line and get back to the south. It seemed to me that the sooner I got in touch with the Foreign Office man, Sir Walter Bullivant, the better. I didn't see how I could get more proof than I had got already. He must just take or leave my story, and anyway, with him I would be in better hands than those devilish Germans. I had begun to feel quite kindly towards the British police.

It was a wonderful starry night, and I had not much difficulty about the road. Sir Harry's map had given me the lie of the land, and all I had to do was to steer a point or two west of south-west to come to the stream where I had met the roadman. In all these travels I never knew the names of the places, but I believe this stream was no less than the upper waters of the River Tweed. I calculated I must be about eighteen miles distant, and that meant I could not get there before morning. So I must lie up a day somewhere, for I was too outrageous a figure to be seen in the sunlight. I had neither coat, waistcoat, collar, nor hat, my trousers were badly torn, and my face and hands were black with the explosion. I daresay I had other beauties, for my eyes felt as if they were furiously bloodshot. Altogether I was no spectacle for God-fearing citizens to see on a highroad.

Very soon after daybreak I made an attempt to clean myself in a hill burn, and then approached a herd's cottage, for I was feeling the need of food. The herd was away from home, and his wife was alone, with no neighbour for five miles. She was a decent old body, and a plucky one, for though she got a fright when she saw me, she had an axe handy, and would have used it on any evil-doer. I told her that I had had a fall—I didn't say how—and she saw by my looks that I was pretty sick. Like a true Samaritan she asked no questions, but gave me a bowl of milk with a dash of whisky in it, and let me sit for a little by her kitchen fire. She would have bathed my shoulder, but it ached so badly that I would not let her touch it.

I don't know what she took me for—a repentant burglar, perhaps; for when I wanted to pay her for the milk and tendered a sovereign, which was the smallest coin I had, she shook her head and said something about "giving it to them that had a right to it." At this I protested so strongly that I think she believed me honest, for she took the money and gave me a warm new plaid for it, and an old hat of her man's. She showed me how to wrap the plaid round my shoulders, and when I left that cottage I was the living image of the kind of Scotsman you see in the illustrations to Burns's poems. But at any rate I was more or less clad.

It was as well, for the weather changed before mid-day to a thick drizzle of rain. I found shelter below an overhanging rock in the crook of a burn, where a drift of dead brackens made a tolerable bed. There I managed to sleep till nightfall, waking very cramped and wretched, with my shoulder gnawing like a toothache. I ate the oatcake and cheese the old wife had given me, and set out again just before the darkening.

I pass over the miseries of that night among the wet hills. There were no stars to steer by, and I had to do the best I could from my memory of the map. Twice I lost my way, and I had some nasty falls into peat-bogs. I had only about ten miles to go as the crow flies, but my mistakes made it nearer twenty. The last bit was completed with set teeth and a very light and dizzy head. But I managed it, and in the early dawn I was knocking at Mr Turnbull's door. The mist lay close and thick, and from the cottage I could not see the highroad.

Mr Turnbull himself opened to me—sober and something

more than sober. He was primly dressed in an ancient but well-tended suit of black; he had been shaved not later than the night before; he wore a linen collar; and in his left hand he carried a pocket Bible. At first he did not recognise me.

"Whae are ye that comes stravaigin' here on the Sabbath mornin'?" he asked.

I had lost all count of the days. So the Sabbath was the reason for this strange decorum.

My head was swimming so wildly that I could not frame a coherent answer. But he recognised me, and he saw that I was ill.

"Hae ye got my specs?" he asked.

I fetched them out of my trouser pocket and gave him them.

"Ye'll hae come for your jaicket and westcoat," he said. "Come in-bye. Losh, man, ye're terrible dune i' the legs. Haud up till I get ye to a chair."

I perceived I was in for a bout of malaria. I had a good deal of fever in my bones, and the wet night had brought it out, while my shoulder and the effects of the fumes combined to make me feel pretty bad. Before I knew, Mr Turnbull was helping me off with my clothes, and putting me to bed in one of the two cupboards that lined the kitchen walls.

He was a true friend in need, that old roadman. His wife was dead years ago, and since his daughter's marriage he lived alone. For the better part of ten days he did all the rough nursing I needed. I simply wanted to be left in peace while the fever took its course, and when my skin was cool again I found that the bout had more or less cured my shoulder. But it was a baddish go, and though I was out of bed in five days, it took me some time to get my legs again.

He went out each morning, leaving me milk for the day, and locking the door behind him; and came in in the evening to sit silent in the chimney corner. Not a soul came near the place. When I was getting better, he never bothered me with a question. Several times he fetched me a two-day's old 'Scotsman,' and I noticed that the interest in the Portland Place murder seemed to have died down. There was no mention of it, and I could find very little about anything except a thing called the General Assembly—some ecclesiastical spree, I gathered.

One day he produced my belt from a lockfast drawer. "There's a terrible heap o' siller in't," he said. "Ye'd better coont it to see it's a' there."

He never even sought my name. I asked him if anybody had been around making inquiries subsequent to my spell at the roadmaking.

"Ay, there was a man in a motor-cawr. He speired whae had ta'en my place that day, and I let on I thocht him daft. But he keepit on at me, and syne I said he maun be thinkin' o' my gude-brither frae the Cleuch that whiles lent me a haun'. He was a wersh-lookin' sowl, and I couldna understand the half o' his English tongue."

I was getting pretty restless those last days, and as soon as I felt myself fit I decided to be off. That was not till the twelfth day of June, and as luck would have it a drover went past that morning taking some cattle to Moffat. He was a man named Hislop, a friend of Turnbull's, and he came in to his breakfast with us and offered to take me with him.

I made Turnbull accept five pounds for my lodging, and a hard job I had of it. There never was a more independent being. He grew positively rude when I pressed him, and shy and red, and took the money at last without a thank you. When I told him how much I owed him, he grunted something about "ae guid turn deservin' anither." You would have thought from our leave-taking that we had parted in disgust.

Hislop was a cheery soul, who chattered all the way over the pass and down the sunny vale of Annan. I talked of

Galloway markets and sheep prices, and he made up his mind I was a "pack-shepherd" from those parts—whatever that may be. My plaid and my old hat, as I have said, gave me a fine theatrical Scots look. But driving cattle is a mortally slow job, and we took the better part of the day to cover a dozen miles.

If I had not had such an anxious heart I would have enjoyed that time. It was shining blue weather, with a constantly changing prospect of brown hills and far green meadows, and a continual sound of larks and curlews and falling streams. But I had no mind for the summer, and little for Hislop's conversation, for as the fateful fifteenth of June drew near I was overweighed with the hopeless difficulties of my enterprise.

I got some dinner in a humble Moffat public-house, and walked the two miles to the junction on the main line. The night express for the south was not due till near midnight, and to fill up the time I went up on the hillside and fell asleep, for the walk had tired me. I all but slept too long, and had to run to the station and catch the train with two minutes to spare. The feel of the hard third-class cushions and the smell of stale tobacco cheered me up wonderfully. At any rate, I felt now that I was getting to grips with my job.

I was decanted at Crewe in the small hours and had to wait till six to get a train for Birmingham. In the afternoon I got to Reading, and changed into a local train which journeyed into the deeps of Berkshire. Presently I was in a land of lush water-meadows and slow reedy streams. About eight o'clock in the evening, a weary and travelled-stained being—a cross between a farm-labourer and a vet—with a checked black-and-white plaid over his arm (for I did not dare to wear it south of the Border), descended at the little station of Artinswell. There were several people on the platform, and I thought I had better wait to ask my way till I was clear of the place.

The road led through a wood of great beeches and then into a shallow valley, with the green backs of downs peeping over the distant trees. After Scotland the air smelt heavy and flat, but infinitely sweet, for the limes and chestnuts and lilac bushes were domes of blossom. Presently I came to a bridge, below which a clear slow stream flowed between snowy beds of water-buttercups. A little above it was a mill; and the lasher made a pleasant cool sound in the scented dusk. Somehow the place soothed me and put me at my ease. I fell to whistling as I looked into the green depths, and the tune which came to my lips was "Annie Laurie."

A fisherman came up from the waterside, and as he neared me he too began to whistle. The tune was infectious, for he followed my suit. He was a huge man in untidy old flannels and a wide-brimmed hat, with a canvas bag slung on his shoulder. He nodded to me, and I thought I had never seen a shrewder or better-tempered face. He leaned his delicate ten-foot split-cane rod against the bridge, and looked with me at the water.

"Clear, isn't it?" he said pleasantly. "I back our Kennet any day against the Test. Look at that big fellow. Four pounds if he's an ounce. But the evening rise is over and you can't tempt 'em."

"I don't see him," said I.

"Look! There! A yard from the reeds just above that stickle."

"I've got him now. You might swear he was a black stone."

"So," he said, and whistled another bar of "Annie Laurie."

"Twisdon's the name, isn't it?" he said over his shoulder, his eyes still fixed on the stream.

"No," I said. "I mean to say, Yes." I had forgotten all about my *alias*.

"It's a wise conspirator that knows his own name," he

observed, grinning broadly at a moor-hen that emerged from the bridge's shadow.

I stood up and looked at him, at the square, cleft jaw and broad, lined brow and the firm folds of cheek, and began to think that here at last was an ally worth having. His whimsical blue eyes seemed to go very deep.

Suddenly he frowned. "I call it disgraceful," he said, raising his voice. "Disgraceful that an able-bodied man like you should dare to beg. You can get a meal from my kitchen, but you'll get no money from me."

A dog-cart was passing, driven by a young man who raised his whip to salute the fisherman. When he had gone, he picked up his rod.

"That's my house," he said, pointing to a white gate a hundred yards on. "Wait five minutes and then go round to the back door." And with that he left me.

I did as I was bidden. I found a pretty cottage with a lawn running down to the stream, and a perfect jungle of guelder-rose and lilac flanking the path. The back door stood open, and a grave butler was awaiting me.

"Come this way, sir," he said, and he led me along a passage and up a back staircase to a pleasant bedroom looking towards the river. There I found a complete outfit laid out for me—dress clothes with all the fixings, a brown flannel suit, shirts, collars, ties, shaving things and hair-brushes, even a pair of patent shoes. "Sir Walter thought as how Mr Reggie's things would fit you, sir," said the butler. "He keeps some clothes 'ere, for he comes regular on the week-ends. There's a bathroom next door, and I've prepared a 'ot bath. Dinner in 'alf an hour, sir. You'll 'ear the gong."

The grave being withdrew, and I sat down in a chintz-covered easy-chair and gaped. It was like a pantomime, to come suddenly out of beggardom into this orderly comfort. Obviously Sir Walter believed in me, though why he did I could not guess. I looked at myself in the mirror and saw a wild, haggard brown fellow, with a fortnight's ragged beard, and dust in ears and eyes, collarless, vulgarly shirted, with shapeless old tweed clothes and boots that had not been cleaned for the better part of a month. I made a fine tramp and a fair drover; and here I was ushered by a prim butler into this temple of gracious ease. And the best of it was that they did not even know my name.

I resolved not to puzzle my head but to take the gifts the gods had provided. I shaved and bathed luxuriously, and got into the dress clothes and clean crackling shirt, which fitted me not so badly. By the time I had finished the looking-glass showed a not unpersonable young man.

Sir Walter awaited me in a dusky dining-room where a little round table was lit with silver candles. The sight of him—so respectable and established and secure, the embodiment of law and government and all the conventions—took me aback and made me feel an interloper. He couldn't know the truth about me, or he wouldn't treat me like this. I simply could not accept his hospitality on false pretences.

"I'm more obliged to you than I can say, but I'm bound to make things clear," I said. "I'm an innocent man, but I'm wanted by the police. I've got to tell you this, and I won't be surprised if you kick me out."

He smiled. "That's all right. Don't let that interfere with your appetite. We can talk about these things after dinner."

I never ate a meal with greater relish, for I had had nothing all day but railway sandwiches. Sir Walter did me proud, for we drank a good champagne and had some uncommon fine port afterwards. It made me almost hysterical to be sitting there, waited on by a footman and a sleek butler, and remember that I had been living for three weeks like a brigand, with every man's hand against me. I told Sir Walter about tiger-fish in the Zambesi that bite off your fingers if you give them a chance, and we discussed sport up and down the globe, for he had hunted a bit in his day.

We went to his study for coffee, a jolly room full of books and trophies and untidiness and comfort. I made up my mind that if ever I got rid of this business and had a house of my own, I would create just such a room. Then when the coffee-cups were cleared away, and we had got our cigars alight, my host swung his long legs over the side of his chair and bade me get started with my yarn.

"I've obeyed Harry's instructions," he said, "and the bribe he offered me was that you would tell me something to wake me up. I'm ready, Mr Hannay."

I noticed with a start that he called me by my proper name.

I began at the very beginning. I told of my boredom in London, and the night I had come back to find Scudder gibbering on my doorstep. I told him all Scudder had told me about Karolides and the Foreign Office conference, and that made him purse his lips and grin. Then I got to the murder, and he grew solemn again. He heard all about the milkman and my time in Galloway, and my deciphering Scudder's notes at the inn.

"You've got them here?" he asked sharply, and drew a long breath when I whipped the little book from my pocket.

I said nothing of the contents. Then I described my meeting with Sir Harry, and the speeches at the hall. At that he laughed uproariously.

"Harry talked dashed nonsense, did he? I quite believe it. He's as good a chap as ever breathed, but his idiot of an uncle has stuffed his head with maggots. Go on, Mr Hannay."

My day as roadman excited him a bit. He made me describe the two fellows in the car very closely, and seemed to be raking back in his memory. He grew merry again when he heard of the fate of that ass Jopley.

But the old man in the moorland house solemnised him. Again I had to describe every detail of his appearance.

"Bland and bald-headed and hooded his eyes like a bird. . . . He sounds a sinister wild-fowl! And you dynamited his hermitage, after he had saved you from the police. Spirited piece of work, that!"

Presently I reached the end of my wanderings. He got up slowly, and looked down at me from the hearth-rug.

"You may dismiss the police from your mind," he said. "You're in no danger from the law of this land."

"Great Scot!" I cried. "Have they got the murderer?"

"No. But for the last fortnight they have dropped you from the list of possibles."

"Why?" I asked in amazement.

"Principally because I received a letter from Scudder. I knew something of the man, and he did several jobs for me. He was half crank, half genius, but he was wholly honest. The trouble about him was his partiality for playing a lone hand. That made him pretty well useless in any Secret Service—a pity, for he had uncommon gifts. I think he was the bravest man in the world, for he was always shivering with fright, and yet nothing would choke him off. I had a letter from him on the 31st of May."

"But he had been dead a week by then."

"The letter was written and posted on the 23rd. He evidently did not anticipate an immediate decease. His communications usually took a week to reach me, for they were sent under cover to Spain and then to Newcastle. He had a mania, you know, for concealing his tracks."

"What did he say?" I stammered.

"Nothing. Merely that he was in danger, but had found shelter with a good friend, and that I would hear from him before the 15th of June. He gave me no address, but said he was living near Portland Place. I think his object was to clear you if anything happened. When I got it I went to Scotland Yard, went over the details of the inquest, and concluded that you were the friend. We made inquiries about you, Mr Hannay, and found you were respectable.

I thought I knew the motives for your disappearance—not only the police, the other one too—and when I got Harry's scrawl I guessed at the rest. I have been expecting you any time this past week."

You can imagine what a load this took off my mind. I felt a free man once more, for I was now up against my country's enemies only, and not my country's law.

"Now let us have the little note-book," said Sir Walter.

It took us a good hour to work through it. I explained the cypher, and he was jolly quick at picking it up. He emended my reading of it on several points, but I had been fairly correct, on the whole. His face was very grave before he had finished, and he sat silent for a while.

"I don't know what to make of it," he said at last. "He is right about one thing—what is going to happen the day after to-morrow. How the devil can it have got known? That is ugly enough in itself. But all this about war and the Black Stone—it reads like some wild melodrama. If only I had more confidence in Scudder's judgment. The trouble about him was that he was too romantic. He had the artistic temperament, and wanted a story to be better than God meant it to be. He had a lot of odd biases, too. Jews, for example, made him see red. Jews and the high finance.

"The Black Stone," he repeated. "*Der Schwarzestein.* It's like a penny novelette. And all this stuff about Karolides. That is the weak part of the tale, for I happen to know that the virtuous Karolides is likely to outlast us both. There is no State in Europe that wants him gone. Besides, he has just been playing up to Berlin and Vienna and giving my Chief some uneasy moments. No! Scudder has gone off the track there. Frankly, Hannay, I don't believe that part of his story. There's some nasty business afoot, and he found out too much and lost his life over it. But I am ready to take my oath that it is ordinary spy work. A certain great European Power makes a hobby of her spy system, and her methods are not too particular. Since she pays by piecework her blackguards are not likely to stick at a murder or two. They want our naval dispositions for their collection at the Marinamt; but they will be pigeon-holed—nothing more."

Just then the butler entered the room.

"There's a trunk-call from London, Sir Walter. It's Mr 'Eath, and he wants to speak to you personally."

My host went off to the telephone.

He returned in five minutes with a whitish face. "I apologise to the shade of Scudder," he said. "Karolides was shot dead this evening at a few minutes after seven."

CHAPTER VIII.

THE COMING OF THE BLACK STONE.

I CAME down to breakfast next morning, after eight hours of blessed dreamless sleep, to find Sir Walter decoding a telegram in the midst of muffins and marmalade. His fresh rosiness of yesterday seemed a thought tarnished.

"I had a busy hour on the telephone after you went to bed," he said. "I got my Chief to speak to the First Lord and the Secretary for War, and they are bringing Royer over a day sooner. This wire clinches it. He will be in London at five. Odd that the code word for a *Sous-chef d'Etat Major-General* should be 'Porker.'"

He directed me to the hot dishes and went on.

"Not that I think it will do much good. If your friends were clever enough to find out the first arrangement they are clever enough to discover the change. I would give my head to know where the leak is. We believed there were only five men in England who knew about Royer's visit, and you may be certain there were fewer in France, for they manage these things better there."

While I ate he continued to talk, making me to my surprise a present of his full confidence.

"Can the dispositions not be changed?" I asked.

"They could," he said. "But we want to avoid that if possible. They are the result of immense thought, and no alteration would be as good. Besides, on one or two points change is simply impossible. Still, something could be done, I suppose, if it were absolutely necessary. But you see the difficulty, Hannay. Our enemies are not going to be such fools as to pick Royer's pocket or any childish game like that. They know that would mean a row and put us on our guard. Their aim is to get the details without any one of us knowing, so that Royer will go back to Paris in the belief that the whole business is still deadly secret. If they can't do that they fail, for, once we suspect, they know that the whole thing must be altered."

"Then we must stick by the Frenchman's side till he is home again," I said. "If they thought they could get the information in Paris they would try there. It means that they have some deep scheme on foot in London which they reckon is going to win out."

"Royer dines with my Chief, and then comes to my house where four people will see him—Whittaker from the Admiralty, myself, Sir Arthur Drew, and General Winstanley. The First Lord is ill, and has gone to Sherringham. At my house he will get a certain document from Whittaker, and after that he will be motored to Portsmouth where a destroyer will take him to Havre. His journey is too important for the ordinary boat-train. He will never be left unattended for a moment till he is safe on French soil. The same with Whittaker till he meets Royer. That is the best we can do, and it's hard to see how there can be any miscarriage. But I don't mind admitting that I'm horribly nervous. This murder of Karolides will play the deuce in the chancelleries of Europe."

After breakfast he asked me if I could drive a car.

" Well, you'll be my chauffeur to-day and wear Hudson's rig. You're about his size. You have a hand in this business and we are taking no risks. There are desperate men against us, who will not respect the country retreat of an over-worked official."

When I first came to London I had bought a car and amused myself with running about the south of England, so I knew something of the geography. I took Sir Walter to town by the Bath Road and made good going. It was a soft breathless June morning, with a promise of sultriness later, but it was delicious enough swinging through the little towns with their freshly watered streets, and past the summer gardens of the Thames valley. I landed Sir Walter at his house in Queen Anne's Gate punctually by half-past eleven. The butler was coming up by train with the luggage.

The first thing he did was to take me round to Scotland Yard. There we saw a prim gentleman, with a clean-shaven, lawyer's face.

" I've brought you the Portland Place murderer," was Sir Walter's introduction.

The reply was a wry smile. " It would have been a welcome present, Bullivant. This, I presume, is Mr Richard Hannay, who for some days greatly interested my department."

" Mr Hannay will interest it again. He has much to tell you, but not to-day. For certain grave reasons his tale must wait for twenty-four hours. Then, I can promise you, you will be entertained and possibly edified. I want you to assure Mr Hannay that he will suffer no further inconvenience."

This assurance was promptly given. " You can take up your life where you left off," I was told. " Your flat, which probably you no longer wish to occupy, is waiting for you, and your man is still there. As you were never publicly accused, we considered that there was no need of a public exculpation. But on that, of course, you must please yourself."

"We may want your assistance later on, MacGillivray," Sir Walter said as we left.

Then he turned me loose.

"Come and see me to-morrow, Hannay. I needn't tell you to keep deadly quiet. If I were you I would go to bed, for you must have considerable arrears of sleep to overtake. You had better lie low, for if one of your Black Stone friends saw you there might be trouble."

I felt curiously at a loose end. At first it was very pleasant to be a free man, able to go where I wanted without fearing anything. I had only been a month under the ban of the law, and it was quite enough for me. I went to the Savoy and ordered very carefully a very good luncheon, and then smoked the best cigar the house could provide. But I was still feeling nervous. When I saw anybody look at me in the lounge, I grew shy, and wondered if they were thinking about the murder.

After that I took a taxi and drove miles away up into North London. I walked back through fields and lines of villas and terraces and then slums and mean streets, and it took me pretty nearly two hours. All the while my restlessness was growing worse. I felt that great things, tremendous things, were happening or about to happen, and I, who was the cog-wheel of the whole business, was out of it. Royer would be landing at Dover, Sir Walter would be making plans with the few people in England who were in the secret, and somewhere in the darkness the Black Stone would be working. I felt the sense of danger and impending calamity, and I had the curious feeling, too, that I alone could avert it, alone could grapple with it. But I was out of the game now. How could it be otherwise? It was not likely that Cabinet Ministers and Admiralty Lords and Generals would admit me to their councils.

I actually began to wish that I could run up against one of my three enemies. That would lead to developments.

I felt that I wanted enormously to have a vulgar scrap with those gentry, where I could hit out and flatten something. I was rapidly getting into a very bad temper.

I didn't feel like going back to my flat. That had to be faced some time, but as I still had sufficient money I thought I would put it off till next morning, and go to a hotel for the night.

My irritation lasted through dinner, which I had at a restaurant in Jermyn Street. I was no longer hungry, and let several courses pass untasted. I drank the best part of a bottle of Burgundy, but it did nothing to cheer me. An abominable restlessness had taken possession of me. Here was I, a very ordinary fellow, with no particular brains, and yet I was convinced that somehow I was needed to help this business through—that without me it would all go to blazes. I told myself it was sheer silly conceit, that four or five of the cleverest people living, with all the might of the British Empire at their back, had the job in hand. Yet I couldn't be convinced. It seemed as if a voice kept speaking in my ear, telling me to be up and doing, or I would never sleep again.

The upshot was that about half-past nine I made up my mind to go to Queen Anne's Gate. Very likely I would not be admitted, but it would ease my conscience to try.

I walked down Jermyn Street, and at the corner of Duke Street passed a group of young men. They were in evening dress, had been dining somewhere, and were going on to a music-hall. One of them was Mr Marmaduke Jopley.

He saw me and stopped short.

"By God, the murderer!" he cried. "Here, you fellows, hold him! That's Hannay, the man who did the Portland Place murder!" He gripped me by the arm, and the others crowded round.

I wasn't looking for any trouble, but my ill-temper made me play the fool. A policeman came up, and I should have told him the truth, and, if he didn't believe it, demanded to be taken to Scotland Yard, or for that matter to the nearest police station. But a delay at that moment seemed to me unendurable, and the sight of Marmie's imbecile face was more than I could bear. I let out with my left, and had the satisfaction of seeing him measure his length in the gutter.

Then began an unholy row. They were all on me at once, and the policeman took me in the rear. I got in one or two good blows, for I think, with fair play, I could have licked the lot of them, but the policeman pinned me behind, and one of them got his fingers on my throat.

Through a black cloud of rage I heard the officer of the law asking what was the matter, and Marmie, between his broken teeth, declaring that I was Hannay the murderer.

"Oh, damn it all," I cried, "make the fellow shut up. I advise you to leave me alone, constable. Scotland Yard knows all about me, and you'll get a proper wigging if you interfere with me."

"You've got to come along of me, young man," said the policeman. "I saw you strike that gentleman crool 'ard. You began it too, for he wasn't doing nothing. I seen you. Best go quietly or I'll have to fix you up."

Exasperation and an overwhelming sense that at no cost must I delay gave me the strength of a bull elephant. I fairly wrenched the constable off his feet, floored the man who was gripping my collar, and set off at my best pace down Duke Street. I heard a whistle being blown, and the rush of men behind me.

I have a very fair turn of speed, and that night I had wings. In a jiffy I was in Pall Mall and had turned down towards St James's Park. I dodged the policeman at the Palace gates, dived through a press of carriages at the entrance to the Mall, and was making for the bridge before my pursuers had crossed the roadway. In the open ways of the Park I put on a spurt. Happily there were few people about and no one tried to stop me. I was staking all on getting to Queen Anne's Gate.

When I entered that quiet thoroughfare it seemed deserted. Sir Walter's house was in the narrow part, and outside it three or four motor-cars were drawn up. I slackened speed some yards off and walked briskly up to the door. If the butler refused me admission, or if he even delayed to open the door, I was done.

He didn't delay. I had scarcely rung before the door opened.

"I must see Sir Walter," I panted. "My business is desperately important."

That butler was a great man. Without moving a muscle he held the door open, and then shut it behind me. "Sir Walter is engaged, sir, and I have orders to admit no one. Perhaps you will wait."

The house was of the old-fashioned kind, with a wide hall and rooms on both sides of it. At the far end was an alcove with a telephone and a couple of chairs, and there the butler offered me a seat.

"See here," I whispered. "There's trouble about and I'm in it. But Sir Walter knows, and I'm working for him. If anyone comes and asks if I am here, tell him a lie."

He nodded, and presently there was a noise of voices in the street, and a furious ringing at the bell. I never admired a man more than that butler. He opened the door, and with a face like a graven image waited to be questioned. Then he gave them it. He told them whose house it was, and what his orders were, and simply froze them off the doorstep. I could see it all from my alcove, and it was better than any play.

I hadn't waited long till there came another ring at the bell. The butler made no bones about admitting this new visitor.

While he was taking off his coat I saw who it was. You couldn't open a newspaper or a magazine without seeing that face—the grey beard cut like a spade, the firm fighting mouth, the blunt square nose, and the keen blue eyes. I recognised the First Sea Lord, the man, they say, that made the new British Navy.

He passed my alcove and was ushered into a room at the back of the hall. As the door opened I could hear the sound of low voices. It shut, and I was left alone again.

For twenty minutes I sat there, wondering what I was to do next. I was still perfectly convinced that I was wanted, but when or how I had no notion. I kept looking at my watch, and as the time crept on to half-past ten I began to think that the conference must soon end. In a quarter of an hour Royer should be speeding along the road to Portsmouth. . . .

Then I heard a bell ring, and the butler appeared. The door of the back room opened, and the First Sea Lord came out. He walked past me, and in passing he glanced in my direction, and for a second we looked each other in the face.

Only for a second, but it was enough to make my heart jump. I had never seen the great man before, and he had never seen me. But in that fraction of time something sprang into his eyes, and that something was recognition. You can't mistake it. It is a flicker, a spark of light, a minute shade of difference which means one thing and one thing only. It came involuntarily, for in a moment it died, and he passed on. In a maze of wild fancies I heard the street door close behind him.

I picked up the telephone book and looked up the number of his house. We were connected at once, and I heard a servant's voice.

"Is his Lordship at home?" I asked.

"His Lordship returned half an hour ago," said the voice, "and has gone to bed. He is not very well to-night. Will you leave a message, sir?"

I rung off and almost tumbled into a chair. My part in this business was not yet ended. It had been a close shave, but I had been in time.

Not a moment could be lost, so I marched boldly to the door of that back room and entered without knocking. Five surprised faces looked up from a round table. There was Sir Walter, and Drew the War Minister, whom I knew from his photographs. There was a slim elderly man, who was probably Whittaker, the Admiralty official, and there was General Winstanley, conspicuous from the long scar on his forehead. Lastly, there was a short stout man with an iron-grey moustache and bushy eyebrows, who had been arrested in the middle of a sentence.

Sir Walter's face showed surprise and annoyance.

"This is Mr Hannay, of whom I have spoken to you," he said apologetically to the company. "I'm afraid, Hannay, this visit is ill-timed."

I was getting back my coolness. "That remains to be seen, sir," I said; "but I think it may be in the nick of time. For God's sake, gentlemen, tell me who went out a minute ago?"

"Lord Alloa," Sir Walter said, reddening with anger.

"It was not," I cried; "it was his living image, but it was not Lord Alloa. It was someone who recognised me, someone I have seen in the last month. He had scarcely left the doorstep when I rang up Lord Alloa's house and was told he had come in half an hour before and had gone to bed."

"Who—who——" someone stammered.

"The Black Stone," I cried, and I sat down in the chair so recently vacated and looked round at five badly scared gentlemen.

CHAPTER IX.

THE THIRTY-NINE STEPS.

"NONSENSE!" said the official from the Admiralty.

Sir Walter got up and left the room while we looked blankly at the table. He came back in ten minutes with a long face. "I have spoken to Alloa," he said. "Had him out of bed—very grumpy. He went straight home after Mulross's dinner."

"But it's madness," broke in General Winstanley. "Do you mean to tell me that that man came here and sat beside me for the best part of half an hour and that I didn't detect the imposture? Alloa must be out of his mind."

"Don't you see the cleverness of it?" I said. "You were too interested in other things to have any eyes. You took Lord Alloa for granted. If it had been anybody else you might have looked more closely, but it was natural for him to be here, and that put you all to sleep."

Then the Frenchman spoke, very slowly and in good English.

"The young man is right. His psychology is good. Our enemies have not been foolish!"

He bent his wise brows on the assembly.

"I will tell you a tale," he said. "It happened many years ago in Senegal. I was quartered in a remote station, and to pass the time used to go fishing for big barbel in the river. A little Arab mare used to carry my luncheon basket—one of the salted dun breed you got at Timbuctoo in the old days. Well, one morning I had good sport, and the mare was unaccountably restless. I could hear her whinnying and squealing and stamping her feet, and I kept soothing her with my voice while my mind was intent on fish. I could see her all the time, as I thought, out of a corner of my eye, tethered to a tree twenty yards away. . . . After a couple of hours I began to think of food. I collected my fish in a tarpaulin bag, and moved down the stream towards the mare, trolling my line. When I got up to her I flung the tarpaulin on her back. . . ."

He paused and looked round.

"It was the smell that gave me warning. I turned my head and found myself looking at a lion three feet off. . . . An old man-eater, that was the terror of the village. . . .

What was left of the mare, a mass of blood and bones and hide, was behind him."

"What happened?" I asked. I was enough of a hunter to know a true yarn when I heard it.

"I stuffed my fishing-rod into his jaws, and I had a pistol. Also my servants came presently with rifles. But he left his mark on me." He held up a hand which lacked three fingers.

"Consider," he said. "The mare had been dead more than an hour, and the brute had been patiently watching me ever since. I never saw the kill, for I was accustomed to the mare's fretting, and I never marked her absence, for my consciousness of her was only of something tawny, and the lion filled that part. If I could blunder thus, gentlemen, in a land where men's senses are keen, why should we busy preoccupied urban folk not err also?"

Sir Walter nodded. No one was ready to gainsay him.

"But I don't see," went on Winstanley. "Their object was to get these dispositions without our knowing it. Now it only required one of us to mention to Alloa our meeting to-night for the whole fraud to be exposed."

Sir Walter laughed dryly. "The selection of Alloa shows their acumen. Which of us was likely to speak to him about to-night? Or was he likely to open the subject?"

I remembered the First Sea Lord's reputation for taciturnity and shortness of temper.

"The one thing that puzzles me," said the General, "is what good his visit here would do that spy fellow? He could not carry away several pages of figures and strange names in his head."

"That is not difficult," the Frenchman replied. "A good spy is trained to have a photographic memory. Like your own Macaulay. You noticed he said nothing, but went through these papers again and again. I think we may assume that he has every detail stamped on his mind. When I was younger I could do the same trick."

"Well, I suppose there is nothing for it but to change the plans," said Sir Walter ruefully.

Whittaker was looking very glum. "Did you tell Lord Alloa what has happened?" he asked. "No? Well, I can't speak with absolute assurance, but I'm nearly certain we can't make any serious change unless we alter the geography of England."

"Another thing must be said," it was Royer who spoke. "I talked freely when that man was here. I told something of the military plans of my Government. I was permitted to say so much. But that information would be worth many millions to our enemies. No, my friends, I see no other way. The man who came here and his confederates must be taken, and taken at once."

"Good God," I cried, "and we have not a rag of a clue."

"Besides," said Whittaker, "there is the post. By this time the news will be on its way."

"No," said the Frenchman. "You do not understand the habits of the spy. He receives personally his reward, and he delivers personally his intelligence. We in France know something of the breed. There is still a chance, *mes amis*. These men must cross the sea, and there are ships to be searched and ports to be watched. Believe me, the need is desperate for both France and Britain."

Royer's grave good sense seemed to pull us together. He was the man of action among fumblers. But I saw no hope in any face, and I felt none. Where among the fifty millions of these islands and within a dozen hours were we to lay hands on the three cleverest rogues in Europe?

Then suddenly I had an inspiration.

"Where is Scudder's book?" I cried to Sir Walter. "Quick, man, I remember something in it."

He unlocked the door of a bureau and gave it to me.

I found the place. "*Thirty-nine steps*," I read, and again, "*Thirty-nine steps—I counted them—High tide*, 10.17 P.M."

The Admiralty man was looking at me as if he thought I had gone mad.

"Don't you see it's a clue," I shouted. "Scudder knew where these fellows laired—he knew where they were going to leave the country, though he kept the name to himself. To-morrow was the day, and it was some place where high tide was at 10.17."

"They may have gone to-night," someone said.

"Not they. They have their own snug secret way, and they won't be hurried. I know Germans, and they are mad about working to a plan. Where the devil can I get a book of Tide Tables?"

Whittaker brightened up. "It's a chance," he said. "Let's go over to the Admiralty."

We got into two of the waiting motor-cars—all but Sir Walter, who went off to Scotland Yard—to "mobilise MacGillivray," so he said.

We marched through empty corridors and big bare chambers where the charwomen were busy, till we reached a little room lined with books and maps. A resident clerk was unearthed, who presently fetched from the library the Admiralty Tide Tables. I sat at the desk and the others stood round, for somehow or other I had got charge of this expedition.

It was no good. There were hundreds of entries, and so far as I could see 10.17 might cover fifty places. We had to find some way of narrowing the possibilities.

I took my head in my hands and thought. There must be some way of reading this riddle. What did Scudder mean by steps? I thought of dock steps, but if he had meant that I didn't think he would have mentioned the number. It must be some place where there were several staircases, and one marked out from the others by having thirty-nine steps.

Then I had a sudden thought, and hunted up all the steamer sailings. There was no boat which left for the Continent at 10.17 P.M.

Why was high tide important? If it was a harbour it must be some little place where the tide mattered, or else it was a heavy-draught boat. But there was no regular steamer sailing at that hour, and somehow I didn't think they would travel by a big boat from a regular harbour. So it must be some little harbour where the tide was important, or perhaps no harbour at all.

But if it was a little port I couldn't see what the steps signified. There were no sets of staircases on any harbour that I had ever seen. It must be some place which a particular staircase identified, and where the tide was full at 10.17. On the whole it seemed to me that the place must be a bit of open coast. But the staircases kept puzzling me.

Then I went back to wider considerations. Whereabouts would a man be likely to leave for Germany, a man in a hurry, who wanted a speedy and a secret passage? Not from any of the big harbours. And not from the Channel or the West Coast or Scotland, for, remember, he was starting from London. I measured the distance on the map, and tried to put myself in the enemy's shoes. I should try for Ostend or Antwerp or Rotterdam, and I should sail from somewhere on the East Coast between Cromer and Dover.

All this was very loose guessing, and I don't pretend it was ingenious or scientific. I wasn't any kind of Sherlock Holmes. But I have always fancied I had a kind of instinct about questions like this. I don't know if I can explain myself, but I used to use my brains as far as they went, and after they came to a blank wall I guessed, and I usually found my guesses pretty right.

So I set out all my conclusions on a bit of Admiralty paper. They ran like this:—

FAIRLY CERTAIN.

(1) Place where there are several sets of stairs; one that matters distinguished by having thirty-nine steps.

(2) Full tide at 10.17 P.M. Leaving shore only possible at full tide.
(3) Steps not dock steps, and so place probably not harbour.
(4) No regular night steamer at 10.17. Means of transport must be tramp (unlikely), yacht, or fishing-boat.

There my reasoning stopped. I made another list, which I headed "Guessed," but I was just as sure of the one as the other.

GUESSED.

(1) Place not harbour but open coast.
(2) Boat small—trawler, yacht, or launch.
(3) Place somewhere on East Coast between Cromer and Dover.

It struck me as odd that I should be sitting at that desk with a Cabinet Minister, a Field-Marshal, two high Government officials, and a French General watching me, while from the scribble of a dead man I was trying to drag a secret which meant life or death for us.

Sir Walter had joined us, and presently MacGillivray arrived. He had sent out instructions to watch the ports and railway stations for the three men whom I had described to Sir Walter. Not that he or anybody else thought that that would do much good.

"Here's the most I can make of it," I said. "We have got to find a place where there are several staircases down to the beach, one of which has thirty-nine steps. I think it's a piece of open coast with biggish cliffs, somewhere between the Wash and the Channel. Also it's a place where full tide is at 10.17 to-morrow night."

Then an idea struck me. "Is there no Inspector of Coastguards or some fellow like that who knows the East Coast?"

Whittaker said there was, and that he lived in Clapham.

He went off in a car to fetch him, and the rest of us sat about the little room and talked of anything that came into our heads. I lit a pipe and went over the whole thing again till my brain grew weary.

About one in the morning the coastguard man arrived. He was a fine old fellow, with the look of a naval officer, and was desperately respectful to the company. I left the War Minister to cross-examine him, for I felt he would think it cheek in me to talk.

"We want you to tell us the places you know on the East Coast where there are cliffs, and where several sets of steps run down to the beach."

He thought for a bit. "What kind of steps do you mean, sir? There are plenty of places with roads cut down through the cliffs, and most roads have a step or two in them. Or do you mean regular staircases — all steps, so to speak?"

Sir Arthur looked towards me. "We mean regular staircases," I said.

He reflected a minute or two. "I don't know that I can think of any. Wait a second. There's a place in Norfolk—Brattlesham—beside a golf-course, where there are a couple of staircases to let the gentlemen get a lost ball."

"That's not it," I said.

"Then there are plenty of Marine Parades, if that's what you mean. Every seaside resort has them."

I shook my head.

"It's got to be more retired than that," I said.

"Well, gentlemen, I can't think of anywhere else. Of course, there's the Ruff——"

"What's that?" I asked.

"The big chalk headland in Kent, close to Bradgate. It's got a lot of villas on the top, and some of the houses have staircases down to a private beach. It's a very high-toned sort of place, and the residents there like to keep by themselves."

I tore open the Tide Tables and found Bradgate. High tide there was at 10.27 P.M. on the 15th of June.

"We're on the scent at last," I cried excitedly. "How can I find out what is the tide at the Ruff?"

"I can tell you that, sir," said the coastguard man. "I once was lent a house there in this very month, and I used to go out at night to the deep-sea fishing. The tide's ten minutes before Bradgate."

I closed the book and looked round at the company.

"If one of those staircases has thirty-nine steps we have solved the mystery, gentlemen," I said. "I want the loan of your car, Sir Walter, and a map of the roads. If Mr MacGillivray will spare me ten minutes, I think we can prepare something for to-morrow."

It was ridiculous in me to take charge of the business like this, but they didn't seem to mind, and after all I had been in the show from the start. Besides, I was used to rough jobs, and these eminent gentlemen were too clever not to see it. It was General Royer who gave me my commission. "I for one," he said, "am content to leave the matter in Mr Hannay's hands."

By half-past three I was tearing past the moonlit hedgerows of Kent, with MacGillivray's best man on the seat beside me.

CHAPTER X.

VARIOUS PARTIES CONVERGING ON THE SEA.

A PINK and blue June morning found me at Bradgate looking from the Griffin Hotel over a smooth sea to the lightship on the Cock sands which seemed the size of a bell-buoy. A couple of miles farther south and much nearer the shore a small destroyer was anchored. Scaife, MacGillivray's man, who had been in the Navy, knew the boat, and told me her name and her commander's, so I sent off a wire to Sir Walter.

After breakfast Scaife got from a house-agent a key for the gates of the staircases on the Ruff. I walked with him along the sands, and sat down in a nook of the cliffs while he investigated the half dozen of them. I didn't want to be seen, but the place at this hour was quite deserted, and all the time I was on that beach I saw nothing but the sea-gulls.

It took him more than an hour to do the job, and when I saw him coming towards me, conning a bit of paper, I can tell you my heart was in my mouth. Everything depended, you see, on my guess proving right.

He read aloud the number of steps in the different stairs. "Thirty-four, thirty-five, thirty-nine, forty-two, forty-seven," and "twenty-one" where the cliffs grew lower. I almost got up and shouted.

We hurried back to the town and sent a wire to MacGillivray. I wanted half a dozen men, and I directed them to divide themselves among different specified hotels. Then Scaife set out to prospect the house at the head of the thirty-nine steps.

He came back with news that both puzzled and reassured me. The house was called Trafalgar Lodge, and belonged to an old gentleman called Appleton—a retired stockbroker, the house-agent said. Mr Appleton was there a good deal in the summer time, and was in residence now—had been for the better part of a week. Scaife could pick up very little information about him, except that he was a decent old fellow, who paid his bills regularly, and was always good for a fiver for a local charity. Then Scaife seems to have penetrated to the back door of the house, pretending he was an agent for sewing-machines. Only three servants were kept, a cook, a parlour-maid, and a housemaid, and they were just the sort that you would find in a respectable middle-class household. The cook was not the gossiping kind, and had pretty soon shut the door in his face, but Scaife said he was positive she knew nothing. Next door there was a new house building which would give good cover for observation, and the villa on the other side was to let, and its garden was rough and shrubby.

I borrowed Scaife's telescope, and before lunch went for a walk along the Ruff. I kept well behind the rows of villas, and found a good observation point on the edge of the golf-course. There I had a view of the line of turf along the cliff top, with seats placed at intervals, and the little square plots, railed in and planted with bushes, whence the staircases descended to the beach. I saw Trafalgar Lodge very plainly, a red-brick villa with a verandah, a tennis lawn behind, and in front the ordinary seaside flower-garden full of marguerites and scraggy geraniums. There was a flagstaff from which an enormous Union Jack hung limply in the still air.

Presently I observed someone leave the house and saunter along the cliff. When I got my glasses on him I saw it was an old man, wearing white flannel trousers, a blue serge jacket, and a straw hat. He carried field-glasses and a newspaper, and sat down on one of the iron seats and began to read. Sometimes he would lay down the paper and turn his glasses on the sea. He looked for a long time at the destroyer. I watched him for half an hour, till he got up and went back to the house for his luncheon, when I returned to the hotel for mine.

I wasn't feeling very confident. This decent commonplace dwelling was not what I had expected. The man might be the bald archæologist of that horrible moorland farm, or he might not. He was exactly the kind of satisfied old bird you will find in every suburb and every holiday place. If you wanted a type of the perfectly harmless person you would probably pitch on that.

But after lunch, as I sat in the hotel porch, I perked up, for I saw the thing I had hoped for and had dreaded to miss.

A yacht came up from the south and dropped anchor pretty well opposite the Ruff. She seemed about a hundred and fifty tons, and I saw she belonged to the Squadron from the white ensign. So Scaife and I went down to the harbour and hired a boatman for an afternoon's fishing.

I spent a warm and peaceful afternoon. We caught between us about twenty pounds of cod and lythe, and out in that dancing blue sea I took a cheerier view of things. Above the white cliffs of the Ruff I saw the green and red of the villas, and especially the great flagstaff of Trafalgar Lodge. About four o'clock, when we had fished enough, I made the boatman row us round the yacht, which lay like a delicate white bird, ready at a moment to flee. Scaife said she must be a fast boat from her build, and that she was pretty heavily engined.

Her name was the *Ariadne*, as I discovered from the cap of one of the men who was polishing brasswork. I spoke to him, and got an answer in the soft dialect of Essex. Another hand that came along passed me the time of day in an unmistakable English tongue. Our boatman had an argument with one of them about the weather, and for a few minutes we lay on our oars close to the starboard bow.

Then the men suddenly disregarded us and bent their heads to their work as an officer came along the deck. He was a pleasant, clean-looking young fellow, and he put a question to us about our fishing in very good English. But there could be no doubt about him. His close-cropped head and the cut of his collar and tie never came out of England.

That did something to reassure me, but as we rowed back to Bradgate my obstinate doubts would not be dismissed. The thing that worried me was the reflection that my enemies knew that I had got my knowledge from Scudder, and it was Scudder who had given me the clue to this place. If they knew that Scudder had this clue, would they not be certain to change their plans ? Too much depended on their success for them to take any risks. The whole question was how much they understood about Scudder's knowledge. I had talked confidently last night about Germans always sticking to a scheme, but if they had any suspicions that I was on their track they would be fools not to cover it. I wondered if the man last night had seen that I recognised him. Somehow I did not think he had, and to that I clung. But the whole business had never seemed so difficult as that afternoon when by all calculations I should have been rejoicing in assured success.

In the hotel I met the commander of the destroyer, to whom Scaife introduced me, and with whom I had a few words. Then I thought I would put in an hour or two watching Trafalgar Lodge.

I found a place farther up the hill, in the garden of an empty house. From there I had a full view of the court, on which two figures were having a game of tennis. One was the old man, whom I had already seen ; the other was a younger fellow, wearing some club colours in the scarf round his middle. They played with tremendous zest, like two city gents who wanted hard exercise to open their pores. You couldn't conceive a more innocent spectacle. They shouted and laughed and stopped for drinks, when a maid brought out two tankards on a salver. I rubbed my eyes and asked myself if I was not the most immortal fool on earth. Mystery and darkness had hung about the men who hunted me over the Scotch moor in aeroplane and motor-car, and notably about that infernal antiquarian. It was easy enough to connect those folk with the knife that pinned Scudder to the floor, and with fell designs on the world's peace. But here were two guileless citizens taking their innocuous exercise, and soon about to go indoors to a humdrum dinner, where they would talk of market prices and the last cricket scores and the gossip of their native Surbiton. I had been making a net to catch vultures and falcons, and lo and behold! two plump thrushes had blundered into it.

Presently a third figure arrived, a young man on a bicycle,

with a bag of golf-clubs slung on his back. He strolled round to the tennis lawn and was welcomed riotously by the players. Evidently they were chaffing him, and their chaff sounded horribly English. Then the plump man, mopping his brow with a silk handkerchief, announced that he must have a tub. I heard his very words—" I've got into a proper lather," he said. " This will bring down my weight and my handicap, Bob. I'll take you on to-morrow and give you a stroke a hole." You couldn't find anything much more English than that.

They all went into the house, and left me feeling a precious idiot. I had been barking up the wrong tree this time. These men might be acting; but if they were, where was their audience? They didn't know I was sitting thirty yards off in a rhododendron. It was simply impossible to believe that these three hearty fellows were anything but what they seemed—three ordinary, game-playing, suburban Englishmen, wearisome, if you like, but sordidly innocent.

And yet there were three of them; and one was old, and one was plump, and one was lean and dark; and their house chimed in with Scudder's notes; and half a mile off was lying a steam yacht with at least one German officer. I thought of Karolides lying dead and all Europe trembling on the edge of earthquake, and the men I had left behind me in London who were waiting anxiously for the events of the next hours. There was no doubt that hell was afoot somewhere. The Black Stone had won, and if it survived this June night would bank its winnings.

There seemed only one thing to do—go forward as if I had no doubts, and if I was going to make a fool of myself to do it handsomely. Never in my life have I faced a job with greater disinclination. I would rather in my then mind have walked into a den of anarchists, each with his Browning handy, or faced a charging lion with a popgun, than enter that happy home of three cheerful Englishmen and tell them that their game was up. How they would laugh at me!

But suddenly I remembered a thing I once heard in Rhodesia from old Peter Pienaar. I have quoted Peter already in this narrative. He was the best scout I ever knew, and before he had turned respectable he had been pretty often on the windy side of the law, when he had been wanted badly by the authorities. Peter once discussed with me the question of disguises, and he had a theory which struck me at the time. He said, barring absolute certainties like finger-prints, mere physical traits were very little use for identification if the fugitive really knew his business. He laughed at things like dyed hair and false beards and such childish follies. The only thing that mattered was what Peter called "ammosphere."

If a man could get into perfectly different surroundings from those in which he had been first observed, and—this is the important part—really play up to these surroundings and behave as if he had never been out of them, he would puzzle the cleverest detectives on earth. And he used to tell a story of how he once borrowed a black coat and went to church and shared the same hymn-book with the man that was looking for him. If that man had seen him in decent company before he would have recognised him; but he had only seen him snuffing the lights in a public-house with a revolver.

The recollection of Peter's talk gave me the first real comfort I had had that day. Peter had been a wise old bird, and these fellows I was after were about the pick of the aviary. What if they were playing Peter's game? A fool tries to look different: a clever man looks the same and *is* different.

Again, there was that other maxim of Peter's which had helped me when I had been a roadman. "If you are playing a part, you will never keep it up unless you convince yourself that you are *it*." That would explain the game of tennis. Those chaps didn't need to act, they just turned a handle and passed into another life, which came as naturally to them as the first. It sounds a platitude, but Peter used to say that it was the big secret of all the famous criminals.

It was now getting on for eight o'clock, and I went back and saw Scaife to give him his instructions. I arranged with him how to place his men, and then I went for a walk, for I didn't feel up to any dinner. I went round the deserted golf-course, and then to a point on the cliffs farther north beyond the line of the villas. On the little trim newly-made roads I met people in flannels coming back from tennis and the beach, and a coastguard from the wireless station, and donkeys and pierrots padding homewards. Out at sea in the blue dusk I saw lights appear on the *Ariadne* and on the destroyer away to the south, and beyond the Cock sands the bigger lights of steamers making for the Thames. The whole scene was so peaceful and ordinary that I got more dashed in spirits every second. It took all my resolution to stroll towards Trafalgar Lodge about half-past nine.

On the way I got a piece of solid comfort from the sight of a greyhound that was swinging along at a nursemaid's heels. He reminded me of a dog I used to have in Rhodesia, and of the time when I took him hunting with me in the Pali hills. We were after rhebok, the dun kind, and I recollected how we had followed one beast, and both he and I had clean lost it. A greyhound works by sight, and my eyes are good enough, but that buck simply leaked out of the landscape. Afterwards I found out how it managed it. Against the grey rock of the kopjes it showed no more than a crow against a thundercloud. It didn't need to run away; all it had to do was to stand still and melt into the background.

Suddenly as these memories chased across my brain I thought of my present case and applied the moral. The Black Stone didn't need to bolt. They were quietly absorbed into the landscape. I was on the right track, and I jammed that down in my mind and vowed never to forget it. The last word was with Peter Pienaar.

Scaife's men would be posted now, but there was no sign of a soul. The house stood as open as a market-place for anybody to observe. A three-foot railing separated it from the cliff road; the windows on the ground-floor were all open, and shaded lights and the low sound of voices revealed where the occupants were finishing dinner. Everything was as public and above-board as a charity bazaar. Feeling the greatest fool on earth, I opened the gate and rang the bell.

A man of my sort, who has travelled about the world in rough places, gets on perfectly well with two classes, what you may call the upper and the lower. He understands them and they understand him. I was at home with herds and tramps and roadmen, and I was sufficiently at my ease with people like Sir Walter and the men I had met the night before. I can't explain why, but it is a fact. But what fellows like me don't understand is the great comfortable, satisfied middle-class world, the folk that live in villas and suburbs. He doesn't know how they look at things, he doesn't understand their conventions, and he is as shy of them as of a black mamba. When a trim parlour-maid opened the door, I could hardly find my voice.

I asked for Mr Appleton, and was ushered in. My plan had been to walk straight into the dining-room, and by a sudden appearance wake in the men that start of recognition which would confirm my theory. But when I found myself in that neat hall the place mastered me. There were the golf-clubs and tennis-rackets, the straw hats and caps, the rows of gloves, the sheaf of walking-sticks, which you will find in ten thousand British homes. A stack of neatly folded coats and waterproofs covered the top of an old oak chest; there was a grandfather clock ticking; and some polished brass warming-pans on the walls, and a barometer, and a print of Chiltern winning the St Leger. The place was as orthodox as an Anglican church. When the maid asked me for my name I gave it automatically, and was shown into the smoking-room, on the right side of the hall.

That room was even worse. I hadn't time to examine it, but I could see some framed group photographs above the mantelpiece, and I could have sworn they were English public school or college. I had only one glance, for I managed to pull myself together and go after the maid. But I was too late. She had already entered the dining-room and given my name to her master, and I had missed the chance of seeing how the three took it.

When I walked into the room the old man at the head of the table had risen and turned round to meet me. He was in evening dress—a short coat and black tie, as was the other, whom I called in my own mind the plump one. The third, the dark fellow, wore a blue serge suit and a soft white collar, and the colours of some club or school.

The old man's manner was perfect. "Mr Hannay?" he said hesitatingly. "Did you wish to see me? One moment, you fellows, and I'll rejoin you. We had better go to the smoking-room."

Though I hadn't an ounce of confidence in me, I forced myself to play the game. I pulled up a chair and sat down on it.

"I think we have met before," I said, "and I guess you know my business."

The light in the room was dim, but so far as I could see their faces, they played the part of mystification very well.

"Maybe, maybe," said the old man. "I haven't a very good memory, but I'm afraid you must tell me your errand, sir, for I really don't know it."

"Well, then," I said, and all the time I seemed to myself to be talking pure foolishness—"I have come to tell you that the game's up. I have here a warrant for the arrest of you three gentlemen."

"Arrest," said the old man, and he looked really shocked. "Arrest! Good God, what for?"

"For the murder of Franklin Scudder in London on the 23rd day of last month."

"I never heard the name before," said the old man in a dazed voice.

One of the others spoke up. "That was the Portland Place murder. I read about it. Good heavens, you must be mad, sir! Where do you come from?"

"Scotland Yard," I said.

After that for a minute there was utter silence. The old man was staring at his plate and fumbling with a nut, the very model of innocent bewilderment.

Then the plump one spoke up. He stammered a little, like a man picking his words.

"Don't get flustered, uncle," he said. "It is all a ridiculous mistake; but these things happen sometimes, and we can easily set it right. It won't be hard to prove our innocence. I can show that I was out of the country on the 23rd of May, and Bob was in a nursing home. You were in London, but you can explain what you were doing."

"Right, Percy! Of course that's easy enough. The 23rd! That was the day after Agatha's wedding. Let me see. What was I doing? I came up in the morning from Woking, and lunched at the club with Charlie Symons. Then—oh yes, I dined with the Fishmongers. I remember, for the punch didn't agree with me, and I was seedy next morning. Hang it all, there's the cigar-box I brought back from the dinner." He pointed to an object on the table, and laughed nervously.

"I think, sir," said the young man, addressing me respectfully, "you will see you are mistaken. We want to assist the law like all Englishmen, and we don't want Scotland Yard to be making fools of themselves. That's so, uncle?"

"Certainly, Bob." The old fellow seemed to be recovering his voice. "Certainly, we'll do anything in our power to assist the authorities. But—but this is a bit too much. I can't get over it."

"How Nellie will chuckle," said the plump man. "She always said that you would die of boredom because nothing ever happened to you. And now you've got it thick and strong," and he began to laugh very pleasantly.

"By Jove, yes. Just think of it! What a story to tell at the club. Really, Mr Hannay, I suppose I should be angry, to show my innocence, but it's too funny! I almost forgive you the fright you gave me! You looked so glum, I thought I might have been walking in my sleep and killing people."

It couldn't be acting, it was too confoundedly genuine. My heart went into my boots, and my first impulse was to apologise and clear out. But I told myself I must see it through, even though I was to be the laughing-stock of Britain. The light from the dinner-table candlesticks was not very good, and to cover my confusion I got up, walked to the door and switched on the electric light. The sudden glare made them blink, and I stood scanning the three faces.

Well, I made nothing of it. One was old and bald, one was stout, one was dark and thin. There was nothing in their appearance to prevent them being the three who had hunted me in Scotland, but there was nothing to identify them. I simply can't explain why I who, as a roadman, had looked into two pair of eyes, and as Ned Ainslie into another pair, why I, who have a good memory and reasonable powers of observation, could find no satisfaction. They seemed exactly what they professed to be, and I could not have sworn to one of them.

There in that pleasant dining-room, with etchings on the walls, and a picture of an old lady in a bib above the mantelpiece, I could see nothing to connect them with the moorland desperadoes. There was a silver cigarette-box beside me, and I saw that it had been won by Percival Appleton, Esq., of the St Bede's Club, in a golf tournament. I had to keep firm hold of Peter Pienaar to prevent myself bolting out of that house.

"Well," said the old man politely, "are you reassured by your scrutiny, sir?"

I couldn't find a word.

"I hope you'll find it consistent with your duty to drop this ridiculous business. I make no complaint, but you'll see how annoying it must be to respectable people."

I shook my head.

"O Lord," said the young man. "This is a bit too thick!"

"Do you propose to march us off to the police station?" asked the plump one. "That might be the best way out of it, but I suppose you won't be content with the local branch. I have the right to ask to see your warrant, but I don't wish to cast any aspersions upon you. You are only doing your duty. But you'll admit it's horribly awkward. What do you propose to do?"

There was nothing to do except to call in my men and have them arrested, or to confess my blunder and clear out. I felt mesmerised by the whole place, by the air of obvious innocence—not innocence merely, but frank honest bewilderment and concern in the three faces.

"Oh, Peter Pienaar," I groaned inwardly, and for a moment I was very near damning myself for a fool and asking their pardon.

"Meantime I vote we have a game of bridge," said the plump one. "It will give Mr Hannay time to think over things, and you know we have been wanting a fourth player. Do you play, sir?"

I accepted as if it had been an ordinary invitation at the club. The whole business had mesmerised me. We went into the smoking-room where a card-table was set out, and I was offered things to smoke and drink. I took my place at the table in a kind of dream. The window was open and the moon was flooding the cliffs and sea with a great tide of yellow light. There was moonshine, too, in my head. The three had recovered their composure, and were talking easily—just the kind of slangy talk you will hear in any golf club-house. I must have cut a rum figure, sitting there knitting my brows with my eyes wandering.

My partner was the young dark one. I play a fair hand at bridge, but I must have been rank bad that night. They saw that they had got me puzzled, and that put them more than ever at their ease. I kept looking at their faces, but they conveyed nothing to me. It was not that they looked different; they *were* different. I clung desperately to the words of Peter Pienaar.

Then something awoke me.

The old man laid down his hand to light a cigar. He didn't pick it up at once, but sat back for a moment in his chair, with his fingers tapping on his knees.

It was the movement I remembered when I had stood before him in the moorland farm, with the pistols of his servants behind me.

A little thing, lasting only a second, and the odds were a thousand to one that I might have had my eyes on my cards at the time and missed it. But I didn't, and, in a flash, the air seemed to clear. Some shadow lifted from my brain, and I was looking at the three men with full and absolute recognition.

The clock on the mantelpiece struck ten o'clock.

The three faces seemed to change before my eyes and reveal their secrets. The young one was the murderer. Now I saw cruelty and ruthlessness, where before I had only seen good-humour. His knife, I made certain, had skewered Scudder to the floor. His kind had put the bullet in Karolides.

The plump man's features seemed to dislimn, and form again, as I looked at them. He hadn't a face, only a hundred masks that he could assume when he pleased. That chap must have been a superb actor. Perhaps he had been Lord Alloa of the night before; perhaps not; it didn't matter. I wondered if he was the fellow who had first tracked Scudder, and left his card on him. Scudder had said he lisped, and I could imagine how the adoption of a lisp might add terror.

But the old man was the pick of the lot. He was sheer brain, icy, cool, calculating, as ruthless as a steam hammer. Now that my eyes were opened I wondered where I had seen the benevolence. His jaw was like chilled steel, and his eyes had the inhuman luminosity of a bird's. I went on playing, and every second a greater hate welled up in my heart. It almost choked me, and I couldn't answer when my partner spoke. Only a little longer could I endure their company.

"Whew! Bob! Look at the time," said the old man. "You'd better think about catching your train. Bob's got to go to town to-night," he added, turning to me. The voice rang now as false as hell.

I looked at the clock, and it was nearly half-past ten.

"I am afraid he must put off his journey," I said.

"Oh, damn," said the young man, "I thought you had dropped that rot. I've simply got to go. You can have my address, and I'll give any security you like."

"No," I said, "you must stay."

At that I think they must have realised that the game was desperate. Their only chance had been to convince me that I was playing the fool, and that had failed. But the old man spoke again.

"I'll go bail for my nephew. That ought to content you, Mr Hannay." Was it fancy, or did I detect some halt in the smoothness of that voice.

There must have been, for as I glanced at him, his eyelids fell in that hawk-like hood which fear had stamped on my memory.

I blew my whistle.

In an instant the lights were out. A pair of strong arms gripped me round the waist, covering the pockets in which a man might be expected to carry a pistol.

"*Schnell, Franz,*" cried a voice, "*der Boot, der Boot!*" As it spoke I saw two of my fellows emerge on the moonlit lawn.

The young dark man leapt for the window, was through it, and over the low fence before a hand could touch him. I grappled the old chap, and the room seemed to fill with figures. I saw the plump one collared, but my eyes were all for the out-of-doors, where Franz sped on over the road towards the railed entrance to the beach stairs. One man followed him, but he had no chance. The gate of the stairs locked behind the fugitive, and I stood staring, with my hands on the old boy's throat, for such a time as a man might take to descend those steps to the sea.

Suddenly my prisoner broke from me and flung himself on the wall. There was a click as if a lever had been pulled. Then came a low rumbling far, far below the ground, and through the window I saw a cloud of chalky dust pouring out of the shaft of the stairway.

Someone switched on the light.

The old man was looking at me with blazing eyes.

"He is safe," he cried. "You cannot follow in time. . . . He is gone. . . . He has triumphed. . . . *Der Schwarzestein ist in der Siegeskrone.*"

There was more in those eyes than any common triumph. They had been hooded like a bird of prey, and now they flamed with a hawk's pride. A white fanatic heat burned in them, and I realised for the first time the terrible thing I had been up against. This man was more than a spy; in his foul way he had been a patriot.

As the handcuffs clinked on his wrists I said my last word to him.

"I hope Franz will bear his triumph well. I ought to tell you that the *Ariadne* for the last hour has been in our hands."

Three weeks later, as all the world knows, we went to war. I joined the New Army the first week, and owing to my Matabele experience got a captain's commission straight off. But I had done my best service, I think, before I put on khaki.

II.

THE POWER-HOUSE

TO

MAJOR-GENERAL

SIR FRANCIS LLOYD, K.C.B.

MY DEAR GENERAL,

A recent tale of mine has, I am told, found favour in the dug-outs and billets of the British front, as being sufficiently short and sufficiently exciting for men who have little leisure to read. My friends in that uneasy region have asked for more. So I have printed this story, written in the smooth days before the war, in the hope that it may enable an honest man here and there to forget for an hour the too urgent realities. I have put your name on it, because among the many tastes which we share one is a liking for precipitous yarns.

J. B.

PREFACE BY THE EDITOR.

We were at Glenaicill—six of us—for the duck-shooting, when Leithen told us this story. Since five in the morning we had been out on the skerries, and had been blown home by a wind which threatened to root the house and its wind-blown woods from their precarious lodgment on the hill. A vast nondescript meal, luncheon and dinner in one, had occupied us till the last daylight departed, and we settled ourselves in the smoking-room for a sleepy evening of talk and tobacco.

Conversation, I remember, turned on some of Jim's trophies which grinned at us from the firelit walls, and we began to spin hunting yarns. Then Hoppy Bynge, who was killed next year on the Bramaputra, told us some queer things about his doings in New Guinea, where he tried to climb Carstensz, and lived for six months in mud. Jim said he couldn't abide mud—anything was better than a country where your boots rotted. (He was to get enough of it last winter in the Ypres Salient.) You know how one tale begets another, and soon the whole place hummed with odd recollections, for five of us had been a good deal about the world.

All except Leithen, the man who was afterwards Solicitor-General, and, they say, will get to the Woolsack in time. I don't suppose he had ever been farther from home than Monte Carlo, but he liked hearing about the ends of the earth.

Jim had just finished a fairly steep yarn about his experiences on a Boundary Commission near Lake Chad, and Leithen got up to find a drink.

"Lucky devils," he said. "You've had all the fun out of life. I've had my nose to the grindstone ever since I left school."

I said something about his having all the honour and glory.

"All the same," he went on, "I once played the chief part in a rather exciting business without ever once budging from London. And the joke of it was that the man who went out to look for adventure only saw a bit of the game, and I who sat in my chambers saw it all and pulled the strings. 'They also serve who only stand and wait,' you know."

Then he told us this story. The version I give is one he afterwards wrote down, when he had looked up his diary for some of the details.

CHAPTER I.

BEGINNING OF THE WILD-GOOSE CHASE.

It all started one afternoon early in May when I came out of the House of Commons with Tommy Deloraine. I had got in by an accident at a by-election, when I was supposed to be fighting a forlorn hope, and as I was just beginning to be busy at the Bar I found my hands pretty full. It was before Tommy succeeded, in the days when he sat for the family seat in Yorkshire, and that afternoon he was in a powerful bad temper. Out-of-doors it was jolly spring weather; there was greenery in Parliament Square and bits of gay colour, and a light wind was blowing up from the river. Inside a dull debate was winding on, and an advertising member had been trying to get up a row with the Speaker. The contrast between the frowsy place and the cheerful world outside would have impressed even the soul of a Government Whip.

Tommy sniffed the spring breeze like a supercilious stag.

"This about finishes me," he groaned. "What a juggins I am to be mouldering here! Joggleberry is the celestial limit, what they call in happier lands the pink penultimate. And the frowst on those back benches! Was there ever such a moth-eaten old museum?"

"It is the Mother of Parliaments," I observed.

"Damned monkey-house," said Tommy. "I must get off for a bit or I'll bonnet Joggleberry or get up and propose a national monument to Guy Fawkes or something silly."

I did not see him for a day or two, and then one morning he rang me up and peremptorily summoned me to dine with him. I went, knowing very well what I should find. Tommy was off next day to shoot lions on the Equator, or something equally unconscientious. He was a bad acquaintance for a placid, sedentary soul like me, for though he could work like a Trojan when the fit took him, he was never at the same job very long. In the same week he would harass an Under-Secretary about horses for the Army, write voluminously to the press about a gun he had invented for potting aeroplanes, give a fancy-dress ball which he forgot to attend, and get into the semi-final of the racquets championship. I waited daily to see him start a new religion.

That night, I recollect, he had an odd assortment of guests. A Cabinet Minister was there, a gentle being for whom Tommy professed public scorn and private affection; a sailor; an Indian cavalry fellow; Chapman, the Labour member, whom Tommy called Chipmunk; myself, and old Milson of the Treasury. Our host was in tremendous form, chaffing everybody, and sending Chipmunk into great rolling gusts of merriment. The two lived adjacent in Yorkshire, and on platforms abused each other like pick-pockets.

Tommy enlarged on the misfits of civilised life. He maintained that none of us, except perhaps the sailor and the cavalryman, were at our proper jobs. He would have had Wytham—that was the Minister—a cardinal of the Roman Church, and he said that Milson should have been the Warden of a college full of port and prejudice. Me he was kind enough to allocate to some reconstructed Imperial General Staff, merely because I had a craze for military history. Tommy's perception did not go very deep. He told Chapman he should have been a lumberman in California. "You'd have made an uncommon good logger, Chipmunk, and you know you're a dashed bad politician."

When questioned about himself he became reticent, as the newspapers say. "I doubt if I'm much good at any job," he confessed, "except to ginger up my friends. Anyhow I'm getting out of this hole. Paired for the rest of the session with a chap who has lockjaw. I'm off to stretch my legs and get back my sense of proportion."

Someone asked him where he was going, and was told "Venezuela, to buy Government bonds and look for birds' nests."

Nobody took Tommy seriously, so his guests did not trouble to bid him the kind of farewell a prolonged journey would demand. But when the others had gone, and we were sitting in the little back smoking-room on the first floor, he became solemn. Portentously solemn, for he wrinkled up his brows and dropped his jaw in the way he had when he fancied he was in earnest.

"I've taken on a queer job, Leithen," he said, "and I want you to hear about it. None of my family know, and I would like to leave someone behind me who could get on to my tracks if things got troublesome."

I braced myself for some preposterous confidence, for I was experienced in Tommy's vagaries. But I own to being surprised when he asked me if I remembered Pitt-Heron.

I remembered Pitt-Heron very well. He had been at Oxford with me, but he was no great friend of mine, though for about two years Tommy and he had been inseparable. He had had a prodigious reputation for cleverness with everybody but the college authorities, and used to spend his vacations doing mad things in the Alps and the Balkans, and writing about them in the halfpenny press. He was enormously rich—cotton-mills and Liverpool ground-rents—and being without a father, did pretty much what his fantastic taste dictated. He was rather a hero for a bit after he came down, for he had made some wild journey in the neighbourhood of Afghanistan, and written an exciting book about it.

Then he married a pretty cousin of Tommy's, who happened

to be the only person that ever captured my stony heart, and settled down in London. I did not go to their house, and soon I found that very few of his friends saw much of him either. His travels and magazine articles suddenly stopped, and I put it down to the common course of successful domesticity. Apparently I was wrong.

"Charles Pitt-Heron," said Tommy, "is blowing up for a most thundering mess."

I asked what kind of mess, and Tommy said he didn't know. "That's the mischief of it. You remember the wild beggar he used to be, always off on the spree to the Mountains of the Moon or somewhere. Well, he has been damping down his fires lately, and trying to behave like a respectable citizen, but God knows what he has been thinking! I go a good deal to Portman Square, and all last year he has been getting queerer."

Questions as to the nature of the queerness only elicited the fact that Pitt-Heron had taken to science with some enthusiasm.

"He has got a laboratory at the back of the house—used to be the billiard-room—where he works away half the night. And Lord! The crew you meet there! Every kind of heathen—Chinese and Turks, and long-haired chaps from Russia, and fat Germans. I've several times blundered into the push. They've all got an odd secretive air about them, and Charlie is becoming like them. He won't answer a plain question or look you straight in the face. Ethel sees it too, and she has often talked to me about it."

I said I saw no harm in such a hobby.

"I do," said Tommy grimly. "Anyhow, the fellow has bolted."

"What on earth——" I began, but was cut short.

"Bolted without a word to a mortal soul. He told Ethel he would be home for luncheon yesterday, and never came. His man knew nothing about him, hadn't packed for him or anything; but he found he had stuffed some things into a kit-bag and gone out by the back through the mews. Ethel was in terrible straits and sent for me, and I ranged all yesterday afternoon like a wolf on the scent. I found he had drawn a biggish sum in gold from the bank, but I couldn't find any trace of where he had gone.

"I was just setting out for Scotland Yard this morning when Tomlin, the valet, rang me up and said he had found a card in the waistcoat of the dress clothes that Charles had worn the night before he left. It had a name on it like Konalevsky, and it struck me that they might know something about the business at the Russian Embassy. Well, I went round there, and the long and short of it was that I found there was a fellow of that name among the clerks. I saw him, and he said he had gone to see Mr Pitt-Heron two days before with a letter from some Embassy chap. Unfortunately the man in question had gone off to New York next day, but Konalevsky told me one thing which helped to clear up matters. It seemed that the letter had been one of those passports that Embassies give to their friends—a higher-powered sort than the ordinary make—and Konalevsky gathered from something he had heard that Charles was aiming at Moscow."

Tommy paused to let his news sink in.

"Well, that was good enough for me. I'm off to-morrow to run him to ground."

"But why shouldn't a man go to Moscow if he wants?" I said feebly.

"You don't understand," said the sage Tommy. "You don't know old Charles as I know him. He's got into a queer set, and there's no knowing what mischief he's up to. He's perfectly capable of starting a revolution in Armenia or somewhere merely to see how it feels like to be a revolutionary. That's the damned thing about the artistic temperament. Anyhow, he's got to chuck it. I won't have Ethel scared to death by his whims. I am going to hale him back from Moscow, even if I have to pretend he's an escaped lunatic.

He's probably like enough one by this time if he has taken no clothes."

I have forgotten what I said, but it was some plea for caution. I could not see the reason for these heroics. Pitt-Heron did not interest me greatly, and the notion of Tommy as a defender of the hearth amused me. I thought that he was working on very slight evidence, and would probably make a fool of himself.

"It's only another of the man's fads," I said. "He never could do things like an ordinary mortal. What possible trouble could there be? Money?"

"Rich as Crœsus," said Tommy.

"A woman?"

"Blind as a bat to female beauty."

"The wrong side of the law?"

"Don't think so. He could settle any ordinary scrape with a cheque."

"Then I give it up. Whatever it is, it looks as if Pitt-Heron would have a companion in misfortune before you are done with the business. I'm all for you taking a holiday, for at present you are a nuisance to your friends and a disgrace to your country's legislature. But for goodness' sake curb your passion for romance. They don't like it in Russia."

Next morning Tommy turned up to see me in Chambers. The prospect of travel always went to his head like wine. He was in wild spirits, and had forgotten his anger at the defaulting Pitt-Heron in gratitude for his provision of an occupation. He talked of carrying him off to the Caucasus when he had found him, to investigate the habits of the Caucasian stag.

I remember the scene as if it were yesterday. It was a hot May morning, and the sun which came through the dirty window in Fountain Court lit up the dust and squalor of my working chambers. I was pretty busy at the time, and my table was well nourished with briefs. Tommy picked up one and began to read it. It was about a new drainage scheme in West Ham. He tossed it down and looked at me pityingly.

"Poor old beggar!" he said. "To spend your days on such work when the world is chock-full of amusing things. Life goes roaring by and you only hear the echo in your stuffy rooms. You can hardly see the sun for the cobwebs on these windows of yours. Charles is a fool, but I'm blessed if he isn't wiser than you. Don't you wish you were coming with me?"

The queer thing was that I did. I remember the occasion, as I have said, for it was one of the few on which I have had a pang of dissatisfaction with the calling I had chosen. As Tommy's footsteps grew faint on the stairs I suddenly felt as if I were missing something, as if somehow I were out of it. It is an unpleasant feeling even when you know that the thing you are out of is foolishness.

Tommy went off at 11 from Victoria, and my work was pretty well ruined for the day. I felt oddly restless, and the cause was not merely Tommy's departure. My thoughts kept turning to the Pitt-Herons—chiefly to Ethel, that adorable child unequally yoked to a perverse egoist, but a good deal to the egoist himself. I have never suffered much from whimsies, but I suddenly began to feel a curious interest in the business—an unwilling interest, for I found it in my heart to regret my robust scepticism of the night before. And it was more than interest. I had a sort of presentiment that I was going to be mixed up in the affair more than I wanted. I told myself angrily that the life of an industrious common-law barrister could have little to do with the wanderings of two maniacs in Muscovy. But, try as I might, I could not get rid of the obsession. That night it followed me into my dreams, and I saw myself with a knout coercing Tommy and Pitt-Heron in a Russian fortress which faded away into the Carlton Hotel.

Next afternoon I found my steps wending in the direction of Portman Square. I lived at the time in Down Street, and I told myself I would be none the worse of a walk in the Park before dinner. I had a fancy to see Mrs Pitt-Heron, for, though I had only met her twice since her marriage, there had been a day when we were the closest of friends.

I found her alone, a perplexed and saddened lady with imploring eyes. Those eyes questioned me as to how much I knew. I told her presently that I had seen Tommy and was aware of his errand. I was moved to add that she might count on me if there were anything she wished done on this side of the Channel.

She was very little changed. There was still the old exquisite slimness, the old shy courtesy. But she told me nothing. Charles was full of business and becoming very forgetful. She was sure the Russian journey was all a stupid mistake. He probably thought he had told her of his departure. He would write; she expected a letter by every post.

But her haggard eyes belied her optimism. I could see that there had been odd happenings of late in the Pitt-Heron household. She either knew or feared something;—the latter, I thought, for her air was more of apprehension than of painful enlightenment.

I did not stay long, and, as I walked home, I had an awkward feeling that I had intruded. Also I was increasingly certain that there was trouble brewing, and that Tommy had more warrant for his journey than I had given him credit for. I cast my mind back to gather recollections of Pitt-Heron, but all I could find was an impression of a brilliant, uncomfortable being, who had been too fond of the byways of life for my sober tastes. There was nothing crooked in him in the wrong sense, but there might be a good deal that was perverse. I remember consoling myself with the thought that, though he might shatter his wife's nerves by his vagaries, he would scarcely break her heart.

To be watchful, I decided, was my business. And I could not get rid of the feeling that I might soon have cause for all my vigilance.

CHAPTER II.

I FIRST HEAR OF MR ANDREW LUMLEY.

A FORTNIGHT later—to be accurate, on the 21st of May—I did a thing I rarely do, and went down to South London on a County Court case. It was an ordinary taxi-cab accident, and, as the solicitors for the company were good clients of mine and the regular County Court junior was ill in bed, I took the case to oblige them. There was the usual dull conflict of evidence. An empty taxi-cab, proceeding slowly on the right side of the road and hooting decorously at the corners, had been run into by a private motor-car which had darted down a side street. The taxi had been swung round and its bonnet considerably damaged, while its driver had suffered a dislocated shoulder. The bad feature in the case was that the motor-car had not halted to investigate the damage, but had proceeded unconscientiously on its way, and the assistance of the London police had been called in to trace it. It turned out to be the property of a Mr Julius Pavia, a retired East India merchant, who lived in a large villa in the neighbourhood of Blackheath, and at the time of the accident it had been occupied by his butler. The company brought an action for damages against its owner.

The butler, Tuke by name, was the only witness for the defence. He was a tall man, with a very long, thin face, and a jaw, the two parts of which seemed scarcely to fit. He was profuse in his apologies on behalf of his master, who was abroad. It seemed that on the morning in question—it was the 8th of May—he had received instructions from Mr Pavia to convey a message to a passenger by the Continental express from Victoria, and had been hot on this errand when he met the taxi. He was not aware that there had been any damage, thought it only a slight grazing of the two cars, and on his master's behalf consented to the judgment of the court.

It was a commonplace business, but Tuke was by no means a commonplace witness. He was very unlike the conventional butler, much liker one of those successful financiers whose portraits you see in the picture papers. His little eyes were quick with intelligence, and there were lines of ruthlessness around his mouth, like those of a man often called to decisive action. His story was simplicity itself, and he answered my questions with an air of serious candour. The train he had to meet was the 11 A.M. from Victoria, the train by which Tommy had travelled. The passenger he had to see was an American gentleman, Mr Wright Davies. His master, Mr Pavia, was in Italy, but would shortly be home again.

The case was over in twenty minutes, but it was something unique in my professional experience. For I took a most intense and unreasoning dislike to that bland butler. I cross-examined with some rudeness, was answered with steady courtesy, and hopelessly snubbed. The upshot was that I lost my temper, to the surprise of the County Court judge. All the way back I was both angry and ashamed of myself. Half-way home I realised that the accident had happened on the very day that Tommy left London. The coincidence merely flickered across my mind, for there could be no earthly connection between the two events.

That afternoon I wasted some time in looking up Pavia in the Directory. He was there sure enough as the occupier of a suburban mansion called the White Lodge. He had no city address, so it was clear that he was out of business. My irritation with the man had made me inquisitive about the master. It was a curious name he bore, possibly Italian, possibly Goanese. I wondered how he got on with his highly competent butler. If Tuke had been my servant I would have wrung his neck or bolted before a week was out.

Have you ever noticed that, when you hear a name that

strikes you, you seem to be constantly hearing it for a bit? Once I had a case in which one of the parties was called Jubber, a name I had never met before, but I ran across two other Jubbers before the case was over. Anyhow, the day after the Blackheath visit I was briefed in a big Stock Exchange case, which turned on the true ownership of certain bearer bonds. It was a complicated business, which I need not trouble you with, and it involved a number of consultations with my lay clients, a famous firm of brokers. They produced their books, and my chambers were filled with glossy gentlemen talking a strange jargon.

I had to examine my clients closely on their practice in treating a certain class of bearer security, and they were very frank in expounding their business. I was not surprised to hear that Pitt-Heron was one of the most valued names on their lists. With his wealth he was bound to be a good deal in the city. Now I had no desire to pry into Pitt-Heron's private affairs, especially his financial arrangements, but his name was in my thoughts at the time, and I could not help looking curiously at what was put before me. He seemed to have been buying these bonds on a big scale. I had the indiscretion to ask if Mr Pitt-Heron had long followed this course, and was told that he had begun to purchase some six months before.

"Mr Pitt-Heron," volunteered the stockbroker, "is very closely connected in his financial operations with another esteemed client of ours, Mr Julius Pavia. They are both attracted by this class of security."

At the moment I scarcely noted the name, but after dinner that night I began to speculate about the connection. I had found out the name of one of Charles's mysterious new friends.

It was not a very promising discovery. A retired East India merchant did not suggest anything wildly speculative, but I began to wonder if Charles's preoccupation, to which Tommy had been witness, might not be connected with financial worries. I could not believe that the huge Pitt-Heron fortunes had been seriously affected, or that his flight was that of a defaulter, but he might have got entangled in some shady city business which preyed on his sensitive soul. Somehow or other I could not believe that Mr Pavia was a wholly innocent old gentleman; his butler looked too formidable. It was possible that he was blackmailing Pitt-Heron, and that the latter had departed to get out of his clutches.

But on what ground? I had no notion as to the blackmailable thing that might lurk in Charles's past, and the guesses which flitted through my brain were too fantastic to consider seriously. After all, I had only the flimsiest basis for conjecture. Pavia and Pitt-Heron were friends; Tommy had gone off in quest of Pitt-Heron; Pavia's butler had broken the law of the land in order, for some reason or other, to see the departure of the train by which Tommy had travelled. I remember laughing at myself for my suspicions, and reflecting that, if Tommy could see into my head, he would turn a deaf ear in the future to my complaints of his lack of balance.

But the thing stuck in my mind, and I called again that week on Mrs Pitt-Heron. She had had no word from her husband, and only a bare line from Tommy, giving his Moscow address. Poor child, it was a wretched business for her. She had to keep a smiling face to the world, invent credible tales to account for her husband's absence, and all the while anxiety and dread were gnawing at her heart. I asked her if she had ever met a Mr Pavia, but the name was unknown to her. She knew nothing of Charles's business dealings, but at my request she interviewed his bankers, and I heard from her next day that his affairs were in perfect order. It was no financial crisis which had precipitated him abroad.

A few days later I stumbled by the merest accident upon what sailors call a "cross-bearing." At the time I used to "devil" a little for the Solicitor-General, and "note" cases sent to him from the different Government offices. It was thankless work, but it was supposed to be good for an ambitious lawyer. By this prosaic channel I received the first hint of another of Charles's friends.

I had sent me one day the papers dealing with the arrest of a German spy at Plymouth, for at the time there was a sort of epidemic of roving Teutons, who got themselves into compromising situations, and gravely troubled the souls of the Admiralty and the War Office. This case was distinguished from the common ruck by the higher social standing of the accused. Generally the spy is a photographer or bagman who attempts to win the bibulous confidence of minor officials. But this specimen was no less than a professor of a famous German university, a man of excellent manners, wide culture, and attractive presence, who had dined with Port officers and danced with Admirals' daughters.

I have forgotten the evidence, or what was the legal point submitted for the Law Officers' opinion; in any case it matters little, for he was acquitted. What interested me at the time were the testimonials as to character which he carried with him. He had many letters of introduction. One was from Pitt-Heron to his wife's sailor uncle; and when he was arrested one Englishman went so far as to wire that he took upon himself the whole costs of the defence. This gentleman was a Mr Andrew Lumley, stated in the papers sent me to be a rich bachelor, a member of the Athenæum and Carlton Clubs, and a dweller in the Albany.

Remember that, till a few weeks before, I had known nothing of Pitt-Heron's circle, and here were three bits of information dropping in on me unsolicited, just when my interest had been awakened. I began to get really keen, for every man at the bottom of his heart believes that he is a born detective. I was on the look-out for Charles's infrequent friends, and I argued that if he knew the spy and the spy knew Mr Lumley, the odds were that Pitt-Heron and Lumley were acquaintances. I hunted up the latter in the Red Book. Sure enough he lived in the Albany, belonged to half a dozen clubs, and had a country house in Hampshire.

I tucked the name away in a pigeon-hole of my memory, and for some days asked everyone I met if he knew the philanthropist of the Albany. I had no luck till the Saturday, when, lunching at the club, I ran against Jenkinson, the art critic.

I forget if you know that I have always been a bit of a connoisseur in a mild way. I used to dabble in prints and miniatures, but at that time my interest lay chiefly in Old Wedgwood, of which I had collected some good pieces. Old Wedgwood is a thing which few people collect seriously, but the few who do are apt to be monomaniacs. Whenever a big collection comes into the market it fetches high prices, but it generally finds its way into not more than half a dozen hands. Wedgwoodites all know each other, and they are less cut-throat in their methods than most collectors. Of all I have ever met Jenkinson was the keenest, and he would discourse for hours on the "feel" of good jasper, and the respective merits of blue and sage-green grounds.

That day he was full of excitement. He babbled through luncheon about the Wentworth sale, which he had attended the week before. There had been a pair of magnificent plaques, with a unique Flaxman design, which had roused his enthusiasm. Urns and medallions and what not had gone to this or that connoisseur, and Jenkinson could quote their prices, but the plaques dominated his fancy, and he was furious that the nation had not acquired them. It seemed that he had been to South Kensington and the British Museum, and all sorts of dignitaries, and he thought he might yet persuade the authorities to offer for them if the purchaser would re-sell. They had been bought by Lutrin for a well-known private collector, by name Andrew Lumley.

I pricked up my ears and asked about Mr Lumley.

Jenkinson said he was a rich old buffer who locked up his things in cupboards and never let the public get a look at them. He suspected that a lot of the best things at recent sales had found their way to him, and that meant that they were put in cold storage for good.

I asked if he knew him.

No, he told me, but he had once or twice been allowed to look at his things for books he had been writing. He had never seen the man, for he always bought through agents, but he had heard of people who knew him. " It is the old silly game," he said. " He will fill half a dozen houses with priceless treasures, and then die, and the whole show will be sold at auction and the best things carried off to America. It's enough to make a patriot swear."

There was balm in Gilead, however. Mr Lumley apparently might be willing to re-sell the Wedgwood plaques if he got a fair offer. So Jenkinson had been informed by Lutrin, and that very afternoon he was going to look at them. He asked me to come with him, and, having nothing to do, I accepted.

Jenkinson's car was waiting for us at the club door. It was closed, for the afternoon was wet. I did not hear his directions to the chauffeur, and we had been on the road ten minutes or so before I discovered that we had crossed the river and were traversing South London. I had expected to find the things in Lutrin's shop, but to my delight I was told that Lumley had taken delivery of them at once.

" He keeps very few of his things in the Albany except his books," I was told. " But he has a house at Blackheath which is stuffed from cellar to garret."

" What is the name of it ? " I asked with a sudden suspicion.

" The White Lodge," said Jenkinson.

" But that belongs to a man called Pavia," I said.

" I can't help that. The things in it belong to old Lumley, all right. I know, for I've been three times there with his permission."

Jenkinson got little out of me for the rest of the ride. Here was excellent corroborative evidence of what I had allowed myself to suspect. Pavia was a friend of Pitt-Heron; Lumley was a friend of Pitt-Heron; Lumley was obviously a friend of Pavia, and he might be Pavia himself, for the retired East India merchant, as I figured him, would not be above an innocent impersonation. Anyhow, if I could find one or the other, I might learn something about Charles's recent doings. I sincerely hoped that the owner might be at home that afternoon when we inspected his treasures, for so far I had found no one who could procure me an introduction to that mysterious old bachelor of artistic and philo-Teutonic tastes.

We reached the White Lodge about half-past three. It was one of those small, square, late-Georgian mansions which you see all around London—once a country-house among fields, now only a villa in a pretentious garden. I looked to see my super-butler Tuke, but the door was opened by a female servant who inspected Jenkinson's card of admission, and somewhat unwillingly allowed us to enter.

My companion had not exaggerated when he described the place as full of treasures. It was far more like the shop of a Bond Street art-dealer than a civilised dwelling. The hall was crowded with Japanese armour and lacquer cabinets. One room was lined from floor to ceiling with good pictures, mostly seventeenth-century Dutch, and had enough Chippendale chairs to accommodate a public meeting. Jenkinson would fain have prowled round, but we were moved on by the inexorable servant to the little back room where lay the objects of our visit. The plaques had been only half-unpacked, and in a moment Jenkinson was busy on them with a magnifying glass, purring to himself like a contented cat.

The housekeeper stood on guard by the door, Jenkinson was absorbed, and after the first inspection of the treasures I had leisure to look about me. It was an untidy little room, full of fine Chinese porcelain in dusty glass cabinets, and in a corner stood piles of old Persian rugs.

Pavia, I reflected, must be an easy-going soul, entirely oblivious of comfort, if he allowed his friend to turn his dwelling into such a pantechnicon. Less and less did I believe in the existence of the retired East India merchant. The house was Lumley's, who chose to pass under another name during his occasional visits. His motive might be innocent enough, but somehow I did not think so. His butler had looked too infernally intelligent.

With my foot I turned over the lid of one of the packing-cases that had held the Wedgwoods. It was covered with a litter of cotton-wool and shavings, and below it lay a crumpled piece of paper. I looked again, and saw that it was a telegraph form. Clearly somebody, with the telegram in his hand, had opened the cases, and had left it on the top of one, whence it had dropped to the floor, and been covered by the lid when it was flung off.

I hope and believe that I am as scrupulous as other people, but then and there came on me the conviction that I must read that telegram. I felt the gimlet eye of the housekeeper on me, so I had recourse to craft. I took out my cigarette-case as if to smoke, and clumsily upset its contents amongst the shavings. Then on my knees I began to pick them up, turning over the litter till the telegram was exposed.

It was in French, and I read it quite clearly. It had been sent from Vienna, but the address was in some code. "*Suivez a Bokhare Saronov*"—these were the words. I finished my collection of the cigarettes, and turned the lid over again on the telegram, so that its owner, if he chose to look for it diligently, might find it.

When we sat in the car going home, Jenkinson absorbed in meditation on the plaques, I was coming to something like a decision. A curious feeling of inevitability possessed me. I had collected by accident a few odd, disjointed pieces of information, and here by the most amazing accident of all was the connecting link. I knew I had no evidence to go upon which would have convinced the most credulous common jury. Pavia knew Pitt-Heron; so probably did Lumley. Lumley knew Pavia, possibly was identical with him. Somebody in Pavia's house got a telegram in which a trip to Bokhara was indicated. It didn't sound much. Yet I was absolutely convinced, with the queer subconscious certitude of the human brain, that Pitt-Heron was or was about to be in Bokhara, and that Pavia-Lumley knew of his being there and was deeply concerned in his journey.

That night after dinner I rang up Mrs Pitt-Heron.

She had had a letter from Tommy, a very dispirited letter, for he had had no luck. Nobody in Moscow had seen or heard of any wandering Englishman remotely like Charles; and Tommy, after playing the private detective for three weeks, was nearly at the end of his tether and spoke of returning home.

I told her to send him the following wire in her own name: "*Go on to Bokhara. Have information you will meet him there.*"

She promised to send the message next day, and asked no further questions. She was a pearl among women.

CHAPTER III.

TELLS OF A MIDSUMMER NIGHT.

HITHERTO I had been the looker-on; now I was to become a person of the drama. That telegram was the beginning of my active part in this curious affair. They say that everybody turns up in time at the corner of Piccadilly Circus if you wait long enough. I was to find myself like a citizen of Baghdad in the days of the great Caliph, and yet never stir from my routine of flat, chambers, club, flat.

I am wrong: there was one episode out of London, and that perhaps was the true beginning of my story.

Whitsuntide that year came very late, and I was glad

of the fortnight's rest, for Parliament and the Law Courts had given me a busy time. I had recently acquired a car and a chauffeur called Stagg, and I looked forward to trying it in a tour in the West Country. But before I left London I went again to Portman Square.

I found Ethel Pitt-Heron in grave distress. You must remember that Tommy and I had always gone on the hypothesis that Charles's departure had been in pursuance of some mad scheme of his own which might get him into trouble. We thought that he had become mixed up with highly undesirable friends, and was probably embarking in some venture which might not be criminal but was certain to be foolish. I had long rejected the idea of blackmail, and convinced myself that Lumley and Pavia were his colleagues. The same general notion, I fancy, had been in his wife's mind. But now she had found something which altered the case.

She had ransacked his papers in the hope of finding a clue to the affair which had taken him abroad, but there was nothing but business letters, notes of investments, and such-like. He seemed to have burned most of his papers in the queer laboratory at the back of the house. But, stuffed into the pocket of a blotter on a bureau in the drawing-room where he scarcely ever wrote, she had found a document. It seemed to be the rough draft of a letter, and it was addressed to her. I give it as it was written; the blank spaces were left blank in the manuscript.

"*You must have thought me mad, or worse, to treat you as I have done. But there was a terrible reason, which some day I hope to tell you all about. I want you as soon as you get this to make ready to come out to me at . . . You will travel by . . . and arrive at . . . I enclose a letter which I want you to hand in deepest confidence to Knowles, the solicitor. He will make all arrangements about your journey and about sending me the supplies of money I want. Darling, you must leave as secretly as I did, and tell nobody anything, not even that I am alive—that least of all. I would not frighten you for worlds, but I am on the edge of a horrible danger, which I hope with God's help and yours to escape . . .*"

That was all—obviously the draft of a letter which he intended to post to her from some foreign place. But can you conceive a missive more calculated to shatter a woman's nerves? It filled me, I am bound to say, with heavy disquiet. Pitt-Heron was no coward, and he was not the man to make too much of a risk. Yet it was clear that he had fled that day in May under the pressure of some mortal fear.

The affair in my eyes began to look very bad. Ethel wanted me to go to Scotland Yard, but I dissuaded her. I have the utmost esteem for Scotland Yard, but I shrank from publicity at this stage. There might be something in the case too delicate for the police to handle, and I thought it better to wait.

I reflected a great deal about the Pitt-Heron business the first day or two of my trip, but the air and the swift motion helped me to forget it. We had a fortnight of superb weather, and sailed all day through a glistening green country under the hazy blue heavens of June. Soon I fell into the blissful state of physical and mental ease which such a life induces. Hard toil, such as deer-stalking, keeps the nerves on the alert and the mind active, but swimming all day in a smooth car through a heavenly landscape mesmerises brain and body.

We ran up the Thames valley, explored the Cotswolds, and turned south through Somerset till we reached the fringes of Exmoor. I stayed a day or two at a little inn high up in the moor, and spent the time tramping the endless ridges of hill or scrambling in the arbutus thickets where the moor falls in steeps to the sea. We returned by Dartmoor and the south coast, meeting with our first rain in

Dorset, and sweeping into sunlight again on Salisbury Plain. The time came when only two days remained to me. The car had behaved beyond all my hopes, and Stagg, a sombre and silent man, was lyrical in its praise.

I wanted to be in London by the Monday afternoon, and to insure this I made a long day of it on the Sunday. It was the long day which brought our pride to a fall. The car had run so well that I resolved to push on and sleep in a friend's house near Farnham. It was about half-past eight, and we were traversing the somewhat confused and narrow roads in the neighbourhood of Wolmer Forest, when, as we turned a sharp corner, we ran full into the tail of a heavy carrier's cart. Stagg clapped on the brakes, but the collision, though it did no harm to the cart, was sufficient to send the butt-end of something through our glass screen, damage the tyre of the near front wheel, and derange the steering-gear. Neither of us suffered much hurt, but Stagg got a long scratch on his cheek from broken glass, and I had a bruised shoulder.

The carrier was friendly but useless, and there was nothing for it but to arrange for horses to take the car to Farnham. This meant a job of some hours, and I found on inquiry at a neighbouring cottage that there was no inn where I could stay within eight miles. Stagg borrowed a bicycle somehow and went off to collect horses, while I morosely reviewed the alternatives before me.

I did not like the prospect of spending the June night beside my derelict car, and the thought of my friend's house near Farnham beckoned me seductively. I might have walked there, but I did not know the road, and I found that my shoulder was paining me, so I resolved to try to find some gentleman's house in the neighbourhood where I could borrow a conveyance. The south of England is now so densely peopled by Londoners that even in a wild district, where there are no inns and few farms, there are certain to be several week-end cottages.

I walked along the white ribbon of road in the scented June dusk. At first it was bounded by high gorse, then came patches of open heath, and then woods. Beyond the woods I found a park-railing, and presently an entrance-gate with a lodge. It seemed to be the place I was looking for, and I woke the lodge-keeper, who thus early had retired to bed. I asked the name of the owner, but was told the name of the place instead—it was High Ashes. I asked if the owner was at home, and got a sleepy nod for answer.

The house, as seen in the half-light, was a long white-washed cottage, rising to two storeys in the centre. It was plentifully covered with creepers and roses, and the odour of flowers was mingled with the faintest savour of wood-smoke, pleasant to a hungry traveller in the late hours. I pulled an old-fashioned bell, and the door was opened by a stolid young parlour-maid.

I explained my errand, and offered my card. I was, I said, a Member of Parliament and of the Bar, who had suffered a motor accident. Would it be possible for the master of the house to assist me to get to my destination near Farnham? I was bidden enter, and wearily seated myself on a settle in the hall.

In a few minutes an ancient house-keeper appeared, a grim dame whom at other times I should have shunned. She bore, however, a hospitable message. There was no conveyance in the place, as the car had gone that day to London for repairs. But if I cared to avail myself of the accommodation of the house for the night it was at my service. Meantime my servant could be looking after the car, and a message would go to him to pick me up in the morning.

I gratefully accepted, for my shoulder was growing trouble-some, and was conducted up a shallow oak staircase to a very pleasant bedroom with a bathroom adjoining. I had a bath, and afterwards found a variety of comforts put at my service from slippers to razors. There was also some

Elliman for my wounded shoulder. Clean and refreshed I made my way downstairs and entered a room from which I caught a glow of light.

It was a library, the most attractive I think I have ever seen. The room was long, as libraries should be, and entirely lined with books, save over the fireplace, where hung a fine picture which I took to be a Raeburn. The books were in glass cases, which showed the beautiful shallow mouldings of a more artistic age. A table was laid for dinner in a corner, for the room was immense, and the shaded candle-sticks on it, along with the late June dusk, gave such light as there was. At first I thought the place was empty, but as I crossed the floor a figure rose from a deep chair by the hearth.

"Good evening, Mr Leithen," a voice said. "It is a kindly mischance which gives a lonely old man the pleasure of your company."

He switched on an electric lamp, and I saw before me—what I had not guessed from the voice—an old man. I was thirty-four at the time, and counted anything over fifty old, but I judged my host to be well on in the sixties. He was about my own size, but a good deal bent in the shoulders, as if from study. His face was clean-shaven and extraordinarily fine, with every feature delicately chiselled. He had a sort of Hapsburg mouth and chin, very long and pointed, but modelled with a grace which made the full lower lip seem entirely right. His hair was silver, brushed so low on the forehead as to give him a slightly foreign air, and he wore tinted glasses, as if for reading.

Altogether it was a very dignified and agreeable figure who greeted me in a voice so full and soft that it belied his obvious age.

Dinner was a light meal, but perfect in its way. There were soles, I remember, an exceedingly well-cooked chicken, fresh strawberries, and a savoury. We drank a '95 Perrier-

Jouet and some excellent Madeira. The stolid parlour-maid waited on us, and, as we talked of the weather and the Hampshire roads, I kept trying to guess my host's profession. He was not a lawyer, for he had not the inevitable lines on the cheek. I thought that he might be a retired Oxford don, or one of the higher civil servants, or perhaps some official of the British Museum. His library proclaimed him a scholar, and his voice a gentleman.

Afterwards we settled ourselves in arm-chairs, and he gave me a good cigar. We talked about many things—books, the right furnishing of a library, a little politics, in deference to my M.P.-ship. My host was apathetic about party questions, but curious about defence matters, and in his way an amateur strategist. I could fancy his inditing letters to 'The Times' on national service.

Then we wandered into foreign affairs, where I found his interest acute, and his knowledge immense. Indeed he was so well informed that I began to suspect that my guesses had been wrong, and that he was a retired diplomat. At that time there was some difficulty between France and Italy over customs duties, and he sketched for me with remarkable clearness the weak points in the French tariff administration. I had been recently engaged in a big South American railway case, and I asked him a question about the property of my clients. He gave me a much better account than I had ever got from the solicitors who briefed me.

The fire had been lit before we finished dinner, and presently it began to burn up and light the figure of my host, who sat in a deep arm-chair. He had taken off his tinted glasses, and as I rose to get a match I saw his eyes looking abstractedly before him.

Somehow they reminded me of Pitt-Heron. Charles had always a sort of dancing light in his, a restless intelligence which was at once attractive and disquieting. My host had this and more. His eyes were paler than I had ever seen in a human head—pale, bright, and curiously wild. But, whereas Pitt-Heron's had only given the impression of reckless youth, this man's spoke of wisdom and power as well as of endless vitality.

All my theories vanished, for I could not believe that my host had ever followed any profession. If he had, he would have been at the head of it, and the world would have been familiar with his features. I began to wonder if my recollection was not playing me false, and I was in the presence of some great man whom I ought to recognise.

As I dived into the recesses of my memory I heard his voice asking if I were not a lawyer.

I told him, Yes. A barrister with a fair common-law practice and some work in Privy Council appeals.

He asked me why I chose the profession.

"It came handiest," I said. "I am a dry creature, who loves facts and logic. I am not a flier, I have no new ideas, I don't want to lead men, and I like work. I am the ordinary educated Englishman, and my sort gravitates to the Bar. We like feeling that, if we are not the builders, at any rate we are the cement of civilisation."

He repeated the words "cement of civilisation" in his soft voice.

"In a sense you are right. But civilisation needs more than the law to hold it together. You see, all mankind are not equally willing to accept as divine justice what is called human law."

"Of course there are further sanctions," I said. "Police and armies and the goodwill of civilisation."

He caught me up quickly. "The last is your true cement. Did you ever reflect, Mr Leithen, how precarious is the tenure of the civilisation we boast about?"

"I should have thought it fairly substantial," I said, "and the foundations grow daily firmer."

He laughed. "That is the lawyer's view, but, believe me, you are wrong. Reflect, and you will find that the foundations are sand. You think that a wall as solid as the earth separates civilisation from barbarism. I tell you the division is a thread, a sheet of glass. A touch here, a push there, and you bring back the reign of Saturn."

It was the kind of paradoxical, undergraduate speculation which grown men indulge in sometimes after dinner. I looked at my host to discover his mood, and at the moment a log flared up again.

His face was perfectly serious. His light wild eyes were intently watching me.

"Take one little instance," he said. "We are a commercial world, and have built up a great system of credit. Without our cheques and bills of exchange and currency the whole of our life would stop. But credit only exists because behind it we have a standard of value. My Bank of England notes are worthless paper unless I can get sovereigns for them if I choose. Forgive this elementary disquisition, but the point is important. We have fixed a gold standard, because gold is sufficiently rare, and because it allows itself to be coined into a portable form. I am aware that there are economists who say that the world could be run equally well on a pure credit basis, with no metal currency at the back of it; but, however sound their argument may be in the abstract, the thing is practically impossible. You would have to convert the whole of the world's stupidity to their economic faith before it would work.

"Now, suppose something happened to make our standard of value useless. Suppose the dream of the alchemists came true, and all metals were readily transmutable. We have got very near it in recent years, as you will know if you interest yourself in chemical science. Once gold and silver lost their intrinsic value, the whole edifice of our commerce would collapse. Credit would become meaningless, because it would be untranslatable. We should be back at a bound in the age of barter, for it is hard to see what other standard of value could take the place of the precious metals. All our civilisation, with its industries and commerce, would come toppling down. Once more, like primitive man, I would plant cabbages for a living, and exchange them for services in kind from the cobbler and the butcher. We should have the simple life with a vengeance—not the self-conscious simplicity of the civilised man, but the compulsory simplicity of the savage."

I was not greatly impressed by the illustration. "Of course there are many key-points in civilisation," I said, "and the loss of them would bring ruin. But those keys are strongly held."

"Not so strongly as you think. Consider how delicate the machine is growing. As life grows more complex, the machinery grows more intricate, and therefore more vulnerable. Your so-called sanctions become so infinitely numerous that each in itself is frail. In the Dark Ages you had one great power—the terror of God and His Church. Now you have a multiplicity of small things, all delicate and fragile, and strong only by our tacit agreement not to question them."

"You forget one thing," I said—"the fact that men really are agreed to keep the machine going. That is what I called the 'goodwill of civilisation.'"

He got up from his chair and walked up and down the floor, a curious dusky figure lit by the rare spurts of flame from the hearth.

"You have put your finger on the one thing that matters. Civilisation is a conspiracy. What value would your police be if every criminal could find a sanctuary across the Channel, or your law courts, if no other tribunal recognised their decisions? Modern life is the silent compact of comfortable folk to keep up pretences. And it will succeed till the day comes when there is another compact to strip them bare."

I do not think that I have ever listened to a stranger conversation. It was not so much what he said—you will hear the same thing from any group of half-baked young men—as the air with which he said it. The room was almost dark, but the man's personality seemed to take shape and bulk in the gloom. Though I could scarcely see him, I knew that those pale strange eyes were looking at me. I wanted more light, but did not know where to look for a switch. It was all so eerie and odd that I began to wonder if my host were not a little mad. In any case, I was tired of his speculations.

"We won't dispute on the indisputable," I said. "But I should have thought that it was the interest of all the best brains of the world to keep up what you call the conspiracy."

He dropped into his chair again.

"I wonder," he said slowly. "Do we really get the best brains working on the side of the compact? Take the business of Government. When all is said, we are ruled by the amateurs and the second-rate. The methods of our departments would bring any private firm to bankruptcy. The methods of Parliament—pardon me—would disgrace any board of directors. Our rulers pretend to buy expert knowledge, but they never pay the price for it that a business man would pay, and if they get it they have not the courage to use it. Where is the inducement for a man of genius to sell his brains to our insipid governors?"

"And yet knowledge is the only power—now as ever. A little mechanical device will wreck your navies. A new chemical combination will upset every rule of war. It is the same with our commerce. One or two minute changes might sink Britain to the level of Ecuador, or give China the key of the world's wealth. And yet we never dream that these things are possible. We think our castles of sand are the ramparts of the universe."

I have never had the gift of the gab, but I admire it in others. There is a morbid charm in such talk, a kind of exhilaration, of which one is half ashamed. I found myself interested, and more than a little impressed.

"But surely," I said, "the first thing a discoverer does is to make his discovery public. He wants the honour and glory, and he wants money for it. It becomes part of the world's knowledge, and everything is readjusted to meet it. That was what happened with electricity. You call our civilisation a machine, but it is something far more flexible. It has the power of adaptation of a living organism."

"That might be true if the new knowledge really became the world's property. But does it? I read now and then in the papers that some eminent scientist had made a great discovery. He reads a paper before some Academy of Science, and there are leading articles on it, and his photograph adorns the magazines. That kind of man is not the danger. He is a bit of the machine, a party to the compact. It is the men who stand outside it that are to be reckoned with, the artists in discovery who will never use their knowledge till they can use it with full effect. Believe me, the biggest brains are without the ring which we call civilisation."

Then his voice seemed to hesitate. "You may hear people say that submarines have done away with the battleship, and that aircraft have annulled the mastery of the sea. That is what our pessimists say. But do you imagine that the clumsy submarine or the fragile aeroplane is really the last word of science?"

"No doubt they will develop," I said, "but by that time the power of the defence will have advanced also."

He shook his head. "It is not so. Even now the knowledge which makes possible great engines of destruction is far beyond the capacity of any defence. You see only the productions of second-rate folk who are in a hurry to get wealth and fame. The true knowledge, the deadly knowledge, is still kept secret. But, believe me, my friend, it is there."

He paused for a second, and I saw the faint outline of the smoke from his cigar against the background of the dark. Then he quoted me one or two cases, slowly, as if in some doubt about the wisdom of his words.

It was these cases that startled me. They were of different kinds—a great calamity, a sudden breach between two nations, a blight on a vital crop, a war, a pestilence. I will not repeat them. I do not think I believed in them then, and now I believe less. But they were horribly impressive, as told in that quiet voice in that sombre room on that dark June night. If he was right, these things had not been the work of Nature or accident, but of a devilish art. The nameless brains that he spoke of, working silently in the background, now and then showed their power by some cataclysmic revelation. I did not believe him, but, as he put the case, showing with strange clearness the steps in the game, I had no words to protest.

At last I found my voice.

"What you describe is super-anarchy, and yet it makes no headway. What is the motive of those diabolical brains?"

He laughed. "How should I be able to tell you? I am a humble inquirer, and in my researches I come on curious bits of fact. But I cannot pry into motives. I only know of the existence of great extra-social intelligences. Let us say that they distrust the machine. They may be idealists and desire to make a new world, or they may simply be artists, loving for its own sake the pursuit of truth. If I were to hazard a guess, I should say that it took both types to bring about results, for the second find the knowledge and the first the will to use it."

A recollection came back to me. It was of a hot upland meadow in Tyrol, where among acres of flowers and beside a leaping stream I was breakfasting after a morning spent in climbing the white crags. I had picked up a German on the way, a small man of the Professor class, who did me the honour to share my sandwiches. He conversed fluently but quaintly in English, and he was, I remember, a Nietzschean and a hot rebel against the established order. "The pity," he cried, "is that the reformers do not know, and those who know are too idle to reform. Some day there will come the marriage of knowledge and will, and then the world will march."

"You draw an awful picture," I said. "But if those extra-social brains are so potent, why after all do they effect so little? A dull police-officer, with the machine behind him, can afford to laugh at most experiments in anarchy."

"True," he said, "and civilisation will win until its enemies learn from it the importance of the machine. The compact must endure until there is a counter-compact. Consider the ways of that form of foolishness which to-day we call nihilism or anarchy. A few illiterate bandits in a Paris slum defy the world, and in a week they are in jail. Half a dozen crazy Russian *intellectuels* in Geneva conspire to upset the Romanovs, and are hunted down by the police of Europe. All the Governments and their not very intelligent police forces join hands, and hey, presto! there is an end of the conspirators. For civilisation knows how to use such powers as it has, while the immense potentiality of the unlicensed is dissipated in vapour. Civilisation wins because it is a world-wide league; its enemies fail because they are parochial. But supposing——"

Again he stopped and rose from his chair. He found a switch and flooded the room with light. I glanced up blinking to see my host smiling down on me, a most benevolent and courteous old gentleman. He had resumed his tinted glasses.

"Forgive me," he said, "for leaving you in darkness while I bored you with my gloomy prognostications. A recluse is apt to forget what is due to a guest."

He handed the cigar-box to me, and pointed to a table where whisky and mineral waters had been set out.

"I want to hear the end of your prophecies," I said. "You were saying——?"

"I said—supposing anarchy learned from civilisation and

became international. Oh, I don't mean the bands of advertising donkeys who call themselves International Unions of Workers and suchlike rubbish. I mean if the real brain-stuff of the world were internationalised. Suppose that the links in the cordon of civilisation were neutralised by other links in a far more potent chain. The earth is seething with incoherent power and unorganised intelligence. Have you ever reflected on the case of China? There you have millions of quick brains stifled in trumpery crafts. They have no direction, no driving power, so the sum of their efforts is futile, and the world laughs at China. Europe throws her a million or two on loan now and then, and she cynically responds by begging the prayers of Christendom. And yet, I say, supposing——"

"It's a horrible idea," I said, "and, thank God, I don't believe it possible. Mere destruction is too barren a creed to inspire a new Napoleon, and you can do with nothing short of one."

"It would scarcely be destruction," he replied gently. "Let us call it iconoclasm, the swallowing of formulas, which has always had its full retinue of idealists. And you do not want a Napoleon. All that is needed is direction, which could be given by men of far lower gifts than a Bonaparte. In a word, you want a Power-House, and then the age of miracles will begin."

I got up, for the hour was late, and I had had enough of this viewy talk. My host was smiling, and I think that smile was the thing I really disliked about him. It was too —what shall I say?—superior and Olympian.

As he led me into the hall he apologised for indulging his whims. "But you, as a lawyer, should welcome the idea. If there is an atom of truth in my fancies, your task is far bigger than you thought. You are not defending an easy case, but fighting in a contest where the issues are still doubtful. That should encourage your professional pride. . . ."

By all the rules I should have been sleepy, for it was past midnight, and I had had a long day in the open air. But that wretched talk had unsettled me, and I could not get my mind off it. I have reproduced very crudely the substance of my host's conversation, but no words of mine could do justice to his eery persuasiveness. There was a kind of magnetism in the man, a sense of vast powers and banked-up fires, which would have given weight to the tritest platitudes. I had a horrible feeling that he was trying to convince me, to fascinate me, to prepare the ground for some proposal. Again and again I told myself it was crazy nonsense, the heated dream of a visionary, but again and again I came back to some detail which had a horrid air of reality. If the man was a romancer he had an uncommon gift of realism.

I flung open my bedroom window and let in the soft air of the June night and the scents from leagues of clover and pines and sweet grasses. It momentarily refreshed me, for I could not believe that this homely and gracious world held such dire portents.

But always that phrase of his, the "Power-House," kept recurring. You know how twisted your thoughts get during a wakeful night, and long before I fell asleep towards morning I had worked myself up into a very complete dislike of that bland and smiling gentleman, my host. Suddenly it occurred to me that I did not know his name, and that set me off on another train of reflection.

I did not wait to be called, but rose about seven, dressed, and went downstairs. I heard the sound of a car on the gravel of the drive, and to my delight saw that Stagg had arrived. I wanted to get away from the house as soon as possible, and I had no desire to meet its master again in this world.

The grim housekeeper, who answered my summons, received my explanation in silence. Breakfast would be ready in twenty minutes; eight was Mr Lumley's hour for it.

"Mr Andrew Lumley?" I asked with a start.

"Mr Andrew Lumley," she said.

So that was my host's name. I sat down at a bureau in the hall and did a wildly foolish thing.

I wrote a letter, beginning "Dear Mr Lumley," thanking him for his kindness and explaining the reason of my early departure. It was imperative, I said, that I should be in London by mid-day. Then I added: "I wish I had known who you were last night, for I think you know an old friend of mine, Charles Pitt-Heron."

Breakfastless I joined Stagg in the car, and soon we were swinging down from the uplands to the shallow vale of the Wey. My thoughts were very little on my new toy or on the midsummer beauties of Surrey. The friend of Pitt-Heron, who knew about his going to Bokhara, was the maniac who dreamed of the "Power-House." There were going to be dark scenes in the drama before it was played out.

CHAPTER IV.

I FOLLOW THE TRAIL OF THE SUPER-BUTLER.

My first thought, as I journeyed towards London, was that I was horribly alone in this business.

Whatever was to be done I must do it myself, for the truth was I had no evidence which any authority would recognise. Pitt-Heron was the friend of a strange being who collected objects of art, probably passed under an *alias* in South London, and had absurd visions of the end of civilisation. That, in cold black and white, was all my story came to. If I went to the police they would laugh at me, and they would be right.

Now I am a sober and practical person, but, slender though my evidence was, it brought to my mind the most absolute conviction. I seemed to know Pitt-Heron's story as if I had heard it from his own lips—his first meeting with Lumley and their growing friendship; his initiation into secret and forbidden things; the revolt of the decent man, appalled that his freakishness had led him so far; the realisation that he could not break so easily with his past, and that Lumley held him in his power; and last, the mad flight under the pressure of overwhelming terror.

I could read, too, the purpose of that flight. He knew the Indian frontier as few men know it, and in the wild tangle of the Pamirs he hoped to baffle his enemy. Then from some far refuge he would send for his wife, and spend the rest of his days in exile. It must have been an omnipotent terror to drive such a man, young, brilliant, rich, successful, to the fate of an absconding felon.

But Lumley was on his trail. So I read the telegram I had picked up on the floor of the Blackheath house, and my business was to frustrate the pursuit. Someone must have gone to Bokhara, some creature of Lumley's, perhaps the super-butler I had met in the County Court. The telegram, for I had noted the date, had been received on the 27th day of May. It was now the 15th of June, so if someone had started immediately on its receipt, in all probability he would by now be in Bokhara.

I must find out who had gone, and endeavour to warn Tommy. I calculated that it would have taken him seven or eight days to get from Moscow by the Transcaspian; probably he would find Pitt-Heron gone, but inquiries would set him on the track. I might be able to get in touch with him through the Russian officials. In any case, if Lumley were stalking Pitt-Heron, I, unknown and unsuspected, would be stalking Lumley.

And then in a flash I realised my folly.

The wretched letter I had written that morning had given the whole show away. Lumley knew that I was a friend of Pitt-Heron, and that I knew that he was a friend of Pitt-Heron. If my guess was right, friendship with

Lumley was not a thing Charles was likely to confess to, and he would argue that my knowledge of it meant that I was in Charles's confidence. I would therefore know of his disappearance and its cause, and alone in London would connect it with the decorous bachelor of the Albany. My letter was a warning to him that he could not play the game unobserved, and I, too, would be suspect in his eyes.

It was no good crying over spilt milk, and Lumley's suspicions must be accepted. But I confess that the thought gave me the shivers. The man had a curious terror for me, a terror I cannot hope to analyse and reproduce for you. My bald words can give no idea of the magnetic force of his talk, the sense of brooking and unholy craft. I was proposing to match my wits against a master's—one, too, who must have at his command an organisation far beyond my puny efforts. I have said that my first feeling was that of loneliness and isolation; my second was one of hopeless insignificance. It was a boy's mechanical toy arrayed against a Power-House with its shining wheels and monstrous dynamos.

My first business was to get into touch with Tommy.

At that time I had a friend in one of the Embassies, whose acquaintance I had made on a dry-fly stream in Hampshire. I will not tell you his name, for he has since become a great figure in the world's diplomacy, and I am by no means certain that the part he played in this tale was strictly in accordance with official etiquette. I had assisted him on the legal side in some of the international worries that beset all Embassies, and we had reached the point of intimacy which is marked by the use of Christian names and by dining frequently together. Let us call him Monsieur Felix. He was a grave young man, slightly my senior, learned, discreet, and ambitious, but with an engaging boyishness cropping up now and then under the official gold lace. It occurred to me that in him I might find an ally.

I reached London about eleven in the morning, and went

straight to Belgrave Square. Felix I found in the little library off the big secretaries' room, a sunburnt sportsman fresh from a Norwegian salmon river. I asked him if he had half an hour to spare, and was told that the day was at my service.

"You know Tommy Deloraine?" I asked.

He nodded.

"And Charles Pitt-Heron?"

"I have heard of him."

"Well, here is my trouble. I have reason to believe that Tommy has joined Pitt-Heron in Bokhara. If he has, my mind will be greatly relieved, for, though I can't tell you the story, I can tell you that Pitt-Heron is in very considerable danger. Can you help me?"

Felix reflected. "That should be simple enough. I can wire in cypher to the Military Governor. The police there are pretty efficient, as you may imagine, and travellers don't come and go without being remarked. I should be able to give you an answer within twenty-four hours. But I must describe Tommy. How does one do that in telegraphese?"

"I want you to tell me another thing," I said. "You remember that Pitt-Heron has some reputation as a Central Asian traveller. Tommy, as you know, is as mad as a hatter. Suppose these two fellows at Bokhara, wanting to make a long trek into wild country—how would they go? You've been there, and know the lie of the land."

Felix got down a big German atlas, and for half an hour we pored over it. From Bokhara, he said, the only routes for madmen ran to the south. East and north you got into Siberia; west lay the Transcaspian desert; but southward you might go through the Hissar range by Pamirski Post to Gilgit and Kashmir, or you might follow up the Oxus and enter the north of Afghanistan, or you might go by Merv into north-eastern Persia. The first he thought the likeliest route, if a man wanted to travel fast.

I asked him to put in his cable a suggestion about watching the Indian roads, and left him with a promise of early enlightenment.

Then I went down to the Temple, fixed some consultations, and spent a quiet evening in my rooms. I had a heavy sense of impending disaster, not unnatural in the circumstances. I really cannot think what it was that held me to the job, for I don't mind admitting that I felt pretty queasy about it. Partly, no doubt, liking for Tommy and Ethel, partly regret for that unfortunate fellow Pitt-Heron, most of all, I think, dislike of Lumley. That bland superman had fairly stirred my prosaic antipathies.

That night I went carefully over every item in the evidence to try and decide on my next step. I had got to find out more about my enemies. Lumley, I was pretty certain, would baffle me, but I thought I might have a better chance with the super-butler. As it turned out, I hit his trail almost at once.

Next day I was in a case at the Old Bailey. It was an important prosecution for fraud, and I appeared, with two leaders, for the bank concerned. The amazing and almost incredible thing about this story of mine is the way clues kept rolling in unsolicited, and I was to get another from this dull prosecution. I suppose that the explanation is that the world is full of clues to everything, and that if a man's mind is sharp-set on any quest, he happens to notice and take advantage of what otherwise he would miss. My leaders were both absent the first day, and I had to examine our witnesses alone.

Towards the close of the afternoon I put a fellow in the box, an oldish, drink-sodden clerk from a Cannon Street bucket-shop. His evidence was valuable for our case, but I was very doubtful how he would stand a cross-examination as to credit. His name was Routh, and he spoke with a strong north-country accent. But what caught my attention was his face. His jaw looked as if it had been made in two pieces which did not fit, and he had little, bright, protuberant eyes. At my first glance I was conscious of a recollection.

He was still in the box when the Court rose, and I informed the solicitors that before going further I wanted a conference with the witness. I mentioned also that I should like to see him alone. A few minutes later he was brought to my Chambers, and I put one or two obvious questions on the case, till the managing clerk who accompanied him announced with many excuses that he must hurry away. Then I shut the door, gave Mr Routh a cigar, and proceeded to conduct a private inquiry.

He was a pathetic being, only too ready to talk. I learned the squalid details of his continuous misfortunes. He had been the son of a dissenting minister in Northumberland, and had drifted through half a dozen occupations till he found his present unsavoury billet. Truth was written large on his statement; he had nothing to conceal, for his foible was folly, not crime, and he had not a rag of pride to give him reticence. He boasted that he was a gentleman and well-educated, too, but he had never had a chance. His brother had advised him badly; his brother was too clever for a prosaic world; always through his reminiscences came this echo of fraternal admiration and complaint.

It was about the brother I wanted to know, and Mr Routh was very willing to speak. Indeed, it was hard to disentangle facts from his copious outpourings. The brother had been an engineer and a highly successful one; had dallied with politics, too, and had been a great inventor. He had put Mr Routh on to a South American speculation, where he had made a little money, but speedily lost it again. Oh, he had been a good brother in his way, and had often helped him, but he was a busy man, and his help never went quite far enough. Besides, he did not like to apply to him too often. I gathered that the brother was not a person to take liberties with.

I asked him what he was doing now.

"Ah," said Mr Routh, "that is what I wish I could tell you. I will not conceal from you that for the moment I am in considerable financial straits, and this case, though my hands are clean enough, God knows, will not make life easier for me. My brother is a mysterious man, whose business often takes him abroad. I have never known even his address, for I write always to a London office from which my communications are forwarded. I only know that he is in some big electrical business, for I remember that he once let drop the remark that he was in charge of some power station. No, I do not think it is in London; probably somewhere abroad. I heard from him a fortnight ago, and he told me he was just leaving England for a couple of months. It is very annoying, for I want badly to get into touch with him."

"Do you know, Mr Routh," I said, "I believe I have met your brother. Is he like you in any way?"

"We have a strong family resemblance, but he is taller and slimmer. He has been more prosperous, and has lived a healthier life, you see."

"Do you happen to know," I asked, "if he ever uses another name? I don't think that the man I knew was called Routh."

The clerk flushed. "I think it highly unlikely that my brother would use an *alias*. He has done nothing to disgrace a name of which we are proud."

I told him that my memory had played me false, and we parted on very good terms. He was an innocent soul, one of those people that clever rascals get to do their dirty work for them. But there was no mistaking the resemblance. There, without the brains and force and virility, went my super-butler of Blackheath, who passed under the name of Tuke.

The clerk had given me the name of the office to whose address he had written to his brother. I was not surprised to find that it was that of the firm of stockbrokers for whom I was still acting in the bearer-bonds case where I had heard Pavia's name.

I rang up the partner whom I knew, and told him a very plausible story of having a message for one of Mr Pavia's servants, and asked him if he were in touch with them and could forward letters. He made me hold the line, and then came back and told me that he had forwarded letters for Tuke, the butler, and one Routh who was a groom or footman. Tuke had gone abroad to join his master and he did not know his address. But he advised me to write to the White Lodge.

I thanked him and rang off. That was settled, anyhow. Tuke's real name was Routh, and it was Tuke who had gone to Bokhara.

My next step was to ring up Macgillivray at Scotland Yard and get an appointment in half an hour's time. Macgillivray had been at the Bar—I had read in his Chambers—and was now one of the heads of the Criminal Investigation Department. I was about to ask him for information which he was in no way bound to give me, but I presumed on our old acquaintance.

I asked him first whether he had ever heard of a secret organisation which went under the name of the Power-House. He laughed out loud at my question.

"I should think we have several hundreds of such pet names on our records," he said. "Everything from the Lodge of the Baldfaced Ravens to Solomon's Seal No. X. Fancy nomenclature is the relaxation of the tired anarchist, and matters very little. The dangerous fellows have no names, no numbers even, which we can get hold of. But I'll get a man to look up our records. There may be something filed about your Power-House."

My second question he answered differently. "Routh! Routh! Why, yes, there was a Routh we had dealings with a dozen years ago when I used to go the North-Eastern Circuit. He was a Trade Union official who bagged the funds, and they couldn't bring him to justice because of the ridiculous extra-legal status they possess. He knew it, and played their own privileges against them. Oh yes, he was a very complete rogue. I once saw him at a meeting in Sunderland, and I remember his face—sneering eyes, diabolically clever mouth, and with it all as smug as a family butler. He has disappeared from England—at least we haven't heard of him for some years, but I can show you his photograph."

Macgillivray took from a lettered cabinet a bundle of cards, selected one, and tossed it towards me. It was that of a man of thirty or so, with short side-whiskers and a drooping moustache. The eyes, the ill-fitting jaw, and the brow were those of my friend Mr Tuke, brother and patron of the sorrowful Mr Routh, who had already that afternoon occupied my attention.

Macgillivray promised to make certain inquiries, and I walked home in a state of elation. Now I knew for certain who had gone to Bokhara, and I knew something, too, of the traveller's past. A discredited genius was the very man for Lumley's schemes—one who asked for nothing better than to use his brains outside the ring-fence of convention. Somewhere in the wastes of Turkestan the ex-Trade Union official was in search of Pitt-Heron. I did not fancy that Mr Tuke would be very squeamish.

I dined at the club and left early. Going home, I had an impression that I was being shadowed.

You know the feeling that someone is watching you, a sort of sensation which the mind receives without actual evidence. If the watcher is behind, where you can't see him, you have a cold feeling between your shoulders. I daresay it is a legacy from the days when the cave-man had to look pretty sharp to keep from getting his enemy's knife between the ribs.

It was a bright summer evening, and Piccadilly had its usual crowd of motor-cars and buses and foot passengers. I halted twice, once in St James's Street and once at the corner of Stratton Street, and retraced my steps for a bit; and each time I had the impression that someone a hundred yards or so off had done the same. My instinct was to turn round and face him, whoever he was, but I saw that that was foolishness. Obviously in such a crowd I could get no certainty in the matter, so I put it out of my mind.

I spent the rest of the evening in my rooms, reading cases and trying to keep my thoughts off Central Asia. About ten I was rung up on the telephone by Felix. He had had his answer from Bokhara. Pitt-Heron had left with a small caravan on June 2nd by the main road through the Hissar range. Tommy had arrived on June 10th, and on the 12th had set off with two servants on the same trail. Travelling the lighter of the two, he should have overtaken Pitt-Heron by the 15th at latest.

That was yesterday, and my mind was immensely relieved. Tommy in such a situation was a tower of strength, for, whatever his failings in politics, I knew no one I would rather have with me to go tiger-shooting.

Next day the sense of espionage increased. I was in the habit of walking down to the Temple by way of Pall Mall and the Embankment, but, as I did not happen to be in Court that morning, I resolved to make a detour and test my suspicions. There seemed to be nobody in Down Street as I emerged from my flat, but I had not walked five yards before, turning back, I saw a man enter from the Piccadilly end, while another moved across the Hertford Street opening. It may have been only my imagination, but I was convinced that these were my watchers.

I walked up Park Lane, for it seemed to me that by taking the Tube at the Marble Arch Station I could bring matters to the proof. I have a knack of observing small irrelevant details, and I happened to have noticed that a certain carriage in the train which left Marble Arch about 9.30 stopped exactly opposite the exit at the Chancery Lane Station, and by hurrying up the passage one could just catch the lift which served an earlier train, and so reach the street before any of the other travellers.

I performed this manœuvre with success, caught the early lift, reached the street, and took cover behind a pillar-box, from which I could watch the exit of passengers from the stairs. I judged that my tracker, if he missed me below, would run up the stairs rather than wait on the lift. Sure enough, a breathless gentleman appeared, who scanned the street eagerly, and then turned to the lift to watch the emerging passengers. It was clear that the espionage was no figment of my brain.

I walked slowly to my Chambers, and got through the day's work as best I could, for my mind was preoccupied with the unpleasant business in which I found myself entangled. I would have given a year's income to be honestly quit of it, but there seemed to be no way of escape. The maddening thing was that I could do so little. There was no chance of forgetting anxiety in strenuous work. I could only wait with the patience at my command, and hope for the one chance in a thousand which I might seize. I felt miserably that it was no game for me. I had never been brought up to harry wild beasts and risk my neck twice a day at polo like Tommy Deloraine. I was a peaceful sedentary man, a lover of a quiet life, with no appetite for perils and commotions. But I was beginning to realise that I was very obstinate.

At four o'clock I left the Temple and walked to the Embassy. I had resolved to banish the espionage from my mind, for that was the least of my difficulties.

Felix gave me an hour of his valuable time. It was something that Tommy had joined Pitt-Heron, but there were other matters to be arranged in that far country. The time had come, in my opinion, to tell him the whole story.

The telling was a huge relief to my mind. He did not laugh at me as I had half feared, but took the whole thing as gravely as possible. In his profession, I fancy, he had found too many certainties behind suspicions to treat anything as trivial. The next step, he said, was to warn the Russian police of the presence of the man called Saronov and the super-butler. Happily we had materials for the description of Tuke or Routh, and I could not believe that such a figure would be hard to trace. Felix cabled again in cypher, asking that the two should be watched, more especially if there was reason to believe that they had followed Tommy's route. Once more we got out the big map and discussed the possible ways. It seemed to me a land created by Providence for surprises, for the roads followed the valleys, and to the man who travelled light there must be many short-cuts through the hills.

I left the Embassy before six o'clock and, crossing the Square engrossed with my own thoughts, ran full into Lumley.

I hope I played my part well, though I could not repress a start of surprise. He wore a grey morning-coat and a white top-hat, and looked the image of benevolent respectability.

"Ah, Mr Leithen," he said, "we meet again."

I murmured something about my regrets at my early departure three days ago, and added the feeble joke that I wished he would hurry on his Twilight of Civilisation, for the burden of it was becoming too much for me.

He looked me in the eyes with all the friendliness in the world. "So you have not forgotten our evening's talk? You owe me something, my friend, for giving you a new interest in your profession."

"I owe you much," I said, "for your hospitality, your advice, and your warnings."

He was wearing his tinted glasses, and peered quizzically into my face.

"I am going to make a call in Grosvenor Place," he said, "and shall beg in return the pleasure of your company. So you know my young friend, Pitt-Heron?"

With an ingenuous countenance I explained that he had been at Oxford with me and that we had common friends.

"A brilliant young man," said Lumley. "Like you, he has occasionally cheered an old man's solitude. And he has spoken of me to you?"

"Yes," I said, lying stoutly. "He used to tell me about your collections." (If Lumley knew Charles well he would find me out, for the latter would not have crossed the road for all treasures of the Louvre.)

"Ah, yes, I have picked up a few things. If ever you should care to see them I should be honoured. You are a connoisseur? Of a sort? You interest me, for I should have thought your taste lay in other directions than the dead things of art. Pitt-Heron is no collector. He loves life better than art, as a young man should. A great traveller, our friend—the Laurence Oliphant or Richard Burton of our day."

We stopped at a house in Grosvenor Place, and he relinquished my arm. "Mr Leithen," he said, "a word from one who wishes you no ill. You are a friend of Pitt-Heron, but where he goes you cannot follow. Take my advice and keep out of his affairs. You will do no good to him, and you may bring yourself into serious danger. You are a man of sense, a practical man, so I speak to you frankly. But, remember, I do not warn twice."

He took off his glasses, and his light, wild eyes looked me straight in the face. All benevolence had gone, and something implacable and deadly burned in them. Before I could say a word in reply he shuffled up the steps of the house and was gone. . . .

CHAPTER V.

I TAKE A PARTNER.

THAT meeting with Lumley scared me badly, but it also clinched my resolution. The most pacific fellow on earth can be gingered into pugnacity. I had now more than my friendship for Tommy and my sympathy with Pitt-Heron to urge me on. A man had tried to bully me, and that roused all the worst stubbornness of my soul. I was determined to see the game through at any cost.

But I must have an ally if my nerves were to hold out, and my mind turned at once to Tommy's friend, Chapman. I thought with comfort of the bluff independence of the Labour Member. So that night at the House I hunted him out in the smoking-room.

He had been having a row with the young bloods of my party that afternoon and received me ungraciously.

"I'm about sick of you fellows," he growled. (I shall not attempt to reproduce Chapman's accent. He spoke rich Yorkshire, with a touch of the drawl of the western dales.) "They went and spoiled the best speech, though I say it as shouldn't, which this old place has heard for a twelvemonth. I've been workin' for days at it in the Library. I was tellin' them how much more bread cost under Protection, and the Jew Hilderstein started a laugh because I said kilometres for kilogrammes. It was just a slip o' the tongue, for I had it right in my notes, and besides, these furrin words don't matter a curse. Then that young lord as sits for East Claygate gets up and goes out as I was gettin' into my peroration, and he drops his topper and knocks off old Higgins's spectacles, and all the idiots laughed. After that I gave it them hot and strong, and got called to order. And then Wattles, him as used to be as good a Socialist as me, replied for the Government and his blamed Board, and said that the Board thought this and the Board thought that, and was blessed if the Board would stir its stumps. Well I mind the day when I was hanging on to the Board's coat-tails in Hyde Park to keep it from talking treason."

It took me a long time to get Chapman settled down and anchored to a drink.

"I want you," I said, "to tell me about Routh—you know the fellow I mean—the ex-Union leader."

At that he fairly blazed up.

"There you are, you Tories," he shouted, causing a pale Liberal Member on the next sofa to make a hurried exit. "You can't fight fair. You hate the Unions, and you rake up any rotten old prejudice to discredit them. You can find out about Routh for yourself, for I'm damned if I help you."

I saw I could do nothing with Chapman unless I made a clean breast of it, so for the second time that day I told the whole story.

I couldn't have wished for a better audience. He got wildly excited before I was half through with it. No doubt of the correctness of my evidence ever entered his head, for, like most of his party, he hated anarchism worse than capitalism, and the notion of a highly capitalised, highly scientific, highly undemocratic anarchism fairly revolted his soul. Besides, he adored Tommy Deloraine.

Routh, he told me, had been a young engineer of a superior type, with a job in a big shop at Sheffield. He had professed advanced political views, and, although he had strictly no business to be there, had taken a large part in Trade Union work, and was treasurer of one big branch. Chapman had met him often at conferences and on platforms, and had been impressed by the fertility and ingenuity of his mind and the boldness of his purpose. He was the leader of the left wing of the movement, and had that gift of half-scientific, half-philosophic jargon which is dear at all times to the hearts of the half-baked. A seat in Parliament had been repeatedly offered him, but he had always declined; wisely, Chapman thought, for he judged him the type which is more effective behind the scenes.

But with all his ability he had not been popular. "He was a cold-blooded, sneering devil," as Chapman put it, "a sort of Parnell. He tyrannised over his followers, and he was the rudest brute I ever met."

Then followed the catastrophe, in which it became apparent that he had speculated with the funds of the Union and had lost a large sum. Chapman, however, was suspicious of these losses, and was inclined to suspect that he had the money all the time in a safe place. A year or two earlier the Unions, greatly to the disgust of old-fashioned folk, had been given certain extra-legal privileges, and this man Routh had been one of the chief advocates of the Unions' claims. Now he had the cool effrontery to turn the tables on them, and use those very privileges to justify his action and escape prosecution.

There was nothing to be done. Some of the fellows, said Chapman, swore to wring his neck, but he did not give them the chance. He had disappeared from England, and was generally believed to be living in some foreign capital.

"What I would give to be even with the swine!" cried my friend, clenching and unclenching his big fist. "But we're up against no small thing in Josiah Routh. There isn't a crime on earth he'd stick at, and he's as clever as the old Devil, his master."

"If that's how you feel, I can trust you to back me up," I said. "And the first thing I want you to do is to come and stay at my flat. God knows what may happen next, and two men are better than one. I tell you frankly, I'm nervous, and I would like to have you with me."

Chapman had no objection. I accompanied him to his Bloomsbury lodgings, where he packed a bag, and we returned to the Down Street flat. The sight of his burly figure and sagacious face was a relief to me in the mysterious darkness where I now found myself walking.

Thus began my housekeeping with Chapman, one of the queerest episodes in my life. He was the best fellow in the world, but I found that I had misjudged his character. To see him in the House you would have thought him a piece of granite, with his Yorkshire bluntness and hard, downright, north-country sense. He had all that somewhere inside him, but he was also as romantic as a boy. The new situation delighted him. He was quite clear that it was another case of the strife between Capital and Labour—Tommy and I standing for Labour, though he used to refer to Tommy in public as a "gilded popinjay," and only a month before had described me in the House as a "viperous lackey of Capitalism." It was the best kind of strife in which you had not to meet your adversary with long-winded speeches, but might any moment get a chance to pummel him with your fists.

He made me ache with laughter. The spying business used to rouse him to fury. I don't think he was tracked as I was, but he chose to fancy he was, and was guilty of assault and battery on one butcher's boy, two cabbies, and a gentleman who turned out to be a bookmaker's assistant. This side of him got to be an infernal nuisance, and I had many rows with him. Among other things, he chose to suspect my man Waters of treachery—Waters, who was the son of a gardener at home, and hadn't wits enough to put up an umbrella when it rained.

"You're not taking this business rightly," he maintained one night. "What's the good of waiting for these devils to down you? Let's go out and down them." And he announced his intention, from which no words of mine could dissuade him, of keeping watch on Mr Andrew Lumley at the Albany.

His resolution led to a complete disregard of his Parliamentary duties. Deputations of constituents waited for him in vain. Of course he never got a sight of Lumley. All that happened was that he was very nearly given in charge more than once for molesting peaceable citizens in the neighbourhood of Piccadilly and Regent Street.

One night on my way home from the Temple I saw in the bills of the evening papers the announcement of the arrest of a Labour Member. It was Chapman, sure enough. At first I feared that he had got himself into serious trouble, and was much relieved to find him in the flat in a state of blazing anger. It seemed that he had found somebody whom he thought was Lumley, for he only knew him from my descriptions. The man was in a shop in Jermyn Street, with a car waiting outside, and Chapman had—politely, as he swore—asked the chauffeur his master's name. The chauffeur had replied abusively, upon which Chapman had haled him from the driver's seat and shaken him till his teeth rattled. The owner came out, and Chapman was arrested and taken off to the nearest police court. He had been compelled to apologise, and had been fined five pounds and costs.

By the mercy of Heaven the chauffeur's master was a money-lender of evil repute, so the affair did Chapman no harm. But I was forced to talk to him seriously. I knew it was no use explaining that for him to spy on the Power-House was like an elephant stalking a gazelle. The only way was to appeal to his incurable romanticism.

"Don't you see," I told him, "that you are playing Lumley's game? He will trap you sooner or later into some escapade which will land you in jail, and where will I be then? That is what he and his friends are out for. We have got to meet cunning with cunning, and lie low till we get our chance."

He allowed himself to be convinced, and handed over to me the pistol he had bought, which had been the terror of my life.

"All right," he said, "I'll keep quiet. But you promise to let me into the big scrap when it comes off."

I promised. Chapman's notion of the grand finale was a Homeric combat in which he would get his fill of fisticuffs.

He was an anxiety, but all the same he was an enormous comfort. His imperturbable cheerfulness and his racy talk were the tonics I wanted. He had plenty of wisdom, too. My nerves were getting bad those days, and, whereas I had rarely touched the things before, I now found myself smoking cigarettes from morning till night. I am pretty abstemious, as you know, but I discovered to my horror that I was drinking far too many whiskys-and-sodas. Chapman knocked me off all that, and got me back to a pipe and a modest nightcap.

He did more, for he undertook to put me in training. His notion was that we should win in the end by superior muscles. He was a square, thick-set fellow, who had been a good middle-weight boxer. I could box a bit myself, but I improved mightily under his tuition. We got some gloves, and used to hammer each other for half an hour every morning. Then might have been seen the shameful spectacle of a rising barrister with a swollen lip and a black eye arguing in Court and proceeding of an evening to his country's legislature, where he was confronted from the opposite benches by the sight of a Leader of the People in the same vulgar condition.

In those days I wanted all the relief I could get, for it was a beastly time. I knew I was in grave danger, so I made my will and went through the other doleful performances consequent on the expectation of a speedy decease. You see I had nothing to grip on, no clear job to tackle, only to wait on the off-chance, with an atmosphere of suspicion thickening around me. The spying went on—there was no mistake about that—but I soon ceased to mind it, though I did my best to give my watchers little satisfaction. There was a hint of bullying about the spying. It is disconcerting at night to have a man bump against you and look you greedily in the face.

I did not go again to Scotland Yard, but one night I ran across Macgillivray in the club.

He had something of profound interest to tell me. I had asked about the phrase, the "Power-House." Well, he had come across it, in the letter of a German friend, a private letter, in which the writer gave the results of his inquiries into a curious affair which a year before had excited Europe.

I have forgotten the details, but it had something to do with the Slav States of Austria and an Italian Students' Union, and it threatened at one time to be dangerous. Macgillivray's correspondent said that in some documents which were seized he found constant allusion to a thing called the *Krafthaus*, evidently the headquarters staff of the plot. And this same word *Krafthaus* had appeared elsewhere—in a sonnet of a poet-anarchist who shot himself in the slums of Antwerp, in the last ravings of more than one criminal, in the extraordinary testament of Professor M—— of Jena, who, at the age of thirty-seven, took his life after writing a strange mystical message to his fellow-citizens.

Macgillivray's correspondent concluded by saying that, in his opinion, if this *Krafthaus* could be found, the key would be discovered to the most dangerous secret organisation in the world. He added that he had some reason to believe that the motive power of the concern was English.

"Macgillivray," I said, "you have known me for some time, and I fancy you think me a sober and discreet person. Well, I believe I am on the edge of discovering the secret of your *Krafthaus*. I want you to promise me that if in the next week I send you an urgent message you will act on it, however fantastic it seems. I can't tell you more. I ask you to take me on trust, and believe that for anything I do I have tremendous reasons."

He knit his shaggy grey eyebrows and looked curiously at me. "Yes, I'll go bail for your sanity. It's a good deal to promise, but if you make an appeal to me, I will see that it is met."

Next day I had news from Felix. Tuke and the man called Saronov had been identified. If you are making inquiries about anybody it is fairly easy to find those who are seeking for the same person, and the Russian police, in tracking Tommy and Pitt-Heron, had easily come on the two gentlemen who were following the same trail. The two had gone by Samarkand, evidently intending to strike into the hills by a shorter route than the main road from Bokhara. The frontier posts had been warned, and the stalkers had become the stalked.

That was one solid achievement, at any rate. I had saved Pitt-Heron from the worst danger, for first I had sent him Tommy, and now I had put the police on guard against his enemies. I had not the slightest doubt that enemies they were. Charles knew too much, and Tuke was the man appointed to reason with him, to bring him back, if possible, or if not—— As Chapman had said, the ex-Union leader was not the man to stick at trifles.

It was a broiling June, the London season was at its height, and I had never been so busy in the Courts before. But that crowded and garish world was little more than a dream to me. I went through my daily tasks, dined out, went to the play, had consultations, talked to my fellows, but all the while I had the feeling that I was watching somebody else perform the same functions. I believe I did my work well, and I know I was twice complimented by the Court of Appeal.

But my real interests were far away. Always I saw two men in the hot glens of the Oxus, with the fine dust of the *loess* rising in yellow clouds behind them. One of these men had a drawn and anxious face, and both rode hard. They passed by the closes of apricot and cherry and the green watered gardens, and soon the Oxus ceased to flow wide among rushes and water-lilies and became a turbid hill-stream. By-and-by the roadside changed, and the horses of the travellers trod on mountain turf, crushing the irises and marigolds and thyme. I could feel the free air blowing from the roof of the world, and see far ahead the snowy saddle of the pass which led to India.

Far behind the riders I saw two others, and they chose a different way, now over waterless plateaux, now in rugged *nullahs*. They rode the faster and their route was the shorter. Sooner or later they must catch up the first riders, and I knew, though how I could not tell, that death would attend the meeting.

I, and only I, sitting in London four thousand miles away, could prevent disaster. The dream haunted me at night, and often, walking in the Strand or sitting at a dinner-table, I have found my eyes fixed clearly on the shining upland with the thin white mountains at the back of it, and the four dots, which were men, hurrying fast on their business.

One night I met Lumley. It was at a big political dinner given by the chief of my party in the House of Lords—fifty or sixty guests, and a blaze of stars and decorations. I sat near the bottom of the table, and he was near the top, sitting between a famous General and an ex-Viceroy of India. I asked my right-hand neighbour who he was, but he could not tell me. The same question to my left-hand neighbour brought an answer.

" It's old Lumley. Have you never met him ? He doesn't go out much, but he gives a man's dinner now and then, which are the best in London. No. He's not a politician, though he favours our side, and I expect has given a lot to our funds. I can't think why they don't make him a Peer. He's enormously rich and very generous, and the most learned old fellow in Britain. My Chief "—my neighbour was an Under-Secretary—" knows him, and told me once that if you wanted any out-of-the-way bit of knowledge you could get it by asking Lumley. I expect he pulls the strings more than anybody living. But he scarcely ever goes out, and it's a feather in our host's cap to have got him to-night. You never see his name in the papers, either. He probably pays the Press to keep him out, like some of those millionaire fellows in America."

I watched him through dinner. He was the centre of the talk at his end of the table. I could see the blue ribbon bulging out on Lord Morecambe's breast as he leaned forward to question him. He was wearing some foreign orders, including the Legion of Honour, and I could hear in the pauses of conversation echoes of his soft rich voice. I could see him beaming through his glasses on his neighbours, and now and then he would take them off and look mildly at a speaker. I wondered why nobody realised, as I did, what was in his light wild eyes.

The dinner, I believe, was excellent, and the company was good, but down at my end I could eat little, and I did not want to talk. Here in this pleasant room, with servants moving softly about, and a mellow light on the silver from the shaded candles, I felt the man was buttressed and defended beyond my reach. A kind of despairing hatred gripped me when I looked his way. For I was always conscious of that other picture—the Asian desert, Pitt-Heron's hunted face, and the grim figure of Tuke on his trail. That, and the great secret wheels of what was too inhuman to be called crime, moving throughout the globe under this man's hand.

There was a party afterwards, but I did not stay. No more did Lumley, and for a second I brushed against him in the hall at the foot of the big staircase.

He smiled on me affectionately.

"Have you been dining here? I did not notice you."

"You had better things to think of," I said. "By the way, you gave me good advice some weeks ago. It may interest you to hear that I have taken it."

"I am so glad," he said softly. "You are a very discreet young man."

But his eyes told me that he knew I lied.

CHAPTER VI.

THE RESTAURANT IN ANTIOCH STREET.

I WAS working late at the Temple next day, and it was nearly seven before I got up to go home. Macgillivray had telephoned to me in the afternoon saying he wanted to see me and suggesting dinner at the club, and I had told him I should come straight there from my Chambers. But just after six he had rung me up again and proposed another meeting-place.

"I've got some very important news for you and want to be quiet. There's a little place where I sometimes dine—Rapaccini's, in Antioch Street. I'll meet you there at half-past seven."

I agreed, and sent a message to Chapman at the flat, telling him I would be out to dinner. It was a Wednesday night, so the House rose early. He asked me where I was dining and I told him, but I did not mention with whom. His voice sounded very cross, for he hated a lonely meal.

It was a hot, still night, and I had had a heavy day in Court, so heavy that my private anxieties had almost slipped from my mind. I walked along the Embankment, and up Regent Street towards Oxford Circus. Antioch Street, as I had learned from the Directory, was in the area between Langham Place and Tottenham Court Road. I wondered vaguely why Macgillivray should have chosen such an out-of-the-way spot, but I knew him for a man of many whims.

The street, when I found it, turned out to be a respectable little place—boarding-houses and architects' offices, with a few antiquity shops, and a picture-cleaner's. The restaurant took some finding, for it was one of those discreet establishments, common enough in France, where no edibles are displayed in the British fashion, and muslin half-curtains deck the windows. Only the door-mat, lettered with the proprietor's name, remained to guide the hungry.

I gave a waiter my hat and stick and was ushered into a garish dining-room, apparently full of people. A single violinist was discoursing music from beside the grill. The occupants were not quite the kind one expects to find in an eating-house in a side street. The men were all in evening dress with white waistcoats, and the women looked either demi-mondaines or those who follow their taste in clothes. Various eyes looked curiously at me as I entered. I guessed that the restaurant had by one of those odd freaks of Londoners become for a moment the fashion.

The proprietor met me half-way up the room. He might call himself Rapaccini, but he was obviously a German.

"Mr Geelvrai," he nodded. "He has engaged a private room. Vill you follow, sir?"

A narrow stairway broke into the wall on the left side of the dining-room. I followed the manager up it and along a short corridor to a door which filled its end. He ushered me into a brightly-lit little room where a table was laid for two.

"Mr Geelvrai comes often here," said the manager. "He vill be late—sometimes. Everything is ready, sir. I hope you vill be pleased."

It looked inviting enough, but the air smelt stuffy. Then I saw that, though the night was warm, the window was shut and the curtains drawn. I pulled back the curtains, and to my surprise saw that the shutters were closed.

"You must open these," I said, "or we'll stifle."

The manager glanced at the window. "I will send a waiter," he said, and departed. The door seemed to shut with an odd click.

I flung myself down in one of the arm-chairs, for I was feeling pretty tired. The little table beckoned alluringly, for I was also hungry. I remember there was a mass of pink roses on it. A bottle of champagne, with the cork loose, stood in a wine-cooler on the sideboard, and there was an unopened bottle beside it. It seemed to me that Macgillivray, when he dined here, did himself rather well.

The promised waiter did not arrive, and the stuffiness was making me very thirsty. I looked for a bell, but could not see one. My watch told me it was now a quarter to eight, but there was no sign of Macgillivray. I poured myself out a glass of champagne from the opened bottle, and was just about to drink it, when my eye caught something in a corner of the room.

It was one of those little mid-Victorian corner tables—I believe they call them "what-nots"—which you will find in any boarding-house littered up with photographs and coral and "Presents from Brighton." On this one stood a photograph in a shabby frame, and I thought I recognised it.

I crossed the room and picked it up. It showed a man of thirty, with short side-whiskers, an ill-fitting jaw, and a drooping moustache. The duplicate of it was in Macgillivray's cabinet. It was Mr Routh, the ex-Union leader.

There was nothing very remarkable about that after all, but it gave me a nasty shock. The room now seemed a sinister place, as well as intolerably close. There was still no sign of the waiter to open the window, so I thought I would wait for Macgillivray downstairs.

But the door would not open. The handle would not turn. It did not seem to be locked, but rather to have shut with some kind of patent spring. I noticed that the whole thing was a powerful piece of oak with a heavy framework, very unlike the usual flimsy restaurant doors.

My first instinct was to make a deuce of a row and attract the attention of the diners below. I own I was beginning to feel badly frightened. Clearly I had got into some sort of trap. Macgillivray's invitation might have been a hoax, for it is not difficult to counterfeit a man's voice on the telephone. With an effort I forced myself into calmness. It was preposterous to think that anything could happen to me in a room not thirty feet from where a score or two of ordinary citizens were dining. I had only to raise my voice to bring inquirers.

Yes, but above all things I did not want a row. It would never do for a rising lawyer and a Member of Parliament to be found shouting for help in an upper chamber of a Bloomsbury restaurant. The worst deductions would be drawn from the open bottle of champagne. Besides, it might be all right after all. The door might have got stuck. Macgillivray at that very moment might be on his way up.

So I sat down and waited. Then I remembered my thirst, and stretched out my hand to the glass of champagne.

But at that instant I looked towards the window, and set down the wine untasted.

It was a very odd window. The lower end was almost flush with the floor, and the hinges of the shutters seemed to be only on one side. As I stared I began to wonder whether it was a window at all.

Next moment my doubts were solved. The window swung open like a door, and in the dark cavity stood a man.

Strangely enough I knew him. His figure was not one that is readily forgotten.

"Good evening, Mr Docken," I said; "will you have a glass of champagne?"

A year before, on the South-Eastern Circuit, I had appeared for the defence in a burglary case. Criminal Law was not my province, but now and then I took a case to keep my hand in, for it is the best training in the world for the handling of witnesses. This case had been peculiar. A certain Bill Docken was the accused, a gentleman who bore a bad reputation in the eyes of the police. The evidence against him was strong, but it was more or less tainted, being chiefly that of two former accomplices—a proof that there is small truth in the proverbial honour among thieves. It was an ugly business, and my sympathies were with the accused, for though he may very well have been guilty, yet he had been the victim of a shabby trick. Anyhow I put my back into the case, and after a hard struggle got a verdict of "Not Guilty." Mr Docken had been kind enough to express his appreciation of my efforts, and to ask in a hoarse whisper how I had "squared the old bird," meaning the Judge. He did not understand the subtleties of the English law of evidence.

He shambled into the room, a huge hulking figure of a man, with the thickness of chest which under happier circumstances might have made him a terror in the prize-ring. His features wore a heavy scowl which slowly cleared to a flicker of recognition.

"By God, it's the lawyer-chap," he muttered.

I pointed to the glass of champagne.

"I don't mind if I do," he said. "'Ere's 'ealth!" He swallowed the wine at a gulp and wiped his mouth on his sleeve. "'Ave a drop yourself, guv'nor," he added. "A glass of bubbly will cheer you up."

"Well, Mr Docken," I said, "I hope I see you fit." I was getting wonderfully collected now that the suspense was over.

"Pretty fair, sir. Pretty fair. Able to do my day's work like an honest man."

"And what brings you here?"

"A little job I'm on. Some friends of mine wants you out of the road for a bit and they've sent me to fetch you. It's a bit of luck for you that you've struck a friend. We needn't 'ave no unpleasantness seein' we're both what you might call men of the world."

"I appreciate the compliment," I said. "But where do you propose to take me?"

"Dunno. It's some lay near the Docks. I've got a motor-car waitin' at the back of the 'ouse."

"But supposing I don't want to go?"

"My orders admits no excuse," he said solemnly. "You're

a sensible chap, and can see that in a scrap I could down you easy."

"Very likely," I said. "But, man, you must be mad to talk like that. Downstairs there is a dining-room full of people. I have only to lift my voice to bring the police."

"You're a kid," he said scornfully. "Them geysers downstairs are all in the job. That was a flat-catching rig to get you up here so as you wouldn't suspect nothing. If you was to go down now—which you ain't going to be allowed to do—you wouldn't find a blamed soul in the place. I must say you're a bit softer than I 'oped after the 'andsome way you talked over yon old juggins with the wig at Maidstone."

Mr Docken took the bottle from the wine-cooler and filled himself another glass.

It sounded horribly convincing. If I was to be kidnapped and smuggled away, Lumley would have scored half a success. Not the whole; for, as I swiftly reflected, I had put Felix on the track of Tuke, and there was every chance that Tommy and Pitt-Heron would be saved. But for myself it looked pretty black. The more my scheme succeeded the more likely the Power-House would be to wreak its vengeance on me once I was spirited from the open-air world into its dark labyrinths.

I made a great effort to keep my voice even and calm.

"Mr Docken," I said, "I once did you a good turn. But for me you might be doing time now instead of drinking champagne like a gentleman. Your pals played you a pretty low trick and that was why I stuck out for you. I didn't think you were the kind of man to forget a friend."

"No more I am," said he. "The man who says Bill Docken would go back on a pal is a liar."

"Well, here's your chance to pay your debts. The men who employ you are my deadly enemies and want to do me in. I'm not a match for you. You're a stronger fellow and can drag me off and hand me over to them. But if you do I'm done with. Make no mistake about that. I put it to you as a decent fellow. Are you going to go back on the man who has been a good friend to you?"

He shifted from one foot to another with his eyes on the ceiling. He was obviously in difficulties. Then he tried another glass of champagne.

"I dursn't, guv'nor. I dursn't let you go. Them I work for would cut my throat as soon as look at me. Besides, it ain't no good. If I was to go off and leave you there'd be plenty more in this 'ouse as would do the job. You're up against it, guv'nor. But take a sensible view and come with me. They don't mean you no real 'arm. I'll take my Bible oath on it. Only to keep you quiet for a bit, for you've run across one of their games. They won't do you no 'urt if you speak 'em fair. Be a sport and take it smiling-like——"

"You're afraid of them," I said.

"Yuss. I'm afraid. Black afraid. So would you be if you knew the gents. I'd rather take on the whole Rat Lane crowd—you know them as I mean—on a Saturday night when they're out for business than go back to my gents and say as 'ow I had shirked the job."

He shivered. "Good Lord, they'd freeze the 'eart out of a bull-pup."

"You're afraid," I said slowly. "So you're going to give me up to the men you're afraid of to do as they like with me. I never expected it of you, Bill. I thought you were the kind of lad who would send any gang to the devil before you'd go back on a pal."

"Don't say that," he said almost plaintively. "You don't 'alf know the 'ole I'm in." His eye seemed to be wandering, and he yawned deeply.

Just then a great noise began below. I heard a voice speaking, a loud peremptory voice. Then my name was shouted: "Leithen! Leithen! Are you there?"

There could be no mistaking that stout Yorkshire tongue.

By some miracle Chapman had followed me and was raising Cain downstairs.

My heart leaped with the sudden revulsion. "I'm here," I yelled. "Upstairs. Come up and let me out!"

Then I turned with a smile of triumph to Bill.

"My friends have come," I said. "You're too late for the job. Get back and tell your masters that."

He was swaying on his feet, and he suddenly lurched towards me. "You come along. By God, you think you've done me. I'll let you see."

His voice was growing thick and he stopped short. "What the 'ell's wrong with me?" he gasped. "I'm goin' all queer. I . . ."

He was like a man far gone in liquor, but three glasses of champagne would never have touched a head like Bill's. I saw what was up with him. He was not drunk, but drugged.

"They've doped the wine," I cried. "They put it there for me to drink it and go to sleep."

There is always something which is the last straw to any man. You may insult and outrage him and he will bear it patiently, but touch the quick in his temper and he will turn. Apparently for Bill drugging was the unforgivable sin. His eye lost for a moment its confusion. He squared his shoulders and roared like a bull.

"Doped, by God!" he cried. "Who done it?"

"The men who shut me in this room. Burst that door and you will find them."

He turned a blazing face on the locked door and hurled his huge weight on it. It cracked and bent, but the lock and hinges held. I could see that sleep was overwhelming him and that his limbs were stiffening, but his anger was still strong enough for another effort. Again he drew himself together like a big cat and flung himself on the woodwork. The hinges tore from the jambs and the whole outfit fell forward into the passage in a cloud of splinters and dust and broken plaster.

It was Mr Docken's final effort. He lay on the top of the wreckage he had made, like Samson among the ruins of Gaza, a senseless and slumbering hulk.

I picked up the unopened bottle of champagne—it was the only weapon available—and stepped over his body. I was beginning to enjoy myself amazingly.

As I expected, there was a man in the corridor, a little fellow in waiter's clothes with a tweed jacket instead of a dress-coat. If he had a pistol I knew I was done, but I gambled upon the disinclination of the management for the sound of shooting.

He had a knife, but he never had a chance to use it. My champagne bottle descended on his head and he dropped like a log.

There were men coming upstairs—not Chapman, for I still heard his hoarse shouts in the dining-room. If they once got up they could force me back through that hideous room by the door through which Docken had come, and in five minutes I should be in their motor-car.

There was only one thing to do. I jumped from the stair-head right down among them. I think there were three, and my descent toppled them over. We rolled in a wild whirling mass and cascaded into the dining-room, where my head bumped violently on the parquet.

I expected a bit of a grapple, but none came. My wits were pretty woolly, but I managed to scramble to my feet. The heels of my enemies were disappearing up the staircase. Chapman was pawing my ribs to discover if there were any bones broken. There was not another soul in the room except two policemen who were pushing their way in from the street.

Chapman was flushed and breathing heavily: his coat had a big split down the seams at the shoulder, but his face was happy as a child's.

I caught his arm and spoke in his ear. "We've got to get

out of this at once. How can we square these policemen? There must be no inquiry and nothing in the papers. Do you hear?"

"That's all right," said Chapman. "These bobbies are friends of mine, two good lads from Wensleydale. On my road here I told them to give me a bit of law and follow me, for I thought they might be wanted. They didn't come too soon to spoil sport, for I've been knocking furriners about for ten minutes. You seem to have been putting up a tidy scrap yourself."

"Let's get home first," I said, for I was beginning to think of the bigger thing.

I wrote a chit for Macgillivray which I asked one of the constables to take to Scotland Yard. It was to beg that nothing should be done yet in the business of the restaurant, and above all, that nothing should get into the papers. Then I asked the other to see us home. It was a queer request for two able-bodied men to make on a summer evening in the busiest part of London, but I was taking no chances. The Power-House had declared war on me, and I knew it would be war without quarter.

I was in a fever to get out of that place. My momentary lust of battle had gone, and every stone of that building seemed to me a threat. Chapman would have liked to spend a happy hour rummaging through the house, but the gravity of my face persuaded him. The truth is, I was bewildered. I could not understand the reason of this sudden attack. Lumley's spies must long ago have told him enough to connect me with the Bokhara business. My visits to the Embassy alone were proof enough. But now he must have found out something new, something which startled him, or else there had been wild doings in Turkestan.

I won't forget that walk home in a hurry. It was a fine July twilight. The streets were full of the usual crowd, shop-girls in thin frocks, promenading clerks, and all the flotsam of a London summer. You would have said it was the safest place on earth. But I was glad we had the policeman with us, who at the end of one beat passed us on to his colleague, and I was glad of Chapman. For I am morally certain I would never have got home alone.

The queer thing is that there was no sign of trouble till we got into Oxford Street. Then I became aware that there were people on these pavements who knew all about me. I first noticed it at the mouth of one of those little dark side-alleys which run up into mews and small dingy courts. I found myself being skilfully edged away from Chapman into the shadow, but I noticed it in time and butted my way back to the pavement. I couldn't make out who the people were who hustled me. They seemed nondescripts of all sorts, but I fancied there were women among them.

This happened twice, and I got wary, but I was nearly caught before we reached Oxford Circus. There was a front of a big shop rebuilding, and the usual wooden barricade with a gate. Just as we passed it there was a special throng on the pavement, and I, being next the wall, got pushed against the gate. Suddenly it gave, and I was pressed inward. I was right inside before I realised my danger, and the gate was closing. There must have been people there, but I could see nothing in the gloom.

It was no time for false pride. I yelled to Chapman, and the next second his burly shoulder was in the gap. The hustlers vanished, and I seemed to hear a polite voice begging my pardon.

After that Chapman and I linked arms and struck across Mayfair. But I did not feel safe till I was in the flat with the door bolted.

We had a long drink, and I stretched myself in an arm-chair, for I was as tired as if I had come out of a big game of Rugby football.

"I owe you a good deal, old man," I said. "I think I'll join the Labour Party. You can tell your fellows to send me their whips. What possessed you to come to look for me?"

The explanation was simple. I had mentioned the restaurant in my telephone message, and the name had awakened a recollection in Chapman's mind. He could not fix it at first, but by-and-by he remembered that the place had cropped up in the Routh case. Routh's London headquarters had been at the restaurant in Antioch Street. As soon as he remembered this he got into a taxi and descended at the corner of the street, where by sheer luck he fell in with his Wensleydale friends.

He said he had marched into the restaurant and found it empty, but for an ill-favoured manager, who denied all knowledge of me. Then, fortunately, he chose to make certain by shouting my name, and heard my answer. After that he knocked the manager down, and was presently assaulted by several men whom he described as "furrin muck." They had knives, of which he made very little, for he seems to have swung a table as a battering-ram and left sore limbs behind him.

He was on the top of his form. "I haven't enjoyed anything so much since I was a lad at school," he informed me. "I was beginning to think your Power-House was a wash-out, but Lord! it's been busy enough to-night. This is what I call life!"

My spirits could not keep pace with his. The truth is that I was miserably puzzled—not afraid so much as mystified. I couldn't make out this sudden dead-set at me. Either they knew more than I bargained for, or I knew far too little.

"It's all very well," I said, "but I don't see how this is going to end. We can't keep up the pace long. At this rate it will be only a matter of hours till they get me."

We pretty well barricaded ourselves in the flat, and, at his earnest request, I restored to Chapman his revolver.

Then I got the clue I had been longing for. It was about eleven o'clock, while we were sitting smoking, when the telephone bell rang. It was Felix who spoke.

"I have news for you," he said. "The hunters have met the hunted, and one of the hunters is dead. The other is a prisoner in our hands. He has confessed."

It had been black murder in intent. The frontier police had shadowed the two men into the cup of a glen, where they met Tommy and Pitt-Heron. The four had spoken together for a little, and then Tuke had fired deliberately at Charles and had grazed his ear. Whereupon Tommy had charged him and knocked the pistol from his hand. The assailant had fled, but a long shot from the police on the hillside had toppled him over. Tommy had felled Saronov with his fists, and the man had abjectly surrendered. He had confessed, Felix said, but what the confession was he did not know.

CHAPTER VII.

I FIND SANCTUARY.

My nervousness and indecision dropped from me at the news. I had won the first round, and I would win the last, for it suddenly became clear to me that I had now evidence which would blast Lumley. I believed that it would not be hard to prove his identity with Pavia and his receipt of the telegram from Saronov; Tuke was his creature, and Tuke's murderous mission was his doing. No doubt I knew little and could prove nothing about the big thing, the Power-House, but conspiracy to murder is not the lightest of criminal charges. I was beginning to see my way to checkmating my friend, at least so far as Pitt-Heron was concerned. Provided—and it was a pretty big proviso—that he gave me the chance to use my knowledge.

That, I foresaw, was going to be the difficulty. What I knew now Lumley had known hours before. The reason of the affair at Antioch Street was now only too clear. If he believed that I had damning evidence against him—and there was no doubt he suspected it—then he would do his best to stop my mouth. I must get my statement lodged in the proper quarter at the earliest possible moment.

The next twenty-four hours, I feared, were going to be too sensational for comfort. And yet I cannot say that I was afraid. I was too full of pride to be in a funk. I had lost my awe of Lumley through scoring a point against him. Had I known more I should have been less at my ease. It was this confidence which prevented me doing the obvious safe thing—ringing up Macgillivray, telling him the gist of my story, and getting him to put me under police protection. I thought I was clever enough to see the thing through myself. And it must have been the same over-confidence which prevented Lumley getting at me that night. An organisation like his could easily have got into the flat and done for us both. I suppose the explanation is that he did not yet know how much I knew, and was not ready to take the last steps in silencing me.

I sat up till the small hours, marshalling my evidence in a formal statement and making two copies of it. One was destined for Macgillivray and the other for Felix, for I was taking no risks. I went to bed and slept peacefully, and was awakened as usual by Waters. My man slept out, and used to turn up in the morning about seven. It was all so normal and homely that I could have believed my adventures of the night before a dream. In the summer sunlight the ways of darkness seemed very distant. I dressed in excellent spirits and made a hearty breakfast.

Then I gave the docile Chapman his instructions. He must take the document to Scotland Yard, ask to see Macgillivray, and put it into his hands. Then he must ring me up at once at Down Street and tell me that he had done this. I had already telephoned to my clerk that I would not be at the Temple that day.

It seems a simple thing to travel less than a mile in the most frequented part of London in broad daylight and perform an easy act like carrying a letter; but I knew that

Lumley's spies would be active, and would connect Chapman sufficiently with me to think him worth following. In that case there might be an attempt at violence. I thought it my duty to tell him this, but he laughed me to scorn. He proposed to walk, and he begged to be shown the man who would meddle with him. Chapman, after last night, was prepared to take on all comers. He put my letter to Macgillivray in his inner pocket, buttoned his coat, crushed down his felt hat on his head, and defiantly set forth.

I expected a message from him in half an hour, for he was a rapid walker. But the half-hour passed, then the three-quarters, and nothing happened. At eleven I rang up Scotland Yard, but they had no news of him.

Then I became miserably anxious, for it was clear that some disaster had overtaken my messenger. My first impulse was to set out myself to look for him, but a moment's reflection convinced me that that would be playing into the enemy's hands. For an hour I wrestled with my impatience, and then a few minutes after twelve I was rung up by St Thomas's Hospital.

A young doctor spoke, and said that Mr Chapman had asked him to tell me what had happened. He had been run down by a motor-car at the corner of Whitehall—nothing serious—only a bad shake and some scalp wounds. In a day or so he would be able to leave.

Then he added what drove the blood from my heart. "Mr Chapman personally wished me to tell you," he said, "that the letter has gone." I stammered some reply asking his meaning. "He said he thinks," I was told, "that, while he was being assisted to his feet, his pocket was picked and a letter taken. He said you would know what he meant."

I knew only too well what he meant. Lumley had got my statement, and realised precisely how much I knew and what was the weight of evidence against him. Before he had only suspected, now he knew. He must know, too, that there would be a copy somewhere which I would try to deliver. It was going to be harder than I had fancied to get my news to the proper ears, and I had to anticipate the extreme of violence on the part of my opponents.

The thought of the peril restored my coolness. I locked the outer door of my flat, and telephoned to the garage where I kept my car, bidding Stagg call for me at two o'clock precisely. Then I lit a pipe and strove to banish the whole business from my thoughts, for fussing would do me no good.

Presently it occurred to me to ring up Felix and give him some notion of the position. But I found that my telephone was now broken and connection was impossible. The spoken as well as the written word was to be denied me. That had happened in the last half-hour, and I didn't believe it was by accident. Also my man Waters, whom I had sent out on an errand after breakfast, had never returned. The state of siege had begun.

It was a blazing hot midsummer day. The water-carts were sprinkling Piccadilly, and looking from my window I could see leisurely and elegant gentlemen taking their morning stroll. A florist's cart full of roses stood below me in the street. The summer smell of town—a mixture of tar, flowers, dust, and patchouli—rose in gusts through the hot air. It was the homely London I knew so well, and I was somehow an exile from it. I was being shepherded into a dismal isolation, which, unless I won help, might mean death. I was cool enough now, but I will not deny that I was miserably anxious. I cursed my false confidence the night before. By now I might have had Macgillivray and his men by my side. As it was, I wondered if I should ever see them.

I changed into a flannel suit, lunched off sandwiches and a whisky-and-soda, and at two o'clock looked for Stagg and my car. He was five minutes late, a thing which had never happened before. But I never welcomed anything so gladly as the sight of that car. I had hardly dared to hope that it would reach me.

My goal was the Embassy in Belgrave Square, but I was convinced that if I approached it directly I should share the fate of Chapman. Worse, for from me they would not merely snatch the letter. What I had once written I could write again, and if they wished to ensure my silence it must be by more drastic methods. I proposed to baffle my pursuers by taking a wide circuit round the western suburbs of London, returning to the Embassy when I thought the coast clear.

It was a tremendous relief to go down the stairs and emerge into the hot daylight. I gave Stagg his instructions, and lay back in the closed car with a curious fluttering sense of anticipation. I had begun the last round in the wild game. There was a man at the corner of Down Street who seemed to peer curiously at the car. He was doubtless one of my watchers.

We went up Park Lane into the Edgware Road, my instructions to Stagg being to make a circuit by Harrow and Brentford. Now that I was ensconced in my car I felt a trifle safer, and my tense nerves relaxed. I grew drowsy and allowed myself to sink into a half doze. The stolid back of Stagg filled my gaze, as it had filled it a fortnight ago on the western road, and I admired lazily the brick-red of his neck. He had been in the Guards, and a Boer bullet at Modder River had left a long scar at the nape of his neck, which gave to his hair the appearance of being badly cut. He had told me the story on Exmoor.

Suddenly I rubbed my eyes. There was no scar there; the hair of the chauffeur grew regularly down to his coat-collar. The resemblance had been perfect, the voice was Stagg's, but clearly it was not Stagg who now drove my car.

I pulled the blind down over the front window as if to shelter myself from the sun. Looking out, I saw that we were some distance up the Edgware Road, nearing the point where the Marylebone Road joins it. Now or never was my chance, for at the corner there is always a block in the traffic.

The car slowed down in obedience to a policeman's uplifted hand, and very gently I opened the door on the left side. Since the car was new it opened softly, and in two seconds I had stepped out, shut it again, and made a dive between a butcher's cart and a motor-bus for the side-walk. I gave one glance back and saw the unconscious chauffeur still rigid at the wheel.

I dodged unobtrusively through the crowd on the pavement, with my hand on my breast-pocket to see that my paper was still there. There was a little picture-shop near-by to which I used to go occasionally, owned by a man who was an adept at cleaning and restoring. I had sent him customers and he was likely to prove a friend. So I dived into his doorway, which made a cool pit of shade after the glaring street, and found him, spectacles on nose, busy examining some dusty prints.

He greeted me cordially and followed me into the back shop.

"Mr Levison," I said, "have you a back door?"

He looked at me in some surprise. "Why, yes; there is the door into the lane which runs from Edgeley Street into Connaught Mews."

"Will you let me use it? There is a friend outside whom I wish to avoid. Such things happen, you know."

He smiled comprehendingly. "Certainly, sir. Come this way." And he led me through a dark passage hung with dingy Old Masters to a little yard filled with the debris of picture frames. There he unlocked a door in the wall and I found myself in a narrow alley. As I emerged I heard the bell of the shop-door ring. "If anyone inquires, you have not seen me here, remember," I said, and Mr Levison nodded. He was an artist in his small way and liked the scent of a mystery.

I ran down the lane and by various cross streets made my way into Bayswater. I believed that I had thrown my trackers for the moment off the scent, but I had got to get to the Embassy, and that neighbourhood was sure to be closely watched. I came out on the Bayswater Road pretty far west, and resolved to strike south-east across the Park. My reason was that the neighbourhood of Hyde Park Corner was certain at that time of day to be pretty well crowded, and I felt more security in a throng than in the empty streets of Kensington. Now that I come to think of it, it was a rash thing to do, for since Lumley knew the full extent of my knowledge, he was likely to deal more violently with me than with Chapman, and the seclusion of the Park offered him too good a chance.

I crossed the riding-track, and struck over the open space where the Sunday demonstrations are held. There was nothing there but nurses and perambulators, children at play, and dogs being exercised. Presently I reached Grosvenor Gate, where on the little green chairs well-dressed people were taking the air. I recognised several acquaintances, and stopped for a moment to talk to one of them. Then I emerged in Park Lane, and walked down it to Hamilton Place.

So far I thought I had not been followed, but now once more I had the indefinable but unerring sensation of being watched. I caught a man looking eagerly at me from the other side of the street, and it seemed to me that he made a sign to someone farther off. There was now less than a quarter of a mile between me and Belgrave Square, but I saw that it would be a hard course to cover.

Once in Piccadilly, there could be no doubt about my watchers. Lumley was doing the thing in style this time. Last night it had only been a trial trip, but now the whole energies of the Power-House were on the job. The place was filled with the usual mid-season crowd, and I had to take off my hat several times. Up in the bow-window of the Bachelors' Club a young friend of mine was writing a letter and sipping a long drink with an air of profound boredom. I would have given much for his *ennui*, for my life at the moment was painfully exciting. I was alone in that crowd, isolated and proscribed, and there was no help save in my own wits. If I spoke to a policeman he would think me drunk or mad, and yet I was on the edge of being made the victim of a far subtler crime than fell within the purview of the Metropolitan force.

Now I saw how thin is the protection of civilisation. An accident and a bogus ambulance—a false charge and a bogus arrest—there were a dozen ways of spiriting me out of this gay, bustling world. I foresaw that, if I delayed, my nerve would break, so I boldly set off across the road.

I jolly nearly shared the fate of Chapman. A car which seemed about to draw up at a club door suddenly swerved across the street, and I had to dash to an island to escape it. It was no occasion to hesitate, so, dodging a bus and missing a motor-bicycle by a hair's-breadth, I rushed across the remaining distance and reached the railings of the Green Park.

Here there were fewer people, and several queer things began to happen. A little group of workmen with their tools were standing by the kerb, and they suddenly moved towards me. A pavement artist, who looked like a cripple, scrambled to his feet and moved in the same direction. There was a policeman at the corner, and I saw a well-dressed man go up to him, say something and nod in my direction, and the policeman too began to move towards me.

I did not await them. I took to my heels and ran for my life down Grosvenor Place.

Long ago at Eton I had won the school mile, and at Oxford I was a second string for the quarter. But never at Eton or at Oxford did I run as I ran then. It was blisteringly hot, but I did not feel it, for my hands were clammy and my heart felt like a cold stone. I do not know how the pursuit got on, for I did not think of it. I did not reflect what kind of spectacle I must afford running like a thief in a London thoroughfare on a June afternoon. I only knew that my enemies were around and behind me, and that in front, a few hundred yards away, lay safety.

But even as I ran I had the sense to think out my movements, and to realise that the front door of the Embassy was impossible. For one thing, it would be watched, and for another, before the solemn footmen opened it, my pursuers would be upon me. My only hope was the back door.

I twisted into the Mews behind the north side of the Square, and as I turned I saw two men run up from the Square as if to cut me off. A whistle was blown, and more men appeared—one entering from the far end of the Mews, one darting from a public-house door, and one sliding down a ladder from a stable-loft. This last was nearest me, and tried to trip me, but I rejoice to say that a left-hander on the chin sent him sprawling on the cobbles. I remembered that the Embassy was the fifth house from the end, and feverishly I tried to count the houses by their backs. It is not so easy as it sounds, for the modern London householder studs his back premises with excrescences which seem to melt into his neighbour's. In the end I had to make a guess at the door, which, to my joy, was unlocked. I rushed in and banged it behind me.

I found myself in a stone passage, with on one side a door opening on a garage. There was a wooden staircase leading to an upper floor, and a glass door in front, which opened into a large disused room full of boxes. Beyond were two doors, one of which was locked. The other abutted on a steep iron stairway, which obviously led to the lower regions of the house.

I ran down the stair—it was no more than a ladder—crossed a small courtyard, traversed a passage, and burst into the kitchen, where I confronted an astonished white-capped *chef* in the act of lifting a pot from the fire.

His face was red and wrathful, and I thought that he was going to fling the pot at my head. I had disturbed him in some delicate operation, and his artist's pride was outraged.

"Monsieur," I stammered in French, "I seek your pardon for my intrusion. There were circumstances which compelled me to enter this house by the back premises. I am an acquaintance of his Excellency, your patron, and an old friend of Monsieur Felix. I beg you of your kindness to direct me to Monsieur Felix's room, or to bid someone take me there."

My abject apologies mollified him.

"It is a grave offence, monsieur," he said, "an unparalleled offence, to enter my kitchen at this hour. I fear you have irremediably spoiled the new casserole dish that I was endeavouring to compose."

I was ready to go on my knees to the offended artist.

"It grieves me indeed to have interfered with so rare an art, which I have often admired at his Excellency's table. But there is danger behind me, and an urgent mission in front. Monsieur will forgive me? Necessity will sometimes overrule the finest sensibility."

He bowed to me, and I bowed to him, and my pardon was assured.

Suddenly a door opened, another than that by which I had entered, and a man appeared whom I took to be a footman. He was struggling into his livery coat, but at the sight of me he dropped it. I thought I recognised the face as that of the man who had emerged from the public-house and tried to cut me off.

"'Ere, Mister Alphonse," he cried, "'elp me to collar this man. The police are after 'im."

"You forget, my friend," I said, "that an Embassy is privileged ground which the police can't enter. I desire to be taken before his Excellency."

"So that's yer game," he shouted. "But two can play at that. 'Ere, give me an 'and, moosoo, and we'll 'ave him in the street in a jiffy. There's two 'undred of the best in our pockets if we 'ands 'im over to them as wants 'im."

The cook looked puzzled and a little frightened.

"Will you allow them to outrage your kitchen—an Embassy kitchen, too—without your consent?" I said.

"What have you done?" he asked in French.

"Only what your patron will approve," I replied in the same tongue. "*Messieurs les assassins* have a grudge against me."

He still hesitated, while the young footman advanced on me. He was fingering something in his trousers-pocket which I did not like.

Now was the time when, as they say in America, I should have got busy with my gun; but alas! I had no gun. I feared supports for the enemy, for the footman at the first sight of me had run back the way he had come, and I had heard a low whistle.

What might have happened I do not know, had not the god appeared from the machine in the person of Hewins, the butler.

"Hewins," I said, "you know me. I have often dined here, and you know that I am a friend of Monsieur Felix. I am on my way to see him on an urgent matter, and for various reasons I had to enter by Monsieur Alphonse's kitchen. Will you take me at once to Monsieur Felix?"

Hewins bowed, and on his imperturbable face there appeared no sign of surprise. "This way, sir," was all he said.

As I followed him I saw the footman plucking nervously at the something in his trousers-pocket. Lumley's agents apparently had not always the courage to follow his instructions to the letter, for I made no doubt that the order had been to take me alive or dead.

I found Felix alone, and flung myself into an arm-chair. "My dear chap," I said, "take my advice and advise his Excellency to sack the red-haired footman."

From that moment I date that sense of mastery over a

situation which drives out fear. I had been living for weeks under a dark pall, and suddenly the skies had lightened. I had found sanctuary. Whatever happened to me now the worst was past, for I had done my job.

Felix was looking at me curiously, for, jaded, scarlet, dishevelled, I was an odd figure for a London afternoon. "Things seem to have been marching fast with you," he said.

"They have, but I think the march is over. I want to ask several favours. First, here is a document which sets out certain facts. I shall ring up Macgillivray at Scotland Yard and ask him to come here at 9.30 this evening. When he comes I want you to give him this and ask him to read it at once. He will know how to act on it."

Felix nodded. "And the next?"

"Give me a telegraph form. I want a wire sent at once by someone who can be trusted." He handed me a form and I wrote out a telegram to Lumley at the Albany, saying that I proposed to call upon him that evening at eight sharp, and asking him to receive me.

"Next?" said Felix.

"Next and last, I want a room with a door which will lock, a hot bath, and something to eat about seven. I might be permitted to taste Monsieur Alphonse's new casserole dish."

I rang up Macgillivray, reminded him of his promise, and told him what awaited him at 9.30. Then I had a wash, and afterwards at my leisure gave Felix a sketch of the day's doings. I have never felt more completely at my ease, for whatever happened I was certain that I had spoiled Lumley's game. He would know by now that I had reached the Embassy, and that any further attempts on my life and liberty were futile. My telegram would show him that I was prepared to offer terms, and I would certainly be permitted to reach the Albany unmolested. To the meeting with my adversary I looked forward without qualms, but with the most lively interest. I had my own theories about that distinguished criminal, and I hoped to bring them to the proof.

Just before seven I had a reply to my wire. Mr Lumley said he would be delighted to see me. The telegram was directed to me at the Embassy, though I had put no address on the one I sent. Lumley, of course, knew all my movements. I could picture him sitting in his chair, like some Chief of Staff, receiving every few minutes the reports of his agents. All the same, Napoleon had fought his Waterloo.

CHAPTER VIII.

THE POWER-HOUSE.

I LEFT Belgrave Square about a quarter to eight and retraced my steps along the route which for me that afternoon had been so full of tremors. I was still being watched—a little observation told me that—but I would not be interfered with, provided my way lay in a certain direction. So completely without nervousness was I that at the top of Constitution Hill I struck into the Green Park and kept to the grass till I emerged into Piccadilly opposite Devonshire House. A light wind had risen, and the evening had grown pleasantly cool. I met several men I knew going out to dinner on foot, and stopped to exchange greetings. From my clothes they thought I had just returned from a day in the country.

I reached the Albany as the clock was striking eight. Lumley's rooms were on the first floor, and I was evidently expected, for the porter himself conducted me to them and waited by me till the door was opened by a manservant.

You know those *rococo*, late Georgian, Albany rooms, large, square, clumsily corniced. Lumley's was lined with books, which I saw at a glance were of a different type from those in his working library at his country house. This was the collection of a bibliophile, and in the light of the summer evening the rows of tall volumes in vellum and morocco lined the walls like some rich tapestry.

The valet retired and shut the door, and presently from a little inner chamber came his master. He was dressed for dinner, and wore more than ever the air of the eminent diplomat. Again I had the old feeling of incredulity. It was the Lumley I had met two nights before at dinner, the friend of Viceroys and Cabinet Ministers. It was hard to connect him with Antioch Street or the red-haired footman with a pistol. Or with Tuke? Yes, I decided, Tuke fitted into the frame. Both were brains cut loose from the decencies that make life possible.

"Good evening, Mr Leithen," he said pleasantly. "As you have fixed the hour of eight, may I offer you dinner?"

"Thank you," I replied, "but I have already dined. I have chosen an awkward time, but my business need not take long."

"So?" he said. "I am always glad to see you at any hour."

"And I prefer to see the master rather than the subordinates who have been infesting my life during the past week."

We both laughed. "I am afraid you have had some annoyance, Mr Leithen," he said. "But remember, I gave you fair warning."

"True. And I have come to do the same kindness to you. That part of the game, at any rate, is over."

"Over?" he queried, raising his eyebrows.

"Yes, over," I said, and took out my watch. "Let us be quite frank with each other, Mr Lumley. There is really very little time to waste. As you have doubtless read the paper which you stole from my friend this morning, you know more or less the extent of my information."

"Let us have frankness by all means. Yes, I have read

your paper. A very creditable piece of work, if I may say so. You will rise in your profession, Mr Leithen. But surely you must realise that it carries you a very little way."

"In a sense you are right. I am not in a position to reveal the full extent of your misdeeds. Of the Power-House and its doings I can only guess. But Pitt-Heron is on his way home, and he will be carefully safeguarded on that journey. Your creature, Saronov, has confessed. We shall know more very soon, and meantime I have clear evidence which implicates you in a conspiracy to murder."

He did not answer, but I wished I could see behind his tinted spectacles to the look in his eyes. I think he had not been quite prepared for the line I took.

"I need not tell you, as a lawyer, Mr Leithen," he said at last, "that what seems good evidence on paper is often feeble enough in Court. You cannot suppose that I will tamely plead guilty to your charges. On the contrary, I will fight them with all the force that brains and money can give. You are an ingenious young man, but you are not the brightest jewel of the English Bar."

"That also is true. I do not deny that some of my evidence may be weakened at the trial. It is even conceivable that you may be acquitted on some technical doubt. But you have forgotten one thing. From the day you leave the Court you will be a suspected man. The police of all Europe will be on your trail. You have been highly successful in the past, and why? Because you have been above suspicion, an honourable and distinguished gentleman, belonging to the best clubs, counting as your acquaintances the flower of our society. Now you will be a suspect, a man with a past, a centre of strange stories. I put it to you—how far you are likely to succeed under these conditions?"

He laughed.

"You have a talent for character-drawing, my friend. What makes you think that I can work only if I live in the limelight of popularity?"

"The talent you mention," I said. "As I read your character—and I think I am right—you are an artist in crime. You are not the common cut-throat who acts out of passion or greed. No, I think you are something subtler than that. You love power, hidden power. You flatter your vanity by despising mankind and making them your tools. You scorn the smattering of inaccuracies which passes for human knowledge, and I will not venture to say you are wrong. Therefore, you use your brains to frustrate it. Unhappily the life of millions is built on that smattering, so you are a foe to society. But there would be no flavour in controlling subterranean things if you were yourself a mole working in the dark. To get the full flavour, the irony of it all, you must live in the light. I can imagine you laughing in your soul as you move about our world, praising it with your lips, patting it with your hands, and kicking its props away with your feet. I can see the charm of it. But it is over now."

"Over?" he asked.

"Over," I repeated. "The end has come—the utter, final, and absolute end."

He made a sudden, odd, nervous movement, pushing his glasses close back upon his eyes.

"What about yourself?" he said hoarsely. "Do you think you can play against me without suffering desperate penalties?"

He was holding a cord in his hand with a knob on the end of it. He now touched a button in the knob, and there came the faint sound of a bell.

The door was behind me, and he was looking beyond me towards it. I was entirely at his mercy, but I never budged an inch. I do not know how I managed to keep calm, but I did it, and without much effort. I went on speaking, conscious that the door had opened and that someone was behind me.

"It is really quite useless trying to frighten me. I am

safe because I am dealing with an intelligent man, and not with the ordinary half-witted criminal. You do not want my life in silly revenge. If you call in your man and strangle me between you what earthly good would it do you?"

He was looking beyond me, and the passion—a sudden white-hot passion like an epilepsy—was dying out of his face.

"A mistake, James," he said. "You can go."

The door closed softly at my back.

"Yes. A mistake. I have a considerable admiration for you, Mr Lumley, and should be sorry to be disappointed."

He laughed quite like an ordinary mortal. "I am glad this affair is to be conducted on a basis of mutual respect. Now that the melodramatic overture is finished let us get to the business."

"By all means," I said. "I promised to deal with you frankly. Well, let me put my last cards on the table. At half-past nine precisely the duplicate of that statement of mine which you annexed this morning will be handed to Scotland Yard. I may add that the authorities there know me, and are proceeding under my advice. When they read that statement they will act on it. You have therefore about one hour and a half, or say one and three-quarters, to make up your mind. You can still secure your freedom, but it must be elsewhere than in England."

He had risen to his feet, and was pacing up and down the room.

"Will you oblige me by telling me one thing," he said. "If you believe me to be, as you say, a dangerous criminal, how do you reconcile it with your conscience to give me a chance of escape? It is your duty to bring me to justice."

"I will tell you why," I said. "I, too, have a weak joint in my armour. Yours is that you can only succeed under the disguise of high respectability. That disguise, in any case, will be stripped from you. Mine is Pitt-Heron. I do not know how far he has entangled himself with you, but I know something of his weakness, and I don't want his career ruined and his wife's heart broken. He has learned his lesson, and will never mention you and your schemes to a mortal soul. Indeed, if I can help it, he will never know that anyone shares his secret. The price of the chance of escape I offer you is that Pitt-Heron's past be buried for ever."

He did not answer. He had his arms folded, walking up and down the room, and suddenly seemed to have aged enormously. I had the impression that I was dealing with a very old man.

"Mr Leithen," he said at last, "you are bold. You have a frankness which almost amounts to genius. You are wasted in your stupid profession, but your speculative powers are not equal to your other endowments, so you will probably remain in it, deterred by an illogical scruple from following your true bent. Your true *métier*, believe me, is what shallow people call crime. Speaking 'without prejudice,' as the idiot solicitors say, it would appear that we have both weak spots in our cases. Mine, you say, is that I can only work by using the conventions of what we agreed to call the Machine. There may be truth in that. Yours is that you have a friend who lacks your iron-clad discretion. You offer a plan which saves both our weaknesses. By the way, what is it?"

I looked at my watch again. "You have ample time to catch the night express to Paris."

"And if not?"

"Then I am afraid there may be trouble with the police between ten and eleven o'clock."

"Which, for all our sakes, would be a pity. Do you know you interest me uncommonly, for you confirm the accuracy of my judgment. I have always had a notion that some day I should run across, to my sorrow, just such a man as you. A man of very great intellectual power I can deal with, for that kind of brain is usually combined with the sort of high-strung imagination on which I can work. The same with your over-imaginative man. Yes, Pitt-Heron was of that type. Ordinary brains do not trouble me, for I puzzle them. Now, you are a man of good commonplace intelligence. Pray forgive the lukewarmness of the phrase ; it is really a high compliment, for I am an austere critic. If you were that and no more you would not have succeeded. But you possess also a quite irrelevant gift of imagination. Not enough to upset your balance, but enough to do what your mere lawyer's talent could never have done. You have achieved a feat which is given to few—you have partially understood me. Believe me, I rate you high. You are the kind of foursquare being bedded in the concrete of our civilisation, on whom I have always felt I might some day come to grief. . . . No, no, I am not trying to wheedle you. If I thought I could do that I should be sorry, for my discernment would have been at fault."

"I warn you," I said, "that you are wasting precious time."

He laughed quite cheerfully.

"I believe you are really anxious about my interests," he said. "That is a triumph indeed. Do you know, Mr Leithen, it is a mere whimsy of fate that you are not my disciple. If we had met earlier, and under other circumstances, I should have captured you. It is because you have in you a capacity for discipleship that you have succeeded in your opposition."

"I abominate you and all your works," I said, "but I admire your courage."

He shook his head gently.

"It is the wrong word. I am not courageous. To be brave means that you have conquered fear, but I have never had any fear to conquer. Believe me, Mr Leithen, I am quite impervious to threats. You come to me to-night and hold a pistol to my head. You offer me two alternatives, both of which mean failure. But how do you know that I regard them as failure ? I have had what they call a good run for my money. No man since Napoleon has tasted such power. I may be willing to end it. Age creeps on and power may grow burdensome. I have always sat loose from common ambitions and common affections. For all you know I may regard you as a benefactor."

All this talk looks futile when it is written down, but it was skilful enough, for it was taking every atom of exhilaration out of my victory. It was not idle brag. Every syllable rang true, as I knew in my bones. I felt myself in the presence of something enormously big, as if a small barbarian was desecrating the colossal Zeus of Pheidias with a coal hammer. But I also felt it inhuman, and I hated it, and I clung to that hatred.

"You fear nothing and you believe nothing," I said. "Man, you should never have been allowed to live."

He raised a deprecating hand. "I am a sceptic about most things," he said, "but, believe me, I have my own worship. I venerate the intellect of man. I believe in its undreamed-of possibilities, when it grows free like an oak in the forest and is not dwarfed in a flower-pot. From that allegiance I have never wavered. That is the God I have never forsworn."

I took out my watch.

"Permit me again to remind you that time presses."

"True," he said, smiling. "The continental express will not wait upon my confession. Your plan is certainly conceivable. There may be other and easier ways. I am not certain. I must think. . . . Perhaps it would be wiser if you left me now, Mr Leithen. If I take your advice there will be various things to do. . . . In any case there will be much to do. . . ."

He led me to the door as if he were an ordinary host speeding an ordinary guest. I remember that on my way he pointed out a set of Aldines and called my attention to their beauty. He shook hands quite cordially and remarked on the fineness of the weather. That was the last I saw of this amazing man.

It was with profound relief that I found myself in Piccadilly in the wholesome company of my kind. I had carried myself boldly enough in the last hour, but I would not have gone through it again for a king's ransom. Do you know what it is to deal with a pure intelligence, a brain stripped of every shred of humanity? It is like being in the company of a snake.

I drove to the club and telephoned to Macgillivray, asking him to take no notice of my statement till he heard from me in the morning. Then I went to the hospital to see Chapman.

That Leader of the People was in a furious temper, and he was scarcely to be appeased by my narrative of the day's doings. Your Labour Member is the greatest of all sticklers for legality, and the outrage he had suffered that morning had grievously weakened his trust in public security. The Antioch Street business had seemed to him eminently right; if you once got mixed up in melodrama you had to expect such things. But for a Member of Parliament to be robbed in broad daylight next door to the House of Commons upset the foundations of his faith. There was little the matter with his body, and the doctor promised that he would be allowed up next day, but his soul was a mass of bruises.

It took me a lot of persuasion to get him to keep quiet. He wanted a public exposure of Lumley, a big trial, a general ferreting out of secret agents, the whole winding up with a speech in Parliament by himself on this latest outrage of Capitalism. Gloomily he listened to my injunction to silence. But he saw the reason of it, and promised to hold his tongue out of loyalty to Tommy. I knew that Pitt-Heron's secret was safe with him.

As I crossed Westminster Bridge on my way home, the night express to the Continent rumbled over the river. I wondered if Lumley was on board, or if he had taken one of the other ways of which he had spoken. . . .

CHAPTER IX.

RETURN OF THE WILD GEESE.

I DO not think I was surprised at the news I read in 'The Times' next morning.

Mr Andrew Lumley had died suddenly in the night of heart failure, and the newspapers woke up to the fact that we had been entertaining a great man unawares. There was an obituary in "leader" type of nearly two columns. He had been older than I thought—close on seventy—and 'The Times' spoke of him as a man who might have done anything he pleased in public life, but had chosen to give to a small coterie of friends what was due to the country. I read of his wit and learning, his amazing connoisseurship, his social gifts, his personal charm. According to the writer, he was the finest type of cultivated amateur, a Beckford with more than a Beckford's wealth and none of his folly. Large private charities were hinted at, and a hope was expressed that some part at least of his collections might come to the nation.

The halfpenny papers said the same thing in their own way. One declared he reminded it of Atticus, another of Mæcenas, another of Lord Houghton. There must have been a great run on biographical dictionaries in the various offices. Chapman's own particular rag said that, although this kind of philanthropist was a dilettante and a back number, yet Mr Lumley was a good specimen of the class and had been a true friend to the poor. I thought Chapman would have a fit when he read this. After that he took in the 'Morning Post.'

It was no business of mine to explode the myth. Indeed I couldn't even if I had wanted to, for no one would have believed me unless I produced proofs, and these proofs were not to be made public. Besides, I had an honest compunction. He had had, as he expressed it, a good run for his money, and I wanted the run to be properly rounded off.

Three days later I went to the funeral. It was a wonderful occasion. Two eminent statesmen were among the pall-bearers, Royalty was represented, and there were wreaths from learned societies and scores of notable people. It was a queer business to listen to that stately service, which was never read over stranger dust. I was thinking all the time of the vast subterranean machine which he had controlled, and which now was so much old iron. I could dimly imagine what his death meant to the hosts who had worked blindly at his discretion. He was a Napoleon who left no Marshals behind him. From the Power-House came no wreaths or newspaper tributes, but I knew that it had lost its power. . . .

De mortuis, &c. My task was done, and it only remained to get Pitt-Heron home.

Of the three people in London besides myself who knew the story—Macgillivray, Chapman, and Felix—the two last might be trusted to be silent, and Scotland Yard is not in the habit of publishing its information. Tommy, of course, must some time or other be told; it was his right; but I knew that Tommy would never breathe a word of it. I wanted Charles to believe that his secret died with Lumley, for otherwise I don't think he would have ever come back to England.

The thing took some arranging, for we could not tell him directly about Lumley's death without giving away the fact that we knew of the connection between the two. We had to approach it by a roundabout road. I got Felix to arrange to have the news telegraphed to and inserted by special order in a Russian paper which Charles could not avoid seeing.

The device was successful. Calling at Portman Square a few days later, I learned from Ethel Pitt-Heron's glowing face that her troubles were over. That same evening a cable to me from Tommy announced the return of the wanderers.

It was the year of the Chilian Arbitration, in which I held a junior brief for the British Government, and that and the late sitting of Parliament kept me in London after the end of the term. I had had a bad reaction from the excitements of the summer, and in these days I was feeling pretty well hipped and overdone. On a hot August afternoon I met Tommy again.

The sun was shining through my Temple chambers, much as it had done when he started. So far as I remember, the West Ham brief which had aroused his contempt was still adorning my table. I was very hot and cross and fagged, for I had been engaged in the beastly job of comparing half a dozen maps of a despicable little bit of South American frontier.

Suddenly the door opened, and Tommy, lean and sunburnt, stalked in.

"Still at the old grind," he cried, after we had shaken hands. "Fellows like you give me a notion of the meaning of Eternity."

"The same uneventful, sedentary life," I replied. "Nothing happens except that my scale of fees grows. I suppose nothing *will* happen till the conductor comes to take the tickets. I shall soon grow fat."

"I notice it already, my lad. You want a bit of waking up or you'll get a liver. A little sensation would do you a pot of good."

"And you?" I asked. "I congratulate you on your success. I hear you have retrieved Pitt-Heron for his mourning family."

Tommy's laughing eyes grew solemn.

"I have had the time of my life," he said. "It was like a chapter out of the Arabian Nights with a dash of Fenimore Cooper. I feel as if I had lived years since I left England in May. While you have been sitting among your musty papers we have been riding like mosstroopers and seeing men die. Come and dine to-night and hear about our adventures. I can't tell you the full story, for I don't know it, but there is enough to curl your hair."

Then I achieved my first and last score at the expense of Tommy Deloraine.

"No," I said, "you will dine with me instead, and *I* will tell you the full story. All the papers on the subject are over there in my safe."

III.

THE WATCHER BY THE THRESHOLD

"Among idle men there be some who tarry in the outer courts, speeding the days joyfully with dance and song. But the other sort dwell near the portals of the House, and are ever anxious and ill at ease that they may see something of the Shadows which come and go. Wherefore night and day they are found watching by the threshold, in fearfulness and joy, not without tears."—*Extract from the Writings of* DONISARIUS OF PADUA, *circa* 1310.

TO

STAIR AGNEW GILLON.

MY DEAR STAIR,

We have travelled so many roads together, highland and lowland, pleasant and dreary, that I ask you to accept this book of travellers' tales. For Scotland is a wide place to travel in for those who believe that it is not bounded strictly by kirk and market-place, and who have an ear for old songs and lost romances. It is of the back-world of Scotland that I write, the land behind the mist and over the seven bens, a place hard of access for the foot-passenger but easy for the maker of stories. Meantime, to you, who have chosen the better part, I wish many bright days by hill and loch in the summers to come.

J. B.

R.M.S. Briton, at sea.

I. NO-MAN'S-LAND.

CHAPTER I.

THE SHIELING OF FARAWA.

It was with a light heart and a pleasing consciousness of holiday that I set out from the inn at Allermuir to tramp my fifteen miles into the unknown. I walked slowly, for I carried my equipment on my back—my basket, fly-books and rods, my plaid of Grant tartan (for I boast myself a distant kinsman of that house), and my great staff, which had tried ere then the front of the steeper Alps. A small valise with books and some changes of linen clothing had been sent on ahead in the shepherd's own hands. It was yet early April, and before me lay four weeks of freedom—twenty-eight blessed days in which to take fish and smoke the pipe of idleness. The Lent term had pulled me down, a week of modest enjoyment thereafter in town had finished the work; and I drank in the sharp moorish air like a thirsty man who has been forwandered among deserts.

I am a man of varied tastes and a score of interests. As an undergraduate I had been filled with the old mania for the complete life. I distinguished myself in the Schools, rowed in my college eight, and reached the distinction of practising for three weeks in the Trials. I had dabbled in a score of learned activities, and when the time came that I won the inevitable St Chad's fellowship on my chaotic acquirements, and I found myself compelled to select if I would pursue a scholar's life, I had some toil in finding my vocation. In the end I resolved that the ancient life of the North, of the Celts and the Northmen and the unknown Pictish tribes, held for me the chief fascination. I had acquired a smattering of Gaelic, having been brought up as a boy in Lochaber, and now I set myself to increase my store of languages. I mastered Erse and Icelandic, and my first book—a monograph on the probable Celtic elements in the Eddic songs—brought me the praise of scholars and the deputy-professor's chair of Northern Antiquities. So much for Oxford. My vacations had been spent mainly in the North—in Ireland, Scotland, and the Isles, in Scandinavia and Iceland, once even in the far limits of Finland. I was a keen sportsman of a sort, an old-experienced fisher, a fair shot with gun and rifle, and in my hillcraft I might well stand comparison with most men. April has ever seemed to me the finest season of the year even in our cold northern altitudes, and the memory of many bright Aprils had brought me up from the South on the night before to Allerfoot, whence a dogcart had taken me up Glen Aller to the inn at Allermuir; and now the same desire had set me on the heather with my face to the cold brown hills.

You are to picture a sort of plateau, benty and rock-strewn, running ridge-wise above a chain of little peaty lochs and a vast tract of inexorable bog. In a mile the ridge ceased in a shoulder of hill, and over this lay the head of another glen, with the same doleful accompaniment of sunless lochs, mosses, and a shining and resolute water. East and west and north, in every direction save the south, rose walls of gashed and serrated hills. It was a grey day with blinks of sun, and when a ray chanced to fall on one of the great dark faces, lines of light and colour sprang into being which told of mica and granite. I was in high spirits, as on the eve of holiday; I had breakfasted excellently on eggs and salmon-steaks; I had no cares to speak of, and my prospects were not uninviting. But in spite of myself the landscape began to take me in thrall and crush me. The silent vanished peoples of the hills seemed to be stirring; dark primeval faces seemed to stare at me from behind boulders and jags of rock. The place was so still, so free from the cheerful clamour of nesting birds, that it seemed a *temenos* sacred to some old-world god. At my feet the lochs lapped ceaselessly; but the waters were so dark that one could not see bottom a foot from the edge. On my right the links of green told of snake-like mires waiting to crush the unwary wanderer. It seemed to me for the moment a land of death, where the tongues of the dead cried aloud for recognition.

My whole morning's walk was full of such fancies. I lit a pipe to cheer me, but the things would not be got rid of. I thought of the Gaels who had held those fastnesses; I thought of the Britons before them, who yielded to their advent. They were all strong peoples in their day, and now they had gone the way of the earth. They had left their mark on the levels of the glens and on the more habitable uplands, both in names and in actual forts, and graves where men might still dig curios. But the hills—that black stony amphitheatre before me—it seemed strange that the hills bore no traces of them. And then with some uneasiness I reflected on that older and stranger race who were said to have held the hill-tops. The Picts, the Picti—what in the name of goodness were they? They had troubled me in all my studies, a sort of blank wall to put an end to speculation. We knew nothing of them save certain strange names which men called Pictish, the names of those hills in front of me—the Muneraw, the Yirnie, the Calmarton. They were the *corpus vile* for learned experiment; but Heaven alone knew what dark abyss of savagery once yawned in the midst of this desert.

And then I remembered the crazy theories of a pupil of mine at St Chad's, the son of a small landowner on the Aller, a young gentleman who had spent his substance too freely at Oxford, and was now dreeing his weird in the

Backwoods. He had been no scholar; but a certain imagination marked all his doings, and of a Sunday night he would come and talk to me of the North. The Picts were his special subject, and his ideas were mad. "Listen to me," he would say, when I had mixed him toddy and given him one of my cigars; "I believe there are traces—ay, and more than traces—of an old culture lurking in those hills and waiting to be discovered. We never hear of the Picts being driven from the hills. The Britons drove them from the lowlands, the Gaels from Ireland did the same for the Britons; but the hills were left unmolested. We hear of no one going near them except outlaws and tinklers. And in that very place you have the strangest mythology. Take the story of the Brownie. What is that but the story of a little swart man of uncommon strength and cleverness, who does good and ill indiscriminately, and then disappears? There are many scholars, as you yourself confess, who think that the origin of the Brownie was in some mad belief in the old race of the Picts, which still survived somewhere in the hills. And do we not hear of the Brownie in authentic records right down to the year 1756? After that, when people grew more incredulous, it is natural that the belief should have begun to die out; but I do not see why stray traces should not have survived till late."

"Do you not see what that means?" I had said in mock gravity. "Those same hills are, if anything, less known now than they were a hundred years ago. Why should not your Picts or Brownies be living to this day?"

"Why not, indeed?" he had rejoined, in all seriousness.

I laughed, and he went to his rooms and returned with a large leather-bound book. It was lettered, in the rococo style of a young man's taste, 'Glimpses of the Unknown,' and some of the said glimpses he proceeded to impart to me. It was not pleasant reading; indeed, I had rarely heard anything so well fitted to shatter sensitive nerves. The early part consisted of folk-tales and folk-sayings, some of them wholly obscure, some of them with a glint of meaning, but all of them with some hint of a mystery in the hills. I heard the Brownie story in countless versions. Now the thing was a friendly little man, who wore grey breeches and lived on brose; now he was a twisted being, the sight of which made the ewes miscarry in the lambing-time. But the second part was the stranger, for it was made up of actual tales, most of them with date and place appended. It was a most Bedlamite catalogue of horrors, which, if true, made the wholesome moors a place instinct with tragedy. Some told of children carried away from villages, even from towns, on the verge of the uplands. In almost every case they were girls, and the strange fact was their utter disappearance. Two little girls would be coming home from school, would be seen last by a neighbour just where the road crossed a patch of heath or entered a wood and then—no human eye ever saw them again. Children's cries had startled outlying shepherds in the night, and when they had rushed to the door they could hear nothing but the night wind. The instances of such disappearances were not very common—perhaps once in twenty years—but they were confined to this one tract of country, and came in a sort of fixed progression from the middle of last century, when the record began. But this was only one side of the history. The latter part was all devoted to a chronicle of crimes which had gone unpunished, seeing that no hand had ever been traced. The list was fuller in last century; [1] in the earlier years of the present it had dwindled; then came a revival about the 'Fifties; and now again in our own time it had sunk low. At the little cottage of Auchterbrean, on the roadside in Glen Aller, a labourer's wife had been found pierced to the heart. It was thought to be a case of a woman's jealousy, and her neighbour was accused, convicted, and hanged. The woman, to be sure, denied the charge with her last breath; but circumstantial evidence seemed sufficiently

[1] The narrative of Mr Graves was written in the year 1898.

strong against her. Yet some people in the glen believed her guiltless. In particular, the carrier who had found the dead woman declared that the way in which her neighbour received the news was a sufficient proof of innocence; and the doctor who was first summoned professed himself unable to tell with what instrument the wound had been given. But this was all before the days of expert evidence, so the woman had been hanged without scruple. Then there had been another story of peculiar horror, telling of the death of an old man at some little lonely shieling called Carrickfey. But at this point I had risen in protest, and made to drive the young idiot from my room.

"It was my grandfather who collected most of them," he said. "He had theories,[1] but people called him mad, so he was wise enough to hold his tongue. My father declares the whole thing mania; but I rescued the book, had it bound, and added to the collection. It is a queer hobby; but, as I say, I have theories, and there are more things in heaven and earth——"

But at this he heard a friend's voice in the Quad., and dived out, leaving the banal quotation unfinished.

Strange though it may seem, this madness kept coming back to me as I crossed the last few miles of moor. I was

[1] In the light of subsequent events I have jotted down the materials to which I refer. The last authentic record of the Brownie is in the narrative of the shepherd of Clachlands, taken down towards the close of last century by the Reverend Mr Gillespie, minister of Allerkirk, and included by him in his 'Songs and Legends of Glen Aller.' The authorities on the strange carrying-away of children are to be found in a series of articles in a local paper, the 'Allerfoot Advertiser,' September and October 1878, and a curious book published anonymously at Edinburgh in 1848, entitled 'The Weathergaw.' The records of the unexplained murders in the same neighbourhood are all contained in Mr Fordoun's 'Theory of Expert Evidence,' and an attack on the book in the 'Law Review' for June 1881. The Carrickfey case has a pamphlet to itself—now extremely rare—a copy of which was recently obtained in a bookseller's shop in Dumfries by a well-known antiquary, and presented to the library of the Supreme Court in Edinburgh.

now on a rough tableland, the watershed between two lochs, and beyond and above me rose the stony backs of the hills. The burns fell down in a chaos of granite boulders, and huge slabs of grey stone lay flat and tumbled in the heather. The full waters looked prosperously for my fishing, and I began to forget all fancies in anticipation of sport.

Then suddenly in a hollow of land I came on a ruined cottage. It had been a very small place, but the walls were still half-erect, and the little moorland garden was outlined on the turf. A lonely apple-tree, twisted and gnarled with winds, stood in the midst.

From higher up on the hill I heard a loud roar, and I knew my excellent friend the shepherd of Farawa, who had come thus far to meet me. He greeted me with the boisterous embarrassment which was his way of prefacing hospitality. A grave reserved man at other times, on such occasions he thought it proper to relapse into hilarity. I fell into step with him, and we set off for his dwelling. But first I had the curiosity to look back to the tumble-down cottage and ask him its name.

A queer look came into his eyes. "They ca' the place Carrickfey," he said. "Naebody has daured to bide there this twenty year sin'—but I see ye ken the story." And, as if glad to leave the subject, he hastened to discourse on fishing.

CHAPTER II.

TELLS OF AN EVENING'S TALK.

THE shepherd was a masterful man; tall, save for the stoop which belongs to all moorland folk, and active as a wild goat. He was not a new importation, nor did he belong to the place; for his people had lived in the remote Borders, and he had come as a boy to this shieling of Farawa. He was unmarried, but an elderly sister lived with him and cooked his meals. He was reputed to be extraordinarily skilful in his trade; I know for a fact that he was in his way a keen sportsman; and his few neighbours gave him credit for a sincere piety. Doubtless this last report was due in part to his silence, for after his first greeting he was wont to relapse into a singular taciturnity. As we strode across the heather he gave me a short outline of his year's lambing. "Five pair o' twins yestreen, twae this morn; that makes thirty-five yowes that hae lambed since the Sabbath. I'll dae weel if God's willin'." Then, as I looked towards the hill-tops whence the thin mist of morn was trailing, he followed my gaze. "See," he said with uplifted crook—"see that sicht. Is that no what is written of in the Bible when it says, 'The mountains do smoke.'" And with this piece of exegesis he finished his talk, and in a little we were at the cottage.

It was a small enough dwelling in truth, and yet large for a moorland house, for it had a garret below the thatch, which was given up to my sole enjoyment. Below was the wide kitchen with box-beds, and next to it the inevitable second room, also with its cupboard sleeping-places. The interior was very clean, and yet I remember to have been struck with the faint musty smell which is inseparable from moorland dwellings. The kitchen pleased me best, for there the great rafters were black with peat-reek, and the uncovered stone floor, on which the fire gleamed dully, gave an air of primeval simplicity. But the walls spoiled all, for tawdry things of to-day had penetrated even there. Some grocers' almanacs—years old—hung in places of honour, and an extraordinary lithograph of the Royal Family in its youth. And this, mind you, between crooks and fishing-rods and old guns, and horns of sheep and deer.

The life for the first day or two was regular and placid. I was up early, breakfasted on porridge (a dish which I detest), and then off to the lochs and streams. At first my sport prospered mightily. With a drake-wing I killed a salmon of seventeen pounds, and the next day had a fine basket of trout from a hill-burn. Then for no earthly reason the weather changed. A bitter wind came out of the north-east, bringing showers of snow and stinging hail, and lashing the waters into storm. It was now farewell to fly-fishing. For a day or two I tried trolling with the minnow on the lochs, but it was poor sport, for I had no boat, and the edges were soft and mossy. Then in disgust I gave up the attempt, went back to the cottage, lit my biggest pipe, and sat down with a book to await the turn of the weather.

The shepherd was out from morning till night at his work, and when he came in at last, dog-tired, his face would be set and hard, and his eyes heavy with sleep. The strangeness of the man grew upon me. He had a shrewd brain beneath his thatch of hair, for I had tried him once or twice, and found him abundantly intelligent. He had some smattering of an education, like all Scottish peasants, and, as I have said, he was deeply religious. I set him down as a fine type of his class, sober, serious, keenly critical, free from the bondage of superstition. But I rarely saw him, and our talk was chiefly in monosyllables—short interjected accounts of the number of lambs dead or alive on the hill. Then he would produce a pencil and note-book, and be immersed in some calculation; and finally he would be revealed sleeping heavily in his chair, till his sister wakened him, and he stumbled off to bed.

So much for the ordinary course of life; but one day—the second I think of the bad weather—the extraordinary happened. The storm had passed in the afternoon into a resolute and blinding snow, and the shepherd, finding it hopeless on the hill, came home about three o'clock. I could make out from his way of entering that he was in a great temper. He kicked his feet savagely against the door-post. Then he swore at his dogs, a thing I had never heard him do before. "Hell!" he cried, "can ye no keep out o' my road, ye britts?" Then he came sullenly into the kitchen, thawed his numbed hands at the fire, and sat down to his meal.

I made some aimless remark about the weather.

"Death to man and beast," he grunted. "I hae got the sheep doun frae the hill, but the lambs will never thole this. We maun pray that it will no last."

His sister came in with some dish. "Margit," he cried, "three lambs away this morning, and three deid wi' the hole in the throat."

The woman's face visibly paled. "Guid help us, Adam; that hasna happened this three year."

"It has happened noo," he said surlily. "But, by God! if it happens again I'll gang mysel' to the Scarts o' the Muneraw."

"O Adam!" the woman cried shrilly, "haud your tongue. Ye kenna wha hears ye." And with a frightened glance at me she left the room.

I asked no questions, but waited till the shepherd's anger should cool. But the cloud did not pass so lightly. When he had finished his dinner he pulled his chair to the fire and sat staring moodily. He made some sort of apology to me for his conduct. "I'm sore troubled, sir; but I'm vexed ye should see me like this. Maybe things will be better the morn." And then, lighting his short black pipe, he resigned himself to his meditations.

But he could not keep quiet. Some nervous unrest seemed to have possessed the man. He got up with a start and went to the window, where the snow was drifting unsteadily past. As he stared out into the storm I heard him mutter to himself, "Three away, God help me, and three wi' the hole in the throat."

Then he turned round to me abruptly. I was jotting down notes for an article I contemplated in the 'Revue Celtique,' so my thoughts were far away from the present. The man recalled me by demanding fiercely, "Do ye believe in God?"

I gave him some sort of answer in the affirmative.

"Then do ye believe in the Devil?" he asked.

The reply must have been less satisfactory, for he came forward and flung himself violently into the chair before me.

"What do ye ken about it?" he cried. "You that bides in a southern toun, what can ye ken o' the God that works in thae hills and the Devil—ay, the manifold devils—that He suffers to bide here? I tell ye, man, that if ye had seen what I have seen ye wad be on your knees at this moment praying to God to pardon your unbelief. There are devils at the back o' every stane and hidin' in every cleuch, and it's by the grace o' God alone that a man is alive upon the earth." His voice had risen high and shrill, and then suddenly he cast a frightened glance towards the window and was silent.

I began to think that the man's wits were unhinged, and the thought did not give me satisfaction. I had no relish for the prospect of being left alone in this moorland dwelling with the cheerful company of a maniac. But his next movements reassured me. He was clearly only dead-tired, for he fell sound asleep in his chair, and by the time his sister brought tea and wakened him, he seemed to have got the better of his excitement.

When the window was shuttered and the lamp lit, I set myself again to the completion of my notes. The shepherd had got out his Bible, and was solemnly reading with one great finger travelling down the lines. He was smoking, and whenever some text came home to him with power he would make pretence to underline it with the end of the stem. Soon I had finished the work I desired, and, my mind being full of my pet hobby, I fell into an inquisitive mood, and began to question the solemn man opposite on the antiquities of the place.

He stared stupidly at me when I asked him concerning monuments or ancient weapons.

"I kenna," said he. "There's a heap o' queer things in the hills."

"This place should be a centre for such relics. You know that the name of the hill behind the house, as far as I can make it out, means the 'Place of the Little Men.' It is a good Gaelic word, though there is some doubt about its exact interpretation. But clearly the Gaelic peoples did not speak of themselves when they gave the name; they must have referred to some older and stranger population."

The shepherd looked at me dully, as not understanding.

"It is partly this fact—besides the fishing, of course—which interests me in this countryside," said I gaily.

Again he cast the same queer frightened glance towards the window. "If ye'll tak the advice of an aulder man," he said slowly, "ye'll let well alane and no meddle wi' uncanny things."

I laughed pleasantly, for at last I had found out my hard-headed host in a piece of childishness. "Why, I thought that you of all men would be free from superstition."

"What do ye call supersteetion?" he asked.

"A belief in old wives' tales," said I, "a trust in the crude supernatural and the patently impossible."

He looked at me beneath his shaggy brows. "How do ye ken what is impossible? Mind ye, sir, ye're no in the toun just now, but in the thick of the wild hills."

"But, hang it all, man," I cried, "you don't mean to say that you believe in that sort of thing? I am prepared for many things up here, but not for the Brownie—though, to be sure, if one could meet him in the flesh, it would be rather pleasant than otherwise, for he was a companionable sort of fellow."

"When a thing pits the fear o' death on a man he aye speaks well of it."

It was true—the Eumenides and the Good Folk over again; and I awoke with interest to the fact that the conversation was getting into strange channels.

The shepherd moved uneasily in his chair. "I am a man that fears God, and has nae time for daft stories; but I havena traivelled the hills for twenty years wi' my een shut. If I say that I could tell ye stories o' faces seen in the mist, and queer things that have knocked against me in the snaw, wad ye believe me? I wager ye wadna. Ye wad say I had been drunk, and yet I am a God-fearing temperate man."

He rose and went to a cupboard, unlocked it, and brought out something in his hand, which he held out to me. I took it with some curiosity, and found that it was a flint arrow-head.

Clearly a flint arrow-head, and yet like none that I had ever seen in any collection. For one thing it was larger, and the barb less clumsily thick. More, the chipping was new, or comparatively so; this thing had not stood the wear of fifteen hundred years among the stones of the hill-side. Now there are, I regret to say, institutions which manufacture primitive relics; but it is not hard for a practised eye to see the difference. The chipping has either a regularity and a balance which is unknown in the real thing, or the rudeness has been overdone, and the result is an implement incapable of harming a mortal creature. But this was the real thing if it ever existed; and yet—I was prepared to swear on my reputation that it was not half a century old.

"Where did you get this?" I asked with some nervousness.

"I hae a story about that," said the shepherd. "Outside the door there ye can see a muckle flat stane aside the buchts. One simmer nicht I was sitting there smoking till the dark, and I wager there was naething on the stane then. But that same nicht I awoke wi' a queer thocht, as if there were folk moving around the hoose—folk that didna mak' muckle noise. I mind o' lookin' out o' the windy, and I could hae sworn I saw something black movin' amang the heather and intil the buchts. Now I had maybe three-score o' lambs there that nicht, for I had to tak' them many miles off in the early morning. Weel, when I gets up about four o'clock and gangs out, as I am passing the muckle stane I finds this bit errow. 'That's come here in the nicht,' says I, and I wunnered a wee and put it in my pouch. But when I came to my faulds what did I see? Five o' my best hoggs were away, and three mair were lying deid wi' a hole in their throat."

"Who in the world——?" I began.

"Dinna ask," said he. "If I aince sterted to speir about thae maitters, I wadna keep my reason."

"Then that was what happened on the hill this morning?"

"Even sae, and it has happened mair than aince sin' that time. It's the most uncanny slaughter, for sheep-stealing I can understand, but no this pricking o' the puir beasts' wizands. I kenna how they dae't either, for it's no wi' a knife or ony common tool."

"Have you never tried to follow the thieves?"

"Have I no?" he asked grimly. "If it had been common sheep-stealers I wad hae had them by the heels, though I had followed them a hundred miles. But this is no common. I've tracked them, and it's ill they are to track; but I never got beyond ae place, and that was the Scarts o' the Muneraw that ye've heard me speak o'."

"But who in Heaven's name are the people? Tinklers or poachers or what?"

"Ay," said he drily. "Even so. Tinklers and poachers whae work wi' stane erroes and kill sheep by a hole in their throat. Lord, I kenna what they are, unless the Muckle Deil himsel'."

The conversation had passed beyond my comprehension. In this prosaic hard-headed man I had come on the dead-rock of superstition and blind fear.

"That is only the story of the Brownie over again, and he is an exploded myth," I said, laughing.

"Are ye the man that exploded it?" said the shepherd

rudely. "I trow no, neither you nor ony ither. My bonny man, if ye lived a twalmonth in thae hills, ye wad sing safter about exploded myths, as ye call them."

"I tell you what I would do," said I. "If I lost sheep as you lose them, I would go up the Scarts of the Muneraw and never rest till I had settled the question once and for all." I spoke hotly, for I was vexed by the man's childish fear.

"I daresay ye wad," he said slowly. "But then I am no you, and maybe I ken mair o' what is in the Scarts o' the Muneraw. Maybe I ken that whilk, if ye kenned it, wad send ye back to the South Country wi' your hert in your mouth. But, as I say, I am no sae brave as you, for I saw something in the first year o' my herding here which put the terror o' God on me, and makes me a fearfu' man to this day. Ye ken the story o' the gudeman o' Carrickfey?"

I nodded.

"Weel, I was the man that fand him. I had seen the deid afore and I've seen them since. But never have I seen aucht like the look in that man's een. What he saw at his death I may see the morn, so I walk before the Lord in fear."

Then he rose and stretched himself. "It's bedding-time, for I maun be up at three," and with a short good-night he left the room.

CHAPTER III.

THE SCARTS OF THE MUNERAW.

THE next morning was fine, for the snow had been intermittent, and had soon melted except in the high corries. True, it was deceptive weather, for the wind had gone to the rainy south-west, and the masses of cloud on that horizon boded ill for the afternoon. But some days' inaction had made me keen for a chance of sport, so I rose with the shepherd and set out for the day.

He asked me where I proposed to begin.

I told him the tarn called the Loch o' the Threshes, which lies over the back of the Muneraw on another watershed. It is on the ground of the Rhynns Forest, and I had fished it of old from the Forest House. I knew the merits of the trout, and I knew its virtues in a south-west wind, so I had resolved to go thus far afield.

The shepherd heard the name in silence. "Your best road will be ower that rig, and syne on to the water o' Caulds. Keep abune the moss till ye come to the place they ca' the Nick o' the Threshes. That will take ye to the very lochside, but it's a lang road and a sair."

The morning was breaking over the bleak hills. Little clouds drifted athwart the corries, and wisps of haze fluttered from the peaks. A great rosy flush lay over one side of the glen, which caught the edge of the sluggish bog-pools and turned them to fire. Never before had I seen the mountain-land so clear, for far back into the east and west I saw mountain-tops set as close as flowers in a border, black crags seamed with silver lines which I knew for mighty waterfalls, and below at my feet the lower slopes fresh with the dewy green of spring. A name stuck in my memory from the last night's talk.

"Where are the Scarts of the Muneraw?" I asked.

The shepherd pointed to the great hill which bears the name, and which lies, a huge mass, above the watershed.

"D'ye see yon corrie at the east that runs straucht up the side? It looks a bit scart, but it's sae deep that it's aye derk at the bottom o't. Weel, at the tap o' the rig it meets anither corrie that runs doun the ither side, and that one they ca' the Scarts. There is a sort o' burn in it that flows intil the Dule and sae intil the Aller, and, indeed, if ye were gaun there it wad be from Aller Glen that your best road wad lie. But it's an ill bit, and ye'll be sair guidit if ye try't."

There he left me and went across the glen, while I struck upwards over the ridge. At the top I halted and looked down on the wide glen of the Caulds, which there is little better than a bog, but lower down grows into a green pastoral valley. The great Muneraw still dominated the landscape, and the black scaur on its side seemed blacker than before. The place fascinated me, for in that fresh morning air the shepherd's fears seemed monstrous. "Some day," said I to myself, "I will go and explore the whole of that mighty hill." Then I descended and struggled over the moss, found the Nick, and in two hours' time was on the loch's edge.

I have little in the way of good to report of the fishing. For perhaps one hour the trout took well; after that they sulked steadily for the day. The promise, too, of fine weather had been deceptive. By mid-day the rain was falling in that soft soaking fashion which gives no hope of clearing. The mist was down to the edge of the water, and I cast my flies into a blind sea of white. It was hopeless work, and yet from a sort of ill-temper I stuck to it long after my better judgment had warned me of its folly. At last, about three in the afternoon, I struck my camp, and prepared myself for a long and toilsome retreat.

And long and toilsome it was beyond anything I had ever encountered. Had I had a vestige of sense I would have followed the burn from the loch down to the Forest House. The place was shut up, but the keeper would gladly have given me shelter for the night. But foolish pride was too strong in me. I had found my road in mist before, and could do it again.

Before I got to the top of the hill I had repented my decision; when I got there I repented it more. For below me was a dizzy chaos of grey; there was no landmark visible; and before me I knew was the bog through which the Caulds Water twined. I had crossed it with some trouble in the morning, but then I had light to pick my steps. Now I could only stumble on, and in five minutes I might be in a bog-hole, and in five more in a better world.

But there was no help to be got from hesitation, so with a rueful courage I set off. The place was if possible worse than I had feared. Wading up to the knees with nothing before you but a blank wall of mist and the cheerful consciousness that your next step may be your last—such was my state for one weary mile. The stream itself was high, and rose to my armpits, and once again I only saved myself by a violent leap backwards from a pitiless green slough. But at last it was past, and I was once more on the solid ground of the hillside.

Now, in the thick weather I had crossed the glen much lower down than in the morning, and the result was that the hill on which I stood was one of the giants which, with the Muneraw for centre, guard the watershed. Had I taken the proper way, the Nick o' the Threshes would have led me to the Caulds, and then once over the bog a little ridge was all that stood between me and the glen of Farawa. But instead I had come a wild cross-country road, and was now, though I did not know it, nearly as far from my destination as at the start.

Well for me that I did not know, for I was wet and dispirited, and had I not fancied myself all but home, I should scarcely have had the energy to make this last ascent. But soon I found it was not the little ridge I had expected. I looked at my watch and saw that it was five o'clock. When, after the weariest climb, I lay on a piece of level ground which seemed the top, I was not surprised to find that it was now seven. The darkening must be at hand, and sure enough the mist seemed to be deepening into a greyish black. I began to grow desperate. Here was I on the summit of some infernal mountain, without any certainty where my road lay. I was lost with a vengeance, and at the thought I began to be acutely afraid.

I took what seemed to me the way I had come, and began to descend steeply. Then something made me halt, and the next instant I was lying on my face trying painfully to retrace my steps. For I had found myself slipping, and before I could stop, my feet were dangling over a precipice with Heaven alone knows how many yards of sheer mist between me and the bottom. Then I tried keeping the ridge, and took that to the right, which I thought would bring me nearer home. It was no good trying to think out a direction, for in the fog my brain was running round, and I seemed to stand on a pin-point of space where the laws of the compass had ceased to hold.

It was the roughest sort of walking, now stepping warily over acres of loose stones, now crawling down the face of some battered rock, and now wading in the long dripping heather. The soft rain had begun to fall again, which completed my discomfort. I was now seriously tired, and, like all men who in their day have bent too much over books, I began to feel it in my back. My spine ached, and my breath came in short broken pants. It was a pitiable state of affairs for an honest man who had never encountered much grave discomfort. To ease myself I was compelled to leave my basket behind me, trusting to return and find it, if I should ever reach safety and discover on what pathless hill I had been strayed. My rod I used as a staff, but it was of little use, for my fingers were getting too numb to hold it.

Suddenly from the blankness I heard a sound as of human speech. At first I thought it mere craziness—the cry of a weasel or a hill-bird distorted by my ears. But again it came, thick and faint, as through acres of mist, and yet clearly the sound of "articulate-speaking men." In a moment I lost my despair and cried out in answer. This was some forwandered traveller like myself, and between us we could surely find some road to safety. So I yelled back at the pitch of my voice and waited intently.

But the sound ceased, and there was utter silence again. Still I waited, and then from some place much nearer came the same soft mumbling speech. I could make nothing of it. Heard in that drear place it made the nerves tense and the heart timorous. It was the strangest jumble of vowels and consonants I had ever met.

A dozen solutions flashed through my brain. It was some maniac talking Jabberwock to himself. It was some belated traveller whose wits had given out in fear. Perhaps it was only some shepherd who was amusing himself thus, and whiling the way with nonsense. Once again I cried out and waited.

Then suddenly in the hollow trough of mist before me, where things could still be half discerned, there appeared a figure. It was little and squat and dark; naked, apparently, but so rough with hair that it wore the appearance of a skin-covered being. It crossed my line of vision, not staying for a moment, but in its face and eyes there seemed to lurk an elder world of mystery and barbarism, a troll-like life which was too horrible for words.

The shepherd's fear came back on me like a thunderclap. For one awful instant my legs failed me, and I had almost fallen. The next I had turned and ran shrieking up the hill.

If he who may read this narrative has never felt the force of an overmastering terror, then let him thank his Maker and pray that he never may. I am no weak child, but a strong grown man, accredited in general with sound sense and little suspected of hysterics. And yet I went up that brae-face with my heart fluttering like a bird and my throat aching with fear. I screamed in short dry gasps; involuntarily, for my mind was beyond any purpose. I felt that beast-like clutch at my throat; those red eyes seemed to be staring at me from the mist; I heard ever behind and before and on all sides the patter of those inhuman feet.

Before I knew I was down, slipping over a rock and falling

some dozen feet into a soft marshy hollow. I was conscious of lying still for a second and whimpering like a child. But as I lay there I awoke to the silence of the place. There was no sound of pursuit; perhaps they had lost my track and given up. My courage began to return, and from this it was an easy step to hope. Perhaps after all it had been merely an illusion, for folk do not see clearly in the mist, and I was already done with weariness.

But even as I lay in the green moss and began to hope, the faces of my pursuers grew up through the mist. I stumbled madly to my feet; but I was hemmed in, the rock behind and my enemies before. With a cry I rushed forward, and struck wildly with my rod at the first dark body. It was as if I had struck an animal, and the next second the thing was wrenched from my grasp. But still they came no nearer. I stood trembling there in the centre of those malignant devils, my brain a mere weathercock, and my heart crushed shapeless with horror. At last the end came, for with the vigour of madness I flung myself on the nearest, and we rolled on the ground. Then the monstrous things seemed to close over me, and with a choking cry I passed into unconsciousness.

CHAPTER IV.

THE DARKNESS THAT IS UNDER THE EARTH.

THERE is an unconsciousness that is not wholly dead, where a man feels numbly and the body lives without the brain. I was beyond speech or thought, and yet I felt the upward or downward motion as the way lay in hill or glen, and I most assuredly knew when the open air was changed for the close underground. I could feel dimly that lights were flared in my face, and that I was laid in some bed on the earth. Then with the stopping of movement the real sleep of weakness seized me, and for long I knew nothing of this mad world.

. . . .

Morning came over the moors with bird-song and the glory of fine weather. The streams were still rolling in spate, but the hill-pastures were alight with dawn, and the little seams of snow were glistening like white fire. A ray from the sunrise cleft its path somehow into the abyss, and danced on the wall above my couch. It caught my eye as I wakened, and for long I lay crazily wondering what it meant. My head was splitting with pain, and in my heart was the same fluttering nameless fear. I did not wake to full consciousness; not till the twinkle of sun from the clean bright out-of-doors caught my senses did I realise that I lay in a great dark place with a glow of dull firelight in the middle.

In time things rose and moved around me, a few ragged shapes of men, without clothing, shambling with their huge feet and looking towards me with curved beast-like glances. I tried to marshal my thoughts, and slowly, bit by bit, I built up the present. There was no question to my mind of dreaming; the past hours had scored reality upon my brain. Yet I cannot say that fear was my chief feeling. The first crazy terror had subsided, and now I felt mainly a sickened disgust with just a tinge of curiosity. I found that my knife, watch, flask, and money had gone, but they had left me a map of the countryside. It seemed strange to look at the calico, with the name of a London printer stamped on the back, and lines of railway and highroad running through every shire. Decent and comfortable civilisation! And here was I a prisoner in this den of nameless folk, and in the midst of a life which history knew not.

Courage is a virtue which grows with reflection and the absence of the immediate peril. I thought myself into some sort of resolution, and lo! when the Folk approached me and bound my feet I was back at once in the most miserable terror. They tied me, all but my hands, with some strong cord, and carried me to the centre, where the fire was glowing. Their soft touch was the acutest torture to my nerves, but I stifled my cries lest someone should lay his hand on my mouth. Had that happened, I am convinced my reason would have failed me.

So there I lay in the shine of the fire, with the circle of unknown things around me. There seemed but three or four, but I took no note of number. They talked huskily among themselves in a tongue which sounded all gutturals. Slowly my fear became less an emotion than a habit, and I had room for the smallest shade of curiosity. I strained my ear to catch a word, but it was a mere chaos of sound. The thing ran and thundered in my brain as I stared dumbly into the vacant air. Then I thought that unless I spoke I should certainly go crazy, for my head was beginning to swim at the strange cooing noise.

I spoke a word or two in my best Gaelic, and they closed round me inquiringly. Then I was sorry I had spoken, for my words had brought them nearer, and I shrank at the thought. But as the faint echoes of my speech hummed in the rock-chamber, I was struck by a curious kinship of sound. Mine was sharper, more distinct, and staccato; theirs was blurred, formless, but still with a certain root-resemblance.

Then from the back there came an older being, who seemed to have heard my words. He was like some foul grey badger, his red eyes sightless, and his hands trembling on a stump of bog-oak. The others made way for him with such deference as they were capable of, and the thing squatted down by me and spoke.

To my amazement his words were familiar. It was some manner of speech akin to the Gaelic, but broadened, lengthened, coarsened. I remembered an old book-tongue, commonly supposed to be an impure dialect once used in Brittany, which I had met in the course of my researches. The words recalled it, and as far as I could remember the thing, I asked him who he was and where the place might be.

He answered me in the same speech—still more broadened, lengthened, coarsened. I lay back with sheer amazement. I had found the key to this unearthly life.

For a little an insatiable curiosity, the ardour of the scholar, prevailed. I forgot the horror of the place, and thought only of the fact that here before me was the greatest find that scholarship had ever made. I was precipitated into the heart of the past. Here must be the fountainhead of all legends, the chrysalis of all beliefs. I actually grew light-hearted. This strange folk around me were now no more shapeless things of terror, but objects of research and experiment. I almost came to think them not unfriendly.

For an hour I enjoyed the highest of earthly pleasures. In that strange conversation I heard—in fragments and suggestions—the history of the craziest survival the world has ever seen. I heard of the struggles with invaders, preserved as it were in a sort of shapeless poetry. There were bitter words against the Gaelic oppressor, bitterer words against the Saxon stranger, and for a moment ancient hatreds flared into life. Then there came the tale of the hill-refuge, the morbid hideous existence preserved for centuries amid a changing world. I heard fragments of old religions, primeval names of god and goddess, half-understood by the Folk, but to me the key to a hundred puzzles. Tales which survive to us in broken disjointed riddles were intact here in living form. I lay on my elbow and questioned feverishly. At any moment they might become morose and refuse to speak. Clearly it was my duty to make the most of a brief good fortune.

And then the tale they told me grew more hideous. I heard of the circumstances of the life itself and their daily shifts for existence. It was a murderous chronicle—a history of lust and rapine and unmentionable deeds in the darkness. One thing they had early recognised—that the race could not be maintained within itself; so that ghoulish carrying away of little girls from the lowlands began, which

I had heard of but never credited. Shut up in those dismal holes, the girls soon died, and when the new race had grown up the plunder had been repeated. Then there were bestial murders in lonely cottages, done for God knows what purpose. Sometimes the occupant had seen more than was safe, sometimes the deed was the mere exuberance of a lust of slaying. As they gabbled their tales my heart's blood froze, and I lay back in the agonies of fear. If they had used the others thus, what way of escape was open for myself? I had been brought to this place, and not murdered on the spot. Clearly there was torture before death in store for me, and I confess I quailed at the thought.

But none molested me. The elders continued to jabber out their stories, while I lay tense and deaf. Then to my amazement food was brought and placed beside me—almost with respect. Clearly my murder was not a thing of the immediate future. The meal was some form of mutton—perhaps the shepherd's lost ewes—and a little smoking was all the cooking it had got. I strove to eat, but the tasteless morsels choked me. Then they set drink before me in a curious cup, which I seized on eagerly, for my mouth was dry with thirst. The vessel was of gold, rudely formed, but of the pure metal, and a coarse design in circles ran round the middle. This surprised me enough, but a greater wonder awaited me. The liquor was not water, as I had guessed, but a sort of sweet ale, a miracle of flavour. The taste was curious, but somehow familiar; it was like no wine I had ever drunk, and yet I had known that flavour all my life. I sniffed at the brim, and there rose a faint fragrance of thyme and heather honey and the sweet things of the moorland. I almost dropped it in my surprise; for here in this rude place I had stumbled upon that lost delicacy of the North, the heather ale.

For a second I was entranced with my discovery, and then the wonder of the cup claimed my attention. Was it a mere relic of pillage, or had this Folk some hidden mine of the precious metal ? Gold had once been common in these hills. There were the traces of mines on Cairnsmore ; shepherds had found it in the gravel of the Gled Water ; and the name of a house at the head of the Clachlands meant the " Home of Gold."

Once more I began my questions, and they answered them willingly. There and then I heard that secret for which many had died in old time, the secret of the heather ale. They told of the gold in the hills, of corries where the sand gleamed and abysses where the rocks were veined. All this they told me, freely, without a scruple. And then, like a clap, came the awful thought that this, too, spelled death. These were secrets which this race aforetime had guarded with their lives ; they told them generously to me because there was no fear of betrayal. I should go no more out from this place.

The thought put me into a new sweat of terror—not at death, mind you, but at the unknown horrors which might precede the final suffering. I lay silent, and after binding my hands they began to leave me and go off to other parts of the cave. I dozed in the horrible half-swoon of fear, conscious only of my shaking limbs, and the great dull glow of the fire in the centre. Then I became calmer. After all, they had treated me with tolerable kindness : I had spoken their language, which few of their victims could have done for many a century ; it might be that I had found favour in their eyes. For a little I comforted myself with this delusion, till I caught sight of a wooden box in a corner. It was of modern make, one such as grocers use to pack provisions in. It had some address nailed on it, and an aimless curiosity compelled me to creep thither and read it. A torn and weather-stained scrap of paper, with the nails at the corner rusty with age ; but something of the address might still be made out. Amid the stains my feverish eyes read, " To Mr M——, Carrickfey, by Allerfoot Station."

The ruined cottage in the hollow of the waste with the

single gnarled apple-tree was before me in a twinkling. I remembered the shepherd's shrinking from the place and the name, and his wild eyes when he told me of the thing that had happened there. I seemed to see the old man in his moorland cottage, thinking no evil; the sudden entry of the nameless things; and then the eyes glazed in unspeakable terror. I felt my lips dry and burning. Above me was the vault of rock; in the distance I saw the fire-glow and the shadows of shapes moving around it. My fright was too great for inaction, so I crept from the couch, and silently, stealthily, with tottering steps and bursting heart, I began to reconnoitre.

But I was still bound, my arms tightly, my legs more loosely, but yet firm enough to hinder flight. I could not get my hands at my leg-straps, still less could I undo the manacles. I rolled on the floor, seeking some sharp edge of rock, but all had been worn smooth by the use of centuries. Then suddenly an idea came upon me like an inspiration. The sounds from the fire seemed to have ceased, and I could hear them repeated from another and more distant part of the cave. The Folk had left their orgy round the blaze, and at the end of the long tunnel I saw its glow fall unimpeded upon the floor. Once there, I might burn off my fetters and be free to turn my thoughts to escape.

I crawled a little way with much labour. Then suddenly I came abreast an opening in the wall, through which a path went. It was a long straight rock-cutting, and at the end I saw a gleam of pale light. It must be the open air; the way of escape was prepared for me; and with a prayer I made what speed I could towards the fire.

I rolled on the verge, but the fuel was peat, and the warm ashes would not burn the cords. In desperation I went farther, and my clothes began to singe, while my face ached beyond endurance. But yet I got no nearer my object. The strips of hide warped and cracked, but did not burn. Then in a last effort I thrust my wrists bodily into the glow and held them there. In an instant I drew them out with a groan of pain, scarred and sore, but to my joy with the band snapped in one place. Weak as I was, it was now easy to free myself, and then came the untying of my legs. My hands trembled, my eyes were dazed with hurry, and I was longer over the job than need have been. But at length I had loosed my cramped knees and stood on my feet, a free man once more.

I kicked off my boots, and fled noiselessly down the passage to the tunnel mouth. Apparently it was close on evening, for the white light had faded to a pale yellow. But it was daylight, and that was all I sought, and I ran for it as eagerly as ever runner ran to a goal. I came out on a rock-shelf, beneath which a moraine of boulders fell away in a chasm to a dark loch. It was all but night, but I could see the gnarled and fortressed rocks rise in ramparts above, and below the unknown screes and cliffs which make the side of the Muneraw a place only for foxes and the fowls of the air.

The first taste of liberty is an intoxication, and assuredly I was mad when I leaped down among the boulders. Happily at the top of the gully the stones were large and stable, else the noise would certainly have discovered me. Down I went, slipping, praying, my charred wrists aching, and my stockinged feet wet with blood. Soon I was in the jaws of the cleft, and a pale star rose before me. I have always been timid in the face of great rocks, and now, had not an awful terror been dogging my footsteps, no power on earth could have driven me to that descent. Soon I left the boulders behind, and came to long spouts of little stones, which moved with me till the hillside seemed sinking under my feet. Sometimes I was face downwards, once and again I must have fallen for yards. Had there been a cliff at the foot, I should have gone over it without resistance; but by the providence of God the spout ended in a long curve into the heather of the bog.

When I found my feet once more on soft boggy earth, my strength was renewed within me. A great hope of escape sprang up in my heart. For a second I looked back. There was a great line of shingle with the cliffs beyond, and above all the unknown blackness of the cleft. There lay my terror, and I set off running across the bog for dear life. My mind was clear enough to know my road. If I held round the loch in front I should come to a burn which fed the Farawa stream, on whose banks stood the shepherd's cottage. The loch could not be far; once at the Farawa I would have the light of the shieling clear before me.

Suddenly I heard behind me, as if coming from the hillside, the patter of feet. It was the sound which white hares make in the winter-time on a noiseless frosty day as they patter over the snow. I have heard the same soft noise from a herd of deer when they changed their pastures. Strange that so kindly a sound should put the very fear of death in my heart. I ran madly, blindly, yet thinking shrewdly. The loch was before me. Somewhere I had read or heard, I do not know where, that the brutish aboriginal races of the North could not swim. I myself swam powerfully; could I but cross the loch I should save two miles of a desperate country.

There was no time to lose, for the patter was coming nearer, and I was almost at the loch's edge. I tore off my coat and rushed in. The bottom was mossy, and I had to struggle far before I found any depth. Something plashed in the water before me, and then something else a little behind. The thought that I was a mark for unknown missiles made me crazy with fright, and I struck fiercely out for the other shore. A gleam of moonlight was on the water at the burn's exit, and thither I guided myself. I found the thing difficult enough in itself, for my hands ached, and I was numb from my bonds. But my fancy raised a thousand phantoms to vex me. Swimming in that black bog water, pursued by those nameless things, I seemed to be in a world of horror far removed from the kindly world of men. My strength seemed inexhaustible from my terror. Monsters at the bottom of the water seemed to bite at my feet, and the pain of my wrists made me believe that the loch was boiling hot, and that I was in some hellish place of torment.

I came out on a spit of gravel above the burn mouth, and set off down the ravine of the burn. It was a strait place, strewn with rocks; but now and then the hill turf came in stretches, and eased my wounded feet. Soon the fall became more abrupt, and I was slipping down a hillside, with the water on my left making great cascades in the granite. And then I was out in the wider vale where the Farawa water flowed among links of moss.

Far in front, a speck in the blue darkness, shone the light of the cottage. I panted forward, my breath coming in gasps and my back shot with fiery pains. Happily the land was easier for the feet as long as I kept on the skirts of the bog. My ears were sharp as a wild beast's with fear, as I listened for the noise of pursuit. Nothing came but the rustle of the gentlest hill-wind and the chatter of the falling streams.

Then suddenly the light began to waver and move athwart the window. I knew what it meant. In a minute or two the household at the cottage would retire to rest, and the lamp would be put out. True, I might find the place in the dark, for there was a moon of sorts and the road was not desperate. But somehow in that hour the lamplight gave a promise of safety which I clung to despairingly.

And then the last straw was added to my misery. Behind me came the pad of feet, the pat-patter, soft, eerie, incredibly swift. I choked with fear, and flung myself forward in a last effort. I give my word it was sheer mechanical shrinking that drove me on. God knows I would have lain down to die in the heather, had the things behind me been a common terror of life.

I ran as man never ran before, leaping hags, scrambling

through green well-heads, straining towards the fast-dying light. A quarter of a mile and the patter sounded nearer. Soon I was not two hundred yards off, and the noise seemed almost at my elbow. The light went out, and the black mass of the cottage loomed in the dark.

Then, before I knew, I was at the door, battering it wearily and yelling for help. I heard steps within and a hand on the bolt. Then something shot past me with lightning force and buried itself in the wood. The dreadful hands were almost at my throat, when the door was opened and I stumbled in, hearing with a gulp of joy the key turn and the bar fall behind me.

CHAPTER V.

THE TROUBLES OF A CONSCIENCE.

My body and senses slept, for I was utterly tired, but my brain all the night was on fire with horrid fancies. Again I was in that accursed cave; I was torturing my hands in the fire; I was slipping barefoot among jagged boulders; and then with bursting heart I was toiling the last mile with the cottage light—now grown to a great fire in the heavens—blazing before me.

It was broad daylight when I awoke, and I thanked God for the comfortable rays of the sun. I had been laid in a box-bed off the inner room, and my first sight was the shepherd sitting with folded arms in a chair regarding me solemnly. I rose and began to dress, feeling my legs and arms still tremble with weariness. The shepherd's sister bound up my scarred wrists and put an ointment on my burns; and, limping like an old man, I went into the kitchen.

I could eat little breakfast, for my throat seemed dry and narrow; but they gave me some brandy-and-milk, which put strength into my body. All the time the brother and sister sat in silence, regarding me with covert glances.

"Ye have been delivered from the jaws o' the Pit," said the man at length. "See that," and he held out to me a thin shaft of flint. "I fand that in the door this morning."

I took it, let it drop, and stared vacantly at the window. My nerves had been too much tried to be roused by any new terror. Out-of-doors it was fair weather, flying gleams of April sunlight and the soft colours of spring. I felt dazed, isolated, cut off from my easy past and pleasing future, a companion of horrors and the sport of nameless things. Then suddenly my eye fell on my books heaped on a table, and the old distant civilisation seemed for the moment inexpressibly dear.

"I must go—at once. And you must come too. You cannot stay here. I tell you it is death. If you knew what I know you would be crying out with fear. How far is it to Allermuir? Eight, fifteen miles; and then ten down Glen Aller to Allerfoot, and then the railway. We must go together while it is daylight, and perhaps we may be untouched. But quick, there is not a moment to lose." And I was on my shaky feet, and bustling among my possessions.

"I'll gang wi' ye to the station," said the shepherd, "for ye're clearly no fit to look after yourself. My sister will bide and keep the house. If naething has touched us this ten year, naething will touch us the day."

"But you cannot stay. You are mad," I began; but he cut me short with the words, "I trust in God."

"In any case let your sister come with us. I dare not think of a woman alone in this place."

"I'll bide," said she. "I'm no feared as lang as I'm indoors and there's steeks on the windies."

So I packed my few belongings as best I could, tumbled my books into a haversack, and, gripping the shepherd's arm nervously, crossed the threshold. The glen was full of sunlight. There lay the long shining links of the Farawa burn, the rough hills tumbled beyond, and far over all the scarred and distant forehead of the Muneraw. I had always looked on moorland country as the freshest on earth—clean, wholesome, and homely. But now the fresh uplands seemed like a horrible pit. When I looked to the hills my breath choked in my throat, and the feel of soft heather below my feet set my heart trembling.

It was a slow journey to the inn at Allermuir. For one thing, no power on earth would draw me within sight of the shieling of Carrickfey, so we had to cross a shoulder of hill and make our way down a difficult glen, and then over a treacherous moss. The lochs were now gleaming like fretted silver; but to me, in my dreadful knowledge, they seemed more eerie than on that grey day when I came. At last my eyes were cheered by the sight of a meadow and a fence; then we were on a little byroad; and soon the fir-woods and corn-lands of Allercleuch were plain before us.

The shepherd came no farther, but with brief good-bye turned his solemn face hillwards. I hired a trap and a man to drive, and down the ten miles of Glen Aller I struggled to keep my thoughts from the past. I thought of the kindly South Country, of Oxford, of anything comfortable and civilised. My driver pointed out the objects of interest as in duty bound, but his words fell on unheeding ears. At last he said something which roused me indeed to interest—the interest of the man who hears the word he fears most in the world. On the left side of the river there suddenly sprang into view a long gloomy cleft in the hills, with a vista of dark mountains behind, down which a stream of considerable size poured its waters.

"That is the Water o' Dule," said the man in a reverent voice. "A graund water to fish, but dangerous to life, for it's a' linns. Awa' at the heid they say there's a terrible wild place called the Scarts o' Muneraw,—that's a shouther o' the muckle hill itsel' that ye see,—but I've never been there, and I never kent ony man that had either."

At the station, which is a mile from the village of Allerfoot, I found I had some hours to wait on my train for the south. I dared not trust myself for one moment alone, so I hung about the goods-shed, talked vacantly to the porters, and when one went to the village for tea I accompanied him, and to his wonder entertained him at the inn. When I returned I found on the platform a stray bagman who was that evening going to London. If there is one class of men in the world which I heartily detest it is this; but such was my state that I hailed him as a brother, and besought his company. I paid the difference for a first-class fare, and had him in the carriage with me. He must have thought me an amiable maniac, for I talked in fits and starts, and when he fell asleep I would wake him up and beseech him to speak to me. At wayside stations I would pull down the blinds in case of recognition, for to my unquiet mind the world seemed full of spies sent by that terrible Folk of the Hills. When the train crossed a stretch of moor I would lie down on the seat in case of shafts fired from the heather. And then at last with utter weariness I fell asleep, and woke screaming about midnight to find myself well down in the cheerful English midlands, and red blast-furnaces blinking by the railwayside.

In the morning I breakfasted in my rooms at St Chad's with a dawning sense of safety. I was in a different and calmer world. The lawn-like quadrangles, the great trees, the cawing of rooks, and the homely twitter of sparrows—all seemed decent and settled and pleasing. Indoors the oak-panelled walls, the shelves of books, the pictures, the faint fragrance of tobacco, were very different from the gimcrack adornments and the accursed smell of peat and heather in that deplorable cottage. It was still vacation-time, so most of my friends were down; but I spent the day hunting out the few cheerful pedants to whom term and vacation were the same. It delighted me to hear again their precise talk, to hear them make a boast of their work, and narrate the childish little accidents of their life. I yearned for the childish once more; I craved for women's drawing-rooms, and women's chatter, and everything which makes life an elegant game. God knows I had had enough of the other thing for a lifetime!

That night I shut myself in my rooms, barred my windows, drew my curtains, and made a great destruction. All books or pictures which recalled to me the moorlands were ruthlessly doomed. Novels, poems, treatises I flung into an old box, for sale to the second-hand bookseller. Some prints and water-colour sketches I tore to pieces with my own hands. I ransacked my fishing-book, and condemned all tackle for moorland waters to the flames. I wrote a letter to my solicitors, bidding them go no further in the purchase of a place in Lorn I had long been thinking of. Then, and not till then, did I feel the bondage of the past a little loosed from my shoulders. I made myself a nightcap of rum-punch instead of my usual whisky-toddy, that all associations with that dismal land might be forgotten, and to complete the renunciation I returned to cigars and flung my pipe into a drawer.

But when I woke in the morning I found that it is hard to get rid of memories. My feet were still sore and wounded, and when I felt my arms cramped and reflected on the causes, there was that black memory always near to vex me.

In a little term began, and my duties—as deputy-Professor of Northern Antiquities—were once more clamorous. I can well believe that my hearers found my lectures strange, for instead of dealing with my favourite subjects and matters, which I might modestly say I had made my own, I confined myself to recondite and distant themes, treating even these cursorily and dully. For the truth is, my heart was no more in my subject. I hated—or I thought that I hated—all things Northern with the virulence of utter fear. My reading was confined to science of the most recent kind, to abstruse philosophy, and to foreign classics. Anything which savoured of romance or mystery was abhorrent; I pined for sharp outlines and the tangibility of a high civilisation.

All the term I threw myself into the most frivolous life of the place. My Harrow schooldays seemed to have come back to me. I had once been a fair cricketer, so I played again for my college, and made decent scores. I coached an indifferent crew on the river. I fell into the slang of the place, which I had hitherto detested. My former friends looked on me askance, as if some freakish changeling had possessed me. Formerly I had been ready for pedantic discussion, I had been absorbed in my work, men had spoken of me as a rising scholar. Now I fled the very mention of things I had once delighted in. The Professor of Northern Antiquities, a scholar of European reputation, meeting me once in the Parks, embarked on an account of certain novel rings recently found in Scotland, and to his horror found that, when he had got well under weigh, I had slipped off unnoticed. I heard afterwards that the good old man was found by a friend walking disconsolately with bowed head in the middle of the High Street. Being rescued from among the horses' feet, he could only murmur, "I am thinking of Graves, poor man! And a year ago he was as sane as I am!"

. . . .

But a man may not long deceive himself. I kept up the illusion valiantly for the term; but I felt instinctively that the fresh schoolboy life, which seemed to me the extreme opposite to the ghoulish North, and as such the most desirable of things, was eternally cut off from me. No cunning affectation could ever dispel my real nature or efface the memory of a week. I realised miserably that sooner or later I must fight it out with my conscience. I began to call myself a coward. The chief thoughts of my mind began to centre themselves more and more round that unknown life waiting to be explored among the wilds.

One day I met a friend—an official in the British Museum

—who was full of some new theory about primitive habitations. To me it seemed inconceivably absurd; but he was strong in his confidence, and without flaw in his evidence. The man irritated me, and I burned to prove him wrong, but I could think of no argument which was final against his. Then it flashed upon me that my own experience held the disproof; and without more words I left him, hot, angry with myself, and tantalised by the unattainable.

I might relate my *bona-fide* experience, but would men believe me? I must bring proofs, I must complete my researches, so as to make them incapable of disbelief. And there in those deserts was waiting the key. There lay the greatest discovery of the century—nay, of the millennium. There, too, lay the road to wealth such as I had never dreamed of. Could I succeed, I should be famous for ever. I would revolutionise history and anthropology; I would systematise folk-lore; I would show the world of men the pit whence they were digged and the rock whence they were hewn.

And then began a game of battledore between myself and my conscience.

"You are a coward," said my conscience.

"I am sufficiently brave," I would answer. "I have seen things and yet lived. The terror is more than mortal, and I cannot face it."

"You are a coward," said my conscience.

"I am not bound to go there again. It would be purely for my own aggrandisement if I went, and not for any matter of duty."

"Nevertheless you are a coward," said my conscience.

"In any case the matter can wait."

"You are a coward."

. . . .

Then came one awful midsummer night, when I lay sleepless and fought the thing out with myself. I knew that the strife was hopeless, that I should have no peace in this world again unless I made the attempt. The dawn was breaking when I came to the final resolution ; and when I rose and looked at my face in a mirror, lo ! it was white and lined and drawn like a man of sixty.

CHAPTER VI.

SUMMER ON THE MOORS.

THE next morning I packed a bag with some changes of clothing and a collection of notebooks, and went up to town. The first thing I did was to pay a visit to my solicitors. "I am about to travel," said I, "and I wish to have all things settled in case any accident should happen to me." So I arranged for the disposal of my property in case of death, and added a codicil which puzzled the lawyers. If I did not return within six months, communications were to be entered into with the shepherd at the shieling of Farawa —post-town Allerfoot. If he could produce any papers, they were to be put into the hands of certain friends, published, and the cost charged to my estate. From my solicitors I went to a gunmaker's in Regent Street and bought an ordinary six-chambered revolver, feeling much as a man must feel who proposed to cross the Atlantic in a skiff and purchased a small life-belt as a precaution.

I took the night express to the North, and, for a marvel, I slept. When I awoke about four we were on the verge of Westmorland, and stony hills blocked the horizon. At first I hailed the mountain-land gladly ; sleep for the moment had caused forgetfulness of my terrors. But soon a turn of the line brought me in full view of a heathery moor, running far to a confusion of distant peaks. I remembered my mission and my fate, and if ever condemned criminal felt a more bitter regret I pity his case. Why should I alone among the millions of this happy isle be singled out as the repository of a ghastly secret, and be cursed by a conscience which would not let it rest?

I came to Allerfoot early in the forenoon, and got a trap to drive me up the valley. It was a lowering grey day, hot and yet sunless. A sort of heat-haze cloaked the hills, and every now and then a smurr of rain would meet us on the road, and in a minute be over. I felt wretchedly dispirited; and when at last the white-washed kirk of Allermuir came into sight and the broken-backed bridge of Aller, man's eyes seemed to have looked on no drearier scene since time began.

I ate what meal I could get, for, fears or no, I was voraciously hungry. Then I asked the landlord to find me some man who would show me the road to Farawa. I demanded company, not for protection—for what could two men do against such brutish strength?—but to keep my mind from its own thoughts.

The man looked at me anxiously.

"Are ye acquaint wi' the folks, then?" he asked.

I said I was, that I had often stayed in the cottage.

"Ye ken that they've a name for being queer. The man never comes here forbye once or twice a-year, and he has few dealings wi' other herds. He's got an ill name, too, for losing sheep. I dinna like the country ava. Up by yon Muneraw—no that I've ever been there, but I've seen it afar off—is enough to put a man daft for the rest o' his days. What's taking ye thereaways? It's no the time for the fishing?"

I told him that I was a botanist going to explore certain hill-crevices for rare ferns. He shook his head, and then after some delay found me an ostler who would accompany me to the cottage.

The man was a shock-headed, long-limbed fellow, with fierce red hair and a humorous eye. He talked sociably about his life, answered my hasty questions with deftness, and beguiled me for the moment out of myself. I passed the melancholy lochs, and came in sight of the great stony hills without the trepidation I had expected. Here at my side was one who found some humour even in those uplands. But one thing I noted which brought back the old uneasiness. He took the road which led us farthest from Carrickfey, and when to try him I proposed the other, he vetoed it with emphasis.

After this his good spirits departed, and he grew distrustful.

"What mak's ye a freend o' the herd at Farawa?" he demanded a dozen times.

Finally, I asked him if he knew the man, and had seen him lately.

"I dinna ken him, and I hadna seen him for years till a fortnicht syne, when a' Allermuir saw him. He cam doun one afternoon to the public-hoose, and begood to drink. He had aye been kenned for a terrible godly kind o' a man, so ye may believe folk wondered at this. But when he had stuck to the drink for twae days, and filled himsel' blind-fou half-a-dozen o' times, he took a fit o' repentance, and raved and blethered about siccan a life as he led in the muirs. There was some said he was speakin' serious, but maist thocht it was juist daftness."

"And what did he speak about?" I asked sharply.

"I canna verra weel tell ye. It was about some kind o' bogle that lived in the Muneraw—that's the shouthers o't ye see yonder—and it seems that the bogle killed his sheep and frichted himsel'. He was aye bletherin', too, about something or somebody ca'd Grave; but oh! the man wasna wise." And my companion shook a contemptuous head.

And then below us in the valley we saw the shieling, with a thin shaft of smoke rising into the rainy grey weather. The man left me, sturdily refusing any fee. "I wantit my legs stretched as weel as you. A walk in the hills is neither here nor there to a stoot man. When will ye be back, sir?"

The question was well-timed. "To-morrow fortnight," I

said, "and I want somebody from Allermuir to come out here in the morning and carry some baggage. Will you see to that?"

He said "Ay," and went off, while I scrambled down the hill to the cottage. Nervousness possessed me, and though it was broad daylight and the whole place lay plain before me, I ran pell-mell, and did not stop till I reached the door.

The place was utterly empty. Unmade beds, unwashed dishes, a hearth strewn with the ashes of peat, and dust thick on everything, proclaimed the absence of inmates. I began to be horribly frightened. Had the shepherd and his sister, also, disappeared? Was I left alone in this bleak place, with a dozen lonely miles between me and human dwellings? I could not return alone; better this horrible place than the unknown perils of the out-of-doors. Hastily I barricaded the door, and to the best of my power shuttered the windows; and then with dreary forebodings I sat down to wait on fortune.

In a little I heard a long swinging step outside and the sound of dogs. Joyfully I opened the latch, and there was the shepherd's grim face waiting stolidly on what might appear.

At the sight of me he stepped back. "What in the Lord's name are ye daein' here?" he asked. "Didna ye get enough afore?"

"Come in," I said, sharply. "I want to talk."

In he came with those blessed dogs,—what a comfort it was to look on their great honest faces! He sat down on the untidy bed and waited.

"I came because I could not stay away. I saw too much to give me any peace elsewhere. I must go back, even though I risk my life for it. The cause of scholarship demands it as well as the cause of humanity."

"Is that a' the news ye hae?" he said. "Weel, I've mair to tell ye. Three weeks syne my sister Margit was lost, and I've never seen her mair."

My jaw fell, and I could only stare at him.

"I cam hame from the hill at nightfa' and she was gone. I lookit for her up hill and doun, but I couldna find her. Syne I think I went daft. I went to the Scarts and huntit them up and doun, but no sign could I see. The Folk can bide quiet enough when they want. Syne I went to Allermuir and drank mysel' blind,—me, that's a God-fearing man and a saved soul; but the Lord help me, I didna ken what I was at. That's my news, and day and night I wander thae hills, seekin' for what I canna find."

"But, man, are you mad?" I cried. "Surely there are neighbours to help you. There is a law in the land, and you had only to find the nearest police-office and compel them to assist you."

"What guid can man dae?" he asked. "An army o' sodgers couldna find that hidey-hole. Forby, when I went into Allermuir wi' my story the folk thocht me daft. It was that set me drinking, for—the Lord forgive me!—I wasna my ain maister. I threepit till I was hairse, but the bodies just lauch'd." And he lay back on the bed like a man mortally tired.

Grim though the tidings were, I can only say that my chief feeling was of comfort. Pity for the new tragedy had swallowed up my fear. I had now a purpose, and a purpose, too, not of curiosity but of mercy.

"I go to-morrow morning to the Muneraw. But first I want to give you something to do." And I drew roughly a chart of the place on the back of a letter. "Go into Allermuir to-morrow, and give this paper to the landlord at the inn. The letter will tell him what to do. He is to raise at once all the men he can get, and come to the place on the chart marked with a cross. Tell him life depends on his hurry."

The shepherd nodded. "D'ye ken the Folk are watching for you? They let me pass without trouble, for they've nae use for me, but I see fine they're seeking you. Ye's no gang half a mile the morn afore they grip ye."

"So much the better," I said. "That will take me quicker to the place I want to be at."

"And I'm to gang to Allermuir the morn," he repeated, with the air of a child conning a lesson. "But what if they'll no believe me?"

"They'll believe the letter."

"Maybe," he said and relapsed into a doze.

I set myself to put that house in order, to rouse the fire, and prepare some food. It was dismal work; and meantime outside the night darkened, and a great wind rose, which howled round the walls and lashed the rain on the windows.

CHAPTER VII.

IN TUAS MANUS, DOMINE!

I HAD not gone twenty yards from the cottage door ere I knew I was watched. I had left the shepherd still dozing, in the half-conscious state of a dazed and broken man. All night the wind had wakened me at intervals, and now in the half-light of morn the weather seemed more vicious than ever. The wind cut my ears, the whole firmament was full of the rendings and thunders of the storm. Rain fell in blinding sheets, the heath was a marsh, and it was the most I could do to struggle against the hurricane which stopped my breath. And all the while I knew I was not alone in the desert.

All men know—in imagination or in experience—the sensation of being spied on. The nerves tingle, the skin grows hot and prickly, and there is a queer sinking of the heart. Intensify this common feeling a hundredfold, and you get a tenth part of what I suffered. I am telling a plain tale, and record bare physical facts. My lips stood out from my teeth as I heard, or felt, a rustle in the heather, a scraping among stones. Some subtle magnetic link seemed established between my body and the mysterious world around. I became sick—acutely sick—with the ceaseless apprehension.

My fright became so complete that when I turned a corner of rock, or stepped in deep heather, I seemed to feel a body rub against mine. This continued all the way up the Farawa water, and then up its feeder to the little lonely loch. It kept me from looking forward; but it likewise kept me in such a sweat of fright that I was ready to faint. Then the notion came upon me to test this fancy of mine. If I was tracked thus closely, clearly the trackers would bar my way if I turned back. So I wheeled round and walked a dozen paces down the glen.

Nothing stopped me. I was about to turn again, when something made me take six more paces. At the fourth something rustled in the heather, and my neck was gripped as in a vice. I had already made up my mind on what I would do. I would be perfectly still, I would conquer my fear, and let them do as they pleased with me so long as they took me to their dwelling. But at the touch of the hands my resolutions fled. I struggled and screamed. Then something was clapped on my mouth, speech and strength went from me, and once more I was back in the maudlin childhood of terror.

. . . .

In the cave it was always a dusky twilight. I seemed to be lying in the same place, with the same dull glare of firelight far off, and the same close stupefying smell. One of the creatures was standing silently at my side, and I asked him some trivial question. He turned and shambled down the passage, leaving me alone.

Then he returned with another, and they talked their guttural talk to me. I scarcely listened till I remembered that in a sense I was here of my own accord, and on a definite mission. The purport of their speech seemed to be that, now I had returned, I must beware of a second flight. Once I had been spared; a second time I should be killed without mercy.

I assented gladly. The Folk, then, had some use for me. I felt my errand prospering.

Then the old creature which I had seen before crept out of some corner and squatted beside me. He put a claw on my shoulder, a horrible, corrugated, skeleton thing, hairy to the finger-tips and nailless. He grinned, too, with toothless gums, and his hideous old voice was like a file on sandstone.

I asked questions, but he would only grin and jabber, looking now and then furtively over his shoulder towards the fire.

I coaxed and humoured him, till he launched into a narrative of which I could make nothing. It seemed a mere string of names, with certain words repeated at fixed intervals. Then it flashed on me that this might be a religious incantation. I had discovered remnants of a ritual and a mythology among them. It was possible that these were sacred days, and that I had stumbled upon some rude celebration.

I caught a word or two and repeated them. He looked at me curiously. Then I asked him some leading question, and he replied with clearness. My guess was right. The midsummer week was the holy season of the year, when sacrifices were offered to the gods.

The notion of sacrifices disquieted me, and I would fain have asked further. But the creature would speak no more. He hobbled off, and left me alone in the rock-chamber to listen to a strange sound which hung ceaselessly about me. It must be the storm without, like a park of artillery rattling among the crags. A storm of storms surely, for the place echoed and hummed, and to my unquiet eye the very rock of the roof seemed to shake!

Apparently my existence was forgotten, for I lay long before anyone returned. Then it was merely one who brought food, the same strange meal as before, and left hastily. When I had eaten I rose and stretched myself. My hands and knees still quivered nervously; but I was strong and perfectly well in body. The empty, desolate, tomb-like place was eerie enough to scare anyone; but its emptiness was comfort when I thought of its inmates. Then I wandered down the passage towards the fire which was burning in loneliness. Where had the Folk gone? I puzzled over their disappearance.

Suddenly sounds began to break on my ear, coming from some inner chamber at the end of that in which the fire burned. I could scarcely see for the smoke; but I began to make my way towards the noise, feeling along the sides of rock. Then a second gleam of light seemed to rise before me, and I came to an aperture in the wall which gave entrance to another room.

This in turn was full of smoke and glow—a murky orange glow, as if from some strange flame of roots. There were the squat moving figures, running in wild antics round the fire. I crouched in the entrance, terrified and yet curious, till I saw something beyond the blaze which held me dumb. Apart from the others and tied to some stake in the wall was a woman's figure, and the face was the face of the shepherd's sister.

My first impulse was flight. I must get away and think,—plan, achieve some desperate way of escape. I sped back to the silent chamber as if the gang were at my heels. It was still empty, and I stood helplessly in the centre, looking at the impassable walls of rock as a wearied beast may look at the walls of its cage. I bethought me of the way I had escaped before and rushed thither, only to find it blocked by a huge contrivance of stone. Yards and yards of solid rock were between me and the upper air, and yet through it all came the crash and whistle of the storm. If I were at my wits' end in this inner darkness, there was also high commotion among the powers of the air in that upper world.

As I stood I heard the soft steps of my tormentors. They seemed to think I was meditating escape, for they flung themselves on me and bore me to the ground. I did not struggle, and when they saw me quiet, they squatted round and began to speak. They told me of the holy season and its sacrifices. At first I could not follow them; then when I caught familiar words I found some clue, and they became intelligible. They spoke of a woman, and I asked, "What woman?" With all frankness they told me of the custom which prevailed—how every twentieth summer a woman was sacrificed to some devilish god, and by the hand of one of the stranger race. I said nothing, but my whitening face must have told them a tale, though I strove hard to keep my composure. I asked if they had found the victims. "She is in this place," they said; "and as for the man, thou art he." And with this they left me.

I had still some hours; so much I gathered from their talk, for the sacrifice was at sunset. Escape was cut off for ever. I have always been something of a fatalist, and at the prospect of the irrevocable end my cheerfulness returned. I had my pistol, for they had taken nothing from me. I took out the little weapon and fingered it lovingly. Hope of the lost, refuge of the vanquished, ease to the coward,—blessed be he who first conceived it!

The time dragged on, the minutes grew to hours, and still I was left solitary. Only the mad violence of the storm broke the quiet. It had increased in fury, for the stones at the mouth of the exit by which I had formerly escaped seemed to rock with some external pressure, and cutting shafts of wind slipped past and cleft the heat of the passage. What a sight the ravine outside must be, I thought, set in the forehead of a great hill, and swept clean by every breeze! Then came a crashing, and the long hollow echo of a fall. The rocks are splitting, said I; the road down the corrie will be impassable now and for evermore.

I began to grow weak with the nervousness of the waiting, and by-and-by I lay down and fell into a sort of doze. When I next knew consciousness I was being roused by two of the Folk, and bidden get ready. I stumbled to my feet, felt for the pistol in the hollow of my sleeve, and prepared to follow.

When we came out into the wider chamber the noise of the storm was deafening. The roof rang like a shield which has been struck. I noticed, perturbed as I was, that my guards cast anxious eyes around them, alarmed, like myself, at the murderous din. Nor was the world quieter when we entered the last chamber, where the fire burned and the remnant of the Folk waited. Wind had found an entrance from somewhere or other, and the flames blew here and there, and the smoke gyrated in odd circles. At the back, and apart from the rest, I saw the dazed eyes and the white old drawn face of the woman.

They led me up beside her to a place where there was a rude flat stone, hollowed in the centre, and on it a rusty iron knife, which seemed once to have formed part of a scythe-blade. Then I saw the ceremonial which was marked out for me. It was the very rite which I had dimly figured as current among a rude people, and even in that moment of horror I had something of the scholar's satisfaction.

The oldest of the Folk, who seemed to be a sort of priest, came to my side and mumbled a form of words. His fetid breath sickened me; his dull eyes, glassy like a brute's with age, brought my knees together. He put the knife in my hands, dragged the terror-stricken woman forward to the altar, and bade me begin.

I began by sawing her bonds through. When she felt herself free she would have fled back, but stopped when I bade her. At that moment there came a noise of rending and crashing as if the hills were falling, and for one second the eyes of the Folk were averted from the frustrated sacrifice.

Only for a moment. The next they saw what I had done, and with one impulse rushed towards me. Then began the last scene in the play. I sent a bullet through the right eye of the first thing that came on. The second shot went wide; but the third shattered the hand of an elderly ruffian with a club. Never for an instant did they stop, and now they were clutching at me. I pushed the woman behind, and fired three rapid shots in blind panic, and then, clutching the scythe, I struck right and left like a madman.

Suddenly I saw the foreground sink before my eyes. The roof sloped down, and with a sickening hiss a mountain of rock and earth seemed to precipitate itself on the foremost of my assailants. One, nipped in the middle by a rock, caught my eye by his hideous writhings. Two only remained in what was now a little suffocating chamber, with embers from the fire still smoking on the floor.

The woman caught me by the hand and drew me with her, while the two seemed mute with fear. "There's a road at the back," she screamed. "I ken it. I fand it out." And she pulled me up a narrow hole in the rock.

. . . .

How long we climbed I do not know. We were both fighting for air, with the tightness of throat and chest, and the craziness of limb which mean suffocation. I cannot tell when we first came to the surface, but I remember the woman, who seemed to have the strength of extreme terror, pulling me from the edge of a crevasse and laying me on a flat rock. It seemed to be the depth of winter, with sheer-falling rain and a wind that shook the hills.

Then I was once more myself and could look about me. From my feet yawned a sheer abyss, where once had been a hill-shoulder. Some great mass of rock on the brow of the mountain had been loosened by the storm, and in its fall had caught the lips of the ravine and blocked the upper outlet from the nest of dwellings. For a moment I feared that all had been destroyed.

My feeling—Heaven help me !—was not thankfulness for God's mercy and my escape, but a bitter mad regret. I rushed frantically to the edge, and when I saw only the blackness of darkness I wept weak tears. All the time the storm was tearing at my body, and I had to grip hard by hand and foot to keep my place.

Suddenly on the brink of the ravine I saw a third figure.

We two were not the only fugitives. One of the Folk had escaped.

I ran to it, and to my surprise the thing as soon as it saw me rushed to meet me. At first I thought it was with some instinct of self-preservation, but when I saw its eyes I knew the purpose of fight. Clearly one or other should go no more from the place.

We were some ten yards from the brink when I grappled with it. Dimly I heard the woman scream with fright, and saw her scramble across the hillside. Then we were tugging in a death-throe, the hideous smell of the thing in my face, its red eyes burning into mine, and its hoarse voice muttering. Its strength seemed incredible ; but I, too, am no weakling. We tugged and strained, its nails biting into my flesh, while I choked its throat unsparingly. Every second I dreaded lest we should plunge together over the ledge, for it was thither my adversary tried to draw me. I caught my heel in a nick of rock, and pulled madly against it.

And then, while I was beginning to glory with the pride of conquest, my hope was dashed in pieces. The thing seemed to break from my arms, and, as if in despair, cast itself headlong into the impenetrable darkness. I stumbled blindly after it, saved myself on the brink, and fell back, sick and ill, into a merciful swoon.

. . . .

CHAPTER VIII.

NOTE IN CONCLUSION BY THE EDITOR.

At this point the narrative of my unfortunate friend, Mr Graves of St Chad's, breaks off abruptly. He wrote it shortly before his death, and was prevented from completing it by the attack of heart failure which carried him off. In accordance with the instructions in his will, I have prepared it for publication, and now in much fear and hesitation give it to the world. First, however, I must supplement it by such facts as fall within my knowledge.

The shepherd seems to have gone to Allermuir and by the help of the letter convinced the inhabitants. A body of men was collected under the landlord, and during the afternoon set out for the hills. But unfortunately the great midsummer storm—the most terrible of recent climatic disturbances—had filled the mosses and streams, and they found themselves unable to proceed by any direct road. Ultimately late in the evening they arrived at the cottage of Farawa, only to find there a raving woman, the shepherd's sister, who seemed crazy with brain-fever. She told some rambling story about her escape, but her narrative said nothing of Mr Graves. So they treated her with what skill they possessed, and sheltered for the night in and around the cottage. Next morning the storm had abated a little, and the woman had recovered something of her wits. From her they learned that Mr Graves was lying in a ravine on the side of the Muneraw in imminent danger of his life. A body set out to find him; but so immense was the landslip, and so dangerous the whole mountain, that it was nearly evening when they recovered him from the ledge of rock. He was alive, but unconscious, and on bringing him back to the cottage it was clear that he was, indeed, very ill. There he lay for three months, while the best skill that could be got was procured for him. By dint of an uncommon toughness of constitution he survived; but it was an old and feeble man who returned to Oxford in the early winter.

The shepherd and his sister immediately left the countryside, and were never more heard of, unless they are the pair of unfortunates who are at present in a Scottish pauper asylum, incapable of remembering even their names. The people who last spoke with them declared that their minds seemed weakened by a great shock, and that it was hopeless to try to get any connected or rational statement.

The career of my poor friend from that hour was little short of a tragedy. He awoke from his illness to find the world incredulous; even the country-folk of Allermuir set down the story to the shepherd's craziness and my friend's credulity. In Oxford his argument was received with polite scorn. An account of his experiences which he drew up for the 'Times' was refused by the editor; and an article on "Primitive Peoples of the North," embodying what he believed to be the result of his discoveries, was unanimously rejected by every responsible journal in Europe. At first he bore the treatment bravely. Reflection convinced him that the colony had not been destroyed. Proofs were still awaiting his hand, and with courage and caution he might yet triumph over his enemies. But unfortunately, though the ardour of the scholar burned more fiercely than ever and all fear seemed to have been purged from his soul, the last adventure had grievously sapped his bodily strength. In the spring following his accident he made an effort to reach the spot—alone, for no one could be persuaded to follow him in what was regarded as a childish madness. He slept at the now deserted cottage of Farawa, but in the morning found himself unable to continue, and with difficulty struggled back to the shepherd's cottage at Allercleuch, where he was confined to bed for a fortnight. Then it became necessary for him to seek health abroad, and it was not till the following autumn that he attempted the journey again. He fell sick a second time at the inn of Allermuir, and during his convalescence had himself carried to a knoll in the inn garden, whence a glimpse can be obtained of the shoulder of the Muneraw. There he would sit for hours with his eyes fixed on the horizon, and at times he would be found weeping with weakness and vexation. The last attempt was made but two months before his last illness. On this occasion he got no farther than Carlisle, where he was taken ill with what proved to be a premonition of death. After that he shut his lips tightly, as though recognising the futility of his hopes. Whether he had been soured by the treatment he received, or whether his brain had already been weakened, he had become a morose silent man, and for the two years before his death had few friends and no society. From the obituary notice in the 'Times' I take the following paragraph, which shows in what light the world had come to look upon him:—

"At the outset of his career he was regarded as a rising scholar in one department of archæology, and his Taffert lectures were a real contribution to an obscure subject. But in after-life he was led into fantastic speculations; and when he found himself unable to convince his colleagues, he gradually retired into himself, and lived practically a hermit's life till his death. His career, thus broken short, is a sad instance of the fascination which the recondite and the quack can exercise even over men of approved ability."

And now his own narrative is published, and the world can judge as it pleases about the amazing romance. The view which will doubtless find general acceptance is that the whole is a figment of the brain, begotten of some harmless moorland adventure and the company of such religious maniacs as the shepherd and his sister. But some who knew the former sobriety and calmness of my friend's mind may be disposed timorously and with deep hesitation to another verdict. They may accept the narrative, and believe that somewhere in those moorlands he met with a horrible primitive survival, passed through the strangest adventure, and had his fingers on an epoch-making discovery. In this case they will be inclined to sympathise with the loneliness and misunderstanding of his latter days. It is not for me to decide the question. Though a fellow-historian, the Picts are outside my period, and I dare not advance an opinion on a matter with which I am not fully familiar. But I would point out that the means of settling the question are still extant, and I would call upon some young archæologist, with a reputation to make, to seize upon the chance of the century. Most of the expresses for the North stop at Allerfoot; a ten-miles' drive will bring him to Allermuir; and then with a fifteen-miles' walk he is at Farawa and on the threshold of discovery. Let him follow the burn and cross the ridge and ascend the Scarts of the Muneraw, and, if he return at all, it may be with a more charitable judgment of my unfortunate friend.

II. THE FAR ISLANDS.

> "Lady Alice, Lady Louise,
> Between the wash of the tumbling seas—"

I.

When Bran the Blessed, as the story goes, followed the white bird on the Last Questing, knowing that return was not for him, he gave gifts to his followers. To Heliodorus he gave the gift of winning speech, and straightaway the man went south to the Italian seas, and, becoming a scholar, left many descendants who sat in the high places of the Church. To Raymond he gave his steel battle-axe, and bade him go out to the warrior's path and hew his way to a throne; which the man forthwith accomplished, and became an ancestor in the fourth degree of the first king of Scots. But to Colin, the youngest and the dearest, he gave no gift, whispering only a word in his ear and laying a finger on his eyelids. Yet Colin was satisfied, and he alone of the three, after their master's going, remained on that coast of rock and heather.

In the third generation from Colin, as our elders counted years, came one Colin the Red, who built his keep on the cliffs of Acharra and was a mighty sea-rover in his day. Five times he sailed to the rich parts of France, and a good score of times he carried his flag of three stars against the easterly vikings. A mere name in story, but a sounding piece of nomenclature well garnished with tales. A master-mind by all accounts, but cursed with a habit of fantasy; for, hearing in his old age of a land to the westward, he forthwith sailed into the sunset, and three days later was washed up, a twisted body, on one of the outer isles.

So far it is but legend, but with his grandson, Colin the Red, we fall into the safer hands of the chroniclers. To him God gave the unnumbered sorrows of story-telling, for he was a bard, cursed with a bard's fervours, and none the less a mighty warrior among his own folk. He it was who wrote the lament called 'The White Waters of Usna,' and the exquisite chain of romances, 'Glede-red Gold and Grey Silver.' His tales were told by many fires, down to our grandfathers' time, and you will find them still pounded at by the folklorists. But his airs—they are eternal. On harp and pipe they have lived through the centuries; twisted and tortured, they survive in many song-books; and I declare that the other day I heard the most beautiful of them all murdered by a band at a German watering-place. This Colin led the wanderer's life, for he disappeared at middle-age, no one knew whither, and his return was long looked for by his people. Some thought that he became a Christian monk, the holy man living in the sea-girt isle of Cuna, who was found dead in extreme old age, kneeling on the beach, with his arms, contrary to the fashion of the Church, stretched to the westward.

As history narrowed into bonds and forms the descendants of Colin took Raden for their surname, and settled more firmly on their lands in the long peninsula of crag and inlets which runs west to the Atlantic. Under Donald of the Isles they harried the Kings of Scots, or, on their own authority, made war on Macleans and Macranalds, till their flag of the three stars, their badge of the grey-goose feather, and their on-cry of "Cuna" were feared from Lochalsh to Cantire. Later they made a truce with the king, and entered into the royal councils. For years they warded the western coast, and as king's lieutenants smoked out the inferior pirates of Eigg and Toronsay. A Raden was made a Lord of Sleat, another was given lands in the low country and the name

Baron of Strathyre, but their honours were transitory and short as their lives. Rarely one of the house saw middle age. A bold, handsome, and stirring race, it was their fate to be cut off in the rude warfare of the times, or, if peace had them in its clutches, to man vessel and set off once more on those mad western voyages which were the weird of the family. Three of the name were found drowned on the far shore of Cuna; more than one sailed straight out of the ken of mortals. One rode with the Good Lord James on the pilgrimage of the Heart of Bruce, and died by his leader's side in the Saracen battle. Long afterwards a Raden led the western men against the Cheshire archers at Flodden, and was slain himself in the steel circle around the king.

But the years brought peace and a greater wealth, and soon the cold stone tower was left solitary on the headland, and the new house of Kinlochuna rose by the green links of the stream. The family changed its faith, and an Episcopal chaplain took the place of the old mass-priest in the tutoring of the sons. Radens were in the '15 and the '45. They rose with Bute to power, and they long disputed the pride of Dundas in the northern capital. They intermarried with great English houses till the sons of the family were Scots only in name, living much abroad or in London, many of them English landowners by virtue of a mother's blood. Soon the race was of the common over-civilised type, graceful, well-mannered, with abundant good looks, but only once in a generation reverting to the rugged northern strength. Eton and Oxford had in turn displaced the family chaplain, and the house by the windy headland grew emptier and emptier save when grouse and deer brought home its fickle masters.

II.

A childless illness brought Colin to Kinlochuna when he had reached the mature age of five, and delicate health kept him there for the greater part of the next six years. During the winter he lived in London, but from the late northern spring, through all the long bright summers, he lived in the great tenantless place without company—for he was an only child. A French nurse had the charge of his doings, and when he had passed through the formality of lessons there were the long pinewoods at his disposal, the rough moor, the wonderful black holes with the rich black mud in them, and best of all the bay of Acharra, below the headland, with Cuna lying in the waves a mile to the west. At such times his father was busy elsewhere; his mother was dead; the family had few near relatives; so he passed a solitary childhood in the company of seagulls and the birds of the moor.

His time for the beach was the afternoon. On the left as you go down through the woods from the house there runs out the great headland of Acharra, red and grey with mosses, and with a nimbus always of screaming sea-fowl. To the right runs a low beach of sand, passing into rough limestone boulders and then into the heather of the wood. This in turn is bounded by a reef of low rocks falling by gentle breaks to the water's edge. It is crowned with a tangle of heath and fern, bright at most seasons with flowers, and dwarf pine-trees straggle on its crest till one sees the meaning of its Gaelic name, "The Ragged Cock's-Comb." This place was Colin's playground in fine weather. When it blew rain or snow from the north he dwelt indoors among dogs and books, puzzling his way through great volumes from his father's shelves. But when the mild west-wind weather fell on the sea, then he would lie on the hot sand—Amelie the nurse reading a novel on the nearest rock—and kick his small heels as he followed his fancy. He built great sand castles to the shape of Acharra old tower, and peopled them with preposterous knights and ladies; he drew great moats and rivers for the tide to fill; he fought battles innumerable with crackling seaweed, till Amelie, with her sharp cry of "Colin, Colin," would carry him houseward for tea.

Two fancies remained in his mind through those boyish years. One was about the mysterious shining sea before him. In certain weathers it seemed to him a solid pathway. Cuna, the little ragged isle, ceased to block the horizon, and his own white road ran away down into the west, till suddenly it stopped and he saw no farther. He knew he ought to see more, but always at one place, just when his thoughts were pacing the white road most gallantly, there came a baffling mist to his sight, and he found himself looking at a commonplace sea with Cuna lying very real and palpable in the offing. It was a vexatious limitation, for all his dreams were about this pathway. One day in June, when the waters slept in a deep heat, he came down the sands barefoot, and lo! there was his pathway. For one moment things seemed clear, the mist had not gathered on the road, and with a cry he ran down to the tide's edge and waded in. The touch of water dispelled the illusion, and almost in tears he saw the cruel back of Cuna blotting out his own magic way.

The other fancy was about the low ridge of rocks which bounded the bay on the right. His walks had never extended beyond it, either on the sands or inland, for that way lay a steep hillside and a perilous bog. But often on the sands he had come to its foot and wondered what country lay beyond. He made many efforts to explore it, difficult efforts, for the vigilant Amelie had first to be avoided. Once he was almost at the top when some seaweed to which he clung gave way, and he rolled back again to the soft warm sand. By-and-by he found that he knew what was beyond. A clear picture had built itself up in his brain of a mile of reefs, with sand in bars between them, and beyond all a sea-wood of alders slipping from the hill's skirts to the water's edge. This was not what he wanted in his explorations, so he stopped, till one day it struck him that the westward view might reveal something beyond the hog-backed Cuna. One day, pioneering alone, he scaled the steepest heights of the seaweed and pulled his chin over the crest of the ridge. There, sure enough, was his picture —a mile of reefs and the tattered sea-wood. He turned eagerly seawards. Cuna still lay humped on the waters, but beyond it he seemed to see his shining pathway running far to a speck which might be an island. Crazy with pleasure he stared at the vision, till slowly it melted into the waves, and Cuna the inexorable once more blocked the skyline. He climbed down, his heart in a doubt between despondency and hope.

It was the last day of such fancies, for on the morrow he had to face the new world of school.

. . . .

At Cecil's Colin found a new life and a thousand new interests. His early delicacy had been driven away by the sea-winds of Acharra, and he was rapidly growing up a tall, strong child, straight of limb like all his house, but sinewy and alert beyond his years. He learned new games with astonishing facility, became a fast bowler with a genius for twists, and a Rugby three-quarters full of pluck and cunning. He soon attained to the modified popularity of a private school, and, being essentially clean, strong, and healthy, found himself a mark for his juniors' worship and a favourite with masters. The homage did not spoil him, for no boy was ever less self-possessed. On the cricket-ground and the football-field he was a leader, but in private he had the nervous, sensitive manners of the would-be recluse. No one ever accused him of "side"—his polite, halting address was the same to junior and senior; and the result was that wild affection which simplicity in the great is wont to inspire.

He spoke with a pure accent, in which lurked no northern trace; in a little he had forgotten all about his birthplace and his origin. His name had at first acquired for him the sobriquet of "Scottie," but the title was soon dropped from its manifest inaptness.

In his second year at Cecil's he caught a prevalent fever, and for days lay very near the brink of death. At his worst he was wildly delirious, crying ceaselessly for Acharra and the beach at Kinlochuna. But as he grew convalescent the absorption remained, and for the moment he seemed to have forgotten his southern life. He found himself playing on the sands, always with the boundary ridge before him, and the hump of Cuna rising in the sea. When dragged back to his environment by the inquiries of Bellew, his special friend, who came to sit with him, he was so abstracted and forgetful that the good Bellew was seriously grieved. "The chap's a bit cracked, you know," he announced in hall. "Didn't know me. Asked me what 'footer' meant when I told him about the Bayswick match, and talked about nothing but a lot of heathen Scotch names."

One dream haunted Colin throughout the days of his recovery. He was tormented with a furious thirst, poorly assuaged at long intervals by watered milk. So when he crossed the borders of dreamland his first search was always for a well. He tried the brushwood inland from the beach, but it was dry as stone. Then he climbed with difficulty the boundary ridge, and found little pools of salt water, while far on the other side gleamed the dark black bog-holes. Here was not what he sought, and he was in deep despair, till suddenly over the sea he caught a glimpse of his old path running beyond Cuna to a bank of mist. He rushed down to the tide's edge, and to his amazement found solid ground. Now was the chance for which he had long looked, and he ran happily westwards, till of a sudden the solid earth seemed to sink with him, and he was in the waters struggling. But two curious things he noted. One was that the far bank of mist seemed to open for a pin-point of time, and he had a gleam of land. He saw nothing distinctly, only a line which was not mist and was not water. The second was that the water was fresh, and as he was drinking from this curious new fresh sea he awoke. The dream was repeated three times before he left the sick-room. Always he wakened at the same place, always he quenched his thirst in the fresh sea, but never again did the mist open for him and show him the strange country.

. . . .

From Cecil's he went to the famous school which was the tradition in his family. The Head spoke to his house-master of his coming. "We are to have another Raden here," he said, "and I am glad of it, if the young one turns out to be anything like the others. There's a good deal of dry-rot among the boys just now. They are all too old for their years and too wise in the wrong way. They haven't anything like the enthusiasm in games they had twenty years ago when I first came here. I hope this young Raden will stir them up." The house-master agreed, and when he first caught sight of Colin's slim, well-knit figure, looked into the handsome kindly eyes, and heard his curiously diffident speech, his doubts vanished. "We have got the right stuff now," he told himself, and the senior for whom the new boy fagged made the same comment.

From the anomalous insignificance of fagdom Colin climbed up the School, leaving everywhere a record of honest good-nature. He was allowed to forget his cricket and football, but in return he was initiated into the mysteries of the river. Water had always been his delight, so he went through the dreary preliminaries of being coached in a tub-pair till he learned to swing steadily and get his arms quickly forward. Then came the stages of scratch fours and scratch eights, till after a long apprenticeship he was promoted to the dignity of a thwart in the Eight itself. In his last year he was Captain of Boats, a position which joins the responsibility of a Cabinet

Minister to the rapturous popular applause of a successful warrior. Nor was he the least distinguished of a great band. With Colin at seven the School won the Ladies' after the closest race on record.

The Head's prophecy fell true, for Colin was a born leader. For all his good-humour and diffidence of speech, he had a trick of shutting his teeth which all respected. As Captain he was the idol of the School, and he ruled it well and justly. For the rest, he was a curious boy with none of the ordinary young enthusiasms, reserved for all his kindliness. At house "shouters" his was not the voice which led the stirring strains of "Stroke out all you know," though his position demanded it. He cared little about work, and the School-house scholar, who fancied him from his manner a devotee of things intellectual, found in Colin but an affected interest. He read a certain amount of modern poetry with considerable boredom; fiction he never opened. The truth was that he had a romance in his own brain which, willy nilly, would play itself out, and which left him small relish for the pale second-hand inanities of art. Often, when with others he would lie in the deep meadows by the river on some hot summer's day, his fancies would take a curious colour. He adored the soft English landscape, the lush grasses, the slow streams, the ancient secular trees. But as he looked into the hazy green distance a colder air would blow on his cheek, a pungent smell of salt and pines would be for a moment in his nostrils, and he would be gazing at a line of waves on a beach, a ridge of low rocks, and a shining sea-path running out to—ah, that he could not tell! The envious Cuna would suddenly block all the vistas. He had constantly the vision before his eyes, and he strove to strain into the distance before Cuna should intervene. Once or twice he seemed almost to achieve it. He found that by keeping on the top of the low rock-ridge he could cheat Cuna by a second or two, and get a glimpse of a misty something out in the west. The vision took odd times for recurring,

—once or twice in lecture, once on the cricket-ground, many times in the fields of a Sunday, and once while he paddled down to the start in a Trials race. It gave him a keen pleasure: it was his private domain, where at any moment he might make some enchanting discovery.

At this time he began to spend his vacations at Kinlochuna. His father, an elderly ex-diplomat, had permanently taken up his abode there, and was rapidly settling into the easy life of the Scots laird. Colin returned to his native place without enthusiasm. His childhood there had been full of lonely hours, and he had come to like the warm south country. He found the house full of people, for his father entertained hugely, and the talk was of sport and sport alone. As a rule, your very great athlete is bored by Scots shooting. Long hours of tramping and crouching among heather cramp without fully exercising the body; and unless he has the love of the thing ingrained in him, the odds are that he will wish himself home. The father, in his new-found admiration for his lot, was content to face all weathers; the son found it an effort to keep pace with such vigour. He thought upon the sunlit fields and reedy water-courses with regret, and saw little in the hills but a rough waste scarred with rock and sour with mosses.

He read widely throughout these days, for his father had a taste for modern letters, and new books lay littered about the rooms. He read queer Celtic tales which he thought "sickening rot," and mild Celtic poetry which he failed to understand. Among the guests was a noted manufacturer of fiction, whom the elder Raden had met somewhere and bidden to Kinlochuna. He had heard the tale of Colin's ancestors and the sea headland of Acharra, and one day he asked the boy to show him the place, as he wished to make a story of it. Colin assented unwillingly, for he had been slow to visit this place of memories, and he did not care to make his first experiment in such company. But the gentleman would not be gainsaid, so the two scrambled through the sea-wood and climbed the low ridge which looked over the bay. The weather was mist and drizzle; Cuna had wholly hidden herself, and the bluff Acharra loomed hazy and far. Colin was oddly disappointed: this reality was a poor place compared with his fancies. His companion stroked his peaked beard, talked nonsense about Colin the Red and rhetoric about "the spirit of the misty grey weather having entered into the old tale." "Think," he cried; "to those old warriors beyond that bank of mist was the whole desire of life, the Golden City, the Far Islands, whatever you care to call it." Colin shivered, as if his holy places had been profaned, set down the man in his mind most unjustly as an "awful little cad," and hurried him back to the house.

. . . .

Oxford received the boy with open arms, for his reputation had long preceded him. To the majority of men he was the one freshman of his year, and gossip was busy with his prospects. Nor was gossip disappointed. In his first year he rowed seven in the Eight. The next year he was captain of his college boats, and a year later the O.U.B.C. made him its president. For three years he rowed in the winning Eight, and old coaches agreed that in him the perfect seven had been found. It was he who in the famous race of 18— caught up in the last three hundred yards the quickened stroke which gave Oxford victory. As he grew to his full strength he became a splendid figure of a man—tall, supple, deep-chested for all his elegance. His quick dark eyes and his kindly hesitating manners made people think his face extraordinarily handsome, when really it was in no way above the common. But his whole figure, as he stood in his shorts and sweater on the raft at Putney, was so full of youth and strength that people involuntarily smiled when they saw him—a smile of pleasure in so proper a piece of manhood.

Colin enjoyed life hugely at Oxford, for to one so frank and well equipped the place gave of its best. He was the most distinguished personage of his day there, but, save to school friends and the men he met officially on the river, he was little known. His diffidence and his very real exclusiveness kept him from being the centre of a host of friends. His own countrymen in the place were utterly nonplussed by him. They claimed him eagerly as a fellow, but he had none of the ordinary characteristics of the race. There were Scots of every description around him—pale-faced Scots who worked incessantly, metaphysical Scots who talked in the Union, robustious Scots who played football. They were all men of hearty manners and many enthusiasms,—who quoted Burns and dined to the immortal bard's honour every 25th of January; who told interminable Scotch stories, and fell into fervours over national sports, dishes, drinks, and religions. To the poor Colin it was all inexplicable. At the remote house of Kinlochuna he had never heard of a Free Kirk or a haggis. He had never read a line of Burns, Scott bored him exceedingly, and in all honesty he thought Scots games inferior to southern sports. He had no great love for the bleak country, he cared nothing for the traditions of his house, so he was promptly set down by his compatriots as "denationalised and degenerate."

He was idle, too, during these years as far as his "schools" were concerned, but he was always very intent upon his own private business. Whenever he sat down to read, when he sprawled on the grass at river picnics, in chapel, in lecture—in short, at any moment when his body was at rest and his mind at leisure—his fancies were off on the same old path. Things had changed, however, in that country. The boyish device of a hard road running over the waters had gone, and now it was invariably a boat which he saw beached on the shingle. It differed in shape. At first it was an ugly salmon-coble, such as the fishermen used for the nets at Kinlochuna. Then it passed, by rapid transitions, through a canvas skiff which it took good watermanship to sit, a whiff, an ordinary dinghy, till at last it settled itself into a long rough boat, pointed at both ends, with oar-holes in the sides instead of row-locks. It was the devil's own business to launch it, and launch it anew he was compelled to for every journey; for though he left it bound in a little rock hollow below the ridge after landing, yet when he returned, lo! there was the clumsy thing high and dry upon the beach.

The odd point about the new venture was that Cuna had ceased to trouble him. As soon as he had pulled his first stroke the island disappeared, and nothing lay before him but the sea-fog. Yet, try as he might, he could come little nearer. The shores behind him might sink and lessen, but the impenetrable mist was still miles to the westward. Sometimes he rowed so far that the shore was a thin line upon the horizon, but when he turned the boat it seemed to ground in a second on the beach. The long laboured journey out and the instantaneous return puzzled him at first, but soon he became used to them. His one grief was the mist, which seemed to grow denser as he neared it. The sudden glimpse of land which he had got from the ridge of rock in the old boyish days was now denied him, and with the denial came a keener exultation in the quest. Somewhere in the west, he knew, must be land, and in this land a well of sweet water—for so he had interpreted his feverish dream. Sometimes, when the wind blew against him, he caught scents from it—generally the scent of pines, as on the little ridge on the shore behind him.

One day on his college barge, while he was waiting for a picnic party to start, he seemed to get nearer than before. Out on that western sea, as he saw it, it was fresh, blowing weather, with a clear hot sky above. It was hard work rowing, for the wind was against him, and the sun scorched his forehead. The air seemed full of scents—and sounds, too, sounds of far-away surf and wind in trees. He rested for a moment on his oars and turned his head. His heart beat quickly, for there was a rift in the mist, and far through a line of sand ringed with snow-white foam.

Somebody shook him roughly,—"Come on, Colin, old man. They're all waiting for you. Do you know you've been half asleep?"

Colin rose and followed silently, with drowsy eyes. His mind was curiously excited. He had looked inside the veil of mist. Now he knew what was the land he sought.

. . . .

He made the voyage often, now that the spell was broken. It was short work to launch the boat, and, whereas it had been a long pull formerly, now it needed only a few strokes to bring him to the Rim of the Mist. There was no chance of getting farther, and he scarcely tried. He was content to rest there, in a world of curious scents and sounds, till the mist drew down and he was driven back to shore.

The change in his environment troubled him little. For a man who has been an idol at the University to fall suddenly into the comparative insignificance of Town is often a bitter experience; but Colin, whose thoughts were not ambitious, scarcely noticed it. He found that he was less his own master than before, but he humbled himself to his new duties without complaint. Many of his old friends were about him; he had plenty of acquaintances; and, being "sufficient unto himself," he was unaccustomed to ennui. Invitations showered upon him thick and fast. Match-making mothers, knowing his birth and his father's income, and reflecting that he was the only child of his house, desired him as a son-in-law. He was bidden welcome everywhere, and the young girls, for whose sake he was thus courted, found in him an attractive mystery. The tall good-looking athlete, with the kind eyes and the preposterously nervous manner, wakened their maidenly sympathies. As they danced with him or sat next to him at dinner, they talked fervently of Oxford, of the north, of the army, of his friends. "Stupid, but nice, my dear," was Lady Afflint's comment; and Miss Clara Etheridge, the beauty of the year, declared to her friends that he was a "dear boy, but so awkward." He was always forgetful, and ever apologetic; and when he forgot the Shandwicks' theatre-party, the Herapaths' dance, and at least a dozen minor matters, he began to acquire the reputation of a cynic and a recluse.

"You're a queer chap, Col," Lieutenant Bellew said in expostulation.

Colin shrugged his shoulders; he was used to the description.

"Do you know that Clara Etheridge was trying all she knew to please you this afternoon, and you looked as if you weren't listening? Most men would have given their ears to be in your place."

"I'm awfully sorry, but I thought I was very polite to her."

"And why weren't you at the Marshams' show?"

"Oh, I went to polo with Collinson and another man. And, I say, old chap, I'm not coming to the Logans to-morrow. I've got a fence on with Adair at the school."

Little Bellew who was a tremendous mirror of fashion and chevalier in general, looked up curiously at his tall friend.

"Why don't you like the women, Col, when they're so fond of you?"

"They aren't," said Colin hotly, "and I don't dislike 'em. But, Lord! they bore me. I might be doing twenty things when I talk nonsense to one of 'em for an hour. I come back as stupid as an owl, and besides there's heaps of things better sport."

The truth was that, while among men he was a leader and at his ease, among women his psychic balance was so oddly upset that he grew nervous and returned unhappy. The boat on the beach, ready in general to appear at the slightest call, would delay long after such experiences, and its place would be taken by some woman's face for which he cared not a straw. For the boat, on the other hand, he cared a very great deal. In all his frank wholesome existence there was this enchanting background, this pleasure-garden which he cherished more than anything in life. He had come of late to look at it with somewhat different eyes. The eager desire to search behind the mist was ever with him, but now he had also some curiosity about the details of the picture. As he pulled out to the Rim of the Mist, sounds seemed to shape themselves on his lips, which by-and-by grew into actual words in his memory. He wrote them down in scraps, and after some sorting they seemed to him a kind of Latin. He remembered a college friend of his, one Medway, now reading for the Bar, who had been the foremost scholar of his acquaintance; so with the scrap of paper in his pocket he climbed one evening to Medway's rooms in the Temple.

The man read the words curiously, and puzzled for a bit. "What's made you take to Latin comps so late in life, Colin? It's baddish, you know, even for you. I thought they'd have licked more into you at Eton."

Colin grinned with amusement. "I'll tell you about it later," he said. "Can you make out what it means?"

"It seems to be a kind of dog-Latin or monkish Latin or something of the sort," said Medway. "It reads like this: '*Soles occidere solent*' (that's cribbed from Catullus, and besides it's the regular monkish pun) . . . *qua* . . . then *blandula* something. Then there's a lot of Choctaw, and then *illæ insulæ dilectæ in quas festinant somnia animulæ gaudia.* That's pretty fair rot. Hullo, by George! here's something better—*Insula pomorum insula vitæ.* That's Geoffrey of Monmouth."

He made a dive to a bookcase and pulled out a battered little calf-bound duodecimo. "Here's all about your Isle of Apple-trees. Listen. 'Situate far out in the Western ocean, beyond the Utmost Islands, beyond even the little Isle of Sheep where the cairns of dead men are, lies the Island of Apple-trees where the heroes and princes of the nations live their second life.'" He closed the book and put it back. "It's the old ancient story, the Greek Hesperides, the British Avilion, and this Apple-tree Island is the northern equivalent."

Colin sat entranced, his memory busy with a problem. Could he distinguish the scents of apple-trees among the perfumes of the Rim of the Mist? For the moment he thought he could. He was roused by Medway's voice asking the story of the writing.

"Oh, it's just some nonsense that was running in my head, so I wrote it down to see what it was."

"But you must have been reading. A new exercise for you, Colin!"

"No, I wasn't reading. Look here. You know the sort of pictures you make for yourself of places you like."

"Rather! Mine is a Yorkshire moor with a little red shooting-box in the heart of it."

"Well, mine is different. Mine is a sort of beach with a sea and a lot of islands somewhere far out. It is a jolly place, fresh, you know, and blowing, and smells good. 'Pon my word, now I think of it, there's always been a scent of apples."

"Sort of cider-press? Well, I must be off. You'd better come round to the club and see the telegrams about the war. *You* should be keen about it."

One evening, a week later, Medway met a friend called Tillotson at the club, and, being lonely, they dined together. Tillotson was a man of some note in science, a dabbler in psychology, an amateur historian, a ripe genealogist. They talked of politics and the war, of a new book, of Mrs Runnymede, and finally of their hobbies.

"I am writing an article," said Tillotson. "Craikes asked me to do it for the 'Monthly.' It's on a nice point in psychics. I call it 'The Transmission of Fallacies,' but I do not mean the logical kind. The question is, Can a particular form of hallucination run in a family for generations? The proof must, of course, come from my genealogical studies. I maintain it can. I instance the Douglas-Ernotts, not one of whom can see straight with the left eye. That is one side. In another class of examples I take the Drapiers, who hate salt water and never go on board ship if they can help it. Then you remember the Durwards? Old Lady Balcrynie used to tell me that no one of the lot could ever stand the sight of a green frock. There's a chance for the romancer. The Manorwaters have the same madness, only their colour is red."

A vague remembrance haunted Medway's brain.

"I know a man who might give you points from his own case. Did you ever meet a chap Raden—Colin Raden?"

Tillotson nodded. "Long chap—in the Guards? 'Varsity oar, and used to be a crack bowler? No, I don't know him. I know him well by sight, and I should like to meet him tremendously—as a genealogist, of course."

"Why?" asked Medway.

"Why? Because the man's family is unique. You never hear much about them nowadays, but away up in that north-west corner of Scotland they have ruled since the days of Noah. Why, man, they were aristocrats when our Howards and Nevilles were greengrocers. I wish you would get this Raden to meet me some night."

"I am afraid there's no chance of it just at present," said Medway, taking up an evening paper. "I see that his regiment has gone to the front. But remind me when he comes back, and I'll be delighted."

III.

AND now there began for Colin a curious divided life,—without, a constant shifting of scene, days of heat and bustle and toil,—within, a slow, tantalising, yet exquisite adventure. The Rim of the Mist was now no more the goal of his journeys, but the starting-point. Lying there, amid cool, fragrant sea-winds, his fanciful ear was subtly alert for the sounds of the dim land before him. Sleeping and waking the quest haunted him. As he flung himself on his bed the kerosene-filled air would change to an ocean freshness, the old boat would rock beneath him, and with clear eye and a boyish hope he would be waiting and watching. And then suddenly he would be back on shore, Cuna and the Acharra headland shining grey in the morning light, and with gritty mouth and sand-filled eyes he would awaken to the heat of the desert camp.

He was kept busy, for his good-humour and energy made him a willing slave, and he was ready enough for volunteer work when others were weak with heat and despair. A thirty-mile ride left him untired; more, he followed the campaign with a sharp intelligence and found a new enthusiasm for his profession. Discomforts there might be, but the days were happy; and then—the cool land, the bright land, which was his for the thinking of it.

Soon they gave him reconnoitring work to do, and his wits were put to the trial. He came well out of the thing, and earned golden praise from the silent colonel in command. He enjoyed it as he had enjoyed a hard race on the river or a good cricket match, and when his worried companions marvelled at his zeal he stammered and grew uncomfortable.

"How the deuce do you keep it up, Colin?" the major asked him. "I'm an old hand at the job, and yet I've got a temper like devilled bones. You seem as chirpy as if you were going out to fish a chalk-stream on a June morning."

"Well, the fact is——" and Colin pulled himself up short, knowing that he could never explain. He felt miserably that he had an unfair advantage of the others. Poor Bellew, who groaned and swore in the heat at his side, knew nothing of the Rim of the Mist. It was really rough luck on the poor beggars, and who but himself was the fortunate man?

As the days passed a curious thing happened. He found fragments of the Other world straying into his common life. The barriers of the two domains were falling, and more than once he caught himself looking at a steel-blue sea when his eyes should have found a mustard-coloured desert. One day, on a reconnoitring expedition, they stopped for a little on a hillock above a jungle of scrub, and, being hot and tired, scanned listlessly the endless yellow distances.

"I suppose yon hill is about ten miles off," said Bellew with dry lips.

Colin looked vaguely. "I should say five."

"And what's that below it—the black patch? Stones or scrub?"

Colin was in a day-dream. "Why do you call it black? It's blue, quite blue."

"Rot," said the other. "It's grey-black."

"No, it's water with the sun shining on it. It's blue, but just at the edges it's very near sea-green."

Bellew rose excitedly. "Hullo, Col, you're seeing the mirage! And you the fittest of the lot of us! You've got the sun in your head, old man!"

"Mirage!" Colin cried in contempt. He was awake now, but the thought of confusing his own bright western sea with a mirage gave him a curious pain. For a moment he felt the gulf of separation between his two worlds, but only for a moment. As the party remounted he gave his fancies the rein, and ere he reached camp he had felt the oars in his hand and sniffed the apple-tree blossom from the distant beaches.

The major came to him after supper.

"Bellew told me you were a bit odd to-day, Colin," he said. "I expect your eyes are getting baddish. Better get your sand-spectacles out."

Colin laughed. "Thanks. It's awfully good of you to bother, but I think Bellew took me up wrong. I never was fitter in my life."

. . . .

By-and-by the turn came for pride to be humbled. A low desert fever took him, and though he went through the day as usual, it was with dreary lassitude; and at night, with hot hands clasped above his damp hair, he found sleep a hard goddess to conquer.

It was the normal condition of the others, so he had small cause to complain, but it worked havoc with his fancies. He had never been ill since his childish days, and this little fever meant much to one whose nature was poised on a needle-point. He found himself confronted with a hard bare world, with the gilt rubbed from its corners. The Rim of the Mist seemed a place of vague horrors; when he reached it his soul was consumed with terror; he struggled impotently to advance; behind him Cuna and the Acharra coast seemed a place of evil dreams. Again, as in his old fever, he was tormented with a devouring thirst, but the sea beside him was not fresh, but brackish as a rock-pool. He yearned for the apple-tree beaches in front; there, he knew, were cold springs of water; the fresh smell of it was blown towards him in his nightmare.

But as the days passed and the misery for all grew more intense, an odd hope began to rise in his mind. It could not last, coolness and health were waiting near, and his reason for the hope came from the odd events at the Rim of the Mist. The haze was clearing from the foreground, the surf-lined coast seemed nearer, and though all was obscure save the milk-white sand and the foam, yet here was earnest enough for him. Once more he became cheerful; weak and light-headed he rode out again; and the major, who was recovering from sun-stroke, found envy take the place of pity in his soul.

The hope was near fulfilment. One evening when the heat was changing into the cooler twilight, Colin and Bellew were sent with a small picked body to scour the foot-hills above the river in case of a flank attack during the night-march. It was work they had done regularly for weeks, and it is possible that precautions were relaxed. At any rate, as they turned a corner of hill, in a sandy pass where barren rocks looked down on more barren thorn thickets, a couple of rifle-shots rang out from the scarp, and above them appeared a line of dark faces and white steel. A mere handful, taken at a disadvantage, they could not hope to disperse numbers, so Colin gave the word to wheel about and return. Again shots rang out, and little Bellew had only time to catch at his friend's arm to save him from falling from the saddle.

The word of command had scarcely left Colin's mouth when a sharp pain went through his chest, and his breath seemed to catch and stop. He felt as in a condensed moment of time the heat, the desert smell, the dust in his eyes and throat, while he leaned helplessly forward on his horse's mane. Then the world vanished for him. . . . The boat was rocking under him, the oars in his hand. He pulled and it moved, straight, arrow-like towards the forbidden shore. As if under a great wind the mist furled up and fled. Scents of pines, of apple-trees, of great fields of thyme and heather, hung about him ; the sound of wind in a forest, of cool waters falling in showers, of old moorland music, came thin and faint with an exquisite clearness. A second and the boat was among the surf, its gunwale ringed with white foam, as it leaped to the still waters beyond. Clear and deep and still the water lay, and then the white beaches shelved downward, and the boat grated on the sand. He turned, every limb alert with a strange new life, crying out words which had shaped themselves on his lips and which an echo seemed to catch and answer. There was the green forest before him, the hills of peace, the cold white waters. With a passionate joy he leaped on the beach, his arms outstretched to this new earth, this light of the world, this old desire of the heart—youth, rapture, immortality.

. . . .

Bellew brought the body back to camp, himself half-dead with fatigue and whimpering like a child. He almost fell from his horse, and when others took his burden from him and laid it reverently in his tent, he stood beside it, rubbing sand and sweat from his poor purblind eyes, his teeth chattering with fever. He was given something to drink, but he swallowed barely a mouthful.

"It was some d-d-damned sharpshooter," he said. "Right through the breast, and he never spoke to me again. My poor old Col! He was the best chap God ever created, and I do-don't care a dash what becomes of me now. I was at school with him, you know, you men."

"Was he killed outright?" asked the major hoarsely.

"N-no. He lived for about five minutes. But I think the sun had got into his head or he was mad with pain, for he d-d-didn't know where he was. He kept crying out about the smell of pine-trees and heather and a lot of pure nonsense about water."

"*Et dulces reminiscitur Argos*," somebody quoted mournfully, as they went out to the desert evening.

III. THE WATCHER BY THE THRESHOLD.

CHAPTER I.

THE HOUSE OF MORE.

I.

I HAVE told this story to many audiences with diverse results, and once again I take my reputation in my hands and brave the perils. To the common circle of my friends it was a romance for a winter's fire, and I, the most prosaic of men, was credited with a fancy. Once I repeated it to an acquaintance, who, scenting mystery, transcribed it in a note-book, and, with feigned names, it figured in the publications of a Learned Society. One man only heard me with true appreciation; but he was a wandering spirit with an ear open to marvels, and I hesitate to advance his security. He received it simply, saying that God was great, and I cannot improve upon his comment.

A chill evening in the early October of the year 189– found me driving in a dogcart through the belts of antique woodland which form the lowland limits of the hilly parish of More. The Highland express, which brought me from the north, took me no farther than Perth. Thence it had been a slow journey in a disjointed local train, till I emerged on the platform at Morefoot, with a bleak prospect of pit-stalks, coal-heaps, certain sour corn-lands, and far to the west a line of moor where the sun was setting. A neat groom and a respectable trap took the edge off my discomfort, and soon

I had forgotten my sacrifice and found eyes for the darkening landscape. We were driving through a land of thick woods, cut at rare intervals by old long-frequented highways. The More, which at Morefoot is an open sewer, became a sullen woodland stream, where the brown leaves of the season drifted. At times we would pass an ancient lodge, and through a gap in the trees would come a glimpse of a chipped crow-step gable. The names of such houses, as told me by my companion, were all famous. This one had been the home of a drunken Jacobite laird, and a kind of north-country Medmenham. Unholy revels had waked the old halls, and the Devil had been toasted at many a hell-fire dinner. The next was the property of a great Scots law family, and there the old Lord of Session who built the place, in his frowsy wig and carpet slippers, had laid down the canons of Taste for his day and society. The whole country had the air of faded and bygone gentility. The mossy roadside walls had stood for two hundred years, the few wayside houses were toll-bars or defunct hostelries. The names, too, were great—Scots baronial with a smack of France—Chatelray and Reiverslaw, Black Holm and Champertoun. The place had a cunning charm, mystery dwelt in every cranny, and yet it did not please me. The earth smelt heavy and raw, the roads were red underfoot, all was old, sorrowful, and uncanny. Compared with the fresh Highland glen I had left, where wind and sun and flying showers were never absent, all was chilly and dull and dead. Even when the sun sent a shiver of crimson over the crests of certain firs, I felt no delight in the prospect. I admitted shamefacedly to myself that I was in a very bad temper.

I had been staying at Glenaicill with the Clanroydens, and for a week had found the proper pleasure in life. You know the house with its old rooms and gardens, and the miles of heather which defend it from the world. The shooting had been extraordinary for a wild place far on in the season, for there are few partridges and the woodcock are notoriously late. I had done respectably in my stalking, more than respectably on the river, and creditably on the moors. Moreover, there were pleasant people in the house—and there were the Clanroydens. I had had a hard year's work, sustained to the last moment of term, and a fortnight in Norway had been disastrous. It was therefore with real comfort that I had settled myself down for another ten days in Glenaicill, when all my plans were shattered by Sybil's letter. Sybil is my cousin and my very good friend, and in old days when I was briefless I had fallen in love with her many times. But she very sensibly chose otherwise, and married a man Ladlaw—Robert John Ladlaw—who had been at school with me. He was a cheery, good-humoured fellow, a great sportsman, a justice of the peace and deputy-lieutenant for his county, and something of an antiquary in a mild way. He had a box in Leicestershire to which he went in the hunting season; but from February till October he lived in his moorland home. The place was called the House of More, and I had shot there once or twice in recent years. I remembered its loneliness and its comfort, the charming diffident Sybil and Ladlaw's genial welcome. And my recollections set me puzzling again over the letter which that morning had broken into my comfort. "You promised us a visit this autumn," Sybil had written, "and I wish you would come as soon as you can." So far common politeness. But she had gone on to reveal the fact that Ladlaw was ill, she did not know how exactly, but something, she thought, about his heart. Then she had signed herself my affectionate cousin, and then had come a short violent postscript, in which, as it were, the fences of convention had been laid low. "For heaven's sake come and see us!" she scrawled below. "Bob is terribly ill, and I am crazy. Come at once." And then she finished with an afterthought, "Don't bother about bringing doctors. It is not their business."

She had assumed that I would come, and dutifully I set

out. I could not regret my decision, but I took leave to upbraid my luck. The thought of Glenaicill with the woodcock beginning to arrive, and the Clanroydens imploring me to stay, saddened my journey in the morning, and the murky, coally midland country of the afternoon completed my depression. The drive through the woodlands of More failed to raise my spirits. I was anxious about Sybil and Ladlaw, and the accursed country had always given me a certain eeriness on my first approaching it. You may call it silly; but I have no nerves, and am little susceptible to vague sentiment. It was sheer physical dislike of the rich deep soil, the woody and antique smells, the melancholy roads and trees, and the flavour of old mystery. I am aggressively healthy and wholly Philistine. I love clear outlines and strong colours, and More, with its half-tints and hazy distances, depressed me miserably. Even when the road crept uphill and the trees ended, I found nothing to hearten me in the moorland which succeeded. It was genuine moorland, close on 800 feet above the sea, and through it ran this old grass-grown coach-road. Low hills rose to the left, and to the right after some miles of peat flared the chimneys of pits and oil-works. Straight in front the moor ran out into the horizon, and there in the centre was the last dying spark of the sun. The place was as still as the grave save for the crunch of our wheels on the grassy road; but the flaring lights to the north seemed to endow it with life. I have rarely felt so keenly the feeling of movement in the inanimate world. It was an unquiet place, and I shivered nervously. Little gleams of loch came from the hollows, the burns were brown with peat, and every now and then there rose in the moor jags of sickening red stone. I remembered that Ladlaw had talked about the place as the old Manann, the holy land of the ancient races. I had paid little attention at the time, but now it struck me that the old peoples had been wise in their choice. There was something uncanny in this soil and air. Framed in dank mysterious woods, and a country of coal and ironstone, no great distance, too, from the capital city, it was a sullen relic of a lost barbarism. Over the low hills lay a green pastoral country with bright streams and valleys, but here in this peaty desert there were few sheep and little cultivation. The House of More was the only dwelling, and, save for the ragged village, the wilderness was given over to the wild things of the hills. The shooting was good; but the best shooting on earth would not persuade me to make my abode in such a place. Ladlaw was ill; well, I did not wonder. You can have uplands without air, moors that are not health-giving, and a country life which is more arduous than a townsman's. I shivered again, for I seemed to have passed in a few hours from the open noon to a kind of dank twilight.

We passed the village and entered the lodge-gates. Here there were trees again, little innocent new-planted firs, which flourished badly. Some large plane-trees grew near the house, and there were thickets upon thickets of the ugly elder. Even in the half-darkness I could see that the lawns were trim and the flower-beds respectable for the season; doubtless Sybil looked after the gardeners. The oblong whitewashed house, more like a barrack than ever, opened suddenly on my sight, and I experienced my first sense of comfort since I left Glenaicill. Here I should find warmth and company, and, sure enough, the hall-door was wide open, and in the great flood of light which poured from it Sybil stood to welcome me.

She ran down the steps as I dismounted, and, with a word to the groom, caught my arm and drew me into the shadow. "Oh, Henry, it was so good of you to come. You mustn't let Bob think that you know he is ill. We don't talk about it. I'll tell you afterwards. I want you to cheer him up. Now we must go in, for he is in the hall expecting you."

While I stood blinking in the light, Ladlaw came forward with outstretched hand and his usual cheery greeting. I looked at him and saw nothing unnatural in his appearance:

a little drawn at the lips, perhaps, and heavy below the eyes, but still fresh-coloured and healthy. It was Sybil who showed change. She was very pale, her pretty eyes were deplorably mournful, and in place of her delightful shyness there was the self-confidence and composure of pain. I was honestly shocked and, as I dressed, my heart was full of hard thoughts about Ladlaw. What could his illness mean? He seemed well and cheerful, while Sybil was pale, and yet it was Sybil who had written the postscript. As I warmed myself by the fire, I resolved that this particular family difficulty was my proper business.

II.

The Ladlaws were waiting for me in the drawing-room. I noticed something new and strange in Sybil's demeanour. She looked to her husband with a motherly protective air, while Ladlaw, who had been the extreme of masculine independence, seemed to cling to his wife with a curious appealing fidelity. In conversation he did little more than echo her words. Till dinner was announced he spoke of the weather, the shooting, and Mabel Clanroyden. Then he did a queer thing, for, when I was about to offer my arm to Sybil, he forestalled me, and, clutching her right arm with his left hand, led the way to the dining-room, leaving me to follow in some bewilderment.

I have rarely taken part in a more dismal meal. The House of More has a pretty Georgian panelling through most of the rooms; but in the dining-room the walls are level, and painted a dull stone colour. Abraham offered up Isaac in a ghastly picture in front of me. Some photographs of the Quorn hung over the mantelpiece, and five or six drab ancestors filled up the remaining space. But one thing was new and startling. A great marble bust, a genuine antique, frowned on me from a pedestal. The head was in the late Roman style, clearly of some emperor, and in its commonplace environment the great brows, the massive neck, and the mysterious solemn lips had a surprising effect. I nodded towards the thing, and asked what it represented.

Ladlaw grunted something which I took for "Justinian," but he never raised his eyes from his plate. By accident I caught Sybil's glance. She looked towards the bust, and laid a finger on her lips.

The meal grew more doleful as it advanced. Sybil scarcely touched a dish, but her husband ate ravenously of everything. He was a strong, thick-set man, with a square, kindly face, burned brown by the sun. Now he seemed to have suddenly coarsened. He gobbled with undignified haste, and his eye was extraordinarily vacant. A question made him start, and he would turn on me a face so strange and inert that I repented the interruption.

I asked him about the autumn's sport, and he collected his wits with difficulty. He thought it had been good on the whole, but he had shot badly. He had not been quite so fit as usual. No, he had had nobody staying with him—Sybil had wanted to be alone. He was afraid the moor might have been under-shot, but he would make a big day with keepers and farmers before the winter.

"Bob has done pretty well," Sybil said. "He hasn't been out often, for the weather has been very bad here. You can have no idea, Henry, how horrible this moorland place of ours can be when it tries. It is one great sponge sometimes, with ugly red burns, and mud to the ankles."

"I don't think it's healthy," said I.

Ladlaw lifted his face. "Nor do I: I think it's intolerable; but I am so busy, I can't get away."

Once again I caught Sybil's warning eye as I was about to question him on his business.

Clearly the man's brain had received a shock, and he was beginning to suffer from hallucinations. This could be the only explanation, for he had always led a temperate life. The *distrait* wandering manner was the only sign of his malady, for otherwise he seemed normal and mediocre as ever. My heart grieved for Sybil, alone with him in this wilderness.

Then he broke the silence. He lifted his head and looked nervously around till his eye fell on the Roman bust.

"Do you know that this countryside is the old Manann?" he said.

It was an odd turn to the conversation, but I was glad of a sign of intelligence. I answered that I had heard so.

"It's a queer name," he said oracularly; "but the thing it stood for was queerer. Manann, Manaw," he repeated, rolling the words on his tongue. As he spoke, he glanced sharply, and, as it seemed to me, fearfully, at his left side.

The movement of his body made his napkin slip from his left knee and fall on the floor. It leaned against his leg, and he started from its touch as if he had been stung by a snake. I have never seen a more sheer and transparent terror on a man's face. He got to his feet, his strong frame shaking like a rush. Sybil ran round to his side, picked up the napkin, and flung it on a sideboard. Then she stroked his hair as one would stroke a frightened horse. She called him by his old boy's name of Robin, and at her touch and voice he became quiet. But the particular course then in progress was removed untasted.

In a few minutes he seemed to have forgotten his behaviour, for he took up the former conversation. For a time he spoke well and briskly.

"You lawyers," he said, "understand only the dry framework of the past. You cannot conceive the rapture, which only the antiquary can feel, of constructing in every detail an old culture. Take this Manann. If I could explore the secret of these moors, I would write the world's greatest book. I would write of that prehistoric life when man was knit close to nature. I would describe the people who were brothers of the red earth and the red rock and the red streams of the hills. Oh, it would be horrible, but superb, tremendous!

It would be more than a piece of history; it would be a new gospel, a new theory of life. It would kill materialism once and for all. Why, man, all the poets who have deified and personified nature would not do an eighth part of my work. I would show you the unknown, the hideous, shrieking mystery at the back of this simple nature. Men would see the profundity of the old crude faiths which they affect to despise. I would make a picture of our shaggy, sombre-eyed forefather, who heard strange things in the hill-silences. I would show him brutal and terror-stricken, but wise, wise, God alone knows how wise! The Romans knew it, and they learned what they could from him, but he did not tell them much. But we have some of his blood in us, and we may go deeper. Manann! A queer land nowadays! I sometimes love it and sometimes hate it, but I always fear it. It is like that statue, inscrutable."

I would have told him that he was talking mystical nonsense; but I had looked towards the bust, and my rudeness was checked on my lips. The moor might be a common piece of ugly waste land, but the statue was inscrutable—of that there was no doubt. I hate your cruel, heavy-mouthed Roman busts; to me they have none of the beauty of life, and little of the interest of art. But my eyes were fastened on this as they had never before looked on marble. The oppression of the heavy woodlands, the mystery of the silent moor, seemed to be caught and held in this face. It was the intangible mystery of culture on the verge of savagery, a cruel, lustful wisdom, and yet a kind of bitter austerity which laughed at the game of life and stood aloof. There was no weakness in the heavy-veined brow and slumbrous eyelids. It was the face of one who had conquered the world and found it dust and ashes, one who had eaten of the tree of the knowledge of good and evil and scorned human wisdom. And at the same time it was the face of one who knew uncanny things, a man who was the intimate of the half-world and the dim background of life. Why on earth I should connect the Roman grandee [1] with the moorland parish of More, I cannot say; but the fact remains, that there was that in the face which I knew had haunted me through the woodlands and bogs of the place, a sleepless, dismal, incoherent melancholy.

"I bought that at Colenzo's," Ladlaw said, "because it took my fancy. It matches well with this place."

I thought it matched very ill with his drab walls and Quorn photographs, but I held my peace.

"Do you know who it is?" he asked. "It is the head of the greatest man the world has ever seen. You are a lawyer and know your Justinian."

The Pandects are scarcely part of the daily work of a common-law barrister. I had not looked into them since I left college.

"I know that he married an actress," I said, "and was a sort of all-round genius. He made law and fought battles and had rows with the Church. A curious man! And wasn't there some story about his selling his soul to the Devil and getting law in exchange? Rather a poor bargain!"

I chattered away sillily enough, to dispel the gloom of that dinner-table. The result of my words was unhappy. Ladlaw gasped, and caught at his left side as if in pain. Sybil, with tragic eyes, had been making signs to me to hold my peace. Now she ran round to her husband's side and comforted him like a child. As she passed me she managed to whisper in my ear to talk to her only and let her husband alone.

For the rest of dinner I obeyed my orders to the letter. Ladlaw ate his food in gloomy silence, while I spoke to Sybil of our relatives and friends, of London, Glenaicill, and any

[1] I have identified the bust, which, when seen under other circumstances, had little power to affect me. It was a copy of the head of Justinian in the Tesci Museum at Venice, and several duplicates exist, dating apparently from the seventh century, and showing traces of Byzantine decadence in the scrollwork on the hair. It is engraved in M. Delacroix's 'Byzantium,' and, I think, in Windscheid's 'Pandektenlehrbuch.'

random subject. The poor girl was dismally forgetful, and her eye would wander to her husband with wifely anxiety. I remember being suddenly overcome by the comic aspect of it all. Here were we three fools alone in this dank upland, one of us sick and nervous, talking out-of-the-way nonsense about Manann and Justinian, gobbling his food and getting scared at his napkin, another gravely anxious, and myself at my wits' end for a solution. It was a Mad Tea-party with a vengeance, Sybil the melancholy little Dormouse, and Ladlaw the incomprehensible Hatter. I laughed aloud, but checked myself when I caught my cousin's eye. It was really no case for finding humour. Ladlaw was very ill, and Sybil's face was getting deplorably thin.

I welcomed the end of that meal with unmannerly joy, for I wanted to speak seriously with my host. Sybil told the butler to have the lamps lit in the library. Then she leaned over to me and spoke low and rapidly: "I want you to talk with Bob. I'm sure you can do him good. You'll have to be very patient with him and very gentle. Oh please try and find out what is wrong with him. He won't tell me, and I can only guess."

The butler returned with word that the library was ready to receive us, and Sybil rose to go. Ladlaw half rose, protesting, making the most curious, feeble clutches at his side. His wife quieted him. "Henry will look after you, dear," she said. "You are going into the library to smoke." Then she slipped from the room, and we were left alone.

He caught my arm fiercely with his left hand, and his grip nearly made me cry out. As we walked down the hall I could feel his arm twitching from the elbow to the shoulder. Clearly he was in pain, and I set it down to some form of cardiac affection, which might possibly issue in paralysis.

I settled him in the biggest arm-chair, and took one of his cigars. The library is the pleasantest room in the house, and at night, when a peat-fire burned on the old hearth and the great red curtains were drawn, it used to be the place for comfort and good talk. Now I noticed changes. Ladlaw's book-shelves had been filled with the proceedings of antiquarian societies and many light-hearted works in *belles-lettres*. But now the Badminton Library had been cleared out of a shelf where it stood most convenient to the hand, and its place taken by an old Leyden reprint of Justinian. There were books on Byzantine subjects of which I never dreamed he had heard the names. There were volumes of history and speculation, all of a slightly bizarre kind; and to crown everything, there were several bulky medical works with gaudily coloured plates. The old atmosphere of sport and travel had gone from the room, with the medley of rods, whips, and gun-cases which used to cumber the tables. Now the place was moderately tidy and slightly learned—and I did not like it.

Ladlaw refused to smoke, and sat for a little while in silence. Then of his own accord he broke the tension,—

"It was devilish good of you to come, Harry. This is a lonely place for a man who is a bit seedy."

"I thought you might be alone," I said, "so I looked you up on my way down from Glenaicill. I'm sorry to find you looking ill."

"Do you notice it?" he asked sharply.

"It's tolerably patent," I said. "Have you seen a doctor?"

He said something uncomplimentary about doctors, and kept looking at me with his curious dull eyes.

I remarked the strange posture in which he sat—his head screwed round to his right shoulder, and his whole body a protest against something at his left hand.

"It looks like your heart," I said. "You seem to have pains in your left side."

Again a spasm of fear. I went over to him and stood at the back of his chair.

"Now, for goodness' sake, my dear fellow, tell me what

is wrong? You're scaring Sybil to death. It's lonely work for the poor girl, and I wish you would let me help you."

He was lying back in his chair now, with his eyes half shut, and shivering like a frightened colt. The extraordinary change in one who had been the strongest of the strong kept me from realising its gravity. I put a hand on his shoulder, but he flung it off.

"For God's sake sit down!" he said hoarsely. "I'm going to tell you; but I'll never make you understand."

I sat down promptly opposite him.

"It's the Devil," he said very solemnly.

I am afraid that I was rude enough to laugh. He took no notice, but sat with the same tense, miserable air, staring over my head.

"Right," said I. "Then it is the Devil. It's a new complaint, so it's as well I did not bring a doctor. How does it affect you?"

He made the old impotent clutch at the air with his left hand. I had the sense to become grave at once. Clearly this was some mental affection, some hallucination born of physical pain.

Then he began to talk in a low voice, very rapidly, with his head bent forward like a hunted animal's. I am not going to set down what he told me in his own words, for they were incoherent often, and there was much repetition. But I am going to write the gist of the odd story which took my sleep away on that autumn night, with such explanations and additions as I think needful. The fire died down, the wind arose, the hour grew late, and still he went on in his mumbling recitative. I forgot to smoke, forgot my comfort,—everything but the odd figure of my friend and his inconceivable romance. And the night before I had been in cheerful Glenaicill!

. . . .

He had returned to the House of More, he said, in the latter part of May, and shortly after he fell ill. It was a trifling sickness—influenza or something—but he had never quite recovered. The rainy weather of June depressed him, and the extreme heat of July made him listless and weary. A kind of insistent sleepiness hung over him, and he suffered much from nightmare. Towards the end of July his former health returned; but he was haunted with a curious oppression. He seemed to himself to have lost the art of being alone. There was a perpetual sound in his left ear, a kind of moving and rustling at his left side, which never left him by night or day. In addition he had become the prey of nerves and an insensate dread of the unknown.

Ladlaw, as I have explained, was a commonplace man, with fair talents, a mediocre culture, honest instincts, and the beliefs and incredulities of his class. On abstract grounds I should have declared him an unlikely man to be the victim of a hallucination. He had a kind of dull, bourgeois rationalism, which used to find reasons for all things in heaven and earth. At first he controlled his dread with proverbs. He told himself it was the sequel of his illness, or the light-headedness of summer heat on the moors. But it soon outgrew his comfort. It became a living second presence, an *alter ego* which dogged his footsteps. He became acutely afraid of it. He dared not be alone for a moment, and clung to Sybil's company despairingly. She went off for a week's visit in the beginning of August, and he endured for seven days the tortures of the lost. His malady advanced upon him with swift steps. The presence became more real daily. In the early dawning, in the twilight, and in the first hours of the morning it seemed at times to take a visible bodily form. A kind of amorphous featureless shadow would run from his side into the darkness, and he would sit palsied with terror. Sometimes in lonely places his footsteps sounded double, and something would brush elbows with him. Human society alone exorcised it. With Sybil at his side he was happy; but as soon as she left him the thing came slinking back from the unknown to watch by him. Company might have saved him, but joined to his affliction was a crazy dread of his fellows. He would not leave his moorland home, but must bear his burden alone among the wild streams and mosses of that dismal place.

The Twelfth came, and he shot wretchedly, for his nerve had gone to pieces. He stood exhaustion badly, and became a dweller about the doors. But with this bodily inertness came an extraordinary intellectual revival. He read widely in a blundering way, and he speculated unceasingly. It was characteristic of the man that, as soon as he left the paths of the prosaic, he should seek his supernatural in a very concrete form. He assumed that he was haunted by the Devil—the visible, personal Devil in whom our fathers believed. He waited hourly for the shape at his side to speak, but no words came. The Accuser of the Brethren in all but tangible form was his ever-present companion. He felt, he declared, the spirit of old evil entering subtly into his blood. He sold his soul many times over, and yet there was no possibility of resistance. It was a Visitation more undeserved than Job's, and a thousandfold more awful.

For a week or more he was tortured with a kind of religious mania. When a man of a healthy, secular mind finds himself adrift on the terrible ocean of religious troubles, he is peculiarly helpless, for he has not the most rudimentary knowledge of the winds and tides. It was useless to call up his old carelessness; he had suddenly dropped into a new world where old proverbs did not apply. And all the while, mind you, there was the shrieking terror of it—an intellect all alive to the torture and the most unceasing physical fear. For a little he was on the near edge of idiocy.

Then by accident it took a new form. While sitting with Sybil one day in the library, he began listlessly to turn over the leaves of an old book. He read a few pages, and found the hint of a story like his own. It was some French life of Justinian, one of the unscholarly productions of last century, made up of stories from Procopius and tags of Roman law.

Here was his own case written down in black and white; and the man had been a king of kings! This was a new comfort, and for a little—strange though it may seem—he took a sort of pride in his affliction. He worshipped the great emperor and read every scrap he could find on him, not excepting the Pandects and the Digest. He sent for the bust in the dining-room, paying a fabulous price. Then he settled himself to study his imperial prototype, and the study became an idolatry. As I have said, Ladlaw was a man of ordinary talents and certainly of meagre imaginative power. And yet from the lies of the 'Secret History' and the crudities of German legalists he had constructed a marvellous portrait of a man. Sitting there in the half-lit room, he drew the picture,—the quiet, cold king with his inheritance of Dacian mysticism, holding the great world in fee, giving it law and religion, fighting its wars, building its churches, and yet all the while intent upon his own private work of making his peace with his soul. The churchman and warrior whom all the world worshipped, and yet one going through life with his lip quivering, the Watcher by the Threshold ever at his left side. Sometimes at night in the great Brazen Palace, warders heard the emperor walking in the dark corridors, alone and yet not alone; for once, when a servant entered with a lamp, he saw his master with a face as of another world, and something beside him which had no face or shape, but which he knew to be that hoary Evil which is older than the stars. Crazy nonsense! I had to rub my eyes to assure myself that I was not sleeping. No! There was my friend with his suffering face, and it was the library of More.

And then he spoke of Theodora—actress, harlot, *devoté*, empress. For him the lady was but another part of the uttermost horror, a form of the shapeless thing at his side. I felt myself falling under the fascination. I have no nerves and little imagination, but in a flash I seemed to realise something of that awful featureless face, crouching ever at a man's hand, till darkness and loneliness comes and it rises to its mastery. I shivered as I looked at the man in the chair before me. Those dull eyes of his were looking upon things I could not see, and I saw their terror. I realised that it was grim earnest for him. Nonsense or no, some devilish fancy had usurped the place of sanity, and he was being slowly broken upon the wheel. And then, when his left hand twitched, I almost cried out. I had thought it comic before; now it seemed the last proof of tragedy.

He stopped, and I got up with loose knees and went to the window. Better the black night than the intangible horror within. I flung up the sash and looked out across the moor. There was no light, nothing but an inky darkness and the uncanny rustle of elder-bushes. The sound chilled me, and I closed the window.

"The land is the old Manann," Ladlaw was saying. "We are beyond the pale here. Do you hear the wind?"

I forced myself back into sanity and looked at my watch. It was nearly one o'clock.

"What ghastly idiots we are!" I said. "I am off to bed."

Ladlaw looked at me helplessly. "For God's sake don't leave me alone!" he moaned. "Get Sybil."

We went together back to the hall, while he kept the same feverish grip on my arm. Someone was sleeping in a chair by the hall-fire, and to my distress I recognised my hostess. The poor child must have been sadly wearied. She came forward with her anxious face.

"I'm afraid Bob has kept you very late, Henry," she said. "I hope you will sleep well. Breakfast at nine, you know." And then I left them.

Over my bed there was a little picture, a reproduction of some Italian work of Christ and the Demoniac. Some impulse made me hold my candle up to it. The madman's face was torn with passion and suffering, and his eye had the pained furtive look which I had come to know. And by his left side there was a dim shape crouching.

I got into bed hastily, but not to sleep. I felt that my reason must be going. I had been pitchforked from our clear and cheerful modern life into the mists of old superstition. Old tragic stories of my Calvinist upbringing returned to haunt me. The man dwelt in by a devil was no new fancy; but I believed that Science had docketed and analysed and explained the Devil out of the world. I remembered my dabblings in the occult before I settled down to law—the story of Donisarius the monk of Padua, the unholy legend of the Face of Proserpina, the tales of *succubi* and *incubi*, the Leannain Sith and the Hidden Presence. But here was something stranger still. I had stumbled upon that very possession which fifteen hundred years ago had made the monks of New Rome tremble and cross themselves. Some devilish occult force, lingering through the ages, had come to life after a long sleep. God knows what earthly connection there was between the splendid Emperor of the World and my prosaic friend, or between the glittering shores of the Bosphorus and this moorland parish! But the land was the old Manann! The spirit may have lingered in the earth and air, a deadly legacy from Pict and Roman. I had felt the uncanniness of the place; I had augured ill of it from the first. And then in sheer disgust I rose and splashed my face with cold water.

I lay down again, laughing miserably at my credulity. That I, the sober and rational, should believe in this crazy fable, was too palpably absurd. I would steel my mind resolutely against such harebrained theories. It was a mere bodily ailment,—liver out of order, weak heart, bad circulation, or something of that sort. At the worst it might be some affection of the brain to be treated by a specialist. I vowed to myself that next morning the best doctor in Edinburgh should be brought to More.

The worst of it was that my duty compelled me to stand

my ground. I foresaw the few remaining weeks of my holiday blighted. I should be tied to this moorland prison, a sort of keeper and nurse in one, tormented by silly fancies. It was a charming prospect, and the thought of Glenaicill and the woodcock made me bitter against Ladlaw. But there was no way out of it. I might do Ladlaw good, and I could not have Sybil worn to death by his vagaries.

My ill-nature comforted me, and I forgot the horror of the thing in its vexation. After that, I think I fell asleep and dozed uneasily till morning. When I awoke I was in a better frame of mind. The early sun had worked wonders with the moorland. The low hills stood out fresh-coloured and clear against the pale October sky, the elders sparkled with frost, the raw film of morn was rising from the little loch in tiny clouds. It was a cold rousing day, and I dressed in good spirits and went down to breakfast.

I found Ladlaw looking ruddy and well, very different from the broken man I remembered of the night before. We were alone, for Sybil was breakfasting in bed. I remarked on his ravenous appetite, and he smiled cheerily. He made two jokes during the meal, he laughed often, and I began to forget the events of the previous day. It seemed to me that I might still flee from More with a clear conscience. He had forgotten about his illness. When I touched distantly upon the matter he showed a blank face.

It might be that the affection had passed: on the other hand, it might return to him at the darkening—I had no means to decide. His manner was still a trifle *distrait* and peculiar, and I did not like the dulness in his eye. At any rate, I should spend the day in his company, and the evening would decide the question.

I proposed shooting, which he promptly vetoed. He was no good at walking, he said, and the birds were wild. This seriously limited the possible occupations. Fishing there was none, and hill-climbing was out of the question. He proposed a game at billiards, and I pointed to the glory of the morning. It would have been sacrilege to waste such sunshine in knocking balls about. Finally we agreed to drive somewhere and have lunch, and he ordered the dogcart.

In spite of all forebodings I enjoyed the day. We drove in the opposite direction from the woodland parts, right away across the moor to the coal-country beyond. We lunched at the little mining town of Borrowmuir, in a small and noisy public-house. The roads made bad going, the country was far from pretty, and yet the drive did not bore me. Ladlaw talked incessantly, talked as I had never heard man talk before. There was something indescribable in all he said,—a different point of view, a lost groove of thought, a kind of innocence and archaic shrewdness in one. I can only give you a hint of it by saying that it was like the mind of an early ancestor placed suddenly among modern surroundings. It was wise with a remote wisdom, and silly (now and then) with a quite antique and distant silliness.

I will give you instances of both. He provided me with a theory of certain early fortifications, which must be true, which commends itself to the mind with overwhelming conviction, and yet which is so out of the way of common speculation that no man could have guessed it. I do not propose to set down the details, for I am working at it on my own account. Again, he told me the story of an old marriage custom, which till recently survived in this district,—told it with full circumstantial detail and constant allusions to other customs which he could not possibly have known of. Now for the other side. He explained why well-water is in winter warmer than a running stream, and this was his explanation. At the Antipodes our winter is summer; consequently the water of a well which comes through from the other side of the earth must be warm in winter and cold in summer, since in our summer it is winter there. You perceive what this is. It is no mere silliness, but a genuine effort of an early mind which had just grasped the fact of the Antipodes, to use it in explanation.

Gradually I was forced to the belief that it was not Ladlaw who was talking to me, but something speaking through him, something at once wiser and simpler. My old fear of the Devil began to depart. This spirit, this exhalation, whatever it was, was ingenuous in its way, at least in its daylight aspect. For a moment I had an idea that it was a real reflex of Byzantine thought, and that by cross-examining I might make marvellous discoveries. The ardour of the scholar began to rise in me, and I asked a question about that much-debated point, the legal status of the *apocrisiarii*. To my vexation he gave no response. Clearly the intelligence of this familiar had its limits.

It was about three in the afternoon, and we had gone half of our homeward journey, when signs of the old terror began to appear. I was driving, and Ladlaw sat on my left. I noticed him growing nervous and silent, shivering at the flick of the whip, and turning half-way round towards me. Then he asked me to change places, and I had the unpleasant work of driving from the wrong side. After that I do not think he spoke once till we arrived at More, but sat huddled together with the driving-rug almost up to his chin—an eccentric figure of a man.

I foresaw another such night as the last, and I confess my heart sank. I had no stomach for more mysteries, and somehow with the approach of twilight the confidence of the day departed. The thing appeared in darker colours, and I could have found it in my mind to turn coward. Sybil alone deterred me. I could not bear to think of her alone with this demented being. I remembered her shy timidity, her innocence. It was monstrous that the poor thing should be called on thus to fight alone with phantoms. So I braced myself for another evening.

When we came to the House it was almost sunset. Ladlaw got out very carefully on the right side, and for a second stood by the horse. The sun was making our shadows long, and as I stood beyond him, it seemed for a moment that his shadow was double. It may have been mere fancy, for I had not time to look twice. He was standing, as I have said, with his left side next the horse. Suddenly the harmless elderly cob fell into a very panic of fright, reared upright, and all but succeeded in killing its master. I was in time to pluck Ladlaw from under its feet, but the beast had become perfectly unmanageable, and we left a groom struggling to quiet it.

In the hall the butler gave me a telegram. It was from my clerk, summoning me back at once to an important consultation.

CHAPTER II.

THE MINISTER INTERVENES.

HERE was a prompt removal of my scruples! There could be no question of my remaining, for the case was one of the first importance, which I had feared might break up my holiday. The consultation fell in vacation-time to meet the convenience of certain people who were going abroad, and there was the most instant demand for my presence. I must go, and at once; and, as I hunted in the time-table, I found that in five hours' time a night-train for the South would pass Borrowmuir, which might be stopped by special wire. This would give me time for dinner and a comfortable departure.

But I had no pleasure in my freedom, for I was in despair about Sybil. I must return to More—that was clear; and I must find someone to look after Ladlaw. I found my cousin in the drawing-room alone and told her my plans.

She was very pale and fragile, and she seemed to shiver as the prospect of solitude returned to her. I spoke with all the carelessness I could muster. "I am coming back," I said. "Don't think you have got rid of me so easily. It is most unpleasant to have to travel eight hundred miles in thirty-six hours, but there is no help for it. I ought to be back again by Friday morning. And you know Bob is much better. He was quite like his old self driving to-day."

My words comforted the poor child, and I went away with the novel feeling of a good conscience. Frankly, I hate the sordid and unpleasant. I am honestly a sun-worshipper; I have small taste for arduous duty, and the quixotic is my abhorrence. My professional success is an accident, for Lord knows I had no impulse to contend and little ambition. But somewhere or other I have the rudiments of an austere conscience. It gives me no peace, and as I love a quiet life, I do its bidding with a grumble. Now I grumbled fiercely in spirit, but outwardly I was a model of virtuous cheerfulness.

But to find somebody to keep Ladlaw company—there was the rub. I racked my brains to think of a substitute. It must be a man of some education and not a mere servant, and it must be somebody in the parish of More; the conjunction seemed for the moment impossible. Then a brilliant idea struck me. There was the minister of Morebrig, the ugly village by the roadside. I remembered him on previous visits. He was a burly young man, with a high complexion and a drooping blonde moustache, who smoked cheap cigarettes incessantly, and spat. He had been what they call a "brilliant student," and he was reported to be something of an orator, eagerly sought after by city congregations, but at present hiding his light under the bushel of Morebrig to allow him time to prepare some great theological work. Ladlaw had liked him in a half-amused and tolerant way, and he used to come sometimes to dine. His name was Bruce Oliphant, and he inhabited a dark manse at the outskirts of the village.

I had an hour before dinner, and I set out for Mr Oliphant's dwelling. I remember the curious dull village street, without colour or life, drab women looking out of dingy doorways, and a solitary child playing in the red mud. The manse stood at the back of the usual elder thicket, a little place with small windows and a weather-stained front door. A gaunt old servant ushered me into Mr Oliphant's study, where I found that young man smoking and reading a weekly paper. It was a room well stocked with books in the popular religious vein, and the Poets in gilt editions adorned his shelves. Mr Oliphant greeted me with the nervous ease of one who would fain cultivate a good manner. The first sight of him sent my hopes down. He had a large calf-like face, mildly arrogant eyes, and a chin which fell sharply away beneath the eaves of his moustache. This was not one to do Ladlaw much good; indeed I questioned if I could ever make him understand, for the man before me had an impenetrable air of omniscience.

"I have come to ask you a great favour on behalf of the Ladlaws," said I. "You are the only other gentleman in the parish of More, and it is your duty to help your neighbours."

He bowed, with pleased eyes. "Anything," he said, "I'll be very glad."

"I am staying there just now, you know, and as it happens I must go back to town by the night-train. I'll only be gone a day, but you know that Ladlaw is a melancholy beggar and gets low-spirited. Now I want you to go up and stay at the House for a couple of nights while I am away."

It was an odd request, and he stared at me. "Why, what's wrong with Mr Ladlaw?" he asked. "I should never have called him melancholy. Now, his lady is different. She always looks a little pale. Did she send you to ask me?" Mr Oliphant was a stickler for the usages of polite society.

I sat down in a chair and took one of his cigarettes. "Now, look here, Oliphant," I said. "You are a man of education and common-sense, and I am going to do you the honour to tell you a story which I would not tell to a stupid man. A stupid man would laugh at me. I hope you will see the gravity of the thing."

I told him briefly the points in Ladlaw's case. His eyes

grew very round as I went on, and when I finished he laughed nervously. He was clearly impressed; but he was too ignorant and unimaginative to understand fully, and he had his credit as a representative of modern thought to support. "Oh, come now! You don't mean all that; I never heard the like of it. You can't expect me as a Christian man to believe in a Pagan spirit. I might as well believe in ghosts at once. What has the familiar of a heathen emperor to do with this parish?"

"Justinian was a Christian," I said.

He looked puzzled. "It's all preposterous. Meaning no disrespect to you, I must decline to believe it. My profession compels me to discourage such nonsense."

"So does mine," I said wearily. "Good Lord! man, do you think I came here to tell you a fairy tale? It's the most terrible earnest. Now I want you to give me an answer, for I have very little time."

He was still incredulous and inclined to argue. "Do you know if Mr Ladlaw has been—eh—a strictly temperate man?" he asked.

With this my patience departed. I got up to go, with rude thoughts on the stupidity of the clergy. But Mr Oliphant was far from a refusal. He had no objection to exchange the barren comfort of the manse for the comparative luxury of the House, and he had no distrust of his power to enliven. As he accompanied me to the door he explained his position. "You see, if they really want me I will come. Tell Mrs Ladlaw that I shall be delighted. Mrs Ladlaw is a lady for whom I have a great respect."

"So have I," I said crossly. "Very well. A trap shall be sent for you after dinner. Good evening, Mr Oliphant. It is a pleasure to have met you."

When I reached the House, I told Sybil of my arrangement. For the first time since my arrival she smiled. "It's very kind of him, but I am afraid he won't do much good. Bob will frighten him away."

"I fancy he won't. The man is strong in his self-confidence and remarkably dense. He'll probably exasperate Bob into sanity. In any case I'll be back by Friday morning."

As I drove away the trap arrived at the door, bringing Mr Oliphant and his portmanteau.

. . . .

The events of the next twenty-four hours, during which I was travelling in the Scotch express or transacting dreary business in my chambers, are known only from the narrative of the minister. He wrote it out some weeks after at my request, for I wished to have all the links in the tale. I propose to give the gist of it, as he wrote it, stripped of certain reflections on human life and an inscrutable Providence, with which he had garnished it.

Narrative of the Reverend Mr Oliphant.

I arrived at the House of More at a quarter-past eight on the Wednesday evening. The family had dined early, as Mr Grey was leaving for London, and when I arrived I was taken to the library, where I found Mr Ladlaw. I had not seen him for some time, and thought him looking pale and a little haggard. He seemed glad to see me, and made me sit down in a chair on his left and draw it up close to him. I wondered at his manner, for though we had always been on good terms he had never admitted me to any close intimacy. But now he was more than amiable. He made me ring for toddy, and though he refused to taste it himself, he pressed the beverage on me. Then he gave me a large cigar, at which I trembled, and finally he said that we should play at picquet. I declined resolutely, for it is part of my conscience to refuse to join in any card games ; but he made no trouble, and indeed in a moment seemed to have forgotten his proposition.

The next thing he did startled my composure. For he

asked abruptly, "Do you believe in a living personal Devil, Oliphant?"

I was taken aback, but answered that to the best of my light I did not.

"And why not?" he asked sharply.

I explained that it was an old, false, anthropomorphic fiction, and that the modern belief was infinitely more impressive. I quoted the words of Dr Rintoul, one of our Church leaders. I am sorry to say that Mr Ladlaw's words were, "Dr Rintoul be d—d!"

"Who the deuce are you to change the belief of centuries?" he cried. "Our forefathers believed in him. They saw him at evening slinking about the folds and peat-stacks, or wrapped up in a black gown standing in the pulpits of the Kirk. Are we wiser men than they?"

I answered that culture had undoubtedly advanced in our day.

Mr Ladlaw replied with blasphemous words on modern culture. I had imagined him to be a gentleman of considerable refinement, and I knew he had taken a good degree at college. Consequently, I was disagreeably surprised at his new manner.

"You are nothing better than an ignorant parson,"—these were his words,—"and you haven't even the merits of your stupid profession. The old Scots ministers were Calvinists to the backbone, and they were strong men—strong men, do you hear?—and they left their mark upon the nation. But your new tea-meeting kind of parson, who has nothing but a smattering of bad German to commend him, is a nuisance to God and man. And they don't believe in the Devil! Well, he'll get them safe enough some day."

I implored him to remember my cloth, and curb his bad language.

"I say the Devil will get you all safe enough some day," he repeated.

I rose to retire in as dignified a manner as possible, but he was before me and closed the door. I began to be genuinely frightened.

"For God's sake, don't go!" he cried. "Don't leave me alone. Do sit down, Oliphant, like a good chap, and I promise to hold my tongue. You don't know how horrible it is to be left alone."

I sat down again, though my composure was shaken. I remembered Mr Grey's words about the strange sickness.

Then Mr Ladlaw fell into an extraordinary moodiness. He sat huddled up in his chair, his face turned away from me, and for some time neither of us spoke a word. I thought that I had seriously offended him, and prepared to apologise, so I touched his left shoulder to attract his attention. Instantly he jumped to his feet, screaming, and turned on me a face of utter terror. I could do nothing but stare at him, and in a second he quieted down and returned to his seat.

Then he became partially sane, and murmured a sort of excuse. I thought that I would discover what truth lay in Mr Grey's singular hypothesis. I did not ask him bluntly, as an ordinary man would have done, what was his malady, but tactfully, as I thought then, I led the conversation to demoniacal possession in the olden time, and quoted Pellinger's theory on the Scriptural cases. He answered with extraordinary vehemence, showing a childish credulity I little expected from an educated man.

"I see that you hold to the old interpretation," I said pleasantly. "Nowadays, we tend to find the solution in natural causes."

"Heavens, man!" he cried. "What do you mean by natural? You haven't the most rudimentary knowledge of nature. Listen to me, and I will tell you something."

And with this he began a long rambling account of something which I could not understand. He talked much about a name which sounded like Canaan, and then he wandered to another subject and talked about Proserpina, whom I remembered from Mr Matthew Arnold's poem. I would have thought him trying to ridicule me, if I had not seen his face, which was white and drawn with pain; and, again, I would have thought him drunk, but for his well-known temperate habits. By-and-by even my nerves, which are very strong, began to suffer. I understood fragments of his talk, and the understanding did not reassure me. It was poisonous nonsense, but it had a terrible air of realism. He had a queer habit of catching at his heart like a man with the heart disease, and his eyes were like a mad dog's I once saw, the pupil drawn to a pin-point with fear. I could not bear it, so I tried to break the spell. I offered, against my conscience, to play a card game, but his face showed that he did not understand me. I began to feel a sort of languor of terror. I could hardly rise from my chair, and when at last I got up the whole room seemed haunted. I rushed to the bell and rang it violently, and then tried to open the door. But he was before me again, and gripped my arm so fiercely that I cried out between the pain and my dread of him.

"Come back!" he cried hoarsely. "Don't leave me alone. For God's sake, Oliphant!"

Just then the man-servant opened the door, and found the two of us standing like lunatics. I had the sense to save the situation, and I asked him to bring more coals for the fire. Then as soon as he turned to go, I stepped out of the open door before Mr Ladlaw could prevent me.

The hall seemed empty, but to my surprise I found Mrs Ladlaw sleeping in a chair by the fire. I did not like to waken her, but I was at my wits' end with fright. If I had known the way to the kitchen, I should have sought the servants' company. I ran down a passage, but it seemed to end in a blind wall, and in a great fear I turned and ran upstairs. But the upper lobbies seemed to be unlit, and I was turning back when I heard Ladlaw's voice behind me. It was muffled and queer, and the sound drove me into the darkness. When

I turned a corner, to my relief I saw a lamp burning on a table and recognised my bedroom door. Here was sanctuary at last, and I ran in and shut it behind me.

My nerves were so shaken by the evening's performances that I found it impossible to get to sleep. I sat up the better part of the night by the fire, and smoked several cigarettes, which in ordinary circumstances I should never have dared to do in a strange bedroom. About four o'clock, I think, I dozed off in my chair, and awoke about nine, very stiff and cold, to find Ladlaw laughing at me in the doorway.

I was at first so confused that I did not remember what had scared me the night before. Then, as it came back to me, I was amazed at my host's appearance. He looked fresh and well, and in excellent spirits. He laughed immoderately when he found I had not gone to bed.

"You do look cheap," he said. "Breakfast's in half an hour. You will feel better when you have had a tub."

I bathed reluctantly, feeling ill and bitterly cold; but I was comforted by a good breakfast. Then I had an opportunity of talking to Mrs Ladlaw. As I remembered her, she had been full of gaiety, and even, I thought, a little frivolous; but now she was so pale and silent that I pitied her sincerely. I began to feel an intense dislike of her husband, partly for the fright he had given me the night before, and partly for the effect his silliness seemed to be having on his wife. The day was a fine one, but after breakfast he showed no intention of going out. I expected to be asked to shoot, a sport which I sometimes try; but he never spoke of it, and insisted on my coming to the billiard-room. As we were leaving the table Mrs Ladlaw touched my arm, and asked me in a low tone if I would promise to stay all day with her husband. "I want to go down to Morefoot," she said, "and you know he cannot be left alone." I promised willingly, for in the daylight Mr Ladlaw had no terrors for me. I thought that Mrs Ladlaw looked relieved. Poor thing! she badly needed a respite.

We hung aimlessly about the place till lunch, playing a few games of billiards, and inthe intervals looking at stables and harness-rooms and the now barren gardens. At lunch Mrs Ladlaw appeared, but immediately after I heard wheels on the gravel and knew that she had gone to Morefoot. Then I began to feel nervous again. I was the only responsible person left in the place, and Mr Ladlaw might at any moment relapse into craziness. I watched his moods anxiously, and talked all the nonsense I knew to keep him in good humour. I told him stories, I talked wildly of sport, I made ridiculous jokes at which I felt myself blushing. At first he seemed amused, but soon I felt that my words were falling on deaf ears. He himself began to talk, violently, incessantly, and, I may say, brilliantly. If my memory had been better and my balance less upset, I might have made my reputation, though it would have been a reputation, perhaps, that a minister of the Gospel might well look askance at. I could have written a terrible romance from that man's babbling. Nay, I could have done more: I could have composed a new philosophy which would have cast Nietzsche in the shade for ever. I do not wish to exaggerate, but I have never been so impressed with a sense of a crazy intellectual acumen. This Mr Ladlaw, whom I had known as a good landlord and a respectable country gentleman, now appeared as a kind of horrible genius, a brilliant and malignant satyr. I was shocked and confounded, and at the same time filled with admiration. I remember that we passed through the dining-room, where there was a great marble bust of a Roman emperor, an old discoloured thing, but wonderful in its way. Mr Ladlaw stopped before it and pointed out its merits. The thing seemed simple enough, and yet after the description I fled from it as if it had been a devil. He followed me, still talking, and we found ourselves in the library.

I remember that I suggested tea, but he scarcely heeded me. The darkness was falling, Mrs Ladlaw had not returned, and I felt horribly uncomfortable. I tried to draw him away from the room which I feared, but he made no sign of understanding. I perceived that the malady of the last night was returning. I hated that library, with its low fire, its ghastly white books, and its dreary outlook. I picked up one volume, and it was lettered on the back ' Sancti Adelberti Certamina.' I dropped it, only to feel Mr Ladlaw clutching my right arm and dragging me to one of those horrible arm-chairs.

" The night is coming on, the old Nox Atra that the monks dreaded. Promise me that you won't go away."

I promised feebly, and prayed for Mrs Ladlaw's return. I suggested that the lamps should be lit. He rose and tried to light the hanging central one, and I noticed how his hands trembled. His awkwardness upset the thing, and it fell with a crash on the floor. He jumped back with a curious scream like an animal.

I was so miserably scared that I had not the heart to do the work for him, so we sat on in the darkness. Any sound from the out-of-doors would have comforted me, but the whole world was as silent as death. I felt that a little more would drive me mad, and the thought roused me to make a final effort after safety. In spite of all my promises I must get away. A man's first duty was to himself, and the hour had come for me. I thought with longing of my little bare manse and my solemn housekeeper. And yet how was I to escape, for this man was the stronger, and he would never let me go.

I begged him to come into the hall, but he refused. Then I became very cunning. I suggested that we should go to the door and receive Mrs Ladlaw. He did not know that she had gone, and the news made him so nervous that he accepted my proposal. He caught my arm as before, and, leaning heavily upon me, went into the hall. There was no one about, and the fire had died down; but at the far end there was a pale glimmer from the glass door. We opened it and stood on the top step, looking over the dark lawns. Now was the time for an effort for freedom. If I could only get rid of his hand I might escape across the fields. I believed him to be too weak on his legs to follow me, and in any case I was a respectable runner. Out-of-doors he seemed less formidable: it was only in that haunted room that I shuddered.

I took the only way of escape which presented itself. There was a flowering-shrub in a pot on the top of the parapet. I caught this with my elbow and knocked it over, so that it broke with a clatter on the stone. As I expected, he screamed and jumped aside, letting go my arm for one instant. The next I was down the steps and running hard across the lawns to the park beyond.

For a little I heard him stumbling after me, breathing heavily and with little short cries. I ran with the speed of fear, for till I was within my own doors I could feel no security. Once I turned, and there he was, a field behind me, running with his head down like a blind dog. I skirted the village, broke through the little fir plantation, and came out on the highway. I saw the light from Jean's little window, and it was like a beacon of hope. In a few minutes I was at the door, and my servant stared as I rushed in, without hat or overcoat, and wet with perspiration. I insisted on barring the doors, and bolting and shuttering every window. Then I had the unusual luxury of a fire in my bedroom, and there I supped, and sat till I fell asleep.

End of Mr Oliphant's Statement.

CHAPTER III.

EVENTS ON THE UPLANDS.

I RETURNED from town by the night express, which landed me at Borrowmuir about seven on the Friday morning. To my surprise there was no dogcart to meet me, as had been arranged, and I was compelled to hire from the inn. The omission filled me with forebodings. Things must have gone badly at More in my absence, or the careful Sybil would never have forgotten. I grudged the time occupied in that weary drive. The horse seemed intolerably slow, the roads unaccountably steep. It was a sharp morning, with haze on the fields and promise of bright sunshine at mid-day; but, tired as I was with my two days' journey, I was in the humour to see little good in my case. I was thankful when we drew up at the house-door, and, cold and stiff, I hobbled up the steps.

The door was open, and I entered. The hall was empty, there was no sign of any servant, and all the doors were wide to the wall. I tried one room after another without success. Then I made my voice heard in that place. I shouted for Ladlaw, and then I shouted for Sybil. There came no answer, and in despair I rushed to the kitchen wing. There I found a cluster of frightened maids, and by dint of much questioning learned the truth.

Ladlaw, it seemed, had disappeared from the house about a quarter-past six on the previous night. The minister had decamped and found sanctuary in the manse; but there was no trace of the other. Sybil had gone to Morefoot in the afternoon, and, returning about half-past six, found her husband gone. She had been distracted with anxiety, had gone to the manse, where she found Mr Oliphant in a state of nervous collapse and quite unable to make any coherent statement, and had then roused some of the neighbouring shepherds and organised a search-party. They had searched all night, but so far no word had come of the result. Meanwhile, Sybil, utterly wearied and a little hysterical, was in bed, sleeping, for her anxiety of the past week had culminated in a sort of deep languor, which in the circumstances was the best thing that could have happened. There was no question of wakening her; but, as I snatched a hurried breakfast, it seemed to me that I must at once follow the search. They were to meet in the morning at a farm called Mossrigging, beneath a hill of the same name, and if I went there I might get word of them. In the meantime I must interview Mr Oliphant.

I found him in bed, unshaven, and very hollow about the eyes. He told me a lame story, and indeed his fright was so palpable that I had not the heart to blame him. But I insisted that he should get up and come with me, for every man would be needed to search those mossy uplands. I was dog-tired, sleepy, and irritable, and yet I must go: why should not this man, who had had his night's rest?

He made some feeble objection; but he had a conscience of his own and rose obediently. We set out to the nearest part of the moor, he in his clergyman's garb, and I in a dark suit and a bowler; and I remember thinking how oddly unsuited was our dress for this stalking-game. I was wretchedly anxious, for I liked Ladlaw, and God alone knew where he might have got to in the night. There were deep bogs and ugly old pit-shafts on the moor, and there were ravines with sheer red sides. At any moment we might find tragedy, and I dreaded the report of the searchers at Mossrigging. When we left the road, we followed an old cart-track up a shallow glen, where stood some curious old stone chimneys, which had been built by a speculator who hoped to make a fortune from peat. The sun was beginning to break through the haze, and miles of low moorland were disclosed to left and right. But the hills in front were still cloudy, and we were close on the cottage before we knew its whereabouts. It stood high in a crinkle of hill, with a wide prospect north and east to the sea, and as I turned I saw Morebrig smoking clear in the autumn light, and the chimneys of the House above the fir-trees. Out on the waters three ships were sailing like toy-boats, a reminder of the bustling modern life beyond this antique place of horrors.

The house was full of men, devouring their morning porridge. They were shepherds of the neighbourhood, and two boys from the village, as well as John Ker, the head-keeper from More. One man, Robert Tod by name, answered my unspoken question. "We havena gotten him, but we've gotten his whereabouts. We got a glisk o' him about six this mornin' on the backside o' the Lowe Moss. I kent him fine by the way he ran. Lord, but he was souple! Nane o' us could come within a hunner yairds o' him. We'll hae to wyse him gently, sir, and some o' us'll hae to tak a lang cast round the hill."

I had no ambition to "tak a lang cast round the hill"; but these men had been abroad all night, and I and the minister must undertake the duty. Tod agreed to come with us, and the shaggy silent men of the party expounded the plan of campaign. The Lowe Moss was impassable on one side, on another bounded by a steep hill-shoulder, and on the others by two narrow glens. They would watch the glens; we three should make a circuit and come back over the hill, driving the fugitive before us. Once enclosed between the moss and our three parties, he should be an easy capture. I implored them to go to work gently, for I feared that he might be driven into the bog. They shook their heads and laughed: it was all a kind of crazy sport to them, and their one idea was to carry out their orders.

I confess I was desperately tired before we had forded the upper waters of the More, crossed the Redscaurhead, and looked over the green pasture-lands to the south. It was a most curious sight; for whereas one side of the range was rough and mossy and hideous with red scaurs, the other was a gentle slope with sweet hill-grass and bright shallow waters. It was a new country where the old curse could not reign, and an idea took possession of me that if once Ladlaw came into the place he would be healed of his malady. The air seemed clearer, the sky softer, the whole world simple and clean. We fetched a circuit down one of the little streams till we came to the back of the hill which on its face is called Mossrigging. I was abominably tired, but in better spirits. As for the minister, he groaned occasionally, but never spoke a word.

At the foot we separated to the distance of half a mile, and began the ascent. So far there was no sign of our man. Tod was on the far east, I was in the centre, and Mr Oliphant took the west. I cannot profess to remember exactly all the incidents of that climb. I was too stupid with sleep and exertion, and the little distant figures of my companions danced in a kind of haze. The ascent was simple,—short grass, varied by short heather, with at wide intervals a patch of shingle. The shepherd walked with an easy swing, the minister stumbled and groaned, while I, in sheer bravado and irritation at my weakness, kept up a kind of despairing trot. The Devil and Ladlaw combined might confront me, but I was too tired to care. Indeed, in a little I had forgotten all about the purpose of our quest.

Then, quite suddenly, almost at the summit, in a little hollow of the ridge, I saw our man. He was sitting on the ground, directly in the minister's line, and his head was sunk on his breast. I remember being taken with a horrid thought that he was dead, and quickened my trot to a run. Meanwhile the minister was approaching very near, but apparently quite unconscious of his presence. His eyes were in the ends of the earth, and he ambled along with no purpose in the world.

What happened rests mainly on my authority; but Robert Tod, shepherd in Nether Mossrigging, is ready to swear to the essentials. Mr Oliphant stumbled on into the hollow till he was within ten yards of the sitting figure. Ladlaw never moved; but the subtle influence which tells of human presence came suddenly upon the minister's senses, for he lifted his eyes and started. The man was still scared to death, and he naturally turned to run away, when something happened which I cannot well explain. Ladlaw was still sitting with his head on his breast, and yet it was clear to my mind that Ladlaw had somehow risen and was struggling with the minister. I could see the man's wrists strained and twisted as if in a death-grapple, and his white face reddening with exertion. He seemed to be held round the middle, for his feet tottered several times, and once he lurched to the left side, so that I thought he was thrown. And yet he was only battling with the air, for there was Ladlaw sitting quietly some yards from him.

And then suddenly the contest seemed to cease. Mr Oliphant ran straight past the sitting man and over the brow of the hill. Surprise had held Tod and myself motionless. Now the spell was broken, and from our several places we ran towards Ladlaw. I heard the shepherd's loud voice crying, "Look at Oliphant! Oliphant's no wise!" and I thought I heard a note of sardonic mirth. In any case, it was the minister he was after, for a moment later he disappeared down the farther slope.

Mr Oliphant might go where he pleased, but my business was with my friend. I caught Ladlaw by the shoulder and shook him fiercely. Then I pulled him to his feet, let him go, and he rolled over. The sight was so comic that I went into a fit of nervous laughter; but the shock seemed to have restored his wits, for he opened sleepy eyes and regarded me solemnly. I do not propose to analyse my reasons, but I was conscious that it was the old Ladlaw who was looking at me. I knew he was healed of his malady, but how I knew it I do not know. He stuck both fists into his eyes like a sleepy child. Then he yawned, and looked down ruefully at soaked, soiled, and ragged clothing. Then he looked reproachfully at me.

"What's up?" he asked. "Stop that hideous row and tell me what has happened. Have I had an accident?"

Then I spoke cunningly. "Nothing much. A little bit of a fall, but you'll be all right soon. Why, you look better already." And again I went into a fit of laughter.

He grew wholesomely cross. "Oh, don't be a confounded

jackass!" he cried. "I feel as if I hadn't slept for a week, and I'm hungry and thirsty."

He swallowed the contents of my flask, and wolfed my sandwiches in a disgusting way. Then he proposed that we should go home. "I'm tired, and I'm sick of shooting for the day. By-the-by, where's my gun?"

"Broken," I said, "broken in the fall. The keeper is going to look after it." And with the aid of my arm he began with feeble steps his homeward journey.

. . . .

The minister—this is the tale of Robert Tod and his colleagues—ran down the precipitous part of Mossrigging like a thing inspired. Tod, labouring heavily in his wake, declared that he went down the hillside like a loose stone, slipping, stumbling, yet never altogether losing his feet, and clearing dangers solely by the grace of God. As he went, said the men, he made clutches at the air, and his face was the face of one distraught. They ran together from their different places to intercept him on the edge of the bog, for at first they thought he was Ladlaw. When they saw their mistake they did not stop, for Tod was making frantic signals for pursuit. John Ker, the More keeper, was nearest, and he declared afterwards that he never approached a business so unwillingly. "I wad hae grippit a wild stot or a daft staig suner nor yon man," he said. But the business was too public for sheer cowardice. John assaulted him on the left flank while the other attacked in front, and John was bowled over like a ninepin. It was not the minister, he said, but something else, something with an arm two yards long, which flew out like a steam-hammer. But the others were more fortunate. One caught Mr Oliphant's right arm, another hung on to the flaps of his coat, while a third tripped him up gallantly, till the whole body of them rolled on the ground. Then ensued an indescribable fray. Tod got a black eye from some unknown source, and one of the boys lost several front teeth. Howls of rage filled the moorland air, and all the while, they declared, the minister was praying with an unction which was never heard in the kirk. "Lord, give me peace!" he cried. "Lord, take the thing away!" and then again, "Get thee behind me, Satan!"

The end came very suddenly, for the company rolled into the bog. The minister, being lowest, saved the others, but he floundered in the green slime up to his middle. The accident seemed to inspire sobriety. He ceased his prayers, his face lost its horror, and took on a common human fear. Then Tod and his friends laboured heroically to rescue him, and all the while, they declared, something was pommelling them and bruising them, and they showed for long black marks on their bodies. Slowly they raised Mr Oliphant from the slough, and on a bridge of coats he crept back to solid land. And then something happened which was the crowning marvel of the business. It was a still sharp day; but suddenly there came a wind, hot and harsh, and like nothing they had ever known. It stung them like nettles, played for a moment in their midst, and then in a kind of visible cloud passed away from them over the bog in the direction of the Red Loch. And with the wind went the Thing which had so long played havoc in the place; and the men were left with an unkempt figure, coated with slime and shivering with fright, but once more the sane and prosaic Mr Oliphant, the minister of the parish of More.

. . . .

We got Ladlaw and the minister back to the house with much trouble, for both were weak on their legs, and one was still in a pitiable fright. The two kept eyeing each other, one with a sort of disgusted amusement, the other with a wondering fear. The shepherds were mystified; but they were matter-of-fact beings, who, having fulfilled their orders, gave no more thought to the business. The wounded nursed their bruises and swore cheerfully, and the boy with the broken teeth whistled his complaints. A good dinner restored them to humour, and the last I saw was Ker and Tod going over the Odyssey of their adventures to a circle of critical spectators.

When Ladlaw and the minister had washed and fed, and sat smoking in the library, I went to talk to Sybil. I have often wondered how much she understood. At any rate she took my word that the trouble had passed, and in a fit of tears thanked me for my labours. Then she said she would go to her husband, and I led her to the library, where the two heroes were smoking the pipe of peace.

Ladlaw greeted her cheerily as if nothing had happened. "I feel a bit shaken," he said, "but I'll be all right after a night's rest. You needn't be nervous, Sib. By-the-bye, Harry, where's that gun?"

Then he wandered round the room, casting an unfriendly eye on his new acquisitions. "Look here! Somebody has been playing the fool in this place. I can't see a single Badminton, and where did this stuff come from?" And he tapped a row of books in old vellum. "I never remember the things before. St Adelbert! Who on earth was he? Why, anyone who came in suddenly and did not know me might think I was a minor poet. I wish you'd tell Harrison to clear all this truck away."

The minister sat by the fire and said nothing. The marvellous had intruded upon his easy life and spoiled the balance. I was sorry for the man as I thanked him in a low tone and asked how he felt.

The words came from between chattering teeth.

"I am getting b-better," he said, "but I have had a terrible sh-shock.—I am a Christian man and I have been tempted. I thought we lived in a progressive age, but now I know that we d-d-don't. And I am going to write to Dr Rintoul."

IV. THE OUTGOING OF THE TIDE.[1]

" Between the hours of twelve and one, even at the turning of the tide."

MEN come from distant parts to admire the tides of Solloway, which race in at flood and retreat at ebb with a greater speed than a horse can follow. But nowhere are there queerer waters than in our own parish of Caulds at the place called the Sker Bay, where between two horns of land a shallow estuary receives the stream of the Sker. I never daunder by its shores, and see the waters hurrying like messengers from the great deep, without solemn thoughts and a memory of Scripture words on the terror of the sea. The vast Atlantic may be fearful in its wrath, but with us it is no clean open rage, but the deceit of the creature, the unholy ways of quicksands when the waters are gone, and their stealthy return like a thief in the night-watches. But in the times of which I write there were more awful fears than any from the violence of nature. It was before the day of my ministry in Caulds, for then I was a bit callant in short clothes in my native parish of Lesmahagow; but the worthy Doctor Chrystal, who had charge of spiritual things, has told me often of the power of Satan and his emissaries in that lonely place. It was the day of warlocks and apparitions, now happily driven out by the zeal of the General Assembly. Witches pursued their wanchancy calling, bairns were spirited away, young lassies selled their souls to the evil one, and the

[1] From the unpublished Remains of the Reverend John Dennistoun, sometime minister of the Gospel in the parish of Caulds, and author of ' Satan's Artifices against the Elect.'

Accuser of the Brethren in the shape of a black tyke was seen about cottage-doors in the gloaming. Many and earnest were the prayers of good Doctor Chrystal, but the evil thing, in spite of his wrestling, grew and flourished in his midst. The parish stank of idolatry, abominable rites were practised in secret, and in all the bounds there was no one had a more evil name for this black traffic than one Alison Sempill, who bode at the Skerburnfoot.

The cottage stood nigh the burn in a little garden with lilyoaks and grosart-bushes lining the pathway. The Sker ran by in a linn among hollins, and the noise of its waters was ever about the place. The highroad on the other side was frequented by few, for a nearer-hand way to the west had been made through the Lowe Moss. Sometimes a herd from the hills would pass by with sheep, sometimes a tinkler or a wandering merchant, and once in a long while the laird of Heriotside on his grey horse riding to Gledsmuir. And they who passed would see Alison hirpling in her garden, speaking to herself like the ill wife she was, or sitting on a cutty-stool by the doorside with her eyes on other than mortal sights. Where she came from no man could tell. There were some said she was no woman, but a ghost haunting some mortal tenement. Others would threep she was gentrice, come of a persecuting family in the west, that had been ruined in the Revolution wars. She never seemed to want for siller; the house was as bright as a new preen, the yaird better delved than the manse garden; and there was routh of fowls and doos about the small steading, forbye a wheen sheep and milk-kye in the fields. No man ever saw Alison at any market in the countryside, and yet the Skerburnfoot was plenished yearly in all proper order. One man only worked on the place, a doited lad who had long been a charge to the parish, and who had not the sense to fear danger or the wit to understand it. Upon all other the sight of Alison, were it but for a moment, cast a cold grue, not to be remembered without terror. It seems she was not ordinarily ill-faured, as men use the word. She was maybe sixty years in age, small and trig, with her grey hair folded neatly under her mutch. But the sight of her eyes was not a thing to forget. John Dodds said they were the een of a deer with the devil ahint them, and indeed they would so appal an onlooker that a sudden unreasoning terror came into his heart, while his feet would impel him to flight. Once John, being overtaken in drink on the roadside by the cottage, and dreaming that he was burning in hell, woke, and saw the old wife hobbling towards him. Thereupon he fled soberly to the hills, and from that day became a quiet-living humble-minded Christian. She moved about the country like a wraith, gathering herbs in dark loanings, lingering in kirk-yairds, and casting a blight on innocent bairns. Once Robert Smillie found her in a ruinous kirk on the Lang Muir where of old the idolatrous rites of Rome were practised. It was a hot day, and in the quiet place the flies buzzed in crowds, and he noted that she sat clothed in them as with a garment, yet suffering no discomfort. Then he, having mind of Beelzebub, the god of flies, fled without a halt homewards; but, falling in the Coo's Loan, broke two ribs and a collar-bone, the whilk misfortune was much blessed to his soul. And there were darker tales in the countryside, of weans stolen, of lassies misguided, of innocent beasts cruelly tortured, and in one and all there came in the name of the wife of the Skerburnfoot. It was noted by them that kenned best that her cantrips were at their worst when the tides in the Sker Bay ebbed between the hours of twelve and one. At this season of the night the tides of mortality run lowest, and when the outgoing of these unco waters fell in with the setting of the current of life, then indeed was the hour for unholy revels. While honest men slept in their beds, the auld rudas carlines took their pleasure. That there is a delight in sin no man denies, but to most it is but a broken glint in the pauses of their conscience. But what must be the hellish joy of those lost beings who have forsworn God and trysted with the Prince of Darkness, it is not for a Christian to say. Certain it is that it must be great, though their master waits at the end of the road to claim the wizened things they call their souls. Serious men, notably Gidden Scott in the Back of the Hill and Simon Wauch in the Shieling of Chasehope, have seen Alison wandering on the wet sands, dancing to no earthly music, while the heavens, they said, were full of lights and sounds which betokened the presence of the prince of the powers of the air. It was a season of heart-searching for God's saints in Caulds, and the dispensation was blessed to not a few.

It will seem strange that in all this time the presbytery was idle, and no effort was made to rid the place of so fell an influence. But there was a reason, and the reason, as in most like cases, was a lassie. Forbye Alison there lived at the Skerburnfoot a young maid, Ailie Sempill, who by all accounts was as good and bonnie as the other was evil. She passed for a daughter of Alison's, whether born in wedlock or not I cannot tell; but there were some said she was no kin to the auld witch-wife, but some bairn spirited away from honest parents. She was young and blithe, with a face like an April morning and a voice in her that put the laverocks to shame. When she sang in the kirk folk have told me that they had a foretaste of the music of the New Jerusalem, and when she came in by the village of Caulds old men stottered to their doors to look at her. Moreover, from her earliest days the bairn had some glimmerings of grace. Though no minister would visit the Skerburnfoot, or if he went, departed quicker than he came, the girl Ailie attended regular at the catechising at the Mains of Sker. It may be that Alison thought she would be a better offering for the devil if she were given the chance of forswearing God, or it may be that she was so occupied in her own dark business that she had no care of the bairn. Meanwhile the lass grew up in the nurture and admonition of the Lord. I have heard Doctor Chrystal say that he never had a communicant more full of the things of the Spirit. From the day when she first declared her wish to come forward to the hour when she broke bread at the table, she walked like one in a dream. The lads of the parish might cast admiring eyes on her bright cheeks and yellow hair as she sat in her white gown in the kirk, but well they knew she was not for them. To be the bride of Christ was the thought that filled her heart; and when at the fencing of the tables Doctor Chrystal preached from Matthew nine and fifteen, "Can the children of the bride-chamber mourn, as long as the bridegroom is with them?" it was remarked by sundry that Ailie's face was liker the countenance of an angel than of a mortal lass.

It is with the day of her first communion that this narrative of mine begins. As she walked home after the morning table she communed in secret and her heart sang within her. She had mind of God's mercies in the past, how He had kept her feet from the snares of evil-doers which had been spread around her youth. She had been told unholy charms like the seven south streams and the nine rowan berries, and it was noted when she went first to the catechising that she prayed "Our Father which wert in heaven," the prayer which the ill wife Alison had taught her, meaning by it Lucifer who had been in heaven and had been cast out therefrom. But when she had come to years of discretion she had freely chosen the better part, and evil had ever been repelled from her soul like Gled water from the stones of Gled brig. Now she was in a rapture of holy content. The drucken bell—for the ungodly fashion lingered in Caulds—was ringing in her ears as she left the village, but to her it was but a kirk-bell and a goodly sound. As she went through the woods where the primroses and the whitethorn were blossoming, the place seemed as the land of Elam, wherein there were twelve wells and three-score and ten palm-trees. And then, as it might be, another thought came into her head, for it is ordained that frail mortality cannot long continue in holy joy. In the kirk she had been only the bride of Christ;

but as she came through the wood, with the birds lilting and the winds of the world blowing, she had mind of another lover. For this lass, though so cold to men, had not escaped the common fate. It seemed that the young Heriotside, riding by one day, stopped to speir something or other, and got a glisk of Ailie's face, which caught his fancy. He passed the road again many times, and then he would meet her in the gloaming or of a morning in the field as she went to fetch the kye. "Blue are the hills that are far away" is an owercome in the countryside, and while at first on his side it may have been but a young man's fancy, to her he was like the god Apollo descending from the skies. He was good to look on, brawly dressed, and with a tongue in his head that would have wiled the bird from the tree. Moreover, he was of gentle kin, and she was a poor lass biding in a cot-house with an ill-reputed mother. It seems that in time the young man, who had begun the affair with no good intentions, fell honestly in love, while she went singing about the doors as innocent as a bairn, thinking of him when her thoughts were not on higher things. So it came about that long ere Ailie reached home it was on young Heriotside that her mind dwelt, and it was the love of him that made her eyes glow and her cheeks redden.

Now it chanced that at that very hour her master had been with Alison, and the pair of them were preparing a deadly pit. Let no man say that the devil is not a cruel tyrant. He may give his folk some scrapings of unhallowed pleasure; but he will exact tithes, yea of anise and cummin, in return, and there is aye the reckoning to pay at the hinder end. It seems that now he was driving Alison hard. She had been remiss of late, fewer souls sent to hell, less zeal in quenching the Spirit, and above all the crowning offence that her bairn had communicated in Christ's kirk. She had waited overlong, and now it was like that Ailie would escape her toils. I have no skill of fancy to tell of that dark collogue, but the upshot was that Alison swore by her lost soul and the pride of sin to bring the lass into thrall to her master. The fiend had bare departed when Ailie came over the threshold to find the auld carline glunching by the fire.

It was plain she was in the worst of tempers. She flyted on the lass till the poor thing's cheek paled. "There you gang," she cried, "troking wi' thae wearifu' Pharisees o' Caulds, whae daurna darken your mither's door. A bonnie dutiful child, quotha! Wumman, hae ye nae pride?—no even the mense o' a tinkler-lass?" And then she changed her voice, and would be as soft as honey. "My puir wee Ailie! was I thrawn till ye? Never mind, my bonnie. You and me are a' that's left, and we maunna be ill to ither." And then the two had their dinner, and all the while the auld wife was crooning over the lass. "We maun 'gree weel," she says, "for we're like to be our lee-lane for the rest o' our days. They tell me Heriotside is seeking Joan o' the Croft, and they're sune to be cried in Gledsmuir kirk."

It was the first the lass had heard of it, and you may fancy she was struck dumb. And so with one thing and other the auld witch raised the fiends of jealousy in that innocent heart. She would cry out that Heriotside was an ill-doing wastrel, and had no business to come and flatter honest lassies. And then she would speak of his gentle birth and his leddy mother, and say it was indeed presumption to hope that so great a gentleman could mean all that he said. Before long Ailie was silent and white, while her mother rhymed on about men and their ways. And then she could thole it no longer, but must go out and walk by the burn to cool her hot brow and calm her thoughts, while the witch indoors laughed to herself at her devices.

For days Ailie had an absent eye and a sad face, and it so fell out that in all that time young Heriotside, who had scarce missed a day, was laid up with a broken arm and never came near her. So in a week's time she was beginning to hearken to her mother when she spoke of incantations and charms for restoring love. She kenned it was sin ; but though not seven days syne she had sat at the Lord's table, so strong is love in a young heart that she was on the very brink of it. But the grace of God was stronger than her weak will. She would have none of her mother's runes and philters, though her soul cried out for them. Always when she was most disposed to listen some merciful power stayed her consent. Alison grew thrawner as the hours passed. She kenned of Heriotside's broken arm, and she feared that any day he might recover and put her stratagems to shame. And then it seems that she collogued with her master and heard word of a subtler device. For it was approaching that uncanny time of year, the festival of Beltane, when the auld pagans were wont to sacrifice to their god Baal. In this season warlocks and carlines have a special dispensation to do evil, and Alison waited on its coming with graceless joy. As it happened, the tides in the Sker Bay ebbed at this time between the hours of twelve and one, and, as I have said, this was the hour above all others when the powers of darkness were most potent. Would the lass but consent to go abroad in the unhallowed place at this awful season and hour of the night, she was as firmly handfasted to the devil as if she had signed a bond with her own blood. For there, it seemed, the forces of good fled far away, the world for one hour was given over to its ancient prince, and the man or woman who willingly sought the spot was his bond-servant for ever. There are deadly sins from which God's people may recover. A man may even communicate unworthily, and yet, so be it he sin not against the Holy Ghost, he may find forgiveness. But it seems that for this Beltane sin there could be no pardon, and I can testify from my own knowledge that they who once committed it became lost souls from that day. James Deuchar, once a promising professor, fell thus out of sinful bravery and died blaspheming ; and of Kate Mallison, who went the same road, no man can tell. Here, indeed, was the witch-wife's chance, and she was the more keen, for her master had warned her that this was her last chance. Either Ailie's soul would be his, or her auld wrinkled body and black heart would be flung from this pleasant world to their apportioned place.

Some days later it happened that young Heriotside was stepping home over the Lang Muir about ten at night—it being his first jaunt from home since his arm had mended. He had been to the supper of the Forest Club at the Cross Keys in Gledsmuir, a clamjamfry of wild young blades who passed the wine and played at cartes once a fortnight. It seems he had drunk well, so that the world ran round about and he was in the best of tempers. The moon came down and bowed to him, and he took off his hat to it. For every step he travelled miles, so that in a little he was beyond Scotland altogether and pacing the Arabian desert. He thought he was the Pope of Rome, so he held out his foot to be kissed, and rolled twenty yards to the bottom of a small brae. Syne he was the King of France, and fought hard with a whin-bush till he had banged it to pieces. After that nothing would content him but he must be a bogle, for he found his head dunting on the stars and his legs were knocking the hills together. He thought of the mischief he was doing to the auld earth, and sat down and cried at his wickedness. Then he went on, and maybe the steep road to the Moss Rig helped him, for he began to get soberer and ken his whereabouts.

On a sudden he was aware of a man linking along at his side. He cried "A fine night," and the man replied. Syne, being merry from his cups, he tried to slap him on the back. The next he kenned he was rolling on the grass, for his hand had gone clean through the body and found nothing but air.

His head was so thick with wine that he found nothing droll in this. "Faith, friend," he says, "that was a nasty fall for a fellow that has supped weel. Where might your road be gaun to?"

"To the World's End," said the man; "but I stop at the Skerburnfoot."

"Bide the night at Heriotside," says he. "It's a thought out of your way, but it's a comfortable bit."

"There's mair comfort at the Skerburnfoot," said the dark man.

Now the mention of the Skerburnfoot brought back to him only the thought of Ailie and not of the witch-wife, her mother. So he jaloused no ill, for at the best he was slow in the uptake.

The two of them went on together for a while, Heriotside's fool head filled with the thought of the lass. Then the dark man broke silence. "Ye're thinkin' o' the maid Ailie Sempill," says he.

"How ken ye that?" asked Heriotside.

"It is my business to read the herts o' men," said the other.

"And who may ye be?" said Heriotside, growing eerie.

"Just an auld packman," said he—"nae name ye wad ken, but kin to mony gentle houses."

"And what about Ailie, you that ken sae muckle?" asked the young man.

"Naething," was the answer—"naething that concerns you, for ye'll never get the lass."

"By God, and I will!" says Heriotside, for he was a profane swearer.

"That's the wrong name to seek her in, anyway," said the man.

At this the young laird struck a great blow at him with his stick, but found nothing to resist him but the hill-wind.

When they had gone on a bit the dark man spoke again. "The lassie is thirled to holy things," says he. "She has nae care for flesh and blood, only for devout contemplation."

"She loves me," says Heriotside.

"Not you," says the other, "but a shadow in your stead."

At this the young man's heart began to tremble, for it

seemed that there was truth in what his companion said, and he was ower drunk to think gravely.

"I kenna whatna man ye are," he says, "but ye have the skill of lassies' hearts. Tell me truly, is there no way to win her to common love?"

"One way there is," said the man, "and for our friendship's sake I will tell it you. If ye can ever tryst wi' her on Beltane's Eve on the Sker sands, at the green link o' the burn where the sands begin, on the ebb o' the tide when the midnight is bye but afore cockcrow, she'll be yours, body and soul, for this world and for ever."

And then it appeared to the young man that he was walking his lone up the grass walk of Heriotside with the house close by him. He thought no more of the stranger he had met, but the word stuck in his heart.

It seems that about this very time Alison was telling the same tale to poor Ailie. She cast up to her every idle gossip she could think of. "It's Joan o' the Croft," was aye her owercome, and she would threep that they were to be cried in kirk on the first Sabbath of May. And then she would rhyme on about the black cruelty of it, and cry down curses on the lover, so that her daughter's heart grew cauld with fear. It is terrible to think of the power of the world even in a redeemed soul. Here was a maid who had drunk of the well of grace and tasted of God's mercies, and yet there were moments when she was ready to renounce her hope. At those awful seasons God seemed far off and the world very nigh, and to sell her soul for love looked a fair bargain. At other times she would resist the devil and comfort herself with prayer; but aye when she woke there was the sore heart, and when she went to sleep there were the weary eyes. There was no comfort in the goodliness of spring or the bright sunshine weather, and she who had been wont to go about the doors lightfoot and blithe was now as dowie as a widow woman.

And then one afternoon in the hinder end of April came young Heriotside riding to the Skerburnfoot. His arm was healed, he had got him a fine new suit of green, and his horse was a mettle beast that well set off his figure. Ailie was standing by the doorstep as he came down the road, and her heart stood still with joy. But a second thought gave her anguish. This man, so gallant and braw, would never be for her; doubtless the fine suit and the capering horse were for Joan o' the Croft's pleasure. And he in turn, when he remarked her wan cheek and dowie eyes, had mind of what the dark man said on the muir, and saw in her a maid sworn to no mortal love. Yet the passion for her had grown fiercer than ever, and he swore to himself that he would win her back from her phantasies. She, one may believe, was ready enough to listen. As she walked with him by the Sker Water his words were like music to her ears, and Alison within-doors laughed to herself and saw her devices prosper.

He spoke to her of love and his own heart, and the girl hearkened gladly. Syne he rebuked her coldness and cast scorn upon her piety, and so far was she beguiled that she had no answer. Then from one thing and another he spoke of some true token of their love. He said he was jealous, and craved something to ease his care. "It's but a small thing I ask," says he; "but it will make me a happy man, and nothing ever shall come atween us. Tryst wi' me for Beltane's Eve on the Sker sands, at the green link o' the burn where the sands begin, on the ebb o' the tide when midnight is bye but afore cockcrow. For," said he, "that was our forebears' tryst for true lovers, and wherefore no for you and me?"

The lassie had grace given her to refuse, but with a woful heart, and Heriotside rode off in black discontent, leaving poor Ailie to sigh her lone. He came back the next day and the next, but aye he got the same answer. A season of great doubt fell upon her soul. She had no clearness in her hope, nor any sense of God's promises. The Scriptures were an idle tale to her, prayer brought her no refreshment, and she was convicted in her conscience of the unpardonable sin. Had she been less full of pride she would have taken her troubles to good Doctor Chrystal and got comfort ; but her grief made her silent and timorous, and she found no help anywhere. Her mother was ever at her side, seeking with coaxings and evil advice to drive her to the irrevocable step. And all the while there was her love for the man riving in her bosom and giving her no ease by night or day. She believed she had driven him away and repented her denial. Only her pride held her back from going to Heriotside and seeking him herself. She watched the road hourly for a sight of his face, and when the darkness came she would sit in a corner brooding over her sorrows.

At last he came, speiring the old question. He sought the same tryst, but now he had a further tale. It seemed he was eager to get her away from the Skerburnside and auld Alison. His aunt, the Lady Balcrynie, would receive her gladly at his request till the day of their marriage. Let her but tryst with him at the hour and place he named, and he would carry her straight to Balcrynie, where she would be safe and happy. He named that hour, he said, to escape men's observation for the sake of her own good name. He named that place, for it was near her dwelling, and on the road between Balcrynie and Heriotside, which fords the Sker Burn. The temptation was more than mortal heart could resist. She gave him the promise he sought, stifling the voice of conscience ; and as she clung to his neck it seemed to her that heaven was a poor thing compared with a man's love.

Three days remained till Beltane's Eve, and throughout the time it was noted that Heriotside behaved like one possessed. It may be that his conscience pricked him, or that he had a glimpse of his sin and its coming punishment. Certain it is that, if he had been daft before, he now ran wild in his pranks, and an evil report of him was in every mouth. He drank deep at the Cross Keys, and fought two battles with young lads that had angered him. One he let off with a touch on the shoulder, the other goes lame to this day from a wound he got in the groin. There was word of the procurator-fiscal taking note of his doings, and troth, if they had continued long he must have fled the country. For a wager he rode his horse down the Dow Craig, wherefore the name of the place is the Horseman's Craig to this day. He laid a hundred guineas with the laird of Slipperfield that he would drive four horses through the Slipperfield loch, and in the prank he had his bit chariot dung to pieces and a good mare killed. And all men observed that his eyes were wild and his face grey and thin, and that his hand would twitch as he held the glass, like one with the palsy.

The eve of Beltane was lown and hot in the low country, with fire hanging in the clouds and thunder grumbling about the heavens. It seems that up in the hills it had been an awesome deluge of rain, but on the coast it was still dry and lowering. It is a long road from Heriotside to the Skerburnfoot. First you go down the Heriot Water, and syne over the Lang Muir to the edge of Mucklewhan. When you pass the steadings of Mirehope and Cockmalane you turn to the right and ford the Mire Burn. That brings you on to the turnpike road, which you will ride till it bends inland, while you keep on straight over the Whinny Knowes to the Sker Bay. There, if you are in luck, you will find the tide out and the place fordable dryshod for a man on a horse. But if the tide runs, you will do well to sit down on the sands and content yourself till it turn, or it will be the solans and scarts of the Solloway that will be seeing the next of you. On this Beltane's Eve the young man, after supping with some wild young blades, bade his horse be saddled about ten o'clock. The company were eager to ken his errand, but he waved them back. "Bide here," he says, "and birl the wine till I return. This is a ploy of my own on which no man follows me." And there was that in his face as he spoke which chilled the wildest, and left them well content to keep to the good claret and the soft seat and let the daft laird go his own ways.

Well and on, he rode down the bridle-path in the wood, along the top of the Heriot glen, and as he rode he was aware of a great noise beneath him. It was not wind, for there was none, and it was not the sound of thunder, and aye as he speired at himself what it was it grew the louder till he came to a break in the trees. And then he saw the cause, for Heriot was coming down in a furious flood, sixty yards wide, tearing at the roots of the aiks, and flinging red waves against the drystone dykes. It was a sight and sound to solemnise a man's mind, deep calling unto deep, the great waters of the hills running to meet with the great waters of the sea. But Heriotside recked nothing of it, for his heart had but one thought and the eye of his fancy one figure. Never had he been so filled with love of the lass, and yet it was not happiness but a deadly secret fear.

As he came to the Lang Muir it was geyan dark, though there was a moon somewhere behind the clouds. It was little he could see of the road, and ere long he had tried many moss-pools and sloughs, as his braw new coat bare witness. Aye in front of him was the great hill of Mucklewhan, where the road turned down by the Mire. The noise of the Heriot had not long fallen behind him ere another began, the same eerie sound of burns crying to ither in the darkness. It seemed that the whole earth was overrun with waters. Every little runnel in the bog was astir, and yet the land around him was as dry as flax, and no drop of rain had fallen. As he rode on the din grew louder, and as he came over the top of Mirehope he kenned by the mighty rushing noise that something uncommon was happening with the Mire Burn. The light from Mirehope shieling twinkled on his left, and had the man not been dozened with his fancies he might have observed that the steading was deserted and men were crying below in the fields. But he rode on, thinking of but one thing, till he came to the cot-house of Cockmalane, which is nigh the fords of the Mire.

John Dodds, the herd who bode in the place, was standing at the door, and he looked to see who was on the road so late.

"Stop," says he, "stop, Laird Heriotside. I kenna what your errand is, but it is to no holy purpose that ye're out on Beltane Eve. D'ye no hear the warning o' the waters?"

And then in the still night came the sound of Mire like the clash of armies.

"I must win over the ford," says the laird quietly, thinking of another thing.

"Ford!" cried John in scorn. "There'll be nae ford for you the nicht unless it be the ford o' the river Jordan. The burns are up, and bigger than man ever saw them. It'll be a Beltane's Eve that a' folk will remember. They tell me that Gled valley is like a loch, and that there's an awesome folk drooned in the hills. Gin ye were ower the Mire, what about crossin' the Caulds and the Sker?" says he, for he jaloused he was going to Gledsmuir.

And then it seemed that that word brought the laird to his senses. He looked the airt the rain was coming from, and he saw it was the airt the Sker flowed. In a second, he has told me, the works of the devil were revealed to him. He saw himself a tool in Satan's hands, he saw his tryst a device for the destruction of the body, as it was assuredly meant for the destruction of the soul, and there came on his mind the picture of an innocent lass borne down by the waters with no place for repentance. His heart grew cold in his breast. He had but one thought, a sinful and reckless one—to get to her side, that the two might go together to their account. He heard the roar of the Mire as in a dream, and when John Dodds laid hands on his bridle he felled him to the earth. And the next seen of it was the laird riding the flood like as man possessed.

The horse was the grey stallion he aye rode, the very beast he had ridden for many a wager with the wild lads of the

Cross Keys. No man but himself durst back it, and it had lamed many a hostler lad and broke two necks in its day. But it seemed it had the mettle for any flood, and took the Mire with little spurring. The herds on the hillside looked to see man and steed swept into eternity; but though the red waves were breaking about his shoulders and he was swept far down, he aye held on for the shore. The next thing the watchers saw was the laird struggling up the far bank, and casting his coat from him, so that he rode in his sark. And then he set off like a wildfire across the muir towards the turnpike road. Two men saw him on the road and have recorded their experience. One was a gangrel, by name M'Nab, who was travelling from Gledsmuir to Allerkirk with a heavy pack on his back and a bowed head. He heard a sound like wind afore him, and, looking up, saw coming down the road a grey horse stretched out to a wild gallop and a man on its back with a face like a soul in torment. He kenned not whether it was devil or mortal, but flung himself on the roadside, and lay like a corp for an hour or more till the rain aroused him. The other was one Sim Doolittle, the fish-hawker from Allerfoot, jogging home in his fish-cart from Gledsmuir fair. He had drunk more than was fit for him, and he was singing some light song, when he saw approaching, as he said, the pale horse mentioned in the Revelations, with Death seated as the rider. Thoughts of his sins came on him like a thunder-clap, fear loosened his knees, he leaped from the cart to the road, and from the road to the back of a dyke. Thence he flew to the hills, and was found the next morning far up among the Mire Craigs, while his horse and cart were gotten on the Aller sands, the horse lamed and the cart without the wheels.

At the tollhouse the road turns inland to Gledsmuir, and he who goes to Sker Bay must leave it and cross the wild land called the Whinny Knowes, a place rough with bracken and foxes' holes and old stone cairns. The tollman, John Gilzean, was opening his window to get a breath of air in the lown night when he heard or saw the approaching horse. He kenned the beast for Heriotside's, and, being a friend of the laird's, he ran down in all haste to open the yett, wondering to himself about the laird's errand on this night. A voice came down the road to him bidding him hurry; but John's old fingers were slow with the keys, and so it happened that the horse had to stop, and John had time to look up at the gash and woful face.

"Where away the nicht sae late, laird?" says John.

"I go to save a soul from hell," was the answer.

And then it seems that through the open door there came the chapping of a clock.

"Whatna hour is that?" asks Heriotside.

"Midnicht," says John, trembling, for he did not like the look of things.

There was no answer but a groan, and horse and man went racing down the dark hollows of the Whinny Knowes.

How he escaped a broken neck in that dreadful place no human being will ever tell. The sweat, he has told me, stood in cold drops upon his forehead; he scarcely was aware of the saddle in which he sat; and his eyes were stelled in his head, so that he saw nothing but the sky ayont him. The night was growing colder, and there was a small sharp wind stirring from the east. But, hot or cold, it was all one to him, who was already cold as death. He heard not the sound of the sea nor the peesweeps startled by his horse, for the sound that ran in his ears was the roaring Sker Water and a girl's cry. The thought kept goading him, and he spurred the grey till the creature was madder than himself. It leaped the hole which they call the Devil's Mull as I would step over a thistle, and the next he kenned he was on the edge of the Sker Bay.

It lay before him white and ghastly, with mist blowing in wafts across it and a slow swaying of the tides. It was the better part of a mile wide, but save for some fathoms in the middle where the Sker current ran, it was no deeper even at flood than a horse's fetlocks. It looks eerie at bright mid-day when the sun is shining and whaups are crying among the seaweeds; but think what it was on that awesome night with the powers of darkness brooding over it like a cloud. The rider's heart quailed for a moment in natural fear. He stepped his beast a few feet in, still staring afore him like a daft man. And then something in the sound or the feel of the waters made him look down, and he perceived that the ebb had begun and the tide was flowing out to sea.

He kenned that all was lost, and the knowledge drove him to stark despair. His sins came in his face like birds of night, and his heart shrank like a pea. He knew himself for a lost soul, and all that he loved in the world was out in the tides. There, at any rate, he could go too, and give back that gift of life he had so blackly misused. He cried small and soft like a bairn, and drove the grey out into the waters. And aye as he spurred it the foam should have been flying as high as his head; but in that uncanny hour there was no foam, only the waves running sleek like oil. It was not long ere he had come to the Sker channel, where the red moss-waters were roaring to the sea, an ill place to ford in midsummer heat, and certain death, as folks reputed it, at the smallest spate. The grey was swimming, but it seemed the Lord had other purposes for him than death, for neither man nor horse could drown. He tried to leave the saddle, but he could not; he flung the bridle from him, but the grey held on, as if some strong hand were guiding. He cried out upon the devil to help his own, he renounced his Maker and his God; but whatever his punishment, he was not to be drowned. And then he was silent, for something was coming down the tide.

It came down as quiet as a sleeping bairn, straight for him as he sat with his horse breasting the waters, and as it came the moon crept out of a cloud and he saw a glint of yellow hair. And then his madness died away and he was himself again, a weary and stricken man. He hung down over the tides and caught the body in his arms, and then let the grey make for the shallows. He cared no more for the devil and all his myrmidons, for he kenned brawly he was damned. It seemed to him that his soul had gone from him and he was as toom as a hazel-shell. His breath rattled in his throat, the tears were dried up in his head, his body had lost its strength, and yet he clung to the drowned maid as to a hope of salvation. And then he noted something at which he marvelled dumbly. Her hair was drookit back from her clay-cold brow, her eyes were shut, but in her face there was the peace of a child. It seemed even that her lips were smiling. Here, certes, was no lost soul, but one who had gone joyfully to meet her Lord. It may be in that dark hour at the burn-foot, before the spate caught her, she had been given grace to resist her adversary and flung herself upon God's mercy.

And it would seem that it had been granted, for when he came to the Skerburnfoot there in the corner sat the weird-wife Alison dead as a stone and shrivelled like a heather-birn.

For days Heriotside wandered the country or sat in his own house with vacant eye and trembling hands. Conviction of sin held him like a vice: he saw the lassie's death laid at his door, her face haunted him by day and night, and the word of the Lord dirled in his ears telling of wrath and punishment. The greatness of his anguish wore him to a shadow, and at last he was stretched on his bed and like to perish. In his extremity worthy Doctor Chrystal went to him unasked and strove to comfort him. Long, long the good man wrestled, but it seemed as if his ministrations were to be of no avail. The fever left his body, and he rose to stotter about the doors; but he was still in his torments, and the mercy-seat was far from him. At last in the back-end of the year came Mungo Muirhead to Caulds to the autumn communion, and nothing would serve him but he must try his hand at this storm-tossed soul. He spoke with power and unction, and a blessing came with his words, the black cloud lifted and showed a glimpse of grace, and in a little the man had some assurance of salvation. He became a pillar of Christ's Kirk, prompt to check abominations, notably the sin of witchcraft, foremost in good works; but with it all a humble man, who walked contritely till his death. When I came first to Caulds I sought to prevail upon him to accept the eldership, but he aye put me by, and when I heard his tale I saw that he had done wisely. I mind him well as he sat in his chair or daundered through Caulds, a kind word for everyone and sage counsel in time of distress, but withal a severe man to himself and a crucifier of the body. It seems that this severity weakened his frame, for three years syne come Martinmas he was taken ill with a fever, and after a week's sickness he went to his account, where I trust he is accepted.

V. FOUNTAINBLUE.

I.

ONCE upon a time, as the story-books say, a boy came over a ridge of hill, from which a shallow vale ran out into the sunset. It was a high, wind-blown country, where the pines had a crook in their backs and the rocks were scarred and bitten with winter storms. But below was the beginning of pastoral. Soft birch-woods, shady beeches, meadows where cattle had browsed for generations, fringed the little brown river as it twined to the sea. Farther, and the waves broke on white sands, the wonderful billows of the West which cannot bear to be silent. And between, in a garden wilderness, with the evening flaming in its windows, stood Fountainblue, my little four-square castle which guards the valley and the beaches.

The boy had torn his clothes, scratched his face, cut one finger deeply, and soaked himself with bog-water, but he whistled cheerfully and his eyes were happy. He had had an afternoon of adventure, startling emprises achieved in solitude; assuredly a day to remember and mark with a white stone. And the beginning had been most unpromising. After lunch he had been attired in his best raiment, and, in the misery of a broad white collar, despatched with his cousins to take tea with the small lady who domineered in Fountainblue. The prospect had pleased him greatly, the gardens fed his fancy, the hostess was an old confederate, and there were sure to be excellent things to eat. But his curious temper had arisen to torment him. On the way he quarrelled with his party, and in a moment found himself out of sympathy with the future. The enjoyment crept out of the prospect. He knew that he did not shine in society, he foresaw an afternoon when he would be left out in the cold and his hilarious cousins treated as the favoured guests. He reflected that tea was a short meal at the best, and that games on a lawn were a poor form of sport. Above all, he felt the torture of his collar and the straitness of his clothes. He pictured the dreary return in the twilight, when the afternoon, which had proved, after all, such a dismal failure, had come to a weary end. So, being a person of impulses, he mutinied at the gates of Fountainblue and made for the hills. He knew he should get into trouble, but trouble, he had long ago found out, was his destiny, and he scorned to avoid it. And now, having cast off the fear of God and man, he would for some short hours do exactly as he pleased.

Half-crying with regret for the delights he had forsworn, he ran over the moor to the craggy hills which had always been forbidden him. When he had climbed among the rocks awe fell upon the desolate little adventurer, and he bewailed his choice. But soon he found a blue hawk's nest, and the possession of a coveted egg inspired him to advance. By-and-by he had climbed so high that he could not return, but must needs scale Stob Ghabhar itself. With a quaking heart he achieved it, and then, in the pride of his heroism, he must venture down the Grey Correi where the wild goats lived. He saw a bearded ruffian, and pursued him with stones, stalking him cunningly till he was out of breath. Then he found odd little spleenwort ferns, which he pocketed, and high up in the rocks a friendly raven croaked his encouragement. And then, when the shadows lengthened, he set off cheerily homewards, hungry, triumphant, and very weary.

All the way home he flattered his soul. In one afternoon he had been hunter and trapper, and what to him were girls' games and pleasant things to eat? He pictured himself the hardy outlaw, feeding on oatmeal and goat's-flesh, the terror and pride of his neighbourhood. Could the little mistress of Fountainblue but see him now, how she would despise his prosaic cousins! And then, as he descended on the highway, he fell in with his forsaken party.

For a wonder they were in good spirits—so good that they forgot to remind him, in their usual way, of the domestic terrors awaiting him. A man had been there who had told them stories and shown them tricks, and there had been cocoa-nut cake, and Sylvia had a new pony on which they had ridden races. The children were breathless with excitement, very much in love with each other as common sharers in past joys. And as they talked all the colour went out of his afternoon. The blue hawk's egg was cracked, and it looked a stupid, dingy object as it lay in his cap. His rare ferns were crumpled and withered, and who was to believe his stories of Stob Ghabhar and the Grey Correi? He had been a fool to barter ponies and tea and a man who knew tricks for the barren glories of following his own fancy. But at any rate he would show no sign. If he was to be an outlaw, he would carry his outlawry well; so with a catch in his voice and tears in his eyes he jeered at his inattentive companions, upbraiding himself all the while for his folly.

II.

THE sun was dipping behind Stob Ghabhar when Maitland drove over the ridge of hill, whence the moor-road dips to Fountainblue. Twenty long miles from the last outpost of railway to the western sea-loch, and twenty of the barest, steepest miles in the bleak north. And all the way he had been puzzling himself with the half-painful, half-pleasing memories of a childhood which to the lonely man still overtopped the present. Every wayside bush was the home of recollection. In every burn he had paddled and fished; here he had found the jack-snipe's nest, there he had hidden when the shepherds sought him for burning the heather in May. He lost for a little the burden of his years and cares, and lived again in that old fresh world which had no boundaries, where sleep and food were all his thought at night, and adventure the sole outlook of the morning. The western sea lay like a thin line of gold beyond the moorland, and down in the valley in a bower of trees lights began to twinkle from the little castle. The remote mountains, hiding deep corries and woods in their bosom, were blurred by twilight to a single wall of hazy purple, which shut off this fairy glen impenetrably from the world. Fountainblue—the name rang witchingly in his ears. Fountainblue, the last home of the Good Folk, the last hold of the vanished kings, where the last wolf in Scotland was slain, and, as stories go, the last saint of the Great Ages taught the people,—what had Fountainblue to do with his hard world of facts and figures? The thought woke him to a sense of the present, and for a little he relished the paradox. He had left it long ago, an adventurous child; now he was returning with success behind him and a portion of life's good things his own. He was rich, very rich and famous. Few men of forty had his power, and he had won it all in fair struggle with enemies and rivals and a niggardly world. He had been feared and hated, as he had been extravagantly admired; he had been rudely buffeted by fortune, and had met the blows with a fighter's joy. And out of it all something hard and austere had shaped itself, something very much a man, but a man with little heart and a lack of kindly human failings. He was master of himself in a curious degree, but the mastery absorbed his interests. Nor had he ever regretted it, when suddenly in this outlandish place the past swept over him, and he had a vision of a long avenue of vanished hopes. It pleased and disquieted him, and as the road dipped into the valley he remembered the prime cause of this mood of vagaries.

He had come up into the north with one purpose in view,

he frankly told himself. The Etheridges were in Fountainblue, and ever since, eight months before, he had met Clara Etheridge, he had forgotten his ambitions. A casual neighbour at a dinner-party, a chance partner at a ball,—and then he had to confess that this slim, dark, bright-eyed girl had broken in irrevocably upon his contentment. At first he hated it for a weakness, then he welcomed the weakness with feverish ecstasy. He did nothing by halves, so he sought her company eagerly, and, being a great man in his way, found things made easy for him. But the girl remained shy and distant, flattered doubtless by his attention, but watching him curiously as an intruder from an alien world. It was characteristic of the man that he never thought of a rival. His whole aim was to win her love; for rivalry with other men he had the contempt of a habitual conqueror. And so the uneasy wooing went on till the Etheridges left town, and he found himself a fortnight later with his work done and a visit before him to which he looked forward with all the vehemence of a nature whose strong point had always been its hope. As the road wound among the fir-trees, he tried to forecast the life at Fountainblue, and map out the future in his usual business-like way. But now the future refused to be thus shorn and parcelled: there was an unknown quantity in it which defied his efforts.

The house-party were sitting round the hall-fire when he entered. The high-roofed place, the flagged floor strewn with rugs, and the walls bright with the glow of fire on armour, gave him a boyish sense of comfort. Two men in knickerbockers were lounging on a settle, and at his entrance came forward to greet him. One was Sir Hugh Clanroyden, a follower of his own; the other he recognised as a lawyer named Durward. From the circle of women Miss Etheridge rose and welcomed him. Her mother was out, but would be back for dinner; meantime he should be shown his room. He noticed that her face was browner, her hair a little less neat, and there seemed something franker and kindlier in her smile. So in a very good humour he went to rid himself of the dust of the roads.

Durward watched him curiously, and then turned, laughing, to his companion, as the girl came back to her friends with a heightened colour in her cheeks.

"Romeo the second," he said. "We are going to be spectators of a comedy. And yet, heaven knows! Maitland is not cast for comedy."

The other shook his head. "It will never come off. I've known Clara Etheridge most of my life, and I would as soon think of marrying a dancing-girl to a bishop. She is a delightful person, and my very good friend, but how on earth is she ever to understand Maitland? And how on earth can he see anything in her? Besides, there's another man."

Durward laughed. "Despencer! I suppose he will be a serious rival with a woman; but imagine him Maitland's rival in anything else! He'd break him like a rotten stick in half an hour. I like little Despencer, and I don't care about Maitland; but all the same it is absurd to compare the two, except in love-making."

"Lord, it will be comic," and Clanroyden stretched his long legs and lay back on a cushion. The girls were still chattering beside the fire, and the twilight was fast darkening into evening.

"You dislike Maitland?" he asked, looking up. "Now, I wonder why?"

Durward smiled comically at the ceiling. "Oh, I know I oughtn't to. I know he's supposed to be a man's man, and that it's bad form for a man to say he dislikes him. But I'm honest enough to own to detesting him. I suppose he's great, but he's not great enough yet to compel one to fall down and worship him, and I hate greatness in the making. He goes through the world with his infernal arrogance and expects everybody to clear out of his way. I am told we live in an age of reason, but that fellow has burked reason. He never gives a reason for a thing he does, and if you try to argue he crushes you. He has killed good talk for ever with his confounded rudeness. All the little sophistries and conventions which make life tolerable are so much rubbish to him, and he shows it. The plague of him is that he can never make-believe. He is as hard as iron, and as fierce as the devil, and about as unpleasant. You may respect the sledge-hammer type, but it's confoundedly dull. Why, the man has not the imagination of a rabbit, except in his description of people he dislikes. I liked him when he said that Layden reminded him of a dissipated dove, because I disliked Layden; but when Freddy Alton played the fool and people forgave him, because he was a good sort, Maitland sent him about his business, saying he had no further use for weaklings. He is so abominably cold-blooded and implacable that everyone must fear him, and yet most people can afford to despise him. All the kind simple things of life are shut out of his knowledge. He has no nature, only a heart of stone and an iron will and a terribly subtle brain. Of course he is a great man—in a way, but at the best he is only half a man. And to think that he should have fallen in love, and be in danger of losing to Despencer! It's enough to make one forgive him."

Clanroyden laughed. "I can't think of Despencer. It's too absurd. But, seriously, I wish I saw Maitland well rid of this mood, married or cured. That sort of man doesn't take things easily."

"It reminds one of Theocritus and the Cyclops in love. Who would have thought to see him up in this moorland place, running after a girl? He doesn't care for sport."

"Do you know that he spent most of his childhood in this glen, and that he *is* keen about sport? He is too busy for many holidays, but he once went with Burton to the Caucasus, and Burton said the experience nearly killed him. He said that the fellow was tireless, and as mad and reckless as a boy with nothing to lose."

"Well, that simply bears out what I say of him. He does not understand the meaning of sport. When he gets keen about anything he pursues it as carefully and relentlessly as if it were something on the Stock Exchange. Now little Despencer is a genuine sportsman in his canary-like way. He loves the art of the thing and the being out of doors. Maitland, I don't suppose, ever thinks whether it is a ceiling or the sky above his august head. Despencer——"

But at the moment Clanroyden uncrossed his legs, bringing his right foot down heavily upon his companion's left. Durward looked up and saw a young man coming towards him, smiling.

The newcomer turned aside to say something to the girls round the fire, and then came and sat on an arm of the settle. He was a straight, elegant person, with a well-tanned, regular face, and very pleasant brown eyes.

"I've had such an afternoon," he said. "You never saw a place like Cairnlora. It's quite a little stone tower all alone in a fir-wood, and nothing else between the moor and the sea. It is furnished as barely as a prison, except for the chairs, which are priceless old Dutch things. Oh, and the silver at tea was the sort of thing that only Americans can buy nowadays. Mrs Etheridge is devoured with envy. But the wonder of the house is old Miss Elphinstone. She must be nearly seventy, and she looks forty-five, except for her hair. She speaks broad Scots, and she has the manners of a *marquise.* I would give a lot to have had Raeburn paint her. She reminded me of nothing so much as a hill-wind with her keen high-coloured old face. Yes, I have enjoyed the afternoon."

"Jack has got a new enthusiasm," said Durward. "I wish I were like you to have a new one once a week. By the way, Maitland has arrived at last."

"Really!" said Despencer. "Oh, I forgot to tell you something which you would never have guessed. Miss Elphinstone is Maitland's aunt, and he was brought up a good deal at Cairnlora. He doesn't take his manners from her, but I suppose he gets his cleverness from that side of the family. She disapproves of him strongly, so of course I had to defend him. And what do you think she said? 'He has betrayed his tradition. He has sold his birthright for a mess of pottage, and I wish him joy of his bargain!' Nice one for your party, Hugh."

Miss Etheridge had left the group at the fire and was standing at Despencer's side. She listened to him with a curious air of solicitude, like an affectionate sister. At the mention of Maitland's name Clanroyden had watched her narrowly, but her face did not change. And when Despencer asked, "Where is the new arrival?" she talked of him with the utmost nonchalance.

. . . .

Maitland came down to dinner, ravenously hungry and in high spirits. Nothing was changed in this house since he had stared at the pictures and imagined terrible things about the armour and broken teacups with childish impartiality. His own favourite seat was still there, where, hidden by a tapestry screen, he had quarrelled with Sylvia while their elders gossiped. This sudden flood of memories mellowed him towards the world. He was cordial to Despencer, forbore to think Durward a fool, and answered every one of Mr Etheridge's many questions. For the first time he felt the success of his life. The old house recalled his childhood, and the sight of Clanroyden, his devoted follower, reminded him of his power. Somehow the weariful crying for the moon, which had always tortured him, was exchanged for a glow of comfort, a shade of complacency in his haggard soul. . . . And then the sight of Clara dispelled his satisfaction.

Here in this cheerful homely party of friends he found himself out of place. On state occasions he could acquit himself with credit, for the man had a mind. He could make the world listen to him when he chose, and the choice was habitual. But now his loneliness claimed its lawful consequences, and he longed for the little friendly graces which he had so often despised. Despencer talked of scenery and weather with a tenderness to which this man, who loved nature as he loved little else, was an utter stranger. This elegant and appropriate sentiment would have worried him past endurance, if Miss Clara had not shared it. It was she who told some folk-tale about the Grey Correi with the prettiest hesitancy which showed her feeling. And then the talk drifted to books and people, flitting airily about their petty world. Maitland felt himself choked by their accomplishments. Most of the subjects were ones no sane man would trouble to think of, and yet here were men talking keenly about trifles and disputing with nimble-witted cleverness on the niceties of the trivial. Feeling miserably that he was the only silent one, he plunged desperately into the stream, found himself pulled up by Despencer and deftly turned. The event gave him the feeling of having been foiled by a kitten.

Angry with the world, angrier with his own angularity, he waited for the end of the meal. Times had not changed in this house since he had been saved by Sylvia from social disgrace. But when the women left the room he found life easier. His host talked of sport, and he could tell him more about Stob Ghabhar than any keeper. Despencer, victorious at dinner, now listened like a docile pupil. Durward asked a political question, and the answer came sharp and definite. Despencer demurred gently, after his fashion. "Well, but surely——" and a grimly smiling "What do you know about it?" closed the discussion. The old Maitland had returned for the moment.

The night was mild and impenetrably dark, and the fall of waters close at hand sounded like a remote echo. An open hall-door showed that some of the party had gone out to the garden, and the men followed at random. A glimmer of white frocks betrayed the women on the lawn, standing by the little river which slipped by cascade and glide from the glen to the low pasture-lands. In the featureless dark there was no clue to locality. The place might have been Berkshire or a suburban garden.

Suddenly the scream of some animal came from the near thicket. The women started and asked what it was.

"It was a hill-fox," said Maitland to Clara. "They used to keep me awake at nights on the hill. They come and bark close to your ear and give you nightmare."

The lady shivered. "Thank Heaven for the indoors," she said. "Now, if I had been the daughter of one of your old Donalds of the Isles, I should have known that cry only too well. Wild nature is an excellent background, but give me civilisation in front."

Maitland was looking into the wood. "You will find it creep far into civilisation if you look for it. There is a very narrow line between the warm room and the savage out-of-doors."

"There are miles of luxuries," the girl cried, laughing. "People who are born in the wrong century have to hunt over half the world before they find their savagery. It is all very tame, but I love the tameness. You may call yourself primitive, Mr Maitland, but you are the most complex and modern of us all. What would Donald of the Isles have said to politics and the Stock Exchange ?"

They had strolled back to the house. "Nevertheless I maintain my belief," said the man. "You call it miles of rampart ; I call the division a line, a thread, a sheet of glass. But then, you see, you only know one side, and I only know the other."

"What preposterous affectation !" the girl said, as with a pretty shiver she ran indoors. Maitland stood for a moment looking back at the darkness. Within the firelit hall, with its rugs and little tables and soft chairs, he had caught a glimpse of Despencer smoking a cigarette. As he looked towards the hills he heard the fox's bark a second time, and then somewhere from the black distance came a hawk's scream, hoarse, lonely, and pitiless. The thought struck him that the sad elemental world of wood and mountain was far more truly his own than this cosy and elegant civilisation. And, oddly enough, the thought pained him.

III.

THE day following was wet and windy, when a fire was grateful, and the hills, shrouded in grey mist, had no attractions. The party read idly in arm-chairs during the morning, and in the afternoon Maitland and Clanroyden went down to the stream-mouth after sea-trout. So Despencer remained to talk to Clara, and, having played many games of picquet and grown heartily tired of each other, as tea-time approached they fell to desultory comments on their friends. Maitland was beginning to interest the girl in a new way. Formerly he had been a great person who was sensible enough to admire her, but something remote and unattractive, for whom friendship (much less love) was impossible. But now she had begun to feel his power, his manhood. The way in which other men spoke of him impressed her unconsciously, and she began to ask Despencer questions which were gall and wormwood to that young man. But he answered honestly, after his fashion.

"Isn't he very rich?" she asked. "And I suppose he lives very plainly?"

"Rich as Crœsus, and he sticks in his ugly rooms in the Albany because he never thinks enough about the thing to change. I've been in them once, and you never saw such a place. He's a maniac for fresh air, so they're large enough, but they're littered like a stable with odds and ends of belongings. He must have several thousand books, and yet he hasn't a decent binding among them. He hasn't a photograph of a single soul, and only one picture, which, I believe, was his father. But you never saw such a collection of whips and spurs and bits. It smells like a harness-room, and there you find Maitland, when by any chance he is at home, working half the night and up to the eyes in papers. I don't think the man has any expenses except food and rent, for he wears the same clothes for years. And he has given up horses."

"Was he fond of horses?" Miss Clara asked.

"Oh, you had better ask him. I really can't tell you any more about him."

"But how do his friends get on with him?"

"He has hardly any, but his acquaintances, who are all the world, say he is the one great man of the future. If you want to read what people think of him, you had better look at the 'Monthly.'"

Under cover of this one ungenerous word Despencer made his escape, for he hated the business, but made it the rule of his life "never to crab a fellow." Miss Clara promptly sought out the 'Monthly,' and found twenty pages of superfine analysis and bitter, grudging praise. She read it with interest, and then lay back in her chair and tried to fix her thoughts. It is only your unhealthy young woman who worships strength in the abstract, and the girl tried to determine whether she admired the man as a power or disliked him as a brute. She chose a compromise, and the feeling which survived was chiefly curiosity.

The result of the afternoon was that when the fishermen returned, and Maitland, in dry clothes, appeared for tea, she settled herself beside him and prepared to talk. Maitland, being healthily tired, was in an excellent temper, and he found himself enticed into what for him was a rare performance—talk about himself. They were sitting apart from the others, and, ere ever he knew, he was answering the girl's questions with an absent-minded frankness. In a little she had drawn from him the curious history of his life, which most men knew, but never from his own lips.

"I was at school for a year," he said, "and then my father

died and our affairs went to pieces. I had to come back and go into an office, a sort of bank. I hated it, but it was good for me, for it taught me something, and my discontent made me ambitious. I had about eighty pounds a year, and I saved from that. I worked too at books incessantly, and by-and-by I got an Oxford scholarship, at an obscure college. I went up there, and found myself in a place where everyone seemed well-off, while I was a pauper. However, it didn't trouble me much, for I had no ambition to play the fool. I only cared about two things—horses and metaphysics. I hated all games, which I thought only fit for children. I daresay it was foolish, but then you see I had had a queer upbringing. I managed to save a little money, and one vacation when I was wandering about in Norfolk, sleeping under haystacks and working in harvest-fields when my supplies ran down, I came across a farmer. He was a good fellow and a sort of sportsman, and I took a fancy to him. He had a colt to sell which I fancied more, for I saw it had blood in it. So I bought it for what seemed a huge sum to me in those days, but I kept it at his farm and I superintended its education. I broke it myself and taught it to jump, and by-and-by in my third year I brought it to Oxford and entered for the Grind on it. People laughed at me, but I knew my own business. The little boys who rode in the thing knew nothing about horses, and not one in ten could ride; so I entered and won. It was all I wanted, for I could sell my horse then, and the fellow who rode second bought it. It was decent of him, for I asked a big figure, and I think he had an idea of doing me a kindness. I made him my private secretary the other day."

"You mean Lord Drapier?" she asked.

"Yes—Drapier. That gave me money to finish off and begin in town. Oh, and I had got a first in my schools. I knew very little about anything except metaphysics, and I never went to tutors. I suppose I knew a good deal more than the examiners in my own subject, and anyhow they felt obliged to give me my first after some grumbling. Then I came up to town with just sixty pounds in my pocket, but I had had the education of a gentleman."

Maitland looked out of the window, and the sight of the mist-clad hills recalled him to himself. He wondered why he was telling the girl this story, and he stopped suddenly.

"And what did you do in town?" she asked, with interest.

"I hung round and kept my eyes open. I nearly starved, for I put half my capital on a horse which I thought was safe, and lost it. By-and-by, quite by accident, I came across a curious fellow, Ransome—you probably have heard his name. I met him in some stables where he was buying a mare, and he took a liking to me. He made me his secretary, and then, because I liked hard work, he let me see his business. It was enormous, for the man was a genius after a fashion; and I slaved away in his office and down at the docks for about three years. He paid me just enough to keep body and soul together and cover them with clothes; but I didn't grumble, for I had a sort of idea that I was on my probation. And then my apprenticeship came to an end."

"Yes," said the girl.

"Yes; for you see Ransome was an odd character. He had a sort of genius for finance, and within his limits he was even a great administrator. But in everything else he was as simple as a child. His soul was idyllic: he loved green fields and Herrick and sheep. So it had always been his fancy to back out some day and retire with his huge fortune to some country place and live as he pleased. It seemed that he had been training me from the first day I went into the business, and now he cut the rope and left the whole enormous concern in my hands. I needed every atom of my wits, and the first years were a hard struggle. I became of course very rich; but I had to do more, I had to keep the thing at its old level. I had no natural turn for the work, and I had to acquire capacity by sheer grind. However, I managed it, and then, when I felt my position sure, I indulged myself with a hobby and went into politics."

"You call it a hobby?"

"Certainly. The ordinary political career is simply a form of trifling. There's no trade on earth where a man has to fear so few able competitors. Of course it's very public and honourable and that sort of thing, and I like it; but sometimes it wearies me to death."

The girl was looking at him with curious interest. "Do you always get what you want?" she asked.

"Never," he said.

"Then is your success all disappointment?"

"Oh, I generally get a bit of my ambitions, which is all one can hope for in this world."

"I suppose your ambitions are not idyllic, like Mr Ransome's?"

He laughed. "No, I suppose not. I never could stand your Corot meadows and ivied cottages and village church bells. But I am at home in this glen, or used to be."

"You said that last night, and I thought it was affectation," said the girl; "but perhaps you are right. I'm not at home in this scenery, at any rate in this weather. Ugh, look at that mist driving and that spur of Stob Ghabhar! I really must go and sit by the fire."

IV.

THE next day dawned clear and chill, with a little frost to whiten the heather; but by mid-day the sun had turned August to June, and sea and land drowsed in a mellow heat. Maitland was roused from his meditations witha pipe on a garden-seat by the appearance of Miss Clara, her eyes bright with news. He had taken her in to dinner the night before, and for the first time in his life had found himself talking easily to a woman. Her interest of the afternoon had not departed; and Despencer in futile disgust shunned the drawing-room, his particular paradise, and played billiards with Clanroyden in the spirit of an unwilling martyr.

"We are going out in the yacht," Miss Clara cried, as she emerged from the shadow of a fuchsia-hedge, "to the Isles of the Waves, away beyond the Seal's Headland. Do you know the place, Mr Maitland?"

"Eilean na Cille? Yes. It used to be dangerous for currents, but a steam-yacht does not require to fear them."

"Well, we'll be ready to start at twelve, and I must go in to give orders about lunch."

A little later she came out with a bundle of letters in her hands. "Here are your letters, Mr Maitland; but you mustn't try to answer them, or you'll be late." He put the lot in his jacket pocket and looked up at the laughing girl. "My work is six hundred miles behind me," he said, "and to-day I have only the Eilean na Cille to think of." And, as she passed by, another name took the place of the Eilean, and it seemed to him that at last he had found the link which was to bind together the two natures—his boyhood and his prime.

Out on the loch the sun was beating with that steady August blaze which is more torrid than midsummer. But as the yacht slipped between the horns of the land, it came into a broken green sea with rollers to the north where the tireless Atlantic fretted on the reefs. In a world of cool salt winds and the golden weather of afternoon, with the cries of tern and gull about the bows and the foam and ripple of green water in the wake, the party fell into a mood of supreme contentment. The restless Miss Clara was stricken into a figure of contemplation, which sat in the bows and watched the hazy blue horizon and the craggy mainland hills in silent delight. Maitland was revelling in the loss of his isolation. He had ceased to be alone, a leader, and for the moment felt himself one of the herd, a devotee of humble pleasures. His mind was blank, his eyes filled only with the sea, and the lady of his devotion, in that happy moment of romance, seemed to have come at last within the compass of his hopes.

The Islands of the Waves are low green ridges which rise little above the highest tide-mark. The grass is stiff with salt, the sparse heather and rushes are crooked with the winds, but there are innumerable little dells where a light wild scrub flourishes, and in one a spring of sweet water sends a tiny stream to the sea. The yacht's company came ashore in boats, and tea was made with a great bustle beside the well, while the men lay idly in the bent and smoked. All wind seemed to have died down, a soft, cool, airless peace like a June evening was abroad, and the heavy surging of the tides had sunk to a distant whisper. Maitland lifted his head, sniffed the air, and looked uneasily to the west, meeting the eye of one of the sailors engaged in the same scrutiny. He beckoned the man to him.

"What do you make of the weather?" he asked.

The sailor, an East-coast man from Arbroath, shook his head. "It's ower lown a' of a sudden," he said. "It looks like mair wind nor we want, but I think it'll haud till the morn."

Maitland nodded and lay down again. He smiled at the return of his old sea craft and weather-lore, on which he had prided himself in his boyhood; and when Miss Clara came up to him with tea she found him grinning vacantly at the sky.

"What a wonderful lull in the wind," she said. "When I was here last these were real isles of the waves, with spray flying over them and a great business to land. But now they might be the island in Fountainblue lake."

"Did you ever hear of the Ocean Quiet?" he asked. "I believe it to be a translation of a Gaelic word which is a synonym for death, but it is also a kind of natural phenomenon. Old people at Cairnlora used to talk of it. They said that sometimes fishermen far out at sea in blowing weather came into a place of extraordinary peace, where the whole world was utterly still and they could hear their own hearts beating."

"What a pretty fancy!" said the girl.

"Yes; but it had its other side. The fishermen rarely came home alive, and if they did they were queer to the end of their days. Another name for the thing was the Breathing of God. It is an odd idea, the passing from the wholesome turmoil of nature to the uncanny place where God crushes you by His silence."

"All the things to eat are down by the fire," she said, laughing. "Do you know, if you weren't what you are, people might think you a poet, Mr Maitland. I thought you cared for none of these things."

"What things?" he asked. "I don't care for poetry. I am merely repeating the nonsense I was brought up on. Shall I talk to you about politics?"

"Heaven forbid! And now I will tell you my own story about these isles. There is a hermit's cell on one of them and crosses, like Iona. The hermit lived alone all winter, and was fed by boats from the shore when the weather was calm. When one hermit died another took his place, and no one knew where he came from. Now one day a great lord in Scotland disappeared from his castle. He was the King's Warden of the Marches and the greatest soldier of his day, but he disappeared utterly out of men's sight, and people forgot about him. Long years after the Northmen in a great fleet came down upon these isles, and the little chiefs fled before them. But suddenly among them there appeared an old man, the hermit of the Wave Islands, who organised resistance and gathered a strong army. No one dared oppose him, and the quarrelsome petty chiefs forgot their quarrels under his banner, for he had the air of one born to command. At last he met the invaders in the valley of Fountainblue, and beat them so utterly that few escaped to their ships. He fell himself in the first charge, but not before his followers had heard his battle-cry of 'Saint Bride,' and known that the Hermit of the Isles and the great King's Warden were the same."

"That was a common enough thing in wild times. Men grew tired of murder and glory and waving banners, and wanted quiet to make their peace with their own souls. I should have thought the craving scarcely extinct yet."

"Then here is your chance, Mr Maitland," said the girl, laughing. "A little trouble would make the hut habitable, and you could simply disappear, leaving no address to forward your letters to. Think of the sensation, 'Disappearance of a Secretary of State,' and the wild theories and the obituaries. Then some day when the land question became urgent on the mainland, you would turn up suddenly, settle it with extraordinary wisdom, and die after confiding your life-story to some country reporter. But I am afraid it would scarcely do, for you would be discovered by Scotland Yard, which would be ignominious."

"It is a sound idea, but the old device is too crude. However, it could be managed differently. Some day, when civilisation grows oppressive, Miss Clara, I will remember your advice."

The afternoon shadows were beginning to lengthen, and from the west a light sharp wind was crisping the sea. The yacht was getting up steam, and boats were coming ashore for the party. The deep blue waters were flushing rose-pink as the level westering sun smote them from the summit of a cloudbank. The stillness had gone, and the air was now full of sounds and colour. Miss Clara, with an eye on the trim yacht, declared her disapproval. "It is an evening for the cutter," she cried, and in spite of Mrs Etheridge's protests she gave orders for it to be made ready. Then the self-willed young woman looked round for company. "Will you come, Mr Maitland?" she said. "You can sail a boat, can't you? And Mr Despencer, I shall want you to talk to me when Mr Maitland is busy. We shall race the yacht, for we ought to be able to get through the Scart's Neck with this wind."

"I am not sure if you are wise, Miss Clara," and Maitland pulled down his brows as he looked to the west. "It will be wind—in a very little, and you stand the chance of a wetting."

"I don't mind. I want to get the full good of such an evening. You want to be near the water to understand one of our sunsets. I can be a barbarian too, you know."

It was not for Maitland to grumble at this friendliness; so he followed her into the cutter with Despencer, who had no love for the orders but much for her who gave them. He took the helm and steered, with directions from the lady, from his memory of the intricate coast. Despencer with many rugs looked to Miss Clara's comfort, and, having assured his own, was instantly entranced with the glories of the evening.

The boat tripped along for a little in a dazzle of light into the silvery grey of the open water. Far in front lay the narrow gut called the Scart's Neck, which was the by-way to the loch of Fountainblue. Then Maitland at the helm felt the sheets suddenly begin to strain, and, looking behind, saw that the Isles of the Waves were almost lost in the gloom, and that the roseate heavens were quickly darkening behind. The wind which he had feared was upon them; a few seconds more and it was sending the cutter staggering among billows. He could hardly make himself heard in the din, as he roared directions to Despencer about disposing of his person in another part of the boat. The girl with flushed face was laughing in pure joy of the storm. She caught a glimpse of Maitland's serious eye and looked over the gunwale at the threatening west. Then she too became quiet, and meekly sat down on the thwart to which he motioned her.

The gale made the Scart's Neck impossible, and the murky

sky seemed to promise greater fury ere the morning. Twilight was falling, and the other entrance to the quiet loch meant the rounding of a headland and a difficult course through a little archipelago. It was the only way, for return was out of the question, and it seemed vain to risk the narrow chances of the short-cut. Maitland looked down at his two companions, and reflected with pleasure that he was the controller of their fates. He had sailed much as a boy, and he found in this moment of necessity that his old lore returned to him. He felt no mistrust of his powers: whatever the gale he could land them at Fountainblue, though it might take hours and involve much discomfort. He remembered the coast like his own name; he relished the grim rage of the elements, and he kept the cutter's head out to sea with a delight in the primeval conflict.

The last flickering rays of light, coming from the screen of cloud, illumined the girl's pale face, and the sight disquieted him. There was a hint of tragedy in this game. Despencer, nervously self-controlled, was reassuring Clara. Ploughing onward in the blackening night in a frail boat on a wind-threshed sea was no work for a girl. But it was Despencer who was comforting her! Well, it was his proper work. He was made for the business of talking soft things to women. Maitland, his face hard with spray, looked into the darkness with a kind of humour in his heart. And then, as the boat shore and dipped into the storm, its human occupants seemed to pass out of the picture, and it was only a shell tossed on great waters in the unfathomable night. The evening had come, moonless and starless, and Maitland steered as best he could by the deeper blackness which was the configuration of the shore. Something loomed up that he knew for the headland, and they were drifting in a quieter stretch of sea, with the breakers grumbling ahead from the little tangle of islands.

Suddenly he fell into one of the abstractions which had always dogged him through his strenuous life. His mind was clear, he chose his course with a certain precision, but the winds and waves had become to him echoes of echoes. Wet with spray and shifting his body constantly with the movement of the boat, it yet was all a phantasmal existence, while his thoughts were following an airy morrice in a fairy-land world. The motto of his house, the canting motto of old reivers, danced in his brain—"Parmi ceu haut bois conduyrai m'amie"—"Through the high wood I will conduct my love"—and in a land of green forests, dragon-haunted, he was piloting Clara robed in a quaint medieval gown, himself in speckless plate-armour. His fancy fled through a score of scenes, sometimes on a dark heath, or by a lonely river, or among great mountains, but always the lady and her protector. Clara, looking up from Despencer's side, saw his lips moving, noted that his eyes were glad, and for a moment hoped better things of their chances.

Then suddenly she was dumb with alarm, for the cutter heeled over, and but that Maitland woke to clear consciousness and swung the sheet loose, all would have been past. The adventure nerved him and quickened his senses. The boat seemed to move more violently than the wind drove her, and in the utter blackness he felt for the first time the grip of the waters. The ugly cruel monster had wakened, and was about to wreak its anger on the toy. And then he remembered the currents which raced round Eilean Righ and the scattered isles. Dim shapes loomed up, shapes strange and unfriendly, and he felt miserably that he was as helpless now as Despencer. To the left night had wholly shut out the coast; his one chance was to run for one of the isles and risk a landing. It would be a dreary waiting for the dawn, but safety had come before any comfort. And yet, he remembered, the little islands were rock-bound and unfriendly, and he was hurrying forward in the grip of a black current with a gale behind and unknown reefs before.

And then he seemed to remember something of this current which swept along the isles. In a little—so he recalled a boyish voyage in clear weather—they would come to a place where the sea ran swift and dark beside a kind of natural wharf. Here he had landed once upon a time, but it was a difficult enterprise, needing a quick and a far leap at the proper moment, for the stream ran very fast. But if this leap were missed there was still a chance. The isle was the great Eilean Righ, and the current swung round its southern end, and then, joining with another stream, turned up its far side, and for a moment washed the shore. But if this second chance were missed, then nothing remained but to fall into the great sea-going stream and be carried out to death in the wide Atlantic. He strained his eyes to the right for Eilean Righ. Something seemed to approach, as they bent under an access of the gale. They bore down upon it, and he struggled to keep the boat's head away, for at this pace to grate upon rock would mean upsetting. The sail was down, fluttering amidships like a captive bird, and the gaunt mast bowed with the wind. A horrible fascination, the inertia of nightmare, seized him. The motion was so swift and beautiful; why not go on and onward, listlessly? And then, conquering the weakness, he leaned forward and called to Clara. She caught his arm like a child, and he pulled her up beside him. Then he beckoned Despencer, and, shrieking against the din, told him to follow him when he jumped. Despencer nodded, his teeth chattering with cold and the novel business. Suddenly out of the darkness, a yard on their right, loomed a great flat rock along which the current raced like a mill-lade. The boat made to strike, but Maitland forced her nose out to sea, and then as the stern swung round he seized his chance. Holding Clara with his left arm he stood up, balanced himself for a moment on the gunwale, and jumped. He landed sprawling on his side on some wet seaweed, over which the sea was lipping, but undeniably on land. As he pulled himself up he had a vision of the cutter, dancing like a cork, vanishing down the current into the darkness.

Holding the girl in his arms he picked his way across the rock pools to the edge of the island heather. For a moment he thought Clara had fainted. She lay still and inert, her eyes shut, her hair falling foolishly over her brow. He sprinkled some water on her face, and she revived sufficiently to ask her whereabouts. He was crossing the island to find Despencer, but he did not tell her. "You are safe," he said, and he carried her over the rough ground as lightly as a child. An intense exhilaration had seized him. He ran over the flats and strode up the low hillocks with one thought possessing his brain. To save Despencer, that of course was the far-off aim on his mind's horizon, but all the foreground was filled with the lady. "Parmi ceu haut bois"—the old poetry of the world had penetrated to his heart. The black night and the wild wind and the sea were the ministrants of love. The hollow shams of life with their mincing conventions had departed, and in this savage out-world a man stood for a man. The girl's light tweed jacket was no match for this chill gale, so he stopped for a moment, took off his own shooting-coat and put it round her. And then, as he came over a little ridge, he was aware of a grumbling of waters and the sea.

The beach was hidden in a veil of surf which sprinkled the very edge of the bracken. Beyond, the dark waters were boiling like a caldron, for the tides in this little bay ran with the fury of a river in spate. A moon was beginning to struggle thr ough the windyclouds, and surf, rock, and wave began to shape themselves out of the night. Clara stood on the sand, a slim, desolate figure, and clung to Maitland's arm. She was still dazed with the storm and the baffling suddenness of change. Maitland, straining his eyes out to sea, was in a waking dream. With the lady no toil was too great, no darkness terrible; for her he would scale the blue air and plough the hills and do all the lover's feats of romance. And then suddenly he shook her hand roughly from his arm and ran forward, for he saw something coming down the tide.

Before he left the boat he had lowered the sail, and the cutter swung to the current, an odd amorphous thing, now heeling over with a sudden gust and now pulled back to balance by the strong grip of the water. A figure seemed to sit in the stern, making feeble efforts to steer. Maitland knew the coast and the ways of the sea. He ran through the surf-ring into the oily-black eddies, shouting to Despencer to come overboard. Soon he was not ten yards from the cutter's line, where the current made a turn towards the shore before it washed the iron rocks to the right. He found deep water, and in two strokes was in the grip of the tides and borne wildly towards the reef. He prepared himself for what was coming, raising his feet and turning his right shoulder to the front. And then with a shock he was pinned against the rock-wall, with the tides tugging at his legs, while his hands clung desperately to a shelf. Here he remained, yelling directions to the coming boat. Surf was in his eyes, so that at first he could not see, but at last in a dip of the waves he saw the cutter, a man's form in the stern, plunging not twenty yards away. Now was his chance or never, for while the tide would take a boat far from his present place of vantage, it would carry a lighter thing, such as a man's body, in a circle nearer to the shore. He yelled again, and the world seemed to him quiet for a moment, while his voice echoed eerily in the void. Despencer must have heard it, for the next moment he saw him slip pluckily overboard, making the cutter heel desperately with his weight. And then—it seemed an age—a man, choking and struggling weakly, came down the current, and, pushing his right arm out against the rush of water, he had caught the swimmer by the collar and drawn him in to the side of the rock.

Then came the harder struggle. Maitland's left hand was numbing, and though he had a foothold, it was too slight to lean on with full weight. A second lassitude oppressed him, a supreme desire to slip into those racing tides and rest. He was in no panic about death, but he had the practical man's love of an accomplished task, and it nerved him to the extreme toil. Slowly by inches he drew himself up the edge of the reef, cherishing jealously each grip and foothold, with Despencer, half-choked and all but fainting, hanging heavily on his right arm. Blind with spray, sick with sea-water, and aching with his labours, he gripped at last the tangles of seaweed, which meant the flat surface, and with one final effort raised himself and Despencer to the top. There he lay for a few minutes with his head in a rock-pool till the first weariness had passed.

He staggered with his burden in his arms along the ragged reef to the strip of sand where Clara was weeping hysterically. The sight of her restored Maitland to vigour, the appeal of her lonely figure there in the wet brackens. She must think them all dead, he reflected, and herself desolate, for she could not have interpreted rightly his own wild rush into the waves. When she heard his voice she started, as if at a ghost, and then seeing his burden, ran towards him. "Oh, he is dead!" she cried. "Tell me! tell me!" and she clasped the inert figure so that her arm crossed Maitland's. Despencer, stupefied and faint, was roused to consciousness by a woman's kisses on his cheek, and still more by his bearer abruptly laying him on the heather. Clara hung over him like a mother, calling him by soft names, pushing his hair from his brow, forgetful of her own wet and sorry plight. And meanwhile Maitland stood watching, while his palace of glass was being shivered about his ears.

Aforetime his arrogance had kept him from any thought of jealousy; now the time and place were too solemn for trifling, and facts were laid bare before him. Sentiment does not bloom readily in a hard nature, but if it once comes to flower it does not die without tears and agonies. The wearied man, who stood quietly beside the hysterical pair, had a moment of peculiar anguish. Then he conquered sentiment, as he had conquered all other feelings of whose vanity he was assured. He was now, as he was used to be, a man among children; and as a man he had his work. He bent over Clara. "I know a hollow in the middle of the island," he said, "where we can camp the night. I'll carry Despencer, for his ankle is twisted. Do you think you could try to walk?"

The girl followed obediently, her eyes only on her lover. Her trust in the other was infinite, her indifference to him impenetrable; while he, hopelessly conscious of his fate, saw in the slim dishevelled figure at his side the lost lady, the mistress for him of all romance and generous ambitions. The new springs in his life were choked; he had still his work, his power, and, thank God, his courage; but the career which ran out to the horizon of his vision was black and loveless. And he held in his arms the thing which had frustrated him, the thing he had pulled out of the deep in peril of his body; and at the thought life for a moment seemed to be only a comic opera with tragedy to shift the scenes.

He found a cleft between two rocks with a soft floor of heather. There had been no rain, so the bracken was dry, and he gathered great armfuls and driftwood logs from the shore. Soon he had a respectable pile of timber, and then in the nick of the cleft he built a fire. His matches, being in his jacket pocket, had escaped the drenchings of salt water, and soon with a smoke and crackling and sweet scent of burning wood, a fire was going cheerily in the darkness. Then he made a couch of bracken, and laid there the still feeble Despencer. The man was more weak than ill; but for his ankle he was unhurt; and a little brandy would have brought him to himself. But this could not be provided, and Clara saw in his condition only the sign of mortal sickness. With haggard eyes she watched by him, easing his head, speaking soft kind words, forgetful of her own cold and soaking clothes. Maitland drew her gently to the fire, shook down the bracken to make a rest for her head, and left a pile of logs ready for use. "I am going to the end of the island," he said, "to light a fire for a signal. It is the only part which they can see on the mainland, and if they see the blaze they will come off for us as soon as it is light." The pale girl listened obediently. This man was the master, and in his charge was the safety of her lover and herself.

Maitland turned his back upon the warm nook, and stumbled along the ridge to the northern extremity of the isle. It was not a quarter of a mile away, but the land was so rough with gullies and crags that the journey took him nearly an hour. Just off the extreme point was a flat rock, sloping northward to a considerable height, a place from which a beacon could penetrate far over the mainland. He gathered brackens for kindling, and driftwood which former tides had heaped on the beach; and then with an armful he splashed through the shallow surf to the rock. Scrambling to the top, he found a corner where a fire might be lit, a place conspicuous and yet sheltered. Here he laid his kindling, and then in many wet journeys he carried his stores of firewood from the mainland to the rock. The lighting was nervous work, for he had few matches; but at last the dampish wood had caught, and tongues of flame shot up out of the smoke. Meantime the wind had sunk lower, the breakers seemed to have been left behind, and the eternal surge of the tides became the dominant sound to the watcher by the beacon.

And then, it seemed to him, the great convulsions of the night died away, and a curious peace came down upon the waters. The fire leaped in the air, the one living thing in a hushed and expectant world. It was not the quiet of sleep but of a sudden cessation, like the lull after a great flood or a snowslip. The tides still eddied and swayed, but it was noiselessly; the world moved, yet without sound or friction. The bitter wind which chilled his face and stirred up the red embers was like a phantom blast, without the roughness of a common gale. For a moment he seemed to be set upon a high mountain with the world infinitely remote beneath his feet. To all men there come moments of loneliness of body, and to some few the mingled ecstasy and grief of loneliness of soul. The child-tale of the Ocean Quiet came back to him, the hour of the Breathing of God. Surely the great silence was now upon the world. But it was an evil presage, for all who sailed into it were homeless wanderers for ever after. Ah well! he had always been a wanderer, and the last gleam of home had been left behind, where by the firelight in the cold cranny a girl was crooning over her lover.

His past, his monotonous, brilliant past, slipped by with the knotless speed of a vision. He saw a boy, haunted with dreams, chafing at present delights, clutching evermore at the faint things of fancy. He saw a man, playing with the counters which others played with, fighting at first for bare existence and then for power and the pride of life. Success came over his path like a false dawn, but he knew in his heart that he had never sought it. What was that remote ineffable thing he had followed? Here in the quiet of the shadowy waters he had the moment of self-revelation which comes to all, and hopes and dim desires seemed to stand out with the clearness of accomplished facts. There had always been something elect and secret at the back of his fiercest ambitions. The ordinary cares of men had been to him but little things to be played with; he had won by despising them; casting them from him, they had fallen into the hollow of his hand. And he had held them at little, finding his reward in his work, and in a certain alertness and freshness of spirit which he had always cherished. There is a story of island-born men who carry into inland places and the streets of cities the noise of sea-water in their ears, and hear continually the tern crying and the surf falling. So from his romantic boyhood this man had borne an arrogance towards the things of the world which had given him a contemptuous empire over a share of them. As he saw the panorama of his life no place or riches entered into it, but only himself, the haggard, striving soul, growing in power, losing, perhaps, in wisdom. And then, at the end of the way, Death, to shrivel the power to dust, and with the might of his sunbeam to waken to life the forgotten world of the spirit.

In the hush he seemed to feel the wheel and the drift of things, the cosmic order of nature. He forgot his weariness and his plashing clothes as he put more wood on the beacon and dreamed into the night. The pitiless sea, infinite, untamable, washing the Poles and hiding Earth's secrets in her breast, spoke to him with a far-remembered voice. The romance of the remote isles, the homes of his people, floating still in a twilight of old story, rose out of the darkness. His life, with its routine and success, seemed in a moment hollow, a child's game, unworthy of a man. The little social round, the manipulation of half-truths, the easy victories over fools—surely this was not the task for him. He was a dreamer, but a dreamer with an iron hand; he was scarcely in the prime of life; the world was wide and his chances limitless. One castle of cards had already been overthrown; the Ocean Quiet was undermining another. He was sick of domesticity of every sort—of town, of home, of civilisation. The sad elemental world was his, the fury and the tenderness of nature, the peace of the wilds which old folk had called the Breathing of God. "Parmi ceu haut bois conduyrai m'amie"—this was still his motto, to carry untarnished to the end an austere and beautiful dream. His little ambitions had been but shreds and echoes and shadows of this supreme reality. And his love had been but another such simulacrum; for what he had sought was no foolish, laughing girl, but the Immortal Shepherdess, who, singing the old songs of youth, drives her flocks to the hill in the first dewy dawn of the world.

Suddenly he started and turned his head. Day was breaking in a red windy sky, and somewhere a boat's oars were plashing in the sea. And then he realised for the first time that he was cold and starving and soaked to the bone.

V.

MR HENRY DURWARD TO LADY CLAUDIA ETHERIDGE.

". . . Things have happened, my dear Clo, since I last wrote; time has passed; to-morrow I leave this place and go to stalk with Drapier; and yet in the stress of departure I take time to answer the host of questions with which you assailed me. I am able to give you the best of news. You have won your bet. Your prophecy about the conduct of the 'other Etheridge girl' has come out right. They are both here, as it happens, having come on from Fountainblue,—both the hero and the heroine, I mean, of this most reasonable romance. You know Jack Despencer, one of the best people in the world, though a trifle given to chirping. But I don't think the grasshopper will become a burden to Miss Clara, for she likes that sort of thing. She must, for there is reason to believe that she refused for its sake the greatest match—I speak with all reverence—which this happy country could offer. I know you like Maitland as little as I do, but we agree in admiring the Colossus from a distance. Well, the Colossus has, so to speak, been laid low by a frivolous member of your sex. It is all a most romantic tale. Probably you have heard the gist of it, but here is the full and circumstantial account.

. . . .

"We found Maitland beside the fire he had been feeding all night, and I shall never forget his figure alone in the dawn on that rock, drenched and dishevelled, but with his haggard white face set like a Crusader's. He took us to a kind of dell in the centre of the island, where we found Clara and Despencer shivering beside a dying fire. He had a twisted ankle and had got a bad scare, while she was perfectly composed, though she broke down when we got home. It must have been an awful business for both, but Maitland never seems to have turned a hair. I want to know two things. First, how in the presence of great danger he managed to get his dismissal from the lady?—for get it he assuredly did, and Despencer at once appeared in the part of the successful lover; second, what part he played in the night's events? Clara remembered little, Despencer only knew that he had been pulled out of the sea, but over all Maitland seems to have brooded like a fate. As usual he told us nothing. It was always his way to give the world results and leave it to find out his methods for itself. . . .

"Despencer overwhelmed him with gratitude. His new happiness made him in love with life, and he included Maitland in the general affection. The night's events seemed to have left their mark on the great man also. He was very quiet, forgot to be rude to anybody, and was kind to both Clara and Despencer. It is his way of acknowledging defeat, the great gentleman's way, for, say what we like about him, he is a tremendous gentleman, one of the last of the breed. . . .

"And then he went away—two days later. Just before he went Hugh Clanroyden and myself were talking in the library, which has a window opening on a flower-garden. Despencer was lying in an invalid's chair under a tree and Clara was reading to him. Maitland was saying good-bye, and he asked for Despencer. We told him that he was with Clara in the garden. He smiled one of those odd scarce smiles of his, and went out to them. When I saw his broad shoulders bending over the chair and the strong face looking down at the radiant Jack with his amiable good looks, confound it, Clo, I had to contrast the pair, and admit with Shakespeare the excellent foppery of the world. Well-a-day! 'Smooth Jacob still robs homely Esau.' And perhaps it is a good thing, for we are most of us Jacobs, and Esau is an uncomfortable fellow in our midst.

"A week later came the surprising, the astounding news that he had taken the African Governorship. A career ruined, everyone said, the finest chance in the world flung away; and then people speculated, and the story came out in bits, and there was only one explanation. It is the right one, as I think you will agree, but it points to some hidden weakness in that iron soul that he could be moved to fling over the ambitions of years because of a girl's choice. He will go and bury himself in the wilds, and our party will have to find another leader. Of course he will do his work well, but it is just as if I were to give up my chances of the Woolsack for a county-court judgeship. He will probably be killed, for he has a million enemies; he is perfectly fearless, and he does not understand the arts of compromise. It was a privilege, I shall always feel, to have known him. He was a great man, and yet—intellect, power, character, were at the mercy of a girl's caprice. As I write, I hear Clara's happy laugh below in the garden, probably at some witticism of the fortunate Jack's. Upon which, with my usual pride in the obvious, I am driven to reflect that the weak things in life may confound the strong, and that, after all, the world is to the young. . . ."

VI.

SIR HUGH CLANROYDEN TO MR HENRY DURWARD.

SOME YEARS LATER.

". . . I am writing this on board ship, as you will see from the heading, and shall post it when I get to the Cape. You have heard of my appointment, and I need not tell you how deep were my searchings of heart before I found courage to accept. Partly I felt that I had got my chance; partly I thought—an inconsequent feeling—that Maitland, if he had lived, would have been glad to see me in the place. But I am going to wear the Giant's Robe, and Heaven knows I have not the shoulders to fill it. Yet I am happy in thinking that I am in a small sense faithful to his memory.

"No further news, I suppose, has come of the manner of his death? Perhaps we shall never know, for it was on one of those Northern expeditions with a few men by which he held the frontier. I wonder if anyone will ever write fully the history of all that he did? It must have been a titanic work, but his methods were always so quiet that people accepted his results like a gift from Providence. He was given, one gathers, a practically free hand, and he made the country—four years' work of a man of genius. They wished to bring his body home, but he made them bury him where he fell—a characteristic last testament. And so he has gone out of the world into the world's history.

"I am still broken by his death, but, now that he is away, I begin to see him more clearly. Most people, I think, misunderstood him. I was one of his nearest friends, and I only knew bits of the man. For one thing—and I hate to use the vulgar word—he was the only aristocrat I ever heard of. Our classes are three-fourths of them of yesterday's growth, without the tradition, character, manner, or any trait of an aristocracy. And the few, who are nominally of the blood, have gone to seed in mind, or are spoilt by coarse marriages, or, worst of all, have the little trifling superior airs of incompetence. But he, he had the most transcendent breeding in mind and spirit. He had no need for self-assertion, for his most casual acquaintances put him at once in a different class from all other men. He had never a trace of a vulgar ideal; men's opinions, worldly honour, the common pleasures of life, were merely degrees of the infinitely small. And yet he was no bloodless mystic. If race means anything, he had it to perfection. Dreams and fancies to him were the realities, while facts were the shadows which he made dance as it pleased him.

"The truth is, that he was that rarest of mortals, the iron dreamer. He thought in æons and cosmic cycles, and because of it he could do what he pleased in life. We call a man practical if he is struggling in the crowd with no knowledge of his whereabouts, and yet in our folly we deny the name to the clear-sighted man who can rule the crowd from above. And here I join issue with you and everybody else. You thought it was Miss Clara's refusal which sent him abroad and interrupted his career. I read the thing otherwise. His love for the girl was a mere accident, a survival of the domestic in an austere spirit. Something, I do not know what, showed him his true desires. She may have rejected him; he may never have spoken to her; in any case the renunciation had to come. You must remember that that visit to Fountainblue was the first that he had paid since his boyhood to his boyhood's home. Those revisitings have often a strange trick of self-revelation. I believe that in that night on the island he saw our indoor civilisation and his own destiny in so sharp a contrast that he could not choose but make the severance. He found work where there could be small hope of honour or reward, but many a chance for a hero. And I am sure that he was happy, and that it was the longed-for illumination that dawned on him with the bullet which pierced his heart.

"But, you will say, the fact remains that he was once in love with Miss Clara, and that she would have none of him. I do not deny it. He was never a favourite with women; but, thank heaven, I have better things to do than study their peculiarities. . . ."

IV.

THE MOON ENDURETH

TALES AND FANCIES

"S. Francis, preaching upon Psalm lxxii., *Deus, judicium*, . . . thus expounded the words, *Orietur in diebus ejus justitia et abundantia pacis donec auferatur luna*,—The moon, he said, signified the dominion of all strange things in earth and air, such as were beyond the comprehension of man's narrow reason or the authority of his temporal will. To the righteous is promised abundance of peace while the moon endureth: that is, peace not from wars and oppressions alone, but likewise from the mysteries which God yet suffereth to cloud His world."—LIVES OF THE SAINTS.

TO THE HAPPY MEMORY OF

MY FATHER.

Requiem aeternam dona ei, Domine,
Et lux perpetua luceat ei.

FROM THE PENTLANDS LOOKING NORTH AND SOUTH.

AROUND my feet the clouds are drawn
In the cold mystery of the dawn ;
No breezes cheer, no guests intrude
My mossy, mist-clad solitude ;
When sudden down the steeps of sky
Flames a long, lightening wind. On high
The steel-blue arch shines clear, and far,
In the low lands where cattle are,
Towns smoke. And swift, a haze, a gleam,—
The Firth lies like a frozen stream,
Reddening with morn. Tall spires of ships,
Like thorns about the harbour's lips,
Now shake faint canvas, now, asleep,
Their salt, uneasy slumbers keep ;
While golden-grey, o'er kirk and wall,
Day wakes in the ancient capital.

Before me lie the lists of strife.
The caravanserai of life,
Whence from the gates the merchants go
On the world's highways ; to and fro
Sail laden ships ; and in the street
The lone foot-traveller shakes his feet,
And in some corner by the fire
Tells the old tale of heart's desire.
Thither from alien seas and skies
Comes the far-quested merchandise :—

Wrought silks of Broussa, Mocha's ware
Brown-tinted, fragrant, and the rare
Thin perfumes that the rose's breath
Has sought, immortal in her death:
Gold, gems, and spice, and haply still
The red rough largess of the hill
Which takes the sun and bears the vines
Among the haunted Apennines.
And he who treads the cobbled street
To-day in the cold North may meet,
Come month, come year, the dusky East,
And share the Caliph's secret feast;
Or in the toil of wind and sun
Bear pilgrim-staff, forlorn, fordone,
Till o'er the steppe, athwart the sand,
Gleam the far gates of Samarkand.
The ringing quay, the weathered face,
Fair skies, dusk hands, the ocean race,
The palm-girt isle, the frosty shore,
Gales and hot suns the wide world o'er,
Grey North, red South, and burnished West,
The goals of the old tireless quest,
Leap in the smoke, immortal, free,
Where shines yon morning fringe of sea.
I turn, and lo! the moorlands high
Lie still and frigid to the sky.
The film of morn is silver-grey
On the young heather, and away,
Dim, distant, set in ribs of hill,
Green glens are shining, stream and mill,
Clachan and kirk and garden-ground,
All silent in the hush profound
Which haunts alone the hills' recess,
The antique home of quietness.
Nor to the folk can piper play
The tune of "Hills and Far Away,"

For they are with them. Morn can fire
No peaks of weary heart's desire,
Nor the red sunset flame behind
Some ancient ridge of longing mind.
For Arcady is here, around,
In lilt of stream, in the clear sound
Of lark and moorbird, in the bold
Gay glamour of the evening gold,
And so the wheel of seasons moves
To kirk and market, to mild loves
And modest hates, and still the sight
Of brown kind faces, and when night
Draws dark around with age and fear
Theirs is the simple hope to cheer.
A land of peace where lost romance
And ghostly shine of helm and lance
Still dwell by castled scarp and lea,
And the last homes of chivalry,
And the good fairy folk, my dear,
Who speak for cunning souls to hear,
In crook of glen and bower of hill
Sing of the Happy Ages still.

O Thou to whom man's heart is known,
Grant me my morning orison.
Grant me the rover's path—to see
The dawn arise, the daylight flee,
In the far wastes of sand and sun!
Grant me with venturous heart to run
On the old highway, where in pain
And ecstasy man strives amain,
Conquers his fellows, or, too weak,
Finds the great rest that wanderers seek!
Grant me the joy of wind and brine,
The zest of food, the taste of wine,

The fighter's strength, the echoing strife,
The high tumultuous lists of life—
May I ne'er lag, nor hapless fall,
Nor weary at the battle-call! . . .
But when the even brings surcease,
Grant me the happy moorland peace;
That in my heart's depth ever lie
That ancient land of heath and sky,
Where the old rhymes and stories fall
In kindly, soothing pastoral.
There in the hills grave silence lies,
And Death himself wears friendly guise;
There be my lot, my twilight stage,
Dear city of my pilgrimage.

I. THE COMPANY OF THE MARJOLAINE.[1]

" Qu'est-c' qui passe ici si tard,
Compagnons de la Marjolaine ? "
—CHANSONS DE FRANCE.

I.

. . . I CAME down from the mountains and into the pleasing valley of the Adige in as pelting a heat as ever mortal suffered under. The way underfoot was parched and white ; I had newly come out of a wilderness of white limestone crags, and a sun of Italy blazed blindingly in an azure Italian sky. You are to suppose, my dear aunt, that I had had enough and something more of my craze for foot-marching. A fortnight ago I had gone to Belluno in a post-chaise, dismissed my fellow to carry my baggage by way of Verona, and with no more than a valise on my back plunged into the fastnesses of those mountains. I had a fancy to see the little sculptured hills which made backgrounds for Gianbellin, and there were rumours of great mountains built wholly of marble which shone like the battlements of the Celestial City. So at any rate reported young Mr Wyndham, who

[1] This extract from the unpublished papers of the Manorwater family has seemed to the Editor worth printing for its historical interest. The famous Lady Molly Carteron became Countess of Manorwater by her second marriage. She was a wit and a friend of wits, and her nephew, the Honourable Charles Hervey-Townshend (afterwards our Ambassador at The Hague), addressed to her a series of amusing letters while making, after the fashion of his contemporaries, the Grand Tour of Europe. Three letters, written at various places in the Eastern Alps and despatched from Venice, contain the following short narrative.

had travelled with me from Milan to Venice. I lay the first night at Pieve, where Titian had the fortune to be born, and the landlord at the inn displayed a set of villainous daubs which he swore were the early works of that master. Thence up a toilsome valley I journeyed to the Ampezzan country, where indeed I saw my white mountains, but, alas! no longer Celestial. For it rained like Westmorland for five endless days, while I kicked my heels in an inn and turned a canto of Ariosto into halting English couplets. By-and-by it cleared, and I headed westward towards Bozen, among the tangle of wild rocks where the Dwarf King had once his rose-garden. The first night I had no inn, but slept in the vile cabin of a forester, who spoke a tongue half Latin, half Dutch, which I failed to master. The next day was a blaze of heat, the mountain-paths lay thick with dust, and I had no wine from sunrise to sunset. Can you wonder that, when the following noon I saw Santa Chiara sleeping in its green circlet of meadows, my thought was only of a deep draught and a cool chamber? I protest that I am a great lover of natural beauty, of rock and cascade, and all the properties of the poet; but the enthusiasm of M. Rousseau himself would sink from the stars to earth if he had marched since breakfast in a cloud of dust with a throat like the nether millstone.

Yet I had not entered the place before Romance revived. The little town—a mere wayside halting-place on the great mountain-road to the North—had the air of mystery which foretells adventure. Why is it that a dwelling or a countenance catches the fancy with the promise of some strange destiny? I have houses in my mind which I know will some day and somehow be intertwined oddly with my life; and I have faces in memory of which I know nothing save that I shall undoubtedly cast eyes again upon them. My first glimpses of Santa Chiara gave me this earnest of romance. It was walled and fortified, the streets were narrow pits of shade, old tenements with bent fronts swayed to meet each other. Melons lay drying on flat roofs, and yet now and then would come a high-pitched northern gable. Latin and Teuton met and mingled in the place, and, as Mr Gibbon has taught us, the offspring of this admixture is something fantastic and unpredictable. I forgot my grievous thirst and my tired feet in admiration and a certain vague expectation of wonders. Here, ran my thought, it is fated, maybe, that Romance and I shall at last compass a meeting. Perchance some princess is in need of my arm, or some affair of high policy is afoot in this jumble of old masonry. You will laugh at my folly, but I had an excuse for it. A fortnight in strange mountains disposes a man to look for something at his next encounter with his kind, and the sight of Santa Chiara would have fired the imagination of a judge in Chancery.

I strode happily into the courtyard of the Tre Croci, and presently had my expectation confirmed. For I found my fellow, Gianbattista,—a faithful rogue I got in Rome on a Cardinal's recommendation,—hot in dispute with a lady's-maid. The woman was old, harsh-featured—no Italian clearly, though she spoke fluently in the tongue. She rated my man like a pickpocket, and the dispute was over a room.

"The signor will bear me out," said Gianbattista. "Was not I sent to Verona with his baggage, and thence to this place of ill manners? Was I not bidden engage for him a suite of apartments? Did I not duly choose these fronting on the gallery, and dispose therein the signor's baggage? And lo! an hour ago I found it all turned into the yard and this woman installed in its place. It is monstrous, unbearable! Is this an inn for travellers, or haply the private mansion of these Magnificences?"

"My servant speaks truly," I said firmly yet with courtesy, having no mind to spoil adventure by urging rights. "He had orders to take these rooms for me, and I know not what higher power can countermand me."

The woman had been staring at me scornfully, for no

doubt in my dusty habit I was a figure of small count; but at the sound of my voice she started, and cried out, "You are English, signor?"

I bowed an admission.

"Then my mistress shall speak with you," she said, and dived into the inn like an elderly rabbit.

Gianbattista was for sending for the landlord and making a riot in that hostelry; but I stayed him, and bidding him fetch me a flask of white wine, three lemons, and a glass of *eau de vie*, I sat down peaceably at one of the little tables in the courtyard and prepared for the quenching of my thirst. Presently, as I sat drinking that excellent compound of my own invention, my shoulder was touched, and I turned to find the maid and her mistress. Alas for my hopes of a glorious being, young and lissom and bright with the warm riches of the south! I saw a short, stout little lady, well on the wrong side of thirty. She had plump red cheeks, and fair hair dressed indifferently in the Roman fashion. Two candid blue eyes redeemed her plainness, and a certain grave and gentle dignity. She was notably a gentlewoman, so I got up, doffed my hat, and awaited her commands.

She spoke in Italian. "Your pardon, signor, but I fear my good Cristine has done you unwittingly a wrong."

Cristine snorted at this premature plea of guilty, while I hastened to assure the fair apologist that any rooms I might have taken were freely at her service.

I spoke unconsciously in English, and she replied in a halting parody of that tongue. "I understand him," she said, "but I do not speak him happily. I will discourse, if the signor pleases, in our first speech."

She and her father, it appeared, had come over the Brenner, and arrived that morning at the Tre Croci, where they purposed to lie for some days. He was an old man, very feeble, and much depending upon her constant care. Wherefore it was necessary that the rooms of all the party should adjoin, and there was no suite of the size in the inn save that which I had taken. Would I therefore consent to forego my right, and place her under an eternal debt?

I agreed most readily, being at all times careless where I sleep, so the bed be clean, or where I eat, so the meal be good. I bade my servant see the landlord and have my belongings carried to other rooms. Madame thanked me sweetly, and would have gone, when a thought detained her.

"It is but courteous," she said, "that you should know the names of those whom you have befriended. My father is called the Count d'Albani, and I am his only daughter. We travel to Florence, where we have a villa in the environs."

"My name," said I, "is Hervey-Townshend, an Englishman travelling abroad for his entertainment."

"Hervey?" she repeated. "Are you one of the family of Miladi Hervey?"

"My worthy aunt," I replied, with a tender recollection of that preposterous woman.

Madame turned to Christine, and spoke rapidly in a whisper.

"My father, sir," she said, addressing me, "is an old frail man, little used to the company of strangers; but in former days he has had kindness from members of your house, and it would be a satisfaction to him, I think, to have the privilege of your acquaintance."

She spoke with the air of a vizier who promises a traveller a sight of the Grand Turk. I murmured my gratitude, and hastened after Gianbattista. In an hour I had bathed, rid myself of my beard, and arrayed myself indecent clothing. Then I strolled out to inspect the little city, admired an altar-piece, chaffered with a Jew for a cameo, purchased some small necessaries, and returned early in the afternoon with a noble appetite for dinner.

The Tre Croci had been in happier days a bishop's lodging, and possessed a dining-hall ceiled with black oak and adorned with frescoes. It was used as a general *salle à manger* for all dwellers in the inn, and there accordingly I sat down to my long-deferred meal. At first there were no other diners, and I had two maids, as well as Gianbattista, to attend on my wants. Presently Madame d'Albani entered, escorted by Cristine and by a tall gaunt serving-man, who seemed no part of the hostelry. The landlord followed, bowing civilly, and the two women seated themselves at the little table at the farther end. "Il Signor Conte dines in his room," said Madame to the host, who withdrew to see to that gentleman's needs.

I found my eyes straying often to the little party in the cool twilight of that refectory. The man-servant was so old and battered, and yet of such a dignity, that he lent a touch of intrigue to the thing. He stood stiffly behind Madame's chair, handing dishes with an air of silent reverence—the lackey of a great noble, if ever I had seen the type. Madame never glanced towards me, but conversed sparingly with Cristine, while she pecked delicately at her food. Her name ran in my head with a tantalising flavour of the familiar. Albani! D'Albani! It was a name not uncommon in the Roman States, but I had never heard it linked to a noble family. And yet I had,—somehow, somewhere; and in the vain effort at recollection I had almost forgotten my hunger. There was nothing bourgeois in the little lady. The austere servants, the high manner of condescension, spake of a stock used to deference, though, maybe, pitifully decayed in its fortunes. There was a mystery in these quiet folk which tickled my curiosity. Romance after all was not destined to fail me at Santa Chiara.

My doings of the afternoon were of interest to myself alone. Suffice it to say that when I returned at nightfall I found Gianbattista the trustee of a letter. It was from Madame, written in a fine thin hand on a delicate paper, and it invited me to wait upon the signor, her father, that evening at eight o'clock. What caught my eye was a coronet stamped in a corner. A coronet, I say, but in truth it was a crown, the same as surmounts the Arms Royal of England on the signboard of a Court tradesman. I marvelled at the ways of foreign heraldry. Either this family of d'Albani had higher pretensions than I had given it credit for, or it employed an unlearned and imaginative stationer. I scribbled a line of acceptance and went to dress.

The hour of eight found me knocking at the Count's door. The grim serving-man admitted me to the pleasant chamber which should have been mine own. A dozen wax candles burned in sconces, and on the table among fruits and the remains of supper stood a handsome candelabra of silver. A small fire of logs had been lit on the hearth, and before it in an arm-chair sat a strange figure of a man. He seemed not so much old as aged. I should have put him at sixty, but the marks he bore were clearly less those of Time than of Life. There sprawled before me the relics of noble looks. The fleshy nose, the pendulous cheek, the drooping mouth, had once been cast in the lines of manly beauty. Heavy eyebrows above and heavy bags beneath spoiled the effect of a choleric blue eye, which age had not dimmed. The man was gross and yet haggard; it was not the padding of good living which clothed his bones, but a heaviness as of some dropsical malady. I could picture him in health a gaunt loose-limbed being, high-featured and swift and eager. He was dressed wholly in black velvet, with fresh ruffles and wristbands, and he wore heeled shoes with antique silver buckles. It was a figure of an older age which rose slowly to greet me, in one hand a snuff-box and a purple handkerchief, and in the other a book with finger marking place. He made me a great bow as Madame uttered my name, and held out a hand with a kindly smile.

"Mr Hervey-Townshend," he said, "we will speak English, if you please. I am fain to hear it again, for 'tis a tongue I love. I make you welcome, sir, for your own sake and for the sake of your kin. How is her honourable ladyship, your aunt? A week ago she sent me a letter."

I answered that she did famously, and wondered what

cause of correspondence my worthy aunt could have with wandering nobles of Italy.

He motioned me to a chair between Madame and himself, while a servant set a candle on a shelf behind him. Then he proceeded to catechise me in excellent English, with now and then a phrase of French, as to the doings in my own land. Admirably informed this Italian gentleman proved himself. I defy you to find in Almack's more intelligent gossip. He inquired as to the chances of my Lord North and the mind of my Lord Rockingham. He had my Lord Shelburne's foibles at his fingers' ends. The habits of the Prince, the aims of their ladyships of Dorset and Buckingham, the extravagance of this noble Duke and that right honourable gentleman were not hid from him. I answered discreetly yet frankly, for there was no ill-breeding in his curiosity. Rather it seemed like the inquiries of some fine lady, now buried deep in the country, as to the doings of a forsaken Mayfair. There was humour in it and something of pathos.

"My aunt must be a voluminous correspondent, sir," I said.

He laughed. "I have many friends in England who write to me, but I have seen none of them for long, and I doubt I may never see them again. Also in my youth I have been in England." And he sighed as at a sorrowful recollection.

Then he showed the book in his hand. "See," he said, "here is one of your English writings, the greatest book I have ever happened on." It was a volume of Mr Fielding.

For a little he talked of books and poets. He admired Mr Fielding profoundly, Dr Smollett somewhat less, Mr Richardson not at all. But he was clear that England had a monopoly of good writers, saving only my friend M. Rousseau, whom he valued, yet with reservations. Of the Italians he had no opinion. I instanced against him the plays of Signor Alfieri. He groaned, shook his head, and grew moody.

"Know you Scotland?" he asked suddenly.

I replied that I had visited Scotch cousins, but had no great estimation for the country. "It is too poor and jagged," I said, "for the taste of one who loves colour and sunshine and suave outlines."

He sighed. "It is indeed a bleak land, but a kindly. When the sun shines at all he shines on the truest hearts in the world. I love its bleakness too. There is a spirit in the misty hills and the harsh sea-wind which inspires men to great deeds. Poverty and courage go often together, and my Scots, if they are poor, are as untamable as their mountains."

"You know the land, sir?" I asked.

"I have seen it, and I have known many Scots. You will find them in Paris and Avignon and Rome, with never a plack in their pockets. I have a feeling for exiles, sir, and I have pitied these poor people. They gave their all for the cause they followed."

Clearly the Count shared my aunt's views of history, those views which have made such sport for us often at Carteron. Stalwart Whig as I am, there was something in the tone of the old gentleman which made me feel a certain majesty in the lost cause.

"I am Whig in blood and Whig in principle," I said, "but I have never denied that those Scots who followed the Chevalier were too good to waste on so trumpery a leader."

I had no sooner spoken the words than I felt that somehow I had been guilty of a *bêtise*.

"It may be so," said the Count. "I did not bid you here, sir, to argue on politics, on which I am assured we should differ. But I will ask you one question. The King of England is a stout upholder of the right of kings. How does he face the defection of his American possessions?"

"The nation takes it well enough, and as for his Majesty's feelings, there is small inclination to inquire into them.

I conceive of the whole war as a blunder out of which we have come as we deserved. The day is gone by for the assertion of monarchic rights against the will of a people."

"May be. But take note that the King of England is suffering to-day as—how do you call him?—the Chevalier suffered forty years ago. 'The wheel has come full circle,' as your Shakespeare says. Time has wrought his revenge."

He was staring into a fire, which burned small and smokily.

"You think the day for kings is ended. I read it differently. The world will ever have need of kings. If a nation cast out one it will have to find another. And mark you, those later kings, created by the people, will bear a harsher hand than the old race who ruled as of right. Some day the world will regret having destroyed the kindly and legitimate line of monarchs and put in their place tyrants who govern by the sword or by flattering an idle mob."

This belated dogma would at other times have set me laughing, but the strange figure before me gave no impulse to merriment. I glanced at Madame, and saw her face grave and perplexed, and I thought I read a warning gleam in her eye. There was a mystery about the party which irritated me, but good breeding forbade me to seek a clue.

"You will permit me to retire, sir," I said. "I have but this morning come down from a long march among the mountains east of this valley. Sleeping in wayside huts and tramping those sultry paths make a man think pleasantly of bed."

The Count seemed to brighten at my words. "You are a marcher, sir, and love the mountains? Once I would gladly have joined you, for in my youth I was a great walker in hilly places. Tell me, now, how many miles will you cover in a day?"

I told him thirty at a stretch.

"Ah," he said, "I have done fifty, without food, over the roughest and mossiest mountains. I lived on what I shot, and for drink I had spring-water. Nay, I am forgetting.

There was another beverage, which I wager you have never tasted. Heard you ever, sir, of that *eau de vie* which the Scots call *usquebagh?* It will comfort a traveller as no thin Italian wine will comfort him. By my soul, you shall taste it. Charlotte, my dear, bid Oliphant fetch glasses and hot water and lemons. I will give Mr Hervey-Townshend a sample of the brew. You English are all *têtes-de-fer*, sir, and are worthy of it."

The old man's face had lighted up, and for the moment his air had the jollity of youth. I would have accepted the entertainment had I not again caught Madame's eye. It said, unmistakably and with serious pleading, "Decline." I therefore made my excuses, urged fatigue, drowsiness, and a delicate stomach, bade my host good-night, and in deep mystification left the room.

Enlightenment came upon me as the door closed. There on the threshold stood the man-servant whom they called Oliphant, erect as a sentry on guard. The sight reminded me of what I had once seen at Basle when by chance a Rhenish Grand Duke had shared the inn with me. Of a sudden a dozen clues linked together—the crowned note-paper, Scotland, my aunt Hervey's politics, the tale of old wanderings.

"Tell me," I said in a whisper, "who is the Count d'Albani, your master?" and I whistled softly a bar of "Charlie is my darling."

"Ay," said the man, without relaxing a muscle of his grim face. "It is the King of England—my king and yours."

II.

In the small hours of the next morning I was awoke by a most unearthly sound. It was as if all the cats on all the roofs of Santa Chiara were sharpening their claws and wailing their battle-cries. Presently out of the noise came a kind of music—very slow, solemn, and melancholy. The notes ran up in great flights of ecstasy, and sunk anon to the tragic deeps. In spite of my sleepiness I was held spellbound, and the musician had concluded with certain barbaric grunts before I had the curiosity to rise. It came from somewhere in the gallery of the inn, and as I stuck my head out of my door I had a glimpse of Oliphant, nightcap on head and a great bagpipe below his arm, stalking down the corridor.

The incident, for all the gravity of the music, seemed to give a touch of farce to my interview of the past evening. I had gone to bed with my mind full of sad stories of the deaths of kings. Magnificence in tatters has always affected my pity more deeply than tatters with no such antecedent, and a monarch out at elbows stood for me the last irony of our mortal life. Here was a king whose misfortunes could find no parallel. He had been in his youth the hero of a high adventure, and his middle age had been spent in fleeting among the courts of Europe, and waiting as pensioner on the whims of his foolish but regnant brethren. I had heard tales of a growing sottishness, a decline in spirit, a squalid taste in pleasures. Small blame, I had always thought, to so ill-fated a princeling. And now I had chanced upon the gentleman in his dotage, travelling with a barren effort at mystery, attended by a sad-faced daughter and two ancient domestics. It was a lesson in the vanity of human wishes which the shallowest moralist would have noted. Nay, I felt more than the moral. Something human and kindly in the old fellow had caught my fancy. The decadence was too tragic to prose about, the decadent too human to moralise on. I had left the chamber of the—shall I say *de jure* King of England? —a sentimental adherent of the cause. But this business of the bagpipes touched the comic. To harry an old valet out of bed and set him droning on pipes in the small hours smacked of a theatrical taste, or at least of an undignified fancy. Kings in exile, if they wish to keep the tragic air, should not indulge in such fantastic serenades.

My mind changed again when after breakfast I fell in with

Madame on the stair. She drew aside to let me pass, and then made as if she would speak to me. I gave her good-morning, and, my mind being full of her story, addressed her as "Excellency."

"I see, sir," she said, "that you know the truth. I have to ask your forbearance for the concealment I practised yesterday. It was a poor requital for your generosity, but it is one of the shifts of our sad fortune. An uncrowned king must go in disguise, or risk the laughter of every stable-boy. Besides, we are too poor to travel in state, even if we desired it."

Honestly, I knew not what to say. I was not asked to sympathise, having already revealed my politics, and yet the case cried out for sympathy. You remember, my dear aunt, the good Lady Culham, who was our Dorsetshire neighbour, and tried hard to mend my ways at Carteron? This poor Duchess—for so she called herself—was just such another. A woman made for comfort, housewifery, and motherhood, and by no means for racing about Europe in charge of a disreputable parent. I could picture her settled equably on a garden seat with a lap-dog and needlework, blinking happily over green lawns and mildly rating an errant gardener. I could fancy her sitting in a summer parlour, very orderly and dainty, writing lengthy epistles to a tribe of nieces. I could see her marshalling a household in the family pew, or riding serenely in the family coach behind fat bay horses. But here, on an inn staircase, with a false name and a sad air of mystery, she was wofully out of place. I noted little wrinkles forming in the corners of her eyes, and the ravages of care beginning in the plump rosiness of her face. Be sure there was nothing appealing in her mien. She spoke with the air of a great lady, to whom the world is matter only for an afterthought. It was the facts that appealed and grew poignant from her courage.

"There is another claim upon your good-nature," she said. "Doubtless you were awoke last night by Oliphant's playing upon the pipes. I rebuked the landlord for his insolence in protesting, but to you, a gentleman and a friend, an explanation is due. My father sleeps ill, and your conversation seems to have cast him into a train of sad memories. It has been his habit on such occasions to have the pipes played to him, since they remind him of friends and happier days. It is a small privilege for an old man, and he does not claim it often."

I declared that the music had only pleased, and that I would welcome its repetition. Whereupon she left me with a little bow and an invitation to join them that day at dinner, while I departed into the town on my own errands. I returned before mid-day, and was seated at an arbour in the garden, busy with letters, when there hove in sight the gaunt figure of Oliphant. He hovered around me, if such a figure can be said to hover, with the obvious intention of addressing me. The fellow had caught my fancy, and I was willing to see more of him. His face might have been hacked out of grey granite, his clothes hung loosely on his spare bones, and his stockinged shanks would have done no discredit to Don Quixote. There was no dignity in his air, only a steady and enduring sadness. Here, thought I, is the one of the establishment who most commonly meets the shock of the world's buffets. I called him by name and asked him his desires.

It appeared that he took me for a Jacobite, for he began a rigmarole about loyalty and hard fortune. I hastened to correct him, and he took the correction with the same patient despair with which he took all things. 'Twas but another of the blows of Fate.

"At any rate," he said in a broad Scotch accent, "ye come of kin that has helpit my maister afore this. I've many times heard tell o' Herveys and Townshends in England, and a' folk said they were on the richt side. Ye're maybe no a freend, but ye're a freend's freend, or I wadna be speirin' at ye."

I was amused at the prologue, and waited on the tale. It soon came. Oliphant, it appeared, was the purse-bearer of the household, and woful straits that poor purse-bearer must have been often put to. I questioned him as to his master's revenues, but could get no clear answer. There were payments due next month in Florence which would solve the difficulties for the winter, but in the meantime expenditure had beaten income. Travelling had cost much, and the Count must have his small comforts. The result in plain words was that Oliphant had not the wherewithal to frank the company to Florence; indeed I doubted if he could have paid the reckoning in Santa Chiara. A loan was therefore sought from a friend's friend, meaning myself.

I was very really embarrassed. Not that I would not have given willingly, for I had ample resources at the moment and was mightily concerned about the sad household. But I knew that the little Duchess would take Oliphant's ears from his head if she guessed that he had dared to borrow from me, and that, if I lent, her back would for ever be turned against me. And yet, what would follow on my refusal? In a day or two there would be a pitiful scene with mine host, and as like as not some of their baggage detained as security for payment. I did not love the task of conspiring behind the lady's back, but if it could be contrived 'twas indubitably the kindest course. I glared sternly at Oliphant, who met me with his pathetic, dog-like eyes.

"You know that your mistress would never consent to the request you have made of me?"

"I ken," he said humbly. "But payin' is *my* job, and I simply havena the siller. It's no' the first time it has happened, and it's a sair trial for them both to be flung out-o'-doors by a foreign hostler because they canna meet his charges. But, sir, if ye can lend to me, ye may be certain that her leddyship will never hear a word o't. Puir thing, she takes nae thocht o' where the siller comes frae, ony mair than the lilies o' the field."

I became a conspirator. "You swear, Oliphant, by all you hold sacred, to breathe nothing of this to your mistress, and if she should suspect, to lie like a Privy Councillor?"

A flicker of a smile crossed his face. "I'll lee like a Scotch packman, and the Father o' lees could do nae mair. You need have no fear for your siller, sir. I've aye repaid when I borrowed, though you may have to wait a bittock." And the strange fellow strolled off.

At dinner no Duchess appeared till long after the appointed hour, nor was there any sign of Oliphant. When she came at last with Cristine, her eyes looked as if she had been crying, and she greeted me with remote courtesy. My first thought was that Oliphant had revealed the matter of the loan, but presently I found that the lady's trouble was far different. Her father, it seemed, was ill again with his old complaint. What that was I did not ask, nor did the Duchess reveal it.

We spoke in French, for I had discovered that this was her favourite speech. There was no Oliphant to wait on us, and the inn servants were always about, so it was well to have a tongue they did not comprehend. The lady was distracted and sad. When I inquired feelingly as to the general condition of her father's health she parried the question, and when I offered my services she disregarded my words. It was in truth a doleful meal, while the faded Cristine sat like a sphinx staring into vacancy. I spoke of England and of her friends, of Paris and Versailles, of Avignon where she had spent some years, and of the amenities of Florence, which she considered her home. But 'twas like talking to a nunnery door. I got nothing but "It is indeed true, sir," or "Do you say so, sir?" till my energy began to sink. Madame perceived my discomfort, and, as she rose, murmured an apology. "Pray forgive my distraction, but I am poor company when my father is ill. I have a foolish mind, easily frightened. Nay, nay!" she went on when I again offered help, "the illness is trifling.

It will pass off by to-morrow, or at the latest the next day. Only I had looked forward to some ease at Santa Chiara, and the promise is belied."

As it chanced that evening, returning to the inn, I passed by the north side where the windows of the Count's rooms looked over a little flower-garden abutting on the courtyard. The dusk was falling, and a lamp had been lit which gave a glimpse into the interior. The sick man was standing by the window, his figure flung into relief by the lamplight. If he was sick, his sickness was of a curious type. His face was ruddy, his eye wild, and, his wig being off, his scanty hair stood up oddly round his head. He seemed to be singing, but I could not catch the sound through the shut casement. Another figure in the room, probably Oliphant, laid a hand on the Count's shoulder, drew him from the window, and closed the shutter.

It needed only the recollection of stories which were the property of all Europe to reach a conclusion on the gentleman's illness. The legitimate King of England was very drunk.

As I went to my room that night I passed the Count's door. There stood Oliphant as sentry, more grim and haggard than ever, and I thought that his eye met mine with a certain intelligence. From inside the room came a great racket. There was the sound of glasses falling, then a string of oaths, English, French, and for all I know, Irish, rapped out in a loud drunken voice. A pause, and then came the sound of maudlin singing. It pursued me along the gallery, an old childish song, delivered as if 'twere a pot-house catch—

" Qu'est-c' qui passe ici si tard,
Compagnons de la Marjolaine——"

One of the late-going company of the Marjolaine hastened to bed. This king in exile, with his melancholy daughter, was becoming too much for him.

III.

It was just before noon next day that the travellers arrived. I was sitting in the shady loggia of the inn, reading a volume of De Thou, when there drove up to the door two coaches. Out of the first descended very slowly and stiffly four gentlemen; out of the second four servants and a quantity of baggage. As it chanced there was no one about, the courtyard slept its sunny noontide sleep, and the only movement was a lizard on the wall and a buzz of flies by the fountain. Seeing no sign of the landlord, one of the travellers approached me with a grave inclination.

"This is the inn called the Tre Croci, sir?" he asked.

I said it was, and shouted on my own account for the host. Presently that personage arrived with a red face and a short wind, having ascended rapidly from his own cellar. He was awed by the dignity of the travellers, and made none of his usual protests of incapacity. The servants filed off solemnly with the baggage, and the four gentlemen sat themselves down beside me in the loggia and ordered each a modest flask of wine.

At first I took them for our countrymen, but as I watched them the conviction vanished. All four were tall and lean beyond the average of mankind. They wore suits of black, with antique starched frills to their shirts; their hair was their own and unpowdered. Massive buckles of an ancient pattern adorned their square-toed shoes, and the canes they carried were like the yards of a small vessel. They were four merchants, I had guessed, of Scotland maybe, or of Newcastle, but their voices were not Scotch, and their air had no touch of commerce. Take the heavy-browed preoccupation of a Secretary of State, add the dignity of a bishop, the sunburn of a fox-hunter, and something of the disciplined erectness of a soldier, and you may perceive the manner of these four gentlemen. By the side of them my assurance vanished. Compared with their Olympian serenity my person seemed fussy and servile. Even so, I mused, must Mr Franklin have looked when baited in Parliament by the Tory pack. The reflection gave me the cue. Presently I caught from their conversation the word "Washington," and the truth flashed upon me. I was in the presence of four of Mr Franklin's countrymen. Having never seen an American in the flesh, I rejoiced at the chance of enlarging my acquaintance.

They brought me into the circle by a polite question as to the length of road to Verona. Soon introductions followed. My name intrigued them, and they were eager to learn of my kinship to Uncle Charles. The eldest of the four, it appeared, was Mr Galloway out of Maryland. Then came two brothers, Sylvester by name, of Pennsylvania, and last Mr Fish, a lawyer of New York. All four had campaigned in the late war, and all four were members of the Convention, or whatever they call their rough-and-ready parliament. They were modest in their behaviour, much disinclined to speak of their past, as great men might be whose reputation was world-wide. Somehow the names stuck in my memory. I was certain that I had heard them linked with some stalwart fight or some moving civil deed or some defiant manifesto. The making of history was in their steadfast eye and the grave lines of the mouth. Our friendship flourished mightily in a brief hour, and brought me the invitation, willingly accepted, to sit with them at dinner.

There was no sign of the Duchess or Cristine or Oliphant. Whatever had happened, that household to-day required all hands on deck, and I was left alone with the Americans. In my day I have supped with the Macaronies, I have held up my head at the Cocoa Tree, I have avoided the floor at hunt dinners, I have drunk glass to glass with Tom Carteron. But never before have I seen such noble consumers of good liquor as those four gentlemen from beyond the

Atlantic. They drank the strong red Cyprus as if it had been spring-water. "The dust of your Italian roads takes some cleansing, Mr Townshend," was their only excuse, but in truth none was needed. The wine seemed only to thaw their iron decorum. Without any surcease of dignity they grew communicative, and passed from lands to peoples and from peoples to constitutions. Before we knew it we were embarked upon high politics.

Naturally we did not differ on the war. Like me, they held it to have been a grievous necessity. They had no bitterness against England, only regrets for her blunders. Of his Majesty they spoke with respect, of his Majesty's advisers with dignified condemnation. They thought highly of our troops in America; less highly of our generals.

"Look you, sir," said Mr Galloway, "in a war such as we have witnessed the Almighty is the only strategist. You fight against the forces of Nature, and a newcomer little knows that the success or failure of every operation he can conceive depends not upon generalship, but upon the conformation of a vast country. Our generals, with this in mind and with fewer men, could make all your schemes miscarry. Had the English soldiery not been of such stubborn stuff, we should have been victors from the first. Our leader was not General Washington, but General America, and his brigadiers were forests, swamps, lakes, rivers, and high mountains."

"And now," I said, "having won, you have the greatest of human experiments before you. Your business is to show that the Saxon stock is adaptable to a republic."

It seemed to me that they exchanged glances.

"We are not pedants," said Mr Fish, "and have no desire to dispute about the form of a constitution. A people may be as free under a king as under a senate. Liberty is not the lackey of any type of government."

These were strange words from a member of a race whom

I had thought wedded to the republicanism of Helvidius Priscus.

"As a loyal subject of a monarchy," I said, "I must agree with you. But your hands are tied, for I cannot picture the establishment of a House of Washington, and—if not, where are you to turn for your sovereign?"

Again a smile seemed to pass among the four.

"We are experimenters, as you say, sir, and must go slowly. In the meantime we have an authority which keeps peace and property safe. We are at leisure to cast our eyes round and meditate on the future."

"Then, gentlemen," said I, "you take an excellent way of meditation in visiting this museum of old sovereignties. Here you have the relics of any government you please—a dozen republics, tyrannies, theocracies, merchant confederations, kingdoms, and more than one empire. You have your choice. I am tolerably familiar with the land, and if I can assist you I am at your service."

They thanked me gravely. "We have letters," said Mr Galloway; "one in especial is to a gentleman whom we hope to meet in this place. Have you heard in your travels of the Count of Albany?"

"He has arrived," said I, "two days ago. Even now he is in the chamber above us at dinner."

The news interested them hugely.

"You have seen him?" they cried. "What is he like?"

"An elderly gentleman in poor health, a man who has travelled much, and, I judge, has suffered something from fortune. He has a fondness for the English, so you will be welcome, sirs; but he was indisposed yesterday, and may still be unable to receive you. His daughter travels with him and tends his old age."

"And you—you have spoken with him?"

"The night before last I was in his company. We talked of many things, including the late war. He is somewhat of your opinion on matters of government."

The four looked at each other, and then Mr Galloway rose.

"I ask your permission, Mr Townshend, to consult for a moment with my friends. The matter is of some importance, and I would beg you to await us." So saying, he led the others out-of-doors, and I heard them withdraw to a corner of the loggia. Now, thought I, there is something afoot, and my long-sought romance approaches fruition. The company of the Marjolaine, whom the Count had sung of, have arrived at last.

Presently they returned and seated themselves at the table.

"You can be of great assistance to us, Mr Townshend, and we would fain take you into our confidence. Are you aware who is this Count of Albany?"

I nodded. "It is a thin disguise to one familiar with history."

"Have you reached any estimate of his character or capabilities? You speak to friends, and, let me tell you, it is a matter which deeply concerns the Count's interests."

"I think him a kindly and pathetic old gentleman. He naturally bears the mark of forty years' sojourn in the wilderness."

Mr Galloway took snuff.

"We have business with him, but it is business which stands in need of an agent. There is no one in the Count's suite with whom we could discuss affairs?"

"There is his daughter."

"Ah, but she would scarcely suit the case. Is there no man—a friend, and yet not a member of the family—who can treat with us?"

I replied that I thought that I was the only being in Santa Chiara who answered the description.

"If you will accept the task, Mr Townshend, you are amply qualified. We will be frank with you and reveal our business. We are on no less an errand than to offer the Count of Albany a crown."

I suppose I must have had some suspicion of their purpose, and yet the revelation of it fell on me like a thunderclap. I could only stare owlishly at my four grave gentlemen.

Mr Galloway went on unperturbed. "I have told you that in America we are not yet republicans. There are those among us who favour a republic, but they are by no means a majority. We have got rid of a king who misgoverned us, but we have no wish to get rid of kingship. We want a king of our own choosing, and we would get with him all the ancient sanctions of monarchy. The Count of Albany is of the most illustrious royal stock in Europe,—he is, if legitimacy goes for anything, the rightful King of Britain. Now, if the republican party among us is to be worsted, we must come before the nation with a powerful candidate for their favour. You perceive my drift? What more potent appeal to American pride than to say: 'We have got rid of King George; we choose of our own free will the older line and King Charles'?"

I said foolishly that I thought monarchy had had its day, and that 'twas idle to revive it.

"That is a sentiment well enough under a monarchical government; but we, with a clean page to write upon, do not share it. You know your ancient historians. Has not the repository of the chief power always been the rock on which republicanism has shipwrecked? If that power is given to the chief citizen, the way is prepared for the tyrant. If it abides peacefully in a royal house, it abides with cyphers who dignify, without obstructing, a popular constitution. Do not mistake me, Mr Townshend. This is no whim of a sentimental girl, but the reasoned conclusion of the men who achieved our liberty. There is every reason to believe that General Washington shares our views, and Mr Hamilton, whose name you may know, is the inspirer of our mission."

"But the Count is an old man," I urged; for I knew

not where to begin in my exposition of the hopelessness of their errand.

"By so much the better. We do not wish a young king who may be fractious. An old man tempered by misfortune is what our purpose demands."

"He has also his failings. A man cannot lead his life for forty years and retain all the virtues."

At that one of the Sylvesters spoke sharply. "I have heard such gossip, but I do not credit it. I have not forgotten Preston and Derby."

I made my last objection. "He has no posterity—legitimate posterity—to carry on his line."

The four gentlemen smiled. "That happens to be his chiefest recommendation," said Mr Galloway. "It enables us to take the House of Stuart on trial. We need a breathing-space and leisure to look around; but unless we establish the principle of monarchy at once the republicans will forestall us. Let us get our king at all costs, and during the remaining years of his life we shall have time to settle the succession problem. We have no wish to saddle ourselves for good with a race who might prove burdensome. If King Charles fails he has no son, and we can look elsewhere for a better monarch. You perceive the reason of my view?"

I did, and I also perceived the colossal absurdity of the whole business. But I could not convince them of it, for they met my objections with excellent arguments. Nothing save a sight of the Count would, I feared, disillusion them.

"You wish me to make this proposal on your behalf?" I asked.

"We shall make the proposal ourselves, but we desire you to prepare the way for us. He is an elderly man, and should first be informed of our purpose."

"There is one person whom I beg leave to consult—the Duchess, his daughter. It may be that the present is an ill moment for approaching the Count, and the affair requires her sanction."

They agreed, and with a very perplexed mind I went forth to seek the lady. The irony of the thing was too cruel, and my heart ached for her. In the gallery I found Oliphant packing some very shabby trunks, and when I questioned him he told me that the family were to leave Santa Chiara on the morrow. Perchance the Duchess had awakened to the true state of their exchequer, or perchance she thought it well to get her father on the road again as a cure for his ailment.

I discovered Cristine, and begged for an interview with her mistress on an urgent matter. She led me to the Duchess's room, and there the evidence of poverty greeted me openly. All the little luxuries of the menage had gone to the Count. The poor lady's room was no better than a servant's garret, and the lady herself sat stitching a rent in a travelling cloak. She rose to greet me with alarm in her eyes.

As briefly as I could I set out the facts of my amazing mission. At first she seemed scarcely to hear me. "What do they want with him?" she asked. "He can give them nothing. He is no friend to the Americans or to any people who have deposed their sovereign." Then, as she grasped my meaning, her face flushed.

"It is a heartless trick, Mr Townshend. I would fain think you no party to it."

"Believe me, dear madame, it is no trick. The men below are in sober earnest. You have but to see their faces to know that theirs is no wild adventure. I believe sincerely that they have the power to implement their promise."

"But it is madness. He is old and worn and sick. His day is long past for winning a crown."

"All this I have said, but it does not move them." And I told her rapidly Mr Galloway's argument.

She fell into a muse. "At the eleventh hour! Nay, too late, too late! Had he been twenty years younger, what a stroke of fortune! Fate bears too hard on us, too hard!"

Then she turned to me fiercely. "You have no doubt heard, sir, the gossip about my father, which is on the lips of every fool in Europe. Let us have done with this pitiful make-believe. My father is a sot. Nay, I do not blame him. I blame his enemies and his miserable destiny. But there is the fact. Were he not old, he would still be unfit to grasp a crown and rule over a turbulent people. He flees from one city to another, but he cannot flee from himself. That is his illness on which you condoled with me yesterday."

The lady's control was at breaking-point. Another moment and I expected a torrent of tears. But they did not come. With a great effort she regained her composure.

"Well, the gentlemen must have an answer. You will tell them that the Count, my father—nay, give him his true title if you care—is vastly obliged to them for the honour they have done him, but would decline on account of his age and infirmities. You know how to phrase a decent refusal."

"Pardon me," said I, "but I might give them that answer till doomsday and never content them. They have not travelled many thousand miles to be put off by hearsay evidence. Nothing will satisfy them but an interview with your father himself."

"It is impossible," she said sharply.

"Then we must expect the renewed attentions of our American friends. They will wait till they see him."

She rose and paced the room.

"They must go," she repeated many times. "If they see him sober he will accept with joy, and we shall be the laughing-stock of the world. I tell you it cannot be. I alone know how immense is the impossibility. He cannot afford to lose the last rags of his dignity, the last dregs of his ease. They must not see him. I will speak with them myself."

"They will be honoured, madame, but I do not think they will be convinced. They are what we call in my land 'men of business.' They will not be content till they get the Count's reply from his own lips."

A new Duchess seemed to have arisen, a woman of quick action and sharp words.

"So be it. They shall see him. Oh, I am sick to death of fine sentiments and high loyalty and all the vapouring stuff I have lived among for years. All I ask for myself and my father is a little peace, and, by heaven! I shall secure it. If nothing will kill your gentlemen's folly but truth, why, truth they shall have. They shall see my father, and this very minute. Bring them up, Mr Townshend, and usher them into the presence of the rightful King of England. You will find him alone." She stopped her walk and looked out of the window.

I went back in a hurry to the Americans. "I am bidden to bring you to the Count's chamber. He is alone and will see you. These are the commands of madame his daughter."

"Good!" said Mr Galloway, and all four, grave gentlemen as they were, seemed to brace themselves to a special dignity as befitted ambassadors to a king. I led them upstairs, tapped at the Count's door, and, getting no answer, opened it and admitted them.

And this was what we saw. The furniture was in disorder, and on a couch lay an old man sleeping a heavy drunken sleep. His mouth was open and his breath came stertorously. The face was purple, and large purple veins stood out on the mottled forehead. His scanty white hair was draggled over his cheek. On the floor was a broken glass, wet stains still lay on the boards, and the place reeked of spirits.

The four looked for a second—I do not think longer—at him whom they would have made their king. They did not look at each other. With one accord they moved out, and Mr Fish, who was last, closed the door very gently behind him.

In the hall below Mr Galloway turned to me. "Our mission is ended, Mr Townshend. I have to thank you for your courtesy." Then to the others. "If we order the coaches now, we may get well on the way to Verona ere sundown."

. . . .

An hour later two coaches rolled out of the courtyard of the Tre Croci. As they passed, a window was half-opened on the upper floor, and a head looked out. A line of a song came down, a song sung in a strange quavering voice. It was the catch I had heard the night before:

"Qu'est-c' qui passe ici si tard,
Compagnons de la Marjolaine—e ?"

It was true. The company came late indeed—too late by forty years. . . .

AVIGNON.

1759.

Hearts to break but nane to sell,
Gear to tine but nane to hain ;—
We maun dree a weary spell
Ere our lad comes back again.

I walk abroad on winter days,
When storms have stripped the wide champaign,
For northern winds have norland ways,
And scents of Badenoch haunt the rain.
And by the lipping river path,
When in the fog the Rhone runs grey,
I see the heather of the Strath,
And watch the salmon leap in Spey.

The hills are feathered with young trees,—
I set them for my children's boys.
I made a garden deep in ease,
A pleasance for my lady's joys.
Strangers have heired them. Long ago
She died,—kind fortune thus to die ;
And my one son by Beauly flow
Gave up the soul that could not lie.

Old, elbow-worn, and pinched I bide
The final toll the gods may take.
The laggard years have quenched my pride ;
They cannot kill the ache, the ache.

Weep not the dead, for they have sleep
  Who lie at home ; but ah, for me
In the deep grave my heart will weep
  With longing for my lost countrie.

Hearts to break but nane to sell,
  Gear to tine but nane to hain ;—
We maun dree a weary spell
  Ere our lad comes back again.

II. A LUCID INTERVAL.

I.

To adopt the opening words of a more famous tale, "The truth of this strange matter is what the world has long been looking for." The events which I propose to chronicle were known to perhaps a hundred people in London whose fate brings them into contact with politics. The consequences were apparent to all the world, and for one hectic fortnight tinged the soberest newspapers with saffron, drove more than one worthy election agent to an asylum, and sent whole batches of legislators to Continental "cures." But no reasonable explanation of the mystery has been forthcoming until now, when a series of chances gave the key into my hands.

Lady Caerlaverock is my aunt, and I was present at the two remarkable dinner-parties which form the main events in this tale. I was also taken into her confidence during the terrible fortnight which intervened between them. Like everybody else, I was hopelessly in the dark, and could only accept what happened as a divine interposition. My first clue came when James, the Caerlaverocks' second footman, entered my service as valet, and being a cheerful youth chose to gossip while he shaved me. I checked him, but he babbled on, and I could not choose but learn something about the disposition of the Caerlaverock household below-stairs. I learned—what I knew before—that his lordship had an inordinate love for curries, a taste acquired during some troubled years as Indian Viceroy. I had often eaten that admirable dish at his table, and had heard him boast of the skill of the Indian cook who prepared it. James, it appeared, did not hold with the Orient in the kitchen. He described the said Indian gentleman as a "nigger," and expressed profound distrust of his ways. He referred darkly to the events of the year before, which in some distorted way had reached the servants' ears. "We always thought as 'ow it was them niggers as done it," he declared; and when I questioned him on his use of the plural, admitted that at the time in question "there 'ad been more nor one nigger 'anging about the kitchen."

Pondering on these sayings, I asked myself if it were not possible that the behaviour of certain eminent statesmen was due to some strange devilry of the East, and I made a vow to abstain in future from the Caerlaverock curries. But last month my brother returned from India, and I got the whole truth. He was staying with me in Scotland, and in the smoking-room the talk turned on occultism in the East. I declared myself a sceptic, and George was stirred. He asked me rudely what I knew about it, and proceeded to make a startling confession of faith. He was cross-examined by the others, and retorted with some of his experiences. Finding an incredulous audience, his tales became more defiant, until he capped them all with one monstrous yarn. He maintained that in a Hindu family of his acquaintance there had been transmitted the secret of a drug, capable of altering a man's whole temperament until the antidote was administered. It would turn a coward into a bravo, a miser into a spendthrift, a rake into a fakir. Then, having delivered his manifesto, he got up abruptly and went to bed.

I followed him to his room, for something in the story had revived a memory. By dint of much persuasion I dragged from the somnolent George various details. The family in question were Beharis, large landholders dwelling near the Nepal border. He had known old Ram Singh for years, and had seen him twice since his return from England. He got the story from him, under no promise of secrecy, for the family drug was as well known in the neighbourhood as the nine incarnations of Krishna. He had no doubt about the truth of it, for he had positive proof. "And others besides me," said George. "Do you remember when Vennard had a lucid interval a couple of years ago and talked sense for once? That was old Ram Singh's doing, for he told me about it."

Three years ago it seems the Government of India saw fit to appoint a commission to inquire into land tenure on the Nepal border. Some of the feudal Rajahs had been "birsing yont," like the Breadalbanes, and the smaller zemindars were gravely disquieted. The result of the commission was that Ram Singh had his boundaries rectified, and lost a mile or two of country which his hard-fisted fathers had won. I know nothing of the rights of the matter, but there can be no doubt about Ram Singh's dissatisfaction. He appealed to the law courts, but failed to upset the commission's finding, and the Privy Council upheld the Indian judgment. Thereupon in a flowery and eloquent document he laid his case before the Viceroy, and was told that the matter was closed. Now Ram Singh came of a fighting stock, so he straightway took ship to England to petition the Crown. He petitioned Parliament, but his petition went into the bag behind the Speaker's chair, from which there is no return. He petitioned the King, but was courteously informed that he must approach the Department concerned. He tried the Secretary of State for India, and had an interview with Abinger Vennard, who was very rude to him, and succeeded in mortally insulting the feudal aristocrat. He appealed to the Prime Minister, and was warned off by a harassed private secretary. The handful of members of Parliament who make Indian grievances their stock-in-trade fought shy of him, for indeed Ram Singh's case had no sort of platform appeal in it, and his arguments were flagrantly undemocratic. But they sent him to Lord Caerlaverock, for the ex-viceroy loved to be treated as a kind of consul-general for India. But this Protector of the Poor proved a broken reed. He told Ram Singh flatly that he was a belated feudalist, which was true; and implied that he was a land-grabber, which was not true, Ram Singh having only enjoyed the fruits of his forebears' enterprise. Deeply incensed, the appellant shook the dust of Caerlaverock House from his feet, and sat down to plan a revenge upon the Government which had wronged him. And in his wrath he thought of the heirloom of his house, the drug which could change men's souls.

It happened that Lord Caerlaverock's cook came from the same neighbourhood as Ram Singh. This cook, Lal Muhammad by name, was one of a large poor family, hangers-on of Ram Singh's house. The aggrieved landowner summoned him, and demanded as of right his humble services. Lal Muhammad, who found his berth to his liking, hesitated, quibbled, but was finally overborne. He suggested a fee for his services, but hastily withdrew when Ram Singh sketched a few of the steps he proposed to take on his return by way of punishing Lal Muhammad's insolence on Lal Muhammad's household. Then he got to business. There was a great dinner next week—so he had learned from Jephson, the butler—and more than one member of the Government would honour Caerlaverock House by his presence. With deference he suggested this as a fitting occasion for the experiment, and Ram Singh was pleased to assent.

I can picture these two holding their meetings in the South Kensington lodgings where Ram Singh dwelt. We know from James, the second footman, that they met also at Caerlaverock House, no doubt that Ram Singh might make certain that his orders were duly obeyed. I can see the little packet of clear grains—I picture them like small granulated sugar—added to the condiments, and soon dissolved out of sight. The deed was done: the cook returned to Bloomsbury and Ram Singh to Gloucester Road, to await with the patient certainty of the East the consummation of a great vengeance.

II.

My wife was at Kissingen, and I was dining with the Caerlaverocks *en garçon*. When I have not to wait upon the adornment of the female person I am a man of punctual habits, and I reached the house as the hall clock chimed the quarter-past. My poor friend, Tommy Deloraine, arrived along with me, and we ascended the staircase together. I call him "my poor friend," for at the moment Tommy was under the weather. He had the misfortune to be a marquis, and a very rich one, and at the same time to be in love with Claudia Barriton. Neither circumstance was in itself an evil, but the combination made for tragedy. For Tommy's twenty-five years of healthy manhood, his cleanly-made upstanding figure, his fresh countenance and cheerful laugh, were of no avail in the lady's eyes when set against the fact that he was an idle peer. Miss Claudia was a charming girl, with a notable bee in her bonnet. She was burdened with the cares of the State, and had no patience with anyone who took them lightly. To her mind the social fabric was rotten beyond repair, and her purpose was frankly destructive. I remember some of her phrases: "A bold and generous policy of social amelioration;" "The development of a civic conscience;" "A strong hand to lop off decaying branches from the trunk of the State." I have no fault to find with her creed, but I objected to its practical working when it took the shape of an inhuman hostility to that devout lover, Tommy Deloraine. She had refused him, I believe, three times, with every circumstance of scorn. The first time she had analysed his character, and described him as a bundle of attractive weaknesses. "The only forces I recognise are those of intellect and conscience," she had said, "and you have neither." The second time—it was after he had been to Canada on the staff—she spoke of the irreconcilability of their political ideals. "You are an

Imperialist," she said, " and believe in an empire of conquest for the benefit of the few. I want a little island with a rich life for all." Tommy declared that he would become a Doukhobor to please her, but she said something about the inability of Ethiopians to change their skin. The third time she hinted vaguely that there was " another." The star of Abinger Vennard was now blazing in the firmament, and she had conceived a platonic admiration for him. The truth is that Miss Claudia, with all her cleverness, was very young and—dare I say it ?—rather silly.

Caerlaverock was stroking his beard, his legs astraddle on the hearthrug, with something appallingly viceregal in his air, when Mr and Mrs Alexander Cargill were announced. The Home Secretary was a joy to behold. He had the face of an elderly and pious bookmaker, and a voice in which lurked the indescribable Scotch quality of " unction." When he was talking you had only to shut your eyes to imagine yourself in some lowland kirk on a hot Sabbath morning. He had been a distinguished advocate before he left the law for politics, and had swayed juries of his countrymen at his will. The man was extraordinarily efficient on a platform. There were unplumbed depths of emotion in his eye, a juicy sentiment in his voice, an overpowering tenderness in his manner, which gave to politics the glamour of a revival meeting. He wallowed in obvious pathos, and his hearers, often unwillingly, wallowed with him. I have never listened to any orator at once so offensive and so horribly effective. There was no appeal too base for him, and none too august: by some subtle alchemy he blended the arts of the prophet and the fishwife. He had discovered a new kind of language. Instead of " the hungry millions," or " the toilers," or any of the numerous synonyms for our masters, he invented the phrase, " Goad's people." " I shall never rest," so ran his great declaration, " till Goad's green fields and Goad's clear waters are free to Goad's people." I remember how on this occasion he pressed my hand with his famous cordiality, looked gravely and earnestly into my face, and then gazed sternly into vacancy. It was a fine picture of genius descending for a moment from its hill-top to show how close it was to poor humanity.

Then came Lord Mulross, a respectable troglodytic peer, who represented the one sluggish element in a swiftly progressing Government. He was an oldish man with bushy whiskers and a reputed mastery of the French tongue. A Whig, who had never changed his creed one iota, he was highly valued by the country as a sober element in the nation's councils, and endured by the Cabinet as necessary ballast. He did not conceal his dislike for certain of his colleagues, notably Mr Vennard and Mr Cargill.

When Miss Barriton arrived with her step-mother the party was almost complete. She entered with an air of apologising for her prettiness. Her manner with old men was delightful, and I watched with interest the unbending of Caerlaverock and the simplifying of Mr Cargill in her presence. Deloraine, who was talking feverishly to Mrs Cargill, started as if to go and greet her, thought better of it, and continued his conversation. The lady swept the room with her eye, but did not acknowledge his presence. She floated off with Mr Cargill to a window-corner, and metaphorically sat at his feet. I saw Deloraine saying things behind his moustache, while he listened to Mrs Cargill's new cure for dyspepsia.

Last of all, twenty minutes late, came Abinger Vennard. He made a fine stage entrance, walking swiftly with a lowering brow to his hostess, and then glaring fiercely round the room as if to challenge criticism. I have heard Deloraine, in a moment of irritation, describe him as a "Pre-Raphaelite attorney," but there could be no denying his good looks. He had a bad, loose figure, and a quantity of studiously neglected hair, but his face was the face of a young Greek. A certain kind of political success gives a man the manners of an actor, and both Vennard and Cargill bristled with self-consciousness. You could see it in the way they patted their hair, squared their shoulders, and shifted their feet to positions loved by sculptors.

"Well, Vennard, what's the news from the House?" Caerlaverock asked.

"Simpson is talking," said Vennard wearily. "He attacks me, of course. He says he has lived forty years in India—as if that mattered! When will people recognise that the truths of democratic policy are independent of time and space? Liberalism is a category, an eternal mode of thought, which cannot be overthrown by any trivial happenings. I am sick of the word 'facts.' I long for truths."

Miss Barriton's eyes brightened, and Cargill said, "Excellent." Lord Mulross, who was a little deaf, and in any case did not understand the language, said loudly to my aunt that he wished there was a close time for legislation. "The open season for grouse should be the close season for politicians."

And then we went down to dinner.

Miss Barriton sat on my left hand, between Deloraine and me, and it was clear she was discontented with her position. Her eyes wandered down the table to Vennard, who had taken in an American duchess, and seemed to be amused at her prattle. She looked with complete disfavour at Deloraine, and turned to me as the lesser of two evils.

I was tactless enough to say that I thought there was a good deal in Lord Mulross's view.

"Oh, how can you?" she cried. "Is there a close season for the wants of the people? It sounds to me perfectly horrible the way you talk of government, as if it were a game for idle men of the upper classes. I want professional politicians, men who give their whole heart and soul to the service of the State. I know the kind of member you and Lord Deloraine like—a rich young man who eats and drinks too much, and thinks the real business of life is killing little birds. He travels abroad and shoots some big game, and then comes home and vapours about the Empire. He knows nothing about realities, and will go down before the men who take the world seriously."

I am afraid I laughed, but Deloraine, who had been listening, was in no mood to be amused.

"I don't think you are quite fair to us, Miss Claudia," he said slowly. "We take things seriously enough, the things we know about. We can't be expected to know about everything, and the misfortune is that the things I care about don't interest you. But they are important enough for all that."

"Hush," said the lady rudely. "I want to hear what Mr Vennard is saying."

Mr Vennard was addressing the dinner-table as if it were a large public meeting. It was a habit he had, for he had no mind to confine the pearls of his wisdom to his immediate neighbours. His words were directed to Caerlaverock at the far end.

"In my opinion this craze for the scientific standpoint is not merely overdone—it is radically vicious. Human destinies cannot be treated as if they were inert objects under the microscope. The cold-blooded logical way of treating a problem is in almost every case the wrong way. Heart and imagination to me are more vital than intellect. I have the courage to be illogical, to defy facts for the sake of an ideal, in the certainty that in time facts will fall into conformity. My creed may be put in the words of Newman's favourite quotation: *Non in dialectica complacuit Deo salvum facere populum suum*—Not in cold logic is it God's will that His people should find salvation."

"It is profoundly true," sighed Mr Cargill, and Miss Claudia's beaming eyes proved her assent.

The moment of destiny, though I did not know it, had arrived. The *entrée* course had begun, and of the two *entrées* one was the famous Caerlaverock curry. Now on a hot July evening in London there are more attractive foods than curry seven times heated, *more Indico*. I doubt if any guest would have touched it, had not our host in his vice-regal voice called the attention of the three Ministers to its merits, while explaining that under doctor's orders he was compelled to refrain for a season. The result was that Mulross, Cargill, and Vennard alone of the men partook of it. Miss Claudia, alone of the women, followed suit in the fervour of her hero-worship. She ate a mouthful, and then drank rapidly two glasses of water.

My narrative of the events which followed is based rather on what I should have seen than on what I saw. I had not the key, and missed much which otherwise would have been plain to me. For example, if I had known the secret, I must have seen Miss Claudia's gaze cease to rest upon Vennard and the adoration die out of her eyes. I must have noticed her face soften to the unhappy Deloraine. As it was, I did not remark her behaviour till I heard her say to her neighbour—

"Can't you get hold of Mr Vennard and forcibly cut his hair?"

Deloraine looked round with a start. Miss Barriton's tone was intimate and her face friendly.

"Some people think it picturesque," he said in serious bewilderment.

"Oh, yes, picturesque—like a hairdresser's young man!" she shrugged her shoulders. "He looks as if he had never been out-of-doors in his life."

Now, whatever the faults of Tommy's appearance, he had a wholesome sunburnt face, and he knew it. This speech of Miss Barriton's cheered him enormously, for he argued that if she had fallen out of love with Vennard's looks she might fall in love with his own. Being a philosopher in his way, he was content to take what the gods gave, and ask for no explanations.

I do not know how their conversation prospered, for my attention was distracted by the extraordinary behaviour of the Home Secretary. Mr Cargill had made himself notorious by his treatment of "political" prisoners. It was sufficient in his eyes for a criminal to confess to political convictions to secure the most lenient treatment and a speedy release. The Irish patriot who cracked skulls in the Scotland Division of Liverpool, the Suffragist who broke windows and the noses of the police, the Social Democrat whose antipathy to the Tzar revealed itself in assaults upon the Russian Embassy, the "hunger-marchers" who had designs on the British Museum,—all were sure of respectful and tender handling. He had announced more than once, amid tumultuous cheering, that he would never be the means of branding earnestness, however mistaken, with the badge of the felon.

He was talking, I recall, to Lady Lavinia Dobson, renowned in two hemispheres for her advocacy of women's rights. And this was what I heard him say. His face had grown suddenly flushed and his eye bright, so that he looked liker than ever to a bookmaker who had had a good meeting. "No, no, my dear lady, I have been a lawyer, and it is my duty in office to see that the law, the palladium of British liberties, is kept sacrosanct. The law is no respecter of persons, and I intend that it shall be no respecter of creeds. If men or women break the laws, to jail they shall go, though their intentions were those of the Apostle Paul. We don't punish them for being Socialists or Suffragists, but for breaking the peace. Why, goodness me, if we didn't, we should have every malefactor in Britain claiming preferential treatment because he was a Christian Scientist or a Pentecostal Dancer."

"Mr Cargill, do you realise what you are saying?" said Lady Lavinia with a scared face.

"Of course I do. I am a lawyer, and may be presumed to know the law. If any other doctrine were admitted, the Empire would burst up in a fortnight."

"That I should live to hear you name that accursed name!" cried the outraged lady. "You are denying your gods,

Mr Cargill. You are forgetting the principles of a lifetime."

Mr Cargill was becoming excited, and exchanging his ordinary Edinburgh-English for a broader and more effective dialect.

"Tut, tut, my good wumman, I may be allowed to know my own principles best. I tell ye I've always maintained these views from the day when I first walked the floor of the Parliament House. Besides, even if I hadn't, I'm surely at liberty to change if I get more light. Whoever makes a fetish of consistency is a trumpery body and little use to God or man. What ails ye at the Empire, too? Is it not better to have a big country than a kailyard, or a house in Grosvenor Square than a but-and-ben in Balham?"

Lady Lavinia folded her hands. "We slaughter our black fellow-citizens, we fill South Africa with yellow slaves, we crowd the Indian prisons with the noblest and most enlightened of the Indian race, and we call it Empire-building!"

"No, we don't," said Mr Cargill stoutly, "we call it common-sense. That is the penal and repressive side of any great activity. D'ye mean to tell me that you never give your maid a good hearing? But would you like it to be said that you spent the whole of your days swearing at the wumman?"

"I never swore in my life," said Lady Lavinia.

"I spoke metaphorically," said Mr Cargill. "If ye cannot understand a simple metaphor, ye cannot understand the rudiments of politics."

Picture to yourself a prophet who suddenly discovers that his God is laughing at him, a devotee whose saint winks and tells him that the devotion of years has been a farce, and you will get some idea of Lady Lavinia's frame of mind. Her sallow face flushed, her lip trembled, and she slewed round as far as her chair would permit her. Meanwhile Mr Cargill, redder than before, went on contentedly with his dinner.

I was glad when my aunt gave the signal to rise. The atmosphere was electric, and all were conscious of it save the three Ministers, Deloraine, and Miss Claudia. Vennard seemed to be behaving very badly. He was arguing with Caerlaverock down the table, and the ex-Viceroy's face was slowly getting purple. When the ladies had gone, we remained oblivious to wine and cigarettes, listening to this heated controversy which threatened any minute to end in a quarrel.

The subject was India, and Vennard was discoursing on the follies of all Viceroys.

"Take this idiot we've got now," he declared. "He expects me to be a sort of wet-nurse to the Government of India and do all their dirty work for them. They know local conditions, and they have ample powers if they would only use them, but they won't take an atom of responsibility. How the deuce am I to decide for them, when in the nature of things I can't be half as well informed about the facts!"

"Do you maintain," said Caerlaverock, stuttering in his wrath, "that the British Government should divest itself of responsibility for the government of our great Indian Dependency?"

"Not a bit," said Vennard impatiently; "of course we are responsible, but that is all the more reason why the fellows who know the business at first hand should do their duty. If I am the head of a bank I am responsible for its policy, but that doesn't mean that every local bank-manager should consult me about the solvency of clients I never heard of. Faversham keeps bleating to me that the state of India is dangerous. Well, for God's sake let him suppress every native paper, shut up the schools, and send every agitator to the Andamans. I'll back him up all right. But don't let him ask me what to do, for I don't know."

"You think such a course would be popular?" asked a large, grave man, a newspaper editor.

"Of course it would," said Vennard cheerily. "The British public hates the idea of letting India get out of hand. But they want a lead. They can't be expected to start the show any more than I can."

Lord Caerlaverock rose to join the ladies with an air of outraged dignity. Vennard pulled out his watch and announced that he must get back to the House.

"Do you know what I am going to do?" he asked. "I am going down to tell Simpson what I think of him. He gets up and prates of having been forty years in India. Well, I am going to tell him that it is to him and his forty-year lot that all this muddle is due. Oh, I assure you, there's going to be a row," said Vennard, as he struggled into his coat.

Mulross had been sitting next me, and I asked him if he was leaving town. "I wish I could," he said, "but I fear I must stick on over the Twelfth. I don't like the way that fellow Von Kladow has been talking. He's up to no good, and he's going to get a flea in his ear before he is very much older."

Cheerfully, almost hilariously, the three Ministers departed, Vennard and Cargill in a hansom, and Mulross on foot. I can only describe the condition of those left behind as nervous prostration. We looked furtively at each other, each afraid to hint his suspicions, but all convinced that a surprising judgment had befallen at least two members of his Majesty's Government. For myself I put the number at three, for I did not like to hear a respected Whig Foreign Secretary talk about giving the Chancellor of a friendly but jealous Power a flea in his ear.

The only unperplexed face was Deloraine's. He whispered to me that Miss Barriton was going on to the Alvanleys' ball, and had warned him to be there. "She hasn't been to a dance for months, you know," he said. "I really think things are beginning to go a little better, old man."

III.

When I opened my paper next morning I read two startling pieces of news. Lord Mulross had been knocked down by a taxi-cab on his way home the night before, and was now in bed suffering from a bad shock and a bruised ankle. There was no cause for anxiety, said the report, but his lordship must keep his room for a week or two.

The second item, which filled leading articles and overflowed into "Political Notes," was Mr Vennard's speech. The Secretary for India had gone down about eleven o'clock to the House, where an Indian debate was dragging out its slow length. He sat himself on the Treasury Bench and took notes, and the House soon filled in anticipation of his reply. His "tail"—progressive young men like himself—were there in full strength, ready to cheer every syllable which fell from their idol. Somewhere about half-past twelve he rose to wind up the debate, and the House was treated to an unparalleled sensation. He began with his critics, notably the unfortunate Simpson, and, pretty much in Westbury's language to the herald, called them silly old men who did not understand their silly old business. But it was the reasons he gave for this abuse which left his followers aghast. He attacked his critics not for being satraps and reactionaries, but because they had dared to talk second-rate Western politics in connection with India. "Have you lived for forty years with your eyes shut," he cried, "that you cannot see the difference between a Bengali, married at fifteen and worshipping a pantheon of savage gods, and the university-extension young Radical at home? There is a thousand years between them, and you dream of annihilating the centuries with a little dubious popular science!" Then he turned to the other critics of Indian administration—his quondam supporters. He analysed the character of these "members for India" with a vigour and acumen which deprived them of speech. The East, he said, had had its revenge upon the West by making certain Englishmen babus. His honourable friends had the same slipshod minds, and they talked the same pigeon-English, as the patriots of Bengal. Then his mood changed, and he delivered a solemn warning against what he called "the treason begotten of restless vanity and proved incompetence." He sat down, leaving a House deeply impressed and horribly mystified.

'The Times' did not know what to make of it at all. In a weighty leader it welcomed Mr Vennard's conversion, but hinted that with a convert's zeal he had slightly overstated his case. 'The Daily Chronicle' talked of "nervous breakdown," and suggested "kindly forgetfulness" as the best treatment. 'The Daily News,' in a spirited article called "The Great Betrayal," washed its hands of Mr Vennard unless he donned the white sheet of the penitent. Later in the day I got 'The Westminster Gazette,' and found an ingenious leader which proved that the speech in no way conflicted with Liberal principles, and was capable of a quite ordinary explanation. Then I went to see Lady Caerlaverock.

I found my aunt almost in tears.

"What has happened?" she cried. "What have we done that we should be punished in this awful way? And to think that the blow fell in this house! Caerlaverock—we all—thought Mr Vennard so strange last night, and Lady Lavinia told me that Mr Cargill was perfectly horrible. I suppose it must be the heat and the strain of the session. And that poor Lord Mulross, who was always so wise, should be stricken down at this crisis!"

I did not say that I thought Mulross's accident a merciful dispensation. I was far more afraid of him than of all the others, for if with his reputation for sanity he chose to run amok, he would be taken seriously. He was better in bed than affixing a flea to Von Kladow's ear.

"Caerlaverock was with the Prime Minister this morning,"

my aunt went on. " He is going to make a statement in the Lords to-morrow to try to cover Mr Vennard's folly. They are very anxious about what Mr Cargill will do to-day. He is addressing the National Convention of Young Liberals at Oldham this afternoon, and though they have sent him a dozen telegrams they can get no answer. Caerlaverock went to Downing Street an hour ago to get news."

There was the sound of an electric brougham stopping in the square below, and we both listened with a premonition of disaster. A minute later Caerlaverock entered the room, and with him the Prime Minister. The cheerful, eupeptic countenance of the latter was clouded with care. He shook hands dismally with my aunt, nodded to me, and flung himself down on a sofa.

" The worst has happened," Caerlaverock boomed solemnly. " Cargill has been incredibly and infamously silly." He tossed me an evening paper.

One glance convinced me that the Convention of Young Liberals had had a waking-up. Cargill had addressed them on what he called the true view of citizenship. He had dismissed manhood suffrage as an obsolete folly. The franchise, he maintained, should be narrowed and given only to citizens, and his definition of citizenship was military training combined with a fairly high standard of rates and taxes. I do not know how the Young Liberals received this creed, but it had no sort of success with the Prime Minister.

" We must disavow him," said Caerlaverock.

" He is too valuable a man to lose," said the Prime Minister. " We must hope that it is only a temporary aberration. I simply cannot spare him in the House."

" But this is flat treason."

" I know, I know. It is all too horrible, and utterly unexpected. But the situation wants delicate handling, my dear Caerlaverock. I see nothing for it but to give out that he was ill."

" Or drunk ? " I suggested.

The Prime Minister shook his head sadly. "I fear it will be the same thing. What we call illness the ordinary man will interpret as intoxication. It is a most regrettable necessity, but we must face it."

The harassed leader rose, seized the evening paper, and departed as swiftly as he had come. "Remember, illness," were his parting words. "An old heart trouble, which is apt to affect the brain. His friends have always known about it."

I walked home, and looked in at the club on my way. There I found Deloraine devouring a hearty tea and looking the picture of virtuous happiness.

"Well, this is tremendous news," I said, as I sat down beside him.

"What news?" he asked with a start.

"This row about Vennard and Cargill."

"Oh, that! I haven't seen the papers to-day. What's it all about?" His tone was devoid of interest.

Then I knew that something of great private moment had happened to Tommy.

"I hope I may congratulate you," I said.

Deloraine beamed on me affectionately. "Thanks very much, old man. Things came all right quite suddenly, you know. We spent most of the time at the Alvanleys together, and this morning in the Park she accepted me. It will be in the papers next week, but we mean to keep it quiet for a day or two. However, it was your right to be told—and, besides, you guessed."

I remember wondering, as I finished my walk home, whether there could not be some connection between the stroke of Providence which had driven three Cabinet Ministers demented and that gentler touch which had restored Miss Claudia Barriton to good sense and a reasonable marriage.

IV.

The next week was an epoch in my life. I seemed to live in the centre of a Mad Tea-party, where everyone was convinced of the madness, and yet resolutely protested that nothing had happened. The public events of those days were simple enough. While Lord Mulross's ankle approached convalescence, the hives of politics were humming with rumours. Vennard's speech had dissolved his party into its parent elements, and the Opposition, as nonplussed as the Government, did not dare as yet to claim the recruit. Consequently he was left alone till he should see fit to take a further step. He refused to be interviewed, using blasphemous language about our free Press; and mercifully he showed no desire to make speeches. He went down to golf at Littlestone, and rarely showed himself in the House. The earnest young reformer seemed to have adopted not only the creed but the habits of his enemies.

Mr Cargill's was a hard case. He returned from Oldham, delighted with himself and full of fight, to find awaiting him an urgent message from the Prime Minister. His chief was sympathetic and kindly. He had long noticed that the Home Secretary looked fagged and ill. There was no Home Office Bill very pressing, and his assistance in general debate could be dispensed with for a little. Let him take a fortnight's holiday—fish, golf, yacht—the Prime Minister was airily suggestive. In vain Mr Cargill declared he was perfectly well. His chief gently but firmly overbore him, and insisted on sending him his own doctor. That eminent specialist, having been well coached, was vaguely alarming, and insisted on a change. Then Mr Cargill began to suspect, and asked the Prime Minister point-blank if he objected to his Oldham speech. He was told that there was no objection —a little strong meat, perhaps, for Young Liberals, a little daring, but full of Mr Cargill's old intellectual power.

Mollified and reassured, the Home Secretary agreed to a week's absence, and departed for a little salmon-fishing in Scotland. His wife had meantime been taken into the affair, and privately assured by the Prime Minister that she would greatly ease the mind of the Cabinet if she could induce her husband to take a longer holiday—say three weeks. She promised to do her best and to keep her instructions secret, and the Cargills duly departed for the North. "In a fortnight," said the Prime Minister to my aunt, "he will have forgotten all this nonsense; but of course we shall have to watch him very carefully in the future."

The Press was given its cue, and announced that Mr Cargill had spoken at Oldham while suffering from severe nervous breakdown, and that the remarkable doctrines of that speech need not be taken seriously. As I had expected, the public put its own interpretation upon this tale. Men took each other aside in clubs, women gossiped in drawing-rooms, and in a week the Cargill scandal had assumed amazing proportions. The popular version was that the Home Secretary had got very drunk at Caerlaverock House, and still under the influence of liquor had addressed the Young Liberals at Oldham. He was now in an Inebriates' Home, and would not return to the House that session. I confess I trembled when I heard this story, for it was altogether too libellous to pass unnoticed. I believed that soon it would reach the ear of Cargill, fishing quietly at Tomandhoul, and that then there would be the deuce to pay.

Nor was I wrong. A few days later I went to see my aunt to find out how the land lay. She was very bitter, I remember, about Claudia Barriton. "I expected sympathy and help from her, and she never comes near me. I can understand her being absorbed in her engagement, but I cannot understand the frivolous way she spoke when I saw her yesterday. She had the audacity to say that both Mr Vennard and Mr Cargill had gone up in her estimation. Young people can be so heartless."

I would have defended Miss Barriton, but at this moment an astonishing figure was announced. It was Mrs Cargill in travelling-dress, with a purple bonnet and a green motor-veil. Her face was scarlet, whether from excitement or the winds of Tomandhoul, and she charged down on us like a young bull.

"We have come back," she said, "to meet our accusers."

"Accusers!" cried my aunt.

"Yes, accusers!" said the lady. "The abominable rumour about Alexander has reached our ears. At this moment he is with the Prime Minister demanding an official denial. I have come to you, because it was here, at your table, that Alexander is said to have fallen."

"I really don't know what you mean, Mrs Cargill."

"I mean that Alexander is said to have become drunk while dining here, to have been drunk when he spoke at Oldham, and to be now in a Drunkards' Home." The poor lady broke down. "Alexander," she cried, "who has been a teetotaller from his youth, and for thirty years an elder in the U.P. Church! No form of intoxicant has ever been permitted at our table. Even in illness the thing has never passed our lips."

My aunt by this time had pulled herself together. "If this outrageous story is current, Mrs Cargill, there was nothing for it but to come back. Your friends know that it is a gross libel. The only denial necessary is for Mr Cargill to resume his work. I trust his health is better."

"He is well, but heartbroken. His is a sensitive nature, Lady Caerlaverock, and he feels a stain like a wound."

"There is no stain," said my aunt briskly. "Every public man is a target for scandals, but no one but a fool believes them. They will die a natural death when he returns to work. An official denial would make everybody look ridiculous, and encourage the ordinary person to think that there may have been something in them. Believe me, dear

Mrs Cargill, there is nothing to be anxious about now that you are back in London again."

On the contrary, I thought, there was more cause for anxiety than ever. Cargill was back in the House and the illness game could not be played a second time. I went home that night acutely sympathetic towards the worries of the Prime Minister. Mulross would be abroad in a day or two, and Vennard and Cargill were volcanoes in eruption. The Government was in a parlous state, with three demented Ministers on the loose.

The same night I first heard the story of *The* Bill. Vennard had done more than play golf at Littlestone. His active mind—for his bitterest enemies never denied his intellectual energy—had been busy on a great scheme. At that time, it will be remembered, a serious shrinkage of unskilled labour existed not only in the Transvaal, but in the new copper fields of East Africa. Simultaneously a famine was scourging Behar, and Vennard, to do him justice, had made manful efforts to cope with it. He had gone fully into the question, and had been slowly coming to the conclusion that Behar was hopelessly overcrowded. In his new frame of mind—unswervingly logical, utterly unemotional, and wholly unbound by tradition—he had come to connect the African and Indian troubles, and to see in one the relief of the other. The first fruit of his meditations was a letter to 'The Times.' In it he laid down a new theory of emigration. The peoples of the Empire, he said, must be mobile, shifting about to suit economic conditions. But if this was true for the white man, it was equally true for the dark races under our tutelage. He referred to the famine, and argued that the recurrence of such disasters was inevitable, unless we assisted the poverty-stricken ryot to emigrate and sell his labour to advantage. He proposed indentures and terminable contracts, for he declared he had no wish to transplant for good. All that was needed was a short season of wage-earning abroad, that the labourer might return home with savings which would set him for the future on a higher economic plane. The letter was temperate and academic in phrasing, the speculation of a publicist rather than the declaration of a Minister. But in Liberals, who remembered the pandemonium raised over the Chinese in South Africa, it stirred up the gloomiest forebodings.

Then, whispered from mouth to mouth, came the news of the Great Bill. Vennard, it was said, intended to bring in a measure at the earliest possible date to authorise a scheme of enforced and State-aided emigration to the African mines. It would apply at first only to the famine districts, but power would be given to extend its working by proclamation to other areas. Such was the rumour, and I need not say it was soon magnified. Questions were asked in the House which the Speaker ruled out of order. Furious articles, inviting denial, appeared in the Liberal Press; but Vennard took not the slightest notice. He spent his time between his office in Whitehall and the links at Littlestone, dropping into the House once or twice for half an hour's slumber while a colleague was speaking. His Under Secretary in the Lords—a young gentleman who had joined the party for a bet, and to his immense disgust had been immediately rewarded with office—lost his temper under cross-examination and swore audibly at the Opposition. In a day or two the story universally believed was that the Secretary for India was about to transfer the bulk of the Indian people to work as indentured labourers for South African Jews.

It was this popular version, I fancy, which reached the ears of Ram Singh, and the news came on him like a thunderclap. He thought that what Vennard proposed Vennard could do. He saw his native province stripped of its people, his fields left unploughed, and his cattle untended; nay, it was possible, his own worthy and honourable self sent to a far country to dig in a hole. It was a grievous and intolerable prospect. He walked home to Gloucester Road in heavy preoccupation, and the first thing he did was to get out the mysterious brass box in which he kept his valuables. From a pocket-book he took a small silk packet, opened it, and spilled a few clear grains on his hand. It was the antidote.

He waited two days, while on all sides the rumour of the Bill grew stronger and its provisions more stringent. Then he hesitated no longer, but sent for Lord Caerlaverock's cook.

V.

I conceive that the drug did not create new opinions, but elicited those which had hitherto lain dormant. Every man has a creed, but in his soul he knows that that creed has another side, possibly not less logical, which it does not suit him to produce. Our most honest convictions are not the children of pure reason, but of temperament, environment, necessity, and interest. Most of us take sides in life and forget the one we reject. But our conscience tells us it is there, and we can on occasion state it with a fairness and fulness which proves that it is not wholly repellent to our reason. During the crisis I write of, the attitude of Cargill and Vennard was not that of roysterers out for irresponsible mischief. They were eminently reasonable and wonderfully logical, and in private conversation they gave their opponents a very bad time. Cargill, who had hitherto been the hope of the extreme Free-traders, wrote an article for the 'Quarterly' on Tariff Reform. It was set up, but long before it could be used it was cancelled and the type scattered. I have seen a proof of it, however, and I confess I have never read a more brilliant defence of a doctrine which the author had hitherto described as a childish heresy. Which proves my contention—that Cargill all along knew that there was a case against Free Trade, but naturally did not choose to admit it, his allegiance being vowed elsewhere. The drug altered temperament, and with it the creed which is based mainly on temperament. It scattered current convictions, roused dormant speculations, and without damaging the reason switched it on to a new track.

I can see all this now, but at the time I saw only stark madness and the horrible ingenuity of the lunatic. While Vennard was ruminating on his Bill, Cargill was going about London arguing like a Scotch undergraduate. The Prime Minister had seen from the start that the Home Secretary was the worse danger. Vennard might talk of his preposterous Bill, but the Cabinet would have something to say to it before its introduction, and he was mercifully disinclined to go near St Stephen's. But Cargill was assiduous in his attendance at the House, and at any moment might blow the Government sky-high. His colleagues were detailed in relays to watch him. One would hale him to luncheon, and keep him till question-time was over. Another would insist on taking him for a motor-ride, which would end in a break-down about Brentford. Invitations to dinner were showered upon him, and Cargill, who had been unknown in society, found the whole social machinery of his party set at work to make him a lion. The result was that he was prevented from speaking in public, but given far too much encouragement to talk in private. He talked incessantly, before, at, and after dinner, and he did enormous harm. He was horribly clever, too, and usually got the best of an argument, so that various eminent private Liberals had their tempers ruined by his dialectic. In his rich and unabashed accent—he had long discarded his Edinburgh-English—he dissected their arguments and ridiculed their character. He had once been famous for his soapy manners: now he was as rough as a Highland stot.

Things could not go on in this fashion: the risk was too great. It was just a fortnight, I think, after the Caerlaverock dinner-party, when the Prime Minister resolved to bring matters to a head. He could not afford to wait for ever on a return of sanity. He consulted Caerlaverock, and it was agreed that Vennard and Cargill should be asked, or rather commanded, to dine on the following evening at Caerlaverock House. Mulross, whose sanity was not suspected, and whose ankle was now well again, was also invited, as were three other members of the Cabinet and myself as *amicus curiæ*. It was understood that after dinner there would be a settling-up with the two rebels. Either they should recant and come to heel, or they should depart from the fold to swell the wolf-pack of the Opposition. The Prime Minister did not conceal the loss which his party would suffer, but he argued very sensibly that anything was better than a brace of vipers in its bosom.

I have never attended a more lugubrious function. When I arrived I found Caerlaverock, the Prime Minister, and the three other members of the Cabinet standing round a small fire in attitudes of nervous dejection. I remember it was a raw, wet evening, but the gloom out-of-doors was sunshine compared to the gloom within. Caerlaverock's viceregal air had sadly altered. The Prime Minister, once famous for his genial manners, was pallid and preoccupied. We exchanged remarks about the weather and the duration of the session. Then we fell silent till Mulross arrived.

He did not look as if he had come from a sickbed. He came in as jaunty as a boy, limping just a little from his accident. He was greeted by his colleagues with tender solicitude,—solicitude, I fear, completely wasted on him.

"Devilish silly thing to do to get run over," he said. "I was in a brown study when a cab came round a corner. But I don't regret it, you know. During the past fortnight I have had leisure to go into this Bosnian Succession business, and I see now that Von Kladow has been playing one big game of bluff. Very well; it has got to stop. I am going to prick the bubble before I am many days older."

The Prime Minister looked anxious. "Our policy towards Bosnia has been one of non-interference. It is not for us, I should have thought, to read Germany a lesson."

"Oh, come now," Mulross said, slapping—yes, actually slapping—his leader on the back; "we may drop that nonsense when we are alone. You know very well that there are limits to our game of non-interference. If we don't read Germany a lesson, she will read us one—and a damned long unpleasant one too. The sooner we give up all this milk-blooded, blue-spectacled, pacificist talk the better. However, you will see what I have got to say to-morrow in the House."

The Prime Minister's face lengthened. Mulross was not the pillar he had thought him, but a splintering reed. I saw that he agreed with me that this was the most dangerous of the lot.

Then Cargill and Vennard came in together. Both looked uncommonly fit, younger, trimmer, cleaner. Vennard, instead of his sloppy clothes and shaggy hair, was groomed like a Guardsman; had a large pearl-and-diamond solitaire in his shirt, and a white waistcoat with jewelled buttons. He had lost all his self-consciousness, grinned cheerfully at the others, warmed his hands at the fire, and cursed the weather. Cargill, too, had lost his sanctimonious look. There was a bloom of rustic health on his cheek, and a sparkle in his eye, so that he had the appearance of some rosy Scotch laird of Raeburn's painting. Both men wore an air of purpose and contentment.

Vennard turned at once on the Prime Minister. "Did you get my letter?" he asked. "No? Well, you'll find it waiting when you get home. We're all friends here, so I can tell you its contents. We *must* get rid of this ridiculous Radical 'tail.' They think they have the whip-hand of us; well, we have got to prove that we can do very well without them. They are a collection of confounded, treacherous, complacent prigs, but they have no grit in them, and will come to heel if we tackle them firmly. I respect an honest fanatic, but I do not respect those sentiment-mongers. They have the impudence to say that the country is with them. I tell you it is rank nonsense. If you take a strong hand with them, you'll double your popularity, and we'll come back next year with an increased majority. Cargill agrees with me."

The Prime Minister looked grave. "I am not prepared to discuss any policy of ostracism. What you call our 'tail' is a vital section of our party. Their creed may be one-sided, but it is none the less part of our mandate from the people."

"I want a leader who governs as well as reigns," said Vennard. "I believe in discipline, and you know as well as I do that the Rump is infernally out of hand."

"They are not the only members who fail in discipline."

Vennard grinned. "I suppose you mean Cargill and myself. But we are following the central lines of British policy. We are on your side, and we want to make your task easier."

Cargill suddenly began to laugh. "I don't want any ostracism. Leave them alone, and Vennard and I will undertake to give them such a time in the House that they will wish they had never been born. We'll make them resign in batches."

Dinner was announced, and, laughing uproariously, the two rebels went arm-in-arm into the dining-room.

Cargill was in tremendous form. He began to tell Scotch stories, memories of his old Parliament House days. He told them admirably, with a raciness of idiom which I had thought beyond him. They were long tales, and some were as broad as they were long, but Mr Cargill disarmed criticism. His audience, rather scandalised at the start, were soon captured, and political troubles were forgotten in old-fashioned laughter. Even the Prime Minister's anxious face relaxed.

This lasted till the *entrée*, the famous Caerlaverock curry.

As I have said, I was not in the secret, and did not detect the transition. As I partook of the dish I remember feeling a sudden giddiness and a slight nausea. The antidote, to those who had not taken the drug, must have been, I suppose, in the nature of a mild emetic. A mist seemed to obscure the faces of my fellow-guests, and slowly the tide of conversation ebbed away. First Vennard, then Cargill, became silent. I was feeling rather sick, and I noticed with some satisfaction that all our faces were a little green. I wondered casually if I had been poisoned.

The sensation passed, but the party had changed. More especially I was soon conscious that something had happened to the three Ministers. I noticed Mulross particularly, for he was my neighbour. The look of keenness and vitality had died out of him, and suddenly he seemed a rather old, rather tired man, very weary about the eyes.

I asked him if he felt seedy.

"No, not specially," he replied, "but that accident gave me a nasty shock."

"You should go off for a change," I said.

"I almost think I will," was the answer. "I had not meant to leave town till just before the Twelfth, but I think I had better get away to Marienbad for a fortnight. There is nothing doing in the House, and work at the Office is at a standstill. Yes, I fancy I'll go abroad before the end of the week."

I caught the Prime Minister's eye and saw that he had forgotten the purpose of the dinner, being dimly conscious that that purpose was now idle. Cargill and Vennard had ceased to talk like rebels. The Home Secretary had subsided into his old, suave, phrasing self. The humour had gone out of his eye, and the looseness had returned to his lips. He was an older and more commonplace man, but harmless, quite harmless. Vennard, too, wore a new air, or rather had recaptured his old one. He was saying little, but his voice had lost its crispness and recovered its half-plaintive unction; his shoulders had a droop in them; once more he bristled with self-consciousness.

We others were still shaky from that detestable curry, and were so puzzled as to be acutely uncomfortable. Relief would come later, no doubt; for the present we were uneasy at this weird transformation. I saw the Prime Minister examining the two faces intently, and the result seemed to satisfy him. He sighed and looked at Caerlaverock, who smiled and nodded.

"What about that Bill of yours, Vennard?" he asked. "There have been a lot of stupid rumours."

"Bill?" Vennard said. "I know of no Bill. Now that my departmental work is over, I can give my whole soul to Cargill's Small Holdings. Do you mean that?"

"Yes, of course. There was some confusion in the popular mind, but the old arrangement holds. You and Cargill will put it through between you."

They began to talk about those weariful small holdings, and I ceased to listen. We left the dining-room and drifted to the library, where a fire tried to dispel the gloom of the weather. There was a feeling of deadly depression abroad, so that, for all its awkwardness, I would really have preferred the former Caerlaverock dinner. The Prime Minister was whispering to his host. I heard him say something about there being "the devil of a lot of explaining" before him.

Vennard and Cargill came last to the library, arm-in-arm as before.

"I should count it a greater honour," Vennard was saying, "to sweeten the lot of one toiler in England than to add a million miles to our territory. While one English household falls below the minimum scale of civic wellbeing, all talk of Empire is sin and folly."

"Excellent!" said Mr Cargill.

Then I knew for certain that at last peace had descended upon the vexed tents of Israel.

THE SHORTER CATECHISM.

(*Revised Version.*)

When I was young and herdit sheep
  I read auld tales o' Wallace wight;
My heid was fou o' sangs and threip
  O' folk that feared nae mortal might.
But noo I'm auld, and weel I ken
  We're made alike o' gowd and mire;
There's saft bits in the stievest men,
  The bairnliest's got a spunk o' fire.

Sae hearken to me, lads,
  It's truth that I tell:
There's nae man a' courage—
  I ken by mysel'.

I've been an elder forty year:
  I've tried to keep the narrow way:
I've walked afore the Lord in fear:
  I've never missed the kirk a day.
I've read the Bible in and oot,
  (I ken the feck o't clean by hert),
But, still and on, I sair misdoot
  I'm better noo than at the stert.

Sae hearken to me, lads,
  It's truth I maintain:
Man's works are but rags, for
  I ken by my ain.

I hae a name for decent trade:
  I'll wager a' the countryside
Wad sweer nae trustier man was made,
  The ford to soom, the bent to bide.
But when it comes to coupin' horse,
  I'm just like a' that e'er were born;
I fling my heels and tak' my course;
  I'd sell the minister the morn.

Sae hearken to me, lads,
  It's truth that I tell:
There's nae man deid honest—
  I ken by mysel'.

III. THE LEMNIAN.

He pushed the matted locks from his brow as he peered into the mist. His hair was thick with salt, and his eyes smarted from the green-wood fire on the poop. The four slaves who crouched beside the thwarts—Carians with thin birdlike faces—were in a pitiable case, their hands blue with oar-weals and the lash marks on their shoulders beginning to gape from sun and sea. The Lemnian himself bore marks of ill-usage. His cloak was still sopping, his eyes heavy with watching, and his lips black and cracked with thirst. Two days before the storm had caught him and swept his little craft into mid-Ægean. He was a sailor, come of sailor stock, and he had fought the gale manfully and well. But the sea had burst his water-jars, and the torments of drought had been added to his toil. He had been driven south almost to Scyros, but had found no harbour. Then a weary day with the oars had brought him close to the Eubœan shore, when a freshet of storm drove him seaward again. Now at last in this northerly creek of Sciathos he had found shelter and a spring. But it was a perilous place, for there were robbers in the bushy hills—mainland men who loved above all things to rob an islander: and out at sea, as he looked towards Pelion, there seemed something adoing which boded little good. There was deep water beneath a ledge of cliff, half covered by a tangle of wildwood. So Atta lay in the bows, looking through the trails of vine at the racing tides now reddening in the dawn.

The storm had hit others besides him, it seemed. The channel was full of ships, aimless ships that tossed between tide and wind. Looking closer, he saw that they were all wreckage. There had been tremendous doings in the north, and a navy of some sort had come to grief. Atta was a prudent man, and knew that a broken fleet might be dangerous. There might be men lurking in the maimed galleys who would make short work of the owner of a battered but navigable craft. At first he thought that the ships were those of the Hellenes. The troublesome fellows were everywhere in the islands, stirring up strife and robbing the old lords. But the tides running strongly from the east were bringing some of the wreckage in an eddy into the bay. He lay closer and watched the spars and splintered poops as they neared him. These were no galleys of the Hellenes. Then came a drowned man, swollen and horrible: then another—swarthy, hook-nosed fellows, all yellow with the sea. Atta was puzzled. They must be the men from the East about whom he had been hearing. Long ere he left Lemnos there had been news about the Persians. They were coming like locusts out of the dawn, swarming over Ionia and Thrace, men and ships numerous beyond telling. They meant no ill to honest islanders: a little earth and water were enough to win their friendship. But they meant death to the ὕβρις of the Hellenes. Atta was on the side of the invaders; he wished them well in their war with his ancient foes. They would eat them up, Athenians, Lacedæmonians, Corinthians, Æginetans, men of Argos and Elis, and none would be left to trouble him. But in the meantime something had gone wrong. Clearly there had been no battle. As the bodies butted against the side of the galley he hooked up one or two and found no trace of a wound. Poseidon had grown cranky, and had claimed victims. The god would be appeased by this time, and all would go well.

Danger being past, he bade the men get ashore and fill the water-skins. "God's curse on all Hellenes," he said, as he soaked up the cold water from the spring in the thicket.

About noon he set sail again. The wind sat in the north-east, but the wall of Pelion turned it into a light stern breeze which carried him swiftly westward. The four slaves, still leg-weary and arm-weary, lay like logs beside the thwarts. Two slept ; one munched some salty figs ; the fourth, the headman, stared wearily forward, with ever and again a glance back at his master. But the Lemnian never looked his way. His head was on his breast as he steered, and he brooded on the sins of the Hellenes. He was of the old Pelasgian stock, the first lords of the land, who had come out of the soil at the call of God. The pillaging northmen had crushed his folk out of the mainlands and most of the islands, but in Lemnos they had met their match. It was a family story how every grown male had been slain, and how the women long after had slaughtered their conquerors in the night. "Lemnian deeds," said the Hellenes, when they wished to speak of some shameful thing : but to Atta the shame was a glory to be cherished for ever. He and his kind were the ancient people, and the gods loved old things, as those new folk would find. Very especially he hated the men of Athens. Had not one of their captains, Miltiades, beaten the Lemnians and brought the island under Athenian sway? True, it was a rule only in name, for any Athenian who came alone to Lemnos would soon be cleaving the air from the highest cliff-top. But the thought irked his pride, and he gloated over the Persians' coming. The Great King from beyond the deserts would smite those outrageous upstarts. Atta would willingly give earth and water. It was the whim of a fantastic barbarian, and would be well repaid if the bastard Hellenes were destroyed. They spoke his own tongue, and worshipped his own gods, and yet did evil. Let the nemesis of Zeus devour them !

The wreckage pursued him everywhere. Dead men shouldered the sides of the galley, and the straits were stuck full of things like monstrous buoys, where tall ships had foundered. At Artemision he thought he saw signs of an anchored fleet with the low poops of the Hellenes, and sheered off to the northern shores. There, looking towards Œta and the

Malian Gulf, he found an anchorage at sunset. The waters were ugly and the times ill, and he had come on an enterprise bigger than he had dreamed. The Lemnian was a stout fellow, but he had no love for needless danger. He laughed mirthlessly as he thought of his errand, for he was going to Hellas, to the shrine of the Hellenes.

It was a woman's doing, like most crazy enterprises. Three years ago his wife had laboured hard in childbirth, and had had the whims of labouring women. Up in the keep of Larisa, on the windy hillside, there had been heart-searching and talk about the gods. The little olive-wood Hermes, the very private and particular god of Atta's folk, was good enough in simple things like a lambing or a harvest, but he was scarcely fit for heavy tasks. Atta's wife declared that her lord lacked piety. There were mainland gods who repaid worship, but his scorn of all Hellenes made him blind to the merits of those potent divinities. At first Atta resisted. There was Attic blood in his wife, and he strove to argue with her unorthodox craving. But the woman persisted, and a Lemnian wife, as she is beyond other wives in virtue and comeliness, excels them in stubbornness of temper. A second time she was with child, and nothing would content her but that Atta should make his prayers to the stronger gods. Dodona was far away, and long ere he reached it his throat would be cut in the hills. But Delphi was but two days' journey from the Malian coast, and the god of Delphi, the Far-Darter, had surprising gifts, if one were to credit travellers' tales. Atta yielded with an ill grace, and out of his wealth devised an offering to Apollo. So on this July day he found himself looking across the gulf to Kallidromos, bound for a Hellenic shrine, but hating all Hellenes in his soul. A verse of Homer consoled him—the words which Phocion spoke to Achilles. "Verily even the gods may be turned, they whose excellence and honour and strength are greater than thine; yet even these do men, when they pray, turn from their purpose with offerings of incense and pleasant vows." The Far-Darter must hate the ὕβρις of those Hellenes, and be the more ready to avenge it since they dared to claim his countenance. "No race has ownership in the gods," a Lemnian song-maker had said when Atta had been questioning the ways of Poseidon.

The following dawn found him coasting past the north end of Eubœa in the thin fog of a windless summer morn. He steered by the peak of Othrys and a spur of Œta, as he had learnt from a slave who had travelled the road. Presently he was in the muddy Malian waters, and the sun was scattering the mist on the landward side. And then he became aware of a greater commotion than Poseidon's play with the ships off Pelion. A murmur like a winter's storm came seawards. He lowered the sail, which he had set to catch a chance breeze, and bade the men rest on their oars. An earthquake seemed to be tearing at the roots of the hills.

The mist rolled up, and his hawk eyes saw a strange sight. The water was green and still around him, but shoreward it changed its colour. It was a dirty red, and things bobbed about in it like the Persians in the creek of Sciathos. On the strip of shore, below the sheer wall of Kallidromos, men were fighting—myriads of men, for away towards Locris they stretched in ranks and banners and tents till the eye lost them in the haze. There was no sail on the queer, muddy, red-edged sea; there was no man on the hills: but on that one flat ribbon of sand all the nations of the earth were warring. He remembered about the place: Thermopylæ they called it, the Gate of the Hot Springs. The Hellenes were fighting the Persians in the pass for their Fatherland.

Atta was prudent and loved not other men's quarrels. He gave the word to the rowers to row seaward. In twenty strokes they were in the mist again. . . .

Atta was prudent, but he was also stubborn. He spent the day in a creek on the northern shore of the gulf, listening to the weird hum which came over the waters out of the haze. He cursed the delay. Up on Kallidromos would be clear dry air and the path to Delphi among the oak woods. The Hellenes could not be fighting everywhere at once. He might find some spot on the shore, far in their rear, where he could land and gain the hills. There was danger indeed, but once on the ridge he would be safe; and by the time he came back the Great King would have swept the defenders into the sea, and be well on the road for Athens. He asked himself if it were fitting that a Lemnian should be stayed in his holy task by the struggles of Hellene and Barbarian. His thoughts flew to his steading at Larisa, and the dark-eyed wife who was awaiting his homecoming. He could not return without Apollo's favour: his manhood and the memory of his lady's eyes forbade it. So late in the afternoon he pushed off again and steered his galley for the south.

About sunset the mist cleared from the sea; but the dark falls swiftly in the shadow of the high hills, and Atta had no fear. With the night the hum sank to a whisper; it seemed that the invaders were drawing off to camp, for the sound receded to the west. At the last light the Lemnian touched a rock-point well to the rear of the defence. He noticed that the spume at the tide's edge was reddish and stuck to his hands like gum. Of a surety much blood was flowing on that coast.

He bade his slaves return to the north shore and lie hidden to await him. When he came back he would light a signal fire on the topmost bluff of Kallidromos. Let them watch for it and come to take him off. Then he seized his bow and quiver, and his short hunting-spear, buckled his cloak about him, saw that the gift to Apollo was safe in the folds of it, and marched sturdily up the hillside.

The moon was in her first quarter, a slim horn which at her rise showed only the faint outline of the hill. Atta plodded steadfastly on, but he found the way hard. This was not like the crisp sea-turf of Lemnos, where among the barrows of the ancient dead sheep and kine could find sweet fodder. Kallidromos ran up as steep as the roof of a barn. Cytisus and thyme and juniper grew rank, but above all the place was strewn with rocks, leg-twisting boulders, and great cliffs where eagles dwelt. Being a seaman, Atta had his bearings. The path to Delphi left the shore road near the Hot Springs, and went south by a rift of the mountain. If he went up the slope in a bee-line he must strike it in time and find better going. Still it was an eerie place to be tramping after dark. The Hellenes had strange gods of the thicket and hillside, and he had no wish to intrude upon their sanctuaries. He told himself that next to the Hellenes he hated this country of theirs, where a man sweltered in hot jungles or tripped among hidden crags. He sighed for the cool beaches below Larisa, where the surf was white as the snows of Samothrace, and the fisher-boys sang round their smoking broth-pots.

Presently he found a path. It was not the mule road, worn by many feet, that he had looked for, but a little track which twined among the boulders. Still it eased his feet, so he cleared the thorns from his sandals, strapped his belt tighter, and stepped out more confidently. Up and up he went, making odd detours among the crags. Once he came to a promontory, and, looking down, saw lights twinkling from the Hot Springs. He had thought the course lay more southerly, but consoled himself by remembering that a mountain path must have many windings. The great matter was that he was ascending, for he knew that he must cross the ridge of Œta before he struck the Locrian glens that led to the Far-Darter's shrine.

At what seemed the summit of the first ridge he halted for breath, and, prone on the thyme, looked back to sea. The Hot Springs were hidden, but across the gulf a single light shone from the far shore. He guessed that by this time his galley had been beached and his slaves were cooking supper. The thought made him homesick. He had beaten and cursed these slaves of his times without number, but now in this strange land he felt them kinsfolk, men of his own household. Then he told himself he was no better than a woman. Had he not gone sailing to Chalcedon and distant Pontus, many months' journey from home, while this was but a trip of days? In a week he would be welcomed by a smiling wife, with a friendly god behind him.

The track still bore west, though Delphi lay in the south. Moreover, he had come to a broader road running through a little tableland. The highest peaks of Œta were dark against the sky, and around him was a flat glade where oaks whispered in the night breezes. By this time he judged from the stars that midnight had passed, and he began to consider whether, now that he was beyond the fighting, he should not sleep and wait for dawn. He made up his mind to find a shelter, and, in the aimless way of the night traveller, pushed on and on in the quest of it. The truth is his mind was on Lemnos, and a dark-eyed, white-armed dame spinning in the evening by the threshold. His eyes roamed among the oak-trees, but vacantly and idly, and many a mossy corner was passed unheeded. He forgot his ill-temper, and hummed cheerfully the song his reapers sang in the barley-fields below his orchard. It was a song of seamen turned husbandmen, for the gods it called on were the gods of the sea. . . .

Suddenly he found himself crouching among the young oaks, peering and listening. There was something coming from the west. It was like the first mutterings of a storm in a narrow harbour, a steady rustling and whispering. It was not wind; he knew winds too well to be deceived. It was the tramp of light-shod feet among the twigs—many feet, for the sound remained steady, while the noise of a few men will rise and fall. They were coming fast and coming silently. The war had reached far up Kallidromos.

Atta had played this game often in the little island wars. Very swiftly he ran back and away from the path up the slope which he knew to be the first ridge of Kallidromos.

The army, whatever it might be, was on the Delphian road. Were the Hellenes about to turn the flank of the Great King?

A moment later he laughed at his folly. For the men began to appear, and they were coming to meet him, coming from the west. Lying close in the brushwood he could see them clearly. It was well he had left the road, for they stuck to it, following every winding—crouching, too, like hunters after deer. The first man he saw was a Hellene, but the ranks behind were no Hellenes. There was no glint of bronze or gleam of fair skin. They were dark, long-haired fellows, with spears like his own, and round Eastern caps, and egg-shaped bucklers. Then Atta rejoiced. It was the Great King who was turning the flank of the Hellenes. They guarded the gate, the fools, while the enemy slipped through the roof.

He did not rejoice long. The van of the army was narrow and kept to the path, but the men behind were straggling all over the hillside. Another minute and he would be discovered. The thought was cheerless. It was true that he was an islander and friendly to the Persian, but up on the heights who would listen to his tale? He would be taken for a spy, and one of those thirsty spears would drink his blood. It must be farewell to Delphi for the moment, he thought, or farewell to Lemnos for ever. Crouching low, he ran back and away from the path to the crest of the sea-ridge of Kallidromos.

The men came no nearer him. They were keeping roughly to the line of the path, and drifted through the oak wood before him, an army without end. He had scarcely thought there were so many fighting men in the world. He resolved to lie there on the crest, in the hope that ere the first light they would be gone. Then he would push on to Delphi, leaving them to settle their quarrels behind him. These were the hard times for a pious pilgrim.

But another noise caught his ear from the right. The

army had flanking squadrons, and men were coming along the ridge. Very bitter anger rose in Atta's heart. He had cursed the Hellenes, and now he cursed the Barbarians no less. Nay, he cursed all war, that spoiled the errands of peaceful folk. And then, seeking safety, he dropped over the crest on to the steep shoreward face of the mountain.

In an instant his breath had gone from him. He slid down a long slope of screes, and then with a gasp found himself falling sheer into space. Another second and he was caught in a tangle of bush, and then dropped once more upon screes, where he clutched desperately for handhold. Breathless and bleeding he came to anchor on a shelf of greensward, and found himself blinking up at the crest which seemed to tower a thousand feet above. There were men on the crest now. He heard them speak, and felt that they were looking down.

The shock kept him still till the men had passed. Then the terror of the place gripped him, and he tried feverishly to retrace his steps. A dweller all his days among gentle downs, he grew dizzy with the sense of being hung in space. But the only fruit of his efforts was to set him slipping again. This time he pulled up at a root of gnarled oak, which overhung the sheerest cliff on Kallidromos. The danger brought his wits back. He sullenly reviewed his case, and found it desperate.

He could not go back, and, even if he did, he would meet the Persians. If he went on he would break his neck, or at the best fall into the Hellenes' hands. Oddly enough he feared his old enemies less than his friends. He did not think that the Hellenes would butcher him. Again, he might sit perched in his eyrie till they settled their quarrel, or he fell off. He rejected this last way. Fall off he should for certain, unless he kept moving. Already he was retching with the vertigo of the heights. It was growing lighter. Suddenly he was looking not into a black world, but to a pearl-grey floor far beneath him. It was the sea, the thing he knew and loved. The sight screwed up his courage. He remembered that he was a Lemnian and a seafarer. He would be conquered neither by rock, nor by Hellene, nor by the Great King. Least of all by the last, who was a barbarian. Slowly, with clenched teeth and narrowed eyes, he began to clamber down a ridge which flanked the great cliff of Kallidromos. His plan was to reach the shore and take the road to the east before the Persians completed their circuit. Some instinct told him that a great army would not take the track he had mounted by. There must be some longer and easier way debouching farther down the coast. He might yet have the good luck to slip between them and the sea.

The two hours which followed tried his courage hard. Thrice he fell, and only a juniper-root stood between him and death. His hands grew ragged, and his nails were worn to the quick. He had long ago lost his weapons; his cloak was in shreds, all save the breast-fold which held the gift to Apollo. The heavens brightened, but he dared not look around. He knew he was traversing awesome places, where a goat could scarcely tread. Many times he gave up hope of life. His head was swimming, and he was so deadly sick that often he had to lie gasping on some shoulder of rock less steep than the rest. But his anger kept him to his purpose. He was filled with fury at the Hellenes. It was they and their folly that had brought him these mischances. Some day . . .

He found himself sitting blinking on the shore of the sea. A furlong off the water was lapping on the reefs. A man larger than human in the morning mist, was standing above him.

"Greeting, stranger," said the voice. "By Hermes, you choose the difficult roads to travel."

Atta felt for broken bones, and, reassured, struggled to his feet.

"God's curse upon all mountains," he said. He staggered

to the edge of the tide and laved his brow. The savour of salt revived him. He turned to find the tall man at his elbow, and noted how worn and ragged he was, and yet how upright.

"When a pigeon is flushed from the rocks there is a hawk near," said the voice.

Atta was angry. "A hawk!" he cried. "Nay, an army of eagles. There will be some rare flushing of Hellenes before evening."

"What frightened you, Islander?" the stranger asked. "Did a wolf bark up on the hillside?"

"Ay, a wolf. The wolf from the East with a multitude of wolflings. There will be fine eating soon in the pass."

The man's face grew dark. He put his hand to his mouth and called. Half a dozen sentries ran to join him. He spoke to them in the harsh Lacedæmonian speech which made Atta sick to hear. They talked with the back of the throat, and there was not an "s" in their words.

"There is mischief in the hills," the first man said. "This islander has been frightened down over the rocks. The Persian is stealing a march on us."

The sentries laughed. One quoted a proverb about island courage. Atta's wrath flared and he forgot himself. He had no wish to warn the Hellenes, but it irked his pride to be thought a liar. He began to tell his story hastily, angrily, confusedly: and the men still laughed.

Then he turned eastward and saw the proof before him. The light had grown and the sun was coming up over Pelion. The first beam fell on the eastern ridge of Kallidromos, and there, clear on the sky-line, was the proof. The Persian was making a wide circuit, but moving shoreward. In a little he would be at the coast, and by noon at the Hellenes' rear.

His hearers doubted no more. Atta was hurried forward through the lines of the Greeks to the narrow throat of the pass, where behind a rough rampart of stones lay the Lacedæmonian headquarters. He was still giddy from the heights and it was in a giddy dream that he traversed the misty shingles of the beach amid ranks of sleeping warriors. It was a grim place, for there were dead and dying in it, and blood on every stone. But in the lee of the wall little fires were burning and slaves were cooking breakfast. The smell of roasting flesh came pleasantly to his nostrils, and he remembered that he had had no meal since he crossed the gulf.

Then he found himself the centre of a group who had the air of kings. They looked as if they had been years in war. Never had he seen faces so worn and so terribly scarred. The hollows in their cheeks gave them the air of smiling, and yet they were grave. Their scarlet vests were torn and muddied, and the armour which lay near was dinted like the scrap-iron before a smithy door. But what caught his attention were the eyes of the men. They glittered as no eyes he had ever seen before glittered. The sight cleared his bewilderment and took the pride out of his heart. He could not pretend to despise a folk who looked like Ares fresh from the wars of the Immortals.

They spoke among themselves in quiet voices. Scouts came and went, and once or twice one of the men, taller than the rest, asked Atta a question. The Lemnian sat in the heart of the group, sniffing the smell of cooking, and looking at the rents in his cloak and the long scratches on his legs. Something was pressing on his breast, and he found that it was Apollo's gift. He had forgotten all about it. Delphi seemed beyond the moon, and his errand a child's dream.

Then the King, for so he thought of the tall man, spoke—

"You have done us a service, Islander. The Persian is at our back and front, and there will be no escape for those who stay. Our allies are going home, for they do not share our vows. We of Lacedæmon wait in the pass. If you go with the men of Corinth you will find a place of safety before noon. No doubt in the Euripus there is some boat to take you to your own land."

He spoke courteously, not in the rude Athenian way; and somehow the quietness of his voice and his glittering eyes roused wild longings in Atta's heart. His island pride was face to face with a greater—greater than he had ever dreamed of.

"Bid yon cooks give me some broth," he said gruffly. "I am faint. After I have eaten I will speak with you."

He was given food, and as he ate he thought. He was on trial before these men of Lacedæmon. More, the old faith of the islands, the pride of the first masters, was at stake in his hands. He had boasted that he and his kind were the last of the men; now these Hellenes of Lacedæmon were preparing a great deed, and they deemed him unworthy to share in it. They offered him safety. Could he brook the insult? He had forgotten that the cause of the Persian was his; that the Hellenes were the foes of his race. He saw only that the last test of manhood was preparing, and the manhood in him rose to greet the trial. An odd wild ecstasy surged in his veins. It was not the lust of battle, for he had no love of slaying, or hate for the Persian, for he was his friend. It was the sheer joy of proving that the Lemnian stock had a starker pride than these men of Lacedæmon. They would die for their fatherland and their vows; but he, for a whim, a scruple, a delicacy of honour. His mind was so clear that no other course occurred to him. There was only one way for a man. He, too, would be dying for his fatherland, for through him the island race would be ennobled in the eyes of gods and men.

Troops were filing fast to the east—Thebans, Corinthians.

"Time flies, Islander," said the King's voice. "The hours of safety are slipping past."

Atta looked up carelessly. "I will stay," he said. "God's curse on all Hellenes! Little I care for your quarrels. It is nothing to me if your Hellas is under the heel of the East. But I care much for brave men. It shall never be said that a man of Lemnos, a son of the old race, fell back when Death threatened. I stay with you, men of Lacedæmon."

The King's eyes glittered; they seemed to peer into his heart.

"It appears they breed men in the islands," he said. "But you err. Death does not threaten. Death awaits us."

"It is all one," said Atta. "But I crave a boon. Let me fight my last fight by your side. I am of older stock than you, and a king in my own country. I would strike my last blow among kings."

There was an hour of respite before battle was joined, and Atta spent it by the edge of the sea. He had been given arms, and in girding himself for the fight he had found Apollo's offering in his breastfold. He was done with the gods of the Hellenes. His offering should go to the gods of his own people. So, calling upon Poseidon, he flung the little gold cup far out to sea. It flashed in the sunlight, and then sank in the soft green tides so noiselessly that it seemed as if the hand of the Sea-god had been stretched to take it. "Hail, Poseidon!" the Lemnian cried. "I am bound this day for the Ferryman. To you only I make prayer, and to the little Hermes of Larisa. Be kind to my kin when they travel the sea, and keep them islanders and seafarers for ever. Hail and farewell, God of my own folk!"

Then, while the little waves lapped on the white sand, Atta made a song. He was thinking of the homestead far up in the green downs, looking over to the snows of Samothrace. At this hour in the morning there would be a tinkle of sheep-bells as the flocks went down to the low pastures. Cool winds would be blowing, and the noise of the surf below the cliffs would come faint to the ear. In the hall the maids would be spinning, while their dark-haired mistress would be casting swift glances to the doorway, lest it might be filled any moment by the form of her returning lord. Outside in the chequered sunlight of the orchard the child would be playing with his nurse, crooning in childish syllables the chanty his father had taught him. And at the thought of his home a great passion welled up in Atta's heart. It was not regret, but joy and pride and aching love. In his antique island creed the death he was awaiting was not other than a bridal. He was dying for the things he loved, and by his death they would be blessed eternally. He would not have long to wait before bright eyes came to greet him in the House of Shadows.

So Atta made the Song of Atta, and sang it then, and later in the press of battle. It was a simple song, like the lays of seafarers. It put into rough verse the thought which cheers the heart of all adventurers—nay, which makes adventure possible for those who have much to leave. It spoke of the shining pathway of the sea which is the Great Uniter. A man may lie dead in Pontus or beyond the Pillars of Herakles, but if he dies on the shore there is nothing between him and his fatherland. It spoke of a battle all the long dark night in a strange place—a place of marshes and black cliffs and shadowy terrors.

"*In the dawn the sweet light comes,*" said the song, "*and the salt winds and the tides will bear me home. . . .*"

When in the evening the Persians took toll of the dead, they found one man who puzzled them. He lay among the tall Lacedæmonians, on the very lip of the sea, and around him were swathes of their countrymen. It looked as if he had been fighting his way to the water, and had been overtaken by death as his feet reached the edge. Nowhere in the pass did the dead lie so thick, and yet he was no Hellene. He was torn like a deer that the dogs have worried, but the little left of his garments and his features spoke of Eastern race. The survivors could tell nothing except that he had fought like a god and had been singing all the while.

The matter came to the ear of the Great King, who was

sore enough at the issue of the day. That one of his men had performed feats of valour beyond the Hellenes was a pleasant tale to tell. And so his captains reported it. Accordingly when the fleet from Artemision arrived next morning, and all but a few score Persians were shovelled into holes, that the Hellenes might seem to have been conquered by a lesser force, Atta's body was laid out with pomp in the midst of the Lacedæmonians. And the seamen rubbed their eyes and thanked their strange gods that one man of the East had been found to match those terrible warriors whose name was a nightmare. Further, the Great King gave orders that the body of Atta should be embalmed and carried with the army, and that his name and kin should be sought out and duly honoured. This latter was a task too hard for the staff, and no more was heard of it till months later, when the King, in full flight after Salamis, bethought him of the one man who had not played him false. Finding that his lieutenants had nothing to tell him, he eased five of them of their heads.

As it happened, the deed was not quite forgotten. An islander, a Lesbian and a cautious man, had fought at Thermopylæ in the Persian ranks, and had heard Atta's singing and seen how he fell. Long afterwards some errand took this man to Lemnos, and in the evening, speaking with the Elders, he told his tale and repeated something of the song. There was that in the words which gave the Lemnians a clue, the mention, I think, of the olive-wood Hermes and the snows of Samothrace. So Atta came to great honour among his own people, and his memory and his words were handed down to the generations. The song became a favourite island lay, and for centuries throughout the Ægean seafaring men sang it when they turned their prows to wild seas. Nay, it travelled farther, for you will find part of it stolen by Euripides and put in a chorus of the *Andromache*. There are echoes of it in some of the epigrams of the *Anthology*; and, though the old days have gone, the simple fisher-folk still sing snatches in their barbarous dialect. The Klephts used to make a catch of it at night round their fires in the hills, and only the other day I met a man in Scyros who had collected a dozen variants, and was publishing them in a dull book on island folklore.

In the centuries which followed the great fight, the sea fell away from the roots of the cliffs and left a mile of marsh-land. About fifty years ago a peasant, digging in a rice-field, found the cup which Atta had given to Poseidon. There was much talk about the discovery, and scholars debated hotly about its origin. To-day it is in the Berlin Museum, and according to the new fashion in archæology it is labelled "Minoan," and kept in the Cretan Section. But anyone who looks carefully will see behind the rim a neat little carving of a dolphin; and I happen to know that that was the private badge of Atta's house.

ATTA'S SONG.

(*Roughly translated.*)

I will sing of thee,
Great Sea-Mother,
Whose white arms gather
Thy sons in the ending :
And draw them homeward
From far sad marches—
Wild lands in the sunset,
Bitter shores of the morning
Soothe them and guide them
By shining pathways
Homeward to thee.

All day I have striven in dark glens
With parched throat and dim eyes,
Where the red crags choke the stream
And dank thickets hide the spear.
I have spilled the blood of my foes
And their wolves have torn my flanks.
I am faint, O Mother,
Faint and aweary.
I have longed for thy cool winds
And thy kind grey eyes
And thy lover's arms.

At the even I came
To a land of terrors,
Of hot swamps where the feet mired
And waters that flowed red with blood.

There I strove with thousands,
Wild-eyed and lost,
As a lion among serpents.
—But sudden before me
I saw the flash
Of the sweet wide waters
That wash my homeland
And mirror the stars of home.
Then sang I for joy,
For I knew the Preserver,
Thee, the Uniter,
The great Sea-Mother.
Soon will the sweet light come,
And the salt winds and the tides
Will bear me home.

Far in the sunrise,
Nestled in thy bosom,
Lies my own green isle.
Thither wilt thou bear me
To where, above the sea-cliffs,
Stretch mild meadows, flower-decked,
 thyme-scented,
Crisp with sea breezes.
There my flocks feed
On sunny uplands,
Looking over thy waters
To where the mount Saos
Raises pure snows to God.

Hermes, guide of souls,
I made thee a shrine in my orchard,
And round thy olive-wood limbs
The maidens twined Spring blossoms—
Violet and helichryse
And the pale wind flowers.

Keep thou watch for me,
For I am coming.
Tell to my lady
And to all my kinsfolk
That I who have gone from them
Tarry not long, but come swift o'er the sea-path,
My feet light with joy,
My eyes bright with longing.
For little it matters
Where a man may fall,
If he fall by the sea-shore;
The kind waters await him,
The white arms are around him,
And the wise Mother of Men
Will carry him home.

I who sing
Wait joyfully on the morning.
Ten thousand beset me
And their spears ache for my heart.
They will crush me and grind me to mire,
So that none will know the man that once was me.
But at the first light I shall be gone,
Singing, flitting, o'er the grey waters,
Outward, homeward,
To thee, the Preserver,
Thee, the Uniter,
Mother the Sea.

IV. SPACE.

"*Est impossible? Certum est.*"
—TERTULLIAN.

LEITHEN told me this story one evening in early September as we sat beside the pony track which gropes its way from Glenavelin up the Correi na Sidhe. I had arrived that afternoon from the south, while he had been taking an off-day from a week's stalking, so we had walked up the glen together after tea to get the news of the forest. A rifle was out on the Correi na Sidhe beat, and a thin spire of smoke had risen from the top of Sgurr Dearg to show that a stag had been killed at the burn-head. The lumpish hill pony with its deer-saddle had gone up the Correi in a gillie's charge, while we followed at leisure, picking our way among the loose granite rocks and the patches of wet bogland. The track climbed high on one of the ridges of Sgurr Dearg, till it hung over a caldron of green glen with the Alt-na-Sidhe churning in its linn a thousand feet below. It was a breathless evening, I remember, with a pale-blue sky just clearing from the haze of the day. West-wind weather may make the North, even in September, no bad imitation of the Tropics, and I sincerely pitied the man who all these stifling hours had been toiling on the screes of Sgurr Dearg. By-and-by we sat down on a bank of heather, and idly watched the trough swimming at our feet. The clatter of the pony's hoofs grew fainter, the drone of bees had gone, even the midges seemed to have forgotten their calling. No place on earth can be so deathly still as a deer-forest early in the season before the stags have begun roaring, for there are no sheep with their homely noises, and only the rare croak of a raven breaks the silence. The hillside was far from sheer—one could have walked down with a little care—but something in the shape of the hollow and the remote gleam of white water gave it an air of extraordinary depth and space. There was a shimmer left from the day's heat, which invested bracken and rock and scree with a curious airy unreality. One could almost have believed that the eye had tricked the mind, that all was mirage, that five yards from the path the solid earth fell away into nothingness. I have a bad head, and instinctively I drew farther back into the heather. Leithen's eyes were looking vacantly before him.

"Did you ever know Hollond?" he asked.

Then he laughed shortly. "I don't know why I asked that, but somehow this place reminded me of Hollond. That glimmering hollow looks as if it were the beginning of eternity. It must be eerie to live with the feeling always on one."

Leithen seemed disinclined for further exercise. He lit a pipe and smoked quietly for a little. "Odd that you didn't know Hollond. You must have heard his name. I thought you amused yourself with metaphysics."

Then I remembered. There had been an erratic genius who had written some articles in 'Mind' on that dreary subject, the mathematical conception of infinity. Men had praised them to me, but I confess I never quite understood their argument. "Wasn't he some sort of mathematical professor?" I asked.

"He was, and, in his own way, a tremendous swell. He wrote a book on Number which has translations in every European language. He is dead now, and the Royal Society founded a medal in his honour. But I wasn't thinking of that side of him."

It was the time and place for a story, for the pony would not be back for an hour. So I asked Leithen about the other side of Hollond which was recalled to him by Correi na Sidhe. He seemed a little unwilling to speak. . . .

"I wonder if you will understand it. You ought to, of course, better than me, for you know something of philosophy. But it took me a long time to get the hang of it, and I can't give you any kind of explanation. He was my fag at Eton, and when I began to get on at the Bar I was able to advise him on one or two private matters, so that he rather fancied my legal ability. He came to me with his story because he had to tell someone, and he wouldn't trust a colleague. He said he didn't want a scientist to know, for scientists were either pledged to their own theories and wouldn't understand, or, if they understood, would get ahead of him in his researches. He wanted a lawyer, he said, who was accustomed to weighing evidence. That was good sense, for evidence must always be judged by the same laws, and I suppose in the long-run the most abstruse business comes down to a fairly simple deduction from certain data. Anyhow, that was the way he used to talk, and I listened to him, for I liked the man, and had an enormous respect for his brains. At Eton he sluiced down all the mathematics they could give him, and he was an astonishing swell at Cambridge. He was a simple fellow, too, and talked no more jargon than he could help. I used to climb with him in the Alps now and then, and you would never have guessed that he had any thoughts beyond getting up steep rocks.

"It was at Chamonix, I remember, that I first got a hint of the matter that was filling his mind. We had been taking an off-day, and were sitting in the hotel garden, watching the Aiguilles getting purple in the twilight. Chamonix always makes me choke a little—it is so crushed in by those great snow masses. I said something about it—said I liked open spaces like the Gornergrat or the Bel Alp better. He asked me why: if it was the difference of the air, or merely the wider horizon? I said it was the sense of not being crowded, of living in an empty world. He repeated the word 'empty' and laughed.

" 'By "empty" you mean,' he said, 'where things don't knock up against you?'

"I told him No. I meant just empty, void, nothing but blank æther.

" 'You don't knock up against things here, and the air is as good as you want. It can't be the lack of ordinary emptiness you feel.'

"I agreed that the word needed explaining. 'I suppose it is mental restlessness,' I said. 'I like to feel that for a tremendous distance there is nothing round me. Why, I don't know. Some men are built the other way and have a terror of space.'

"He said that that was better. 'It is a personal fancy, and depends on your *knowing* that there is nothing between you and the top of the Dent Blanche. And you know because your eyes tell you there is nothing. Even if you were blind, you might have a sort of sense about adjacent matter. Blind men often have it. But in any case, whether got from instinct or sight, the *knowledge* is what matters.'

"Hollond was embarking on a Socratic dialogue in which I could see little point. I told him so, and he laughed.

" 'I am not sure that I am very clear myself. But yes—there *is* a point. Supposing you knew—not by sight or by instinct, but by sheer intellectual knowledge, as I know the truth of a mathematical proposition—that what we call empty space was full, crammed. Not with lumps of what we call matter like hills and houses, but with things as real—as real to the mind. Would you still feel crowded?'

" 'No,' I said, 'I don't think so. It is only what we call matter that signifies. It would be just as well not to feel crowded by the other thing, for there would be no escape from it. But what are you getting at? Do you mean atoms or electric currents or what?'

"He said he wasn't thinking about that sort of thing, and began to talk of another subject.

"Next night, when we were pigging it at the Géant *cabane*,

he started again on the same tack. He asked me how I accounted for the fact that animals could find their way back over great tracts of unknown country. I said I supposed it was the homing instinct.

"'Rubbish, man,' he said. 'That's only another name for the puzzle, not an explanation. There must be some reason for it. They must *know* something that we cannot understand. Tie a cat in a bag and take it fifty miles by train and it will make its way home. That cat has some clue that we haven't.'

"I was tired and sleepy, and told him that I did not care a rush about the psychology of cats. But he was not to be snubbed, and went on talking.

"'How if Space is really full of things we cannot see and as yet do not know? How if all animals and some savages have a cell in their brain or a nerve which responds to the invisible world? How if all Space be full of these landmarks, not material in our sense, but quite real? A dog barks at nothing, a wild beast makes an aimless circuit. Why? Perhaps because Space is made up of corridors and alleys, ways to travel and things to shun? For all we know, to a greater intelligence than ours the top of Mont Blanc may be as crowded as Piccadilly Circus.'

"But at that point I fell asleep and left Hollond to repeat his questions to a guide who knew no English and a snoring porter.

"Six months later, one foggy January afternoon, Hollond rang me up at the Temple and proposed to come to see me that night after dinner. I thought he wanted to talk Alpine shop, but he turned up in Duke Street about nine with a kit-bag full of papers. He was an odd fellow to look at—a yellowish face with the skin stretched tight on the cheek-bones, clean-shaven, a sharp chin which he kept poking forward, and deep-set, greyish eyes. He was a hard fellow, too, always in pretty good condition, which was remarkable considering how he slaved for nine months out of the twelve.

He had a quiet, slow-spoken manner, but that night I saw that he was considerably excited.

" He said that he had come to me because we were old friends. He proposed to tell me a tremendous secret. ' I must get another mind to work on it or I'll go crazy. I don't want a scientist. I want a plain man.'

" Then he fixed me with a look like a tragic actor's. ' Do you remember that talk we had in August at Chamonix—about Space ? I daresay you thought I was playing the fool. So I was in a sense, but I was feeling my way towards something which has been in my mind for ten years. Now I have got it, and you must hear about it. You may take my word that it's a pretty startling discovery.'

" I lit a pipe and told him to go ahead, warning him that I knew about as much science as the dustman.

" I am bound to say that it took me a long time to understand what he meant. He began by saying that everybody thought of Space as an ' empty homogeneous medium.' ' Never mind at present what the ultimate constituents of that medium are. We take it as a finished product, and we think of it as mere extension, something without any quality at all. That is the view of civilised man. You will find all the philosophers taking it for granted. Yes, but every living thing does not take that view. An animal, for instance. It feels a kind of quality in Space. It can find its way over new country, because it perceives certain landmarks, not necessarily material, but perceptible, or if you like intelligible. Take an Australian savage. He has the same power, and, I believe, for the same reason. He is conscious of intelligible landmarks.'

" ' You mean what people call a sense of direction,' I put in.

" ' Yes, but what in Heaven's name is a sense of direction ? The phrase explains nothing. However incoherent the mind of the animal or the savage may be, it is there somewhere, working on some data. I've been all through the psychological and anthropological side of the business, and after you eliminate clues from sight and hearing and smell and half-conscious memory there remains a solid lump of the inexplicable.'

"Hollond's eye had kindled, and he sat doubled up in his chair, dominating me with a finger.

"'Here, then, is a power which man is civilising himself out of. Call it anything you like, but you must admit that it is a power. Don't you see that it is a perception of another kind of reality that we are leaving behind us? . . . Well, you know the way nature works. The wheel comes full circle, and what we think we have lost we regain in a higher form. So for a long time I have been wondering whether the civilised mind could not re-create for itself this lost gift, the gift of seeing the quality of Space. I mean that I wondered whether the scientific modern brain could not get to the stage of realising that Space is not an empty homogeneous medium, but full of intricate differences, intelligible and real, though not with our common reality.'

"I found all this very puzzling, and he had to repeat it several times before I got a glimpse of what he was talking about.

"'I've wondered for a long time,' he went on, 'but now, quite suddenly, I have begun to know.' He stopped and asked me abruptly if I knew much about mathematics.

"'It's a pity,' he said, 'but the main point is not technical, though I wish you could appreciate the beauty of some of my proofs.' Then he began to tell me about his last six months' work. I should have mentioned that he was a brilliant physicist besides other things. All Hollond's tastes were on the borderlands of sciences, where mathematics fades into metaphysics and physics merges in the abstrusest kind of mathematics. Well, it seems he had been working for years at the ultimate problem of matter, and especially of that rarefied matter we call æther or space. I forget what his view was—atoms or molecules or electric waves. If he ever told me I have forgotten, but I'm not certain that I ever knew. However, the point was that these ultimate constituents were dynamic and mobile, not a mere passive medium but a medium in constant movement and change. He claimed to have discovered—by ordinary inductive experiment—that the constituents of æther possessed certain functions, and moved in certain figures obedient to certain mathematical laws. Space, I gathered, was perpetually 'forming fours' in some fancy way.

"Here he left his physics and became the mathematician. Among his mathematical discoveries had been certain curves or figures or something whose behaviour involved a new dimension. I gathered that this wasn't the ordinary Fourth Dimension that people talk of, but that fourth-dimensional inwardness or involution was part of it. The explanation lay in the pile of manuscripts he left with me, but though I tried honestly I couldn't get the hang of it. My mathematics stopped with desperate finality just as he got into his subject.

"His point was that the constituents of Space moved according to these new mathematical figures of his. They were always changing, but the principles of their change were as fixed as the law of gravitation. Therefore, if you once grasped these principles you knew the contents of the void. What do you make of that?"

I said that it seemed to me a reasonable enough argument, but that it got one very little way forward. "A man," I said, "might know the contents of Space and the laws of their arrangement and yet be unable to see anything more than his fellows. It is a purely academic knowledge. His mind knows it as the result of many deductions, but his senses perceive nothing."

Leithen laughed. "Just what I said to Hollond. He asked the opinion of my legal mind. I said I could not pronounce on his argument, but that I could point out that he had established no *trait d'union* between the intellect which understood and the senses which perceived. It was like a blind man with immense knowledge but no eyes, and therefore no peg to hang his knowledge on and make it useful. He had not explained his savage or his cat. 'Hang it, man,' I said, 'before you can appreciate the existence of your Spacial forms you have to go through elaborate experiments and deductions. You can't be doing that every minute. Therefore you don't get any nearer to the *use* of the sense you say that man once possessed, though you can explain it a bit."

"What did he say?" I asked.

"The funny thing was that he never seemed to see my difficulty. When I kept bringing him back to it he shied off with a new wild theory of perception. He argued that the mind can live in a world of realities without any sensuous stimulus to connect them with the world of our ordinary life. Of course that wasn't my point. I supposed that this world of Space was real enough to him, but I wanted to know how he got there. He never answered me. He was the typical Cambridge man, you know—dogmatic about uncertainties, but curiously diffident about the obvious. He laboured to get me to understand the notion of his mathematical forms, which I was quite willing to take on trust from him. Some queer things he said, too. He took our feeling about Left and Right as an example of our instinct for the quality of Space. But when I objected that Left and Right varied with each object, and only existed in connection with some definite material thing, he said that that was exactly what he meant. It was an example of the mobility of the Spacial forms. Do you see any sense in that?"

I shook my head. It seemed to me pure craziness.

"And then he tried to show me what he called the 'involution of Space,' by taking two points on a piece of paper. The points were a foot away when the paper was flat, but they coincided when it was doubled up. He said that there were no gaps between the figures, for the medium was continuous, and he took as an illustration the loops on a cord.

You are to think of a cord always looping and unlooping itself according to certain mathematical laws. Oh, I tell you, I gave up trying to follow him. And he was so desperately in earnest all the time. By his account Space was a sort of mathematical pandemonium."

Leithen stopped to refill his pipe, and I mused upon the ironic fate which had compelled a mathematical genius to make his sole confidant of a philistine lawyer, and induced that lawyer to repeat it confusedly to an ignoramus at twilight on a Scotch hill. As told by Leithen it was a very halting tale.

"But there was one thing I could see very clearly," Leithen went on, "and that was Hollond's own case. This crowded world of Space was perfectly real to him. How he had got to it I do not know. Perhaps his mind, dwelling constantly on the problem, had unsealed some atrophied cell and restored the old instinct. Anyhow, he was living his daily life with a foot in each world.

"He often came to see me, and after the first hectic discussions he didn't talk much. There was no noticeable change in him—a little more abstracted perhaps. He would walk in the street or come into a room with a quick look round him, and sometimes for no earthly reason he would swerve. Did you ever watch a cat crossing a room? It sidles along by the furniture and walks over an open space of carpet as if it were picking its way among obstacles. Well, Hollond behaved like that, but he had always been counted a little odd, and nobody noticed it but me.

"I knew better than to chaff him, and we had stopped argument, so there wasn't much to be said. But sometimes he would give me news about his experiences. The whole thing was perfectly clear and scientific and above-board, and nothing creepy about it. You know how I hate the washy supernatural stuff they give us nowadays. Hollond was well and fit, with an appetite like a hunter. But as he talked, sometimes—well, you know I haven't much in the way of nerves or imagination—but I used to get a little eerie. Used to feel the solid earth dissolving round me. It was the opposite of vertigo, if you understand me—a sense of airy realities crowding in on you—crowding the mind, that is, not the body.

"I gathered from Hollond that he was always conscious of corridors and halls and alleys in Space, shifting, but shifting according to inexorable laws. I never could get quite clear as to what this consciousness was like. When I asked he used to look puzzled and worried and helpless. I made out from him that one landmark involved a sequence, and once given a bearing from an object you could keep the direction without a mistake. He told me he could easily, if he wanted, go in a dirigible from the top of Mont Blanc to the top of Snowdon in the thickest fog and without a compass, if he were given the proper angle to start from. I confess I didn't follow that myself. Material objects had nothing to do with the Spacial forms, for a table or a bed in our world might be placed across a corridor of Space. The forms played their game independent of our kind of reality. But the worst of it was, that if you kept your mind too much in one world you were apt to forget about the other, and Hollond was always barking his shins on stones and chairs and things.

"He told me all this quite simply and frankly. Remember his mind and no other part of him lived in his new world. He said it gave him an odd sense of detachment to sit in a room among people, and to know that nothing there but himself had any relation at all to the infinite strange world of Space that flowed around them. He would listen, he said, to a great man talking, with one eye on the cat on the rug, thinking to himself how much more the cat knew than the man."

"How long was it before he went mad?" I asked.

It was a foolish question, and made Leithen cross. "He

never went mad in your sense. My dear fellow, you're very much wrong if you think there was anything pathological about him—then. The man was brilliantly sane. His mind was as keen as a keen sword. I couldn't understand him, but I could judge of his sanity right enough."

I asked if it made him happy or miserable.

"At first I think it made him uncomfortable. He was restless because he knew too much and too little. The unknown pressed in on his mind, as bad air weighs on the lungs. Then it lightened, and he accepted the new world in the same sober practical way that he took other things. I think that the free exercise of his mind in a pure medium gave him a feeling of extraordinary power and ease. His eyes used to sparkle when he talked. And another odd thing he told me. He was a keen rock-climber, but, curiously enough, he had never a very good head. Dizzy heights always worried him, though he managed to keep hold on himself. But now all that had gone. The sense of the fulness of Space made him as happy—happier I believe—with his legs dangling into eternity, as sitting before his own study fire.

"I remember saying that it was all rather like the mediæval wizards who made their spells by means of numbers and figures.

"He caught me up at once, 'Not numbers,' he said. 'Number has no place in Nature. It is an invention of the human mind to atone for a bad memory. But figures are a different matter. All the mysteries of the world are in them, and the old magicians knew that at least, if they knew no more.'

"He had only one grievance. He complained that it was terribly lonely. 'It is the Desolation,' he would quote, 'spoken of by Daniel the prophet.' He would spend hours travelling those eerie shifting corridors of Space with no hint of another human soul. How could there be? It was a world of pure reason, where human personality had no place. What puzzled me was why he should feel the absence of this. One wouldn't, you know, in an intricate problem of geometry or a game of chess. I asked him, but he didn't understand the question. I puzzled over it a good deal, for it seemed to me that if Hollond felt lonely, there must be more in this world of his than we imagined. I began to wonder if there was any truth in fads like psychical research. Also, I was not so sure that he was as normal as I had thought: it looked as if his nerves might be going bad.

"Oddly enough, Hollond was getting on the same track himself. He had discovered, so he said, that in sleep everybody now and then lived in this new world of his. You know how one dreams of triangular railway platforms with trains running simultaneously down all three sides and not colliding. Well, this sort of cantrip was 'common form,' as we say at the Bar, in Hollond's Space, and he was very curious about the why and wherefore of Sleep. He began to haunt psychological laboratories, where they experiment with the charwoman and the odd-man, and he used to go up to Cambridge for *séances*. It was a foreign atmosphere to him, and I don't think he was very happy in it. He found so many charlatans that he used to get angry, and declare he would be better employed at Mothers' Meetings!"

From far up the Glen came the sound of the pony's hoofs. The stag had been loaded up, and the gillies were returning. Leithen looked at his watch. "We'd better wait and see the beast," he said.

. . . "Well, nothing happened for more than a year. Then one evening in May he burst into my rooms in high excitement. You understand quite clearly that there was no suspicion of horror or fright or anything unpleasant about this world he had discovered. It was simply a series of interesting and difficult problems. All this time Hollond had been rather extra well and cheery. But when he came in I thought I noticed a different look in his eyes, something puzzled and diffident and apprehensive.

" 'There's a queer performance going on in the other world,' he said. 'It's unbelievable. I never dreamed of such a thing. I—I don't quite know how to put it, and I don't know how to explain it, but—but I am becoming aware that there are other beings—other minds—moving in Space besides mine.'

" I suppose I ought to have realised then that things were beginning to go wrong. But it was very difficult, he was so rational and anxious to make it all clear. I asked him how he knew. There could, of course, on his own showing be no *change* in that world, for the forms of Space moved and existed under inexorable laws. He said he found his own mind failing him at points. There would come over him a sense of fear—intellectual fear—and weakness, a sense of something else, quite alien to Space, thwarting him. Of course he could only describe his impressions very lamely, for they were purely of the mind, and he had no material peg to hang them on, so that I could realise them. But the gist of it was that he had been gradually becoming conscious of what he called 'Presences' in his world. They had no effect on Space —did not leave footprints in its corridors, for instance—but they affected his mind. There was some mysterious contact established between him and them. I asked him if the affection was unpleasant, and he said 'No, not exactly.' But I could see a hint of fear in his eyes.

" Think of it. Try to realise what intellectual fear is. I can't, but it is conceivable. To you and me fear implies pain to ourselves or some other, and such pain is always in the last resort pain of the flesh. Consider it carefully and you will see that it is so. But imagine fear so sublimated and transmuted as to be the tension of pure spirit. I can't realise it, but I think it possible. I don't pretend to understand how Hollond got to know about these Presences. But there was no doubt about the fact. He was positive, and he wasn't in the least mad—not in our sense. In that very month he published his book on Number, and gave a German professor who attacked it a most tremendous public trouncing.

"I know what you are going to say,—that the fancy was a weakening of the mind from within. I admit I should have thought of that, but he looked so confoundedly sane and able that it seemed ridiculous. He kept asking me my opinion, as a lawyer, on the facts he offered. It was the oddest case ever put before me, but I did my best for him. I dropped all my own views of sense and nonsense. I told him that, taking all that he had told me as fact, the Presences might be either ordinary minds traversing Space in sleep; or minds such as his which had independently captured the sense of Space's quality; or, finally, the spirits of just men made perfect, behaving as psychical researchers think they do. It was a ridiculous task to set a prosaic man, and I wasn't quite serious. But Hollond was serious enough.

"He admitted that all three explanations were conceivable, but he was very doubtful about the first. The projection of the spirit into Space during sleep, he thought, was a faint and feeble thing, and these were powerful Presences. With the second and the third he was rather impressed. I suppose I should have seen what was happening and tried to stop it; at least, looking back that seems to have been my duty. But it was difficult to think that anything was wrong with Hollond; indeed the odd thing is that all this time the idea of madness never entered my head. I rather backed him up. Somehow the thing took my fancy, though I thought it moonshine at the bottom of my heart. I enlarged on the pioneering before him. 'Think,' I told him, 'what may be waiting for you. You may discover the meaning of Spirit. You may open up a new world, as rich as the old one, but imperishable. You may prove to mankind their immortality and deliver them for ever from the fear of death. Why, man, you are picking at the lock of all the world's mysteries.'

"But Hollond did not cheer up. He seemed strangely languid and dispirited. 'That is all true enough,' he said, 'if you are right, if your alternatives are exhaustive. But suppose they are something else, something . . .' What that 'something' might be he had apparently no idea, and very soon he went away.

"He said another thing before he left. He asked me if I ever read poetry, and I said, Not often. Nor did he: but he had picked up a little book somewhere and found a man who knew about the Presences. I think his name was Traherne, one of the seventeenth-century fellows. He quoted a verse which stuck to my fly-paper memory. It ran something like this:—

> "'Within the region of the air,
> Compassed about with Heavens fair,
> Great tracts of lands there may be found,
>   Where many numerous hosts,
>   In those far distant coasts,
> For other great and glorious ends
> Inhabit, my yet unknown friends.'

Hollond was positive he did not mean angels or anything of the sort. I told him that Traherne evidently took a cheerful view of them. He admitted that, but added: 'He had religion, you see. He believed that everything was for the best. I am not a man of faith, and can only take comfort from what I understand. I'm in the dark, I tell you. . . .'

"Next week I was busy with the Chilian Arbitration case, and saw nobody for a couple of months. Then one evening I ran against Hollond on the Embankment, and thought him looking horribly ill. He walked back with me to my rooms, and hardly uttered one word all the way. I gave him a stiff whisky-and-soda, which he gulped down absent-mindedly. There was that strained, hunted look in his eyes that you see in a frightened animal's. He was always lean, but now he had fallen away to skin and bone.

"'I can't stay long,' he told me, 'for I'm off to the Alps to-morrow and I have a lot to do.' Before then he used to plunge readily into his story, but now he seemed shy about beginning. Indeed I had to ask him a question.

"'Things are difficult,' he said hesitatingly, 'and rather distressing. Do you know, Leithen, I think you were wrong about—about what I spoke to you of. You said there must be one of three explanations. I am beginning to think that there is a fourth. . . .'

"He stopped for a second or two, then suddenly leaned forward and gripped my knee so fiercely that I cried out. 'That world is the Desolation,' he said in a choking voice, 'and perhaps I am getting near the Abomination of the Desolation that the old prophet spoke of. I tell you, man, I am on the edge of a terror, a terror,' he almost screamed, 'that no mortal can think of and live.'

"You can imagine that I was considerably startled. It was lightning out of a clear sky. How the devil could one associate horror with mathematics? I don't see it yet. . . . At any rate, I—— You may be sure I cursed my folly for ever pretending to take him seriously. The only way would have been to have laughed him out of it at the start. And yet I couldn't, you know—it was too real and reasonable. Anyhow, I tried a firm tone now, and told him the whole thing was arrant raving bosh. I bade him be a man and pull himself together. I made him dine with me, and took him home, and got him into a better state of mind before he went to bed. Next morning I saw him off at Charing Cross, very haggard still, but better. He promised to write to me pretty often. . . ."

The pony, with a great eleven-pointer lurching athwart its back, was abreast of us, and from the autumn mist came the sound of soft Highland voices. Leithen and I got up to go, when we heard that the rifle had made direct for the Lodge by a short-cut past the Sanctuary. In the wake of the gillies we descended the Correi road into a glen all swimming with dim purple shadows. The pony minced and boggled; the stag's antlers stood out sharp on the rise against a patch of sky, looking like a skeleton tree. Then we dropped into a covert of birches and emerged on the white glen highway.

Leithen's story had bored and puzzled me at the start, but now it had somehow gripped my fancy. Space a domain of endless corridors and Presences moving in them! The world was not quite the same as an hour ago. It was the hour, as the French say, "between dog and wolf," when the mind is disposed to marvels. I thought of my stalking on the morrow, and was miserably conscious that I would miss my stag. Those airy forms would get in the way. Confound Leithen and his yarns!

"I want to hear the end of your story," I told him, as the lights of the Lodge showed half a mile distant.

"The end was a tragedy," he said slowly. "I don't much care to talk about it. But how was I to know? I couldn't see the nerve going. You see I couldn't believe it was all nonsense. If I could I might have seen. But I still think there was something in it—up to a point. Oh, I agree he went mad in the end. It is the only explanation. Something must have snapped in that fine brain, and he saw the little bit more which we call madness. Thank God, you and I are prosaic fellows. . . .

"I was going out to Chamonix myself a week later. But before I started I got a post-card from Hollond, the only word from him. He had printed my name and address, and on the other side had scribbled six words—'*I know at last—God's mercy.—H. G. H.*' The handwriting was like a sick man of ninety. I knew that things must be pretty bad with my friend.

"I got to Chamonix in time for his funeral. An ordinary climbing accident—you probably read about it in the papers.

The Press talked about the toll which the Alps took from intellectuals—the usual rot. There was an inquiry, but the facts were quite simple. The body was only recognised by the clothes. He had fallen several thousand feet.

"It seems that he had climbed for a few days with one of the Kronigs and Dupont, and they had done some hair-raising things on the Aiguilles. Dupont told me that they had found a new route up the Montanvert side of the Charmoz. He said that Hollond climbed like a '*diable fou,*' and if you know Dupont's standard of madness you will see that the pace must have been pretty hot. 'But monsieur was sick,' he added; 'his eyes were not good. And I and Franz, we were grieved for him and a little afraid. We were glad when he left us.'

"He dismissed the guides two days before his death. The next day he spent in the hotel, getting his affairs straight. He left everything in perfect order, but not a line to a soul, not even to his sister. The following day he set out alone about three in the morning for the Grèpon. He took the road up the Nantillons glacier to the Col, and then he must have climbed the Mummery crack by himself. After that he left the ordinary route and tried a new traverse across the Mer de Glace face. Somewhere near the top he fell, and next day a party going to the Dent du Requin found him on the rocks thousands of feet below.

"He had slipped in attempting the most foolhardy course on earth, and there was a lot of talk about the dangers of guideless climbing. But I guessed the truth, and I am sure Dupont knew, though he held his tongue. . . ."

We were now on the gravel of the drive, and I was feeling better. The thought of dinner warmed my heart, and drove out the eeriness of the twilight glen. The hour between dog and wolf was passing. After all, there was a gross and jolly earth at hand for wise men who had a mind to comfort.

Leithen, I saw, did not share my mood. He looked glum

and puzzled, as if his tale had aroused grim memories. He finished it at the Lodge door.

"... For, of course, he had gone out that day to die. He had seen the something more, the little bit too much, which plucks a man from his moorings. He had gone so far into the land of pure spirit that he must needs go further and shed the fleshly envelope that cumbered him. God send that he found rest! I believe that he chose the steepest cliff in the Alps for a purpose. He wanted to be unrecognisable. He was a brave man and a good citizen. I think he hoped that those who found him might not see the look in his eyes."

STOCKS AND STONES.

[*The Chief* TOPIAWARI *replieth to* Sir WALTER RALEIGH, *who upbraided him for idol worship*.]

My gods, you say, are idols dumb,
  Which men have wrought from wood or clay,
Carven with chisel, shaped with thumb,
  A morning's task, an evening's play.
You bid me turn my face on high
  Where the blue heaven the sun enthrones,
And serve a viewless deity,
  Nor make my bow to stocks and stones.

My lord, I am not skilled in wit
  Nor wise in priestcraft, but I know
That fear to man is spur and bit
  To jog and curb his fancies' flow.
He fears and loves, for love and awe
  In mortal souls may well unite
To fashion forth the perfect law
  Where Duty takes to wife Delight.

But on each man one Fear awaits
  And chills his marrow like the dead.—
He cannot worship what he hates
  Or make a god of naked Dread.
The homeless winds that twist and race,
  The heights of cloud that veer and roll,
The unplumb'd Abyss, the drifts of Space—
  These are the fears that drain the soul.

Ye dauntless ones from out the sea
  Fear nought. Perchance your gods are strong
To rule the air where grim things be,
  And quell the deeps with all their throng.
For me, I dread not fire nor steel,
  Nor aught that walks in open light,
But fend me from the endless Wheel,
  The voids of Space, the gulfs of Night.

Wherefore my brittle gods I make
  Of friendly clay and kindly stone,—
Wrought with my hands, to serve or break,
  From crown to toe my work, my own.
My eyes can see, my nose can smell,
  My fingers touch their painted face,
They weave their little homely spell
  To warm me from the cold of Space.

My gods are wrought of common stuff
  For human joys and mortal tears ;
Weakly, perchance, yet staunch enough
  To build a barrier 'gainst my fears,
Where, lowly but secure, I wait
  And hear without the strange winds blow.—
I cannot worship what I hate,
  Or serve a god I dare not know.

V. STREAMS OF WATER IN THE SOUTH.

"As streams of water in the south,
Our bondage, Lord, recall."
—Psalm cxxvi. (Scots Metrical Version).

I.

It was at the ford of the Clachlands Water in a tempestuous August, that I, an idle boy, first learned the hardships of the Lammas droving. The shepherd of the Redswirehead, my very good friend, and his three shaggy dogs, were working for their lives in an angry water. The path behind was thronged with scores of sheep bound for the Gledsmuir market, and beyond it was possible to discern through the mist the few dripping dozen which had made the passage. Between raged yards of brown foam coming down from murky hills, and the air echoed with the yelp of dogs and the perplexed cursing of men.

Before I knew I was helping in the task, with water lipping round my waist and my arms filled with a terrified sheep. It was no light task, for though the water was no more than three feet deep it was swift and strong, and a kicking hogg is a sore burden. But this was the only road; the stream might rise higher at any moment; and somehow or other those bleating flocks had to be transferred to their fellows beyond. There were six men at the labour, six men and myself, and all were cross and wearied and heavy with water.

I made my passages side by side with my friend the shepherd, and thereby felt much elated. This was a man who had dwelt all his days in the wilds and was familiar with torrents as with his own doorstep. Now and then a swimming dog would bark feebly as he was washed against us, and flatter his fool's heart that he was aiding the work. And so we wrought on, till by mid-day I was dead-beat, and could scarce stagger through the surf, while all the men had the same gasping faces. I saw the shepherd look with longing eye up the long green valley, and mutter disconsolately in his beard.

"Is the water rising?" I asked.

"It's no rising," said he, "but I likena the look o' yon big black clud upon Cairncraw. I doubt there's been a shoor up the muirs, and a shoor there means twae mair feet o' water in the Clachlands. God help Sandy Jamieson's lambs, if there is."

"How many are left?" I asked.

"Three, fower,—no abune a score and a half," said he, running his eye over the lessened flocks. "I maun try to tak twae at a time."

So for ten minutes he struggled with a double burden, and panted painfully at each return. Then with a sudden swift look up-stream he broke off and stood up. "Get ower the water, every yin o' ye, and leave the sheep," he said, and to my wonder every man of the five obeyed his word.

And then I saw the reason of his command, for with a sudden swift leap forward the Clachlands rose, and flooded up to where I had stood an instant before high and dry.

"It's come," said the shepherd in a tone of fate, "and there's fifteen no ower yet, and Lord kens how they'll dae't. They'll hae to gang roond by Gledsmuir Brig, and that's twenty mile o' a differ. 'Deed, it's no like that Sandy Jamieson will get a guid price the morn for sic sair forfochen beasts."

Then with firmly gripped staff he marched stoutly into the tide till it ran hissing below his armpits. "I could dae't alane," he cried, "but no wi' a burden. For, losh, if ye slippit, ye'd be in the Manor Pool afore ye could draw breath."

And so we waited with the great white droves and five

angry men beyond, and the path blocked by a surging flood. For half an hour we waited, holding anxious consultation across the stream, when to us thus busied there entered a newcomer, a helper from the ends of the earth.

He was a man of something over middle size, but with a stoop forward that shortened him to something beneath it. His dress was ragged homespun, the cast-off clothes of some sportsman, and in his arms he bore a bundle of sticks and heather-roots which marked his calling. I knew him for a tramp who long had wandered in the place, but I could not account for the whole-voiced shout of greeting which met him as he stalked down the path. He lifted his eyes and looked solemnly and long at the scene. Then something of delight came into his eye, his face relaxed, and flinging down his burden he stripped his coat and came toward us.

"Come on, Yeddie, ye're sair needed," said the shepherd, and I watched with amazement this grizzled, crooked man seize a sheep by the fleece and drag it to the water. Then he was in the midst, stepping warily, now up, now down the channel, but always nearing the farther bank. At last with a final struggle he landed his charge, and turned to journey back. Fifteen times did he cross that water, and at the end his mean figure had wholly changed. For now he was straighter and stronger, his eye flashed, and his voice, as he cried out to the drovers, had in it a tone of command. I marvelled at the transformation; and when at length he had donned once more his ragged coat and shouldered his bundle, I asked the shepherd his name.

"They ca' him Adam Logan," said my friend, his face still bright with excitement, "but maist folk ca' him 'Streams o' Water.'"

"Ay," said I, "and why 'Streams of Water'?"

"Juist for the reason ye see," said he.

Now I knew the shepherd's way, and I held my peace, for it was clear that his mind was revolving other matters, concerned most probably with the high subject of the morrow's prices. But in a little, as we crossed the moor toward his dwelling, his thoughts relaxed and he remembered my question. So he answered me thus,—

"Oh, ay; as ye were sayin', he's a queer man, Yeddie—aye been; guid kens whaur he cam' frae first, for he's been trampin' the countryside since ever I mind, and that's no' yesterday. He maun be sixty year, and yet he's as fresh as ever. If onything, he's a thocht dafter in his ongaein's, mair silent-like. But ye'll hae heard tell o' him afore?"

I owned ignorance.

"Tut," said he, "ye ken nocht. But Yeddie had aye a queer crakin' for waters. He never gangs on the road. Wi' him it's juist up yae glen and doon anither, and aye keepin' by the burn-side. He kens every water i' the warld, every bit sheuch and burnie frae Gallowa' to Berwick. And then he kens the way o' spates the best I ever seen, and I've heard tell o' him fordin' waters when nae ither thing could leeve i' them. He can weyse and wark his road sae cunnin'ly on the stanes that the roughest flood, if it's no' juist fair ower his heid, canna upset him. Mony a sheep has he saved to me, and it's mony a guid drove wad never hae won to Gledsmuir market but for Yeddie."

I listened with a boy's interest in any romantic narration. Somehow, the strange figure wrestling in the brown stream took fast hold on my mind, and I asked the shepherd for further tales.

"There's little mair to tell," he said, "for a gangrel life is nane o' the liveliest. But d'ye ken the lang-nebbit hill that cocks its tap abune the Clachlands heid? Weel, he's got a wee bit o' grund on the tap frae the Yerl, and there he's howkit a grave for himsel'. He's sworn me and twae-three ithers to bury him there, wherever he may dee. It's a queer fancy in the auld dotterel."

So the shepherd talked, and as at evening we stood by his door we saw a figure moving into the gathering shadows. I knew it at once, and did not need my friend's " There gangs 'Streams o' Water' " to recognise it. Something wild and pathetic in the old man's face haunted me like a dream, and as the dusk swallowed him up, he seemed like some old Druid recalled of the gods to his ancient habitation of the moors.

II.

Two years passed, and April came with her suns and rains, and again the waters brimmed full in the valleys. Under the clear, shining sky the lambing went on, and the faint bleat of sheep brooded on the hills. In a land of young heather and green upland meads, of faint odours of moor-burn, and hill-tops falling in clear ridges to the sky-line, the veriest St Anthony would not abide indoors; so I flung all else to the winds and went a-fishing.

At the first pool on the Callowa, where the great flood sweeps nobly round a ragged shoulder of hill, and spreads into broad deeps beneath a tangle of birches, I began my toils. The turf was still wet with dew and the young leaves gleamed in the glow of morning. Far up the stream rose the grim hills which hem the mosses and tarns of that table-land, whence flow the greater waters of the countryside. An ineffable freshness, as of the morning alike of the day and the seasons, filled the clear hill-air, and the remote peaks gave the needed touch of intangible romance.

But as I fished, I came on a man sitting in a green dell, busy at the making of brooms. I knew his face and dress, for who could forget such eclectic raggedness?—and I remembered that day two years before when he first hobbled into my ken. Now, as I saw him there, I was captivated by the nameless mystery of his appearance. There was something startling to one, accustomed to the lack-lustre gaze of town-bred folk, in the sight of an eye as keen and wild as a hawk's from sheer solitude and lonely travelling. He was so bent and scarred with weather that he seemed as much a part of that woodland place as the birks themselves, and the noise of his labours did not startle the birds that hopped on the branches.

Little by little I won his acquaintance—by a chance reminiscence, a single tale, the mention of a friend. Then he made me free of his knowledge, and my fishing fared well that day. He dragged me up little streams to sequestered pools, where I had astonishing success; and then back to some great swirl in the Callowa where he had seen monstrous takes. And all the while he delighted me with his talk, of men and things, of weather and place, pitched high in his thin, old voice, and garnished with many tones of lingering sentiment. He spoke in a broad, slow Scots, with so quaint a lilt in his speech that one seemed to be in an elder time among people of a quieter life and a quainter kindliness.

Then by chance I asked him of a burn of which I had heard, and how it might be reached. I shall never forget the tone of his answer as his face grew eager and he poured forth his knowledge.

"Ye'll gang up the Knowe Burn, which comes down into the Cauldshaw. It's a wee tricklin' thing, trowin' in and out o' pools i' the rock, and comin' doun out o' the side o' Caerfraun. Yince a merrymaiden bided there, I've heard folks say, and used to win the sheep frae the Cauldshaw herd, and bile them i' the muckle pool below the fa'. They say that there's a road to the Ill Place there, and when the Deil likit he sent up the lowe and garred the water faem and fizzle like an auld kettle. But if ye're gaun to the Colm Burn ye maun haud atower the rig o' the hill frae the Knowe heid, and ye'll come to it wimplin' among green brae faces. It's a bonny bit, rale lonesome, but awfu' bonny, and there's mony braw trout in its siller flow."

Then I remembered all I had heard of the old man's craze, and I humoured him.

"It's a fine countryside for burns," I said.

"Ye may say that," said he gladly, "a weel-watered land.

But a' this braw south country is the same. I've traivelled frae the Yeavering Hill in the Cheviots to the Caldons in Galloway, and it's a' the same. When I was young, I've seen me gang north to the Hielands and doun to the English lawlands, but now that I'm gettin' auld I maun bide i' the yae place. There's no' a burn in the South I dinna ken, and I never cam' to the water I couldna ford."

"No?" said I. "I've seen you at the ford o' Clachlands in the Lammas floods."

"Often I've been there," he went on, speaking like one calling up vague memories. "Yince, when Tam Rorison was drooned, honest man. Yince again, when the brigs were ta'en awa', and the Back House o' Clachlands had nae bread for a week. But oh, Clachlands is a bit easy water. But I've seen the muckle Aller come roarin' sae high that it washed awa' a sheep-fold that stood weel up on the hill. And I've seen this verra burn, this bonny clear Callowa, lyin' like a loch for miles i' the haugh. But I never heeds a spate, for if a man just kens the way o't it's a canny, hairmless thing. I couldna wish to dee better than just be happit i' the waters o' my ain countryside, when my legs fail and I'm ower auld for the trampin'."

Something in that queer figure in the setting of the hills struck a note of curious pathos. And towards evening as we returned down the glen the note grew keener. A spring sunset of gold and crimson flamed in our backs and turned the clear pools to fire. Far off down the vale the plains and the sea gleamed half in shadow. Somehow in the fragrance and colour and the delectable crooning of the stream, the fantastic and the dim seemed tangible and present, and high sentiment revelled for once in my prosaic heart.

And still more in the breast of my companion. He stopped and sniffed the evening air, as he looked far over hill and dale and then back to the great hills above us. "Yon's Crappel, and Caerdon, and the Laigh Law," he said, lingering with relish over each name, "and the Gled comes doun atween them. I haena been there for a twalmonth, and I maun hae anither glisk o't, for it's a braw place." And then some bitter thought seemed to seize him, and his mouth twitched. "I'm an auld man," he cried, "and I canna see ye a' again. There's burns and mair burns in the high hills that I'll never win to." Then he remembered my presence, and stopped. "Ye maunna mind me," he said huskily, "but the sicht o' a' thae lang blue hills makes me daft, now that I've faun i' the vale o' years. Yince I was young and could get where I wantit, but now I am auld and maun bide i' the same bit. And I'm aye thinkin' o' the waters I've been to, and the green heichs and howes and the linns that I canna win to again. I maun e'en be content wi' the Callowa, which is as guid as the best."

And then I left him, wandering down by the stream-side and telling his crazy meditations to himself.

III.

A space of years elapsed ere I met him, for fate had carried me far from the upland valleys. But once again I was afoot on the white moor-roads; and, as I swung along one autumn afternoon up the path which leads from the Glen of Callowa to the Gled, I saw a figure before me which I knew for my friend. When I overtook him, his appearance puzzled and troubled me. Age seemed to have come on him at a bound, and in the tottering figure and the stoop of weakness I had difficulty in recognising the hardy frame of the man as I had known him. Something, too, had come over his face. His brow was clouded, and the tan of weather stood out hard and cruel on a blanched cheek. His eye seemed both wilder and sicklier, and for the first time I saw him with none of the appurtenances of his trade.

He greeted me feebly and dully, and showed little wish to speak. He walked with slow, uncertain step, and his breath laboured with a new panting. Every now and then he would look at me sidewise, and in his feverish glance I could detect none of the free kindliness of old. The man was ill in body and mind.

I asked him how he had done since I saw him last.

"It's an ill world now," he said in a slow, querulous voice. "There's nae need for honest men, and nae leevin'. Folk dinna heed me ava now. They dinna buy my besoms, they winna let me bide a nicht in their byres, and they're no like the kind canty folk in the auld times. And a' the countryside is changin'. Doun by Goldieslaw they're makkin' a dam for takin' water to the toun, and they're thinkin' o' daein' the like wi' the Callowa. Guid help us, can they no let the works o' God alane? Is there no room for them in the dirty lawlands that they maun file the hills wi' their biggins?"

I conceived dimly that the cause of his wrath was a scheme for waterworks at the border of the uplands, but I had less concern for this than his strangely feeble health.

"You are looking ill," I said. "What has come over you?"

"Oh, I canna last for aye," he said mournfully. "My auld body's about dune. I've warkit it ower sair when I had it, and it's gaun to fail on my hands. Sleepin' out o' wat nichts and gangin' lang wantin' meat are no the best ways for a long life;" and he smiled the ghost of a smile.

And then he fell to wild telling of the ruin of the place and the hardness of the people, and I saw that want and bare living had gone far to loosen his wits. I knew the countryside, and I recognised that change was only in his mind. And a great pity seized me for this lonely figure toiling on in the bitterness of regret. I tried to comfort him, but my words were useless, for he took no heed of me; with bent head and faltering step he mumbled his sorrows to himself.

Then of a sudden we came to the crest of the ridge where the road dips from the hill-top to the sheltered valley. Sheer from the heather ran the white streak till it lost itself among the reddening rowans and the yellow birks of the wood. The land was rich in autumn colour, and the shining waters dipped and fell through a pageant of russet and gold. And all around hills huddled in silent spaces, long brown moors crowned with cairns, or steep fortresses of rock and shingle rising to foreheads of steel-like grey. The autumn blue faded in the far sky-line to white, and lent distance to the farther peaks. The hush of the wilderness, which is far different from the hush of death, brooded over the scene, and like faint music came the sound of a distant scythe-swing, and the tinkling whisper which is the flow of a hundred streams.

I am an old connoisseur in the beauties of the uplands, but I held my breath at the sight. And when I glanced at my companion, he, too, had raised his head, and stood with wide nostrils and gleaming eye revelling in this glimpse of Arcady. Then he found his voice, and the weakness and craziness seemed for one moment to leave him.

"It's my ain land," he cried, "and I'll never leave it. D'ye see yon broun hill wi' the lang cairn?" and he gripped my arm fiercely and directed my gaze. "Yon's my bit. I howkit it richt on the verra tap, and ilka year I gang there to mak' it neat and orderly. I've trystit wi' fower men in different pairishes, that whenever they hear o' my death, they'll cairry me up yonder and bury me there. And then I'll never leave it, but lie still and quiet to the warld's end. I'll aye hae the sound o' water in my ear, for there's five burns tak' their rise on that hillside, and on a' airts the glens gang doun to the Gled and the Aller.

Then his spirit failed him, his voice sank, and he was almost the feeble gangrel once more. But not yet, for again his eye swept the ring of hills, and he muttered to himself names which I knew for streams, lingeringly, lovingly, as of old affections. "Aller and Gled and Callowa," he crooned, "braw names, and Clachlands and Cauldshaw and the Lanely Water. And I maunna forget the Stark and the Lin and the bonny streams o' the Creran. And what mair? I canna mind a' the burns, the Howe and the Hollies and the Fawn and the links o' the Manor. What says the Psalmist about them?

> 'As streams o' water in the South,
> Our bondage, Lord, recall.'

Ay, but yon's the name for them. 'Streams o' water in the South.'"

And as we went down the slopes to the darkening vale I heard him crooning to himself in a high, quavering voice the single distich; then in a little his weariness took him again, and he plodded on with no thought save for his sorrows.

IV.

The conclusion of this tale belongs not to me but to the shepherd of the Redswirehead, and I heard it from him in his dwelling, as I stayed the night, belated on the darkening moors. He told me it after supper in a flood of misty Doric, and his voice grew rough at times, and he poked viciously at the dying peat.

In the last back-end I was at Gledfoot wi' sheep, and a weary job I had and little credit. Ye ken the place, a lang dreich shore wi' the wind swirlin' and bitin' to the bane, and the broun Gled water choked wi' Solloway sand. There was nae room in ony inn in the town, so I bude to gang to a bit public on the Harbour Walk, where sailor-folk and fishermen feucht and drank, and nae dacent men frae the hills thocht of gangin'. I was in a gey ill way, for I had sell't my beasts dooms cheap, and I thocht o' the lang miles hame in the wintry weather. So after a bite o' meat I gangs out to get the air and clear my heid, which was a' rammled wi' the auction-ring.

And whae did I find, sittin' on a bench at the door, but

the auld man Yeddie. He was waur changed than ever. His lang hair was hingin' ower his broo, and his face was thin and white as a ghaist's. His claes fell loose about him, and he sat wi' his hand on his auld stick and his chin on his hand, hearin' nocht and glowerin' afore him. He never saw nor kenned me till I shook him by the shoulders, and cried him by his name.

"Whae are ye?" says he, in a thin voice that gaed to my hert.

"Ye ken me fine, ye auld fule," says I. "I'm Jock Rorison o' the Redswirehead, whaur ye've stoppit often."

"Redswirehead," he says, like a man in a dream, "Redswirehead! That's at the tap o' the Clachlands Burn as ye gang ower to the Dreichil."

"And what are ye daein' here? It's no your countryside ava, and ye're no fit noo for lang trampin'."

"No," says he, in the same weak voice and wi' nae fushion in him, "but they winna hae me up yonder noo. I'm ower auld and useless. Yince a'body was gled to see me, and wad keep me as lang's I wantit, and had aye a guid word at meeting and pairting. Noo it's a' changed, and my wark's dune."

I saw fine that the man was daft, but what answer could I gie to his havers? Folk in the Callowa Glens are as kind as afore, but ill weather and auld age had put queer notions intil his heid. Forbye, he was seeck, seeck unto death, and I saw mair in his ee than I likit to think.

"Come in-by and get some meat, man," I said. "Ye're famishin' wi' cauld and hunger."

"I canna eat," he says, and his voice never changed. "It's lang since I had a bite, for I'm no' hungry. But I'm awfu' thirsty. I cam' here yestreen, and I can get nae water to drink like the water in the hills. I maun be settin' out back the morn, if the Lord spares me."

I mindit fine that the body wad tak' nae drink like an honest man, but maun aye draibble wi' burn water, and noo he had got the thing on the brain. I never spak' a word, for the maitter was bye ony mortal's aid.

For lang he sat quiet. Then he lifts his heid and looks awa ower the grey sea. A licht for a moment cam' intil his een.

"Whatna big water's yon?" he said, wi' his puir mind aye rinnin' on waters.

"That's the Solloway," says I.

"The Solloway," says he; "it's a big water, and it wad be an ill job to ford it."

"Nae man ever fordit it," I said.

"But I never yet cam' to the water I couldna ford," says he. "But what's that queer smell i' the air? Something snell and cauld and unfreendly."

"That's the salt, for we're at the sea here, the mighty ocean."

He keepit repeatin' the word ower in his mouth. "The salt, the salt, I've heard tell o' it afore, but I dinna like it. It's terrible cauld and unhamely."

By this time an onding o' rain was comin' up frae the water, and I bade the man come indoors to the fire. He followed me, as biddable as a sheep, draggin' his legs like yin far gone in seeckness. I set him by the fire, and put whisky at his elbow, but he wadna touch it.

"I've nae need o' it," said he. "I'm fine and warm;" and he sits staring at the fire, aye comin' ower again and again, "The Solloway, the Solloway. It's a guid name and a muckle water." But sune I gaed to my bed, being heavy wi' sleep, for I had traivelled for twae days.

. . . .

The next morn I was up at six and out to see the weather. It was a' changed. The muckle tides lay lang and still as our ain Loch o' the Lee, and far ayont I saw the big blue hills o' England shine bricht and clear. I thankit Providence for the day, for it was better to tak' the lang miles back in sic a sun than in a blast o' rain.

But as I lookit I saw some folk comin' up frae the beach cairryin' something atween them. My hert gied a loup and "some puir, drooned sailor-body," says I to mysel', "whae has perished in yesterday's storm." But as they cam' nearer I got a glisk which made me run like daft, and lang ere I was up on them I saw it was Yeddie.

He lay drippin' and white, wi' his puir auld hair lyin' back frae his broo and the duds clingin' to his legs. But out o' the face there had gane a' the seeckness and weariness. His een were stelled, as if he had been lookin' forrit to something, and his lips were set like a man on a lang errand. And mair, his stick was grippit sae firm in his hand that nae man could loose it, so they e'en let it be.

Then they tell't me the tale o't, how at the earliest licht they had seen him wanderin' alang the sands, juist as they were putting out their boats to sea. They wondered and watched him, till of a sudden he turned to the water and wadit in, keeping straucht on till he was oot o' sicht. They rowed a' their pith to the place, but they were ower late. Yince they saw his heid appear abune water, still wi' his face to the other side; and then they got his body, for the tide was rinnin' low in the mornin'. I tell't them a' I kenned o' him, and they were sair affected. "Puir cratur," said yin, "he's shürely better now."

So we brocht him up to the house and laid him there till the folk i' the town had heard o' the business. Syne the procurator-fiscal came and certifeed the death, and the rest was left tae me. I got a wooden coffin made and put him in it, juist as he was, wi' his staff in his hand and his auld duds about him. I mindit o' my sworn word, for I was yin o' the four that had promised, and I ettled to dae his bidding. It was saxteen mile to the hills, and yin-and-twenty to the lanely tap whaur he had howkit his grave. But I never heedit it. I'm a strong man, weel-used to the walkin', and my hert was sair for the auld body. Now that he had gotten deliverance from his affliction, it was for me to leave him in the place he wantit. Forbye, he wasna muckle heavier than a bairn.

It was a long road, a sair road, but I did it, and by seven o'clock I was at the edge o' the muirlands. There was a braw mune, and a' the glens and taps stood out as clear as mid-day. Bit by bit, for I was gey tired, I warstled ower the rigs and up the cleuchs to the Gledhead: syne up the stany Gled-cleuch to the lang grey hill which they ca' the Hurlybackit. By ten I had come to the cairn, and black i' the mune I saw the grave. So there I buried him, and though I'm no' a releegious man, I couldna help sayin' ower him the guid words o' the Psalmist—

> "As streams of water in the South,
> Our bondage, Lord, recall."

So if you go from the Gled to the Aller, and keep far over the north side of the Muckle Muneraw, you will come in time to a stony ridge which ends in a cairn. There you will see the whole hill country of the south, a hundred lochs, a myriad streams, and a forest of hill-tops. There on the very crest lies the old man, in the heart of his own land, at the fountain-head of his many waters. If you listen you will hear a hushed noise as of the swaying in trees or a ripple on the sea. It is the sound of the rising of burns, which, innumerable and unnumbered, flow thence to the silent glens for evermore.

THE GIPSY'S SONG TO THE LADY CASSILIS.

"Whereupon the Faas, coming down from the Gates of Galloway, did so bewitch my lady that she forgat husband and kin, and followed the tinkler's piping."—Chap-book of the *Raid of Cassilis.*

The door is open to the wall,
The air is bright and free;
Adown the stair, across the hall,
And then—the world and me;
The bare grey bent, the running stream,
The fire beside the shore;
And we will bid the hearth farewell,
And never seek it more,
My love,
And never seek it more.

And you shall wear no silken gown,
No maid shall bind your hair;
The yellow broom shall be your gem,
Your braid the heather rare.
Athwart the moor, adown the hill,
Across the world away;
The path is long for happy hearts
That sing to greet the day,
My love,
That sing to greet the day.

When morning cleaves the eastern grey,
And the lone hills are red;
When sunsets light the evening way
And birds are quieted;

In autumn noon and springtide dawn,
  By hill and dale and sea,
The world shall sing its ancient song
  Of hope and joy for thee,
            My love,
  Of hope and joy for thee.

And at the last no solemn stole
  Shall on thy breast be laid ;
No mumbling priest shall speed thy soul,
  No charnel vault thee shade.
But by the shadowed hazel copse,
  Aneath the greenwood tree,
Where airs are soft and waters sing,
  Thou'lt ever sleep by me,
            My love,
  Thou'lt ever sleep by me.

VI. THE GROVE OF ASHTAROTH.

> "*C'est enfin que dans leurs prunelles*
> *Rit et pleure—fastidieux—*
> *L'amour des choses éternelles,*
> *Des vieux morts et des anciens dieux !*"
>
> —Paul Verlaine.

I.

We were sitting around the camp-fire, some thirty miles north of a place called Taqui, when Lawson announced his intention of finding a home. He had spoken little the last day or two, and I had guessed that he had struck a vein of private reflection. I thought it might be a new mine or irrigation scheme, and I was surprised to find that it was a country-house.

"I don't think I shall go back to England," he said, kicking a sputtering log into place. "I don't see why I should. For business purposes I am far more useful to the firm in South Africa than in Throgmorton Street. I have no relations left except a third cousin, and I have never cared a rush for living in town. That beastly house of mine in Hill Street will fetch what I gave for it,—Isaacson cabled about it the other day, offering for furniture and all. I don't want to go into Parliament, and I hate shooting little birds and tame deer. I am one of those fellows who are born Colonial at heart, and I don't see why I shouldn't arrange my life as I please. Besides, for ten years I have been falling in love with this country, and now I am up to the neck."

He flung himself back in the camp-chair till the canvas creaked, and looked at me below his eyelids. I remember glancing at the lines of him, and thinking what a fine make of a man he was. In his untanned field-boots, breeches, and grey shirt he looked the born wilderness-hunter, though less than two months before he had been driving down to the City every morning in the sombre regimentals of his class. Being a fair man, he was gloriously tanned, and there was a clear line at his shirt-collar to mark the limits of his sunburn. I had first known him years ago, when he was a broker's clerk working on half-commission. Then he had gone to South Africa, and soon I heard he was a partner in a mining house which was doing wonders with some gold areas in the North. The next step was his return to London as the new millionaire,—young, good-looking, wholesome in mind and body, and much sought after by the mothers of marriageable girls. We played polo together, and hunted a little in the season, but there were signs that he did not propose to become the conventional English gentleman. He refused to buy a place in the country, though half the Homes of England were at his disposal. He was a very busy man, he declared, and had not time to be a squire. Besides, every few months he used to rush out to South Africa. I saw that he was restless, for he was always badgering me to go big-game hunting with him in some remote part of the earth. There was that in his eyes, too, which marked him out from the ordinary blond type of our countrymen. They were large and brown and mysterious, and the light of another race was in their odd depths.

To hint such a thing would have meant a breach of friendship, for Lawson was very proud of his birth. When he first made his fortune he had gone to the Heralds to discover his family, and these obliging gentlemen had provided a pedigree. It appeared that he was a scion of the house of Lowson or Lowieson, an ancient and rather disreputable clan on the Scottish side of the Border. He took a shooting in Teviotdale on the strength of it, and used to commit lengthy Border ballads to memory. But I had known his father, a financial journalist who never quite succeeded, and I had heard of a grandfather who sold antiques in a back street at Brighton. The latter, I think, had not changed his name, and still frequented the synagogue. The father was a progressive Christian, and the mother had been a blonde Saxon from the Midlands. In my mind there was no doubt, as I caught Lawson's heavy-lidded eyes fixed on me. My friend was of a more ancient race than the Lowsons of the Border.

"Where are you thinking of looking for your house?" I asked. "In Natal or in the Cape Peninsula? You might get the Fishers' place if you paid a price."

"The Fishers' place be hanged!" he said crossly. "I don't want any stuccoed, overgrown Dutch farm. I might as well be at Roehampton as in the Cape."

He got up and walked to the far side of the fire, where a lane ran down through thorn-scrub to a gully of the hills. The moon was silvering the bush of the plains, forty miles off and three thousand feet below us.

"I am going to live somewhere hereabouts," he answered at last.

I whistled. "Then you ve got to put your hand in your pocket, old man. You'll have to make everything, including a map of the countryside."

"I know," he said; "that's where the fun comes in. Hang it all, why shouldn't I indulge my fancy? I'm uncommonly well off, and I haven't chick or child to leave it to. Supposing I'm a hundred miles from railhead, what about it? I'll make a motor-road and fix up a telephone. I'll grow most of my supplies, and start a colony to provide labour. When you come and stay with me, you'll get the best food and drink on earth, and sport that will make your mouth water. I'll put Lochleven trout in these streams,—at 6000 feet you can do anything. We'll have a pack of hounds, too, and we can drive pig in the woods, and if we want big game there are the Mangwe flats at our feet. I tell you I'll make such a country-house as nobody ever dreamed of. A man will come plumb out of stark savagery into lawns and rose-gardens." Lawson flung himself into his chair again and smiled dreamily at the fire.

"But why here, of all places?" I persisted. I was not feeling very well and did not care for the country.

"I can't quite explain. I think it's the sort of land I have always been looking for. I always fancied a house on a green plateau in a decent climate looking down on the tropics. I like heat and colour, you know, but I like hills too, and greenery, and the things that bring back Scotland. Give me a cross between Teviotdale and the Orinoco, and, by Gad! I think I've got it here."

I watched my friend curiously, as with bright eyes and eager voice he talked of his new fad. The two races were very clear in him—the one desiring gorgeousness, the other athirst for the soothing spaces of the North. He began to plan out the house. He would get Adamson to design it, and it was to grow out of the landscape like a stone on the hillside. There would be wide verandahs and cool halls, but great fireplaces against winter-time. It would all be very simple and fresh—"clean as morning" was his odd phrase; but then another idea supervened, and he talked of bringing the Tintorets from Hill Street. "I want it to be a civilised house, you know. No silly luxury, but the best pictures and china and books. . . . I'll have all the furniture made after the old plain English models out of native woods. I don't want second-hand sticks in a new country. Yes, by Jove, the Tintorets are a great idea, and all those Ming pots I bought. I had meant to sell them, but I'll have them out here."

He talked for a good hour of what he would do, and his dream grew richer as he talked, till by the time we went to bed he had sketched something liker a palace than a country-house. Lawson was by no means a luxurious man. At present he was well content with a Wolseley valise, and shaved cheerfully out of a tin mug. It struck me as odd that a man so simple in his habits should have so sumptuous a taste in bric-à-brac. I told myself, as I turned in, that the Saxon mother from the Midlands had done little to dilute the strong wine of the East.

It drizzled next morning when we inspanned, and I mounted my horse in a bad temper. I had some fever on me, I think, and I hated this lush yet frigid tableland, where all the winds on earth lay in wait for one's marrow. Lawson was, as usual, in great spirits. We were not hunting, but shifting our hunting ground, so all morning we travelled fast to the north along the rim of the uplands.

At mid-day it cleared, and the afternoon was a pageant of pure colour. The wind sank to a low breeze; the sun lit the infinite green spaces, and kindled the wet forest to a jewelled coronal. Lawson gaspingly admired it all, as he cantered bareheaded up a bracken-clad slope. "God's country," he said twenty times. "I've found it." Take a piece of Sussex downland; put a stream in every hollow and a patch of wood; and at the edge, where the cliffs at home would fall to the sea, put a cloak of forest muffling the scarp and dropping thousands of feet to the blue plains. Take the diamond air of the Gornergrat, and the riot of colour which you get by a West Highland loch-side in late September. Put flowers everywhere, the things we grow in hothouses, geraniums like sunshades, and arums like trumpets. That will give you a notion of the countryside we were in. I began to see that after all it was out of the common.

And just before sunset we came over a ridge and found something better. It was a shallow glen, half a mile wide, down which ran a blue-grey stream in linns like the Spean, till at the edge of the plateau it leaped into the dim forest in a snowy cascade. The opposite side ran up in gentle slopes to a rocky knoll, from which the eye had a noble prospect of the plains. All down the glen were little copses, half-moons of green edging some silvery shore of the burn, or delicate clusters of tall trees nodding on the hill brow. The place so satisfied the eye that for the sheer wonder of its perfection we stopped and stared in silence for many minutes.

Then "The House," I said, and Lawson replied softly, "The House!"

We rode slowly into the glen in the mulberry gloaming. Our transport waggons were half an hour behind, so we had time to explore. Lawson dismounted and plucked handfuls of flowers from the water-meadows. He was singing to himself all the time—an old French catch about *Cadet Rousselle* and his *trois maisons*.

"Who owns it?" I asked.

"My firm, as like as not. We have miles of land about here. But whoever the man is, he has got to sell. Here I build my tabernacle, old man. Here, and nowhere else!"

In the very centre of the glen, in a loop of the stream, was one copse which even in that half light struck me as different from the others. It was of tall, slim, fairy-like trees, the kind of wood the monks painted in old missals. No, I rejected the thought. It was no Christian wood. It was not a copse, but a "grove,"—one such as Artemis may have flitted through in the moonlight. It was small, forty or fifty yards in diameter, and there was a dark something at the heart of it which for a second I thought was a house.

We turned between the slender trees, and—was it fancy?—an odd tremor went through me. I felt as if I were penetrating the *temenos* of some strange and lovely divinity, the goddess of this pleasant vale. There was a spell in the air, it seemed, and an odd dead silence.

Suddenly my horse started at a flutter of light wings. A flock of doves rose from the branches, and I saw the burnished green of their plumes against the opal sky. Lawson did not seem to notice them. I saw his keen eyes staring at the centre of the grove and what stood there.

It was a little conical tower, ancient and lichened, but, so far as I could judge, quite flawless. You know the famous Conical Temple at Zimbabwe, of which prints are in every guide-book. This was of the same type, but a thousandfold more perfect. It stood about thirty feet high, of solid masonry, without door or window or cranny, as shapely as when it first came from the hands of the old builders. Again I had the sense of breaking in on a sanctuary. What right had I, a common vulgar modern, to be looking at this fair thing, among these delicate trees, which some white goddess had once taken for her shrine?

Lawson broke in on my absorption. "Let's get out of this," he said hoarsely, and he took my horse's bridle (he had left his own beast at the edge) and led him back to the open. But I noticed that his eyes were always turning back, and that his hand trembled.

"That settles it," I said after supper. "What do you want with your mediæval Venetians and your Chinese pots now? You will have the finest antique in the world in your garden—a temple as old as time, and in a land which they say has no history. You had the right inspiration this time."

I think I have said that Lawson had hungry eyes. In his enthusiasm they used to glow and brighten; but now, as he sat looking down at the olive shades of the glen, they seemed ravenous in their fire. He had hardly spoken a word since we left the wood.

"Where can I read about these things?" he asked, and I gave him the names of books.

Then, an hour later, he asked me who were the builders. I told him the little I knew about Phœnician and Sabæan wanderings, and the ritual of Sidon and Tyre. He repeated some names to himself and went soon to bed.

As I turned in, I had one last look over the glen, which lay ivory and black in the moon. I seemed to hear a faint echo of wings, and to see over the little grove a cloud of light visitants. "The Doves of Ashtaroth have come back," I said to myself. "It is a good omen. They accept the new tenant." But as I fell asleep I had a sudden thought that I was saying something rather terrible.

II.

Three years later, pretty nearly to a day, I came back to see what Lawson had made of his hobby. He had bidden me often to Welgevonden, as he chose to call it—though I do not know why he should have fixed a Dutch name to a countryside where Boer never trod. At the last there had been some confusion about dates, and I wired the time of my arrival, and set off without an answer. A motor met me at the queer little wayside station of Taqui, and after many miles on a doubtful highway I came to the gates of the park, and a road on which it was a delight to move. Three years had wrought little difference in the landscape. Lawson had done some planting,—conifers and flowering shrubs and suchlike,—but wisely he had resolved that Nature had for the most part forestalled him. All the same, he must have spent a mint of money. The drive could not have been beaten in England, and fringes of mown turf on either hand had been pared out of the lush meadows. When we came over the edge of the hill and looked down on the secret glen, I could not repress a cry of pleasure. The house stood on the farther ridge, the viewpoint of the whole neighbourhood; and its brown timbers and white rough-cast walls melted into the hillside as if it had been there from the beginning of things. The vale below was ordered in lawns and gardens. A blue lake received the rapids of the stream, and its banks were a maze of green shades and glorious masses of blossom. I noticed, too, that the little grove we had explored on our first visit stood alone in a big stretch of lawn, so that its perfection might be clearly seen. Lawson had excellent taste, or he had had the best advice.

The butler told me that his master was expected home shortly, and took me into the library for tea. Lawson had left his Tintorets and Ming pots at home after all. It was a long, low room, panelled in teak half-way up the walls, and the shelves held a multitude of fine bindings. There were good rugs on the parquet floor, but no ornaments anywhere, save three. On the carved mantelpiece stood two of the old soapstone birds which they used to find at Zimbabwe, and between, on an ebony stand, a half-moon of alabaster, curiously carved with zodiacal figures. My host had altered his scheme of furnishing, but I approved the change.

He came in about half-past six, after I had consumed two cigars and all but fallen asleep. Three years make a difference in most men, but I was not prepared for the change in Lawson. For one thing, he had grown fat. In place of the lean young man I had known, I saw a heavy, flaccid being, who shuffled in his gait, and seemed tired and listless. His sunburn had gone, and his face was as pasty as a city clerk's. He had been walking, and wore shapeless flannel clothes, which hung loose even on his enlarged figure. And the worst of it was, that he did not seem over-pleased to see me. He murmured something about my journey, and then flung himself into an arm-chair and looked out of the window.

I asked him if he had been ill.

"Ill! No!" he said crossly. "Nothing of the kind. I'm perfectly well."

"You don't look as fit as this place should make you. What do you do with yourself? Is the shooting as good as you hoped?"

He did not answer, but I thought I heard him utter something like "shooting be damned."

Then I tried the subject of the house. I praised it extravagantly, but with conviction. "There can be no place like it in the world," I said.

He turned his eyes on me at last, and I saw that they were as deep and restless as ever. With his pallid face they made him look curiously Semitic. I had been right in my theory about his ancestry.

"Yes," he said slowly, "there is no place like it—in the world."

Then he pulled himself to his feet. "I'm going to change," he said. "Dinner is at eight. Ring for Travers, and he'll show you your room."

I dressed in a noble bedroom, with an outlook over the garden-vale and the escarpment to the far line of the plains, now blue and saffron in the sunset. I dressed in an ill temper, for I was seriously offended with Lawson, and also seriously alarmed. He was either very unwell or going out of his mind, and it was clear, too, that he would resent any anxiety on his account. I ransacked my memory for rumours, but found none. I had heard nothing of him except that he had been extraordinarily successful in his speculations, and that from his hill-top he directed his firm's operations with uncommon skill. If Lawson was sick or mad, nobody knew of it.

Dinner was a trying ceremony. Lawson, who used to be rather particular in his dress, appeared in a kind of smoking suit with a flannel collar. He spoke scarcely a word to me, but cursed the servants with a brutality which left me aghast. A wretched footman in his nervousness spilt some sauce over his sleeve. Lawson dashed the dish from his hand, and volleyed abuse with a sort of epileptic fury. Also he, who had been the most abstemious of men, swallowed disgusting quantities of champagne and old brandy.

He had given up smoking, and half an hour after we left the dining-room he announced his intention of going to bed. I watched him as he waddled upstairs with a feeling of angry bewilderment. Then I went to the library and lit a pipe. I would leave first thing in the morning—on that I was determined. But as I sat gazing at the moon of alabaster and the soapstone birds my anger evaporated, and concern took its place. I remembered what a fine fellow Lawson had been, what good times we had had together. I remembered especially that evening when we had found this valley and given rein to our fancies. What horrid alchemy in the place had turned a gentleman into a brute? I thought of drink and drugs and madness and insomnia, but I could fit none of them into my conception of my friend. I did not consciously rescind my resolve to depart, but I had a notion that I would not act on it.

The sleepy butler met me as I went to bed. "Mr Lawson's room is at the end of your corridor, sir," he said. "He don't sleep over well, so you may hear him stirring in the night. At what hour would you like breakfast, sir? Mr Lawson mostly has his in bed."

My room opened from the great corridor, which ran the full length of the front of the house. So far as I could make out, Lawson was three rooms off, a vacant bedroom and his servant's room being between us. I felt tired and cross, and tumbled into bed as fast as possible. Usually I sleep well, but now I was soon conscious that my drowsiness was wearing off and that I was in for a restless night. I got up and laved my face, turned the pillows, thought of sheep coming over a hill and clouds crossing the sky; but none of the old devices were of any use. After about an hour of make-believe I surrendered myself to facts, and, lying on my back, stared at the white ceiling and the patches of moonshine on the walls.

It certainly was an amazing night. I got up, put on a dressing-gown, and drew a chair to the window. The moon was almost at its full, and the whole plateau swam in a radiance of ivory and silver. The banks of the stream were black, but the lake had a great belt of light athwart it, which made it seem like a horizon, and the rim of land beyond it like a contorted cloud. Far to the right I saw the delicate outlines of the little wood which I had come to think of as the Grove of Ashtaroth. I listened. There was not a sound in the air. The land seemed to sleep peacefully beneath the moon, and yet I had a sense that the peace was an illusion. The place was feverishly restless.

I could have given no reason for my impression, but there it was. Something was stirring in the wide moonlit landscape under its deep mask of silence. I felt as I had felt on the evening three years ago when I had ridden into the grove. I did not think that the influence, whatever it was, was maleficent. I only knew that it was very strange, and kept me wakeful.

By-and-by I bethought me of a book. There was no lamp in the corridor save the moon, but the whole house was bright as I slipped down the great staircase and across the hall to the library. I switched on the lights and then switched them off. They seemed a profanation, and I did not need them.

I found a French novel, but the place held me and I stayed. I sat down in an arm-chair before the fireplace and the stone birds. Very odd those gawky things, like prehistoric Great Auks, looked in the moonlight. I remember that the alabaster moon shimmered like translucent pearl, and I fell to wondering about its history. Had the old Sabæans used such a jewel in their rites in the Grove of Ashtaroth?

Then I heard footsteps pass the window. A great house like this would have a watchman, but these quick shuffling footsteps were surely not the dull plod of a servant. They passed on to the grass and died away. I began to think of getting back to my room.

In the corridor I noticed that Lawson's door was ajar, and that a light had been left burning. I had the unpardonable curiosity to peep in. The room was empty, and the bed had not been slept in. Now I knew whose were the footsteps outside the library window.

I lit a reading-lamp and tried to interest myself in 'La Cruelle Enigme.' But my wits were restless, and I could not keep my eyes on the page. I flung the book aside and sat down again by the window. The feeling came over me that I was sitting in a box at some play. The glen was a huge stage, and at any moment the players might appear on it. My attention was strung as high as if I had been waiting for the advent of some world-famous actress. But nothing came. Only the shadows shifted and lengthened as the moon moved across the sky.

Then quite suddenly the restlessness left me, and at the same moment the silence was broken by the crow of a cock and the rustling of trees in a light wind. I felt very sleepy, and was turning to bed when again I heard footsteps without. From the window I could see a figure moving across the garden towards the house. It was Lawson, got up in the sort of towel dressing-gown that one wears on board ship. He was walking slowly and painfully, as if very weary. I did not see his face, but the man's whole air was that of extreme fatigue and dejection.

I tumbled into bed and slept profoundly till long after daylight.

III.

The man who valeted me was Lawson's own servant. As he was laying out my clothes I asked after the health of his master, and was told that he had slept ill and would not rise till late. Then the man, an anxious-faced Englishman, gave me some information on his own account. Mr Lawson was having one of his bad turns. It would pass away in a day or two, but till it had gone he was fit for nothing. He advised me to see Mr Jobson, the factor, who would look to my entertainment in his master's absence.

Jobson arrived before luncheon, and the sight of him was the first satisfactory thing about Welgevonden. He was a big, gruff Scot from Roxburghshire, engaged, no doubt, by Lawson as a duty to his Border ancestry. He had short grizzled whiskers, a weather-worn face, and a shrewd, calm blue eye. I knew now why the place was in such perfect order.

We began with sport, and Jobson explained what I could have in the way of fishing and shooting. His exposition was brief and business-like, and all the while I could see his eye searching me. It was clear that he had much to say on other matters than sport.

I told him that I had come here with Lawson three years before, when he chose the site. Jobson continued to regard me curiously. "I've heard tell of ye from Mr Lawson. Ye're an old friend of his, I understand."

"The oldest," I said. "And I am sorry to find that the place does not agree with him. Why it doesn't I cannot imagine, for you look fit enough. Has he been seedy for long?"

"It comes and goes," said Mr Jobson. "Maybe once a month he has a bad turn. But on the whole it agrees with him badly. He's no' the man he was when I first came here."

Jobson was looking at me very seriously and frankly. I risked a question.

"What do you suppose is the matter?"

He did not reply at once, but leaned forward and tapped my knee.

"I think it's something that doctors canna cure. Look at me, sir. I've always been counted a sensible man, but if I told you what was in my head you would think me daft. But I have one word for you. Bide till to-night is past and then speir your question. Maybe you and me will be agreed."

The factor rose to go. As he left the room he flung me back a remark over his shoulder—"Read the eleventh chapter of the First Book of Kings."

After luncheon I went for a walk. First I mounted to the crown of the hill and feasted my eyes on the unequalled loveliness of the view. I saw the far hills in Portuguese territory, a hundred miles away, lifting up thin blue fingers into the sky. The wind blew light and fresh, and the place was fragrant with a thousand delicate scents. Then I descended to the vale, and followed the stream up through the garden. Poinsettias and oleanders were blazing in coverts, and there was a paradise of tinted water-lilies in the slacker reaches. I saw good trout rise at the fly, but I did not think about fishing. I was searching my memory for a recollection which would not come. By-and-by I found myself beyond the garden, where the lawns ran to the fringe of Ashtaroth's Grove.

It was like something I remembered in an old Italian picture. Only, as my memory drew it, it should have been peopled with strange figures—nymphs dancing on the sward, and a prick-eared faun peeping from the covert. In the warm afternoon sunlight it stood, ineffably gracious and beautiful, tantalising with a sense of some deep hidden loveliness. Very reverently I walked between the slim trees, to where the little conical tower stood half in sun and half in shadow. Then I noticed something new. Round the tower ran a narrow path, worn in the grass by human feet. There had been no such path on my first visit, for I remembered the grass growing tall to the edge of the stone. Had the Kaffirs made a shrine of it, or were there other and stranger votaries?

When I returned to the house I found Travers with a message for me. Mr Lawson was still in bed, but he would like me to go to him. I found my friend sitting up and drinking strong tea,—a bad thing, I should have thought, for a man in his condition. I remember that I looked about the room for some sign of the pernicious habit of which I believed him a victim. But the place was fresh and clean, with the windows wide open, and, though I could not have given my reasons, I was convinced that drugs or drink had nothing to do with the sickness.

He received me more civilly, but I was shocked by his looks. There were great bags below his eyes, and his skin had the wrinkled puffy appearance of a man in dropsy. His voice, too, was reedy and thin. Only his great eyes burned with some feverish life.

"I am a shocking bad host," he said, "but I'm going to be still more inhospitable. I want you to go away. I hate anybody here when I'm off colour."

"Nonsense," I said; "you want looking after. I want to know about this sickness. Have you had a doctor?"

He smiled wearily. "Doctors are no earthly use to me. There's nothing much the matter, I tell you. I'll be all right in a day or two, and then you can come back. I want you to go off with Jobson and hunt in the plains till the end of the week. It will be better fun for you, and I'll feel less guilty."

Of course I pooh-poohed the idea, and Lawson got angry. "Damn it, man," he cried, "why do you force yourself on me when I don't want you? I tell you your presence here makes me worse. In a week I'll be as right as the mail, and then I'll be thankful for you. But get away now; get away, I tell you."

I saw that he was fretting himself into a passion. "All right," I said soothingly; "Jobson and I will go off hunting. But I am horribly anxious about you, old man."

He lay back on his pillows. "You needn't trouble. I only want a little rest. Jobson will make all arrangements, and Travers will get you anything you want. Good-bye."

I saw it was useless to stay longer, so I left the room. Outside I found the anxious-faced servant. "Look here," I said, "Mr Lawson thinks I ought to go, but I mean to stay. Tell him I'm gone if he asks you. And for heaven's sake keep him in bed."

The man promised, and I thought I saw some relief in his face.

I went to the library, and on the way remembered Jobson's remark about 1st Kings. With some searching I found a Bible and turned up the passage. It was a long screed about the misdeeds of Solomon, and I read it through without enlightenment. I began to re-read it, and a word suddenly caught my attention—

"For Solomon went after Ashtaroth, the goddess of the Zidonians."

That was all, but it was like a key to a cipher. Instantly there flashed over my mind all that I had heard or read of that strange ritual which seduced Israel to sin. I saw a sunburnt land and a people vowed to the stern service of Jehovah. But I saw, too, eyes turning from the austere sacrifice to lonely hill-top groves and towers and images, where dwelt some subtle and evil mystery. I saw the fierce prophets, scourging the votaries with rods, and a nation penitent before the Lord ; but always the backsliding again, and the hankering after forbidden joys. Ashtaroth was the old goddess of the East. Was it not possible that in all Semitic blood there remained, transmitted through the dim generations, some craving for her spell ? I thought of the grandfather in the back street at Brighton and of those burning eyes upstairs.

As I sat and mused my glance fell on the inscrutable stone birds. They knew all those old secrets of joy and terror. And that moon of alabaster ! Some dark priest had worn it on his forehead when he worshipped, like Ahab, " all the host of Heaven." And then I honestly began to be afraid. I, a prosaic, modern Christian gentleman, a half-believer in casual faiths, was in the presence of some hoary mystery of sin far older than creeds or Christendom. There was fear in my heart—a kind of uneasy disgust, and above all a nervous eerie disquiet. Now I wanted to go away, and yet I was ashamed of the cowardly thought. I pictured Ashtaroth's Grove with sheer horror. What tragedy was in the air ? what secret awaited twilight ? For the night was coming, the night of the Full Moon, the season of ecstasy and sacrifice.

I do not know how I got through that evening. I was disinclined for dinner, so I had a cutlet in the library and sat smoking till my tongue ached. But as the hours passed a more manly resolution grew up in my mind. I owed it to old friendship to stand by Lawson in this extremity. I could not interfere,—God knows, his reason seemed already rocking,—but I could be at hand in case my chance came. I determined not to undress but to watch through the night. I had a bath, and changed into light flannels and slippers. Then I took up my position in a corner of the library close to the window, so that I could not fail to hear Lawson's footsteps if he passed.

Fortunately I left the lights unlit, for as I waited I grew drowsy, and fell asleep. When I woke the moon had risen, and I knew from the feel of the air that the hour was late. I sat very still, straining my ears, and as I listened I caught the sound of steps. They were crossing the hall stealthily, and nearing the library door. I huddled into my corner as Lawson entered.

He wore the same towel dressing-gown, and he moved swiftly and silently as if in a trance. I watched him take the alabaster moon from the mantelpiece and drop it in his pocket. A glimpse of white skin showed that the gown was his only clothing. Then he moved past me to the window, opened it, and went out.

Without any conscious purpose I rose and followed, kicking off my slippers that I might go quietly. He was running, running fast, across the lawns in the direction of the Grove—an odd shapeless antic in the moonlight. I stopped, for there was no cover, and I feared for his reason if he saw me. When I looked again he had disappeared among the trees.

I saw nothing for it but to crawl, so on my belly I wormed my way over the dripping sward. There was a ridiculous suggestion of deer-stalking about the game which tickled me and dispelled my uneasiness. Almost I persuaded myself I was tracking an ordinary sleep-walker. The lawns were broader than I imagined, and it seemed an age before I reached the edge of the Grove. The world was so still that I appeared to be making a most ghastly amount of noise. I remember that once I heard a rustling in the air, and looked up to see the green doves circling about the tree-tops.

There was no sign of Lawson. On the edge of the Grove I think that all my assurance vanished. I could see between the trunks to the little tower, but it was quiet as the grave, save for the wings above. Once more there came over me the unbearable sense of anticipation I had felt the night before. My nerves tingled with mingled expectation and dread. I did not think that any harm would come to me, for the powers of the air seemed not malignant. But I knew them for powers, and felt awed and abased. I was in the presence of the "host of Heaven," and I was no stern Israelitish prophet to prevail against them.

I must have lain for hours waiting in that spectral place, my eyes riveted on the tower and its golden cap of moonshine. I remember that my head felt void and light, as if my spirit were becoming disembodied and leaving its dew-drenched sheath far below. But the most curious sensation was of something drawing me to the tower, something mild and kindly and rather feeble, for there was some other and stronger force keeping me back. I yearned to move nearer, but I could not drag my limbs an inch. There was a spell somewhere which I could not break. I do not think I was in any way frightened now. The starry influence was playing tricks with me, but my mind was half asleep. Only I never took my eyes from the little tower. I think I could not, if I had wanted to.

Then suddenly from the shadows came Lawson. He was stark-naked, and he wore, bound across his brow, the half-moon of alabaster. He had something, too, in his hand,—something which glittered.

He ran round the tower, crooning to himself, and flinging wild arms to the skies. Sometimes the crooning changed to a shrill cry of passion, such as a mænad may have uttered in the train of Bacchus. I could make out no words, but the sound told its own tale. He was absorbed in some infernal ecstasy. And as he ran, he drew his right hand across his breast and arms, and I saw that it held a knife.

I grew sick with disgust,—not terror, but honest physical loathing. Lawson, gashing his fat body, affected me with an overpowering repugnance. I wanted to go forward and stop him, and I wanted, too, to be a hundred miles away. And the result was that I stayed still. I believe my own will held me there, but I doubt if in any case I could have moved my legs.

The dance grew swifter and fiercer. I saw the blood dripping from Lawson's body, and his face ghastly white above his scarred breast. And then suddenly the horror left me; my head swam; and for one second—one brief second—I seemed to peer into a new world. A strange passion surged up in my heart. I seemed to see the earth peopled with forms—not human, scarcely divine, but more desirable than man or god. The calm face of Nature broke up for me into wrinkles of wild knowledge. I saw the things which brush against the soul in dreams, and found them lovely. There seemed no cruelty in the knife or the blood. It was a delicate mystery of worship, as wholesome as the morning song of birds. I do not know how the Semites found Ashtaroth's ritual; to them it may well have been more rapt and passionate than it seemed to me. For I saw in it only the sweet simplicity of Nature, and all riddles of lust and terror soothed away as a child's nightmares are calmed by a mother. I found my legs able to move, and I think I took two steps through the dusk towards the tower.

And then it all ended. A cock crew, and the homely noises of earth were renewed. While I stood dazed and shivering, Lawson plunged through the Grove towards me. The impetus carried him to the edge, and he fell fainting just outside the shade.

My wits and common-sense came back to me with my bodily strength. I got my friend on my back, and staggered with him towards the house. I was afraid in real earnest now, and what frightened me most was the thought that I had not been afraid sooner. I had come very near the "abomination of the Zidonians."

At the door I found the scared valet waiting. He had apparently done this sort of thing before.

"Your master has been sleep-walking, and has had a fall," I said. "We must get him to bed at once."

We bathed the wounds as he lay in a deep stupor, and I dressed them as well as I could. The only danger lay in his utter exhaustion, for happily the gashes were not serious, and no artery had been touched. Sleep and rest would make him well, for he had the constitution of a strong man. I was leaving the room when he opened his eyes and spoke. He did not recognise me, but I noticed that his face had lost its strangeness, and was once more that of the friend I had known. Then I suddenly bethought me of an old hunting remedy which he and I always carried on our expeditions. It is a pill made up from an ancient Portuguese prescription. One is an excellent specific for fever. Two are invaluable if you are lost in the bush, for they send a man for many hours into a deep sleep, which prevents suffering and madness, till help comes. Three give a painless death. I went to my room and found the little box in my jewel-case. Lawson swallowed two, and turned wearily on his side. I bade his man let him sleep till he woke, and went off in search of food.

IV.

I had business on hand which would not wait. By seven, Jobson, who had been sent for, was waiting for me in the library. I knew by his grim face that here I had a very good substitute for a prophet of the Lord.

"You were right," I said. "I have read the 11th chapter of 1st Kings, and I have spent such a night as I pray God I shall never spend again."

"I thought you would," he replied. "I've had the same experience myself."

" The Grove ? " I said.

" Ay, the wud," was the answer in broad Scots.

I wanted to see how much he understood.

" Mr Lawson's family is from the Scottish Border ? "

" Ay. I understand they come off Borthwick Water side," he replied, but I saw by his eyes that he knew what I meant.

" Mr Lawson is my oldest friend," I went on, " and I am going to take measures to cure him. For what I am going to do I take the sole responsibility. I will make that plain to your master. But if I am to succeed I want your help. Will you give it me ? It sounds like madness, and you are a sensible man and may like to keep out of it. I leave it to your discretion."

Jobson looked me straight in the face. " Have no fear for me," he said ; " there is an unholy thing in that place, and if I have the strength in me I will destroy it. He has been a good master to me, and, forbye, I am a believing Christian. So say on, sir."

There was no mistaking the air. I had found my Tishbite.

" I want men," I said,—" as many as we can get."

Jobson mused. " The Kaffirs will no' gang near the place, but there's some thirty white men on the tobacco farm. They'll do your will, if you give them an indemnity in writing."

" Good," said I. " Then we will take our instructions from the only authority which meets the case. We will follow the example of King Josiah." I turned up the 23rd chapter of 2nd Kings, and read—

" And the high places that were before Jerusalem, which were on the right hand of the Mount of Corruption, which Solomon the king of Israel had builded for Ashtaroth the abomination of the Zidonians . . . did the king defile.

" And he brake in pieces the images, and cut down the groves, and filled their places with the bones of men.

" Moreover the altar that was at Beth-el, and the high place which Jeroboam the son of Nebat, who made Israel to sin, had made, both that altar and the high place he brake down, and burned the high place, and stamped it small to powder, and burned the grove."

Jobson nodded. "It'll need dinnymite. But I've plenty of yon down at the workshops. I'll be off to collect the lads."

Before nine the men had assembled at Jobson's house. They were a hardy lot of young farmers from home, who took their instructions docilely from the masterful factor. On my orders they had brought their shot-guns. We armed them with spades and woodman's axes, and one man wheeled some coils of rope in a handcart.

In the clear, windless air of morning the Grove, set amid its lawns, looked too innocent and exquisite for ill. I had a pang of regret that a thing so fair should suffer; nay, if I had come alone, I think I might have repented. But the men were there, and the grim-faced Jobson was waiting for orders. I placed the guns, and sent beaters to the far side. I told them that every dove must be shot.

It was only a small flock, and we killed fifteen at the first drive. The poor birds flew over the glen to another spinney, but we brought them back over the guns and seven fell. Four more were got in the trees, and the last I killed myself with a long shot. In half an hour there was a pile of little green bodies on the sward.

Then we went to work to cut down the trees. The slim stems were an easy task to a good woodman, and one after another they toppled to the ground. And meantime, as I watched, I became conscious of a strange emotion.

It was as if someone were pleading with me. A gentle voice, not threatening, but pleading—something too fine for the sensual ear, but touching inner chords of the spirit. So tenuous it was and distant that I could think of no personality behind it. Rather it was the viewless, bodiless grace of this delectable vale, some old exquisite divinity of the groves. There was the heart of all sorrow in it, and the soul of all loveliness. It seemed a woman's voice, some lost lady who had brought nothing but goodness unrepaid to the world.

And what the voice told me was that I was destroying her last shelter.

That was the pathos of it—the voice was homeless. As the axes flashed in the sunlight and the wood grew thin, that gentle spirit was pleading with me for mercy and a brief respite. It seemed to be telling of a world for centuries grown coarse and pitiless, of long sad wanderings, of hardly-won shelter, and a peace which was the little all she sought from men. There was nothing terrible in it. No thought of wrong-doing. The spell which to Semitic blood held the mystery of evil, was to me, of the Northern race, only delicate and rare and beautiful. Jobson and the rest did not feel it, I with my finer senses caught nothing but the hopeless sadness of it. That which had stirred the passion in Lawson was only wringing my heart. It was almost too pitiful to bear. As the trees crashed down and the men wiped the sweat from their brows, I seemed to myself like the murderer of fair women and innocent children. I remember that the tears were running over my cheeks. More than once I opened my mouth to countermand the work, but the face of Jobson, that grim Tishbite, held me back.

I knew now what gave the Prophets of the Lord their mastery, and I knew also why the people sometimes stoned them.

The last tree fell, and the little tower stood like a ravished shrine, stripped of all defence against the world. I heard Jobson's voice speaking. "We'd better blast that stane thing now. We'll trench on four sides and lay the dinnymite. Ye're no' looking weel, sir. Ye'd better go and sit down on the brae-face."

I went up the hillside and lay down. Below me, in the waste of shorn trunks, men were running about, and I saw the mining begin. It all seemed like an aimless dream in which I had no part. The voice of that homeless goddess was still pleading. It was the innocence of it that tortured me. Even so must a merciful Inquisitor have suffered from the plea of some fair girl with the aureole of death on her hair. I knew I was killing rare and unrecoverable beauty. As I sat dazed and heart-sick, the whole loveliness of Nature seemed to plead for its divinity. The sun in the heavens, the mellow lines of upland, the blue mystery of the far plains, were all part of that soft voice. I felt bitter scorn for myself. I was guilty of blood; nay, I was guilty of the sin against light which knows no forgiveness. I was murdering innocent gentleness, and there would be no peace on earth for me. Yet I sat helpless. The power of a sterner will constrained me. And all the while the voice was growing fainter and dying away into unutterable sorrow.

. . . .

Suddenly a great flame sprang to heaven, and a pall of smoke. I heard men crying out, and fragments of stone fell around the ruins of the grove. When the air cleared, the little tower had gone out of sight.

The voice had ceased and there seemed to me to be a bereaved silence in the world. The shock moved me to my feet, and I ran down the slope to where Jobson stood rubbing his eyes.

"That's done the job. Now we maun get up the tree-roots. We've no time to howk. We'll just blast the feck o' them."

The work of destruction went on, but I was coming back to my senses. I forced myself to be practical and reasonable. I thought of the night's experience and Lawson's haggard eyes, and I screwed myself into a determination to see the thing through. I had done the deed; it was my business to make it complete. A text in Jeremiah came into my head: "*Their children remember their altars and their groves by the green trees upon the high hills.*" I would see to it that this grove should be utterly forgotten.

We blasted the tree-roots, and, yoking oxen, dragged the debris into a great heap. Then the men set to work with their spades, and roughly levelled the ground. I was getting back to my old self, and Jobson's spirit was becoming mine.

"There is one thing more," I told him. "Get ready a couple of ploughs. We will improve upon King Josiah." My brain was a medley of Scripture precedents, and I was determined that no safeguard should be wanting.

We yoked the oxen again and drove the ploughs over the site of the grove. It was rough ploughing, for the place was thick with bits of stone from the tower, but the slow Afrikander oxen plodded on, and sometime in the afternoon the work was finished. Then I sent down to the farm for bags of rock-salt, such as they use for cattle. Jobson and I took a sack apiece, and walked up and down the furrows, sowing them with salt.

The last act was to set fire to the pile of tree-trunks. They burned well, and on the top we flung the bodies of the green doves. The birds of Ashtaroth had an honourable pyre.

Then I dismissed the much-perplexed men, and gravely shook hands with Jobson. Black with dust and smoke I went back to the house, where I bade Travers pack my bags and order the motor. I found Lawson's servant, and heard from him that his master was sleeping peacefully. I gave him some directions, and then went to wash and change.

Before I left I wrote a line to Lawson. I began by transcribing the verses from the 23rd chapter of 2nd Kings. I told him what I had done, and my reason. "I take the whole responsibility upon myself," I wrote. "No man in the place had anything to do with it but me. I acted as I did for the sake of our old friendship, and you will believe it was no easy task for me. I hope you will understand. Whenever you are able to see me send me word, and I will come back and settle with you. But I think you will realise that I have saved your soul."

The afternoon was merging into twilight as I left the house on the road to Taqui. The great fire, where the Grove had been, was still blazing fiercely, and the smoke made a cloud over the upper glen, and filled all the air with a soft violet haze. I knew that I had done well for my friend, and that he would come to his senses and be grateful. My mind was at ease on that score, and in something like comfort I faced the future. But as the car reached the ridge I looked back to the vale I had outraged. The moon was rising and silvering the smoke, and through the gaps I could see the tongues of fire. Somehow, I know not why, the lake, the stream, the garden-coverts, even the green slopes of hill, wore an air of loneliness and desecration.

And then my heartache returned, and I knew that I had driven something lovely and adorable from its last refuge on earth.

WOOD MAGIC.

(9TH CENTURY.)

I will walk warily in the wise woods on the fringes of eventide,
For the covert is full of noises and the stir of nameless things.
I have seen in the dusk of the beeches the shapes of the lords that ride,
And down in the marish hollow I have heard the lady who sings.
And once in an April gloaming I met a maid on the sward,
All marble-white and gleaming and tender and wild of eye ;—
I, Jehan the hunter, who speak am a grown man, middling hard,
But I dreamt a month of the maid, and wept I knew not why.

Down by the edge of the firs, in a coppice of heath and vine,
Is an old moss-grown altar, shaded by briar and bloom,
Denys, the priest, hath told me 'twas the lord Apollo's shrine
In the days ere Christ came down from God to the Virgin's womb.
I never go past but I doff my cap and avert my eyes—
(Were Denys to catch me I trow I'd do penance for half a year)—
For once I saw a flame there and the smoke of a sacrifice,
And a voice spake out of the thicket that froze my soul with fear.

Wherefore to God the Father, the Son, and the Holy Ghost,
Mary the Blessed Mother, and the kindly Saints as well,
I will give glory and praise, and them I cherish the most,
For they have the keys of Heaven, and save the soul from Hell.

But likewise I will spare for the lord Apollo a grace,
And a bow for the lady Venus—as a friend but not as a thrall.
'Tis true they are out of Heaven, but some day they may win the place;
For gods are kittle cattle, and a wise man honours them all.

VII. THE RIDING OF NINEMILEBURN.

Sim bent over the meal ark and plumbed its contents with his fist. Two feet and more remained: provender—with care—for a month, till he harvested the waterside corn and ground it at Ashkirk mill. He straightened his back, better pleased; and, as he moved, the fine dust flew into his throat and set him coughing. He choked back the sound till his face crimsoned.

But the mischief was done. A woman's voice, thin and weary, came from the ben-end.

The long man tiptoed awkwardly to her side. "Canny, lass," he crooned. "It's me back frae the hill. There's a mune and a clear sky, and I'll hae the lave under thack and rape the morn. Syne I'm for Ninemileburn, and the coo 'ill be i' the byre by Setterday. Things micht be waur, and we'll warstle through yet. There was mair tint at Flodden."

The last rays of October daylight that filtered through the straw lattice showed a woman's head on the pillow. The face was white and drawn, and the great black eyes—she had been an Oliver out of Megget—were fixed in the long stare of pain. Her voice had the high lilt and the deep undertones of the Forest.

"The bairn 'ill be gone ere ye ken, Sim," she said wearily. "He canna live without milk, and I've nane to gie him. Get the coo back or lose the son I bore ye. If I were my ordinar' I wad hae't in the byre, though I had to kindle Ninemileburn ower Wat's heid."

She turned miserably on her pillow and the babe beside her set up a feeble crying. Sim busied himself with relighting the peat fire. He knew too well that he would never see the milk-cow till he took with him the price of his debt or gave a bond on harvested crops. He had had a bad lambing, and the wet summer had soured his shallow lands. The cess to Branksome was due, and he had had no means to pay it. His father's cousin of the Ninemileburn was a brawling fellow, who never lacked beast in byre or corn in bin, and to him he had gone for the loan. But Wat was a hard man, and demanded surety; so the one cow had travelled the six moorland miles and would not return till the bond was cancelled. As well might he try to get water from stone as move Wat by any tale of a sick wife and dying child.

The peat smoke got into his throat and brought on a fresh fit of coughing. The wet year had played havoc with his chest, and his lean shoulders shook with the paroxysms. An anxious look at the bed told him that Marion was drowsing, so he slipped to the door.

Outside, as he had said, the sky was clear. From the plashy hillside came the rumour of swollen burns. Then he was aware of a man's voice shouting.

"Sim," it cried, "Sim o' the Cleuch . . . Sim." A sturdy figure came down through the scrog of hazel and revealed itself as his neighbour of the Dodhead. Jamie Telfer lived five miles off in Ettrick, but his was the next house to the Cleuch shieling.

Telfer was running, and his round red face shone with sweat. "Dod, man, Sim, ye're hard o' hearing. I was routin' like to wake the deid, and ye never turned your neck. It's the fray I bring ye. Mount and ride to the Carewoodrig. The word's frae Branksome. I've but Ranklehope to raise, and then me and William's Tam will be on the road to join ye."

"Whatna fray?" Sim asked blankly.

"Ninemileburn. Bewcastle's marching. They riped the place at cockcrow, and took twenty-six kye, five horse, and a walth o' plenishing. They were seen fordin' Teviot at ten afore noon, but they're gaun round by Ewes Water, for they durstna try the Hermitage Slack. Forbye they move slow, for the bestial's heavy wark to drive. They shut up Wat in the auld peel, and he didna win free till bye mid-day. Syne he was off to Branksome, and the word frae Branksome is to raise a' Ettrick, Teviotdale, Ale Water, and the Muirs o' Esk. We look to win up wi' the lads long ere they cross Liddel, and that at the speed they gang will be gey an' near sunrise. It's a braw mune for the job."

Jamie Telfer lay on his face by the burn and lapped up water like a dog. Then without another word he trotted off across the hillside beyond which lay the Ranklehope.

Sim had a fit of coughing and looked stupidly at the sky. Here was the last straw. He was dog-tired, for he had had little sleep the past week. There was no one to leave with Marion, and Marion was too weak to tend herself. The word was from Branksome, and at another time Branksome was to be obeyed. But now the thing was past reason. What use was there for a miserable careworn man to ride among the swank, well-fed lads in the Bewcastle chase?

And then he remembered his cow. She would be hirpling with the rest of the Ninemileburn beasts on the road to the Border. The case was more desperate than he had thought. She was gone for ever unless he helped Wat to win her back. And if she went, where was the milk for the child?

He stared hopelessly up at a darkening sky. Then he went to the lean-to where his horse was stalled. The beast was fresh, for it had not been out for two days—a rough Forest shelty with shaggy fetlocks and a mane like a thicket. Sim set his old saddle on it, and went back to the house.

His wife was still asleep, breathing painfully. He put water on the fire to boil, and fetched a handful of meal from the ark. With this he made a dish of gruel, and set it by the bedside. He drew a pitcher of water from the well, for she might be thirsty. Then he banked up the fire and steeked the window. When she woke she would find food and drink, and he would be back before the next darkening. He dared not look at the child.

The shelty shied at a line of firelight from the window, as Sim flung himself wearily on its back. He had got his long ash spear from its place among the rafters, and donned his leather jacket with the iron studs on breast and shoulder. One of the seams gaped. His wife had been mending it when her pains took her.

. . . .

He had ridden by Commonside and was high on the Caerlanrig before he saw signs of men. The moon swam in a dim dark sky, and the hills were as yellow as corn. The round top of the Wisp made a clear mark to ride by. Sim was a nervous man, and at another time would never have dared to ride alone by the ruined shieling of Chasehope, where folk said a witch had dwelt long ago and the Devil still came in the small hours. But now he was too full of his cares to have room for dread. With his head on his breast he let the shelty take its own road through the mosses.

But on the Caerlanrig he came on a troop of horse. They were a lusty crowd, well-mounted and armed, with iron basnets and corselets that jingled as they rode. Harden's men, he guessed, with young Harden at the head of them. They cried him greeting as he fell in at the tail. "It's Long Sim o' the Cleuch," one said; "he's sib to Wat or he wadna be here. Sim likes his ain fireside better than the 'Bateable Land."

The companionship of others cheered him. There had been a time, before he brought Marion from Megget, when he was a well-kenned figure on the Borders, a good man at weapon-shows, and a fierce fighter when his blood was up. Those days were long gone; but the gusto of them returned. No man had ever lightlied him without paying scot. He held up his head and forgot his cares and his gaping jacket. In a little they had topped the hill, and were looking down on the young waters of Ewes.

The company grew, as men dropped in from left and right. Sim recognised the wild hair of Charlie of Geddinscleuch, and the square shoulders of Adam of Frodslaw. They passed Mosspaul, a twinkle far down in the glen, and presently came to the long green slope which is called the Carewoodrig, and which makes a pass from Ewes to Hermitage. To Sim it seemed that an army had encamped on it. Fires had been lit in a howe, and wearied men slept by them. These were the runners, who all day had been warning the dales. By one fire stood the great figure of Wat o' the Ninemileburn, blaspheming to the skies and counting his losses. He had girded on a long sword, and for better precaution had slung an axe on his back. At the sight of young Harden he held his peace. The foray was Branksome's and a Scott must lead.

Dimly and stupidly, for he was very weary, Sim heard word of the enemy. The beasts had travelled slow, and would not cross Liddel till sunrise. Now they were high up on Tarras water, making for Liddel at a ford below the Castletown. There had been no time to warn the Elliots, but the odds were that Lariston and Mangerton would be out by morning.

"Never heed the Elliots," cried young Harden. "We can redd our ain frays, lads. Haste and ride, and we'll hae Geordie Musgrave long ere he wins to the Ritterford. Borrowstonemoss is the bit for us." And with a light Scott laugh he was in the saddle.

They were now in a land of low marshy hills, which made ill-going. A companion gave Sim the news. Bewcastle had five-score men and the Scots four-score and three. "It's waur to haud than to win," said the man. "Ae man can take ten beasts when three 'ill no keep them. There'll be bluidy war on Tarras side ere the nicht's dune."

Sim was feeling his weariness too sore for speech. He remembered that he had tasted no food for fifteen hours. He found his meal-poke and filled his mouth, but the stuff choked him. It only made him cough fiercely, so that Wat o' the Ninemileburn, riding before him, cursed him for a broken-winded fool. Also he was remembering about Marion, lying sick in the darkness twenty miles over the hills.

The moon was clouded, for an east wind was springing up. It was ill riding on the braeface, and Sim and his shelty floundered among the screes. He was wondering how long it would all last. Soon he must fall down and be the scorn of the Border men. The thought put Marion out of his head again. He set his mind on tending his horse and keeping up with his fellows.

Suddenly a whistle from Harden halted the company. A man came running back from the crown of the rig. A whisper went about that Bewcastle was on the far side, in the little glen called the Brunt Burn. The men held their breath, and in the stillness they heard far off the sound of hooves on stones and the heavy breathing of cattle.

It was a noble spot for an ambuscade. The Borderers scattered over the hillside, some riding south to hold the convoy as it came down the glen. Sim's weariness lightened. His blood ran quicker; he remembered that the cow, his child's one hope, was there before him. He found himself next his cousin Wat, who chewed curses in his great beard. When they topped the rig they saw a quarter of a mile below them the men they sought. The cattle were driven in the centre, with horsemen in front and rear and flankers on the braeside.

"Hae at them, lads," cried Wat o' the Ninemileburn, as he dug spurs into his grey horse. From farther down the glen he was answered with a great shout of "Branksome."

Somehow or other Sim and his shelty got down the steep braeface. The next he knew was that the raiders had turned to meet him—to meet him alone, it seemed; the moon had come out again, and their faces showed white in it. The cattle, as the driving ceased, sank down wearily in the moss. A man with an iron ged turned, cursing, to receive Wat's sword on his shoulder-bone. A light began to blaze from down the burn—Sim saw the glitter of it out of the corner of an eye—but the men in front were dark figures with white faces.

The Bewcastle lads were stout fellows, well used to hold as well as take. They closed up in line around the beasts, and the moon lit the tops of their spears. Sim brandished his ash-shaft, which had weighed heavily these last hours, and to his surprise found it light. He found his voice, too, and fell a-roaring like Wat.

Before he knew he was among the cattle. Wat had broken the ring, and men were hacking and slipping among the slab sides of the wearied beasts. The shelty came down over the rump of a red bullock, and Sim was sprawling on his face in the trampled grass. He struggled to rise, and someone had him by the throat.

Anger fired his slow brain. He reached out his long arms and grappled a leather jerkin. His nails found a seam and rent it, for he had mighty fingers. Then he was gripping warm flesh, tearing it like a wild beast, and his assailant with a cry slackened his hold.

"Whatna wull-cat . . ." he began, but he got no further. The hoof of Wat's horse came down on his head and brained him. A spatter of blood fell on Sim's face.

The man was half wild. His shelty had broken back for the hill, but his spear lay a yard off. He seized it and got to his feet, to find that Wat had driven the English over the burn. The cattle were losing their weariness in panic, and tossing wild manes among the Scots. It was like a fight in a winter's byre. The glare on the right grew fiercer, and young Harden's voice rose, clear as a bell, above the tumult. He was swearing by the cross of his sword.

On foot, in the old Border way, Sim followed in Wat's wake, into the bog and beyond the burn. He laired to his knees, but he scarcely heeded it. There was a big man before him, a foolish, red-haired fellow, who was making great play with a cudgel. He had shivered two spears and was singing low to himself. Farther off Wat had his axe in hand and was driving the enemy to the brae. There were dead men in the moss. Sim stumbled over a soft body, and a hand caught feebly at his heel. "To me, lads," cried Wat. "Anither birse and we hae them broken."

But something happened. Harden was pushing the van of the raiders up the stream, and a press of them surged in from the right. Wat found himself assailed on his flank, and gave ground. The big man with the cudgel laughed loud and ran down the hill, and the Scots fell back on Sim. Men tripped over him, and as he rose he found the giant above him with his stick in the air.

The blow fell, glancing from the ash-shaft to Sim's side. Something cracked and his left arm hung limp. But the furies of hell had hold of him now. He rolled over, gripped his spear short, and with a swift turn struck upwards. The big man gave a sob and toppled down into a pool of the burn.

Sim struggled to his feet, and saw that the raiders were beginning to hough the cattle. One man was driving a red spear into a helpless beast. It might have been the Cleuch cow. The sight maddened him, and like a destroying angel he was among them. One man he caught full in the throat, and had to set a foot on his breast before he could tug the spear out. Then the head shivered on a steel corselet, and Sim played quarterstaff with the shaft. The violence of his onslaught turned the tide. Those whom Harden drove up were caught in a vice, and squeezed out, wounded and dying and mad with fear, on to the hill above the burn. Both sides were weary men, or there would have been a grim slaughter. As it was, none followed the runners, and every now and again a Scot would drop like a log, not from wounds but from dead weariness.

Harden's flare was dying down. Dawn was breaking, and Sim's wild eyes cleared. He saw the press of cattle, dazed with fright, and the red and miry heather. Queer black things were curled and stretched athwart it. He noticed a dead man beside him, perhaps of his own slaying. It was a shabby fellow, in a jacket that gaped like Sim's. His face was thin and patient, and his eyes, even in death, looked puzzled and reproachful. He would be one of the plain folk who had to ride, willy-nilly, on bigger men's quarrels. Sim found himself wondering if he, also, had a famished wife and child at home. The fury of the night had gone, and Sim began to sob from utter tiredness.

. . . .

He slept in what was half a swoon. When he woke the sun was well up in the sky and the Scots were cooking food. His arm irked him, and his head burned like fire. He felt his body and found nothing worse than bruises, and one long shallow scar where his jacket was torn.

A Teviotdale man brought him a cog of brose. Sim stared at it and sickened: he was too far gone for food. Young Harden passed, and looked curiously at him. "Here's a man that hasna spared himsel'," he said. "A drop o' French cordial is the thing for you, Sim." And out of a leathern flask he poured a little draught which he bade Sim swallow.

The liquor ran through his veins and lightened the ache of his head. He found strength to rise and look round. Surely they were short of men. If these were all that were left Bewcastle had been well avenged.

Jamie Telfer enlightened him. "When we had gotten the victory, there were some o' the lads thocht that Bewcastle sud pay scot in beasts as weel as men. Sae Wat and a score mair rade off to lowse Geordie Musgrave's kye. The road's clear, and they'll be back ower Liddel by this time. Dod, there'll be walth o' plenishin' at the Ninemileburn."

Sim was cheered by the news. If Wat got back more than his own he might be generous. They were cooking meat round the fire, the flesh of the cattle killed in the fight. He went down to the nearest blaze, and was given a strip of roast which he found he could swallow.

"How mony beasts were killed?" he asked incuriously, and was told three. Saugh poles had been set up to hang the skins on. A notion made Sim stagger to his feet and go to inspect them. There could be no mistake. There hung the brindled hide of Marion's cow.

. . . .

Wat returned in a cloud of glory, driving three-and-twenty English beasts before him—great white fellows that none could match on the Scottish side. He and his lads clamoured for food, so more flesh was roasted, till the burnside smelt like a kitchen. The Scots had found better than cattle, for five big skins of ale bobbed on their saddles. Wat summoned all to come and drink, and Harden, having no fear of reprisals, did not forbid it.

Sim was becoming a man again. He had bathed his bruises and scratches in the burn, and Will o' Phawhope, who had skill as a leech, had set his arm and bound it to his side in splints of ash and raw hide. He had eaten grossly of flesh—the first time since the spring, and then it had only been braxy lamb. The ale had warmed his blood and quickened his wits. He began to feel pleased with himself. He had done well in the fray—had not young Harden praised him?—and surly Wat had owned that the salvage of so many beasts was Sim's doing. "Man, Sim, ye wrocht michtily at the burnside," he had said. "The heids crackit like nits when ye garred your staff sing. Better you wi' a stick than anither man wi' a sword." It was fine praise, and warmed Sim's chilly soul. For a year he had fought bitterly for bread, and now glory had come to him without asking.

Men were drawn by lot to drive the cattle, and others to form a rearguard. The rest set off for their homes by the nearest road. The shelty had been recovered, and Sim to his pride found himself riding in the front with Wat and young Harden and others of the Scott and Elliot gentry.

The company rode fast over the green hills in the clear autumn noon. Harden's blue eyes danced, and he sang snatches in his gay voice. Wat rumbled his own praises and told of the raid over Liddel. Sim felt a new being from the broken man who the night before had wearily jogged on the same road. He told himself he took life too gravely and let care ride him too hard. He was too much thirled to the Cleuch and tied to his wife's apron. In the future he would see his friends, and bend the bicker with the rest of them.

By the darkening they had come to Ninemileburn, where Harden's road left theirs. Wat had them all into the bare dwelling, and another skin of ale was broached. A fire was lit and the men sprawled around it, singing songs. Then tales began, and they would have sat till morning, had not Harden called them to the road. Sim, too, got to his feet. He was thinking of the six miles yet before him, and as home grew nearer his spirits sank. Dimly he remembered the sad things that waited his home-coming.

Wat made him a parting speech. " Gude e'en to ye, Cousin Sim. Ye've been a kind man to me the day. May I do as weel by you if ever the fray gangs by the Cleuch. I had a coo o' yours in pledge, and it was ane o' the beasts the Musgraves speared. By the auld law your debt still stands, and if I likit I could seek anither pledge. But there'll be something awin' for rescue-shot, and wi' that and the gude wark ye've dune the day, I'm content to ca' the debt paid."

Wat's words sounded kind, and no doubt Wat thought himself generous. Sim had it on his tongue to ask for a cow —even on a month's loan. But pride choked his speech. It meant telling of the pitiful straits at the Cleuch. After what had passed he must hold his head high amongst those full-fed Branksome lads. He thanked Wat, cried farewell to the rest, and mounted his shelty.

The moon was rising and the hills were yellow as corn. The shelty had had a feed of oats, and capered at the shadows. What with excitement, meat and ale, and the dregs of a great fatigue, Sim's mind was hazy, and his cheerfulness returned. He thought only on his exploits. He had done great things—he, Sim' o the Cleuch—and every man in the Forest would hear of them and praise his courage. There would be ballads made about him ; he could hear the blind violer at the Ashkirk change-house singing songs which told how Sim o' the Cleuch smote Bewcastle in the howe of the Brunt Burn—ash against steel, one against ten. The fancy intoxicated him ; he felt as if he, too, could make a ballad. It would speak of the soft shiny night with the moon high in the heavens. It would tell of the press of men and beasts by the burnside, and the red glare of Harden's fires, and Wat with his axe, and above all of Sim with his ash-shaft and his long arms, and how Harden drove the raiders up the burn and Sim smote them silently among the cattle. Wat's exploits would come in, but the true glory was Sim's. But for him Scots saddles might have been empty and every beast safe over Liddel.

The picture fairly ravished him. It carried him over the six miles of bent and down by the wood of hazel to where the Cleuch lay huddled in its nook of hill. It brought him to the door of his own silent dwelling. As he pushed into the darkness his heart suddenly sank. . . .

With fumbling hands he kindled a rushlight. The peat fire had long gone out and left only a heap of white ashes. The gruel by the bed had been spilled and was lying on the floor. Only the jug of water was drained to the foot.

His wife lay so still that he wondered. A red spot burned in each cheek, and, as he bent down, he could hear her fast breathing. He flashed the light on her eyes and she slowly opened them.

"The coo, Sim," she said faintly. "Hae ye brocht the coo?"

The rushlight dropped on the floor. Now he knew the price of his riding. He fell into a fit of coughing.

PLAIN FOLK.

Since flaming angels drove our sire
From Eden's green to walk the mire,
We are the folk who tilled the plot
And ground the grain and boiled the pot.
We hung the garden terraces
That pleasured Queen Semiramis.
Our toil it was and burdened brain
That set the Pyramids o'er the plain.
We marched from Egypt at God's call
And drilled the ranks and fed them all;
But never Eschol's wine drank we,—
Our bones lay 'twixt the sand and sea.
We officered the brazen bands
That rode the far and desert lands;
We bore the Roman eagles forth
And made great roads from south to north;
White cities flowered for holiday,
But we, forgot, died far away.
And when the Lord called folk to Him,
And some sat blissful at His feet,
Ours was the task the bowl to brim,
For on this earth even saints must eat.
The serfs have little need to think,
Only to work and sleep and drink;
A rover's life is boyish play,
For when cares press he rides away;
The king sits on his ruby throne,
And calls the whole wide world his own.
But we, the plain folk, noon and night

No surcease of our toil we see ;
We cannot ease our cares by flight,
For Fortune holds our loves in fee.
We are not slaves to sell our wills,
We are not kings to ride the hills,
But patient men who jog and dance
In the dull wake of circumstance :
Loving our little patch of sun,
Too weak our homely dues to shun,
Too nice of conscience, or too free,
To prate of rights—if rights there be.

The Scriptures tell us that the meek
The earth shall have to work their will ;
It may be they shall find who seek,
When they have topped the last long hill.
Meantime we serve among the dust
For at the best a broken crust,
A word of praise, and now and then
The joy of turning home again.
But freemen still we fall or stand,
We serve because our hearts command.
Though kings may boast and knights cavort,
We broke the spears at Agincourt.
When odds were wild and hopes were down,
We died in droves by Leipsic town.
Never a field was starkly won
But *ours* the dead that faced the sun.
The slave will fight because he must,
The rover for his ire and lust,
The king to pass an idle hour
Or feast his fatted heart with power ;
But we, because we choose, we choose,
Nothing to gain and much to lose,
Holding it happier far to die
Than falter in our decency.

The serfs may know an hour of pride
When the high flames of tumult ride.
The rover has his days of ease
When he has sacked his palaces.
A king may live a year like God
When prostrate peoples drape the sod.
We ask for little,—leave to tend
Our modest fields : at daylight's end
The fires of home : a wife's caress :
The star of children's happiness.
Vain hope ! 'Tis ours for ever and aye
To do the job the slaves have marred,
To clear the wreckage of the fray,
And please our kings by working hard.
Daily we mend their blunderings,
Swashbucklers, demagogues, and kings !

What if we rose ?—If some fine morn,
Unnumbered as the autumn corn,
With all the brains and all the skill
Of stubborn back and steadfast will,
We rose and, with the guns in train,
Proposed to deal the cards again,
And, tired of sitting up o' nights,
Gave notice to our parasites,
Announcing that in future they
Who paid the piper should call the lay ?
Then crowns would tumble down like nuts,
And wastrels hide in water-butts ;
Each lamp-post as an epilogue
Would hold a pendent demagogue :
Then would the world be for the wise !—

. . . .

But ah ! the plain folk never rise.

VIII. THE KINGS OF ORION.

"An ape and a lion lie side by side in the heart of a man."
PERSIAN PROVERB.

SPRING-FISHING in the North is a cold game for a man whose blood has become thin in gentler climates. All afternoon I had failed to stir a fish, and the wan streams of the Laver, swirling between bare grey banks, were as icy to the eye as the sharp gusts of hail from the north-east were to the fingers. I cast mechanically till I grew weary, and then with an empty creel and a villainous temper set myself to trudge the two miles of bent to the inn. Some distant ridges of hill stood out snow-clad against the dun sky, and half in anger, half in a dismal satisfaction, I told myself that fishing to-morrow would be as barren as to-day.

At the inn door a tall man was stamping his feet and watching a servant lifting rod-cases from a dogcart. Hooded and wrapped though he was, my friend Thirlstone was an unmistakable figure in any landscape. The long, haggard, brown face, with the skin drawn tightly over the cheek-bones, the keen blue eyes finely wrinkled round the corners with staring at many suns, the scar which gave his mouth a humorous droop to the right, made up a whole which was not easily forgotten. I had last seen him on the quay at Funchal bargaining with some rascally boatman to take him after mythical wild goats in Las Desertas. Before that we had met at an embassy ball in Vienna, and still earlier at a hill-station in Persia to which I had been sent post-haste by an anxious and embarrassed Government. Also I had been at school with him, in those far-away days when we rode nine stone and dreamed of cricket averages. He was a soldier of note, who had taken part in two little wars and one big one; had himself conducted a political mission through a hard country with some success, and was habitually chosen by his superiors to keep his eyes open as a foreign attaché in our neighbours' wars. But his fame as a hunter had gone abroad into places where even the name of the British army is unknown. He was the hungriest shikari I have ever seen, and I have seen many. If you are wise you will go forthwith to some library and procure a little book entitled 'Three Hunting Expeditions,' by A. W. T. It is a modest work, and the style is that of a leading article, but all the lore and passion of the Red Gods are in its pages.

The sitting-room at the inn is a place of comfort, and while Thirlstone warmed his long back at the fire I sank contentedly into one of the well-rubbed leather arm-chairs. The company of a friend made the weather and the scarcity of salmon less the intolerable grievance they had seemed an hour ago than a joke to be laughed at. The landlord came in with whisky, and banked up the peats till they glowed beneath a pall of blue smoke.

"I hope to goodness we are alone," said Thirlstone, and he turned to the retreating landlord and asked the question.

"There's naebody bidin' the nicht forbye yoursels," he said, "but the morn there's a gentleman comin'. I got a letter frae him the day. Maister Wiston, they ca' him. Maybe ye ken him?"

I started at the name, which I knew very well. Thirlstone, who knew it better, stopped warming himself and walked to the window, where he stood pulling his moustache and staring at the snow. When the man had left the room, he turned to me with the face of one whose mind is made up on a course but uncertain of the best method.

"Do you know this sort of weather looks infernally unpromising? I've half a mind to chuck it and go back to town."

I gave him no encouragement, finding amusement in his difficulties.

"Oh, it's not so bad," I said, "and it won't last. To-morrow we may have the day of our lives."

He was silent for a little, staring at the fire. "Anyhow," he said at last, "we were fools to be so far up the valley. Why shouldn't we go down to the Forest Lodge? They'll take us in, and we should be deucedly comfortable, and the water's better."

"There's not a pool on the river to touch the stretch here," I said. "I know, for I've fished every inch of it."

He had no reply to this, so he lit a pipe and held his peace for a time. Then, with some embarrassment but the air of having made a discovery, he announced that his conscience was troubling him about his work, and he thought he ought to get back to it at once. "There are several things I have forgotten to see to, and they're rather important. I feel a beast behaving like this, but you won't mind, will you?"

"My dear Thirlstone," I said, "what is the good of hedging? Why can't you say you won't meet Wiston?"

His face cleared. "Well, that's the fact—I won't. It would be too infernally unpleasant. You see, I was once by way of being his friend, and he was in my regiment. I couldn't do it."

The landlord came in at the moment with a basket of peats. "How long is Capt—Mr Wiston staying here?" I asked.

"He's no bidin' ony time. He's just comin' here in the middle o' the day for his denner, and then drivin' up the water to Altbreac. He has the fishin' there."

Thirlstone's face showed profound relief. "Thank God!" I heard him mutter under his breath, and when the landlord had gone he fell to talking of salmon with enthusiasm. "We must make a big day of it to-morrow, dark to dark, you know. Thank heaven, our beat's down-stream, too."

And thereafter he made frequent excursions to the door, and bulletins on the weather were issued regularly.

Dinner over, we drew our chairs to the hearth and fell to talk and the slow consumption of tobacco. When two men from the ends of the earth meet by a winter fire, their thoughts are certain to drift overseas. We spoke of the racing tides off Vancouver, and the lonely pine-clad ridges running up to the snow-peaks of the Selkirks, to which we had both travelled once upon a time in search of sport. Thirlstone on his own account had gone wandering to Alaska, and brought back some bear-skins and a frost-bitten toe as trophies, and from his tales had consorted with the finest band of rogues which survives unhanged on this planet. Then some casual word took our thoughts to the south, and our memories dallied with Africa. Thirlstone had hunted in Somaliland and done mighty slaughter; while I had spent some never-to-be-forgotten weeks long ago in the hinterland of Zanzibar, in the days before railways and game-preserves. I have gone through life with a keen eye for the discovery of earthly paradises, to which I intend to retire when my work is over, and the fairest I thought I had found above the Rift valley, where you have a hundred miles of blue horizon and the weather of Scotland. Thirlstone, not having been there, naturally differed, and urged the claim of a certain glen in Kashmir, where you may hunt two varieties of bear and three of buck in thickets of rhododendron, and see the mightiest mountain-wall on earth from your tent door. The mention of the Indian frontier brought us back to our professions, and for a little we talked "shop" with the unblushing confidence of those who know each other's work and approve it. As a very young soldier Thirlstone had gone shooting in the Pamirs, and had blundered into a Russian party of exploration which contained Kuropatkin. He had in consequence grossly outstayed his leave, having been detained for a fortnight by an arbitrary hospitality; but he had learned many things, and the experience had given him strong views on frontier questions. Half an hour was devoted to a masterly survey of the East, until a word pulled us up.

"I went there in '99," Thirlstone was saying,—"the time Wiston and I were sent——" and then he stopped, and his eager face clouded. Wiston's name cast a shadow over our reminiscences.

"What did he actually do ?" I asked after a short silence.

"Pretty bad! He seemed a commonplace, good sort of fellow, popular, fairly competent, a little bad-tempered perhaps. And then suddenly he did something so extremely blackguardly that everything was at an end. It's no good repeating details, and I hate to think about it. We know little about our neighbours, and I'm not sure that we know much about ourselves. There may be appalling depths of iniquity in every one of us, only most people are fortunate enough to go through the world without meeting anything to wake the devil in them. I don't believe Wiston was bad in the ordinary sense. Only there was something else in him—*somebody else*, if you like,—and in a moment it came uppermost, and he was a branded man. Ugh! it's a gruesome thought."

Thirlstone had let his pipe go out, and was staring moodily into the fire.

"How do you explain things like that ?" he asked. "I have an idea of my own about them. We talk glibly of ourselves and our personality and our conscience, as if every man's nature were a smooth, round, white thing, like a chuckie-stone. But I believe there are two men—perhaps more—in every one of us. There's our ordinary self, generally rather humdrum; and then there's a bit of something else, good, bad, but never indifferent,—and it is that something else which may make a man a saint or a great villain."

"'The Kings of Orion have come to earth,'" I quoted.

Something in the words struck Thirlstone, and he asked me what was the yarn I spoke of.

"It's an old legend," I explained. "When the kings were driven out of Orion, they were sent to this planet and given each his habitation in some mortal soul. There were differences of character in that royal family, and so the *alter ego* which dwells alongside of us may be virtuous or very much the reverse. But the point is that he is always greater than ourselves, for he has been a king. It's a foolish story, but very widely believed. There is something of the sort in Celtic folklore, and there's a reference to it in Ausonius. Also the bandits in the Bakhtiari have a version of it in a very excellent ballad."

"Kings of Orion," said Thirlstone musingly. "I like that idea. Good or bad, but always great! After all, we show a kind of belief in it in our daily practice. Every man is always making fancies about himself; but it is never his workaday self, but something else. The bank clerk who pictures himself as a financial Napoleon knows that his own thin little soul is incapable of it; but he knows, too, that it is possible enough for that other bigger thing which is not his soul, but yet in some odd way is bound up with it. I fancy myself a field-marshal in a European war; but I know perfectly well that if the job were offered me, I should realise my incompetence and decline. I expect you rather picture yourself now and then as a sort of Julius Cæsar and empire-maker, and yet, with all respect, my dear chap, I think it would be rather too much for you."

"There was once a man," I said, "an early Victorian Whig, whose chief ambitions were to reform the criminal law and abolish slavery. Well, this dull, estimable man in his leisure moments was Emperor of Byzantium. He fought great wars and built palaces, and then, when the time for fancy was past, went into the House of Commons and railed against militarism and Tory extravagance. That particular king from Orion had a rather odd sort of earthly tenement."

Thirlstone was all interest. "A philosophic Whig and the throne of Byzantium. A pretty rum mixture! And yet—yet," and his eyes became abstracted. "Did you ever know Tommy Lascelles?"

"The man who once governed Deira? Retired now, and lives somewhere in Kent? Yes, I've met him once or twice. But why?"

"Because," said Thirlstone solemnly, "unless I'm greatly mistaken, Tommy was another such case, though no man ever guessed it except myself. I don't mind telling you the story, now that he is retired and vegetating in his ancestral pastures. Besides, the facts are all in his favour, and the explanation is our own business. . . .

"His wife was my cousin, and when she died Tommy was left a very withered, disconsolate man, with no particular object in life. We all thought he would give up the service, for he was hideously well off; and then one fine day, to our amazement, he was offered Deira, and accepted it. I was short of a job at the time, for my battalion was at home, and there was nothing going on anywhere, so I thought I should like to see what the East Coast of Africa was like, and wrote to Tommy about it. He jumped at me, cabled offering me what he called his Military Secretaryship, and I got seconded, and set off. I had never known him very well, but what I had seen I had liked; and I suppose he was glad to have one of Maggie's family with him, for he was still very low about her loss. I was in pretty good spirits, for it meant new experiences, and I had hopes of big game.

"You've never been to Deira? Well, there's no good trying to describe it, for it's the only place in the world like itself. God made it and left it to its own devices. The town is pretty enough, with its palms and green headland, and little scrubby islands in the river's mouth. It has the usual half-Arab, half-Portugee look—white green-shuttered houses, flat roofs, sallow little men in duck, and every type of nigger from the Somali to the Shangaan. There are some good buildings, and Government House was the mansion of some old Portugee seigneur, and was built when people in

Africa were not in such a hurry as to-day. Inland there's a rolling, forest country, beginning with decent trees and ending in mimosa-thorn, when the land begins to rise to the stony hills of the interior; and that poisonous yellow river rolls through it all, with a denser native population along its banks than you will find anywhere else north of the Zambesi. For about two months in the year the climate is Paradise, and for the rest you live in a Turkish bath, with every known kind of fever hanging about. We cleaned out the town and improved the sanitation, so there were few epidemics, but there was enough ordinary malaria to sicken a crocodile.

"The place was no special use to us. It had been annexed in spite of a tremendous Radical outcry, and, upon my soul, it was one of the few cases where the Radicals had something to say for themselves. All we got by it was half a dozen of the nastiest problems an unfortunate governor can have to face. Ten years before it had been a decaying strip of coast, with a few trading firms in the town, and a small export of ivory and timber. But some years before Tommy took it up there had been a huge discovery of copper in the hills inland, a railway had been built, and there were several biggish mining settlements at the end of it. Deira itself was filled with offices of European firms, it had got a Stock Exchange of its own, and it was becoming the usual cosmopolitan playground. It had a knack, too, of getting the very worst breed of adventurer. I know something of your South African and Australian mining towns, and with all their faults they are run by white men. If they haven't much morals, they have a kind of decency which keeps them fairly straight. But for our sins we got a brand of Levantine Jew who was fit for nothing but making money and making trouble. They were always defying the law, and then, when they got into a hole, they squealed to Government for help, and started a racket in the home papers about the weakness of the Imperial power. The crux of the whole difficulty was the natives, who lived along the river and in the foot-hills. They were a hardy race of Kaffirs, sort of far-away cousins to the Zulu, and till the mines were opened they had behaved well enough. They had arms, which we had never dared to take away, but they kept quiet and paid their hut-taxes like men. I got to know many of the chiefs, and liked them, for they were upstanding fellows to look at and heaven-born shikaris. However, when the Jews came along they wanted labour, and, since we did not see our way to allow them to add to the imported coolie population, they had to fall back upon the Labonga. At first things went smoothly. The chiefs were willing to let their men work for good wages, and for a time there was enough labour for everybody. But as the mines extended, and the natives, after making a few pounds, wanted to get back to their kraals, there came a shortage; and since the work could not be allowed to slacken, the owners tried other methods. They made promises which they never intended to keep, and they stood on the letter of a law which the natives did not understand, and they employed touts who were little better than slave-dealers. They got the labour, of course, but soon they had put the Labonga into a state of unrest which a very little would turn into a rising.

"Into this kettle of fish Tommy was pitchforked, and when I arrived he was just beginning to understand how unpleasant it was. As I said before, I did not know him very well, and I was amazed to find how bad he was at his job. A more curiously incompetent person I never met. He was a long, thin man, with a grizzled moustache, and a mild sleepy eye,—not an impressive figure, except on a horse; and he had an odd lisp which made even a shrewd remark sound foolish. He was the most industrious creature in the world, and a model of official decorum. His papers were always in order, his despatches always neat and correct, and I don't believe anyone ever caught him tripping in office work. But he had no more conception than a child of the kind of trouble that was brewing. He never knew an honest man from a rogue, and the result was that he received all unofficial communications with a polite disbelief. I used to force him to see people—miners, prospectors, traders, anyone who had something to say worth listening to, but it all glided smoothly off his mind. He was simply the most incompetent being ever created, living in the world as not being of it, or rather creating a little official world of his own, where all events happened on lines laid down by the Colonial Office, and men were like papers, to be rolled into packets and properly docketed. He had an Executive Council of people like himself, competent officials and blind bats at anything else. Then there was a precious Legislative Council, intended to represent the different classes of the population. There were several good men on it—one old trader called Mackay, for instance, who had been thirty years in the country,—but most were nominees of the mining firms, and very seedy rascals at that. They were always talking about the rights of the white man, and demanding popular control of the Government, and similar twaddle. The leader was a man who hailed from Hamburg, and called himself Le Foy—descended from a Crusader of the name of Levi,—who was a jackal of one of the chief copper firms. He overflowed with Imperialist sentiment, and when he wasn't waving the flag he used to gush about the beauties of English country life and the grandeur of the English tradition. He hated me from the start, for when he talked of going 'home' I thought he meant Hamburg, and said so; and then a thing happened which made him hate me worse. He was infernally rude to Tommy, who, like the dear sheep he was, never saw it, and, if he had, wouldn't have minded. But one day I chanced to overhear some of his impertinences, so I hunted out my biggest sjambok and lay in wait for Mr Le Foy. I told him that he was a representative of the sovereign people, that I was a member of an effete bureaucracy, and that it would be most painful if unpleasantness arose between us. But, I added, I was prepared, if necessary, to sacrifice my official career to my private feelings, and if he dared to use such language again to His Majesty's representative I would give him a hiding he would remember till he found himself in Abraham's bosom. Not liking my sjambok, he became soap and butter at once, and held his tongue for a month or two.

"But though Tommy was no good at his job, he was a tremendous swell at other things. He was an uncommonly good linguist, and had always about a dozen hobbies which he slaved at; and when he found himself at Deira with a good deal of leisure, he became a bigger crank than ever. He had a lot of books which used to follow him about the world in zinc-lined boxes—your big paper-backed German books which mean research,—and he was a Fellow of the Royal Society, and corresponded with half a dozen foreign shows. India was his great subject, but he had been in the Sudan and knew a good deal about African races. When I went out to him, his pet hobby was the Bantu, and he had acquired an amazing amount of miscellaneous learning. He knew all about their immigration from the North, and the Arab and Phœnician trade-routes, and the Portuguese occupation, and the rest of the history of that unpromising seaboard. The way he behaved in his researches showed the man. He worked hard at the Labonga language—which, I believe, is a linguistic curiosity of the first water,—from missionary books and the conversation of tame Kaffirs. But he never thought of paying them a visit in their native haunts. I was constantly begging him to do it, but it was not Tommy's way. He did not care a straw about political expedience, and he liked to look at things through the medium of paper and ink. Then there were the Phœnician remains in the foot-hills where the copper was mined—old workings, and things which might have been forts or temples. He knew all that was to be known about them, but he had never seen them, and never wanted to. Once only he went to the hills, to open some new reservoirs and make the ordinary Governor's speech ; but he went in a special train and stayed two hours, most of which was spent in lunching and being played to by brass bands.

"But, oddly enough, there was one thing which stirred him with an interest that was not academic. I discovered it by accident one day when I went into his study and found him struggling with a map of Central Asia. Instead of the mild, benevolent smile with which he usually greeted my interruptions, he looked positively furtive, and, I could have sworn, tried to shuffle the map under some papers. Now it happens that Central Asia is the part of the globe that I know better than most men, and I could not help picking up the map and looking at it. It was a wretched thing, and had got the Oxus two hundred miles out of its course. I pointed this out to Tommy, and to my amazement he became quite excited. 'Nonsense,' he said. 'You don't mean to say it goes south of that desert. Why, I meant to——,' and then he stammered and stopped. I wondered what on earth he had meant to do, but I merely observed that I had been there, and knew. That brought Tommy out of his chair in real excitement. 'What ! ' he cried, 'you ! You never told me,' and he started to fire off a round of questions which showed that if he knew very little about the place, he had it a good deal in his mind. I drew some sketch-plans for him, and left him brooding over them.

"That was the first hint I got. The second was a few nights later, when we were smoking in the billiard-room. I had been reading Marco Polo, and the talk got on to Persia and drifted all over the north side of the Himalaya. Tommy, with an abstracted eye, talked of Alexander and Timour and Genghis Khan, and particularly of Prester John, who was a character that took his fancy. I had told him that the natives in the Pamirs were true Persian stock, and this interested him greatly. 'Why was there never a great state built up in those valleys ? ' he asked. 'You get nothing but a few wild conquerors rushing east and west, and then some squalid khanates. And yet all the materials were there —the stuff for a strong race, a rich land, the traditions of an old civilisation, and natural barriers against all invasion.'

"'I suppose they never found the man,' I said.

"He agreed. 'Their princes were sots, or they were barbarians of genius who could devastate to the gates of Peking or Constantinople, but could never build. They did not recognise their limits, and so they went out in a whirlwind. But if there had been a man of solid genius he might have built up the strongest nation on the globe. In time he could have annexed Persia and nibbled at China. He would have been rich, for he could tap all the inland trade-routes of Asia. He would have had to be a conqueror, for his people would be a race of warriors, but first and foremost he must have been a statesman. Think of such a civilisation, *the* Asian civilisation, growing up mysteriously behind the deserts and the ranges! That's my idea of Prester John. Russia would have been confined to the line of the Urals. China would have been absorbed. There would have been no Japan. The whole history of the world for the last few hundred years would have been different. It is the greatest of all the lost chances in history.' Tommy waxed pathetic over the loss.

"I was a little surprised at his eloquence, especially when he seemed to remember himself and stopped all of a sudden. But for the next week I got no peace with his questions. I told him all I knew of Bokhara, and Samarkand, and Tashkend, and Yarkand. I showed him the passes in the Pamirs and the Hindu Kush. I traced out the rivers, and I calculated distances; we talked over imaginary campaigns, and set up fanciful constitutions. It was a childish game, but I found it interesting enough. He spoke of it all with a curious personal tone which puzzled me, till one day when we were amusing ourselves with a fight on the Zarafshan, and I put in a modest claim to be allowed to win once in a while. For a second he looked at me in blank surprise. 'You can't,' he said; 'I've got to enter Samarkand before I can . . .' and he stopped again, with a glimmering sense in his face that he was giving himself away. And then I knew that I had surprised Tommy's secret. While he was muddling his own job, he was salving his pride with fancies of some wild career in Asia, where Tommy, disguised as the lord knows what Mussulman grandee, was hammering the little states into an empire.

"I did not think then as I think now, and I was amused to find so odd a trait in a dull man. I had known something of the kind before. I had met fellows who after their tenth peg would begin to swagger about some ridiculous fancy of their own—their little private corner of soul showing for a moment when the drink had blown aside their common-sense. Now, I had never known the thing appear in cold blood and everyday life, but I assumed the case to be the same. I thought of it only as a harmless fancy, never imagining that it had anything to do with character. I put it down to that kindly imagination which is the old opiate for failures. So I played up to Tommy with all my might, and though he became very discreet after the first betrayal, having hit upon the clue, I knew what to look for, and I found it. When I told him that the Labonga were in a devil of a mess, he would look at me with an empty face and change the subject; but once among the Turcomans his eye would kindle, and he would slave at his confounded folly with sufficient energy to reform the whole East Coast. It was the spark that kept the man alive. Otherwise he would have been as limp as a rag, but this craziness put life into him, and made him carry his head in the air and walk like a free man. I remember he was very keen about any kind of martial poetry. He used to go about crooning Scott and Macaulay to himself, and when we went for a walk or a ride he wouldn't speak for miles, but keep smiling to himself and humming bits of songs. I daresay he was very happy,—far happier than your stolid, competent man, who sees only the one thing to do and does it. Tommy was muddling his particular duty, but building glorious palaces in the air.

"One day Mackay, the old trader, came to me after a sitting of the precious Legislative Council. We were very friendly, and I had done all I could to get the Government to listen to his views. He was a dour, ill-tempered Scotsman, very anxious for the safety of his property, but perfectly careless about any danger to himself.

"'Captain Thirlstone,' he said, 'that Governor of yours is a damned fool.'

"Of course I shut him up very brusquely, but he paid no attention. 'He just sits and grins, and lets yon Pentecostal crowd we've gotten here as a judgment for our sins do what they like wi' him. God kens what'll happen. I would go home to-morrow, if I could realise without an immoderate loss. For the day of reckoning is at hand. Maark my words, Captain—at hand.'

"I said I agreed with him about the approach of trouble, but that the Governor would rise to the occasion. I told him that people like Tommy were only seen at their best in a crisis, and that he might be perfectly confident that when it arrived he would get a new idea of the man. I said this, but of course I did not believe a word of it. I thought Tommy was only a dreamer, who had rotted any grit he ever possessed by his mental opiates. At that time I did not understand about the kings from Orion.

"And then came the thing we had all been waiting for—a Labonga rising. A week before I had got leave and had gone up country, partly to shoot, but mainly to see for myself what trouble was brewing. I kept away from the river, and therefore missed the main native centres, but such kraals as I passed had a look I did not like. The chiefs were almost always invisible, and the young bloods were swaggering about and bukking to each other, while the women were grinding maize as if for some big festival. However, after a bit the country seemed to grow more normal, and I went into the foot-hills to shoot, fairly easy in my mind. I had got up to a place called Shimonwe, on the Pathi River, where I had ordered letters to be sent, and one night coming in from a hard day after kudu I found a post-runner half-dead of fatigue with a chit from Utterson, who commanded a police district twenty miles nearer the coast. It said simply that all the young men round about him had cleared out and appeared to be moving towards Deira, that he was in the devil of a quandary, and that, since the police were under the Governor, he would take his orders from me.

"It looked as if the heather were fairly on fire at last, so I set off early next morning to trek back. About mid-day I met Utterson, a very badly scared little man, who had come to look for me. It seemed that his policemen had bolted in the night and gone to join the rising, leaving him with two white sergeants, barely fifty rounds of ammunition, and no neighbour for a hundred miles. He said that the Labonga chiefs were not marching to the coast, as he had thought, but north along the eastern foot-hills in the direction of the mines. This was better news, for it meant that in all probability the railway would remain open. It was my business to get somehow to my chief, and I was in the deuce of a stew how to manage it. It was no good following the line of the natives' march, for they would have been between me and my goal, and the only way was to try and outflank them by going due east, in the Deira direction, and then turning north, so as to strike the railway about half-way to the mines. I told Utterson we had better scatter, otherwise we should have no chance of getting through a densely populated native country. So, about five in the afternoon I set off with my chief shikari, who, by good luck, was not a Labonga, and dived into the jungly bush which skirts the hills.

"For three days I had a baddish time. We steered by

the stars, travelling chiefly by night, and we showed extraordinary skill in missing the water-holes. I had a touch of fever and got light-headed, and it was all I could do to struggle through the thick grass and wait-a-bit thorns. My clothes were torn to rags, and I grew so footsore that it was agony to move. All the same we travelled fast, and there was no chance of our missing the road, for any route due north was bound to cut the railway. I had the most sickening uncertainty about what was to come next. Hely, who was in command at Deira, was a good enough man, but he had only three companies of white troops, and the black troops were as likely as not to be on their way to the rebels. It looked as if we should have a Cawnpore business on a small scale, though I thanked Heaven there were no women in the case. As for Tommy, he would probably be repeating platitudes in Deira and composing an intelligent despatch on the whole subject.

"About four in the afternoon of the third day I struck the line near a little station called Palala. I saw by the look of the rails that trains were still running, and my hopes revived. At Palala there was a coolie stationmaster, who gave me a drink and a little food, after which I slept heavily in his office till wakened by the arrival of an up train. It contained one of the white companies and a man Davidson, of the 101st, who was Hely's second in command. From him I had news that took away my breath. The Governor had gone up the line two days before with an A.D.C. and old Mackay. 'The sportsman has got a move on him at last,' said Davidson, 'but what he means to do Heaven only knows. The Labonga are at the mines, and a kind of mine-guard has been formed for defence. The joke of it is that most of the magnates are treed up there, for the railway is cut and they can't get away. I don't envy your chief the job of schooling that nervous crowd.'

"I went on with Davidson, and very early next morning we came to a broken culvert and had to stop. There we stuck for three hours till the down train arrived, and with it Hely. He was for ordinary a stolid soul, but I never saw a man in such a fever of excitement. He gripped me by the arm and fairly shook me. 'That old man of yours is a hero,' he cried. 'The Lord forgive me! and I have always crabbed him.'

"I implored him in Heaven's name to tell me what was up, but he would say nothing till he had had his pow-wow with Davidson. It seemed that he was bringing all his white troops up the line for some great demonstration that Tommy had conceived. Davidson went back to Deira, while we mended the culvert and got the men transferred to the other train. Then I screwed the truth out of Hely. Tommy had got up to the mines before the rebels arrived, and had found as fine a chaos as can be imagined. He did not seem to have had any doubts what to do. There were a certain number of white workmen, hard fellows from Cornwall mostly, with a few Australians, and these he got together with Mackay's help and organised into a pretty useful corps. He set them to guard the offices, and gave them strict orders to shoot at sight anyone attempting to leave. Then he collected the bosses and talked to them like a father. What he said Hely did not know, except that he had damned their eyes pretty heartily, and told them what a set of swine they were, making trouble which they had not the pluck to face. Whether from Mackay, or from his own intelligence, or from a memory of my neglected warnings, he seemed to have got a tight grip on the facts at last. Meanwhile the Labonga were at the doors, chanting their battle-songs half a mile away, and shots were heard from the far pickets. If they had tried to rush the place then, all would have been over, but, luckily, that was never their way of fighting. They sat down in camp to make their sacrifices and consult their witch-doctors, and presently Hely arrived with the first troops, having come in on the northern flank when he found the line cut. He had been in time to hear the tail-end of

Tommy's final address to the mine-owners. He told them, in words which Hely said he could never have imagined coming from his lips, that they would be well served if the Labonga cleaned the whole place out. Only, he said, that would be against the will of Britain, and it was his business, as a loyal servant, to prevent it. Then, after giving Hely his instructions, he had put on his uniform, gold lace and all, and every scrap of bunting he possessed—all the orders and 'Golden Stars' of half a dozen Oriental States where he had served. He made Ashurst, the A.D.C., put on his best Hussar's kit, and Mackay rigged himself out in a frock-coat and a topper; and the three set out on horseback for the Labonga. 'I believe he'll bring it off,' said Hely, with wild eyes, 'and, by heaven, if he does, it'll be the best thing since John Nicholson!'

"For the rest of the way I sat hugging myself with excitement. The miracle of miracles seemed to have come. The old, slack, incompetent soul in Tommy seemed to have been driven out by that other spirit, which had hitherto been content to dream of crazy victories on the Oxus. I cursed my folly in having missed it all, for I would have given my right hand to be with him among the Labonga. I envied that young fool Ashurst his luck in being present at that queer transformation scene. I had not a doubt that Tommy would bring it off all right. The kings from Orion don't go into action without coming out on top. As we got near the mines I kept my ears open for the sound of shots; but all was still,—not even the kind of hubbub a native force makes when it is on the move. Something had happened, but what it was no man could guess. When we got to where the line was up, we made very good time over the five miles to the mines. No one interfered with us, and the nearer we got the greater grew my certainty. Soon we were at the pickets, who had nothing to tell us; and then we were racing up the long sandy street to the offices, and there, sitting smoking on the doorstep of the hotel, surrounded by everybody who was not on duty, were Mackay and Ashurst.

"They were an odd pair. Ashurst still wore his uniform; but he seemed to have been rolling about in it on the ground; his sleek hair was wildly ruffled, and he was poking holes in the dust with his sword. Mackay had lost his topper, and wore a disreputable cap, his ancient frock-coat was without buttons, and his tie had worked itself up behind his ears. They talked excitedly to each other, now and then vouchsafing a scrap of information to an equally excited audience. When they saw me they rose and rushed for me, and dragged me between them up the street, while the crowd tailed at our heels.

"'Ye're a true prophet, Captain Thirlstone,' Mackay began, 'and I ask your pardon for doubting you. Ye said the Governor only needed a crisis to behave like a man. Well, the crisis has come; and if there's a man alive in this sinful world, it's that chief o' yours.' And then his emotion overcame him, and, hard-bitten devil as he was, he sat down on the ground and gasped with hysterical laughter, while Ashurst, with a very red face, kept putting the wrong end of a cigarette in his mouth and swearing profanely.

"I never remember a madder sight. There was the brassy blue sky and reddish granite rock and acres of thick red dust. The scrub had that metallic greenness which you find in all copper places. Pretty unwholesome it looked, and the crowd, which had got round us again, was more unwholesome still. Fat Jew boys, with diamond rings on dirty fingers and greasy linen cuffs, kept staring at us with twitching lips; and one or two smarter fellows in riding-breeches, mine-managers and suchlike, tried to show their pluck by nervous jokes. And in the middle was Mackay, with his damaged frocker, drawling out his story in broad Scots.

"'He made this laddie put on his braws, and he commandeered this iniquitous garment for me. I've raxed its seams, and it'll never look again on the man that owns it. Syne he arrayed himself in purple and fine linen till he was like the king's daughter, all glorious without; and says he to me, "Mackay," he says, "we'll go and talk to these uncovenanted deevils in their own tongue. We'll visit them at home, Mackay," he says. "They're none such bad fellows, but they want a little humouring from men like you and me." So we got on our horses and started the procession—the Governor with his head in the air, and the laddie endeavouring to look calm and collected, and me praying to the God of Israel and trying to keep my breeks from working up above my knees. I've been in Kaffir wars afore, but I never thought I would ride without weapon of any kind into such a black Armageddon. I am a peaceable man for ordinar', and a canny one, but I wasna myself in that hour. Man, Thirlstone, I was that overcome by the spirit of your chief, that if he had bidden me gang alone on the same errand, I wouldna say but what I would have gone.

"'We hadna ridden half a mile before we saw the indunas and their men, ten thousand if there was one, and terrible as an army with banners. I speak feeguratively, for they hadna the scrap of a flag among them. They were beating the war-drums, and the young men were dancing with their big skin shields and wagging their ostrich feathers, so I saw they were out for business. I'll no' say but what my blood ran cold, but the Governor's eye got brighter and his back stiffer. "Kings may be blest," I says to myself, "but thou art glorious."

"'We rode straight for the centre of the crowd, where the young men were thickest and the big war-drums lay. As soon as they saw us a dozen lifted their spears and ran out to meet us. But they stopped after six steps. The sun glinted on the Governor's gold lace and my lum hat, and no doubt they thought we were heathen deities descended from the heavens. Down they went on their faces, and then back like rabbits to the rest, while the drums stopped, and the whole body awaited our coming in a silence like the tomb.

"'Never a word we spoke, but just jogged on with our chins cocked up till we were forenent the big drum, where yon old scoundrel Umgazi was standing with his young men looking as black as sin. For a moment their spears were shaking in their hands, and I heard the click of a breech-bolt. If we had winked an eye we would have become pincushions that instant. But some unearthly power upheld us. Even the laddie kept a stiff face, and for me I forgot my breeks in watching the Governor. He looked as solemn as an archangel, and comes to a halt opposite Umgazi, when he glowers at the old man for maybe three minutes, while we formed up behind him. Their eyes fell before his, and by-and-by their spears dropped to their sides. "The father has come to his children," says he in their own tongue. "What do the children seek from their father?"

"'Ye see the cleverness of the thing. The man's past folly came to help him. The natives had never seen the Governor before till they beheld him in gold lace and a cocked hat on a muckle horse, speaking their own tongue and looking like a destroying angel. I tell you the Labonga's knees were loosed under them. They durstna speak a word until the Governor repeated the question in the same quiet, steely voice. "You seek something," he said, "else you had not come out to meet me in your numbers. The father waits to hear the children's desires."

"'Then Umgazi found his tongue and began an uneasy speech. The mines, he said, truly enough, were the abode of devils, who compelled the people to work under the ground. The crops were unreaped and the buck went unspeared, because there were no young men left to him. Their father had been away or asleep, they thought, for no help had come from him; therefore it had seemed good to them, being freemen and warriors, to seek help for themselves.

"'The Governor listened to it all with a set face. Then

he smiled at them with supernatural assurance. They were fools, he said, and people of little wit, and he flung the better part of the Book of Job at their heads. The Lord kens where the man got his uncanny knowledge of the Labonga. He had all their heathen customs by heart, and he played with them like a cat with a mouse. He told them they were damned rascals to make such a stramash, and damned fools to think they could frighten the white man by their demonstrations. There was no brag about his words, just a calm statement of fact. At the same time, he said, he had no mind to let anyone wrong his children, and if any wrong had been done it should be righted. It was not meet, he said, that the young men should be taken from the villages unless by their own consent, though it was his desire that such young men as could be spared should have a chance of earning an honest penny. And then he fired at them some stuff about the British Empire and the King, and you could see the Labonga imbibing it like water. The man in a cocked hat might have told them that the sky was yellow, and they would have swallowed it.

" ' " I have spoken," he says at last, and there was a great shout from the young men, and old Umgazi looked pretty foolish. They were coming round our horses to touch our stirrups with their noses, but the Governor stopped them.

" ' " My children will pile their weapons in front of me," says he, " to show me how they have armed themselves, and likewise to prove that their folly is at an end. All except a dozen," says he, " whom I select as a bodyguard." And there and then he picked twelve lusty savages for his guard, while the rest without a cheep stacked their spears and guns forenent the big drum.

" ' Then he turned to us and spoke in English. " Get back to the mines hell-for-leather, and tell them what's happening, and see that you get up some kind of a show for to-morrow at noon. I will bring the chiefs, and we'll feast them. Get all the bands you can, and let them play me in.

Tell the mines fellows to look active, for it's the chance of their lives." Then he says to the Labonga, "My men will return," he says, "but as for me I will spend the night with my children. Make ready food, but let no beer be made, for it is a solemn occasion."

"'And so we left him. I will not describe how I spent last night mysel', but I have something to say about this remarkable phenomenon. I could enlarge on the triumph of mind over matter. . . .'

"Mackay did not enlarge. He stopped, cocked his ears, and looked down the road, from which came the strains of 'Annie Laurie,' played with much spirit but grievously out of tune. Followed 'The British Grenadiers,' and then an attempt at 'The March of the Priests.' Mackay rose in excitement and began to crane his disreputable neck, while the band—a fine scratch collection of instruments—took up their stand at the end of the street, flanked by a piper in khaki who performed when their breath failed. Mackay chuckled with satisfaction. 'The deevils have entered into the spirit of my instructions,' he said. 'In a wee bit the place will be like Falkirk Tryst for din.'

"Punctually at twelve there came a great hullabaloo up the road, the beating of drums and the yelling of natives, and presently the procession hove in sight. There was Tommy on his horse, and on each side of him six savages with feather head-dress, and shields and war-paint complete. After him trooped about thirty of the great chiefs, walking two by two, for all the world like an Aldershot parade. They carried no arms, but the bodyguard shook their spears, and let yells out of them that would have scared Julius Cæsar. Then the band started in, and the piper blew up, and the mines people commenced to cheer, and I thought the heavens would fall. Long before Tommy came abreast of me I knew what I should see. His uniform looked as if it had been slept in, and his orders were all awry. But he had his head flung back, and his eyes very bright, and his jaw set square. He never looked to right or left, never recognised me or anybody, for he was seeing something quite different from the red road and the white shanties and the hot sky."

The fire had almost died out. Thirlstone stooped for a moment and stirred the peats.

"Yes," he said, "I knew that in his fool's ear the trumpets of all Asia were ringing, and the King of Bokhara was entering Samarkand."

BABYLON.

(*The Song of* NEHEMIAH'S *Workmen.*)

How many miles to Babylon?
Three score and ten.
Can I get there by candle-light?
Yes, and back again.

We are come back from Babylon,
Out of the plains and the glare,
To the little hills of our own country
And the sting of our kindred air;
To the rickle of stones on the red rock's edge
Which Kedron cleaves like a sword.
We will build the walls of Zion again,
To the glory of Zion's Lord.

Now is no more of dalliance
By the reedy waters in spring,
When we sang of home, and sighed, and dreamed,
And wept on remembering.
Now we are back in our ancient hills
Out of the plains and the sun;
But before we make it a dwelling-place
There's a wonderful lot to be done.

The walls are to build from west to east,
  From Gihon to Olivet,
Waters to lead and wells to clear,
  And the garden furrows to set.
From the Sheep Gate to the Fish Gate
  Is a welter of mire and mess;
And southward over the common lands
  'Tis a dragon's wilderness.

The Courts of the Lord are a heap of dust
  Where the hill winds whistle and race,
And the noble pillars of God His House
  Stand in a ruined place.
In the Holy of Holies foxes lair,
  And owls and night-birds build.
There's a deal to do ere we patch it anew
  As our father Solomon willed.

Now is the day of the ordered life
  And the law which all obey.
We toil by rote and speak by note
  And never a soul dare stray.
Ever among us a lean old man
  Keepeth his watch and ward,
Crying, "The Lord hath set you free:
  Prepare ye the way of the Lord."

A goodly task we are called unto,
  A task to dream on o' nights,—
Work for Judah and Judah's God,
  Setting our land to rights;
Everything fair and all things square
  And straight as a plummet string.—
Is it mortal guile, if once in a while
  Our thoughts go wandering? . . .

We were not slaves in Babylon,
For the gate of our souls lay free,
There in that vast and sunlit land
On the edges of mystery.
Daily we wrought and daily we thought,
And we chafed not at rod and power,
For Sinim, Sabæa, and dusky Hind
Talked to us hour by hour.

The man who lives in Babylon
May poorly sup and fare,
But loves and lures from the ends of the earth
Beckon him everywhere.
Next year he too may have sailed strange seas
And conquered a diadem ;
For kings are as common in Babylon
As crows in Bethlehem.

Here we are bound to the common round
In a land which knows not change.
Nothing befalleth to stir the blood
Or quicken the heart to range ;
Never a hope that we cannot plumb
Or a stranger visage in sight,—
At the most a sleek Samaritan
Or a ragged Amorite.

Here we are sober and staid of soul,
Working beneath the law,
Settled amid our fathers' dust,
Seeing the hills they saw.
All things fixed and determinate,
Chiselled and squared by rule ;—
Is it mortal guile once in a while
To try and escape from school ?

We will go back to Babylon,
  Silently one by one,
Out from the hills and the laggard brooks
  To the streams that brim in the sun.
Only a moment, Lord, we crave,
  To breathe and listen and see.—
Then we start anew with muscle and thew
  To hammer trestles for Thee.

IX. THE GREEN GLEN.

I.

I FIRST saw the Glen when I was eleven years old, a small boy consumed with a passion for trout. Adventuring on a rusty bicycle I had penetrated to remote dales, and made baskets in streams which no 'Anglers' Guide' ever heard of. One day I had fished the sources of the Cauldshaw, and, the sun being yet high, bethought me of the Fawn, which flowed on the other side of the narrow watershed. I shouldered my rod and tramped up the mossy spaces of the burn-head, till I waded deep in the bracken of the ridge. There on the summit the heather ended as if ruled by a gardener's line. I was looking into a narrow glen which ran from a round hope till a broad green hill baulked the view. From beginning to end there was no house, not even a sheep-fold or a dyke. I remember my amazement at its indescribable greenness. There was the yellow-green of moss, the old velvet of mountain turf, the grey-green of bent on the hill-brow; but all was green, without tree or crag or heather bush to distract the eye. Through the middle of it ran the Fawn, a very fishable stream to my notion, and I ran down the brae with hope high in my heart.

But I never cast a fly in those waters. Long before I was down the hill the eeriness and the solitariness of the place weighed on my mind. There was no man here, and no sign of man. There were no whaups crying, or grouse to upbraid my presence. It was still as the grave, but for the lilt of the stream; and it was terribly green. I remembered a line of a song that ploughmen used to whistle—"*The wild glen sae green*"—and I thought how much deeper this green wildness was than any rock and heather. The still slopes and folds of hill seemed to my unquiet eye to stretch to eternity.

At the edge of the burn was a rude mound, embanked like some Roman fort. With a fluttering heart I began to put my rod together. The Fawn dashed and swirled in noble pools, but I could not keep my eyes on it. The green hills shut me in, and the awe of them brooded over me. I was mortally afraid, and not ashamed of my fear. I could not give a name to it, but something uncanny was in the air: not terrible exactly, or threatening, but inhumanly strange. I clutched my rod—the butt and middle piece were put together—and fled the way I had come. I do not think I stopped running till I fell panting by the side of the Cauldshaw among the friendly heather.

II.

Twenty years later, when the doings of eleven are a faint memory, chance set me fishing the lower streams of the Fawn. It was a clear June day, but the waters were too low and my basket was light. I fished like an epicure, a cast in each pool sufficing for me; and presently I had rounded the shoulder of the green hill which cuts the valley in two. They call it the Green Dod, and there is no greener hill in that green country. I found myself in an upland glen, where the Fawn had sunk to a mountain burn. The place was very soothing and quiet, and idly I wandered on, drinking in the peace of the hills. Then something in the contours awakened a memory, and I recalled my boyish escapade. The years have their consolations, for what had once terrified now charmed. I laughed at the scared little sinner, whose trembling legs had once twinkled up those braes. I put by my rod and abandoned myself to the delights of the greenness. Far up on the hill shoulders white sheep were dotted, but the water-side was empty. Not even a water-crow was visible, and in the patches of bog there was no sign of snipe. The place was full of a delicious desolation. There were the strait green sides, the Green Dod at the foot, a green hope at the head, and only the clear singing water stirred in the sunny afternoon.

I found a seat on a mound, and basked in deep content. It was the height of pastoral, yet without sheep or shepherd. The Fawn was a true Border stream, jewelled in sunlight, but wan as death under grey skies. I wondered how I had hitherto missed this happy valley. Nature had wrought it in a kindly mood, and hidden it very far from men. It must, I thought, have had a gracious history. There was no terror in its solitude. I could not imagine the cry of death from the burn, or harsh deeds done on those green lawns. Who had owned it in old days? Perhaps some Roman, pushing north with his bronze soldiers against the Picts, had been caught by its grace, and christened it by the name of his woodland god. True Thomas may have walked by its streams. But its story must have been chiefly of elves and fairy folk, for it wore the fairy livery.

I looked at the mound on which I sat, and saw that it had once been the site of a dwelling. It was all crisp moorland turf, gemmed with eyebright and milkwort, but the rampart had been made by man. Scraping with the butt-end of my rod, I laid bare a chiselled block. This had been no sheepfold or shepherd's cot, but a tower.

The discovery stirred a fresh strain of fancy. Some old raider had his keep here, and filled the glen with ill-gotten cattle. I pictured the forays returning over the green hills in some autumn twilight. I saw beacons fired on the tops, and the winter snows reddened with blood. Just then a cloud came over the sun, and the grace of the valley vanished Now the stream ran wan, and I saw that the glen was wild and very lonely. Terror had dwelt here as well as peace. I remembered the boy of eleven, who on this very mound had picked up his rod and run.

That evening at Hardriding I hunted the library for local histories. They could not tell me much, being mostly the casual compilations of local ministers. But I found one thing of interest. I had been right about True Thomas. It seemed that the Rhymer had honoured the Fawn with a couplet of doubtful Latin:

Ubi Faunus fluit
Spes mortalis ruit.

I had no notion what he meant, and suspected the hand of the Reverend Mr Gilfillan *circa* 1780.

III.

Fortune and a broken leg gave me some leisure that winter, and I spent it in searching for the history of what I had come to call the Green Glen. For two hundred years back it was plain going. Along with a dozen other valleys it had been swept into the net of the noble house which had built its fortunes on the fall of the turbulent little Border septs. Earlier it had been by turns in the hands of two families, both long perished—Home of Hardriding and Douglas of Cauldshaw. That took me back to the fourteenth century or thereabouts, where the history stopped short. But I found a charter of Melrose a century before, from which it appeared that the lands of Fawn, "the nether and hither glens thereof," had been in the hands of the monks, who had profited by the good grazing. A chapel of Our Lady had stood by the burn-side, endowed with a hundred merks a year by a certain Simon de Fries in penance for the slaying of an erring wife. There my tale ended, but I hazarded a guess. Fifty years ago a slab was found near Hadrian's Wall with a list of stations on the great road which ran north to the land of the Picts. You will find it copied in the Berlin *Corpus*, and there is much dispute about the identification of the names. One of them is a certain *Fauni Castellum*, which scholars have fastened on a dozen places between Ardoch and Melrose. I was myself convinced that the castellum was the mound in the Green Glen, the more so as Mr Gilfillan reported a find there of gold coins of the Antonines in 1758. It is true that the place was some miles from the main line of transit, but it would command the hill-roads from the West. Besides, might it not have been a sacred place, half fort, half shrine, an outpost of the dying faith? Why, otherwise, the strange name of the woodland god?

These were all my facts,—too few on which to spin the delicate web of history. But my imagination was kindled, and I set to work. If I were right, this glen had a virtue which had drawn to it many races. Little as the recorded history was, it was far more than the due of an inconsiderable howe of the hills. Rome had made it a halting-place and consecrated it to her gods; the Church had built a shrine in it; two famous clans had fought furiously for its sake. My first impression was justified, for it had been no common place. Some ancient *aura* had brooded over its greenness and compelled men's souls.

Bit by bit from monkish Latin, from fragments of ballads, from cumbrous family histories, and from musty chronicles, I built up the shadow of a tale. Rome gave me nothing—the fog of years lay too thick over that greatest of mortal pages; but I hazarded a guess that the broken Satyr's head, found in some unknown Border earthwork and now in the Grange collection, had come from my glen. Perhaps the Melrose monks had found it and copied it in their gargoyles. But of the Christian shrine I had something to tell. The chapel seems to have had an ill reputation for a holy place. The chapter of Melrose in or about 1250 held an inquisition into the doings of a certain John of Fawn, who tended the shrine with unhallowed service. There were complaints of his successor, a monk who bore the name of Lapidarius; and the grand climax was reached in the fate of one Andrew de Faun, a priest, says the record, who had the unpleasing gift "diabolos convocandi." He was hand in glove with Lord Soulis, whose castle of Hermitage lay some twenty miles over the hills. Of his iniquities it is recorded that the country folk grew weary, and one October night surprised him at the business. He confessed his sins under the pressure of boiling lead, was duly burned, and his ashes cast into Tweed to be borne to the cleansing sea.

To the monks succeeded the Barons, the first being the tragically fated house of Home. But side by side with the record of their moorland wars I found a ballad history. Fawn had caught the fancy of the wandering minstrel. The heroine of the ghastly "Riding of Etterick" had eyes "grey as Fawn." (The other reading "grey as a fawn" is obvious nonsense.) The tryst for true love on Beltane's E'en was the Fawn side, and it was in the Green Glen that young Brokyn found himself asleep on his return from Fairyland.

"And when ye come to Fawn water,"

says the wise wife in "May Margaret,"

"I bid ye lout fu' low,
And say three prayers to Christes grace
Afore ye ride the flow."

In the lovely fragment, "The Thorn of Life," there is a variant, not given by Child, which tells how on Midsummer morning the lady washed herself with dew "clear as dawn"—an absurd literary phrase which spoils the poem. My emendation "Fawn" is, I take it, certain. In the later riding ballads the name is still more frequent. The doomed raider in "Carlisle Town" swears that Fawn will run red as blood ere his wrongs are forgotten. In "Castle Gay" the dying Home craves, like King David, for a draught of Fawn water; and in "Lord Archibald's Good-night" there is a strange line about "the holy wells of Fawn." No doubt the line is corrupt, but the form of the corruption testifies to the spell of the Green Glen.

The Homes of Hardriding marched through disorder and violence to catastrophe. Never more than a hill clan, and kin to no powerful house, they persisted for three centuries by sheer audacity and pride. They held the Fawn glen and built a tower in it, but their real seat was Hardriding in the lower valley. The wave of Douglas aggression flowed round them, but they stoutly resisted, and it was only the power of the great Warden of the Marches that seized Fawnside for the Cauldshaw branch of his house. The battle in which Piers Home died by the hand of young Cauldshaw was fought in the Green Glen. Presently the Douglases were in trouble with the King, and a younger Piers, under a King's commission, won back his lands and chased Cauldshaw into Northumberland. The Douglas clan was as often as not in treaty with the English Warden, while the Hardriding folk were vehemently Scottish, and, alone of their name, gave a good account of themselves at Flodden. The fortunes of the two houses see-sawed so long as lands were won and kept by the strong arm alone. By-and-by came the day of smooth things, when a parchment was more potent than the sword, and both Home and Douglas withered, like hill plants brought into a lowland garden.

It was all an unedifying tale of blood and treason, but in reading it I was struck by one curious fact. Every critical event in the fortunes of the two clans befell in the Green Glen. There the leaders died in battle or in duel, and there a shameless victor celebrated his mastery. It was, so to speak, the citadel, of which the possession was the proof of triumph. It can have had but little value in itself, for the tower by the burn was scarcely a fortalice, and was never seriously dwelled in. Indeed it is referred to not as a castle but as a "bower." When a Douglas defied a Home he summoned him to meet him by the "Bower o' Fawn." This same Bower was the centre of a pretty tale, when for once the bloodstained record emerges into the clear air of pastoral. The Fawn glen did not always pass by war; once it fell to the Douglases by marriage. Marjory of Hardriding, walking one evening by the stream, fell in with the young Douglas, sore wounded in a forest hunt. In the Bower she tended his wounds, and hid him from her fierce clan. Love ripened, and one July morn came the heir of Cauldshaw to Hardriding gates on an errand of peace. But the Home was surly, and the Douglas retired with a bitter denial and an arrow in his corselet. Thereupon Maid Marjory took the matter into her own hands, and rode over the hills to her lover. A gallant lass this, for, after a hurried wedding at the Kirk o' Shaws, she returned with her man to the Fawn Bower to confront an angry father and six angrier brothers. She offered peace or war, but declared that, if war it should be, she herself would fight in the first rank of the Douglases. Whereupon, it is said, old Piers, struck with wonder and delight at the courage he had begotten, declared for peace, and the Green Glen was her dowry.

IV.

The thing became an obsession with me, and I could not let this nook of history alone. Weary hours were spent in the search for Homes and Douglases. Why I wasted my time thus I cannot tell. I told myself it was part of the spell of the Green Glen. "The place was silent and *aware*," as Browning says. I could not think that the virtue had departed and that the romance of Fawn was a past tale. Now it had no visitants save a shepherd taking a short-cut or a fisherman with a taste for moorland trout. But some day a horseman on a fateful errand would stir its waters, or the Bower witness a new pastoral. I told myself that the wise years might ordain a long interval, but sooner or later they would ring up the curtain on the play.

A needle in a haystack was a simple quest compared to

mine. History, which loves to leave fringes and loose threads, had cut the record of Home and Douglas with her sharpest shears. The two families disappeared within the same decade. Cauldshaw had chosen the King's side in the Covenant wars, and the head of the house, Sir Adam, had been a noted persecutor of the godly. He came to his end by a bullet of the Black Macmichael's somewhere in the hills of Galloway. His son had fought in the Scots Brigade for the French King, and returned about 1710 to find an estate broken by fines and penalties. We see him last riding south with Mackintosh in the 'Fifteen, but history does not tell us of his fate. He may have died with Derwentwater, or, more likely, he may have escaped and lain low till the hunt passed. Cauldshaw was forfeited and sold, and there was an end of it. Thirty years later I find a Douglas, a locksmith in the High Street of Edinburgh, who may have been his son, since he was gently born and yet clearly of no other known Douglas sept. After that the shears are at work. My note at the end of my researches was, "merged in the burgesses of Edinburgh."

Hardriding showed a similar tale, save that the Homes stood for the Covenant. One of them, Piers or Patrick, swung in the Grassmarket, and was the subject of the eulogies of Wodrow and Patrick Walker. An odd type of saint, his godliness was proved chiefly by his ferocity against the King's officers, for whom he would lie in wait behind a dyke with a musket. He died gallantly, declaiming the 23rd Psalm. The Jacobite rising brought Hardriding round to the side of Cauldshaw. Home and Douglas rode south together, and the fate of the first at any rate is clear. He fell in the rout of Preston, charging with a mouthful of oaths and texts. He left landless sons who disappear into the mist, and the ancient name of Home of Hardriding died in the land. David Hume, the philosopher, in his cups used to claim kin with the house, but it is recorded that David's friends did not take him seriously.

V.

About that time I used to try to analyse the impression the Green Glen made upon me. I went to it often and in all weathers, but especially in the soft June days and the flaming twilights of October. At first I thought that the attraction was the peace of it, Wordsworth's "sleep that is among the lonely hills." Certainly it was very quiet and hallowed, with that brooding stillness which is a positive thing and not a mere absence of unrest. I have gone there, worried and distraught, and returned at ease with the world. Once, I remember, I came to it after fighting a forlorn bye-election in an English slum, with my brain fagged and dull and my nerves a torment. The Glen healed me, plunging me into the deeps of cool old-world shadows. But I soon discovered that the charm was not an opiate, but a stimulant. Its spell was the spell of life. It stirred the blood, comforting failure and nursing hope, but it did not lull to sleep. Once after a bad illness I went to Hardriding to rest, but I could not face the Glen. It only fevered a sick man. Its call was to action, and its ancient genius had no love for weaklings.

Often I tried to test it, to see if others could feel as I did. I was ridiculously unsuccessful. The sportsmen who frequented Hardriding, finding no grouse in the Glen, fought shy of it, and, if chance took them there, lamented the absence of heather. "Pretty place," one young man observed to me, "but no more Scotch than my hat. It might be Sussex. Where's the brown heath and shaggy wood? What! There isn't cover for a tomtit. It's a nasty big slice out of Harry's shooting to have that long bare place taking up room." It was too remote for ladies to picnic in, but one who penetrated as far called it "sweet," and said it reminded her of Dartmoor. The people of the neighbourhood were no better. Keepers took the same view as the Hardriding sportsmen, and the farmer whose lease covered it spoke of it darkly as "Poaverty Neuk." "Food for neither man nor beast," he said. "Something might be done with phosphates, but I've no money to spend. It would make a grand dam if any town wanted a water-supply." Good business-like views, but no hint anywhere of the strangeness which to me had made it a kind of sanctuary.

There was one exception, the shepherd of the Nine Stane Rig. He was a young man, with a fiery red head and a taste for poetry. He would declaim Burns and Hogg with gusto, and was noted at "kirns" and weddings for his robust rendering of songs like "When the Kye come Hame" and "Robin Tamson's Smiddy." I used to accompany him sometimes on his rounds, and he spoke to me of the Green Glen.

"It's a bonny bit," he once said, waving his arm towards the Green Dod. "And there's ae queer thing about it. Sheep'll no bide in it. Ye may pit a hirsel in at nicht, and every beast 'll be on the tap o' the rig by the mornin'. How d'ye account for that? Mr Yellowlees says the feedin's no guid, and that it wants phosphates. I dinna agree wi' him. I've herdit a' my days, and I never saw better feedin' than by yon burn-side. I've no just fawthomed it yet, but I've an idea o' my ain. I think the glen is an auld kirkyaird. I mind when I herdit in Eskdalemuir there was a bit on the hill whaur Covenanters had been buried, and the sheep were aye sweer to gang near it. Some day I'm thinkin' o' gettin' a spade and howkin'. I micht find something queer. . . ."

VI.

I came to regard the Green Glen as my own exclusive property, which shared with me a secret. It was a pleasant intimacy, and I had resigned myself to its limits, conscious that the curtain of the past was drawn too close to allow more than one little chink to be seen. Then one day Fate brought Linford across my path.

I had known him slightly for several years. I can see

him now as I first knew him, a big solemn young man, too heavy for elegance, and an awkward weight for a horse. We met first one spring at Valescure, and a lonely fortnight established a kind of friendship between us. He was a modest being, full of halting sympathies and interests, for which he rarely found words. His family had been settled for two generations in Australia, sheep-farming in the good days when the big profits were made. His father had made a second fortune in a gold mine, and, disliking the land legislation of the country, had sold his farms and brought his boy to England. An undistinguished progress through a public school and Oxford had left him without a profession, and, his father having died, with no near relations and a ridiculous amount of money. He should have been a soldier, but somehow had missed his chance. The man was in no way slack, but he gave me the impression of having no niche to fit into. He was very English in speech and manners, but he seemed to stand outside all the ordinary English occupations and look on. Not that he didn't do most things well. He was a magnificent shot, a first-rate horseman, and the best man to sail a boat I have ever met. He read much, had travelled considerably, and had a keen interest in scientific geography. I thought he had found a job when he took a notion of exploring the Brahmaputra gorges, but the expedition fell through and his interest flagged. He belonged to many clubs, and had a few hundred acquaintances; but beyond myself I don't think he had a friend.

He used to come to see me, and I tried to understand what puzzled him. For puzzled he was—not unhappy or disillusioned, but simply puzzled with life. Somehow he did not fit in with the world around him. I used to think it would have been better if he had never left Australia. There he had a ready-made environment; here in England he had to make his own, and he did not seem to have the knack of it. People liked him, and thought him, for all his stiffness, a good fellow. But he never accepted anybody or anything as his own; he was always the observant and sympathetic stranger. I began to realise that my friend, with all his advantages, was desperately homeless.

To myself, as I thought about him, I prescribed marriage. *Vix ea nostra voco* might have been his motto about most things, but in a wife he would find something his very own. The thing was obvious, but I saw also that he would be a hard fellow to marry. He was hopelessly shy and curiously unimpressionable. I do not remember that he ever spoke to me of any woman, and he avoided every chance of meeting them. I only once saw his tall figure at a dance, when he looked like nothing so much as Marius among the ruins of Carthage.

Hunting was his main hobby, and one January I found myself staying under the same roof with him in the Cottesmore country. He was, as I have said, a bold and fine rider, but he had to know his horse, and on this occasion our host mounted both of us. There was an ugly banked fence where he misjudged his animal's powers, and came down in a heap on a hardish bit of ground. I thought his neck was broken, and prepared for the worst, as I helped three other white-faced men to get him clear. But it was only a slight concussion, a broken finger, and a dislocated shoulder. He had a bad night, but next day was little th worse for his fall, and, frost having set in, I spent most of the afternoon in his bedroom.

He wore a ring which I had often noticed, a little engraved carnelian in a heavy setting of Australian gold. In doctoring his hand it had been removed, and now lay on the dressing table. We were talking idly of runs and spills, and, as we talked, I picked it up and examined it.

The stone was old and curious. There was no motto, and the carving seemed to be a heart transfixed by an arrow. I thought it the ordinary trumpery love-token—Cupid and his darts—when I noticed something more. The heart was crowned, and the barb transfixing it was not an arrow but a spear.

The sight roused me to the liveliest interest. For the cognisance belonged to one house and one house alone. It was Douglas of Cauldshaw who had carried the family badge with this strange difference. Mary of Scots, it was said, had given them the spear, for to the last they had stood by that melancholy lady.

"Where did you get this?" I asked.

"What? The ring? It was my father's. An ugly thing."

I looked at it again. "It has an odd crest. Did you ever inquire about it?"

He said No. He knew little heraldry, and didn't want to pretend to what didn't belong to him. Then he corrected himself. He thought that the thing was a family relic, right enough. His father had got the stone in turn from his mother, and had had it reset. He thought, but he wasn't sure, that it had been a long time in his grandmother's family.

"What was her name?" I asked eagerly.

The answer was disappointing. "Brown," he said. "They had the Wooramanga place."

I asked if they came from Scotland. "No," he said. "They were Yorkshire, I think. But wait a bit. I think—yes—I have heard my father say something about the Browns being Scotch—Brouns, you know."

This was a false scent and I tried again. But Linford had nothing to tell me. He had no family papers or jewels or pictures, nothing but the one ring. I could see that he was puzzled at my interest, and to my horror offered to pay the Heralds' College to investigate matters. I made him promise to let the Heralds alone, and tried to get more about his grandmother. She had been a tall thin old lady, as he remembered her, with a north-country accent. She had disliked Melbourne intensely. That was all he could tell; not a saying or a rhyme or a memory to link her with those who had borne the ring's cognisance.

I heard, however, another startling thing that afternoon. Linford, blushing delightfully, confessed that he was in love.

He had no chance, of course, wasn't good enough, and all the rest of it. When I heard that the lady was Virginia Dasent I was inclined to agree with him. Miss Dasent was very high game for Linford to fly at—or for anybody.

VII.

Language is too coarse a medium in which to give a true portrait of Miss Virginia. Airy diaphanous colours and the sharp fineness of marble are needed; and something more, something to recapture that grace, wild and bird-like and only half mortal, which for three seasons turned all our heads. She was an astounding success. Coming from nowhere, and as innocent as a child of ambition, she made every man her most hopeless and humble servant. I think her charm was her pure girlishness—neither childish nor womanly, you understand. She had the air of one who faces the world frankly but does not accept it. She was a changeling, a wanderer, a dainty solitary figure on the weary old roads of life. I remember thinking, when I first saw her, that she might have stood for a statue of incarnate Wonder.

I knew her a little, well enough to see the hopelessness of my friend's case. She was an American—from one of the Carolinas, I believe; and Lady Amysfort took her about in London. I do not think that they were related. I hope my friends beyond the Atlantic will forgive me for saying that Miss Virginia was like no American I have ever met. Not that she had any of the sad homeless vulgarity of the denationalised. She was a fervent patriot, and had a delicious variety of the national humour. But I could not fit her in with her great continent. Indeed, I could not place her anywhere in any society. She belonged to some fanciful world of her own; but all the time she seemed to me to be looking for something—perhaps for her lost material heritage.

I was more interested, however, in Linford than in Miss Dasent. I could find out no more from him about his forebears, but I wondered if the Glen could tell me anything. Supposing I took him there, unprepared, of course, by any warning of mine, might not he feel the spell of it? If he did, I would be convinced of the Douglas blood; for I was certain that not otherwise would so prosaic a being feel so subtle a charm.

I persuaded him to take the Hardriding shootings; with an option to purchase, too, for Harry's finances were now past praying for. The chance came two days before the Twelfth, when he and I were alone in the house. It was a mild, blue August day, with clear distances and a cool breeze, and as we rounded the Green Dod I thought that my Glen was nobly dressed for us. I had hoped for some cry of delight, but none came. Linford stalked through the bent, muttering something about black-game.

We came to the mound by the waterside, Maid Marjory's Bower, and stretched ourselves on the scented turf. Then a curious thing happened to me. A light wind came up the stream, rippling the pools and sending a grey shiver over the grasses. Suddenly I became oppressed with a mortal fear. I must have lain limp and white, looking dumbly at the opposite hill. I had no notion what I feared, but it was worse than my old boyish adventure, for, though I longed madly to flee, I knew I could not. The Green Glen was trying me, and if I failed I had lost its secret for ever. I shut my teeth, and for a second or two hung at the limit of my endurance. Then it all passed. I found myself lying back on the mound, desperately sleepy and dripping with sweat, as if I had run twenty miles.

I mopped my brow and looked at Linford. He was quite unperturbed, and had got out his pouch and was filling his pipe. He glanced at me curiously.

"You're in pretty bad condition, old chap," he observed. "You'll founder on the Twelfth if you drip like this in an afternoon saunter."

He got up and stretched himself. "Let's go back," he

said. "There isn't a beast or bird in the place. I am glad I came here, for it will keep us from wasting time over it."

I followed him, still shaky and acutely disappointed. The Glen had nothing to say to him. The ring was an accident, and the Cauldshaw stock was still to find. And yet as we walked home, I began to doubt. The Glen had been not for Douglas or Home alone, but for both. What if a Home were needed to complete the circuit?

It was a possible explanation. Besides, the extraordinary seizure which had befallen me that afternoon seemed to argue that the visit had not been meaningless. I was perfectly well and normal, and I had sat on the mound a hundred times before. Might it not be that the Glen had been stirred, and was striving to tell us its secret? Then I began to laugh, and told myself that I was a fool to treat my fancies as solid facts.

VIII.

That winter was made memorable to me, and a good many others, by Virginia Dasent. The Amysforts went to Egypt, leaving her very much to her own devices. She hunted a little and spent some time in country-houses; but mostly she was to be found in London, a city for which she had an inordinate love. This was bad for Linford, who stayed devotedly in town, and being deprived of healthful exercise put on flesh and lost spirits. I found him in the club one afternoon in a very bad temper. I alone knew of his hopeless plight, and with me he did not trouble to keep up appearances.

"I get no forrarder," he groaned. "She tolerates me as she tolerates everybody else. Lord, how I hate that kind smile of hers! She isn't a woman, Jack. She's an adorable sort of bird that flits about and never settles. You know the way she holds her head forward and peers away beyond you. She's always preening for another flight."

Love was making him a psychologist, for Miss Virginia's maddening charm lay in just that bird-like detachment. We had become very good friends, she and I; and often of a late afternoon we talked in the Amysforts' big ugly drawing-room. She liked me because I was interested in old things and odd bypaths, for I found that the child bubbled over with romance. A lonely girlhood in some Carolinian manor had given her fancy rich feeding. Half in a world of books, half in a world of pure dreaming, she took her airy way. She had about as much worldliness as St Theresa, and much less worldly knowledge. Frankly, I was a little afraid for her; some day disillusion would come, and come cruelly. There was a loneliness about her, as about Linford, but it was the loneliness of a happy preoccupation. Some day those wondering eyes would find the world less marvellous, and then her heart would break. Or would she carry her fresh childlike interest undimmed to the end? I could not tell, but I argued badly for Linford's chances. He was far too eligible—young, good-looking, preposterously rich. The man who was to win Miss Virginia's heart, I thought, must come riding in the fearless old fashion. Linford was as romantic in the ordinary sense of the word as a Republican senator of Virginia's native land.

That was my first impression, but I found cause to alter it slightly. As I came to know her better, new avenues opened up in her soul. She had an excellent brain, very clever, shrewd and subtle, and behind all her fancies I was aware of a solid rock of common-sense. She was not a ready talker, and never rhapsodised. Little odd phrases, a shrug and a laugh, gave the key to her whimsical world. But on a matter of prosaic fact I found her amazingly practical. More than once she offered me advice, with a little wise air which spoke of youth, but with a penetration, too, which took my breath away. I put my surprise into words. "Of course I'm practical," she said. "I'm more than half Scotch, you know."

I thought nothing of it at the time, for American girls have a habit of being either Scotch or early Norman. I remember asking her if she had ever been to Scotland, and she said—No: not yet. She had not had time. But some day . . .

I was inclined to be a little angry with both her and Linford. He went about like a sheep, a ridiculous figure of purposeless melancholy, and the deeper he sank in this mood the worse it was for his chances. As for the lady, I began to think her almost inhuman. I wondered if she were not perfectly heartless, hollow within like an Ell-woman. She seemed unconscious of the havoc she was causing everywhere. I think I would have preferred a common flirt to this unearthly aloofness. But her eyes used always to make me revise my judgments: they were so innocent and young. Some day she would awaken, I told myself. Some day the sleeping princess would be kissed into life. But I was pretty certain that, unless a miracle happened, it would be none of Linford's doing.

It was one morning in the Park in early May that she exploded the mine under my feet. She had been riding with Linford, and turned, as I came up, to accompany me. I don't know what they had been talking about, but her eyes were shining, her colour high, and her lips very tight.

"We have been discussing Scotch places," she volunteered. "It is very tiresome. I wanted a place, and Mr Linford seems to have got a long lease of it. He offered to make it over to me, but of course that was impossible. It's a great nuisance, for I had set my heart on it."

I asked the name, and even as I asked I think I guessed the answer.

"Hardriding," she said. "A little old place in the Borders. My family lived there long ago, and I have always meant to make a pilgrimage to it. Caroline Amysfort is going to Bayreuth, so I shall set up as hostess on my own account.

If I can't get Hardriding I must have Cauldshaw. Will you come and stay with me?"

I listened to her, I hope, with an impassive face, but inwardly I was a volcano of excitement. Hardriding and Cauldshaw! Home and Douglas! Was the circuit by some amazing chance to be completed? I wondered how soon I could decently make an appointment with Miss Virginia and get the whole story. She was going away for the week-end, but would be free on Tuesday, rather late. I hugged my impatience for three beastly days.

I had expected a fragment, and found instead a complete and well-authenticated tale. I blessed that lovable American seriousness about genealogies. There was the pedigree neatly inscribed, with excerpts from registers and letters, as business-like, as irrefutable, as a share certificate. After old Sir Piers fell at Preston his eldest son, Gideon, fled to France, and thence to the Canadas. He fought under the French flag, and rose to a colonelcy before he fell at Quebec. He had married a Frenchwoman, and their son—Lewis, I think—took to the sea and did good trade in the smuggling and privateering line along the New England coast. He settled in North Carolina, and, being rich from his ventures, bought a handsome property, and built a manor-house in the colonial style. With his grand-daughter the male line of Home—Miss Virginia pronounced it to rhyme with "loam"—ended. She married a Dasent, son of a neighbouring squire, and was Miss Virginia's grandmother. There it was, all set down in black and white, and very prettily she expounded it to me. I had found the Hardriding stock at last. It had come back to me out of the mist with ample credentials.

Miss Virginia at Cauldshaw, Linford at Hardriding, and between them the Green Glen! Surely the stage was being set at last for the play. My first impulse was to tell her the whole romance. I pictured her delight; I saw the prosaic Linford take on the colour of poetry. But a scruple deterred me. It would be breaking faith with the Green Glen. If the spell were there it needed no preparation of mine for its working. Those starry influences called for respectful treatment. I would go to Hardriding, and some day—some mellow autumn day—Miss Virginia would cross the hills, and Linford would be there by the Bower to meet her!

Meanwhile all that summer the course of true love ran badly. The two were friends after a fashion, but Linford was such a clumsy and uneasy being, and Miss Virginia so swift and evasive, that it seemed impossible that that friendship could ripen. I got very sick of the whole business, angry with Linford, and puzzled about the lady. At one moment I called her inhuman, at another angelic: but, whatever view one took (and after all they came to the same conclusion), she was the most heartbreaking beauty. Her wild childlike eyes looked through one as if to a pleasant country beyond. There is a Greek fable, isn't there? about some hero who needed the touch of his mother the Earth to give him strength. I wondered if she would ever find that earth-kinship, which means common humanity.

IX.

In early August the Lammas floods were high, so that sultriness was purged from the air and the world left clean and rain-washed and sweet-scented. I was staying at Cauldshaw, in a small party which tried in vain to induce its dancing hostess to be still. She was in wild spirits, out at all hours, a crony of shepherds, already learned in the ways of the moors. She had come back, she said, to her own country, and lived every hour in a whirl of delight and wonder. The long round-shouldered hills, the clear burns, the very homely simplicity of the old land ravished her heart. I counted the days till I could take her to the Green Glen.

Then the party melted away, and it was arranged that she should pay a visit of state to Hardriding. I also was bidden, and Linford spent his days in a fever of expectation.

Miss Virginia was scrupulous about the details. She would walk across the hills by the old raiding road from Cauldshaw. I showed her the way, which traversed the Green Glen, and on the map I pointed out the Bower. She clapped her hands with delight at my tale—the barest sketch—of the Home doings. "What an adventure!" she cried. "I shall tell you all about it at dinner. I feel like a princess coming home to her kingdom."

I sincerely hoped that she was. If the Fates were kind this airy spirit should feel the antique spell of earth, and I dared to think that two wanderers might find a home.

To this hour I remember every incident of that autumn day. It was the 3rd of September. The morning broke cold and misty, but by ten o'clock the sun had burned up the rime, and the hills slept in a bright windless calm. I was shooting with Linford, and set out from Cauldshaw at eleven o'clock. Miss Virginia was to leave after luncheon, and, if she followed my directions, would be at Hardriding by six. She would reach the Green Glen about four o'clock, and I laid my plans accordingly.

I shot vilely, for I was full of a curious sense of anticipation. So was Linford, but nothing could impair his skill. We talked very little, I remember; but it took some manœuvring on my part to have the afternoon beat where I wanted it. Linford would have had us try the moors near the house, for his mind was always turning to Hardriding; but after some persuasion I got him to keep to the hills by the Nine Stane Rig, where we looked down on the Green Glen. Had I told him that Miss Virginia was walking, he would have set off then and there to meet her, and spoiled everything. He kept asking me when she would start. "She'll have to go round by the Red Ford," he repeated, "and that means Hardriding at tea-time. We needn't stay too long up here. Hardriding is her family place, so to speak, and I want to be there to welcome her."

Shortly after three we stood on the summit of the Dun Rig, and as I watched the green shoulders of the Fawn Hope I saw a figure cross the sky-line. Then I told Linford the truth. I bade him go up the Glen to meet her and wait for her at the Bower. He looked at me shyly. "You arranged all this?" he asked. "Thanks very much, old man. You've been a pretty good friend to me."

I set off for Hardriding without a glance behind. The Glen was now no place for me. Looking back at my frame of mind, I can see nothing but exhilaration. Some great thing was about to befall two people whom I loved. I had no doubt of the virtue of the place. By devious paths I had brought back to it its old masters. It had whispered its secret to me, and I had repaid it. For the moment I felt that time was not, that death was little, and change a mockery. The wise years let nothing die, and always the circle came full again, bringing back lost hopes and dreams. The still and golden afternoon spoke the same message to my heart. I felt the serene continuance of all things, the sense of something eternal behind the trivial ways of man.

I reached Hardriding a little after four, and according to my plan sat down to read and smoke. But I soon found that idleness was impossible. I was strung too high with expectation. I wandered into the library, and then into the garden, but my eyes were always turning to the shoulder of hill which marked the opening of the Fawn glen. Then I resolved to go to meet Linford. Whatever had happened, it would be right for me to welcome Miss Virginia to Hardriding.

Before I had crossed the lawns my mood changed utterly. I suddenly became a prey to black forebodings. The doggerel Latin of True Thomas rang in my head like the croak of a raven:—

Ubi Faunus fluit
Spes mortalis ruit.

I tried to laugh at it. I told myself that the verses were no doubt the work of a foolish eighteenth-century parson. What harm could follow the meeting of two friends in a hill glen where their forebears had fought and loved? But I reasoned in vain. A deadly depression overmastered me. The light had gone out of the sky, and the bent, all yellow in the westering sun, seemed wan as death.

Where Fawn flows
Man's hope goes.

The dolorous refrain would not leave me.

I emerged from the park into the water meadows where Fawn runs deep among flags and meadow-sweet. Beyond them I came to the lower glen, where the fir-clad slopes leave a thin strip of pasture by the stream. Here I should have met the two, but there was no sign of them. I looked at my watch and found it after five.

Then I began to quicken my pace. My depression had turned to acute anxiety. Before me was half a mile of open strath, and then the Green Dod, where the Glen turned sharply to the right. I ran that half-mile with dread in my heart of what I might see beyond it. But when I came to the Green Dod there was still no sign of a human being. The Fawn flows round the shoulder of hill in a narrow defile, at the upper end of which begins the Green Glen. I resolved to wait there, for I realised that I could not enter the Glen. I can give no reason for this, but I knew the truth of it. My feet could not have carried me round the shoulder of hill.

I did not wait long. Suddenly down the defile came a single figure. It was Linford, but even to my distraught sight a different Linford from him I had known. As I have said, he was a big fellow, a little ungainly, a little afraid of his size. But now he was a noble figure of a man, and as he strode along there was a strange mastery and dignity in him. But why was he alone? I blinked my eyes, for I saw that he was not alone. He carried in his arms something slim and white and very quiet. I crouched behind a boulder as he came near, but he had no eyes for anything but his burden. His head was bent over it, and his face was wild and drawn with grief. Then I saw that a fair head lay limply in the crook of his arm and that the face was very pale. . . .

The doctors called it heart failure. Miss Virginia, said one of them in a moment of poetry, had for years had a frail chariot for her body and the horses of her spirit had driven too fiercely. She must have had heart trouble, though no one had diagnosed it. The hill walk from Cauldshaw had been too much for her. The same man spoke wisely about the evils of our modern life. "Most people to-day," he said, "have temperaments that prey on their bodies. They must live at white heat and the shell cracks. . . ."

Years afterwards, when time had taken the edge off his grief, Linford told me something of what happened. "She met me, looking very well and jolly, and we walked to the place you call the Bower. You may laugh at me, but I tell you I had a presentiment that something was going to happen, but I couldn't be sure whether it was good or bad. . . . She looked all round the Glen and sighed happily, as if she had found something she liked very much. Then suddenly she gave a little cry and went very white. I caught her, and saw that she was all in a shiver. She was staring at the burn, and her eyes were round and frightened like a deer's. Then she smiled again, and turned to me with a look—Oh, my God, I can never forget it! It was so kind and happy and . . . She must have cared for me all the time, and like a blind fool I didn't know it. She put her arms round my neck and said, 'My ain true love'—I suppose she was quoting from a Scotch song. And just as I was bursting with joy I felt that her cheek was cold. . . ."

Now it is a curious thing, but in the 'Scotichronicon' of Hume of Calzeat—it is in manuscript, and I do not think anyone living has read it besides myself—there is a version of the story of Maid Marjory. And according to that version, when the lady confronted her father in the Green Glen, she put her arm around the Douglas's neck and said, "My ain true love."

THE WISE YEARS.

(*The monk,* LAPIDARIUS, *in meditation.*)

I, Lapidarius, priest of the Most High,
(Called, ere Christ sought me, John of Dinlay-burn),
Now in this shadowy twilight of my days
Give laud and make confession. Yester-eve
I cast lots in the Scriptures, for 'tis right,
As Austin teaches, thus to question God.
Twofold the answer: first I found the text,
"The hour is nigh," a token clear that soon
I must put off these tattered mortal weeds
And don the immortal raiment of the blest.
The second was the Psalm, that "to the just
Peace shall be granted while the moon endures."
A fitting benediction, quoth my soul;
For I have ever loved the moon and sought
The gentle lore that dwelleth in her beams.

Here, in this moorland cell, long years I strove
To pierce the veil that hideth Heaven from man.
By fasts and vigils I wore thin the robe,
The fleshly robe that clogs the soul; in prayer
I from the body soared among the stars
And held high converse with the cherubim.
I moved in ecstasy, and all the land
Spake of my sainthood; people thronged from far
To gaze upon the man who walked with God.
Ah, little knew they! In my heart I wept,

For God was ever distant. Not with Him
I communed, but with fancies self-begot,
Half of sick brain and half of fevered flesh.
And then one eve—'twas at the Lammastide
When every twilight is a taste of Heaven,
While half-distraught I laboured, sudden came
The light that shone on Paul; I caught my breath,
Felt on my forehead the cool hand of God,
And heard His holy accents in my ear:—
"Why troublest thou thyself to mount to Me
When I am with thee always. Love My world,
The good green earth I gave thee for thy joy."
Then through the rushes flowered the rose of eve,
And I went forth into the dewy air,
And made my first communion with God's world.

The robe of flesh wears thin, and with the years
God shines through all things. Time and Death are not,
Nor Change, but all endures even as a tree
Bears in its secular trunk the rings of youth.
I walk by stream and hill, at even and dawn,
In noontide's height, in the first joy of spring,
Through the warm hours of summer, in the ripe
Soft fall of autumn, when the winter's spell
Has stilled the earth to sleep; and as I go
The dear unseen companions walk with me;
The birds and beasts attend me, and their speech,
Wise as the hills, hath opened mysteries.
I hold high fellowship with souls long dead
And souls unborn, for I am one with life,
One with the earth, and almost one with God.
They name me saint no more. The abbot scowls,
The brethren flee me, and the country folk
Call me the devil's minion. Soon, belike,—
For God may will I reach Him through the fire—
They seek to burn me as a brand of hell.

All men have shunned me, but the children come
Stealthily on a holy day with flowers
Or autumn berries ; from the hazel shade
They whisper, "Brother John, come play with us,
And tell us stories of your fairy friends."
They know, whose hearts are pure, that mine is kind,
And erreth not in loving all God gave.
They shall have comfort while the moon endures.

The hour is nigh. Behind the wattled strip
Which screens my pallet, lo ! the first grey light
Creeps timorous like a fawn. My limbs are moved
To a strange exaltation. . . . Soon the sun
Will steep the moorlands in a holier dawn,
And my thin veil of sense will fade and fall.
I shall be one with Him, and hear His speech
As friend to friend, and see Him face to face.
He findeth God who finds the earth He made . . .
The Green Glen waits the morning, and I go.

X. THE RIME OF TRUE THOMAS.

(BEING THE TALE OF THE RESPECTABLE WHAUP AND THE GREAT GODLY MAN.)

THIS is a story that I heard from the King of the Numidians, who with his tattered retinue encamps behind the peat-ricks. If you ask me where and when it happened I fear that I am scarce ready with an answer. But I will vouch my honour for its truth; and if anyone seek further proof, let him go east the town and west the town and over the fields of Nomansland to the Long Muir, and if he find not the King there among the peat-ricks, and get not a courteous answer to his question, then times have changed in that part of the country, and he must continue the quest to his Majesty's castle in Spain.

Once upon a time, says the tale, there was a Great Godly Man, a shepherd to trade, who lived in a cottage among heather. If you looked east in the morning, you saw miles of moor running wide to the flames of sunrise, and if you turned your eyes west in the evening, you saw a great confusion of dim peaks with the dying eye of the sun set in a crevice. If you looked north, too, in the afternoon, when the life of the day is near its end and the world grows wise, you might have seen a country of low hills and haughlands with many waters running sweet among meadows. But if you looked south in the dusty forenoon or at hot mid-day, you saw the far-off glimmer of a white road, the roofs of the ugly little clachan of Kilmaclavers, and the rigging of the fine new kirk of Threepdaidle.

It was a Sabbath afternoon in the hot weather, and the

man had been to kirk all the morning. He had heard a grand sermon from the minister (or it may have been the priest, for I am not sure of the date and the King told the story quickly)—a fine discourse with fifteen heads and three parentheses. He held all the parentheses and fourteen of the heads in his memory, but he had forgotten the fifteenth; so for the purpose of recollecting it, and also for the sake of a walk, he went forth in the afternoon into the open heather.

The whaups were crying everywhere, making the air hum like the twanging of a bow. *Poo-eelie, Poo-eelie,* they cried, *Kirlew, Kirlew, Whaup, Wha- -up.* Sometimes they came low, all but brushing him, till they drove settled thoughts from his head. Often had he been on the moors, but never had he seen such a stramash among the feathered clan. The wailing iteration vexed him, and he *shoo'd* the birds away with his arms. But they seemed to mock him and whistle in his very face, and at the flaff of their wings his heart grew sore. He waved his great stick; he picked up bits of loose moor-rock and flung them wildly; but the godless crew paid never a grain of heed. The morning's sermon was still in his head, and the grave words of the minister still rattled in his ear, but he could get no comfort for this intolerable piping. At last his patience failed him and he swore unchristian words. "Deil rax the birds' thrapples!" he cried.

At this all the noise was hushed and in a twinkling the moor was empty. Only one bird was left, standing on tall legs before him with its head bowed upon its breast, and its beak touching the heather.

Then the man repented his words and stared at the thing in the moss. "What bird are ye?" he asked thrawnly.

"I am a Respectable Whaup," said the bird, "and I kenna why ye have broken in on our family gathering. Once in a hundred years we foregather for decent conversation, and here we are interrupted by a muckle, sweerin' man."

Now the shepherd was a fellow of great sagacity, yet he never thought it a queer thing that he should be having talk in the mid-moss with a bird.

"What for were ye making siccan a din, then?" he asked. "D'ye no ken ye were disturbing the afternoon of the holy Sabbath?"

The bird lifted its eyes and regarded him solemnly. "The Sabbath is a day of rest and gladness," it said, "and is it no' reasonable that we should enjoy the like?"

The shepherd shook his head, for the presumption staggered him. "Ye little ken what ye speak of," he said. "The Sabbath is for them that have the chance of salvation, and it has been decreed that salvation is for Adam's race and no for the beasts that perish."

The whaup gave a whistle of scorn. "I have heard all that long ago. In my great-grandmother's time, which 'ill be a thousand years and mair syne, there came a people from the south with bright brass things on their heads and breasts, and terrible swords at their thighs. And with them were some lang-gowned men who kenned the stars and would come out o' nights to talk to the deer and the corbies in their ain tongue. And one, I mind, foregathered with my great-grandmother and told her that the souls o' men flitted in the end to braw meadows where the gods bide or gaed down to the black pit which they ca' Hell. But the souls o' birds, he said, die wi' their bodies, and that's the end o' them. Likewise in my mother's time, when there was a great abbey down yonder by the Threepdaidle Burn which they called the House of Kilmaclavers, the auld monks would walk out in the evening to pick herbs for their distillings, and some were wise and kenned the ways of bird and beast. They would crack often o' nights with my ain family, and tell them that Christ had saved the souls o' men, but that birds and beasts were perishable as the dew o' Heaven. And now ye have a black-gowned man in Threepdaidle who threeps on the same owercome. Ye may a' ken something o' your ain kitchen-midden, but certes! ye ken little o' the warld beyond it."

Now this angered the man, and he rebuked the bird. "These are great mysteries," he said, "which are no' to be mentioned in the ears of an unsanctified creature. What can a thing like you wi' a lang neb and twae legs like stilts ken about the next warld?"

"Weel, weel," said the whaup, "we'll let the matter be. Everything to its ain trade, and I will not dispute with ye on metapheesics. But if ye ken something about the next warld, ye ken terrible little about this."

Now this angered the man still more, for he was a shepherd reputed to have great skill in sheep and esteemed the nicest judge of hogg and wether in all the countryside. "What ken ye about that?" he asked. "Ye may gang east to Yetholm and west to Kells, and no find a better herd."

"If sheep were a'," said the bird, "ye micht be right; but what o' the wide warld and the folk in it? Ye are Simon Etterick o' the Lowe Moss. Do ye ken aucht o' your forebears?"

"My father was a God-fearing man at the Kennel-head, and my grandfather and great-grandfather afore him. One o' our name, folk say, was shot at a dyke-back by the Black Westeraw."

"If that's a'," said the bird, "ye ken little. Have ye never heard o' the little man, the fourth back from yoursel', who killed the Miller o' Bewcastle at the Lammas Fair? That was in my ain time, and from my mother I have heard o' the Covenanter who got a bullet in his wame hunkering behind the divot-dyke and praying to his Maker. There were others o' your name rode in the Hermitage forays and burned Naworth and Warkworth and Castle Gay. I have heard o' an Etterick, Sim o' the Redcleuch, who cut the throat o' Jock Johnstone in his ain house by the Annan side. And my grandmother had tales o' auld Ettericks who rade wi' Douglas and the Bruce and the ancient Kings o' Scots;

and she used to tell o' others in her mother's time, terrible shock-headed men, hunting the deer and rinnin' on the high moors, and bidin' in the broken stane biggings on the hill-taps."

The shepherd stared, and he, too, saw the picture. He smelled the air of battle and lust and foray, and forgot the Sabbath.

"And you yoursel'," said the bird, "are sair fallen off from the auld stock. Now ye sit and spell in books, and talk about what ye little understand, when your fathers were roaming the warld. But little cause have I to speak, for I too am a downcome. My bill is two inches shorter than my mother's, and my grandmother was taller on her feet. The warld is getting weaklier things to dwell in it, even since I mind mysel'."

"Ye have the gift o' speech, bird," said the man, "and I would hear mair." You will perceive that he had no mind of the Sabbath day or the fifteenth head of the forenoon's discourse.

"What things have I to tell ye when ye dinna ken the very horn-book o' knowledge? Besides, I am no clatter-vengeance to tell stories in the middle o' the muir, where there are ears open high and low. There's others than me wi' mair experience and a better skill at the telling. Our clan was well acquaint wi' the reivers and lifters o' the muirs, and could crack fine o' wars and the taking of cattle. But the blue hawk that lives in the corrie o' the Dreichil can speak o' kelpies and the dwarfs that bide in the hill. The heron, the lang solemn fellow, kens o' the greenwood fairies and the wood elfins, and the wild geese that squatter on the tap o' the Muneraw will croak to ye of the merrymaidens and the girls o' the pool. The wren—him that hops in the grass below the birks—has the story of the *Lost Ladies of the Land*, which is ower auld and sad for any but the wisest to hear; and there is a wee bird bides in the heather—hill-lintie men call him—who sings the *Lay of the West Wind* and the

Glee of the Rowan Berries. But what am I talking of? What are these things to you, if ye have not first heard True Thomas's Rime, which is the beginning and end o' all things?"

"I have heard no rime," said the man, "save the sacred psalms o' God's Kirk."

"Bonny rimes," said the bird. "Once I flew by the hinder end o' the Kirk and I keekit in. A wheen auld wives wi' mutches and a wheen solemn men wi' hoasts! Be sure the Rime is no like yon."

"Can ye sing it, bird?" said the man, "for I am keen to hear it."

"Me sing," cried the bird, "me that has a voice like a craw! Na, na, I canna sing it, but maybe I can tak ye where ye may hear it. When I was young an auld bog-blitter did the same to me, and sae began my education. But are ye willing and brawly willing?—for if ye get but a sough of it ye will never mair have an ear for other music."

"I am willing and brawly willing," said the man.

"Then meet me at the Gled's Cleuch Head at the sun's setting," said the bird, and it flew away.

Now it seemed to the man that in a twinkling it was sunset, and he found himself at the Gled's Cleuch Head with the bird flapping in the heather before him. The place was a long rift in the hill, made green with juniper and hazel, where it was said True Thomas came to drink the water.

"Turn ye to the west," said the whaup, "and let the sun fall on your face; then turn ye five times round about and say after me the Rune of the Heather and the Dew." And before he knew, the man did as he was told, and found himself speaking strange words, while his head hummed and danced as if in a fever.

"Now lay ye down and put your ear to the earth," said the bird; and the man did so. Instantly a cloud came over his brain, and he did not feel the ground on which he lay or the keen hill-air which blew about him. He felt himself falling deep into an abysm of space, then suddenly caught up and set among the stars of Heaven. Then slowly from the stillness there welled forth music, drop by drop like the clear falling of rain, and the man shuddered, for he knew that he heard the beginning of the Rime.

High rose the air, and trembled among the tallest pines and the summits of great hills. And in it were the sting of rain and the blatter of hail, the soft crush of snow and the rattle of thunder among crags. Then it quieted to the low sultry croon which told of blazing mid-day when the streams are parched and the bent crackles like dry tinder. Anon it was evening, and the melody dwelled among the high soft notes which mean the coming of dark and the green light of sunset. Then the whole changed to a great pæan which rang like an organ through the earth. There were trumpet notes in it and flute notes and the plaint of pipes. " Come forth," it cried; " the sky is wide and it is a far cry to the world's end. The fire crackles fine o' nights below the firs, and the smell of roasting meat and wood smoke is dear to the heart of man. Fine, too, is the sting of salt and the risp of the north wind in the sheets. Come forth, one and all, to the great lands oversea, and the strange tongues and the fremit peoples. Learn before you die to follow the Piper's Son, and though your old bones bleach among grey rocks, what matter, if you have had your bellyful of life and come to your heart's desire ? " And the tune fell low and witching, bringing tears to the eyes and joy to the heart; and the man knew (though no one told him) that this was the first part of the Rime, the *Song of the Open Road*, the *Lilt of the Adventurer*, which shall be now and ever and to the end of days.

Then the melody changed to a fiercer and sadder note. He saw his forefathers, gaunt men and terrible, run stark among woody hills. He heard the talk of the bronze-clad invader, and the jar and clangour as stone met steel. Then rose the last coronach of his own people, hiding in wild glens, starving in corries, or going hopelessly to the death. He heard the cry of Border foray, the shouts of the famished Scots as they harried Cumberland, and he himself rode in the midst of them. Then the tune fell more mournful and slow, and Flodden lay before him. He saw the flower of the Scots gentry around their King, gashed to the breast-bone, still fronting the lines of the south, though the paleness of death sat on each forehead. "The flowers of the Forest are gone," cried the lilt, and through the long years he heard the cry of the lost, the desperate, fighting for kings over the water and princes in the heather. "Who cares?" cried the air. "Man must die, and how can he die better than in the stress of fight with his heart high and alien blood on his sword? Heigh-ho! One against twenty, a child against a host, this is the romance of life." And the man's heart swelled, for he knew (though no one told him) that this was the *Song of Lost Battles* which only the great can sing before they die.

But the tune was changing, and at the change the man shivered, for the air ran up to the high notes and then down to the deeps with an eldrich cry, like a hawk's scream at night, or a witch's song in the gloaming. It told of those who seek and never find, the quest that knows no fulfilment. "There is a road," it cried, "which leads to the Moon and the Great Waters. No change-house cheers it, and it has no end; but it is a fine road, a braw road—who will follow it?" And the man knew (though no one told him) that this was the *Ballad of Grey Weather*, which makes him who hears it sick all the days of his life for something which he cannot name. It is the song which the birds sing on the moor in the autumn nights, and the old crow on the tree-top hears and flaps his wing. It is the lilt which men and women hear in the darkening of their days, and sigh for the unforgetable; and love-sick girls get catches of it and play pranks with their lovers. It is a song so old that Adam heard it in the Garden before Eve came to comfort him, so young that from it still flows the whole joy and sorrow of earth.

Then it ceased, and all of a sudden the man was rubbing his eyes on the hillside, and watching the falling dusk. "I have heard the Rime," he said to himself, and he walked home in a daze. The whaups were crying, but none came near him, though he looked hard for the bird that had spoken with him. It may be that it was there and he did not know it, or it may be that the whole thing was only a dream; but of this I cannot say.

The next morning the man rose and went to the manse.

"I am glad to see you, Simon," said the minister, "for it will soon be the Communion Season, and it is your duty to go round with the tokens."

"True," said the man, "but it was another thing I came to talk about," and he told him the whole tale.

"There are but two ways of it, Simon," said the minister. "Either ye are the victim of witchcraft, or ye are a self-deluded man. If the former (whilk I am loth to believe), then it behoves ye to watch and pray lest ye enter into temptation. If the latter, then ye maun put a strict watch over a vagrom fancy, and ye'll be quit o' siccan whigmaleeries."

Now Simon was not listening, but staring out of the window. "There was another thing I had it in my mind to say," said he. "I have come to lift my lines, for I am thinking of leaving the place."

"And where would ye go?" asked the minister, aghast.

"I was thinking of going to Carlisle and trying my luck as a dealer, or maybe pushing on with droves to the South."

"But that's a cauld country where there are no faithfu' ministrations," said the minister.

"Maybe so, but I am not caring very muckle about ministrations," said the man, and the other looked after him in horror.

When he left the manse he went to a Wise Woman, who lived on the left side of the kirkyard above Threepdaidle burn-foot. She was very old, and sat by the ingle day and night, waiting upon death. To her he told the same tale.

She listened gravely, nodding with her head. "Ach," she said, "I have heard a like story before. And where will you be going?"

"I am going south to Carlisle to try the dealing and droving," said the man, "for I have some skill of sheep."

"And will ye bide there?" she asked.

"Maybe ay, and maybe no," he said. "I had half a mind to push on to the big toun or even to the abroad. A man must try his fortune."

"That's the way of men," said the old wife. "I, too, have heard the Rime, and many women who now sit decently spinning in Kilmaclavers have heard it. But a woman may hear it and lay it up in her soul and bide at hame, while a man, if he get but a glisk of it in his fool's heart, must needs up and awa' to the warld's end on some daft-like ploy. But gang your ways and fare-ye-weel. My cousin Francie heard it, and he went north wi' a white cockade in his bonnet and a sword at his side, singing 'Charlie's come hame.' And Tam Crichtoun o' the Bourhopehead got a sough o' it one simmer's morning, and the last we heard o' Tam he was fechting like a deil among the Frenchmen. Once I heard a tinkler play a sprig of it on the pipes, and a' the lads were wud to follow him. Gang your ways, for I am near the end o' mine." And the old wife shook with her coughing.

So the man put up his belongings in a pack on his back and went whistling down the Great South Road.

Whether or not this tale have a moral it is not for me to say. The King (who told it me) said that it had, and quoted a scrap of Latin, for he had been at Oxford in his youth before he fell heir to his kingdom. One may hear tunes from the Rime, said he, in the thick of a storm on the scarp of a rough hill, in the soft June weather, or in the sunset silence of a winter's night. But let none, he added, pray to have the full music; for it will make him who hears it a footsore traveller in the ways o' the world and a masterless man till death.

Printed in Great Britain by
WILLIAM BLACKWOOD & SONS LTD.